THE
DARK TIDE

Andrew Gross

The Blue Zone

Novels by Andrew Gross and James Patterson

Judge & Jury

Lifeguard

3rd Degree

The Jester

2nd Chance

THE
DARK TIDE

Andrew Gross

wm

WILLIAM MORROW
An Imprint of HarperCollins*Publishers*

THE DARK TIDE. Copyright © 2008 by Andrew Gross. All rights reserved. Printed in the United States of America. No part of this book may be used or reproduced in any manner whatsoever without written permission except in the case of brief quotations embodied in critical articles and reviews. For information address HarperCollins Publishers, 10 East 53rd Street, New York, NY 10022.

ISBN 978-0-06-114342-7

PART ONE

CHAPTER ONE

6:10 A.M.

As the morning sun canted sharply through the bedroom window, Charles Friedman dropped the baton.

He hadn't had the dream in years, yet there he was, gangly, twelve years old, running the third leg of the relay in the track meet at summer camp, the battle between the Blue and the Gray squarely on the line. The sky was a brilliant blue, the crowd jumping up and down—crew-cut, red-cheeked faces he would never see again, except here. His teammate, Kyle Bregman, running the preceding leg, was bearing down on him, holding on to a slim lead, cheeks puffing with everything he had.

Reach. . . .

Charles readied himself, set to take off at the touch of the baton. He felt his fingers twitch, awaiting the slap of the stick in his palm.

There it was! Now! He took off.

Suddenly there was a crushing groan.

Charles stopped, looked down in horror. The baton lay on the ground. The Gray Team completed the exchange, sprinting past him to an improbable victory, their supporters jumping in glee. Cheers of jubilation mixed with jeers of disappointment echoed in Charles's ears.

That's when he woke up. As he always did. Breathing heavily, sheets damp with sweat. Charles glanced at his hands—empty. He patted the covers as if the baton were somehow still there, after thirty years.

But it was only Tobey, their white West Highland terrier, staring wide-eyed and expectantly, straddled turkey-legged on his chest.

Charles let his head fall back with a sigh.

He glanced at the clock: 6:10 A.M. Ten minutes before the alarm. His wife, Karen, lay curled up next to him. He hadn't slept much at all. He'd been wide awake from 3:00 to 4:00 A.M., staring at the World's Strongest Female Championship on ESPN2 without the sound, not wanting to disturb her. Something was weighing heavily on Charles's mind.

Maybe it was the large position he had taken in Canadian oil sands last Thursday and had kept through the weekend—highly risky with the price of oil leaking the other way. Or how he had bet up the six-month natural-gas contracts, at the same time going short against the one-years. Friday the energy index had continued to decline. He was scared to get out of bed, scared to look at the screen this morning and see what he'd find.

Or was it Sasha?

For the past ten years, Charles had run his own energy hedge fund in Manhattan, leveraged up eight to one. On the outside—his sandy brown hair, the horn-rim glasses, his bookish calm—he seemed more the estate-planner type or a tax consultant than someone whose bowels (and now his dreams as well!) attested to the fact that he was living in high-beta hell.

Charles pushed himself up in his boxers and paused, elbows on knees. Tobey leaped off the bed ahead of him, scratching feverishly at the door.

"Let him out." Karen stirred, rolling over, yanking the covers over her head.

"You're sure?" Charles checked out the dog, ears pinned back, tail quivering, jumping on his hind legs in anticipation, as if he could turn the knob with his teeth. "You know what's going to happen."

"C'mon, Charlie, it's your turn this morning. Just let the little bastard out."

"Famous last words . . ."

Charles got up and opened the door leading to their fenced-in half-acre yard, a block from the sound in Old Greenwich. In a flash Tobey bolted out onto the patio, his nose fixed to the scent of some unsuspecting rabbit or squirrel.

Immediately the dog began his high-pitched yelp.

Karen scrunched the pillow over her head and growled. *"Rrrrggg . . ."*

That's how every day began, Charles trudging into the kitchen, turning on CNN and a pot of coffee, the dog barking outside.

Then going into his study and checking the European spots online before hopping into the shower.

That morning the spots didn't offer much cheer—$72.10. They had continued to decline. Charles did a quick calculation in his head. Three more contracts he'd be forced to sell out. Another couple of million—gone. It was a little after 6:00 A.M., and he was already underwater.

Outside, Tobey was in the middle of a nonstop three-minute barrage.

In the shower, Charles went over his day. He had to reverse his positions. He had these oil-sand contracts to clear up, then a meeting with one of his lenders. *Was it time for him to come clean?* He had a transfer to make into his daughter Sam's college account; she'd be a senior at the high school in the fall.

That's when it hit him. *Shit!*

He had to take in the goddamn car this morning.

The fifteen-thousand-mile service on the Merc. Karen had finally badgered him into making the appointment last week. That meant he'd have to take the train in. It would set him back a bit. He'd hoped to be at his desk by seven-thirty to deal with those positions. Now Karen would have to pick him up at the station later that afternoon.

Dressed, Charles was usually in rush mode by now. The six-thirty wake-up shout to Karen, a knock on Alex's and Samantha's doors to get them rolling for school. Looking over the *Wall Street Journal*'s headlines at the front door.

This morning, thanks to the car, he had a moment to sip his coffee.

They lived in a warm, refurbished Colonial on an affluent tree-lined street in the town of Old Greenwich, a block off the sound. Fully paid for, the damned thing was probably worth more than Charles's father, a tie salesman from Scranton, had earned in his entire life. Maybe he couldn't show it like some of their big-time friends in their megahomes out on North Street, but he'd done well. He'd fought to get himself into Penn from a high-school class of seven hundred, distinguished himself at the energy desk at Morgan Stanley, steered a few private clients away when he'd opened his own firm, Harbor Capital. They had the ski house in Vermont, the kids' college paid for, took fancy vacations.

So what the hell had he done wrong?

Outside, Tobey was scratching at the kitchen's French doors, trying to get back in. *All right, all right.* Charles sighed.

Last week their other Westie, Sasha, had been run over. Right on their quiet street, directly in front of their house. It had been Charles who'd found her, bloodied, inert. Everyone was still upset. And then the note. The note that came to his office in a basket of flowers the very next day. That had left him in such a sweat. And brought on these dreams.

Sorry about the pooch, Charles. Could your kids be next?

How the hell had it gotten this far?

He stood up and checked the clock on the stove: 6:45. With any luck, he figured, he could be out of the dealership by 7:30, catch a ride to the 7:51, be at his desk at Forty-ninth Street and Third Avenue fifty minutes after that. Figure out what to do. He let in the dog, who immediately darted past him into the living room with a yelp and out the front door, which Charles had absentmindedly failed to shut. Now he was waking up the entire neighborhood.

The little bastard was more work than the kids!

"Karen, I'm leaving!" he yelled, grabbing his briefcase and tucking the *Journal* under his arm.

"Kiss, kiss," she called back, wrapped in her robe, dashing out of the shower.

She still looked sexy to him, her caramel-colored hair wet and a little tangled from the shower. Karen was nothing if not beautiful. She had kept her figure toned and inviting from years of yoga, her skin was still smooth, and she had those dreamy, grab-you-and-never-let-go hazel eyes. For a moment Charles regretted not rolling over to her back in bed once Tobey had flown the coop and given them the unexpected opportunity.

But instead he just yelled up something about the car—that he'd be taking in the Metro-North. That maybe he'd call her later and have her meet him on the way home to pick it up.

"Love you!" Karen called over the hum of the hair dryer.

"You, too!"

"After Alex's game we'll go out. . . ."

Damn, that was right, Alex's lacrosse game, his first of the season. Charles went back and scratched out a note to him that he left on the kitchen counter.

To our #1 attacker! Knock 'em dead, champ! BEST OF LUCK!!!

He signed his initials, then crossed it out and wrote *Dad*. He stared at the note for a second. He had to stop this. Whatever was going on, he'd never let anything happen to them.

Then he headed for the garage, and over the sound of the automatic door opening and the dog's barking in the yard, he heard his wife yell above the hair dryer, *"Charlie, would you please let in the goddamn dog!"*

CHAPTER TWO

By eight-thirty Karen was at yoga.

By that time she had already roused Alex and Samantha from their beds, put out boxes of cereal and toast for their breakfasts, found the top that Sam claimed was *"absolutely* missing, Mom" (in her daughter's dresser drawer), and refereed two fights over who was driving whom that morning and whose cooties were in the bathroom sink the kids shared.

She'd also fed the dog, made sure Alex's lacrosse uniform was pressed, and when the shoulder-slapping, finger-flicking spat over who touched whom last began to simmer into a name-calling brawl, pushed them out the door and into Sam's Acura with a kiss and a wave, got a quote from Sav-a-Tree about one of their elms that needed to come down and dashed off two e-mails to board members on the school's upcoming capital campaign.

A start . . . Karen sighed, nodding *"Hey, all,"* to a few familiar faces as she hurriedly joined in with their sun salutations at the Sportsplex studio in Stamford.

The afternoon was going to be a bitch.

Karen was forty-two, pretty; she knew she looked at least five years younger. With her sharp brown eyes, the trace of a few freckles still dotting her cheekbones, people often compared her to a fairer Sela Ward. Her thick, light brown hair was clipped up in back, and as she caught herself in the mirror, she wasn't at all ashamed of how she still looked in her yoga tights for a mom who in a former life had been the leading fund-raiser for the City Ballet.

That's where she and Charlie had first met. At a large-donors dinner. Of course, he was only there to fill out a table for the firm and couldn't tell a plié from the twist. *Still couldn't,* she always ribbed him. But he was shy and a bit self-deprecating—and with his horn-rim glasses and suspenders, his mop of sandy hair, he seemed more like some poli-sci professor than the new hotshot on the Morgan Stanley energy desk. Charlie seemed to like that she wasn't from around here—the hint of a drawl she still carried in her voice. The velvet glove wrapped around her iron fist, he always called it admiringly, because he'd never met anyone, *anyone,* who could get things done like she could.

Well, the drawl was long gone, and so was the perfect slimness of her hips. Not to mention the feeling that she had any control over her life.

She'd lost that one a couple of kids ago.

Karen concentrated on her breathing as she leaned forward into stick pose, which was a difficult one for her, focusing on the extension of her arms, the straightness of her spine.

"Straight back," Cheryl, the instructor, intoned. "Donna, arms by the ears. Karen, *posture.* Engage that thighbone."

"It's my *thighbone* that's about to fall off." Karen groaned, wobbling. A couple of people around her laughed. Then she righted herself and regained her form.

"*Beautiful.*" Cheryl clapped. "Well done."

Karen had been raised in Atlanta. Her father owned a small chain of paint and remodeling stores there. She'd gone to Emory and studied art. At twenty-three she and a girlfriend went up to New York, she got her first job in the publicity department at Sotheby's, and things just seemed to click from there. It wasn't easy at first, after she and Charlie married. Giving up her career, moving up here to the country, starting a family. Charlie was always working back then—or away—and even when he was home, it seemed he had a phone perpetually stapled to his ear.

Things were a little dicey at the beginning. Charlie had made a few wrong plays when he opened his firm and almost "bought the farm." But one of his mentors from Morgan Stanley had stepped in and bailed him out, and since then things had worked out pretty well. It wasn't a big life—like some of the people they knew who lived in those giant Normandy castles in backcountry, with places in Palm Beach and whose kids had never flown commercial. But who even wanted that? They had the place in Vermont, a skiff at a yacht club in Greenwich. Karen still shopped for the groceries and picked up the poop out of the driveway. She solicited auction gifts for the Teen Center, did the household bills. The bloom on her cheeks said she was happy. She loved her family more than anything in the world.

Still, she sighed, shifting into chair pose; it was like heaven that at least for an hour the kids, the dog, the bills piling up on her desk were a million miles away.

Karen's attention was caught by something through the glass partition. People were gathering around the front desk, staring up at the overhead TV.

"Think of a beautiful place. . . ." Cheryl directed them. "Inhale. Use your breath to take you there. . . ."

Karen drifted to the place she always fixed on. A remote cove just outside Tortola, in the Caribbean. She and Charlie and the kids had come upon it when they were sailing nearby. They had waded in and spent the day by themselves in the beautiful turquoise bay. A world without cell phones and Comedy Central. She had never seen her husband so relaxed. When the kids were gone, he always said, when he was able to get it all together, they could go there. *Right*. Karen always smiled inside. Charlie was a lifer. He loved the arbitrage, the risk. The cove could stay away, a lifetime if it had to. She was happy. She caught her face in the mirror. It made her smile.

Suddenly Karen became aware that the crowd at the front desk had grown. A few runners had stepped off their treadmills, focused on the overhead screens. Even the trainers had come over and were watching.

Something had happened!

Cheryl tried clapping them back to attention. "People, focus!" But to no avail.

One by one, they all broke their poses and stared.

A woman from the club ran over, throwing open their door. *"Something's happened!"* she said, her face white with alarm. "There's a fire in Grand Central Station! *There's been some kind of bombing there.*"

CHAPTER THREE

Karen hurried through the glass door and squeezed in front of the screen to watch.

They all did.

There was a reporter broadcasting from the street in Manhattan across from the train station, confirming in a halting tone that some sort of explosion had gone off inside. *"Possibly multiple explosions . . ."*

The screen then cut to an aerial view from a helicopter. A billowing plume of black smoke rose into the sky from inside.

"Oh, Jesus, God," Karen muttered, staring at the scene in horror. "What's happened . . . ?"

"It's down on the tracks," a woman in a leotard standing next to her said. "They think some kind of bomb went off, maybe on one of the trains."

"My son went in by train this morning," a woman gasped, pressing a hand to her lips.

Another, a towel draped around her neck, holding back tears: "My husband, too."

Before Karen could even think, fresh reports came in. An explosion, *several explosions,* on the tracks, just as a Metro-North train was pulling into the station. There was a fire raging down there, the news reporter said. Smoke coming up on the street. Dozens of people still trapped. Maybe hundreds. *This was bad!*

"Who?" people were murmuring all around.

"Terrorists, they're saying." One of the trainers shook his head. "They don't know. . . ."

They'd all been part of this kind of terrible moment before. Karen and Charlie had both known people who'd never made it out on 9/11. At first Karen watched with the empathetic worry of someone whose life was outside the tragedy that was taking place. Nameless, faceless people she might have seen a hundred times— across from her on the train, reading the sports page, hurrying on the street for a cab. Eyes fixed to the screen, now many of them locked fingers with one another's hands.

Then, all of a sudden, it hit Karen.

Not with a flash—a numbing sensation at first, in her chest. Then intensifying, accompanied by a feeling of impending dread.

Charlie had yelled something up to her—about going in by train this morning. Above the drone of the hair dryer.

About having to take in the car and needing her to pick him up later on that afternoon.

Oh, my God . . .

She felt a constriction in her chest. Her eyes darted toward the clock. Frantically, she tried to reconstruct some sort of timeline. Charlie, what time he left, what time it was now . . . It started to scare her. Her heart began to speed up like a metronome set on high.

An updated report came in. Karen tensed. "It appears we are talking about a bomb," the reporter announced. "Aboard a Metro-North train just as it pulled into Grand Central. This has just been confirmed," he said. "It was on the *Stamford branch*."

A collective gasp rose up from the studio.

Most of them were from around there. Everyone knew people— relatives, friends—who regularly took the train. Faces drained of blood—in shock. People turning to each other without even knowing whom they were next to, seeking the comfort of each other's eyes.

"It's horrible, isn't it?" A woman next to Karen shook her head.

Karen could barely answer. A chill had suddenly taken control of her, knifing through her bones.

The Stamford train went through Greenwich.

All she could do was look up at the clock in terror—8:54. Her chest was coiled so tightly she could barely breathe.

The woman stared at her. "Honey, are you okay?"

"I don't know. . . ." Karen's eyes had filled with terror. "I think my husband might be on that train."

CHAPTER FOUR

8:45 A.M.

Ty Hauck was on his way to work.

He cut the engines to five miles per hour as he maneuvered his twenty-four-foot fishing skiff, the *Merrily,* into the mouth of Greenwich Harbor.

Hauck took the boat in from time to time when the weather turned nice. *This* morning, with its clear, crisp April breeze, he looked off his deck and sort of mentally declared it: *Summer hours officially begin!* The twenty-five minutes on the Long Island Sound from where he lived near Cove Island in Stamford were hardly longer than the slow slog this time of the morning down I-95. And the brisk wind whipping through his hair woke him a whole lot faster than any grande at Starbucks. He clicked the portable CD player on. Fleetwood Mac. An old favorite:

Rhiannon rings like a bell through the night / And wouldn't you love to love her.

It was why he'd moved back up here, four years ago. After the accident, after his marriage had broken up. Some said that it was running away. Hiding out. And maybe it was, just a little. *So the hell what?*

He was head of the Violent Crimes Unit on the Greenwich police force. People relied on him. *Was that running away?* Sometimes he took the boat out for an hour or so before work in the rosy predawn calm and fished for blues and striped bass. *Was that?*

He had grown up here. In middle-class Byram, near Port Chester by the New York border, only a few miles but a lifetime away from the massive estates that now lined the way out to backcountry, gates he now drove through to follow up on some rich kid who had tipped over his sixty-thousand-dollar Hummer.

It was all different now. The countrified families who had grown up there in his youth had given way to thirty-something hedge-fund zillionaires who tore the old homes down and built enormous castles behind iron gates, with lake-size pools and movie theaters. Everyone with money was coming in. Now Russian moguls—who even knew where *their* wealth was from?—were buying up horse-country estates in Conyers Farm, putting in helicopter pads.

Billionaires ruining things for millionaires. Hauck shook his head.

Twenty years ago he'd been a running back at Greenwich High. Then he went on and played at Colby, Division III. Not exactly Big Ten, but the fancy degree got him fast-tracked into the NYPD detectives' training program, which made his dad, who worked his whole life for the Town of Greenwich Water Authority, proud. He'd cracked a couple of high-profile cases and moved up. Later on he worked for the department's Information Office when the Trade Towers were hit.

So now he was back.

As he chugged into the harbor, the manicured lawns of Belle Haven to his left, a couple of small boats cruised past him on their way out—doing the same thing he was doing, heading to work on Long Island across the sound, a half hour's ride away.

Hauck waved.

And he liked it here now, though a lot of pain had left its mark in between.

It was lonely since he and Beth had split up. He dated a bit: a pretty secretary to the CEO at General Reinsurance, a marketing gal who worked at Altria for a while. Even one or two gals on the force. But he'd found no one new to share his life with. Though Beth had.

Occasionally he hung out with a few of his old buddies from town, a couple who had made bundles building homes, some who just became plumbers or mortgage brokers or owned a landscaping company. "The Leg," that's what everyone still called him—with a soft *g*, as in "Legend." Old-timers, who still recalled him busting two tackles into the end zone to beat Stamford West for the Lower Fairfield County crown, still toasted that as the best game they'd ever seen anyone play here since Steve Young and bought him beers.

But mostly he simply felt free. That the past hadn't followed him up here. He just tried to do a little good during the day, cut people a break. Be fair. And he had Jessica, who was ten now, up on weekends, and they fished and kicked soccer balls around on Tod's Point and had cookouts there. Sunday afternoons, in his eight-year-old Bronco, he'd drive her back to where she lived now, in Brooklyn. Friday nights in the winter, he played hockey in the local over-forty league.

Basically he tried to push it back a little each day—time, that is—trying to find himself back to that point before everything caved in on him. That moment before the accident. Before his marriage collapsed. Before he gave up.

Why go back there, Ty?

Hard as you tried, you could never quite push it back all the way. Life didn't afford you that.

Hauck caught sight of the marina at the Indian Harbor Yacht Club, where the dock manager, Hank Gordon, an old buddy, always let him put in for the day. He picked up the radio. "Heading in, Gordo . . ."

But the marina manager was waiting for him out on the pier.

"What the hell are you doing here, Ty?"

Hauck yelled to him, "Summer hours, guy!" He reversed and backed the *Merrily* in. Gordo tossed a bowline to him and reeled him in. Hauck cut the engine. He went out to the stern as the boat hit the buoy and hopped onto the pier. "Like a dream out there today."

"A *bad* dream," Hank said. "Lemme take it from here, Ty. You better get your ass up that hill."

There was something on the dock manager's face that Hauck couldn't quite read. He glanced at his watch—8:52. Usually he and Gordo shot the shit a few minutes, about the Rangers or what had made it onto the police blotter the night before.

That's when Hauck's cell phone started to beep. The office. *Two-three-seven.*

Two-thirty-seven was the department's emergency code.

"You didn't have the radio on, did you?" Gordo asked, securing the line.

Hauck shook his head blankly.

"Then you haven't heard what the hell happened out there, have you, Lieutenant?"

CHAPTER FIVE

Karen didn't flip out at first. That wasn't her way. She told herself over and over to stay calm. Charlie could be anywhere. *Anywhere.*

You don't know for sure if he was even on that train.

Like a few years back, when Samantha was four or five, and they thought they'd lost her at Bloomie's. And after a frantic, heart-constricting search, retracing their steps, calling for the manager, and starting to accept the reality that something horrible had happened—*that this wasn't a false alarm!*—there she was, their little Sammy, waving hi to Mommy and Daddy, paging through one of her favorite books atop a pile of Oriental rugs, as innocent as if she were on a stage at school.

This could be just like that, Karen reassured herself now. *Stay calm, Karen. Goddamn it, just stay calm!*

She ran back into the yoga studio, found her purse, and fumbled around for her phone. Heart pumping, she punched in Charlie's number on the speed dial. *C'mon, c'mon. . . .* Her fingers barely complied.

As she waited for the call to connect, she tried her best to flash through her husband's schedule that morning. He'd left the house around seven. She'd been finishing her hair. Ten minutes into town, ten minutes at the dealership dropping off the car, going over what had to be done. So that was, what—7:20? Another ten or so to the station. The news said the explosion had occurred at 8:41. He could have made an earlier train. Or even ended up getting a loaner and driving in. For a second, Karen allowed herself to feel uplifted.

Anything was possible. . . . Charlie was the most resourceful man she knew.

His phone began to ring. Karen saw that her hands were shaking. *C'mon, Charlie, answer. . . .*

To her dismay, his voice recording came on. "This is Charlie Friedman. . . ."

"*Charlie, it's me,*" Karen blurted. "I'm really worried about you. I know you took the train in. You've got to call me as soon as you get this. I don't care what you're doing, Charlie. Just call, hon. . . ."

She pressed the end button feeling totally helpless.

Then she realized—there was a voice-mail message on her phone! Blood racing, she scrolled immediately to Recently Received Calls.

It was Charlie's number! Thank God! Her heart almost climbed up her throat in joy.

Anxiously, Karen punched in her code and pressed the receiver to her ear. His familiar voice came on and it was calm. "Listen, hon, I thought as long as I'm gonna be in Grand Central, I'd pick up some of those marinated steaks you like at Ottomanelli's on the way home and we'd grill instead of going out. . . . Sound good? Lemme know. I'll be in the office by nine. I got hung up. Madhouse at the dealership. *Bye.*"

Karen stared at the message screen—8:34. *He was heading into Grand Central when he made the call. Still on the train.* The sweats began to come over her again. She looked back outside at the monitor, at the pall of smoke building over Grand Central, the chaos and confusion on the screen.

Suddenly she knew in her heart. She couldn't deny it anymore.

Her husband was on that train.

Unable to control herself any longer, Karen punched in the speed code to her husband's office. *C'mon, c'mon,* she said over and over during the agonizing seconds it took for the call to connect. Finally Heather, Charlie's assistant, picked up.

"Charles Friedman's office."

"Heather, it's Karen." She tried to control herself. "By any chance has my husband come in?"

"Not yet, Mrs. Friedman. He left me an e-mail earlier from his BlackBerry saying that he had to take his car in or something. I'm sure I'll be hearing from him soon."

"I know he had to take his car in, Heather! That's what I'm worried about. Have you seen the news? He said he was taking the train."

"Oh, my God!" His assistant gasped, reality setting in. Of course she'd seen it. They *all* had. The whole office was watching it now.

"Mrs. Friedman, let me try and get him on the phone. I'm sure it's got to be crazy around Grand Central. Maybe he's on his way over and the phones just aren't functioning. Maybe he took a later train—"

"I got a call from him, Heather! At eight thirty-four. He said they were pulling into Grand Central in a while. . . ." Her voice was shaking. "That was eight thirty-four, Heather! He was on it. Otherwise he would have called. *I think he was on that train. . . ."*

Heather begged her to stay calm and said she would e-mail him, that she was sure she'd hear from him soon. Karen nodded okay, but when she put down the phone, her heart was racing and her blood was pumping out of control and she had no idea what to do next. She pressed the phone to her heart and dialed his number one more time.

C'mon, Charlie. . . . Charlie, please . . .

Outside Grand Central, the news reporter was confirming that it had been at least one bomb. A few survivors had staggered out of the station. They were gathered on the street, dazed, faces smeared with blood and black with soot. Some were muttering something about Track 109, that there'd been at least two powerful explosions and a fire raging down there, with lots of people still trapped. That something had gone off in the first two cars.

Karen froze. That's when tears finally started to roll down her cheeks.

That's where Charlie always sat. It was like a ritual with him. He always camped out in the first car!

C'mon, Charlie. . . . Karen pleaded silently, watching the screen outside. *People are making it out. Look, they're interviewing them.*

She punched his number in again, her body giving over to full-out panic.

"Answer the fucking phone, Charlie!"

CHAPTER SIX

Her thoughts flashed to Samantha and Alex. Karen realized she had to get home.

What could she possibly tell them? Charlie always drove in. He had a spot in his building's garage. He'd been doing it for years.

That this was the one goddamn morning he picked to take the train!

Karen crumpled her sweat top into her bag and ran out, past the front counter, through the outer glass doors. She hurried over to where her Lexus was parked, the hybrid Charlie had bought her barely a month ago. The console still smelled new. She flicked the automatic lock on her key chain and jumped in.

Her house was about ten minutes away. Pulling out of the lot, Karen kept the Blue Tooth phone on automatic dial to Charlie's cell. *Please, Charlie, please, answer the goddamn phone!*

Her heart kept sinking. "This is Charlie Friedman. . . ."

Tears rolled down her cheeks as she pushed back her worst fears. *This can't be happening!*

Karen made a sharp right out of the Sportsplex's lot onto Prospect, cut the light at the corner, accelerating onto I-95. Traffic was backed up, slowing everything headed into downtown Greenwich.

All sorts of new, conflicting reports were coming in. The radio said that multiple explosions had taken place. That there was a fire on the tracks, burning out of control. That the intense heat and the possibility of noxious fumes made it impossible for firefighters even to get close. That there were significant casualties.

It was starting to scare Karen to death.

He could be trapped down there. *Anywhere*. He could be burned or injured, unable to get out. On his way to a hospital. There were a hundred fucking scenarios that could possibly be playing out. Karen pressed the speed dial again.

"Where are you, goddamn it, Charlie? *Come on, please....*"

Her mind flashed again to Alex and Samantha. They wouldn't have any idea. Even if word had spread to them, it wouldn't occur to them. Charlie always drove.

Karen pulled off the highway at Exit 5, Old Greenwich, and onto the Post Road. Suddenly her car phone beeped. *Thank God!* Her heart almost leaped out of her chest.

But it was only Paula, her best friend, who lived nearby in Riverside, only a few minutes away.

"You hear what's going on?" The sound of the TV was blaring in the background.

"Of course I've heard, Paula. I—"

"They're saying it was from Greenwich. There might even be people we—"

"*Paula.*" Karen interrupted her. She could barely force the words out of her mouth. "I think Charlie was on that train."

"*What?*"

Karen told her about the car and not being able to reach him. She said she was heading home and wanted to keep the lines free, in case he or his office might call.

"Of course, honey. I understand. Kar, he's going to be okay. Charlie always comes out okay. You know that, Kar, don't you?"

"I know," Karen said, though she knew she was lying to herself. "*I know.*"

Karen drove through town, her heart beating madly, then turned onto Shore Road near the sound. Then Sea Wall. Half a block down, she jerked the Lexus into her driveway. Charlie's old Mustang was pulled into the third bay of the garage, just as she'd left it an hour earlier. She ran through the garage and into the kitchen. Her hope was momentarily raised by a message light flashing on the machine. *Please* . . . she prayed to herself, and pushed the play button, her blood pulsing with alarm.

"Hey, Mrs. Friedman . . ." a dull voice came over the speaker. It was Mal, their plumber, droning on and on about the water heater she'd wanted to have fixed, about some goddamn valve he was having a bitch of a time finding. Tears ran down Karen's cheeks as her legs started to give out, and she pressed herself to the wall and sank helplessly onto the floor. Tobey wagged his way up, nuzzling into her. She mashed her tears with the palms of her hands. "Not now, baby. Please, not now. . . ."

Up on the counter, Karen fumbled for the remote. She flicked on the TV. The situation had gotten worse. Matt Lauer was on the screen—with Brian Williams now—and the reports were that there were dozens of casualties down on the tracks, that the fire was spreading and uncontained. That some of the lower part of the building had collapsed, and while they were flashing to some expert about Al Qaeda and terrorism, they split-screened to the dark cloud seeping into the Manhattan sky.

He would've called them, Karen knew, at least Heather at the office—if he was okay. Maybe even before he would've called her. That's what scared her most. She closed her eyes.

Just be okay, Charlie, wherever you are. Just be okay.

A car door slammed outside. Karen heard the doorbell ring. Someone called out her name and came running into the house.

It was Paula. She fixed on Karen huddled on the floor, in a way she had never seen her before. Paula sank down next to her, and they just hugged each other, tears glistening on each other's cheeks.

"It's gonna be okay, honey." Paula stroked Karen's hair. "I know it will. There could be hundreds of people down there. Maybe the phones aren't working. Maybe he needed some medical attention. Charlie's a survivor. If anyone's gonna get out, it's him. You'll see, baby. It's gonna be okay."

And Karen kept nodding back and repeating, "I know, I know," wiping the tears with her sleeve.

They called over and over. What else was there to do? Charlie's cell phone. His office. Maybe thirty, forty times.

At some point Karen even sniffled back a smile. "You know how mad Charlie gets when I bug him at the office?"

By nine forty-five they had settled onto the couch in the family room. That's when they heard the car pull up and more doors slamming. Alex and Samantha burst in through the kitchen with a shout. *"School's closed!"*

They stuck their heads into the TV room. "You heard what happened?" Alex said.

Karen could barely answer. The sight of them struck terror in her heart. She told them to sit down. They could see that her face was raw and worried. That something was terribly wrong was written all over it.

Samantha sat down across from her. "Mom, what's wrong?"

"Daddy took the car in this morning," Karen said, "for service."

"*So?*"

Karen swallowed back a lump, or she was sure she would start to cry. "Afterward," she paused, "I think he went into the city by train."

Both kids' eyes went wide and followed hers, as if drawn, to the wide screen.

"*He's there?*" her son asked. "*At Grand Central?*"

"I don't know, baby. We haven't heard from him. That's what's so worrisome. He called and said he was on the train. That was eight thirty-four. This happened at eight forty-one. I don't know. . . ."

Karen was trying so hard to appear positive and strong, trying with all her heart not to alarm them, because she knew with that same unflinching certainty that any moment Charlie would call, tell them he had made it out, that he was okay. So she didn't even feel the trail of tears carving its way down her cheeks and onto her lap, and Samantha staring at her, jaw parted, about to cry herself. And Alex—her poor, macho Alex, white as parchment—eyes glued to the horrifying plume of smoke elevating into the Manhattan sky.

For a while no one said a word. They just stared, all in their own world between denial and hope. Sam, arms hung loosely around her brother's neck, her chin resting nervously on his shoulder. Alex, grasping Karen's hand for the first time in years, watching, waiting for their father's face to emerge. Paula, elbows on knees, poised to shout and point, *Look, there he is!* Jump up in glee. Waiting with all the certainty in the world to hear the phone she was sure was about to ring.

Alex turned to Karen. "Dad's gonna make it out of there? Isn't he, Mom?"

"Of course he is, baby." Karen squeezed his hand. "You know your father. If anyone will, it's him. He'll make it out."

That was when they heard a rumble. On the screen the camera shook from another muffled explosion. Onlookers gasped and screamed as a fresh cloud of dense black smoke emerged from the station.

Samantha wailed, "*Oh, God . . .*"

Karen felt her stomach fall. She cupped Alex's fist tightly and squeezed. "Oh, Charlie, Charlie, Charlie . . ."

"Secondary explosions . . ." muttered a fire chief coming out of the station, his head shaking with a kind of finality. "There are many, many bodies down there. We can't even get our people close."

CHAPTER SEVEN

Around noon

When the call came in, Hauck was on the phone with the NYPD's Emergency Management Office in the city.

Possible 634. Leaving the scene of an accident. *West Street and the Post Road.*

All morning long he'd kept a close tab on the mess going on in the city. Panicked people had been calling in all day, unable to reach their loved ones, not knowing what else to do. When the Trade Towers were hit, he'd been working for the department's Office of Information, and it had been his job for weeks afterward to track down the fates of people unaccounted for—through the hospitals, the wreckage, the network of first responders. Hauck still had friends down there. He stared at the list of Greenwich names he'd taken down: Pomeroy. Bashtar. Grace. O'Connor.

The first time around, out of the hundreds unaccounted for, they had found only two.

"Possible 634, Ty!" the day sergeant buzzed in a second time. Hit and Run. Down on the Post Road, by West Street, near the fast-food outlets and car dealerships.

"Can't," Hauck said back to her. "Get Muñoz on it. I'm on something."

"Muñoz is already on the scene, Lieutenant. It's a homicide. It seems you got a body down there."

It took only minutes for Hauck to grab his Grand Corona out of the lot outside, shoot straight up Mason, his top hat flashing, to the top of the avenue by the Greenwich Office Park, then down the Post Road to West Street, across from the Acura dealership.

As he was the head of Violent Crimes in town, this was his call. Mostly his department broke up spats at the high school, the occasional report of a break-in, marital rows. Dead bodies were rare up here in Greenwich.

Stock fraud was a lot more common.

At the bottom of the avenue, four local blue-and-whites had blocked off the busy commercial thoroughfare, their lights ablaze. Traffic was being routed into one lane. Hauck slowed, nodding to a couple of patrolmen he recognized. Freddy Muñoz, one of the detectives on his staff, came over as Hauck got out.

"You gotta be kidding, Freddy." Hauck shook his head in disbelief. "Today of all days . . ."

The detective made a grim motion toward a covered mound in the middle of West Street, which intersected the Post Road and cut up to Railroad Avenue and I-95.

"It look like we're kidding, LT?"

The patrol cars had parked in a way that formed sort of a protective circle around the body. An EMS truck had arrived, but the tech was standing around waiting for the regional medical team out of Farmington. Hauck knelt and peeled back the plastic tarp.

Christ! His cheeks puffed out a blast of air.

The guy was just a kid—twenty-two, twenty-three at most—white, wearing a brown work uniform, long red locks braided in cornrows in the manner of a Jamaican *rasta*. His body was twisted so that his hips were swung over slightly and raised off the pavement, while his back was flat, face upward. The eyes were open, wide, the moment of impact still frozen in their pupils. A trickle of blood ran onto the pavement from the corner of the victim's mouth.

"You got a name?"

"Raymond. First name Abel. Middle name John. Went by AJ, his boss at the auto-customizing shop over there said. That's where he worked."

A young uniformed officer was standing nearby with a notepad. His nameplate read STASIO. Hauck assumed he'd been first on the scene.

"He was just off-shift," Muñoz said. "Said he was going out to buy some smokes and make a call." He pointed across the street. "Seems like he was headed into the diner over there."

Hauck glanced over to a place he knew called the Fairfield Diner, an occasional police hangout. He'd grabbed a meal there a couple of times himself.

"What do we know about the car?"

Muñoz called over Officer Stasio, who looked about a month removed from training, and who read, a little nervously, from his spiral pad. "It appears like the hit-car was a white SUV, Lieutenant. It was traveling north up the Post Road and turned sharply onto West Street here. . . . Ran into the vic just as he was crossing the street. We got two eyewitnesses who saw the whole thing."

Stasio pointed to two men, one stocky, sport coat, mustached, sitting in the front seat of an open patrol car rubbing his hair. The other in a blue fleece top talking to another officer, somberly shaking his head. "We located one in the parking lot of the Arby's over there. An ex-cop, it turns out. The other came from the bank across the street."

The kid had put it together pretty good. "Good work, Stasio."

"Thank you, sir."

Hauck slowly raised himself up, his knees cracking. A parting gift from his football days.

He looked back at the rutted gray asphalt on West Street—the two extended streaks of rubber about twenty feet farther along than the victim's cell phone and glasses. Skid marks. Well past the point of impact. Hauck sucked in an unpleasant breath, and his stomach shifted.

Son of a bitch hadn't even tried to stop.

He looked over at Stasio. "You doin' okay, son?" That this was the young officer's first fatality was plainly written all over his face.

Stasio nodded back. "Yessir."

"Never easy." Hauck patted the young patrolman on the shoulder. "That's true for any of us."

"Thank you, Lieutenant."

Hauck pulled Muñoz aside. He guided his detective's eye along the Post Road south, the route that the hit-car traveled, then in the direction of the tire marks on the pavement.

"Seeing what I'm seeing, Freddy?"

The detective nodded grimly. "Bastard never made a move to stop."

"Yeah." Hauck pulled out a latex glove from his jacket pocket and threaded it over his fingers.

"Okay." He knelt back down to the inert body. "Let's see what she says. . . ."

Hauck lifted Abel Raymond's torso just enough to remove a black wallet from the victim's trouser pocket. A Florida driver's license: Abel John Raymond. There was also a laminated photo ID from Seminole Junior College, dating back two years. Same bright-eyed grin as on the license, hair a little shorter. Maybe the kid had dropped out.

There was a MasterCard in his name, a card from Sears, others from Costco, ExxonMobil, Social Security. Forty-two dollars in cash. A ticket stub from the 1996 Orange Bowl. Florida State–Notre Dame. Hauck recalled the game. From out of the wallet's divider he unfolded a snapshot of an attractive dark-haired woman who appeared to be in her twenties holding a young boy. Hauck handed it up to Muñoz.

"Doesn't look like a sister." The detective shrugged. The victim wasn't wearing a wedding ring. "Girlfriend, maybe."

They'd have to track down who it was.

"*Someone's* not going to be very happy tonight." Freddy Muñoz sighed.

Hauck tucked the photo back into the wallet and exhaled. "Long list, I'm afraid, Freddy."

"It's crazy, isn't it, Lieutenant?" Muñoz shook his head. He was no longer talking about the accident. "You know my wife's brother took in the 7:57 this morning. Got out just before it happened. My sister-in-law was going crazy. She couldn't reach him till he got into the office. You roll over in bed for a few more minutes, get stuck at a light, miss your train. . . . You know how lucky he is?"

Hauck thought of the list of names back on his desk, the nervous, hopeful voices of those who had called in about them. He glanced over to Stasio's witnesses.

"C'mon, Freddy, let's get an ID on that car."

CHAPTER EIGHT

Hauck took the guy in the sport jacket, Freddy the North Face fleece.

Hauck's turned out to be a retired cop from South Jersey, name of Phil Dietz. He claimed he was up here cold-canvassing for state-of-the-art security systems—"You know, 'smart' homes, thumb-print, ID sensors, that sort of thing"—which he'd been handling since turning in the badge three years before. He had just pulled into the Arby's up the street to grab a sandwich when he saw the whole thing.

"He came down the street moving pretty good," Dietz said. He was short, stocky, graying hair a little thin on top, with a thick mustache, and he moved his stubby hands excitedly. "I heard the engine pick up. He accelerated down the street and made this turn *there*." He pointed toward the intersection of West Street and the Post Road. "SOB hit that kid without even touching the brakes. I didn't see it until it was too late."

"Can you give me a make on the car?" Hauck asked.

Dietz nodded. "It was a white late-model SUV. A Honda or an Acura, I think, something like that. I could look at some pictures. Plates were white, too—I think blue lettering, or maybe green." He shook his head. "Too far away. My eyes aren't what they were when I was on the job." He jiggled a set of reading glasses in his breast pocket. "Now all I have to do is to be able to read POs."

Hauck smiled, then made a notation on his pad. "Not local?"

Dietz shook his head. "No. Maybe New Hampshire or Massachusetts. Sorry, I couldn't get a solid read. The bastard stopped for a second—*after.* I yelled, 'Hey, you!' and started to run down the hill. But he just took off up the road. I tried to grab a picture with my cell phone, but it happened too fast. He was gone."

Dietz pointed up the hill, toward the heights of Railroad Avenue. West Street went into a curve as it bent past an open lot, an office building. Once you were up there, I-95 was only a minute or two away. Hauck knew they'd have to be lucky if anyone up there saw him.

He turned back to the witness. "You said you heard the engine accelerate?"

"That's right. I was stepping out of my car. Thought I'd kill some time before my next appointment." Dietz pressed his interlocked hands around the back of his head. "Cold calls . . . Don't ever quit."

"I'll try not to." Hauck grinned, then redirected him, motioning south. "It was coming from down there? You were able to follow it before it turned?"

"Yup. It caught my eyes as it sped up." Dietz nodded.

"The driver was male?"

"Definitely."

"Any chance you caught a description?"

He shook his head. "After the vehicle stopped, the guy looked back for an instant through the glass. Maybe had a second thought at what he'd done. I couldn't get a read on his face. Tinted windows. Believe me, I wish I had."

Hauck looked back up the hill and followed what he imagined was the victim's path. If he worked at J&D Tint and Rims, he'd have to walk across West Street, then cross the Post Road at the light to get to the diner.

"You say you used to be on the force?"

"Township of Freehold." The witness's eyes lit up. "South Jersey. Near Atlantic City. Twenty-three years."

"Good for you. So what I'm going to ask you, Mr. Dietz, you may understand. Did you happen to notice if the vehicle was traveling at a consistently high rate of speed prior to making the turn? Or did it speed up as the victim stepped into the street?'

"You're trying to decide if this was an accident or intentional?" The ex-cop cocked his head.

"I'm just trying to get a picture of what took place," Hauck replied.

"I heard him from up there." Dietz pointed up the block toward the Arby's. "He shot down the hill, then spun into the turn—

outta control. To me it was like he must've been drunk. I don't know, I just looked up when I heard the impact. He dragged the poor kid's body like a sack of wheat. You can still see the marks. Then he stopped. I think the kid was underneath him at that point, before he sped away."

Dietz said he'd be happy to look at some photos of white SUVs, to try to narrow down the make and model. "You find this SOB, Lieutenant. Anything I can do, you let me know. I wanna be the hammer that drives the nail into his coffin."

Hauck thanked him. Not as much to go on as he would have liked. Muñoz stepped over. The guy he'd been talking to saw the incident from across the street. A track coach from up in Wilton, twenty miles away. Hodges. He identified the same white vehicle and same out-of-state plates. "AD or something. Maybe eight . . ." He was just stepping out of the bank after using the ATM. It had happened so quickly that he, too, couldn't get much of a read. He gave roughly the same sketchy picture Dietz had of what had taken place.

Muñoz shrugged, disappointed. "Not a whole lot to go on, is it, Lieutenant?"

Hauck pressed his lips in frustration. "No."

He went back to his car and called in an APB. A white late-model SUV driven by a white male, "possibly Honda or Acura, possibly Massachusetts or New Hampshire plates, possibly beginning AD8. Likely front-end body damage." They'd put it out to the state police and the auto-repair shops all over the Northeast. They'd canvass people farther up along West Street to see if anyone spotted him racing by. There might be some speed-control cameras along the highway. That was their best hope.

Unless, of course, it turned out someone had it in for Abel Raymond.

There was a guy in a Yankees cap standing nearby, huddled against the chill. Stasio brought him over. Dave Corso, the owner of the auto custom shop where AJ Raymond worked.

"He was a good kid." Corso shook his head, visibly distressed. "He'd been working with me for about a year. He was talented. He remodeled old cars himself. He was up from Florida."

Hauck recalled his license. "You know where?"

The body-shop owner shrugged. "I don't know. Tallahassee, Pensacola . . . He always wore these T-shirts, the Florida State Seminoles. I think he took everyone out for a beer when they won that college bowl last year. I think his father was a sailor or something down there."

"You mean like in the navy?"

"No. Tugboat or something. He had his picture tacked up on the board. It's still inside."

Hauck nodded. "Where did Mr. Raymond live?"

"Up in Bridgeport, I'm pretty sure. I know we have it on file inside, but you know how it is—things change. But I know he banked over at First City. . . ." He told them that AJ got this call, maybe twenty minutes before he left. He was in the middle of doing this tinting. Then he came and said he was going on early break. "Marty something, I think the guy said. AJ said he was going across the street to grab some smokes. The diner, I think. It has a machine." Corso glanced over at the covered mound in the street. "Then *this* . . . How the hell do you figure?"

Hauck removed the victim's wallet from out of a bag and showed Corso the photo of the girl and her son. "Any idea who this is?"

The auto-body manager shrugged. "I think he had some gal up there. . . . Or maybe Stamford. She picked him up here once or twice. Lemme look. . . . Yeah, I think that's her. AJ was into working on classic cars. You know, restoring them. Corvettes, LeSabres, Mustangs. I think he'd just been up at a show this past weekend. *Man . . .*"

"Mr. Corso." Hauck took the man aside. "Is there anyone you can think of who'd possibly want to do Mr. Raymond harm? Did he have debts? Did he gamble? Do drugs? Anything you can think of would help."

"You're thinking this wasn't an accident?" The victim's employer's eyes widened in surprise.

"Just doing our job," Muñoz said.

"Jeez, I don't know. To me he was just a solid kid. He showed up. Did his job. People liked him here. But now that you mention it, this gal . . . I think she was married or recently split up from her husband. I know somewhere back I heard AJ mention he was having trouble with her ex. Maybe Jackie would know. Inside. He was closer to him."

Hauck nodded. He signaled to Muñoz to follow that up.

"While we're in there, Mr. Corso, you mind if we check where the phone call he received came from, too?"

There was something in Hauck's gut that wasn't sitting well about this.

He went out to the side of the road, looking back down the knoll to the accident site. It was visible—clearly. The West Street turnoff. Nothing obstructing the view. The assailant's car hadn't slowed. It hadn't made a move to stop or avoid him. A DUI would have had to have been drop-dead out of his gourd on a Monday at noon to have hit this kid head-on.

The medical team from upstate had finally arrived. Hauck went back down the hill. He picked up the victim's cell phone. He'd check the recently dialed numbers. It wouldn't surprise him if the number that had called in would be traced to the same guy.

Things like this often worked that way.

Hauck knelt over Abel Raymond's body a last time, taking a good look at the kid's face. *I'm gonna find out for you, son,* he vowed. His thoughts flashed back to the bombing. There were a lot of people in town who weren't going to be coming home tonight. This would only be one. But this one he could do something about.

This one—Hauck stared at the locks of long red hair, the ache of a long-untended wound rising up inside him—this one had a face.

As he was about to get up, Hauck checked the victim's pockets a final time. In the guy's trousers, he found some change, a gas receipt. Then he reached into the chest pocket under the embroidered patch that bore his initials. AJ.

He poked his finger around and brought out a yellow scrap of paper, a standard Post-it note. It had a name written on it with a number, a local phone exchange.

It could've been the person AJ Raymond was on his way to meet. Or it could've been in there for weeks. Hauck dropped it in the evidence bag with the other things he had pulled, one more link to check out.

Charles Friedman.

CHAPTER NINE

I never heard from my husband again. I never knew what happened.

The fires raged underground in Grand Central for most of the day. There'd been a powerful accelerant used in the blast. Four blasts. One in each of the first two cars of the 7:51 out of Greenwich, exploding just as it came to a stop. The others in trash baskets along the platform packed with a hundred pounds of hexagen, enough to bring a good-sized building down. A splinter cell, they said. Over Iraq. Can you imagine? Charlie hated the war in Iraq. They found names, pictures of the station, traces of chemicals where the bombs were made. The fire that burned there for most of two days had reached close to twenty-three hundred degrees.

We waited. We waited all day that first day to hear something. Anything. Charlie's voice. A message from one of the hospitals that he was there. It seemed like we called the whole world: the NYPD, the hotline that had been set up. Our local congressman, whom Charlie knew.

We never did.

One hundred and eleven people died. That included three of the bombers, who, they suspected, were in the first two cars. Where Charlie always sat. Many of them couldn't even be identified. No distinguishable remains. They just went to work one morning and disappeared from the earth. That was Charlie. My husband of eighteen years. He just yelled good-bye over the hum of the hair dryer and went to take in the car.

And disappeared.

What they did find was the handle of the leather briefcase the kids had given him last year—the charred top piece still attached, blown clear from the blast site, the gold-embossed monogram, CMF, which made it final for the first time and brought our tears.

Charles Michael Friedman.

Those first days I was sure he was going to crawl out of that mess. Charlie could pull himself out of anything. He could fall off the damn roof trying to fix the satellite and he'd land on his feet. You could just count on him so much.

But he didn't. There was never a call, or a piece of his clothing, even a handful of ashes.

And I'll never know.

I'll never know if he died from the initial explosion or in the flames. If he was conscious or if he felt pain. If he had a final thought of us. If he called out our names.

Part of me wanted one last chance to take him by the shoulders and scream, "How could you let yourself die in there, Charlie?" How?

Now I guess I have to accept that he's gone. That he won't be coming back. Though it's so effing hard. . . .

That he'll never get to drive Samantha to college that first time. Or watch Alex score a goal. Or see the people they become. Things that would have made him so proud.

We were going to grow old together. Sail off to that Caribbean cove. Now he's gone, in a flash.

Eighteen years of our lives.

Eighteen years . . .

And I don't even get to kiss him good-bye.

CHAPTER TEN

A few days later—Friday, Saturday, Karen had lost track—a police detective came by the house.

Not from the city. People from the police in New York and the FBI had been by a few times trying to trace Charlie's movements that day. This one was local. He called ahead and asked if he could talk with Karen for just a few moments on a matter unrelated to the bombing. She said sure. Anything that helped take her mind off things for a few moments was a godsend to her now.

She was in the kitchen arranging flowers that had come in from one of the outfits that Charlie cleared through when he stopped by.

Karen knew she looked a mess. She wasn't exactly keeping up appearances right now. Her dad, Sid, who was up from Atlanta and who was being very protective of her, brought him in.

"I'm Lieutenant Hauck," he said. He was nicely dressed, for a cop, in a tweed sport jacket and slacks and a tasteful tie. "I saw you at the meeting in town Monday night. I'll only take a few moments of your time. I'm very sorry for your loss."

"Thank you." Karen nodded and pushed her hair back as they sat down in the sunroom, trying to shift the mood with an appreciative smile.

"My daughter's not feeling so well," her father cut in, "so maybe, whatever it is you have to go over . . ."

"Dad, I'm fine." She smiled. She rolled her eyes affectionately, then caught the lieutenant's gaze. "It's okay. Let me talk to the policeman."

"Okay, okay," he said. "I'm out here. If you need me . . ." He went back into the TV room and shut the door.

"He doesn't know what to do," Karen said with a deep sigh. "No one does. It's tough for everyone right now."

"Thank you for seeing me," the detective said. "I won't take long." He sat across from her and took something out of his pocket. "I don't know if you heard, but there was another incident in town on Monday. A hit-and-run accident, down on the Post Road. A young man was killed."

"No, I didn't," Karen said, surprised.

"His name was Raymond. Abel John Raymond." The lieutenant handed her a photo of a smiling, well-built young man with red dreadlocks, standing next to a surfboard on the beach. "AJ, he was called. He worked in a custom-car shop here in town. He was crossing West Street when he was run over at a high speed by an SUV making a right turn. Whoever it was didn't even bother to stop. The guy dragged him about fifty feet, then took off."

"That's horrible," Karen said, staring at the face again, feeling a stab of sorrow. Whatever had happened to her, it was still a small town. It could have been anybody. Anybody's son. The same day she'd lost Charlie.

She looked back at him. "What does this have to do with me?"

"Any chance you've seen this person before?"

Karen looked again. A handsome face, full of life. The long red locks would've made it hard to forget. "I don't think so. No."

"You never heard the name Abel Raymond or maybe AJ Raymond?"

Karen stared again at the photo once again and shook her head. "I don't think so, Lieutenant. Why?"

The detective seemed disappointed. He reached back into his jacket again, this time removing a yellow slip of paper, a wrinkled Post-it note contained in a plastic bag. "We found this in the victim's work uniform, at the crime scene."

As Karen looked, she felt her insides tighten and her eyes grow wide.

"That is your husband's name, isn't it? Charles Friedman. And his cell number?"

Karen looked up, completely mystified, and nodded. "Yes. It is."

"And you're sure you never heard your husband mention his name? Raymond? He did tinting and custom painting at a car shop in town."

"*Tinting?*" Karen shook her head and smiled with her eyes. "Unless he was gearing up for some kind of midlife crisis he didn't tell me about."

Hauck smiled back at her. But Karen could see he was disappointed.

"I wish I could help you, Lieutenant. Are you thinking this was intentional, this hit-and-run?"

"Just being thorough." He took back the photo and the slip of paper with Charlie's name. He was handsome, Karen thought. In a rugged sort of way. Serious blue eyes. But something caring in them. It must have been hard for him to come here today. It was clear he wanted to do right by this boy.

She shrugged. "It's a bit of a coincidence, isn't it? Charlie's name on that paper. In that boy's pocket. The same day . . . you having to come here like this."

"A bad one"—he nodded, forcing a tight smile—"yes. I'll be out of your way." They both stood up. "If you think of anything, you'll let me know. I'll leave a card."

"Of course." Karen took it and stared at it: CHIEF OF DETECTIVES. VIOLENT CRIMES. GREENWICH POLICE DEPARTMENT.

"I'm very sorry about your husband," the lieutenant repeated.

His eyes seemed to drift to a photo she kept on the shelf. She and Charlie, dressed up formal. At her cousin Meredith's wedding. Karen always loved the way the two of them looked in that picture.

She smiled wistfully. "Eighteen years together, I don't even get to kiss him good-bye."

For a second they just stood there, she wishing she hadn't said that, he shifting on the balls of his feet, seemingly contemplating something and a little strained. Then he said, "On 9/11, I was working in the city at the NYPD's Office of Information. It was my job to try and track down people who were missing. You know, presumed to be inside the buildings, lost. It was tough. I saw a lot of families"—he wet his lips—"in this same situation. I guess all I'm trying to say is, I have a rough idea of what you're going through. . . ."

Karen felt a sting at the back of her eyes. She looked up and tried to smile, not knowing what else to say.

"You'll let me know if there's anything I can do." He took a step to the door. "I still keep a few friends down there."

"I appreciate that, Lieutenant." She walked him through the kitchen to the back door in order to avoid the crowd in front. "It's awful. I wish you luck with finding this guy. I wish I could be more help."

"You have your own things to be thinking about," he said, opening the door.

Karen looked at him. A tone of hopefulness rose in her voice. "So did anyone ever turn up? When you were looking?"

"Two." He shrugged. "One at St. Vincent's Hospital. She had been struck by debris. The other, he never even made it in to work that morning. He witnessed what happened and just couldn't go home for a few days."

"Not the best odds." Karen smiled, looking at him as if she knew what he must be thinking. "It would just be good, you know, to have something. . . ."

"My best to you and your family, Mrs. Friedman." The lieutenant opened the door. "I'm very sorry for your loss."

OUTSIDE, HAUCK STOOD a moment on the walkway.

He had hoped the name and number in AJ Raymond's pocket would prove more promising. It was pretty much all he had left.

A check of the phone records where the victim worked hadn't panned out at all. The call that he'd received—*Marty something,* the manager had said—was designated a private caller. From a cell phone. Totally untraceable now.

Nor had the girlfriend's ex. The guy turned out to be a lowlife, maybe a wife beater, but his alibi checked. He'd been at a conference at his kid's school at the time of the accident, and anyway he drove a navy Toyota Corolla, not an SUV. Hauck had double-checked.

Now all he was left with were the conflicting reports from the two eyewitnesses and his APB on the white SUVs.

Next to nothing.

It burned in him. Like AJ Raymond's red hair.

Someone out there was getting away with murder. He just couldn't prove it.

Karen Friedman was attractive, nice. He wished he could help in some way. It hurt a little, seeing the strain and uncertainty in her eyes. Knowing exactly what she would be going through. What she was going to face.

The heaviness in his heart, he knew it wasn't tied quite as closely to 9/11 victims as he'd said. But to something deeper, something never very far away.

Norah. *She'd be eight now, right?*

The thought of her came back to him with a stab, as it always did. A child in a powder blue sweatshirt and braces, playing with her sister on the pavement. A Tugboat Annie toy.

He could still hear the trill of her sweet voice. *Merrily, merrily, merrily, merrily . . .*

He could still see her red, braided hair.

A car door slammed at the curb, rocketing him back. Hauck looked up and saw a nicely dressed couple holding flowers walking up to Karen Friedman's front door.

Something caught his eye.

One of the garage doors had been opened in the time since he'd arrived. A housekeeper was lugging out a bag of trash.

There was a copper-colored Mustang parked in one of the bays—'65 or '66, he guessed. A convertible. A red heart decal on the rear fender and a white racing stripe running down the side.

The license plate read CHRLYS BABY.

Hauck went over and knelt, running his hand along the smooth chrome trim.

Son of a bitch . . .

That's what AJ Raymond did! He restored old cars. For a second it almost made Hauck laugh out loud. He wasn't sure how it made him feel, disappointed or relieved, the last of his leads slipping away.

Still, he decided, heading back across the driveway to his car, at least he now knew what the guy was doing with Charles Friedman's number.

CHAPTER ELEVEN

Pensacola, Florida

The huge gray tanker emerged from the mist and cut its engines at the mouth of the harbor.

The shadows of heavy industry: steel-gray trestles, the refinery tanks, the gigantic hydraulic pumps awaiting gas and oil, all lay quiet in the vessel's approach.

A single launch motored out to meet it.

At the helm the pilot, who was called Pappy, fixed on the waiting ship. As assistant harbormaster, Pensacola Port Authority, his job was to guide the football-field-size craft through the sandy limestone shoals around Singleton Point and then through the busy lanes of the inner harbor, which bustled with commercial traffic as the day wore on. He'd been bringing home large ships like this since he was twenty-two, a job—more like a rite, handed down from his own father, who had done it himself since *he* was twenty-two. For close to thirty years, Pappy had done this so many times he could pretty much guide home a ship in his sleep, which in the darkened calm before the dawn this morning—if it were a normal morning and this just another tanker—would be exactly what he was about to do.

She's tall there, Pappy noted, focused on the ship's hull.

Too tall. The draft line was plainly visible. He stared at the logo on the tanker's bow.

He'd seen these ships before.

Normally the real skill lay in gauging what the large tanker was drawing and navigating it through the sandbars at the outer rim of the harbor. Then simply follow the lanes, which by 10:00 A.M. could be livelier than the loop into downtown, and make the wide, sweeping arc into Pier 12, which was where the *Persephone,* according to its papers carrying a full load of Venezuelan crude, was slotted to put in.

But not this morning.

Pappy's launch approached the large tanker from the port side. As he neared, he focused on the logo of a leaping dolphin on the *Persephone*'s hull.

Dolphin Oil.

He scratched a weathered hand across his beard and scanned over his entry papers from Maritime Control: 2.3 million barrels of crude aboard. The ship had made the trip up from Trinidad in barely fourteen hours. *Fast,* Pappy noted, especially for an out-dated 1970 ULCC-class piece of junk like this, weighed down with a full load.

They always made it up here fast.

Dolphin Oil.

The first time he'd just been curious. It had come in from Jakarta. He had wondered, how could a ship loaded with slime be riding quite that high? The second time, just a few weeks back, he'd actually snuck below after it docked—inside the belly of the ship, making his way past the distracted crew, and checked out the forward tanks.

Empty. Came as no surprise. At least not to him.

Clean as a newborn's ass.

He'd brought this up to the harbormaster, not once but twice. But he just patted Pappy on the back like he was some old fool and asked him what his plans were when he retired. This time, though, no glorified paper pusher was going to slip this under a stack of forms. Pappy knew people. People who worked in the right places. People who'd be interested in this kind of thing. This time, when he brought the ship in, he'd prove it.

2.3 million barrels . . .

2.3 million barrels, my ass.

Pappy sounded the horn and pulled the launch along the ship's bow. His mate, Al, took over the wheel. A retractable gangway was lowered from the main deck. He prepared to board.

That's when his cell phone vibrated. He grabbed it off his belt. It was 5:10 in the morning. Anyone not insane was still asleep. The screen read PRIVATE. Text message.

Some kind of picture coming through.

Pappy yelled forward to Al to hold it and jumped back from

the *Persephone*'s gangway. In the predawn light, he squinted at the image on the screen.

He froze.

It was a body. Twisted and contorted on the street. A dark pool beneath the head that Pappy realized was blood.

He brought the screen closer and tried to find the light.

"Oh, Lord God, no . . ."

His eyes were seized by the image of the victim's long red dreadlocks. His chest filled up with pain as if he'd been stabbed. He fell back, an inner vice cracking his ribs.

"Pappy!" Al called back from the bridge. "You all right there?"

No. He wasn't all right.

"That's Abel," he gasped, his airways closing. *"That's my son!"*

Suddenly, he felt the vibration of another message coming through.

Same: PRIVATE NUMBER.

This time it was just three words that flashed on the screen.

Pappy ripped open his collar and tried to breathe. But it was sorrow knifing at him there, not a heart attack. And anger—at his own pride.

He sank to the deck, the three words flashing in his brain.

SEEN ENOUGH NOW?

CHAPTER TWELVE

A month later—a few days after they'd finally held a memorial for Charlie, Karen trying to be upbeat, but it was so, so hard—the UPS man dropped off a package at her door.

It was during the day. The kids were at school. Karen was getting ready to leave. She had a steering-committee meeting at the kids' school. She was trying as best she could to get back to some kind of normal routine.

Rita, their housekeeper, brought it in, knocking on the bedroom door.

It was a large padded envelope. Karen checked out the sender. The label said it was from a Shipping Plus outlet in Brooklyn. No return name or address. Karen couldn't think of anyone she knew in Brooklyn.

She went into the kitchen and took a package blade and opened the envelope. Whatever was inside was protected in bubble wrap, which Karen carefully slit open. Curious, she lifted out the contents.

It was a frame. Maybe ten by twelve inches. Chrome. Someone had gone to a lot of trouble.

Inside the frame was what appeared to be a page from some kind of notepad, charred, dirt marks on it, torn on the upper right edge. There were a bunch of random numbers scratched all over it, and a name.

Karen felt her breath stolen away.

The page read *From the desk of Charles Friedman.*

The writing on it was Charlie's.

"Ees a gift?" asked Rita, picking up the wrappings.

Karen nodded, barely able to even speak. "*Yes.*"

She took it into the sunroom and sat with it on the window seat, rain coming down outside.

It was her husband's notepad. The stationery Karen had given him herself a few years back. The sheet was torn. The numbers didn't make sense to her and the name scrawled there was one Karen didn't recognize. Megan Walsh. A corner of it was charred. It looked as if it had been on the ground for a long time.

But it was Charlie—his writing. Karen felt a tingling sensation all over.

There was a note taped to the frame. Karen pulled it off. It read: *I found this, three days after what happened, in the main terminal of Grand Central. It must have floated there. I held on to it, because I didn't know if it would hurt or help. I pray it helps.*

It was unsigned.

Karen couldn't believe it. On the news she'd heard there were thousands of papers blown all over the station after the explosion. They had settled everywhere. Like confetti after a parade.

Karen fixed intently on Charlie's writing. It was just a bunch of meaningless numbers and a name she didn't recognize, scribbled at odd angles. Dated 3/22, weeks before his death. A bunch of random messages, no doubt.

But it was from Charlie. His writing. It was a part of him the day he died.

They had never given her back the piece of his briefcase they'd recovered. This was all she had. Holding it to her, for a moment it was almost as if she felt him there.

Her eyes filled up with tears. "Oh, Charlie . . ."

In a way it was like he was saying good-bye.

I didn't know if it would hurt or help, the sender had written.

Oh, yes, it helps. It more than helps. . . . Karen held it close. *A thousand times more.*

It was just a jumble of stupid numbers and a name scratched out in his hand. But it was all she had.

She hadn't been able to cry at his memorial. Too many people. Charlie's blown-up photo looming above them. And they all wanted it to be upbeat, not sad. She'd tried to be so strong.

But there, sitting by the window, her husband's writing pressed against her heart, she felt it was okay. *I'm here with you, Charlie,* Karen thought. She finally let herself really cry.

CHAPTER THIRTEEN

Down the street a man hunched in a darkened car, rain streaming on the windshield. He smoked as he watched the house and cracked the window a shade to flick the ashes onto the street.

The UPS truck had just left. He knew that what it brought would send things spinning. A short while later, Karen Friedman rushed out, a rain jacket over her head, and climbed into her Lexus.

Things promised to get interesting.

She backed out of the driveway and onto the street, reversed, and headed back toward him. The man hunched lower in the car, the Lexus's headlights hitting his windshield, glistening sharply in the rain as it went by.

Hybrid, he noted, impressed, watching in the rearview mirror as it went down the block.

He picked up his phone, which was sitting on the passenger seat across from him, next to his Walther P38, punching in a private number. His gaze fell to his hands. They were thick, coarse, workman's hands.

Time to get them dirty again, he sighed.

"Plan A doesn't seem to be moving," he said into the phone when the voice he was expecting finally answered.

"We don't have forever," the person on the other end replied.

"Exactamente." He exhaled. He started his ignition, flicked an ash out the window, and took off at a slow pace, following the Lexus. "I'm already on Plan B."

CHAPTER FOURTEEN

One of the things Karen had to deal with in the weeks that followed was the liquidation of Charlie's firm.

She'd never gotten deeply involved in her husband's business. Harbor was what was termed "a general limited partnership." The share agreement maintained that in case the principal partner ever became deceased or unable to perform, the assets of the firm were to be redistributed back to the other partners. Charlie managed a modest-size fund, with assets of around $250 million. The lead investors were Goldman Sachs, where he had started out years before, and a few wealthy families he'd attracted over the years.

Saul Lennick, Charlie's first boss at Goldman, who had helped put him in business, acted as the firm's trustee.

It was hard for Karen to go through. Bittersweet. Charlie had only seven people working for him: a junior trader and a bookkeeper, Sally, who ran the back office and had been with him since he'd first opened shop. His assistant, Heather, handled a lot of their personal stuff. Karen pretty much knew them all.

It would take a few months, Lennick advised her, for everything to be finalized. And that was fine with her. Charlie would've wanted them all to be well taken care of. "Hell, you know better than anyone that he practically spent more time with them over the years than he did with me," she said, smiling knowingly at Saul. Anyway, money wasn't exactly the issue right now.

She and the kids were okay financially. She had the house, which they owned clear, the ski place in Vermont. Plus, Charlie had been able to pull out some money over the years.

But it was tough, seeing his baby dismantled. The positions were sold. The office on Park Avenue was put up for lease. One by one, people found new jobs and began to leave.

That was like the final straw. The final imprint of him gone.

About that time the junior trader Charlie had brought into the firm just a few months before, Jonathan Lauer, called her at home. Karen wasn't around. He left a message on her machine: "I'd like to speak with you, Mrs. Friedman. At your convenience. There are some things you ought to know."

Some things . . . Whatever they were, she wasn't up to it right then. Jonathan was new; he had started working for Charles only this past year. Charlie had lured him from Morgan. She passed the message on to Saul.

"Don't worry, I'll handle it," he told her. "All kinds of sticky issues, closing down a firm. People are looking out for their own arrangements. There may have been some bonus agreements discussed. Charlie wasn't the best at recording those things. You shouldn't have to deal with any of that right now."

He was right. She *couldn't* deal with that right now. In July she went away for a well-needed week at Paula and Rick's house in Sag Harbor. She rejoined her book group, started doing yoga again. God, how she needed that. Her body began to resemble itself once again and feel alive. Gradually her spirits did, too.

August came, and Samantha had a job at a local beach club. Alex was away at lacrosse camp. Karen was thinking maybe she'd look into getting a real-estate license.

Jonathan Lauer contacted her again.

This time Karen was at home. Still, she didn't pick up. She heard the same cryptic message on the machine: "Mrs. Friedman, I think it's important that we talk. . . ."

But Karen just let the message tape go on. She didn't like avoiding him. Charlie had always spoken highly of the young man. *People are looking out for their own arrangements. . . .*

She just couldn't answer. Hearing his voice trail off, she felt bad.

CHAPTER FIFTEEN

It was September, the kids were back in school when Karen ran into Lieutenant Hauck, the Greenwich detective, again.

It was halftime of a high-school football game at Greenwich Field. They were playing Stamford West. Karen had volunteered to sell raffle tickets for the Teen Center drive for the athletic department. The stands were packed. It was a crisp, early-autumn Saturday morning. The Huskies band was on the field. She went over to the refreshment stand to grab herself a cup of coffee against the chill.

She almost didn't recognize him at first. He was dressed in a navy polar-fleece pullover and jeans, a young, pretty girl who looked no more than nine or ten to Karen hoisted on his shoulders. They sort of bumped into each other in the crowd.

"Lieutenant . . . ?"

"Hauck." He turned and stopped, a pleased glimmer in his eye.

"Karen Friedman." She nodded, shielding the sun out of her eyes.

"Of course I remember." He let the girl down. "Jess, say hi to Mrs. Friedman."

"Hi." The pretty girl waved, a little shy. "Nice to meet you."

"It's nice to meet you too, sweetie." Karen smiled. "Your daughter?"

The lieutenant nodded. "Just as well," he groaned, clutching his back, "she's getting way too big for me to do this for very long. Right, honey? Why don't you go ahead and find your friends. I'll be over in a while."

"Okay." The girl ran off and melded into the crowd, heading in the direction of the far sidelines.

"Nine?" Karen guessed, an inquisitive arch of her eyebrows.

"*Ten*. Somehow she still pushes for the Big Ride. I figure I've got another year or two at best before she'll start to cringe if I ever offer to do it again."

"Not girls and their daddies." Karen shook her head and grinned. "Anyway, it's sort of like a bell curve. At some point they come all the way back. At least that's what I'm told. *I'm* still waiting."

They stood around for a minute, bucking the flow of the crowd. A heavyset guy in a Greenwich sweatshirt slapped Hauck on the shoulder as he went by. "Hey, *Leg* . . ."

"Rollie." The lieutenant waved back.

"I was just headed to get some coffee," Karen said.

"Let me," Hauck offered. "Trust me, you won't be able to beat the price."

They stepped over to the refreshment line. A woman who was running the coffee station seemed to recognize him. "Hey, Ty! How's it going, Lieutenant? Looks like we could use you out there today."

"Yeah, just gimme about twenty of these straight up plus a shot of cortisone in both knees and you can put me in." He pulled out a couple of bills.

"On the house, Lieutenant." She waved him away. "Booster program."

"Thanks, Mary." Hauck winked back. He handed a cup to Karen. There was a table free, and Hauck motioned her toward it and they each grabbed a metal chair.

"See what I mean?" He took a sip. "One of the few legal perks I have left."

"Rank has its privilege." Karen winked, pretending to be impressed.

"Nah." Hauck shrugged. "Tailback. Greenwich High, 1975. Went all the way to the state finals that year. They never forget."

Karen grinned. She brushed her hair back from under her hooded Greenwich High sweatshirt and cupped her hands on the steaming cup.

"So how are you doing?" the detective asked. "I actually meant to call a couple of times. When I last saw you, things were pretty raw."

"I know." Karen shrugged again. "They were then. I'm doing better. Time . . ." She sighed, tilting her cup.

"As they say . . ." The lieutenant did the same and smiled. "So you have kids in the high school?"

"Two. Samantha's graduating this year. Alex is a sophomore. He plays lacrosse. He's still taking things pretty hard."

"'Course he is," the lieutenant said. Someone brushed him in the back, rushing by. He nodded, pressing his lips together. What could you say?

"You were looking into a hit-and-run then," Karen said, shifting gears. "Some kid out of Florida. You ever find that guy?"

"No. But I did find out why your husband's name was in his pocket."

He told Karen about the Mustang.

"'Charlie's Baby.'" She nodded and smiled. "Figures. Still have it. Charlie asked in his will not to sell it. How about it, Lieutenant? You want your own American icon, only year they made the color Emberglow. Only costs about eight grand a year to take it out of the garage a couple of times?"

"Sorry. I have my own American icon. College account." He grinned.

The PA announced that the teams were heading back on the field. The Huskies band marched off to a brassy version of Bon Jovi's "Who Says You Can't Go Home?" The lieutenant's daughter ran out of the crowd and yelled, "*Daddy,* come on! I want to sit with Elyse!"

"Second half's starting up," the lieutenant said.

"She's pretty," Karen said. "Oldest?"

"*My only,*" the detective replied after a short pause. "Thanks."

Their eyes met for a second. There was something Karen felt hiding behind his deep-set eyes.

"So how about a raffle ticket?" she asked. "It's for a good cause. Booster program." She chuckled. "C'mon, I'm running behind."

"I'm afraid I already paid my dues." Hauck sighed resignedly, patting his knees.

She tore one off the pad and penciled his name in the blank. "It's on the house. You know, it was nice what you said to me that day. About how you knew how I felt. I guess I needed something then. I appreciated that."

"Man . . ." Hauck shook his head, taking the raffle slip out of her hand, their fingers momentarily touching. "The gifts just don't stop coming today."

"Price you have to pay for doing a good deed, Lieutenant."

They stood up. The lieutenant's daughter called out impatiently, "Daddy, c'mon!"

"Good luck with the raffles," he said. "You know, it might be good if you actually ended up *selling* a few of them today."

Karen laughed. "Nice to see you, Lieutenant." She shook her fists like imaginary pom-poms. *"Go Huskies!"*

Hauck waved, backing into the crowd. "See you around."

CHAPTER **SIXTEEN**

It took him by surprise that night, Hauck decided as he dabbed at the canvas in the small two-bedroom home he rented on Euclid Avenue in Stamford, overlooking Holly Cove.

Another marina scene. A sloop in a harbor, sails down. Pretty much the same scene from his deck. It was all he ever painted. Boats . . .

Jessie was in her room, watching TV, sending text messages. They'd had a pizza at Mona Lisa in town and went to the new animated release. Jess pretended to be bored. He'd enjoyed it.

"It's for, like, three-year-olds, Daddy." She rolled her eyes.

"Oh." He stopped pushing it. "The penguins were cool."

Hauck liked it here. A block from the small cove. His little two-story sixties Cape. The owner had fixed it up. From the deck off the second floor, where the living room was, you could see Long Island Sound. A French couple lived next door, Richard and Jacqueline, custom furniture restorers—their workshop was out in their garage—and they always invited him to their parties, full of lots of people with crazy accents and not-half-bad wine.

Yes, it took him by surprise. What he was feeling. How he had noticed her eyes—brown and fetchingly wide. How laughter seemed a natural fit in them. The little lilt in her voice, as if she weren't from around here. Her auburn hair tied back in a youthful ponytail.

How she stuffed that raffle ticket into his pocket and tried to make him smile.

Unlike Beth. When *her* world fell apart.

Hauck traced a narrow line from the sailboat's mast and blended it into the blue of the sea. He stared. It sucked.

No one would exactly confuse him with Picasso.

She had asked him if Jess was his youngest, and he had replied, pausing for what seemed an eternity—*my only*. He could have told her. She would have understood. She was going through it, too.

C'mon, Ty, why does it always have to come back to this?

They'd had everything then. He and Beth. It was hard to remember how they were once so in love. How she once thought he was the sexiest man alive. And he, her.

My only . . .

What had he forgotten at the store that made him rush back in? Pudding Snacks. . . .

Jamming the van hastily into park. How many times had he done that—and it stayed? A thousand? *A hundred thousand?*

"Watch out, guys. Daddy's got to back out of the garage. . . ."

As he headed back to the garage, receipt in hand, wallet in hand, they heard the shriek. Jessie's.

Beth's frozen eyes—*"Oh, my God, Ty, no!"*—as through the kitchen window they watched the van roll back.

Norah never even uttered a sound.

Hauck laid down his brush. He rested his forehead on the heel of his hand. It had cost him his marriage. It had cost him ever being able to look in the mirror without starting to cry. For the longest time, being able to put his arms around Jess and hug her.

Everything.

His mind came back to that morning. The freckles dancing on her cheek. It made him smile.

Get real, Ty. . . . She probably drives a car worth more than your 401(k). She's just lost her husband. A different life, maybe.

A different time.

But it surprised him as he picked up the brush again. What he was thinking . . . what it made him feel.

Awakened.

And that was strange, he decided. Because nothing surprised him anymore.

CHAPTER SEVENTEEN

December

Their lives had just begun to get back on some kind of even keel. Sam was applying to colleges, Tufts and Bucknell, her top choices. Karen had made the obligatory visits with her.

That was when the two men from Archer knocked on her door.

"Mrs. Friedman?" the shorter one stood at the door and inquired. He had a chiseled face and close-cropped light hair, was wearing a gray business suit under a raincoat. The other was gaunt and taller with horn-rim glasses, carrying a leather lawyer's briefcase.

"We're from a private auditing firm, Mrs. Friedman. Do you mind if we come in?"

At first it flashed through Karen's mind that they might be from the government fund that was being set up for victims' families. She'd heard through her support group that these people could be pretty officious and cold. She opened the door.

"Thank you." The light-haired one had a slight European accent and handed her a card. Archer and Bey Associates. Johannesburg, South Africa. "My name is Paul Roos, Mrs. Friedman. My partner is Alan Gillespie. We won't take too much of your time. Do you mind if we sit down?"

"Of course . . ." Karen said, a little hesitant. There *was* something cool and impersonal about them. She glanced closer at their cards. "If this is about my husband, you know Saul Lennick of the Whiteacre Capital Group is overseeing the disposition of the funds."

"We've been in touch with Mr. Lennick," answered Roos, a little matter-of-factly. He took a step toward the living room. "If you wouldn't mind . . ."

She took them over to the couch.

"You have a lovely home, Mrs. Friedman," Roos told her, looking around intently.

"Thank you. You said you were auditors," Karen replied. "I think my husband was handled by someone out of the city. Ross and Weiner—I don't recall your firm's name."

"We're actually not here on behalf of your husband, Mrs. Friedman"—the South African crossed his legs—"but on the part of some of his investors."

"Investors?"

Karen knew that Morgan Stanley was Charlie's largest by far. Then came the O'Flynns and the Hazens, who had been with him since he began.

"Which ones?" Karen stared at him, puzzled.

Roos looked at her with a hesitant smile. "Just . . . *investors.*" That smile began to make Karen feel ill at ease.

His partner, Gillespie, opened his briefcase. "You received proceeds from the liquidation of your husband's firm assets, did you not, Mrs. Friedman?"

"This sounds more like an audit." Karen tightened. "Yes. Is there something wrong?" The funds had just been finalized. Charlie's share, after some final expenses to close down the firm, came to a little less than $4 million. "Maybe if you just told me what this is about."

"We're looking back through certain transactions," Gillespie said, dropping a large bound report in front of him on the coffee table.

"Look, I never got very involved at all in my husband's business," Karen answered. This was starting to make her worried. "I'm sure if you spoke to Mr. Lennick—"

"*Shortfalls,* actually," the accountant corrected himself, clear-eyed.

Karen didn't like these people. She didn't know why they were here. She peered at the business cards again. "You said you were auditors?"

"Auditors, and forensic investigators, Mrs. Friedman," Paul Roos told her.

"Investigators . . . ?"

"We're trying to piece through certain aspects of your husband's firm," Gillespie explained. "The records are proving to be a little . . . shall we call it *hazy*. We realize that as an independent hedge fund, he was not bound by certain formalities."

"Listen, I think you'd better go. I think you'd be better off if you took this to—"

"But what is clearly inescapable," the accountant continued, "is that there seems to be a considerable amount of money *missing*."

"*Missing* . . ." Karen met his eyes, holding back anger. Saul had never mentioned anything about any missing money. "That's why you're here? Well, isn't that just too bad, Mr. Gillespie? My husband's dead, as you seem to know. He went in to work one morning eight months ago and never came home again. So please, tell me"—her eyes burned through him like X-rays, and she stood up—"just how much money are we talking about, Mr. Gillespie? I'll go get my purse."

"We're speaking of two hundred and fifty million dollars, Mrs. Friedman," the accountant said. "Do you happen to keep that much in cash?"

Karen's heart almost stopped. She sat back down, the words striking her like bullets. The accountant's expression never changed.

"What the hell are you saying?"

Roos took over again, edging slightly forward. "What we're saying is that there's a hell of a lot of money unaccounted for in your husband's firm, Mrs. Friedman. And our clients want us to find out where it is."

Two hundred and fifty million. Karen was too stunned to even laugh. The proceeds had been finalized without a hitch. Charlie's entire business was barely larger than that.

She looked back into their dull, unchanging eyes. She knew they were implying something about her husband. Charlie was dead. He couldn't defend himself.

"I'm not sure we have anything further to discuss, Mr. Gillespie, Mr. Roos." Karen stood again. She wanted these men to leave. She wanted them out of her house. Now. "I told you, I never got involved in my husband's business. You'll have to address your concerns to Mr. Lennick. I'd like you to go."

The accountants looked at each other. Gillespie folded his file back into his briefcase and clasped it shut. They rose.

"We don't mean any insult, Mrs. Friedman," Roos said in a more conciliatory tone. "What I would tell you, though, is that there may well be some sort of investigation launched. I wouldn't be spending any of those proceeds you received just yet." He smiled transparently and glanced around.

"Like I said, you have a lovely home. . . . But it's only fair to warn you." He turned at the door. "Your personal accounts may have to be looked at, too."

The hairs on Karen's arms stood on edge.

CHAPTER EIGHTEEN

It took just minutes, frantic ones, for Karen to get Saul Lennick on the phone.

It was hard for his office to find him. He was out of the country, on business. But his secretary heard the agitation in Karen's voice. Finally they tracked him down.

"Karen . . . ?"

"Saul, I'm sorry to bother you." She was almost on the verge of tears. She told him about the upsetting visit she'd had with two men from Archer.

"*Who?*"

"They're from something called Archer and Bey Associates. They're auditors, forensic investigators. It's says they're out of South Africa. They said they spoke with you."

He made her go through every detail again, injecting a few sharp questions about their names and specifically what they said.

"Karen, listen. First, I want to assure you this is nothing you have to be concerned about. Harbor's partnership dissolution is moving along smoothly, and I promise you it's one hundred percent by the book. For the record, yes, Charlie may have taken a few losses at the end. He bet pretty heavily on some Canadian oil leases that took a hit."

"Who *are* these people, Saul?"

"I don't know. Some overseas accounting group, I suspect, but I'll find out. They could have been hired by some of Charles's investors over there, hoping to hold up the process."

"They're talking about hundreds of millions of dollars, Saul! You know Charlie didn't handle money like that. They were making these insinuations, warning me not to spend any of the proceeds. That's Charlie's money, Saul! It was creepy. They told me our personal accounts might be examined, too."

"That's not going to happen, Karen. Look, there are some details pending that someone could make some issues on if they wanted—"

"What kind of details, Saul?" She hadn't heard any of that before.

"Maybe some plays one could question. A glitch or two in one of Charles's lending agreements. But I don't want to get ahead of ourselves. This isn't the time."

"Charlie's dead, Saul! He can't defend himself. I mean, how many times did I hear him fretting over goddamn nickels and dimes for his clients? Fractions of a fucking point. And *these* people, making innuendos like that . . . They had no right to come here, Saul."

"Karen, I want to assure you there's no basis at all to what they're talking about. Whoever they are, they're just trying to stir up trouble. And they just went about it the wrong way."

"Yeah, Saul, they did." The fury in her blood began to recede. "They damn well did go about it the wrong way. I don't want them back in my house again. Thank God Samantha and Alex weren't here."

"Listen, I want you to fax me that card, Karen. I'll look into it from here. I promise, I'll make sure it doesn't happen again."

"Charlie was a reputable guy, Saul. You know that better than anyone."

"I know that, Karen. Charlie was like a second son to me. You realize I always have your interests at heart."

She pushed the hair off her face to cool herself down. "I do. . . ."

"Send me the card, Karen. And I want to be the first to know if they contact you again."

"Thank you, Saul."

Suddenly something strange came over Karen, an unexplainable rush of tears. Sometimes it just happened like that. Out of nowhere. The thought of having to defend her husband. She let a few seconds elapse on the line while she regained control.

"I mean it, Saul. . . . Really, thank you."

Her husband's mentor told her softly, "You don't even have to say it, Karen."

He didn't have the heart to tell her now. Or the will.

Lennick replaced the house phone in its cradle in the Old World lobby of the Vier Jahreszeiten Hotel in Munich.

A week ago his contact from the Royal Bank of Scotland had called, one of the lenders he had arranged for Charlie, who advanced his firm funds. It sounded perfunctory. The banker had a tone of slight concern.

A random check of an oil tanker by a customs official in Jakarta had reached their attention.

Lennick's heart had come to a stop. He wheeled around back to his desk. "Why?"

"Some kind of discrepancy," the banker explained, "in the stated contents of the cargo." Which was declared to have been 1.4 million barrels of oil.

The tanker was found to be empty, the bank official declared.

Lennick had turned ashen.

"I'm sure there's simply been some kind of mistake," the Scottish banker said to him. It seemed that 1.4 million barrels at sixty-six dollars per had been previously pledged by Charles Friedman as collateral against their loan.

The banker cleared his throat. "Is there any cause for alarm?"

Lennick felt a shiver of concern race down his spine. He'd look into it, he told the man, and that was enough to make the banker feel appeased. But as soon as he put down the phone, Lennick closed his eyes.

He thought of Charlie's recent losses, the pressure he'd been under. The pressure they'd all been under. How heavily he'd leveraged up on his funds.

You stupid son of a bitch, Charlie. Lennick sighed. He reached for the phone and started to dial a number. *How could you be so desperate, you fool, so careless? Don't you have any idea who these people are?*

People who didn't like to be looked into. Or have their affairs examined. Now everything had to be reconstructed. *Everything, Charlie.*

Even now, weeks later, in the Vier Jahreszeiten's lobby, the banker's all-too-delicate question made Lennick's mouth go dry.

Is there any cause for alarm?

CHAPTER NINETEEN

It was the second day of field-hockey practice, near the end of February. Sam Friedman tossed her stick into the bottom of her locker.

She played right forward for the girls' team. They'd lost a couple of their best attackers from last year, so this season it was going to be tough. Sam grabbed her parka off the hook and scanned over a few books. She had an English quiz tomorrow on a story by Tobias Wolfe, a chapter to skim on Vietnam. Since she'd gotten into Tufts, Early Decision 2 in January, she'd pretty much been coasting. Tonight a bunch of them were meeting in town at Thataways for wings and maybe sneak a beer.

Senior slump was in full throttle.

Outside, Sam ran over to her blue Acura SUV, which she'd parked in the west lot after lunch. She jumped in and tossed her bag onto the seat, and started up the engine. Then she plugged her iPod into the port and scrolled to her favorite tune.

"And I am telling you I'm not going . . . ," she sang, belting it out as closely as she could to Jennifer Hudson in *Dreamgirls.* She went to slip the Acura into drive.

That's when the hand wrapped around her mouth and jerked her head back to the headrest.

Samantha's eyes peeled back and she tried to let out a muffled scream.

"Don't make a sound, Samantha," a voice from behind her said.

Oh my God! That scared her even more, that the person knew her name. She felt a bolt of fear race down her spine, her eyes darting around, straining to glance at him in the rearview mirror.

"Uh-uh, Samantha." The assailant redirected her face forward. "Don't try to look at me. It'll be better for you that way."

How did he know her name?

This was bad. She ratcheted through a million things she had always heard in case something like this occurred. *Don't fight back. Let him do what he wants. Give him your money, jewelry, even if it's something important. Let him have his way.*

Anything.

"You're scared, Samantha, aren't you?" the man asked in a subdued voice. He had his hand wrapped tightly over her mouth, her eyes stretched wide.

She nodded.

"I don't blame you. I'd be scared, too."

She glanced outside, praying someone might come by. But it was late, and dark. The lot was empty. She felt his breath, hot on the back of her neck. She closed her eyes. *Oh, God, he's going to rape me. Or worse . . .*

"But it's your lucky day. I'm not going to hurt you, Samantha. I just want you to deliver a message to someone. Will you do that for me?"

Yes, Samantha nodded, yes. *Stay together, stay together,* she begged herself. *He's going to let you go.*

"To your mom."

My mom . . . What did her mom have to do with this?

"I want you to tell her, Sam, that the investigation is going to start very soon. And that it's going to get very personal. She'll understand. And that we're not the types to wait around patiently— forever. I think you can see that, can't you? Do you understand that, Sam?"

She shut her eyes. Shaking. Nodded.

"Good. Be sure and tell her that the clock's ticking. And she doesn't want it to run out, I can promise that. Do you hear me, Sam?" He loosened his hand just slightly from her mouth.

"*Yes,*" Sam whispered, her voice quaking.

"Now, don't look around," he said. "I'm going to slip out the back." The man had a hooded sweatshirt pulled over his face. "Trust me, the less you see, the better for you."

Samantha sat rigid. Her head moved up and down. "I understand."

"Good." The door opened. The man slipped out. She didn't look. Or turn to follow. She just sat there staring. Exactly as she was told.

"You are your father's little girl, aren't you, Sam?"

Her eyes shot wide.

"Remember about the sum. Two hundred and fifty million dollars. You tell your mom we won't wait long."

CHAPTER TWENTY

Karen clung to her daughter on the living-room couch. Samantha was sobbing, her head buried against her mother's shoulder, barely able to speak. She'd called Karen after the man had left, then driven home in a panic. Karen immediately called the police. Outside, the quiet street was ablaze in flashing lights.

Karen went through it with the first officers who'd arrived. "How could there be no protection at the school? How could they just let anyone in there?" Then to Sam, in total frustration, "Baby, how could you not have locked the car?"

"I don't know, Mom."

But inside she knew—her daughter's fingers tight and trembling, her face smeared with tears—that this wasn't about Samantha. Or more protection at school. Or locking the car door.

It was about Charlie.

This was about something he had done. Something she was growing more and more afraid that he had withheld from her.

They would have found Samantha at the mall, or at someone's house, or at the club where she worked. But they weren't trying to get to Samantha, she knew.

They were trying to get to her.

And the scariest part was, Karen had no idea what these people wanted from her.

When she spotted Lieutenant Hauck come through the front door, her body almost gave out all at once. She leaped up and ran over to him. She had to hold herself back from hugging him.

He placed a hand on her shoulder. "Is she all right?"

"Yes." Karen nodded in relief. "I think so."

"I know she's already been through it a couple of times, but I need to talk with her, too."

Karen took him over to her daughter. "Okay."

Hauck sat down on the coffee table directly across from Samantha. "Sam, my name's Lieutenant Hauck. I'm the head of detectives with the Greenwich police here in town. I know your mom a little from when your dad died. I want you to tell me exactly what took place."

Karen nodded to her, sitting next to her on the couch and taking her hand.

Sniffling back tears, Sam went through it all again. Coming out of the gym after practice, stepping into her car, putting on her iPod. The man in the backseat, completely surprising her from behind. Cupping her mouth so she couldn't scream, his voice so chilling and close to her ear that his words seemed to tingle down her spine.

"It was so scary, Mom."

Karen squeezed. "I know, baby, I know. . . ."

She told Hauck that she'd never gotten a good look at him. "He told me not to." She was certain she was about to be raped or killed.

"You did right, honey," Hauck said.

"He said that the investigation was going to start soon. And that it was going to get very personal. He said something about two hundred and fifty million dollars." Samantha looked up at Karen. *"What the hell did he mean by that, Mom?"*

Karen fitfully shook her head. "I don't know."

When they'd finished, Karen eased herself away from her daughter. She asked Hauck if he would come outside with her. The awning on the patio wasn't up yet. Still too cold. In the darkness there were lights flashing out on the sound.

"Do you have any idea what she's talking about?" he asked.

Karen drew a sharp breath and nodded. "Yes."

And no . . .

She took him through the visit she'd received. The two men from Archer and Bey, who had pressured her about all that missing money. "Two hundred and fifty million dollars," she admitted.

Now this.

"I don't know what the hell is going on." She shook her head, eyes glistening. "Charlie's trustee—he's a friend—he promises that everything in the partnership was one hundred percent by the book. And I'm sure it was. These people . . ." Karen looked at Hauck, flustered. "Charlie was a good man. He didn't handle that kind of money. It's like they've targeted the wrong person, Lieutenant. My husband had a handful of clients. Morgan Stanley, a few well-to-do families he'd known a long time."

"You understand I have to look into this," Hauck said.

Karen nodded.

"But I need to tell you that without a physical description from your daughter, it's going to be very tough. There are cameras at the school entrances. Maybe someone around spotted a car. But it was dark and pretty much deserted at that time. And whoever these people are, they're clearly professional."

Karen nodded again. "I know."

She leaned toward him, suddenly so full of questions she felt light-headed, her knees on the verge of buckling.

The lieutenant placed his hand on her shoulder. She didn't pull away.

She'd handled Charlie's death, the long months of uncertainty and loneliness, the breakup of his business. But this was too much. Tears rushed in her eyes—burning. Tears of mounting fear and confusion. The fear that her children had suddenly become involved. The fear of what she did not know. More tears started to flow. She hated this feeling. This doubt that had so abruptly sprung up about her husband. She hated these people who had invaded their lives.

"I'll make sure you have some protection," the lieutenant said, squeezing Karen's shoulder. "I'll station someone outside the house. We'll see that someone follows the kids to school for a while."

She looked at him, sucking in a tense breath. "I have this feeling that my husband might have done something, Lieutenant. In his business. Charlie always took risks, and now one of them has come back to haunt us. But he's dead. He can't untangle this for us." She wiped her eyes with the heel of her hand. "He's gone, and we're still here."

"I'll need a list of his clients," Hauck said, his hand still perched upon her shoulder.

"Okay."

"And I'll need to talk to Lennick, your husband's trustee."

"I understand." Karen pulled back, taking in a breath, trying to compose herself. Her mascara had run. She dabbed her eyes.

"I'll find something. I promise you. I'll do my best to make sure you're safe."

"Thank you, Lieutenant." She leaned against him. "For everything."

Static from her sweater rippled against his hand as he took it away.

"Listen." He smiled. "I'm not exactly a Wall Street guy. But somehow I don't think this is how Morgan Stanley goes about collecting its debts."

CHAPTER TWENTY-ONE

The call came in at eleven-thirty that night. The limo had just dropped Saul Lennick at his Park Avenue apartment, home from the opera. His wife, Mimi, was in the bathroom removing her makeup.

"Can you get that, Saul?"

Lennick had just pulled off his shoes and removed his tie. Calls this late, he knew what they were usually about. He picked up the phone in frustration. *Couldn't it wait for the morning?* "Hello."

"Saul?"

It was Karen Friedman. Her voice was cracking and upset. He knew that something was wrong. "What's happened, Karen?"

Exasperated, she told him what had happened to Samantha leaving school.

Lennick stood up. Sam was like a grandniece to him. He had been at her bat mitzvah. He had set up accounts for her, and for Alex, at his firm. Every bone in his tired body became rigid.

"Jesus, Karen, is she all right?"

"She's okay. . . ." Karen sniffed back a sob in frustration. "But . . ." She told him what the man who had accosted her said, about wanting their money. The same two hundred and fifty million dollars as before. The part about how she was her father's little girl.

"What the hell did they mean by that Saul? Was that some kind of threat?"

In his underwear and socks, Lennick sank down on the bed. His mind ran back to Charles. The avalanche he had unleashed.

You stupid son of a bitch. He shook his head and sighed.

"Something's going on, Saul. You were about to tell me something a couple of weeks back. You said it wasn't the right time. . . . Well I just put my daughter in my own bed," Karen said, her voice stiffening. "She was scared within an inch of her life. What do you think, Saul—*is it the right time now?*"

CHAPTER **TWENTY-TWO**

Archer and Bey turned out to be phony.

Just a name on a business card. A call to an old contact at Interpol and a quick scan over the Internet for companies registered in South Africa determined that. Even the address and telephone number in Johannesburg were bogus.

Someone was trying to extort her, Hauck knew. Someone familiar with her husband's dealings. Even his trustee, Lennick, whom Hauck had spoken with earlier and who appeared like a stand-up guy, agreed.

"*Incoming*, Lieutenant!"

The call rang out from the outside squad room, followed by the low, pretend *whoosh* of a mortar round exploding.

"Incoming" was how they referred to it when Hauck's ex-wife was on the line.

Hauck paused a second, phone in hand, before picking up. "Hey, Beth, how's it going?"

"I'm okay, Ty, fine. You?"

"How's Rick?"

"He's good. He just got an increase in territory. Now he's got Pennsylvania and Maryland, too." Beth's new husband was a district manager in a mortgage firm.

"That's real good. Congratulations. Jess mentioned something like that."

"It's sort of why I'm calling. We thought we'd take this long-overdue trip. You know how we've been promising Jessie we'd take her down to Orlando? The theme-park thing."

Hauck straightened. "You know I was sort of hoping she and *I* could do that together, Beth."

"Yeah, I know how you've always been saying that, Ty. But, um . . . this trip's for real."

The dig cut sharply into his ribs. But she was probably right. "So when are you planning on doing this, Beth?"

Another pause. "We were thinking about Thanksgiving, Ty."

"Thanksgiving?" This time the cut dug all the way through his intestines. "I thought we agreed Thanksgiving's mine this year, Beth. I was going to take Jess up to Boston to my sister's. To see her cousins. She hasn't been up there in a while."

"I'm sure she'd like that, Ty. But this came up. And it's Disney World."

He sniffed, annoyed. "What, does Rick have a sales conference down there then or something?"

Beth didn't answer. "It's Disney World, Ty. You can take her Christmas."

"No." He tossed his pen on his desk. "I can't take her Christmas, Beth. We discussed this. We had this planned. I'm going away Christmas." He'd made these plans to go bonefishing with a group of school buddies off the Bahamas, the first time he'd been away in a long time. "We went over this, Beth."

"Oh, yeah." She sighed as if it had somehow slipped her mind. "You're right. I remember now."

"Why not ask Jess?"

"Ask Jess what, Ty?"

"Ask her where *she'd* like to go."

"I don't have to ask her, Ty. I'm her mother."

He was about to snap back, *Goddamn it, Beth, I'm her father,* but he knew where that would lead.

"We actually sort of already booked the tickets, Ty. I'm sorry. I really didn't call you to fight."

He let out a long, frustrated exhale. "You know she likes it up there, Beth. With her cousins. They're expecting us. It's good for her now—for her to see them once or twice a year."

"I know, Ty. You're right. Next time, I promise, she will." Another pause. "Listen, I'm glad you understand."

They hung up. He swiveled around in his chair, his eyes settling on the picture of Jessie and Norah he kept on the credenza. Five and three. A year before the accident. All smiles.

It was hard to remember they had once been in love.

There was a knock against Hauck's office door, startling him. *"Hey, Loo!"*

It was Steve Christofel, who handled bunko and fraud.

"What, Steve?"

The detective shrugged, apologetic, notepad in hand. "You want me to come back, boss? Maybe this isn't a good time."

"No, it's fine. Come on in." Hauck swiveled back around, mad at himself. "Sorry. You know the routine."

"Always something, right? But, hey, Lieutenant, you mind if I see that case file you always keep in here?"

"Case file?"

"You know, the one you always keep hidden on your desk over there." The detective grinned. "That old hit-and-run thing. *Raymond.*"

"Oh, that." Hauck shrugged as if exposed. He always kept it buried under a stack of open cases. Not forgotten, not for a second. Just not solved. He lifted the stack and fished out the yellow case file from the bottom. "What's going on?"

"My memory's a little fuzzy, Lieutenant, but wasn't there a name that was connected to it somewhere? Marty something?"

Hauck nodded.

The person who had called up AJ Raymond at the shop, just before he'd left to cross the street. *Something like Marty,* his boss had said. It had just never led anywhere.

"Why?"

"This wire just came in." Christofel came around and placed his notepad on Hauck's desk. "Some credit-card-fraud division has been trying to chase it down after all this time. An Amex card belonging to a Thomas *Mardy*—that's M-A-R-D-Y—was used to pay for a limo ride up to Greenwich. Dropped him off at the Fairfield Diner at a little before noon, Lieutenant. April ninth."

Hauck looked up, his blood starting to course.

April 9. That was the morning of the hit-and-run. *Mardy,* not Marty—*that fit!* A Thomas Mardy had been dropped off across the street from where AJ Raymond was killed.

Now every cell in Hauck's body sprang alive.

"There's just one catch, Lieutenant." The detective scratched his head. "Get this. . . . The Thomas Mardy the Amex card belonged to was actually *killed* on April ninth. In the Grand Central bombing. On the tracks . . ."

Hauck stared.

"And that was three full hours," the detective said, "before the Greenwich hit-and-run."

CHAPTER **TWENTY-THREE**

That night Hauck couldn't sleep. It was a little after twelve. He climbed out of bed. Letterman was on the TV, but he hadn't been watching. He went to the window and stared out at the sound. A stubborn chill knifed through the air. His mind was racing.

How?

How was it possible someone had died on the tracks and yet hours later his card had been used to pay for a ride to the Fairfield Diner? To the very spot where the Raymond kid was killed.

Someone had called him right before he left to cross the street. *Something like Marty . . .*

Mardy.

How did Charles and AJ Raymond fit together. *How?*

He was missing something.

He threw on a sweatshirt and some jeans and slipped on some old moccasins. Outside, the air was sharp and chilly. He hopped into his Bronco. The block was dark.

He drove.

They had kept the protection on for four days now. He'd had a car in front of the house, another that followed the kids to school. Nothing had happened. Not surprising. Maybe whoever was bothering her had backed off? The temperature had already been turned up pretty high.

Hauck pulled off the highway at Exit 5. Old Greenwich. As if by some inner GPS.

He headed onto Sound Beach and into town. Main Street was totally dark and deserted. He turned right on Shore toward the water. Another right onto Sea Wall.

Hauck pulled up twenty yards down from her house. The rookie, Stasio, was on duty tonight. Hauck spotted the patrol car, lights out, parked across from the house.

He went up and rapped on the window. The young officer rolled it down, surprised. "Lieutenant."

"You look tired, Stasio. You married, son?"

"Yessir," the rookie answered. "Two years."

"Go home. Grab some sleep," Hauck said. "I'll take over here."

"You? I'm fine, Lieutenant," the kid protested.

"It's okay. Go on home." Hauck winked at him. "I appreciate your doing the job."

It took a final remonstration, but Stasio, outranked, finally gave in.

Alone, Hauck balled his fists inside his sweatshirt against the cold.

Across the street the house was completely dark, other than a dim light upstairs shining through a curtain. He looked at his watch. He had meeting with Chief Fitzpatrick at 9:00 A.M. A replacement shift wouldn't be on until 6:00. He inhaled the crisp, damp air from off the sound.

You're crazy, Ty.

He went back to his Bronco and opened the door. As he was about to climb in, he noticed that the drapes had parted upstairs. Someone looked out. For a moment, in the darkness, their gazes met.

Hauck thought he made out the faint outline of a smile.

It's Ty, he mouthed, looking up. He had wanted to tell her that every time she called him "Lieutenant."

It's *Ty.*

And about your husband. What you're feeling, what you're going through now . . . *I know.*

I damn well know.

He waved, a wink of recognition he wasn't sure she could even read. Then he pulled himself inside the Bronco, shutting the door. When he looked back up, the drapes had closed.

But that was okay.

He knew she felt safe, knowing he was there. Somehow he did, too.

He hunkered down in the seat and turned the radio on.

It's Ty. He chuckled. *That was all I wanted to say.*

CHAPTER TWENTY-FOUR

April

And then it was a year.

A year without her husband. A year spent bringing up her kids by herself. A year of sleeping in her bed alone. An anniversary Karen dreaded.

Time heals, right? That's what everyone always says. And at first, Karen wouldn't allow herself to believe it. Everything reminded her of Charlie. Everything she picked up around the house. Every time she went out with friends. TV. Songs. The pain was still too raw.

But day by day, month into month, the pain seemed to lessen each morning. You just got used to it. Almost against your will.

Life just went on.

Sam went to Acapulco with her senior classmates and had a blast. Alex scored a game-winning goal in lacrosse, his stick raised high in the air. It was nice to see life in their faces again. Karen had to do something. She decided to get her real-estate license. She even dated, once or twice. A couple of divorced, well-heeled Greenwich financial types. Not exactly her type. One wanted to fly her to Paris for the weekend. On his jet. After meeting him the kids rolled their eyes and went "yick," too old, giving her a big thumbs-down.

It was still too soon, too creepy. It just didn't seem right.

The best news was that the whole situation with Archer gradually just died down. Maybe there was too much heat. Maybe whoever was trying to extort money from them got cold feet and gave up. Gradually things relaxed. The protection came off, their fears subsided. It was as if the whole frightening episode just went away.

Or at least that's what Karen always prayed, every night as she turned off the lights.

April 8 there was a TV documentary airing on the bombing, the night before the one-year anniversary. Shot by some camera crew that had been embedded with one of the fire teams that had responded, along with footage from handheld cameras by people who just happened to be in Grand Central at the time, or on the street.

Even still, Karen had never watched anything about that day.

She couldn't. It wasn't an event to her—it was the day her husband was killed. And it perpetually seemed to be around: On the news. *Law & Order* episodes. Even ball games.

So they all talked it over—as a family. They made plans to be together the following night, by themselves, to recognize the real anniversary of Charlie's death. The night before was just a distraction. Sam and Alex didn't want to see it, so they hung out with friends. Paula and Rick had invited Karen out. But she said no.

She wasn't even sure why.

Maybe because she wanted to show she was strong enough. Not to have to hide. Charlie had gone through it. He'd gone through it for *real*.

So could she.

Maybe there was just the slightest urge to be part of it. She was going to have to deal with it sometime. It might as well be now.

Whatever it was, Karen made herself a salad that night. Read through a couple of magazines that had piled up, did a little work on some competitive real-estate listings on the computer. With a glass of wine. All the while it was like she had some anxious inner eye fixed to the clock.

You can do this, Karen. Not to hide.

As it approached nine, Karen switched off the computer. She flicked the TV remote to NBC.

As the program came on, Karen felt anxious. She steeled herself. *Charlie went through this,* she told herself. *So can you.*

One of the news anchors introduced it. The show began by tracing the 7:51 train to Grand Central, docudrama style, starting with its departure out of the Stamford station. People reading the papers, doing crossword puzzles, talking about the Knicks game the night before.

Karen felt her heart start to pound.

She could almost see Charlie in the lead car, immersed in the *Journal*. Then the camera switched to two Middle Eastern types with knapsacks, one stowing a suitcase on the luggage rack. Karen brought Tobey up into her arms and squeezed him close. Her stomach felt hollow. Maybe this wasn't such a good idea.

Then on the screen, the timeline suddenly read 8:41. The time of the explosion. Karen looked away. *Oh, God . . .*

A security camera on the tracks in Grand Central captured the moment. A shudder, then a flash of blinding light. The lights on the train went out. Camera phones in cars farther back recorded it. A tremor. Darkness. People screaming.

Concrete collapsing from a hundred pounds of hexagen and accelerant—the fire raging near two thousand degrees, smoke billowing into the main concourse of the station and onto the street. Aerial shots from traffic helicopters circling. The same pictures Karen saw that terrible morning, all hurtling back. Panicked people stumbling out of the station, coughing. The deadly plume of black smoke billowing into the sky.

No, this was a mistake. Karen clenched her fists and shook her head. She squeezed Tobey, tears flooding her eyes. *It's wrong*. She couldn't watch this. Her mind flashed to Charlie down there. What he must have been going through. Karen sat, frozen, thrust back to the horror of that first day. It was almost unbearable. People were dying. Her husband was down there dying. . . .

No. I'm sorry, honey, I can't do this.

She reached for the remote and went to turn it off.

That was when the footage shifted up to the street level. One of the remote entrances on Forty-eighth and Madison. Handheld cameras: people staggering onto the street, shell-shocked, gagging, blackened with char and ash, collapsing onto the pavement. Some were weeping, some just glassy-eyed, grateful to be alive.

Horrible. She couldn't watch.

She went to flick it off just as something caught her eye.

She blinked.

It was only an instant—the briefest moment flashing by. Her eyes playing tricks on her. A cruel one. *It couldn't be. . . .*

Karen hit the reverse button on the remote with her thumb, waiting a few seconds for it to rewind. Then she pressed the play arrow again, moving a little closer to the screen. The people staggering out of the station . . .

Every cell in her body froze.

Frantically, Karen rewound it again, her heart slamming to a complete stop. When she got back to the spot a third time, she took a breath and pressed pause.

Oh, my God . . .

Her eyes stretched wide, as if her lids were stapled open. A paralyzing tightness squeezed her chest. Karen stood up, her mouth like sandpaper, drawing closer to the screen. *This cannot be. . . .*

It was a face.

A face that her mind was screaming to her couldn't be real.

Outside the station. Amid the chaos. *After* the explosion. Averted from the camera.

Charlie's face.

Karen's stomach started to crawl up her throat.

No one might have ever noticed it, no one but her. And if she had so much as blinked, turned away for just an instant, it would have been gone.

But it was real. Captured there. No matter how much she might want to deny it!

Charlie's face.

Karen was staring at her husband.

PART *TWO*

CHAPTER TWENTY-FIVE

The morning was clear and bright, the suburban New Jersey road practically deserted of traffic, except for about thirty bikers cruising in unison in their colorful jerseys.

Coasting near the front of the pack, Jonathan Lauer cast a quick glance behind, searching out the bright green jersey of his friend Gary Eddings, a bond trader at Merrill. He caught a glimpse of him, boxed in. *The perfect chance!* Crouching into a tuck, Jonathan began to pump his legs and weave a path through the maze of lead riders of the peloton. When a path opened up in front of him, he broke free.

Lauer, the imaginary announcer exclaimed in his head, *a bold, confident move!*

While for the most part they were just a bunch of thirty-something dads sweating off a few carbs on a Sunday morning, privately he and Gary had this game. More than a game, a challenge. They always pushed each other to the limit. Raced each other in the final straightaway. Waited for the other to make the first move. The winner got to brag for a week and wear the pretend yellow jersey. The loser bought the beers.

Calves pistoning, leaning over the handlebar of his brand-new carbon-fiber LeMond, Jonathan built a margin of about twenty yards, then coasted freely into the curve.

The finish line, the bend after the intersection with 287, was a half mile ahead.

Looking back, Jonathan caught a glimpse of Gary trying to free himself from the pack. His blood started to pump, accelerating as the country road turned into a perfect straightaway in the last half mile. He'd moved at the right time!

Pedaling fiercely now, Jonathan's thighs were burning. He wasn't thinking about the new job he had started just a few weeks before—on the energy desk at Man Securities, one of the real biggies—a chance to earn some real numbers after the mess at Harbor.

Nor was he thinking about the deposition he had to make that week. With that auditor from the Bank of Scotland and the lawyer from Parker, Kegg forcing him to testify against his former company after taking the attractive payout deal that had been offered him when the firm shut down.

No, all that was in Jonathan's mind that morning was racing to that imaginary line ahead of his friend. Gary had maneuvered out of the pack and had made up some distance. The intersection was just a hundred yards ahead. Jonathan went at it, his quads aching and his lungs on fire. He snuck a final peek back. Gary had pulled up. Game over. The rest of the pack was barely in sight. No way he could catch him now.

Jonathan coasted underneath the 287 overpass and cruised around the bend, raising his arms with a triumphant whoop.

He'd dusted him!

A short time later, Jonathan was pedaling home through the residential streets in Upper Montclair.

The traffic was light. His mind drifted to some complex energy index play someone had described at work. He was relishing his win and how he could tell his eight-year-old son, Stevie, how his old dad had smoked everyone today.

As he neared his neighborhood, the streets turned a little winding and hilly. He coasted down the straightaway on Westerly, then turned up, Mountain View, the final hill. He huffed, thinking how he'd promised he'd take Stevie to buy some soccer shoes. His house was just a quarter mile away.

That was when he spotted the car. More like a large black façade, a Navigator or an Escalade or something with a shiny chrome grille.

It was heading right for his path.

For a second, Jonathan Lauer was annoyed. *Hit the brakes, dude.* It was a residential street. There was plenty of distance between them. No one else was around. It flashed through his head that maybe he had taken the turn a little wide.

But Jonathan Lauer didn't hear the sound of brakes.

He heard something else.

Something crazy, his annoyance twisting into something else. Something horrifying, as the SUV's grille came closer and closer.

He heard acceleration.

CHAPTER TWENTY-SIX

Over the next few days, Karen must have watched that two-second clip a hundred times.

Horrified. Confused. Unable to comprehend what she was seeing.

The face of the man she had lived with for eighteen years. The man she'd mourned and missed and cried over. Whose pillow she still sometimes crept over to at night and hugged, whose name she still whispered.

It was Charlie, her husband, caught in an unexpected freeze-frame as the camera randomly swept by.

Outside Grand Central. *After* the attack.

How the hell can that be you, Charlie . . . ?

Karen didn't know what to do. Whom she could possibly tell? She went for a jog with Paula out on Tod's Point, and listened to her friend going on about some dinner party she and Rick had attended, at this amazing house out on Stanwich, when all the while she just wanted to stop. Face her friend. Tell her: *I saw Charlie, Paula.*

The kids? It would shatter them to see their father there. They would die. Her folks? How could she possibly explain? Until she knew.

Saul? The person he owed everything to. No.

So she kept it to herself. She watched the captured moment, over and over, until she was driving herself crazy. Confusion hardening into anger. Anger into hurt and pain.

Why? Why, Charlie? How can that be you? How could you have done this to us, Charlie?

Karen went over what she knew. Charlie's name had been on the Mercedes dealer's transit sheet. They had found the remnants of his briefcase blown apart, the charred slip of paper from his notepad she had received. He'd called her! *8:34.* It didn't make any sense to Karen.

He was there on that train!

At first she tried to convince herself that it couldn't be him. He would never, ever do this to her. Or to the kids. Not Charlie. . . . And why? *Why?* She stared at him. People look alike. Eyes, hopes—they can play crazy tricks. The picture was a little fuzzy. But every time she went back to that screen, replayed the image she had saved for maybe the thousandth time—there it was. Unmistakable. The sweats coming over her. Accusation knifing up in her belly. Her legs giving out like jelly.

Why?

Days passed. She tried to pretend to be herself, but the experience made her so sick and so confused, all Karen could do was hide in her bed. She told the kids she had come down with something. The anniversary of Charlie's death. All those feelings rushing back at her. One night they even brought dinner up to her. Chicken soup they had bought at the store, a cup of green tea. Karen thanked them and looked into their bolstering eyes. "C'mon, Mom, you'll be fine." As soon as they left, she cried.

Then later, when they were asleep or at school, she'd go around the house, studying her husband's face in the photos that were everywhere. The ones that meant everything to Karen. All she had. The one of him in his beach shirt and Ray-Bans that they'd blown up for the memorial. Of him and Karen dressed in black tie at her cousin's wedding. The personal items she had never cleared off his dresser in his closet: business cards, receipts, his watches.

You couldn't do this to me, could you, Charlie? To us . . .

Not you . . .

It had to be some kind of coincidence. A freakish one. *I trust you, Charlie. . . . I trusted you in life, and I'm goddamned going to trust you now.* In a million years, he would never hurt her this way.

Karen kept coming back to the one thing she still had of him. The torn sheet from his notepad someone had found in Grand Central. *From the Desk of Charlie Friedman.*

She felt him there. Trust had to win out here. The trust of eighteen years. Whatever she saw on that screen, she knew damn well in her heart just who her husband was.

For the first time, Karen looked at the note sheet. Really looked at it. Not just as a keepsake. Megan Walsh. The random name scrawled there in Charlie's barely legible script. The scribbled phone number: 964-1650. And another number, underlined in his bold, broad strokes:

B1254.

Karen closed her eyes.

Don't even go there, she admonished herself, suspicion snaking through her. *That wasn't Charlie. It couldn't be.*

But suddenly Karen stared wide-eyed at the scribbled numbers. The doubts kept tearing at her. Seeing his face up on that screen. It was like a piece of his past, a link to him—the only link.

Crazy as it is, you've got to go ahead and call, Karen.

If only to stop yourself from totally going insane.

CHAPTER TWENTY-SEVEN

It took everything Karen had to do it.

In a way it made her feel like she was cheating on him, on his memory. What if that wasn't even *him* up on that screen? What if she was making all this up, over someone who simply looked like him?

Her husband had been dead for over a year!

But she dialed, secretly praying inside that the number wasn't to some hotel and B1254 a room there, and this was how she would have to think of him. The weirdest doubts crossed Karen's mind.

"JP Morgan Chase. Fortieth and Third Avenue branch," a woman on the line answered.

Karen exhaled, relief mixed with a little shame. But as long as she'd gone this far, she might as well go all the way. "I'd like to speak with Megan Walsh, please."

"One moment, please."

It turned out Megan Walsh was the manager in charge of the Private Banking Department there. And after she'd explained that her husband was now deceased and that Karen was the sole beneficiary of his estate, B1254 turned out to be a safe-deposit box that had been opened at the branch a year before.

In Charlie's name.

Karen drove into town the following morning. The bank was a large, high-ceilinged branch, only a few blocks from Charlie's office. Megan Walsh was an attractive woman in her thirties, with long dark hair and dressed in a tasteful suit. She took Karen back to her cubicle office along a row with the other managers.

"I remember Mr. Friedman," she told Karen, her lips pressed tightly in sympathy. "I opened the account with him myself. I'm very sorry for your loss."

"I was just piecing through some of his things," Karen said. "This wasn't even listed as part of his estate. I never even knew it existed."

The bank manager perused Karen's copy of Charlie's death certificate and the letter of execution from the estate. She asked her a couple of questions: First, the name of their dog. Karen smiled. (It turned out he had listed Sasha.) His mother's maiden name. Then she took Karen back into a private room near the vault.

"The account was opened about eighteen months ago, last September." Ms. Walsh handed Karen the paperwork. The signature on the box was plainly Charlie's.

Probably just business stuff, Karen assumed. She'd see what was in there and turn whatever it was over to Saul.

Megan Walsh excused herself and returned shortly with a large metal container.

"Feel free to take as much time as you need," she explained. She placed it on the table, unlocking the clasp in Karen's presence with her own duplicate key. "If there's anything you need, or if you'd care to transfer anything into an account, I'll be happy to help you when you're done."

"Thank you." Karen nodded.

She hesitated over it for a few moments, after the door had closed and she was left alone with this piece of her husband he had never shared with her.

There was the shock of seeing his face up on that screen. Now this box that had never been mentioned as part of the estate or even come up in any of Charlie's business files. She ran her hand a little cautiously along the metal sides. *What could he be keeping from her in here?*

Karen drew open the large container from the top and peered inside.

Her eyes stretched wide.

The box was filled with neatly arranged bundles of cash. Wrapped packets of hundred-dollar bills. Bearer-bond notes bound with rubber bands with denominations scrawled on the top sheet in Charlie's handwriting: $76,000, $210,000. Karen lifted a couple of packets, catching her breath.

There's at least a couple of million dollars here.

She knew immediately this wasn't right. Where would Charlie get his hands on this kind of cash? They shared everything. Numbly, she let the packets of bundled cash drop back into the case. Why would he have kept all this from her?

Her stomach knotted. She flashed back to the two men from Archer two months before. *A considerable amount of money missing.* And the incident with Samantha in her car. *Two hundred and fifty million dollars.* This was only a fraction of that amount.

She was still gaping at the contents of the box—it started to scare her. *What the hell is going on, Charlie?*

Toward the bottom of the container, there was more. Karen dug around and came out with a manila envelope. She unfastened the clasp and slid out what was inside. She couldn't believe what she saw.

A passport.

New, unused. Karen flipped through it. It had Charlie's face inside.

Charlie's face—but with a completely different name. A fake one.

Weitzman. Alan Weitzman.

In addition, she slid out a couple of credit cards, all made out to the same false name. Karen's jaw fell slack. Her head started to ache. *What are you hiding from me, Charlie?*

Confused, Karen sank back into the chair. There had to be some reason for all this that would make sense. Maybe the face she'd seen on that screen was *not* really Charlie's.

But here it was. . . . Suddenly it seemed impossible to pretend anything else. She ran her eyes down the activity sheet again. The box had been opened two years before. October 24. Six months before he died. Charlie's signature, plain as day. All the entries had been his. A couple shortly after the box was opened. Then once or twice a month, seemingly like clockwork, almost as if he were preparing for something. Karen skimmed to the bottom, her gaze locking on the final entry.

There was Charlie's signature. His quick, forward-leaning scrawl.

But the date . . . *April 9.* The day of the Grand Central bombing.

Her eyes fastened on the time—1:35 P.M. Karen felt the sweats come over her.

That was four and a half hours after her husband had supposedly died.

CHAPTER **TWENTY-EIGHT**

Karen held back the urge to retch.

She felt dizzy. Light-headed. She grabbed onto the edge of the table to steady herself, unable to free her eyes from what she saw on that sheet.

1:35 P.M.

Suddenly, there was very little that made sense to Karen in that moment. But one thing did, flashing back to his grainy image from that handheld camera up on that screen.

Her husband was definitely alive.

Reeling, Karen ran through the contents of the safe-deposit box once again, accepting in that moment that everything she had felt and taken for granted over the past year, every shudder of grief and loss, every time she'd wondered empathetically what Charlie must have felt, every time she'd crawled over to his side of the bed at night and hugged his pillow, asking, *Why . . . why?*—it had all been nothing but a lie.

He had kept it all from her. He had planned this.

He didn't die there that day. In the blast. In the hellish flames. *He was alive.*

Karen's mind shot back to that morning . . . Charlie hollering to her over the dryer, about taking in the car. In her haste, words she had barely heard.

He's alive.

Then to the shock that had gripped her at the yoga studio as, glued to the screen, panic taking over her, she slowly came to accept that he was on that train. His call—the very last sound of his voice—about bringing home dinner that night. That was 8:34 A.M.

The blown-apart top piece of the briefcase with his initials on it. The sheet from his notepad that someone had sent.

It all came tumbling back—deepening with the force of a storm circling in her mind. All the pain and anguish she had felt, every tear . . .

He was there. On that train.

He just hadn't died.

At first it was like the cramp of a stomach flu forcing her insides up. She fought back the urge to gag. She should be jubilant. *He was alive!* But then she just stared blankly at the cash and the fake passport. He hadn't let her know. He'd let her suffer with the thought all the past year. Her confusion turned to anger. She sat there staring at the fake passport photo. Weitzman. *Why, Charlie, why? What were you devising? How could you do something like this to me?*

To us, Charlie?

They had loved each other. They had a life together. A family. They traveled. They talked about things they were going to do once the kids were gone. They still made love. *How do you fake that? How do you possibly do this to someone you loved?*

Suddenly Karen felt jelly-legged. All that money, that passport, what did it mean? Had Charlie committed some kind of crime? The room began to close in on her.

She felt she had to get out of there. *Now.*

Karen clasped the box shut and called outside. In a moment Megan Walsh came back in.

"I'd like to just leave this here if I could for now," Karen said, brushing the perspiration off her cheeks.

"Of course," Ms. Walsh replied. "I'll just give you my card."

Karen asked her, "Did anyone else have access to this box?"

"No, just your husband." The bank official looked back quizzically. "Is everything all right?"

"Yes," Karen lied. She took her purse but before running out requested a copy of the activity sheet. "I'll be back in a few days to decide what to do."

"That's fine, Mrs. Friedman, just let me know."

Out on the street, Karen sucked a breath of cooling air into her lungs. She steadied herself against a signpost. Slowly, her equilibrium began to return.

What the hell is going on here, Charlie? She turned away from people passing by on the sidewalk, afraid they would think her a lunatic to be reeling around in such a distraught state.

Didn't I take care of you? Wasn't I good to you, baby? I loved you. I trusted you. I mourned you, Charlie. It tore me fucking apart when I thought you were dead.

How can you possibly be alive?

CHAPTER **TWENTY-NINE**

Saul Lennick's office was close by, on the forty-second floor of one of those tall glass office towers on Forty-seventh and Park.

Karen hurried over, without even calling, praying he was there. His secretary, Maureen, came out and immediately saw the distress and nerves all over Karen's face.

"Can I get you anything, Ms. Friedman?" she asked solicitously. "A glass of water?"

Karen shook her head.

"Please come on back. Mr. Lennick's available. He can see you now."

"Thank you." Karen exhaled with relief. *Thank God!*

Saul Lennick's office was large and important-looking, filled with a collection of African masks and Balinese burial artifacts, with a view of the Manhattan skyline and, to the north, Central Park.

He had just hung up from a call, and he stood with a look of concern as Maureen rang Karen in.

"Karen?"

"Something's going on, Saul. I don't know what it is. But Charlie's done something . . . in his business."

"What?" Lennick inquired. He came around and pulled out a chair for her in front of his large desk, then sat back down.

She was about to blurt out everything she knew and had discovered—starting with seeing Charlie's face in the documentary. And that he was alive!

But she managed to catch herself at the last second, worried that maybe Saul might think he was talking to a raving lunatic, and decided to tell him only what she'd seen today.

"I came across something, Saul. Something Charlie wrote out before he died. I don't know how to even begin to explain, but I do know it fits into all these crazy things that have been happening. Those people from Archer. Samantha. I didn't know what to do with it, Saul."

"With what?"

Agitated, Karen told him about finding the safe-deposit box. The cash and bonds. The passport. Charlie's photograph next to the fake name.

"At first I thought maybe it was another woman, but it wasn't another woman, Saul. It's worse. Look at me, Saul, I'm a goddamn wreck." She took in a breath. "Charlie's done something. I don't know what. He was my husband, Saul. And I'm scared. I feel like those people are going to come back. People are coming after us, and now I find this box full of cash and a false ID. I'm not going to put my kids in danger, Saul. Why would Charlie be hiding this stuff from me? I know you know something. What the hell's going on here? You owe that much to me, Saul—*what?*"

Lennick rocked back in his leather chair. Behind him the vast skyline of New York spread out like a giant panoramic photo.

He exhaled.

"All right, Karen. I was hoping I'd never have to bring this up. That it had somehow all gone away."

"What, Saul? That *what* had gone away?"

He leaned forward. "Did Charles ever mention someone by the name of Coombs? Ian Coombs?"

"Coombs?" Karen shook her head. "I don't think so. I don't recall."

"What about an investment outfit called Baltic Securities? Did he ever mention them?"

"Why are you asking me all these things, Saul? I didn't exactly get involved in my husband's business. You of all people know that."

"I do know that, Karen, it's just that . . ."

"It's just that *what,* Saul? Charlie's not here. All of a sudden, everybody's making these innuendos about him. *What the hell has my husband done?*"

Lennick stood up, dressed in a navy pinstripe suit with gold cuff links at his wrists. He came around the desk in front of Karen and sat back down on a corner of it. "Karen, by any chance did Charlie ever mention any other accounts he might have been managing?"

"Other accounts?"

Lennick nodded. "Completely separate from Harbor. Maybe offshore—the Bahamas or the Cayman Islands, perhaps? Things aren't governed by the SEC or the U.S. accounting laws down there." His gaze was measured, serious.

"You're scaring me a little, Saul. Charlie was a stand-up guy. He didn't keep things from anyone. Least of all you."

"I know that, Karen. And I wouldn't have brought it up. Except . . ."

She stared. "Except . . . ?"

"Except you found what you found, Karen. The cash, that passport. Which together don't look exactly stand-up to me."

Karen tensed. Her thoughts flashed to the face on that screen. Their entire lives together, they had shared pretty much everything. Stuff with the kids, their finances. When they were angry with each other. Even what was going on with the dogs. That was how they did things. It was a matter of trust. Now, in the pit of her stomach, Karen felt this doubt. Chilling her. Over Charlie. It was a feeling she'd never had before.

"Whose money are we talking about, Saul?"

He didn't answer. He simply pressed his lips together and brushed back his thinning gray hair.

"*Whose money?*" Karen stared at him directly.

Her husband's mentor let out a breath. His fingers drummed on the top of his walnut desk like a funeral dirge.

He shrugged. "That's the trouble, Karen. No one's exactly sure."

CHAPTER THIRTY

Karen was frantic. The next few days, she barely dragged herself out of bed, not knowing what the hell to do. Samantha was starting to act concerned. It had been almost a week since Karen hadn't been herself, since she'd seen Charlie on that screen. Her daughter's eyes reflected that they knew that something wasn't right. "What's going on, Mom?"

As much as she wanted to, how could Karen possibly tell her?

That the person she admired most in the world, who had always provided for her and kept her strong, had deceived them in this way. What had Saul said? Setting up accounts. Running money, for people she didn't know. Offshore?

What kind of people?

All that money, it terrified Karen. What was it for? She began to think that maybe Charlie had committed some kind of crime. *Did Charlie ever mention any other accounts he might be managing?*

No, she had told him. *You know Charlie, he was an honest guy. He fretted over nickels and dimes for his clients.*

Had she been kidding herself all these years?

A few more days went by. Karen was driving herself half crazy, thinking about Charlie being out there somewhere, what all this meant. It was late one night. The kids' lights had long been turned off. Tobey was asleep on her bed. Karen went downstairs to the kitchen to make herself some tea.

Charlie's photo was on the counter. The one from the memorial: in his white polo shirt and khaki shorts, Topsiders and aviator Ray-Bans. They had always thought it was vintage Charlie, kicking back on a boat in the middle of the Caribbean—a cell phone stapled to his ear.

You knew him, Saul. . . .

Karen picked it up, for the first time restraining an urge to shatter it in anger against the wall. But then the strangest memory came to mind. From deep in the vault of their life together.

Charlie—waving.

It had been the end of a glorious week in the Caribbean, sailing. St. Bart's. Virgin Gorda. They ended up in Tortola. The kids had to be back to school the following day.

Then, strangely, Charlie announced he needed to stay on. A change of plans. Someone he had to see down there.

Out of the blue?

So he accompanied them to the local airport, the little twelve-seater shuttling them back to San Juan. It had always made Karen a bit nervous to fly those tiny planes. On takeoff and landing, she always held Charlie's hand. Everyone made a little fun of her. . . .

Why was all this coming back now?

Charlie said good-bye to them at the makeshift gate, more like a glass door leading out onto the tarmac. "You'll be fine," he told her with a hug. "I'll be back up north in two days." But buckling herself in, in the two-engine plane, Karen felt an inexplicable jolt of fear shoot through her—like she might never see him again. She had thought, *Why aren't you with me, Charlie?* a flash of being alone, reaching out for Alex's hand.

As the plane's propellers whirred, Karen's eyes went to the window, and she saw him, on the balcony of the tiny terminal, in his beach shirt and Ray-Bans, his eyes reflecting back the sun.

Waving.

Waving, with his cell phone stapled to his ear, watching the tiny plane pull away.

Offshore, Saul had said to her. *Tortola or the Cayman Islands.*

Now that same fear rippled through Karen, staring at his photo. That she somehow didn't really know him. Not the way it mattered. His eyes dark now, not reflecting the sun but deeper, unfamiliar—like a cave that led to many chasms. Chasms she had never explored before.

It scared her. Karen put down the photo. She was thinking, *He's out there.* Maybe thinking of her now. Maybe wondering, at this very moment, if she knew, if she suspected, felt him. It gave her the chills. *What the hell have you done, Charlie?*

She knew she couldn't keep bottling this up forever. She'd go insane. She had to know. Why he had done this. Where he was.

Karen sank down on a stool at the counter. She put her head in her hands. She'd never felt so confused or so isolated.

There was only one place she could think to go.

CHAPTER THIRTY-ONE

Hauck headed back upstairs to his office from the holding cells down in the basement. He and Freddy Muñoz had just taken a statement from a scared Latino kid who was part of this group from up in Norwalk who had been heisting fancy cars from back-country Greenwich homes, a statement that could now blow the case wide open. Joe Horner, a detective from the Norwalk police department, was holding on the phone for him.

As Hauck turned in from the hallway, Debbie, his unit's secretary, flagged his attention.

"Someone's here to see you, Ty."

She was seated on the bench in the outer office, wearing an orange turtleneck and a lightweight beige jacket, a tote bag on the bench next to her. Hauck made no attempt to conceal that he was pleased to see her.

"Tell Horner I'll get back to him in a minute, Deb."

Karen stood up. She smiled, a little nervous to be here. Hauck hadn't seen her for a couple of months, since that other situation, the people harassing her, had quieted down and they'd pulled the protection. He had called once or twice to make sure everything was okay. Smiling, he went up to her. Her face was pallid and drawn.

"You said I should call." She shrugged. "If anything ever came up."

"Of course."

She looked up at him. "Something did."

"Come on in my office," he said, taking her by the arm.

Hauck called to Debbie that he'd ring the Norwalk detective back, then led Karen past the row of detectives' desks through the glass partition into his office. He pulled out a cheap metal chair at the round conference table across from his desk. "Sit down."

It was clear she was upset. "You want something? Some water? A cup of coffee?" She shook her head. Hauck pulled another chair around and sat, facing her, arms across the back. "So tell me what's going on."

Karen sucked in a breath and pressed her lips tightly together, then reached inside her purse, the expression on her face somewhere between grateful and relieved. "Do you have a computer in here, Lieutenant?"

"Sure." Hauck nodded, wheeling around to a credenza by his desk.

She handed him a small DVR disc. "Can you put this in?"

He reached down and inserted it into the computer beneath the credenza. The disc kicked in and came to life, some kind of TV show or news report in mid-airing on the screen. A mass of people on the streets of New York. In unrest. Amateur footage, a handheld camera in the crowd. It became immediately clear he was watching the aftermath of the Grand Central bombing.

Karen asked him, "Did you happen to watch that documentary, Lieutenant? Last Wednesday night?"

He shook his head. "I was working. No."

"I did." She brought his attention back to the disc: people running out of the station onto the street. "It was very hard for me. A mistake. It was like living the whole thing all over again."

"I can understand."

Karen pointed. "Just about here I couldn't watch it anymore. I went to turn it off." She stood up and came behind his back, leaning over his shoulder, facing the screen. "It was like I was going crazy inside. Watching Charlie's death. All over."

Hauck didn't see where this was heading. She reached her hand across him for the mouse. She waited, letting the action on the screen unfold, people staggering up onto the street out of a remote entrance to the station, gagging, coughing out smoke, faces blackened. The handheld camera jiggled.

"That's when I saw it." Karen pointed.

She positioned the mouse on the toolbar and clicked. The picture on the screen came to a stop. 9:16 A.M.

The frame captured a woman reaching out to comfort some-one on the street who had collapsed. In front of her was someone else, a man, his jacket dusty, his face slightly averted from the cam-era, rushing by. Karen's eyes fixed on the screen, something almost steely about them, hardened, yet at the same time, Hauck couldn't help but notice, sad.

"That's my husband," she said, trying to keep her voice from cracking. She looked him in the eye. *"That's Charlie, Lieuten-ant."*

Hauck's pulse came to a stop. It took a second for it to fully sink in just what she meant. Her husband had died there. A year ago. He had been to her home, to the memorial. That much was clear. He turned again to the screen. The features seemed a bit fa-miliar from the photos he'd seen at her house. He blinked back at her.

"What do you mean?"

"I don't know *what I mean,"* Karen said. "He was on that train—that much I'm sure. He called me from it, just before the blast. They found pieces of his briefcase in the wreckage. . . ." She shook her head. "But somehow he didn't die."

Hauck pushed back from the desk, his eyes intent on the screen again. "A hundred people might look like that. He's covered in ash. There's no way you can be sure."

"That's what I told *myself,*" she said. "At first. At least it's what I was hoping." Karen moved back to the table. "Over the past week, I must have looked at that scene a thousand times."

She reached in and drew a sheet of paper out of her bag. "Then I found something. It doesn't matter what. All that matters is that it led me to this safe-deposit box at a bank in Manhattan that I never knew my husband had."

She slid the sheet across the table to Hauck.

It was a photocopy of an account-activation form from Chase. For a safe-deposit box and, attached, what appeared to be an ac-count history. There was a lot of activity, going back a couple of years. All the entries bore the same signature.

Charles Friedman.

Hauck scanned down.

"Check out the last date," Karen Friedman told him. "And the time."

Hauck did, and felt a sharp pain stick him in the chest. His eyes flashed back at her, not understanding. *Can't be . . .*

"He's alive." Karen Friedman met his eyes. Her pupils glistened. "He was there, at that bank, four and a half hours *after* the bombing. Four and a half hours after I thought he was dead.

"That's Charlie." She nodded to him, glancing at the screen. *"That's my husband, Lieutenant."*

CHAPTER THIRTY-TWO

"Who have you told?"

"No one." She stared back at him. "How could I? My kids . . . after what they've been through, it would kill them, Lieutenant. How could they even begin to understand? *My friends?*" She shook her head, glassy-eyed. "What am I possibly supposed to say to them, Lieutenant? That it was all some kind of crazy mistake? 'Sorry, Charlie's not really dead. He's just been fucking deceiving me over the past year. Deceiving all of us!' At first I thought maybe you hear about people who come out of these life-altering situations, you know, *affected*. . . . " She placed her finger on the bank forms. "But then I found *these*. I thought about taking everything to Saul Lennick. Charlie was like a second son to him. But I got scared. I thought, what if he's really done something? You know, something bad. What if I was doing the wrong thing . . . ? How it would affect everybody. I got all scared. *Do you understand what I mean?*"

Hauck nodded, the stress clear in her voice.

"So I came here."

Hauck picked up the bank papers. Because he was a cop, he had learned over the years to withhold his reactions. Gather the facts, be a little circumspect, until a picture of the truth becomes clear. He looked at the bank form. *Charles Friedman was there.*

"What is it you want me to do?"

"I don't know." Karen shook her head in consternation. "I don't even know what he's done. But it's something. . . . Charlie wouldn't just do this to us. I knew him. He wasn't that kind of man, Lieutenant." She pushed a wisp of hair out of her face and wiped her eyes with the heel of her hand, tears smearing. "The truth is, I don't have any fucking idea what I want you to do."

"It's okay," he said, squeezing her arm. Hauck stared back at the screen. He ran through the usual responses. Some crazy shock reaction—amnesia—from the bombing. But the bank form dismissed that one fast. Another woman? Embezzlement? He flashed to the scene in the parking lot with Karen's daughter. *Two hundred and fifty million dollars.* Yet Saul Lennick had assured him Charles's hedge fund was perfectly intact.

"If you don't mind my asking, what did you find in there?" Hauck asked, pointing to the record for the safe-deposit box.

"Money." Karen exhaled. "Lots of money. And a passport. Charlie's picture, with a totally assumed name. A few credit cards . . ."

"He left this all behind?" A year ago. "This may have been just some kind of backup." Hauck shrugged. "I guess you understand, this wasn't unpremeditated. He was planning this."

She nodded, biting her lower lip. "I realize that."

But what Charles could never have planned, Hauck knew, was how he would execute this. Until the moment came.

His thoughts settled on another name. *Thomas Mardy.*

"Listen." Hauck swiveled to her. "I have to ask, did your husband have any history of . . . you know . . ."

"Did he *what*?" Karen stared at him. "Did he play around? I don't know. A week ago I would have said that was impossible. Now I'd be almost happy to hear that's what it was. He had that passport, those cards. . . . He was planning all this. While we were sleeping in the same bed. While he was rooting for the kids at school. He somehow managed to get away from that train in the midst of the chaos and say, '*Now* it's happening. Now's the time. *Now's the time I'm going to walk out on my entire life.*'"

For a few seconds, there was only silence.

Hauck pressed his lips together and asked again, "What do you want me to do?"

"*I don't know.* Part of me wants to just put my arms around him and tell him that I'm happy he's alive. This other part . . . I opened that box and realized he's kept a whole part of his life secret from me. From the person he supposedly loved. I don't know what the hell I want to do, Lieutenant! Slap him in the face. Throw him in jail. I don't even know if he's committed a crime. Other than hurting me. But it doesn't matter. That's not why I'm here."

Hauck wheeled his chair closer. "Why are you here?"

"*Why am I here?*" Tears rushed into her eyes again. She clenched her fists and tapped them helplessly against the table. Then she looked back up at him. "Isn't it pretty obvious? *I'm here because I can't think of anywhere else to go!*"

Hauck went over to her as she just folded, weightlessly, into his arms. She buried her head on his shoulder and dug her fists into him. He held her, feeling her trembling in his grasp, and she didn't pull away.

"*He was dead!* I mourned him. I missed him. I agonized on whether his last thoughts were about us. There wasn't a day when I didn't wish I just could have talked to him one last time. To tell him I hoped that he was okay. And now he's *alive*. . . ."

She sucked back a breath, wiping the tears off her dampened cheeks. "I don't want him hunted down. He did what he did, and he must have had some reason. He's not a bastard, Lieutenant—whatever you might think. I don't even want him back. It's too late now. I have no idea what I even feel. . . .

"I guess I just want to know . . . I just want to know why he did this to me, Lieutenant. I want to know what he's done. I want to see his face and have him tell me. The truth. That's all."

Hauck nodded. He squeezed her arms and let go. He kept a tissue box by his desk. He pulled a couple for her.

She sniffled back a smile. "Thanks."

"Part of the job. People always seem to be crying in here."

She laughed and dabbed her eyes and nose. "I must be like a goddamn train wreck to you. Every time you see me . . ."

"No." He winked. "Anything but. However, you do seem to present some intriguing situations."

Karen tried to laugh again. "I don't even know what the hell I'm asking you to do."

"*I* know what you want me to do," he replied.

"I'm not sure where else to turn, Lieutenant."

"It's *Ty*."

What he said seemed to take her by surprise. For a second they just stood there, drawn to each other. She brushed a wave of auburn hair away from her still-raw eyes.

"Okay." She sucked in a breath and nodded. "*Ty* . . ."

"And the answer's yes." He sat back on the edge of his desk and nodded. "I'll help."

CHAPTER THIRTY-THREE

He'd said yes. Hauck went over the scene again.

Yes, he would help her. Yes, he knew what she needed him to do. Even though he knew in that instant it could never be accomplished with him on the job.

He took the *Merrily* out on the sound that night. He sat in the dark with the engines off, the water calm, the lights of downtown Stamford flickering on the shore.

Why? he asked himself.

Because he couldn't get the image of her out of his mind? Or the feel of her softness when she leaned into him. Her sweet scent still vibrant in his nostrils, every hair on his arm on edge, every nerve awakened from its long slumber.

Was that what it was, Ty? Is that all?

Or maybe it was the face that crept into his head as he sat with his Topsiders up on the gunnels, drinking a Harpoon Ale. A face Hauck had not brought into mind for months but that now once again came back to life for him, frighteningly real.

Abel Raymond.

The blood trickling out from under his long red hair. Hauck kneeling over him, promising he'd find out who had done this.

Charles Friedman hadn't died.

That changed everything now.

Thomas Mardy. He'd been a supervisor at a credit-checking business. He'd gotten on the 7:57 that day out of Cos Cob and had died on the tracks in Grand Central, in the blast.

Yet somehow one of his credit cards had been used for a limo ride up to Greenwich three hours later.

Now Hauck knew how.

He wondered, could the Mustang just have been a coincidence? *Charlie's Baby* . . . It had thrown him off. It would have thrown anyone off.

But now, seeing Charlie's face on the screen, he knew—more clearly than Karen Friedman could ever know—just how her husband had spent the hours between being caught by that camera coming out of that station and ending up hours later in the vault of that bank.

The son of a bitch hadn't died.

That afternoon Hauck had run Charlie's name through the NCIC system. The usual asset check—credit cards, bank accounts, even immigration. Freddy Muñoz brought it back, knocked on the door wearing a quizzical expression. "This guy's deceased, LT. On April ninth." His look sort of summed it up. "In the Grand Central bombing."

Nothing. But Hauck wasn't surprised.

Charles Friedman and AJ Raymond had been connected. And not by the copper Mustang. That much he now knew. They had lived different lives, a universe apart. Yet they had been connected.

What the hell could it be?

Hauck drained the last of his IPA. The answer wasn't here. The kid had family. Pensacola, right? His brother had come up to claim his things. His father was a harbor captain. Hauck remembered the old man's photo among AJ's things.

Yes, he would help her, he had said. Hauck pulled himself up out of the chair. He started the ignition. The *Merrily* coughed to life.

He'd help her. He only hoped she wouldn't regret whatever he found.

"CARL, I'M GOING to need a little time." Hauck knocked on his boss's door. "I have a bunch built up."

Carl Fitzpatrick, Greenwich's chief of police, was at his desk, preparing for an upcoming meeting. "Sure, Ty. C'mon in, sit down." He swiveled his chair around his desk and came back with a scheduling folder. "What are we talking about, a few days?"

"A couple of weeks," Hauck said, unconfiding. "Maybe more."

"*Couple of weeks?*" Fitzpatrick gazed at him over his reading glasses. "I can't authorize that kind of time."

Hauck shrugged. "Maybe more."

"Jesus, Ty . . ." The chief tossed his glasses on his desk, looked at him directly. "What's going on?"

"Can't say. Things are pretty clean right now. Whatever comes up, Freddy and Zaro can cover. I haven't taken more than a week in five years."

"Is everything all right, Ty? This isn't something about Jess, is it?"

"No, Carl, everything's fine." Fitzpatrick and he were friends, and he hated being vague. "It's just something that's come up I have to see through."

"Couple of weeks . . ." The chief scratched the back of his head. He pieced through the file. "Gimme a few days. I'll shuffle things around. When did you need to leave?"

"Tomorrow."

"*Tomorrow.*" Fitzpatrick's eyes stretched wide. "Tomorrow's impossible, Ty. This is totally out of the blue."

"To you, maybe." Hauck slowly stood up. "To me it's long overdue."

CHAPTER THIRTY-FOUR

The doorbell rang. Barking, Tobey scampered to the door. Alex was at a friend's, studying for an exam. Samantha was on the phone in the family room, her legs dangling over the back of the couch, *Heroes* on the TV.

"Can you get that, Mom?"

Karen had just finished up cleaning in the kitchen. She tossed down the cloth and went to answer the door.

When she saw who it was, she lit up in surprise.

"There's a couple of things you can do for me," the lieutenant said, huddled in a beige nylon jacket against a slight rain.

"My daughter's at home," Karen said, glancing back into the family room, not wanting to involve her. She grabbed a rain jacket off the bench and threw it over her shoulders and stepped outside. "What?"

"You can look through any of your husband's personal belongings. Notes from his desk. Canceled checks, credit-card receipts. Whatever might still be around. Are you still able to access his computer?"

Karen nodded. She'd never had the urge to remove it from his study. It had never been quite the right time. "I think so."

"Good. Go through his old e-mails, any travel sites he may have visited before he left, phone records. What about his work-related things? Are they still around?"

"I have some stuff of his that was given back to me in a box downstairs. I'm not sure where his office computer ended up. What am I looking for?"

"Anything that might prove useful in determining where he might go. Even if it ends up it's not where he is now, it could at least be a starting point. Something to go on . . ."

Karen covered her head against the raindrops. "It's been over a year."

"I know it's been a year. But there are still records. Get in touch with his ex-secretary or the travel agency he used to use. Maybe they sent him brochures or made some reservations that no one would have even thought were important then. Try to think yourself, where would he go? You lived with him for eighteen years."

"You don't think I haven't already racked my brain?" The rain intensified. Karen wrapped her arms against the chill. "I'll look again."

"I'll help you arrange to get some of it done if you need," Hauck said, "when I get back."

"When you get back? Back from where?"

"Pensacola."

"Pensacola?" Karen squinted at him. "What's down there? Is that for me?"

"I'll let you know," Hauck said with a smile, "as soon as it's clear to me. In the meantime I want you to go through whatever you can find. Think back. There's always some clue. Something someone's left behind. I'll be in touch when I get back."

"Thank you," Karen said. She placed her hand against his slicker, rain going down her face. Her eyes suddenly full.

It had been a long time since she'd felt the presence of someone in her life, and here was this man, this man she barely knew who had come into her life in the mayhem after Charlie had died, and he'd seen her, rootless as a craft foundering in the waves of a storm. And now he was the one person she could cling to in this world, the one anchor. It was strange.

"I'm sorry I dragged you into all this, Lieutenant. I'm sure you have enough to do in your job."

"You didn't drag me into it." Hauck shook his head. "And anyway, I'm not doing this on the job."

"What do you mean?"

"You didn't want this out in the open, did you? You didn't want me to have to deal with whatever came back. I'd never be able to do that if I was there."

She looked at him, confused. "I don't understand."

"I took a few weeks," he said, rain streaming down his collar. Then he winked. "Don't worry about it. I had no idea what to do with the time anyway. But it's only me. No badge. No one else." His blue eyes glimmered in a soft smile. "I hope that's okay."

Was it okay? Karen didn't know what she was expecting when she went to him. Maybe only someone to listen to. But now her heart melted a bit at what he was willing to do.

"Why . . . ?"

He shrugged. "Everybody else—they were either really busy or just needed the paycheck."

Karen smiled, gazing back at him, a warming, grateful sensation filling up her chest. "I meant, why are you doing this, Lieutenant?"

Hauck shifted his weight from one foot to another. "I don't really know."

"*You know.*" Karen looked at him. She pushed back a lock of wet hair that had fallen into her eyes. "You'll let *me* know when it's time. But thank you anyway, Lieutenant. Whatever it is."

"I thought we went through that one already," he said. "It's *Ty.*"

"All right, *Ty.*"

A glow of grateful warmth came into her gaze. Karen held out her hand. He took it. They stood there like that, rain pelting down on them.

"It's *Karen.*" Her eyes met his. "I'm happy to meet you, Ty."

CHAPTER THIRTY-FIVE

Gregory Khodoshevsky gunned the engine on his three-wheeled, seventy-thousand-dollar T-Rex sport cycle, and the three-hundred-horsepower vehicle shot over the makeshift course he had set up on the grounds of his twenty-acre Greenwich estate.

Trailing close behind, his fourteen-year-old son, Pavel, in his own bright red T-Rex, gamely tried to keep up.

"C'mon, boy!" Khodoshevsky laughed through the helmet mike as he maneuvered around a cone, passing his son back on the other side. "You're not going to let an old *starik* like me take you, are you?"

Pavel cut the turn sharply, almost flipping his machine. Then he righted himself and sped up to almost sixty miles per hour, going airborne over a knoll.

"I'm right behind you, old man!"

They sped around the man-made pond, past the helicopter pad, then bounced back onto a long straightaway on Khodoshevsky's vast property. On the rise, his eighteen-thousand-square-foot redbrick Georgian stood like a castle with its enormous fountained courtyard and sprawling eight-car garage. Which Khodoshevsky filled with a Lamborghini Murciélago, a yellow Hummer that his wife, Ludmila, paraded around town, and a customized black Maybach Mercedes complete with bulletproof windows and a Bloomberg satellite setup. That cost him over half a million alone.

Though he was only forty-eight, the "Black Bear," as Khodoshevsky was sometimes known, was one of the most powerful people in the world, though his name would not be found on any list. In the *kleptocracy* that became the privatization spree in Russia of the 1990s, Khodoshevsky convinced a French investment bank to buy a run-down automotive-parts plant in Irkutsk, then leveraged it into a controlling seat on the board of Tazprost, Russia's largest— and ailing—automobile manufacturer, which, upon the sudden demise of two of its more uncompliant board members, dropped in Khodoshevsky's lap at the age of thirty-six. From there he obtained the rights to open Mercedes and Nissan dealerships in Estonia and Latvia, along with hundreds of Gaznost filling stations all over Russia to fill them up.

Under Yeltsin the Russian economy was carved up by a handful of eager *kapitalisti*. One big fucking candy store, Khodoshevsky always called it. In the free-for-all that became the public finance sector, he opened department stores modeled after Harrods that sold pricey Western brands. He bought liquor distributorships for expensive French champagnes and wines. Then banks, radio stations. Even a low-cost airline.

Today, through a holding company, Khodoshevksy was now the largest single private landlord on the Champs-Élysées!

In the course of growing his empire, he had done many questionable things. Public ministers on Putin's economic trade councils were on his payroll. Many of his rivals were known to have been arrested and imprisoned. More than a few had been disposed of, suffering untimely falls from their office windows or unexplained car accidents on the way home. These days Khodoshevsky generated more free cash flow than a medium-size economy. In Russia today what he could not buy, he stole.

Fortunately, his was not a conscience that kept him troubled or awake at night. He was in touch daily through emissaries with a handful of powerful people—Europeans, Arabs, South Americans—whose capital had become so vast it basically ran the world. Wealth that had created the equivalent of a supereconomy, keeping real-estate prices booming, luxury brands flourishing, yacht makers busy, Wall Street indices high. They developed economies the way the International Monetary Fund once developed nations: buying up coal deposits in Smolensk, sugarcane fields for ethanol in Costa Rica, steel factories in Vietnam. However the coin fell, theirs always ended up on top. It was the ultimate arbitrage Khodoshevsky had crafted. The hedge fund of hedge funds! There was no way to lose.

Except maybe, as he relaxed a bit on the accelerator, today, to his son.

"C'mon, Pavel, let me see what you're made of. *Gun it now!*"

Laughing, they sped into the final straightaway, then did a lap around the massive fountain in the courtyard in front of the house. The T-Rexes' superheated engines spurted like souped-up go-carts. They bounced over the Belgian cobblestones in a father-son race to the finish.

"I've got you, Pavel!" Khodoshevsky called, pulling even.

"Believe it, old man!" His determined son gunned the engine and grinned.

In the final turn, they both went all out. Their wheels bumped together and scraped. Sparks flew, and Khodoshevsky lurched into the basin of the gigantic baroque fountain they had brought over from France. His T-Rex's fiberglass chassis caved in like crepe paper. Pavel threw up his hands in victory as he raced by. *"I win!"*

Stiffly, Khodoshevsky squeezed himself out of the mangled machine. A total loss, he noted glumly. Seventy thousand dollars down the drain.

Pavel jumped out of his and ran over. "Father, are you all right?"

"Am I all right?" He took off his helmet and patted himself around to make sure. He had a scrape on his elbow. "Nothing broken. A good pass, boy! That was fun, eh? You'll make a race driver yet. Now, help me drag this piece of junk into the garage before your mother sees what we've done." He mussed his boy's hair. "Who else has toys like this, eh?"

That was when his cell phone rang. The Russian reached in and pulled his BlackBerry out of his jeans. He recognized the number. "I'll be with you in a second." He waved to Pavel. "I'm afraid it's business, boy." He sat on the edge of the stone fountain and flipped open his phone. He ran a hand through his tousled black hair.

"Khodo here."

"I just want you to know," the caller, a private banker Khodoshevsky knew, began, "the assets we spoke of have been transferred. I'm bringing him the final shipment myself."

"That's good." Khodoshevsky snorted. "He must have pictures of you, my friend, for you to trust him after that mess he made of things last year. You just be sure you explain to him the price of doing business with us. This time you see to it he fully understands."

"You can be certain I will," the German banker said. "I'll remember to pass along your best regards."

Khodoshevsky hung up. It wouldn't be the first time, he thought, he had gotten his hands dirty. Surely not the last. The man was a good friend. Khodoshevsky had shared many meals with him, and a lot of good wine. Not that it mattered. Khodoshevsky clenched his jaw. No one loses that kind of money of theirs and doesn't feel it.

No one.

"Come, boy." He got up and went over to pat Pavel on the back. "Help me drag this piece of shit into the garage. I have a brand-new one in there. What do you say, maybe you'd like to give your old man another turn?"

CHAPTER THIRTY-SIX

"Mr. Raymond?"

Hauck knocked at the small white, shingle-roofed home with a cheap green awning over the door in a middle-class section of Pensacola. There was a small patch of dry lawn in front, a black GMC pickup with an EVEN JESUS LOVED A GOOD BEER bumper sticker parked in the one-car garage.

The door opened, and a dark, sun-flayed man peered back. "Who're you?"

"My name's Hauck. I'm a lieutenant with the police department up in Greenwich, Connecticut. I handled your son's case."

Raymond was strongly built, of medium height, with a rough gray stubble. Hauck figured him for around sixty. His gnarled, cedar-colored skin looked more like a hide of leather and offset his clear blue eyes. He had a faded blue and red military tattoo on his thick right arm.

"Everyone knows me as Pappy," he grunted, throwing open the door. "Only people who want money call me Mr. Raymond. That's why I wasn't sure."

Hauck stepped through the screen door into a cramped, sparely furnished living room. There was a couch that looked like it had been there for forty years, a wooden table with a couple of Budweiser cans on it. The TV was on—a *CSI* rerun. There were a couple of framed pictures arranged on the wall. Kids. In baseball and football uniforms.

Hauck recognized one.

"Take yourself a seat," Pappy Raymond said. "I'd offer you something, but my wife's at her sister over in Destin, so there's nothing here but week-old casserole and warm beer. What brings you all the way down here, Lieutenant Hauck?"

"Your son."

"My son?" Raymond reached for the remote and flicked off the TV. "My son's been dead over a year now. Hit-and-run. Never solved. I understood the case was closed."

"Some information's come out," Hauck said, stepping over a pile of newspapers, "that might shed some new light on it."

"*New light...*" The old man bunched his lips together and mocked being impressed. "Just in fucking time."

Hauck stared at him. He pointed to the wall. "That's AJ over there, isn't it?"

"That's Abel." Raymond nodded and released a breath.

"He played defensive backfield, huh?"

Raymond took a long time before saying, "Listen, son, I know you came a long way down here and that somehow you're just trying to help my boy—" He stopped, looked at Hauck with hooded eyes. "But just why in hell are you here?"

"*Charles Friedman,*" Hauck answered. He moved a stack of local sports pages off the chair and sat down across from Raymond. "Any chance you know that name?"

"Friedman. Nope. Never heard it before."

"You're sure?"

"Said it, didn't I? My right hand's got a bit of a tremor in it, but not my brain."

Hauck smiled. "Any chance AJ . . . *Abel* ever mentioned it?"

"Not to me. 'Course, we weren't exactly in regular conversation over the past year after he moved up north." He rubbed his face. "I don't know if you know, but I worked thirty years down at the port."

"I was told that, sir. By your other son when he came to claim AJ's things."

"Rough life." Pappy Raymond exhaled. "Just look at me." He picked up a photo of himself at the wheel of what appeared to be like a tug and handed it to Hauck. "Still, it provided some. Abel got what I never got—meaning a little school, not that he ever had cause to do much with it. He chose to go his own way. . . . We all make our choices, don't we, Lieutenant Hauck?" He put the photo down. "Anyway, no, I don't think he ever mentioned the name Charles Friedman to me. Why?"

"He had a connection to AJ."

"That so?"

Hauck nodded. "He was a hedge-fund manager. He was thought to have been killed at the bombing at Grand Central Station in New York last April. But that wasn't the case. Afterward, I believe he found a ride up to Greenwich and contacted your son."

"Contacted Abel? Why?"

"That's why I'm here. To find out."

The father's eyes narrowed, circumspect, a look Hauck knew. He laughed. "Now, that's a pickle. One dead man going to meet another."

"AJ never mentioned being involved in anything before he was killed? Drugs, gambling—maybe even some kind of blackmail?"

Raymond brought back his legs off the table and sat up. "I know you came down here a long way, Lieutenant, but I don't see how you can go implying things about my boy."

"I didn't mean to," Hauck said. "I apologize. I'm not interested in whatever he may have done, except if it sheds any light on who killed him. But what I *am* interested in is why a man who's just gone through a life-threatening situation and whose life is a world apart from your son's finds his way up to Greenwich and gets in touch with your boy directly after."

Pappy Raymond shrugged. "I'm not a cop. I expect the normal course would be to ask him."

"I wish I could," Hauck said. "But he's gone. For over a year. Disappeared."

"Then that's where I'd be putting my best efforts, son, if I were you. You're wasting your time here."

Hauck handed Pappy Raymond back the photo. Stood up.

"You think that man killed Abel?" Pappy Raymond said. "This Charles Friedman? Ran him down."

"I don't know. I think he knows what happened."

"He was a good boy." Raymond blew out air. A gleam showed in his clear blue eyes. "Headstrong. Did things his own way. Like you-know-who. I wish we'd had more time." He drew in a breath. "But I'll tell you this: That boy wouldn't have harmed the wings on a goddamn fly, Lieutenant. No reason . . ." He shook his head. "No reason he had to die like that."

"Maybe there's someone else I could ask," Hauck pressed. "Who might know. I'd like to help you."

"Help *me*?"

"Solve AJ's killing, Mr. Raymond, 'cause that's what I damn well feel it was."

The old man chuckled, a wheezy laugh escaping. "You seem like a good man, Lieutenant, and you've come a long way. What'd you say your name was?"

"Hauck."

"Hauck." Pappy Raymond flicked on the TV. "You go on back, Luh-tenant Hauck. Back to wherever you're from. *Connecticut.* 'Cause there ain't no way in hell, whatever 'new light' you may have turned up, sir, that it's ever gonna be of any help to me."

CHAPTER **THIRTY-SEVEN**

Pappy Raymond was holding back. Why else would he push Hauck away so completely? Hauck also knew the old guy would be a tough one to crack.

He went back to the Harbor Inn hotel overlooking Pensacola Bay, where he was staying, stopped in the gift shop to buy a T-shirt for Jess that said PENSACOLA ROCKS, then fished out a Seminole beer from the minibar and threw himself onto the bed, turning on CNN.

Something had happened. An explosion at an oil refinery in Lagos, Nigeria. Over a hundred people killed. It had spiked the price of oil all day.

He reached over and fished out the number of AJ Raymond's brother, Pete, who had come up to Greenwich after the accident to take possession of his things.

Hauck called him. Pete said he would meet him at a bar after his shift the next day.

The Bow Line was down near the port, where Pete, who had come out of the Coast Guard two years before, was a harbor pilot like his father.

"It was like something just turned off in Pop," Pete said, drawing from a bottle of Bud. "AJ was killed. No one ever called my dad a teddy bear, but one day he went to work, wanting to do everything he could about what happened. The next day it was like it was all in the past. Off-limits to even bring it up. He never shared what he was feeling."

"You think part of it's guilt?"

"Guilt?"

Hauck took a swig of beer. "I've interviewed my share of people, Pete. I think he's holding something back."

"About AJ?" Pete shrugged, pushed back his hair under a Jacksonville Jaguars cap. "Something was going on. . . . People who he talked to tell me he had this thing—this cover-up he'd stumbled into. Some ships he thought were falsifying their cargo. Like some big national-security thing. He was all worked up.

"Then the thing with AJ happened. And that was it. It was over for him." He snapped his finger. "Lights out. Whatever it was, I never heard squat about it ever again. It was as if the whole thing just got buried the next day."

"I don't mean to push it," Hauck said, tilting his beer. "All I want to do is find your brother's killer, which is precisely what I believe it was. Anyone you know who can tell me any more on this?"

Pete thought a moment. "I could give you a few names. His old pals. I'm not sure what makes you think it's all related, though."

Hauck tossed a couple of bills on the counter. "That would be a big help."

"Thirty years . . ." Pete got up and drained the last of his beer. "Pop was like a god down there in the harbor. There was nothing went on he didn't know about or hadn't done. Now look at him. He was always a hard man, but I would never call him bitter. He took it rough, what happened to my brother. Rougher than I would expect. Given that they never saw eye to eye for a goddamned second while AJ was alive."

THE FOLLOWING DAY Hauck made the rounds at the docks. A couple of large freighters had come in early that morning. Huge unloading trestles and hydraulic lifts were hissing, off-loading massive containers.

He found Mack Tyler, a sunburned, broad-chested tug's mate at the pilots' station. He had just come in from a launch.

Tyler was a bit guarded at first. People protected their own down there, and here was this cop from up north asking all kinds of questions. It took a little finesse for Hauck to get him to open up.

"I remember I was out with him one day," Tyler said. He leaned against a retaining wall and lit up a cigarette. "He was about to board some oil tanker we were bringing in. Pappy was always going on about these ships he'd seen before, making false declarations.

How they were riding so high in the water, no way they could possibly be full, like their papers said. I think he even snuck down into the holds of one once.

"Anyway"—Tyler blew out smoke—"this one time we had pulled up alongside and the gangway was lowered to us, and Pappy was getting ready to go aboard. And he gets this cell-phone call. Five in the fucking A.M. He takes it, and all of a sudden his legs just give out and his face gets all pale and pasty—it was like he was having some kind of heart attack. We called in another launch. I had to bring the old man in. He wouldn't take any medical attention. Just a panic attack, he claimed. Why, he wouldn't say. Panic attack, my ass."

"You remember when that was?" asked Hauck.

"Sure, I remember." The big sailor exhaled another plume of smoke. "It wasn't too long after the death of his boy up there."

Later, Hauck met with Ray Dubose, one of the other harbor pilots, at a coffee stand near the navy yard.

"It was getting crazy," said Dubose, a big man with curly gray hair, scratching the bald spot on his head. "Pappy was going around making all kinds of claims that some oil company was falsifying its cargo. About how these ships were riding so high in the water. How he'd seen them before. The same company. Same logo—some kind of a whale or shark, maybe. Can't recall."

"What happened then?"

"The harbormaster told him to back off." Dubose took a sip of coffee. "That's what happened! That this was one for customs, not us. 'We just pull 'em in, Pappy.' He'd pass it along. But Pappy, God bless, he just kept on pushing. Raised a big stink with the customs people. Tried to contact some business reporter he knew from the bar, like it was some big national-security story he was uncovering and Pappy was Bruce Willis or someone."

"Go on."

Dubose shrugged. "Everyone kept telling him just to back off, that's all. But Pappy was never one to listen. Stubborn old fool. You know the type? Came out of the womb that way. I miss the son of a bitch, though. Pretty soon after his boy died up there, he packed it in with his thirty years and called it quits. Took it hard.

"Funny thing, though . . ." Dubose crumpled his cup and tossed it into a trash bin against a wall. "After that happened, I never heard another peep out of him about those stupid tankers again."

Hauck thanked him and drove back to the hotel. For the rest of the afternoon, he sat around on the small balcony overlooking the beautiful Gulf blue of Pensacola Bay.

The old man was hiding something. Hauck felt it for sure. He'd seen that haunted face a hundred times before. *There's nothing you can do that's gonna help me now. . . .*

It might only be guilt, that he had pushed his youngest son away. And what happened afterward.

Or it could be more. That the hit-and-run up north hadn't been so accidental after all. That that was why they were unable to ever find anything resembling the SUV the witnesses had described. Why no one else ever saw it. Maybe someone had deliberately killed Pappy Raymond's son.

And Hauck felt sure those tankers were connected.

He nursed a beer. He thought about placing a call to Karen to see what she had found.

But he kept coming back to the hardened look in the old sailor's eyes.

CHAPTER THIRTY-EIGHT

Karen went back through all of Charlie's things as Hauck had asked her. She opened the cartons she had kept piled in the basement, doing her best to avoid the attention of the kids. Heavy, boxed-up files that Heather, his secretary, had sent with a note: *You never know what's in them. Maybe something you'll want to keep.* Brochures for trips they had taken as a family. The ski house they rented one year at Whistler. Letters. A kazillion letters. A bunch of things on the Mustang, which Charlie had asked her in the will he left not to sell.

Basically, the sum of their lives together. Stuff Karen had never had the heart to go through. But nothing that helped. At some point she sat in frustration with her back against the concrete basement wall and silently swore at him. *Charlie, why the hell did you do this to us?*

Then she went through the computer that was still sitting at his desk. She turned it on for the first time since the incident. It felt weird, invasive—as if she were prying into him. His signature was everywhere. In a million years she would never have done this when he was alive. Charlie never kept a password. Karen was able to get right in. What on earth had there ever been to hide?

She scrolled through his stored Word documents. Mostly they were letters he'd written from home—to industry people, trade publications. The draft of a speech or two he'd given. She went on his AOL account. Any e-mails he might've written before he disappeared had probably long since been wiped away.

It felt futile. And dirty, going through his things. She sat there at his desk, in the messy study, much of it still just as he'd left it a year before, where he'd paid the bills and read over his trade journals and checked his positions, the desk still piled with trade sheets and prospectuses.

There was nothing. He didn't want to be found. He could be anywhere in the fucking world.

And the truth was, Karen had no idea what she was gong to do if she even found him.

She contacted Heather, who was working at a small law firm now. And Linda Edelstein, whom Karen still occasionally used as a travel agent. She asked them both to think back on whether Charlie had made any unusual purchases ("a condo somewhere, as crazy as that sounds, or a car?") or booked any travel plans in the weeks before he died. She concocted this inane story about discovering something in his office about a surprise trip he'd been planning, an anniversary thing.

How in the world could she possibly tell them what was really in her mind?

As a friend, Linda scrolled back through her travel computer. "I don't think so, Kar. I would have remembered at the time. I'm sorry, hon. There's nothing here."

This was insane. Karen sat there among her husband's things at her wits' end, growing angry, wishing she never had watched that documentary. It had changed everything. *Why would you do this to us, Charlie? What could you possibly have done?*

Tell me, Charlie!

She picked up a stack of loose papers and went to throw them against the wall. Just then her gaze fell to a memo from Harbor that was still there from a year before. Her eye ran down the office distribution list. Maybe they knew. She spotted a name there— a name that hadn't crossed her mind in months.

Along with a voice. A voice she had never responded to, but one that now suddenly echoed in her ears with the same ringing message:

I'd like to speak with you, Mrs. Friedman. . . . There are some things you ought to know.

CHAPTER THIRTY-NINE

The address was 3135 Mountain View Drive, a hilly residential road. In Upper Montclair, New Jersey.

Karen found Jonathan Lauer's address in one of Charlie's folders. She checked to make sure it was still valid. She didn't want to talk with him on the phone. It was a Saturday afternoon.

There are some things you ought to know. . . .

Saul had said it was just a matter of personnel issues, compensation. Karen had never heard from him again. And it wasn't that she didn't trust Saul. It was just that if they were turning over every stone, the way Ty wanted to, she thought she might as well hear it from Lauer directly. She had never called him back. It had been an awfully long time.

But suddenly Charlie's trader's cryptic words took on a more important meaning.

Karen pulled into the driveway. There was a white minivan parked in the open two-car garage. The house was a cedar and glass contemporary with a large double-story window in the front. A kid's bike lay on the front lawn. Next to a portable soccer net. Rows of pachysandra and boxwood flanked the flagstone walkway leading up to the front door.

Karen felt a little nervous and embarrassed, after so much time. She rang the bell.

"I got it, Mommy!"

A young girl in pigtails who appeared around five or six opened the door.

"Hey." Karen smiled. "Is your daddy or mommy at home?"

A woman's voice called out from inside, "Lucy, who's there?"

Kathy Lauer came to the door, holding a rolling pin. Karen had met her once or twice—first at an office gathering and, later, at Charlie's memorial. She was petite, with shoulder-length dark hair, wearing a green Nantucket sweatshirt. She stared at Karen in surprise.

"I don't know if you remember me—" Karen started in.

"Of course I remember you, Mrs. Friedman," Kathy Lauer replied, cradling her daughter's face to her thigh.

"*Karen,*" Karen replied. "I'm sorry to bother you. I know you must be wondering what I'm doing here, out of the blue. I was just wondering if your husband might be at home."

Kathy Lauer looked at her a bit strangely. "My husband?"

There was a bit of an awkward pause.

Karen nodded. "Jon called me a couple of times, after Charlie—" She stopped herself before she said the word. "I'm a little embarrassed. I never got back to him. I was all caught up then. I know it's a while back. But he mentioned some things. . . ."

"*Some things?*" Kathy Lauer stared. Karen couldn't quite read her reaction, nervousness or annoyance. Kathy asked her daughter to go back into the kitchen, said she'd be along in a second to finish rolling the cookie dough with her. The little girl ran off.

"Some things about my husband's business," Karen clarified. "By any chance is he around? I know it's a little strange to be coming here now. . . ."

"Jon's dead," Kathy Lauer said. "I thought you knew."

"*Dead?*" Karen felt her heart come to a stop and the blood rush out of her face. She shook her head numbly. "My God, I'm so sorry. . . . No . . ."

"About a month ago," his wife said. "He was on his bike coming back up the road, up Mountain View. A car ran into him. Just like that. A hit-and-run. The guy who hit him never even stopped."

CHAPTER FORTY

Dock 39 was a dingy, nautical-style bar in the harbor, not far from the navy yard. A shorted-out Miller sign flickered on and off in the window, while a carving of a ship's bow hung above the entrance on the wooden façade. From the street Hauck could see a TV on inside. A basketball game. It was playoff time. A crowd of people gathered whooping around the bar.

Hauck stepped inside.

The place was dark, smoky, jammed with bodies fresh from the docks. A noisy throng at the bar was following the game. The Pistons versus the Heat. People were still in their work clothes, blowing off steam. Dock workers and seamen. No office crowd here. Ray Dubose had told Hauck that this was where he could find him.

Hauck caught the barman's eye and asked him for a Bass ale. He spotted Pappy, huddled with a few guys drinking beer down at the end of the bar. The old man seemed disinterested in the game. He stared ahead, ignoring the sudden shouts that occasionally rang out or the jab of his neighbor's elbow when someone made a play. At some point Pappy turned around and noticed Hauck, Pappy's eyes narrowing balefully and his jaw growing tight. He picked up his beer and stood up, pushing himself away from his crew.

He came over to Hauck, pushing through the crowd. "I heard you been asking about me. I thought I told you to head back to where you came."

"I'm trying to solve a murder," Hauck told him.

"I don't need you to solve no murder. I need you to leave me alone and go back home."

"What did you stumble into?" Hauck asked. "That's why you won't talk to me, isn't it? That's why you quit your job—or were pressured to. Someone threatened you. You can't keep pretending it's going to go away. It won't go away now. Your son is dead. That's what that 'accident' up in Greenwich was about, wasn't it? Why AJ was killed."

"Get the hell away from me." Pappy Raymond pushed away Hauck's arm. Hauck could see he was drunk.

"I'm trying to solve your son's murder, Mr. Raymond. And I will, whether you help me or not. Why don't you make it easy and tell me what you found?"

The more Hauck said, the more the anger seemed to build in Pappy Raymond's eyes. "You're not hearing me, are you, son?" He thrust his beer mug into Hauck's chest. "I don't want your help. I don't need it. Go on out of here. Go back home."

Hauck grabbed his arm. "I'm not your enemy, old man. But letting your son's death eat away at you by doing nothing is. Those ships were falsifying something. They were empty, right? There was some kind of fraud going on. That's why AJ was killed. It wasn't any 'accident' up there. I know it—you know it, too. And I'm not backing off. You don't tell me, someone will. I'll pitch a tent on your goddamn lawn until I know."

A roar went up from the bar. "C'mon, Pappy!" one of his buddies yelled to him. "Wade just hit a three. We're back down by six."

"This is the last time I'm telling you." Pappy glared. His gaze burned into Hauck's eyes. "Go on home."

"No." Hauck shook his head. "I'm not."

That was when the old guy raised his arm and took a swing at him. A wild one, his fist catching on the shoulder of a man nearby, but the punch of a man who was used to throwing them, and it surprised Hauck, catching him on the side of his face. The mug shot out of his hands, crashing to the floor, spilling beer.

People spun around to them. "*Whoa . . . !*"

"What is it you want from me, mister?" Pappy grabbed Hauck by the collar. He raised his fist again. "Can't you just go back to wherever the hell you're from and let what's happened here die out? You want to be a hero, solve someone else's crime. Leave my family alone."

"Why are you protecting these people? Whoever they are, they killed your son."

Pappy's face was barely an inch away from Hauck's, the smell of beer and anger all over him. He raised his fist back again.

"Why?" Hauck stared at him. "*Why . . . ?*"

"Because I have other children," Pappy said, anguish burning in his eyes. His fist hesitated. "Don't you understand? *They* have children."

Suddenly the wrath in the old man's eyes began to diminish, and what was left there, in his hot, tremoring irises, was something else. Helplessness. The desperation of someone boxed in, with nowhere to turn.

"You don't know." Pappy glared at him, lowering his fist, releasing Hauck's collar. "You just don't know. . . ."

"I do know." Hauck met the old man's eyes. "I know exactly. I lost a child, too."

Hauck pressed something into Pappy's hand as a couple of his friends finally came over and pulled him away, saying the old man had had one too many, offering to buy Hauck another beer. They dragged him back to the bar, where he sat, his face flushed with alcohol and incoherence, amid the hollering and smoke.

Dejected, Pappy opened his fist and stared. His eyes widened. Then he looked back at Hauck.

Please, his expression said, this time with desperation. *Just go away.*

CHAPTER FORTY-ONE

"Mom?"

Samantha knocked on the bedroom door.

Karen turned. "Yes, hon."

Karen was on the bed with the TV going. She didn't even know what she was watching. The whole ride back to Greenwich, it beat on her—Jonathan was dead. Struck by a car coming down from the hill while cycling back to his home. Charlie's trader had been trying to tell her something. He had a family, two young kids. And just like that boy who had Charlie's name in his pocket, who had died in Greenwich the same day Charlie disappeared—Jonathan had died the same way. A hit-and-run. If she hadn't had the thought to go and see him, she would never have known.

Samantha sat beside her. "Mom, what's going on?"

Karen turned down the volume. "What do you mean?"

"Mom, please, we're not idiots. You haven't been yourself for over a week. You don't exactly have to have a medical degree to see that you don't have the flu. Something's going on. Are you okay?"

"Of course I'm okay, honey." Karen knew that her face was saying something different. *How could she possibly tell her daughter this?*

Sam stared. "I don't believe you. Look at you. You've barely left the house in days. You haven't been working out or gone to yoga. You're pale as a ghost. You can't keep things from us. If they're important. You're not sick, are you?"

"No, baby." Karen reached for her daughter's hand. "I'm not sick. I promise."

"So what is it, then?"

What could she possibly say? That things were starting to piece together that were really scaring her? That she had seen her husband's face after he'd supposedly died? That she had come upon phony passports and money? That he may have been doing something illegal? That two people who might've shed some light on it were dead? How do you drag your children into the truth that their father had deceived them all in such a monstrous way? Karen asked herself. How do you unleash that kind of hurt and pain onto someone you love so much?

"*Pregnant,* then?" Sam pressed her, with a sheepish grin.

"No, honey"—Karen smiled back—"I'm not pregnant." A tear built up in her eye.

"Are you sad about me going off to college? Because if you are, I won't go. I could go somewhere local. Stay here with you and Alex . . ."

"Oh, Samantha." Karen pulled her daughter close and squeezed. "I would never, ever do that to you. I'm so proud of you, hon. How you've dealt with all this. I know how hard it's been. I'm proud of both of you. You've got lives to live. What's happened to your father can't change that."

"So what *is* it then, Mom?" Sam curled up her knee. "I saw that detective here the other night. The one from Greenwich. You guys were outside in the rain. Please, you can tell me. You always want honesty from me. Now it's your turn."

"I know," Karen said. She lifted the hair out of Sam's eyes. "I've always asked that from you, and you've given it, haven't you?"

"Pretty much." Samantha shrugged. "I've held a few things back."

"Pretty much." Karen smiled again, looking in her daughter's eyes. "That's about all I could ask for, isn't it, honey?"

Samantha smiled in return.

"I know it's my turn, Sam. But I just can't tell you, honey. Not just yet. I'm sorry. There are some things—"

"It's about Dad, isn't it? I've seen you looking through his old things."

"Sam, please, you have to trust me. I can't—"

"I know he loved you, Mom." Samantha's eyes shone brightly. "Loved all of us. I just hope that in my life I'm lucky enough to find someone who loved me the same way."

"Yes, baby." Karen held her close. Tears wound their way down her cheeks as they clung to each other there. "I know, baby, I know—"

Then in mid-sentence she stopped. Something unsettling crossed her mind.

Lauer's wife had said he was set to testify regarding Harbor the week he was killed. Saul Lennick would have known that. *Let me handle it, Karen. . . .* He had never told her anything.

All of a sudden, Karen wondered, *Did he know?*

Did he know Charlie was alive?

"Yes, baby . . ." Karen kept brushing her daughter's hair. "I hope to God one day you do."

CHAPTER FORTY-TWO

Saul Lennick waited on the Charles Bridge in Prague overlooking the Vltava River.

The bridge teemed with tourists and afternoon pedestrians. Artists sat at easels capturing the view. Violinists played Dvořák and Smetana. Spring had left a festive mood in the city. He looked up at the Gothic spires of St. Vitus and Prague Castle. This was one of his favorite views.

Three men in business attire stepped onto the span from the Linhart Ulice entrance and paused underneath the east tower.

The sandy-haired one, in a topcoat and brown felt hat, wearing wire-rimmed spectacles, and with a ruddy, cheerful face, came forward holding a metal briefcase, while the others waited a few steps behind.

Lennick knew him well.

Johann-Pieter Fichte was German. He had worked in the private banking departments of Credit Suisse and the Bundesbank. Fichte possessed a doctorate in economics from the University of Basel. Now he was a private banker, catering to the highest financial circles.

He was also known to represent some of the most unsavory people in the world.

The banker was what was known in the trade as a "money trafficker." His particular skill was to be able to shift sizable assets from any part of the world in no matter what form: cash, stones, arms—even drugs on occasion—until they emerged in a completely different currency as clean and perfectly investable funds. He did this through a network of currency traders and shell corporations, a labyrinthine web of relationships that stretched from the dark corners of the underworld to boardrooms across the globe. Among Fichte's less visible clients were Iraqi clerics and Afghani warlords who had looted American reconstruction funds; a Kazakh oil minister, a cousin of the president, who had diverted a tenth of his country's reserves; Russian oligarchs, who dealt primarily in drugs and prostitution; even the Colombian drug cartels.

Fichte waved, angling through the crowd. His two associates—bodyguards, Lennick assumed—stayed a few paces behind.

"Saul!" Fichte said, embracing Lennick with a broad smile, placing his case at Lennick's feet. "It's always a pleasure to see you, my friend. And for you to come all this way."

"The price of a service job." Lennick grinned, grasping the banker's hand.

"Yes, we are only the high-priced errand boys and accountants of the rich"—the banker shrugged—"available at their beck and call. So how is your lovely wife? And your daughter? She's still up in Boston, is she not? Lovely city."

"All fine, Johann. Thank you for asking. Shall we get on?"

"Ah, business." Fichte sighed, turning to face the river. "The American way . . . His Excellency Major General Mubuto sends you his highest regards."

"I'm honored," Lennick said, lying. "And you will return them, of course."

"Of course." The German banker amped up his smile. Then, in a soft voice, staring ahead, as if his gaze were tracking a far-off bird that had landed on the Vltava, he explained. "The funds we discussed will be in the form of four separate deliveries. The first is already on account at Zurich Bank, ready to be transferred upon your say-so to anywhere in the world. The second is currently held at the BalticBank in Estonia. It is in the form of a charitable trust designed to sponsor UN grain shipments to needy populations in East Africa."

Lennick smiled. Fichte always had a cultivated sense of irony.

"I thought you'd appreciate that. The third delivery is presently in non-cash form. Military hardware. Some of it your own, I am told. It should be leaving the country within the week. The general is quite insistent on the timing."

"Why the rush?"

"Pending the status of the Ethiopian military buildup on the Sudanese border, it's conceivable His Excellency and his family may be forced to leave the country at fairly short notice." He winked.

"I'll see to it the funds don't sit unproductive for too long," Lennick promised with a smile.

"That would be greatly appreciated." The German bowed. Then his tone turned businesslike again. "As discussed, each of the deliveries will be in the amount of two hundred and fifty million euros."

Well over a billion dollars. Even Lennick had to marvel. It crossed his mind just how many heads had had to roll and thousands of fortunes wiped out to assemble such a sum.

The banker said, "I think we've already gone over the general agreement."

"The mix of products is quite diversified and fully transparent if need be," Lennick replied. "A combination of U.S. and worldwide equities, real-estate trusts, hedge funds. Twenty percent will be retained in our private equity fund. As you know, we've been able to achieve a twenty-two and a half percent average portfolio return over the past seven years, net of any unforeseen fluctuations, of course."

"*Fluctuations . . .*" The German nodded, the warmth in his blue eyes suddenly dimmed. "I assume you're speaking of that energy hedge fund that collapsed last year. I hope it won't be necessary to revisit my clients' unhappiness over that development, will it, Saul?"

"As said"—Lennick swallowed a lump, trying to redirect the subject—"an unforeseen fluctuation, Johann. It won't happen again."

The truth was, with the amount of capital available in today's world, Lennick had learned to make money in every conceivable market environment. In times of economic strength or stagnation. Good markets or bad. Even following acts of terrorism. The panic after 9/11 would never occur again. He had billions invested on all sides of the economic ledger, impervious to the vagaries of whoever won or lost. Today geopolitical trends and shifts were merely hiccups in the global transfer of capital. Yes, there were always blips—blips like Charlie, betting on the price of oil so stubbornly and unable to cover his spots on the way down. But behind that, all one had to do was look at the vast Saudi and Kuwaiti investment funds, the world's greatest oil producers, hedging their bets by buying up all the ethanol-producing sugarcane fields in the world.

It was the greatest capital-enlarging engine in the world.

"So it doesn't bother you, my friend?" the German banker suddenly asked. "You are a Jew, yes, and yet you know that this money you take regularly finds its way into the hands of interests that are unfriendly to your own race."

"Yes, I'm a Jew." Lennick looked at him and shrugged. "But I learned a long time ago that money is neutral, Johann."

"Yes, money is neutral," Fichte agreed. "Still, my client's patience is not." His expression sharpened again. "The loss of over half a billion dollars of their funds does not sit easily with these kinds of people, Saul. They asked me to remind you—your daughter has children up in Boston, does she not?" He met Lennick's eye. "Ages two and four?"

The blood seeped from Lennick's face.

"I was asked to inquire as to their general health, Saul. I hope they're well. Just a thought, my old friend, from my own employers. Please, do not dwell. Still . . ." His smile returned with an affable tap of Lennick's arm. "A small incentive to keep those—how was it you phrased it?—*fluctuations* to a minimum, yes?"

A cold bead of sweat traveled down Lennick's back underneath his six-hundred-dollar Brioni pinstripe shirt.

"Your man lost us a considerable amount of money," Fichte said. "You shouldn't be so surprised, Saul. You know who you're playing with here. No one is above accountability, my friend—*even you*."

Fichte put on his hat.

Lennick felt a constriction in his chest. His palms, suddenly slick with sweat, pressed deeply onto the bridge's railing. He nodded. "You spoke of four new deliveries, Johann. Two hundred and fifty million euros each. So far you've only mentioned three."

"Ah, *the fourth* . . . " The German banker smiled and patted Lennick briskly on the back. He drew his gaze to the metal case at his feet.

"The fourth I'm giving you *today*, Herr Lennick. In bearer bonds. My men will be happy to escort you to wherever you would like it placed."

CHAPTER FORTY-THREE

By morning the welt on Hauck's face had gone down a bit. He had packed his bags, set to check out in a couple of minutes. There was no need to press the old man any longer. He had other ways to find out what he needed to know. He glanced at his watch. He had a ten o'clock plane.

When he opened the door to leave, Pappy Raymond was leaning on the outside railing.

The old man's face was haggard, eyes bloodshot and drawn. He looked like he'd spent the night curled up in some alley. Or like he'd been in a street fight with a ferret. And the ferret had won!

"How's the eye?" He looked at Hauck. Somewhere in his tone was the hint of an apology.

"Works." Hauck shrugged, rubbing the side of his face. "I was a little peeved about the beer, though."

"Yeah." Pappy smiled sheepishly. "Guess I owe you one of those." The blue in his hooded eyes shone through. "You heading home?"

"Somehow I got the sense you'd be okay with that."

"Hmphh," Pappy snorted. "How'd I ever give you that idea?"

Hauck waited. He set down his bags.

"I was a fool my whole life," Pappy said finally. He eased off the railing. "Stubborn with the best of them. Problem is, it takes getting old to find that out. Then it's too late."

From his coverall pocket, he took out the Orange Bowl ticket stub Hauck had placed in his hand the night before. He bunched up his lips. "We drove all day to see that game. Might as well have been the Super Bowl for all my son cared. It was to him. Seminoles were always his team." He scratched his head, suddenly clear-eyed. "I guess I should say thanks. I remember last night you said . . ."

"My daughter was four." Hauck gazed back at him. "She was run over by our car, in our own driveway. Five years ago. I'd been driving. I thought I'd left it in park. I was bitter, after the pain finally eased. My ex-wife still can't look me in the eyes without seeing it all over. So I know. . . . That's all I meant to say."

"Never goes away, does it?" Raymond shifted his weight on the railing.

Hauck shook his head. "Never does."

Raymond let out a breath. "I watched those goddamn tankers come in three, four times. From Venezuela, the Philippines, Trinidad. Twice I even brought 'em in myself. Even a fool could see those ships were riding way too high. Didn't have a lick of oil. Even snuck inside the holds once to see for myself." He shook his head. "Clean as a baby's ass. It's not right what they were trying to do. . . ."

Hauck asked, "You took it to your boss?"

"My boss, the harbormaster, the customs people . . . No duty on oil, so what the hell do they care? No telling who was getting paid. I kept hearing, 'You just bring 'em in and park 'em, old man. Don't stir it up.' But I kept stirring. Then I got this call."

"To push you to stop?"

Pappy nodded. " 'Don't make waves, mister. You never know where they might fall.' Finally I got this visit, too."

"You remember from whom?"

"Met me outside the bar, just like you. Square jaw, dark hair, mustache. The kind of SOB who looked like he meant trouble. Mentioned my boy up north. Even showed me a picture. AJ and some gal up there with a kid. I knew what he was telling me. Still I kept at it. Called up this reporter I knew. I said I'd get him proof. That's when I went aboard. A week later they sent me *this*."

Pappy dug into his trousers, the kind of navy blue work pants he'd worn on the job, and came out with his cell phone, scanning it until he found a stored call. He handed it to Hauck.

A photo. Hauck exhaled. AJ Raymond lying in the road.

Pappy pointed. "You see what they wrote to me there?"

SEEN ENOUGH NOW?

A screw of anger and understanding tightened in Hauck's chest. "Who sent this to you?"

Pappy shook his head. "Never knew."

"You take this to the police?"

Another shake of the head. "They won. No."

"I'd like to send this picture to myself, if that's okay?"

"Go ahead. I'm not standing by any longer. It's yours now."

Hauck forwarded the image to himself. Felt his phone vibrate.

"He was a good boy, my son." Pappy looked Hauck in the eye. "He liked surfing and fishing. Cars. He'd never hurt a fly. He didn't deserve to die like that. . . ."

Hauck handed Pappy back the phone. He moved next to the old man on the railing. "These people, it was they that did this to him, not you. You were just trying to do what you thought was right."

Pappy gazed at him. "Why are you doing all this, mister? You never showed me no badge. It can't just be for AJ."

"My daughter," Hauck said, shrugging back at him, "she had red hair, too."

"So we're the same." Pappy smiled. "Sort of. I was wrong, Lieutenant, the way I treated you. I was scared for Pete and my other boy, Walker, their families. Bringing all this up again. But you get them. You get those sons of bitches who killed my boy. I don't know why they did. I don't know what they were protecting. But whatever it was, it wasn't worth this. You get them, you hear? Wherever this leads. And when you do"—he winked, a glimmer in his eye—"you don't think about throwin' 'em in no jail, you understand?"

Hauck smiled. He squeezed the man on the arm. "So what was the name?"

Pappy squinted. "The *name*?"

"Of the tanker?" Hauck asked.

"Some Greek word." Pappy sniffed. "I looked it up. Goddess of the underworld. *Persephone,* it was called."

CHAPTER FORTY-FOUR

Vito Collucci could find anything, if the matter was about money. He made his living as a forensic accountant, tracking down the buried assets of philandering husbands for vengeful ex-wives. The hidden profits of large companies trying to fend off class-action suits. Before putting out a shingle, he had been a detective on the Stamford police force for fifteen years, which was where Hauck knew him from.

Vito Collucci could spot a bad seed in a sperm bank, he liked to say.

"Vito, I need a favor," Hauck said over the phone, heading out to the airport for his flight from Pensacola.

These days Vito ran a good-size company. He was a frequent "guest expert" on MSNBC, but he had never forgotten how Hauck had thrown him cases when he first got started.

"When?" he asked. When Hauck called, Vito knew it usually involved information. Information that was hard to find.

"Today," Hauck said. "I guess, tomorrow, if you need it."

"Today's fine."

Hauck landed at two, taking his Bronco up from La Guardia. As he passed Greenwich heading to Stamford, the station a mile away, it occurred to him that he was getting deeper into something and a little further outside the law than he liked. He thought about giving Karen Friedman a call but decided to wait. There was a text message on his phone.

Usual place. From Vito. Three P.M. was fine.

The usual place was the Stamford Restaurant & Pizzeria, a no-frills cops' haunt on Main Street, past downtown, close to the Darien border.

Vito was already there, at one of the long tables covered in checkered cloths. He was short, barrel-chested, with thick wrestler's forearms and wiry graying hair. A plate of ziti with sauce was set before him, and a bowl of escarole and cannellini beans.

"I'd run up the check," he said as Hauck came in, "but you're lucky, Ellie's got me on this cholesterol thing."

"I can see." Hauck grinned and sat down. He ordered the same. "So how've you been?"

"Good," Vito said. "Busy."

"You look thinner on TV."

"And you don't seem to age," Vito said. "Except for that shiner you're carrying. You gotta realize, Ty, you can't tussle with the young dudes anymore."

"I'll keep that in mind."

Vito had a manila envelope beside him on the table. He pushed it over to Hauck. "Take a peek. I'll let you know what I found."

Hauck gazed at the contents.

"The ship was easy. I looked it up in Jane's. *Persephone,* right?" Vito stabbed at a few ziti with his fork. "ULCC-class supertanker. Built in Germany, 1978. Pretty much outdated now. What're you thinking, maybe of trading up to something a bit more seaworthy, Ty?"

"Might look good on the sound." Hauck nodded. "Be a bit of a bitch to dock, though." He scanned a photocopied page from the nautical manual that displayed an image of the ship. Sixty-two thousand tons.

"Been sold around a couple of times over the years," Vito went on. "The last time to some Greek shipping company—Argos Maritime. That mean anything to you?"

Hauck shook his head.

"Didn't think it would. So I kept at it. Pretended that I was a lawyer's assistant to the company, tracking down a claim. The past four years this scrap heap's been leased to some oil-exploration outfit I can't bring up anything on anywhere. Dolphin Oil."

Hauck scratched his head. "Who's Dolphin?"

"Fuck if I know." Vito shrugged. "Believe me, I checked. No record of them anywhere in the D&B. Then I tried a trade list of petroleum-exploration and -development companies, and it didn't show up either. If Dolphin's a player in the oil and gas business, they're keeping it pretty much on the QT."

"You think they're a real company?"

"My thoughts exactly," Vito said, pushing his plate away. "So I kept digging. I tried a directory of offshore-company listings. No record of them in Europe or Asia. I'm thinking, how does a company with no record in the industry lease a goddamn supertanker? Guess what came up? Feel free to turn the page."

Hauck did.

Vito grinned widely. "Out of Tortola—in the BVIs . . . Whaddaya know about that—*Dolphin fucking Oil!*"

"In *Tortola?*"

Vito nodded. "A lot of companies are being set up there now. It's like a mini–Cayman Islands. Avoids taxes. Keeps the funds out from under the eye of the U.S. government. As well as the SEC, if they're public. Far as I can tell, and I've only been at it a couple of hours, Dolphin's basically just a holding company. No revenues or profits of any kind. No transactions. A shell. The management seems to be just a bunch of fancy barristers down there. Check out the board—everybody's got an LLC behind his name. Far as I can tell, it basically belongs to this investment company that's situated down there as well. Falcon Partners."

"*Falcon* . . . never heard of it." Hauck shook his head.

"You're not supposed to have heard of it, Ty. That's why the hell it's there! It's some kind of private investment partnership. Or at least *was*. The fund was dissolved and the assets redistributed back to its limited partners earlier this year. Took me a while to figure out why. I was hoping to try to get a list of who the partners were, but it's totally private—buttoned up. Whoever they are, the money's probably long back to wherever it came from by now."

Hauck scanned over the one-page company summary of Falcon. He knew in his gut he was getting close.

Whoever owned Dolphin had been engaged in some kind of cover-up. They had used empty tankers but declared that they were filled with oil. Pappy had stumbled onto it, and they'd tried to shut him up, but whatever they were hiding, he wasn't the kind that shut up easily, and it had ended up costing him his son. *Seen enough now?* Dolphin led to Falcon.

Close enough, Hauck felt, the hairs raised expectantly on his arms. "How the hell do we get to Falcon, Vito?"

The detective was staring at him. "What's the point of all this, Ty?"

"The point?"

Vito shrugged. "First time since I've known you you're not up front with me. My spies tell me you're on leave from the department."

"Maybe your spies told you why."

"Something personal, is all. Some kind of case that's consuming you."

"It's called murder, Vito, no matter who I'm working for. And if this was all just so personal"—Hauck looked back at him, curling a smile—"I'd have called Match.com, not you."

Vito grinned. "Just warning an old friend to stay within the boundaries, that's all."

The private investigator took out a folded piece of paper from his jacket pocket and pushed it across the table. "Whoever Falcon is, Ty, they wanted to keep it secret. The board's pretty much the same legal functionaries as Dolphin."

Hauck scanned down the page. Nothing. Fucking close.

"One thing, though," Vito added. "I mentioned that Falcon was comprised of a bunch of limited partners who want to remain secret. But the general partner *is* listed. In the investment agreement, plain as day. It's the outfit who manages the funds."

Hauck turned the page. Staring back at him, there was a name. Vito had highlighted it in yellow.

When Hauck's gaze fell on it, his heart sank a little, as opposed to the leap he'd always imagined. He knew where this was about to lead.

Harbor Capital. The general partner.

Harbor was the firm that belonged to Karen Friedman's husband.

"That what you're looking for?" Vito asked, watching Hauck dwell on the page.

"Yeah, that's what I'm looking for, buddy." Hauck sighed.

CHAPTER **FORTY-FIVE**

The man broke through the surface of the glistening turquoise water in the remote Caribbean cove.

No one around. Not even a name for this place, just a speck on the map. The only sounds were the caws of a handful of frigate birds as they tumbled out of the sky into the sea searching for prey. The man looked back at the perfect half circle of white sand beach, palm trees swaying in the languid breeze on the shore.

He could be anywhere. Anywhere in the world.

Why did he choose here?

Twenty yards away, his boat bobbed on the tranquil tide. What seemed like a lifetime ago, it occurred to him, he had told his wife he could spend the rest of his life in just such a place as this. A place without markets or indices. Without cell phones or TV. A place where no one looked for you.

And where there was no one to find you.

Every day that part of his life became a more distant part of his mind. The thought had a strange appeal to him.

The rest of his life.

He raised his face into the warm rays of the sun. His hair was cut short now, shaved in a way that might make his children roll their eyes, some old guy trying to appear cool. His body was fit and trim. He no longer wore glasses. His face was covered in a stubbly growth. He had a local's tan.

And money.

Enough money to last forever. If he could manage it right. And a new name. Hanson. Steven Hanson. A name he had paid for. A name no one knew.

Not his wife, his kids.

Not those who might want to find him.

In this complicated world of computers and personal histories, he had simply gone, *poof.* Disappeared. One life ended—with remorse, regret, at the pain he knew he'd caused, the trust he'd broken. Still, he'd had to do it. It had been necessary. To save them. To save himself.

One life ended—and another sprang up.

When the moment had presented itself, he could not turn it down.

He hardly even thought of it now. The blast. One minute he had gone back from the front of the car to make a call, then flash! A black, rattling cloud with a core of orange heat. Like a furnace. The clothes burned off your back. Hurled against the wall. In a tangle of people screaming. Black smoke everywhere, the dark tide rushing over him. He was sure he was dead. He remembered thinking, through the haze, this way was best. It solved everything.

Just die.

When he came to, he looked at the ravaged train car. Every place he had been just a moment before was gone. Obliterated. The car in which he'd sat. The people around him, who were reading the paper, listening to their iPods. Gone. In a horrifying ocean of flame. He coughed up smoke. *Got to get out of here,* he thought. His brain was ringing. Numb. He staggered out, onto the platform. Horrible sights—blood everywhere, the smell of cordite and charred flesh. People moaning, calling out for help. *What could he do?* He had to get out, let Karen know he was alive.

Then it all became startlingly clear.

This was how. This was what had been presented to him.

He could die.

He stumbled over something. A body. Its face almost unrecognizable. In the chaos he knew he needed to be someone else. He felt around in the man's trousers. In the smoke-filled darkness, the whole station black. He found it. He didn't even look at the name. What did it matter? Then he began to run. His wits suddenly clearer than they'd ever been. *This was how!* Running, stumbling over the flow, not toward the entrance but to the other end of the tracks. Away from the flames. People from the rear cars were rushing there. The uptown entrances. Away from the flames. The one thing he had to do, resonating in his mind. Abel Raymond. He took a last look back at the smoldering car.

He could die.

"Mr. Hanson!" A voice suddenly brought him back, interrupting his dark memory. Leaning back in the water, Charles looked over at the boat. His Trinidadian captain was bending over the bow. "Mr. Hanson, w'ought to be pushing off about now. If we want to make it there by night."

There. Wherever it was they were heading. Another dot on the map. With a bank. A rare-stone dealer. What did it matter?

"Right, I'll be along in a moment," he called back.

Treading water, he looked at the idyllic cove one last time.

Why had he come here? The memories only hurt him. The happy voices and recollections only filled him with regret and shame. He prayed she had found a new life, someone new to love her. And Sam and Alex . . . That was the only hope open to him now. *We could spend the rest of our lives here,* he had told her once.

The rest of our lives.

Charles Friedman swam toward the anchored boat, its name painted on the stern in gold script. The only attachment he allowed himself, the only reminder.

Emberglow.

PART *THREE*

THREE

Twice a week, Tuesday and Thursday, Ronald Torbor generally took his lunch at home. Those days Mr. Carty, the senior bank manager, covered his desk from one to three.

As assistant manager of the First Caribbean Bank on the isle of Nevis, Ronald lived in a comfortable three-bedroom stone house just off the airport road, large enough to fit his own family—his wife, Edith, along with Alya and Peter and Ezra, and his wife's mother, too. At the bank, people came to him to open accounts, apply for loans—the position came, to the view of his fellow locals, with a certain air of importance. He also took pleasure in catering to the needs of some of the island's wealthier clientele. Though he had grown up kicking around a soccer ball on dirt fields, Ronald now liked golf on the weekends over on St. Kitts. And when the general manager, who was soon to be transferred, went back home, Ronald felt sure he had a good chance of becoming the bank's first local-born manager.

That Tuesday, Edith had prepared him his favorite—stewed chicken in a green curry sauce. It was May. Not much going on at the office. Once the tourist season died, Nevis was basically a sleepy little isle. These kinds of days, other than waving to Mr. Carty that he was back, he felt there was no urgency to hurry back to his desk.

At the table, Ronald glanced over the paper: the results from the Caribbean cricket championships being held in Jamaica. His six-year-old, Ezra, was home from school. After lunch, Edith was taking him to the doctor. The boy had what they called Asperger's syndrome, a mild form of autism. And on Nevis, despite the rush of new money and developers, the care wasn't very good.

"After work you can come watch Peter play soccer," said Edith, seated in the chair next to Ezra. The boy was playing with a toy truck, making noise.

"Yes, Edith." Ronald sighed, enjoying his peace. He focused on the box score. Matson, for Barbados, wrong-foots Anguilla for six!

"And you can bring me back some fresh-baked roti from Mrs. Williams, if you please." Her bakery was directly across from the bank, best on the island. "You know the kind I like, onion and—"

"Yes, mum," Ronald muttered again.

"And don't be 'mumming' me in front of your boy like I'm some kind of schoolmarm, Ronald."

Ronald looked up from the paper and flashed Ezra a wink.

The six-year-old started to laugh.

Outside, they heard the sound of gravel crunching, as a car drove up the road to their house.

"That is probably Mr. P.," Edith said. Paul Williams, her cousin. "I said he could come by about a loan."

"Jeez, Edith," Ronald groaned, "couldn't you have him just come by the bank?"

But it wasn't Mr. P. It was two white men, who got out of the Jeep and stepped up to the front door. One was short and stocky, with wraparound sunglasses and a thick mustache. The other was taller, wearing a light sport jacket with a colorful beach shirt underneath with a baseball cap.

Ronald shrugged. "Who's this?"

"I don't know." Edith opened the door.

"Afternoon, ma'am." The mustached man politely took off his hat. His eyes drifted past her. "Mind if we speak to your husband? I can see he's at home."

Ronald stood up. He'd never seen them before. "What's this about?"

"Banking business," the man said, stepping around Ronald's wife and into the house.

"Banking hours are closed—for lunch." Ronald tried not to seem unfriendly. "I'll be back down there at three."

"No." The mustached man lifted his glasses and smiled. "I'm afraid the bank is open, Mr. Torbor. *Right here.*"

The man shut the door. "Just look at these as extra hours."

A shudder of fear rippled through Ronald's body. Edith met his gaze as if to find out what was going on, then moved back around to the table, next to her son.

The mustached man nodded to Ronald. "Sit down."

Ronald did, the man flipping a chair around and pulling it up to him, smiling strangely. "We're really sorry to interrupt your lunch, Mr. Torbor. You can get back to it, though, once you tell us what we need."

"What you need . . . ?"

"That's right, Mr. Torbor." The man reached into his jacket and removed a folded sheet. "This is the number of a private account at your bank. It should be familiar. A sizable amount of money was wired into it several months back, from Tortola, the Barclays bank there."

Ronald stared at the number. His eyes grew wide. The numbers were from his bank, First Caribbean. The taller man had pulled up a chair next to Ezra, winking and making mugging faces at the boy, which made him laugh. Ronald glanced fearfully toward Edith. *What the hell are they doing here?*

"This particular account is no longer active, Mr. Torbor," the man with the mustache acknowledged. "The funds are no longer in your bank. But what we want to know, and what you're going to help us find out, Mr. Torbor, if you hope to ever get back to your lunch and this happy little life of yours, is precisely where the funds were wired—once they left here. And also under what name."

Perspiration was starting to soak through Ronald's newly pressed white shirt. "You must know I can't give out that kind of information. That's all private. Covered by banking regulations—"

"Private." The mustached man nodded, glancing toward his partner.

"Regulations." The man in the beach shirt sighed. "Always a bitch. We sort of anticipated that."

With a sudden motion, he reached over and jerked Ezra up out of his chair. Surprised, the child whimpered. The man put him on his lap. Edith tried to stop him, but he just elbowed her, knocking her to the floor.

"Ezra!" she cried out.

The small boy started crying. Ronald leaped up.

"Sit down!" The mustached man grabbed him by the arm. He also took something out of his jacket and placed it on the table.

Something black and metallic. Ronald felt his heart seize as he saw what it was. "Sit down."

Frantic, Ronald lowered himself back into the chair. He looked at Edith helplessly. "Whatever you want. Please, don't hurt Ezra."

"No reason to, Mr. Torbor." The mustached man smiled. "But no point beating around the bush. What you're going to do now is call in to your office, and I want you to have your secretary or whomever the fuck you talk to down there look up that account. Make up whatever excuse or justification you need. We know you don't get those kinds of funds in your sleepy little bank very often. I want to know where it went, which country, what bank, and under what name. Do you understand?"

Ronald sat silent.

"Your father understands what I mean, doesn't he, boy?" He tickled Ezra's ear. "Because if he doesn't"—his eyes now shifted darkly—"I promise that your lives will not be happy, and you will remember this little moment with regret and anguish for as long as you live. I'm clear on that, aren't I, Mr. Torbor?"

"*Do it, Ronald, please, do it,*" Edith pleaded, pulling herself up off the floor.

"I can't. I can't," he said, trembling. "There are procedures for this sort of thing. Even if I agreed, it's governed by international banking regulations. Laws . . ."

"Back to those regulations again." The mustached man shook his head and sighed loudly.

The taller man holding Ezra removed something from *his* jacket pocket.

Ronald's eyes bulged wide.

It was a tin of lighter fluid.

Ronald dove out of the chair to stop him, but the mustached man hit him on the side of the head with the gun, sending him sprawling onto the floor.

"*Oh, Jesus Lord, no!*" Edith screamed, trying to wrench the man off her son. He elbowed her away.

Then, smiling, the man holding Ezra took the crying boy by the collar and began to douse him with fluid.

Ronald launched himself again, but the mustached man had cocked his gun and raised it to Ronald's forehead. "I keep remembering asking you to sit down."

Ezra was bawling now.

"Here's your cell phone, Mr. Torbor," pushing Ronald his phone from across the table. "Make the call and we just go away. Now."

"*I can't.*" Ronald held out trembling hands. "Jesus God in heaven, don't. I . . . can't."

"I know he's a bit off, Mr. Torbor." The man shook his head. "But he's just an innocent boy. Shame to hurt him in this way. For a bunch of silly regulations . . . Anyway, not a pretty thing at all for your wife to witness, is it?"

"*Ronald!*"

The man holding Ezra took out a plastic lighter. He flicked it, sparking up a steady flame. He brought it close to the child's damp shirt.

"*No!*" Edith shrieked. "Ronald, please, don't let them do this! For God's sake, do whatever the hell they're asking. *Ronald, please . . .* "

Ezra was screaming. The man holding him drew the flame closer. The man with the mustache pushed the phone in front of Ronald and looked steadily at him.

"*Exactamente*, Mr. Torbor. Fuck the regulations. It's time to make that call."

CHAPTER **FORTY-SEVEN**

Karen rushed to drop Alex off at the Arch Street Teen Center that Tuesday afternoon, for a youth fund-raiser for the Kids in Crisis shelter in town.

She was excited when Hauck had called. They agreed to meet in the bar at L'Escale, overlooking Greenwich Harbor, which was virtually next door. She was eager to tell him what she'd found.

Hauck was sitting at a table near the bar and waved when she came in.

"Hi." She waved, folding her leather jacket over the back of her chair.

For a moment she moaned about how traffic was getting crazy in town this time of day. "Try to find a parking space on the avenue." She rolled her eyes in mock frustration. "You have to be a cop!"

"Seems fair to me." Hauck shrugged, suppressing a smile.

"I forgot who I was talking to!" Karen laughed. "Can't you do anything about this?"

"I'm on leave, remember? When I'm back, I promise that'll be the very first thing."

"Good!" Karen nodded brightly, as if pleased. "Don't let me down. I'm relying on you."

The waitress came over, and it took Karen about a second to order a pinot grigio. Hauck was already nursing a beer. She'd put on some makeup and a nice beige sweater over tight-fitting pants. Something made her want to look good. When her wine came, Hauck tilted his glass at her.

"We ought to think of something," she said.

"To simpler times," he proposed.

"Amen." Karen grinned. They touched glasses lightly.

It was a little awkward at first, and they just chatted. She told him about Alex's involvement on the Kids in Crisis board, which Hauck was impressed with and called "a pretty admirable thing."

Karen smiled. "Community-service requirement, Lieutenant. All the kids have to do it. It's a college application rite of spring."

She asked him where his daughter went to school and he said, "Brooklyn," the short version, leaving out Norah and Beth. "She's growing up pretty fast," he said. "Pretty soon I'll be doing the community-service thing."

Karen's eyes lit up. "Just wait for the SATs!"

Gradually Hauck grew relaxed, the lines between them softening just a little, suddenly feeling alive in the warm glow of her bright hazel eyes, the cluster of freckles dotting her cheeks, the trace of her accent, the fullness of her lips, the honey color of her hair. He decided to hold back what he'd learned about Dolphin and Charles's connection to it. About Thomas Mardy and how he'd been at the hit-and-run that day. Until he knew for sure. It would only hurt her more—send things down a path he would one day regret. Still, when he gazed at Karen Friedman, he was transported back to a part of his life that had not been wounded by loss. And he imagined—in the ease of her laugh, the second glass of wine, how she laughed at all the lines he had hoped she would— she was feeling the same way, too.

At a lull, Karen put down her wine. "So you said you made a little headway down there?"

He nodded. "You remember that hit-and-run that happened the day of the bombing, when I came by?"

"Of course I remember."

Hauck put down his beer. "I found out why the kid died."

Her eyes widened. "Why?"

He had thought carefully about this before she arrived, what he might say, and he heard himself retelling how some company was carrying on a fraud of some kind down there, a petroleum company, and how the kid's father—a harbor pilot—had stumbled right into the middle of it.

"It was a warning"—Hauck shrugged—"if you can believe it. To get him to back off."

"It was *murder*?" Karen said, a jolt of shock shooting through her.

Hauck nodded. "Yeah."

She sat back, stunned. "That's so terrible. You never thought it was an accident. My God . . ."

"And it worked."

"What do you mean?"

"The old man stopped. He buried it. It never would have come out if I didn't go down."

Karen's face turned pallid. "You said you went down there for me. How does this relate to Charles?"

How could he tell her? About Charles, Dolphin, the empty ships? Or how Charles had been in Greenwich that day? How could he hurt her more, more than she'd already been, until he knew? Knew for sure.

And being with her now, he knew why.

"The company," Hauck said, "the one that was doing this down there, had a connection to Harbor."

The color drained from Karen's face. "To Charlie?"

Hauck nodded. "Dolphin Petroleum. You know the name?"

She shook her head.

"It may have been part of a group of investments he owned."

Karen hesitated. "What do you mean, investments?"

"Offshore."

Karen put a hand to her mouth and looked at him. It only echoed what Saul had said. "You think Charles was involved? In this hit-and-run?"

"I don't want to get ahead of ourselves, Karen."

"Please don't protect me, Ty. You're thinking he was involved?"

"I don't know." He exhaled. He held back the fact that Charles had been up there that day. "There are still a lot more leads I have to run down."

"Leads?" Karen sat back. Her eyes had a strange, confused look to them. She pressed her palms together in front of her lips and nodded. "I found something, too, Ty."

"What?"

"I don't know, but it's scaring me a little—like you are now."

She described how she'd been going through some of Charles's old things, as he'd asked, his old files, had spoken to his old secretary and travel agent but been unable to find anything.

Until she came across a name.

"The guy had called me a couple of times, just after Charles died. Someone who worked for him." She described how Jonathan

Lauer had tried to contact her, the cryptic messages he'd left. *Some things you ought to know* . . . "I just couldn't deal with it back then. It was too much. I mentioned them to Saul. He said it was just personnel stuff and he'd take care of it."

Hauck nodded. "Okay . . ."

"But then I thought of it in light of all that's come up, and it began to gnaw at me. So I went out to see him while you were gone. To New Jersey. To see him. I didn't know where he worked now, and all I had was this address from when he worked for Charles, with a private number. I just took a chance. His wife answered the door." Karen's eyes turned glassy. "She told me the most horrible thing."

"What?"

"*He's dead.* He was killed. In a cycling accident, a few months back. What made it all a little creepy was that he'd been scheduled to give a deposition in some matter related to Harbor later in the week."

"What kind of matter?"

"I don't know. But it wasn't just that. It was the way he was killed. Coupled with the way your Raymond kid was killed, who had Charlie's name on him."

Hauck put down his glass, his antennae for these sorts of things beginning to buzz.

"A car hit him," Karen said. "Just like your guy. It was a hit-and-run."

A group of office people seated next to them suddenly grew louder. Karen leaned forward, her knees pressed together, her face a little blank.

"You did good," Hauck said, showing he was pleased. "Real good."

Some of the color returned to her cheeks.

"You hungry?" Hauck asked, taking a chance.

Karen shrugged, casting a quick glance at her watch. "Alex has a ride home with a neighbor. I guess I have a little time."

CHAPTER FORTY-EIGHT

On the way home, Hauck rang up Freddy Muñoz.

"LT!" his detective exclaimed in surprise. "Long time no hear. How's vacation?"

"I'm not on vacation, Freddy. Listen, I need a favor. I need you to get a copy of the file on an unsolved homicide in New Jersey. Upper Montclair. The victim's name is Lauer. L-A-U-E-R, like Matt. First name Jonathan. There may be a parallel investigation by the Jersey State Police."

Muñoz was writing it down. "Lauer. And what do I say is the reason we need it, LT?"

"Similar pattern to a case we've been looking at up here."

"And which case is that, Lieutenant?"

"It's an unsolved hit-and-run."

Muñoz paused. In the background there was the sound of young kids shouting, maybe the Yankees game on TV. "Jesus, Ty, this becoming an MO with you now?"

"Have someone drop it off at my home tomorrow. If I was active, I'd do it myself. And Freddy . . ." Hauck heard the sound of Freddy's son, Will, cheering. "This stays just between us, okay?"

"Yeah, LT," the detective answered. "Sure."

New leads, Hauck was thinking.

One definitely ran through Charlie Friedman's trustee, Lennick. Karen trusted him. Almost like a member of the family. He would have known about Lauer. Did he know about Dolphin and Falcon, too?

Did Charlie ever mention he was managing any accounts off-shore?

The other ran through New Jersey, this second hit-and-run. Hauck had never been one to have much faith in coincidences.

As he drove, his thoughts kept straying back to Karen. Off the top of his head, he came up with ten good, solid reasons he should stop now, before things went any further between them.

Starting with the fact that her husband was alive. And how Hauck had made a pledge to find him. And how he didn't want to cause her any more needless hurt by holding things back than she had already been through.

And how she was rich. Used to different things. Traveled in a totally different league.

Jesus, Ty, you're not exactly playing the strongest hand here.

Still, he couldn't deny that he felt something with her. The electricity when their hands brushed once or twice at dinner. The same sensation coursing through his veins right now.

He pulled his Bronco off the exit of 95 back in Stamford. It occurred to him why he couldn't tell her. Why he was holding back the whole truth. That Charles had returned to Greenwich after the bombing. That he had a hand in killing that boy. Maybe the other one, too.

Why he didn't want to bring the police into the matter. Get other people involved.

Because Hauck realized that for the last four years he'd been essentially rootless, alone. And Karen Friedman was the one thing he felt connected to right now.

CHAPTER FORTY-NINE

There was a knock on the door the following afternoon, and Hauck went over to answer.

Freddy Muñoz was there.

He handed Hauck one of those large, string-bound interoffice envelopes. "Hope I'm not bothering you. Thought I'd bring it up to you myself, Lieutenant, if that's okay?"

Hauck had just come back from a run. He was sweaty. He was in a gray Colby College T-shirt and gym shorts. He had spent most of the morning working on the computer.

"You're not bothering me."

"Place looks nice." The detective nodded approvingly. "Needs a bit of a woman's touch, don't you think? Maybe make a little sense of that kitchen over there?"

Hauck glanced at the dishes piled in the sink, a few open containers of takeout on the counter. "Care to volunteer?"

"Can't." Muñoz snapped his fingers, feigning disappointment. "Working tonight, Lieutenant. But I thought I'd just hang around a minute while you took a look through that, if that's okay?"

Buoyed, Hauck opened the envelope's flap and slid the contents on the coffee table, while Muñoz threw himself into a cushy living-room chair.

The first thing he came upon was the incident report. The report of the accident by the lead officer on the scene. From the Essex County PD. Details on the deceased. His name, Lauer. Address: 3135 Mountain View. DOB. Description: white male, approximately thirty, wearing a yellow biking uniform, severe body trauma and bleeding. Eyewitness described a red SUV, make undetermined, speeding away. New Jersey plates, number undetermined. Time: 10:07 A.M. Date. Eyewitness report attached.

It all seemed to have a familiar feel.

Hauck glanced through the photos. Photostats of them. The victim. In his biking jersey. Hit head-on. Severe blunt trauma to the face and torso. There was a shot of the bike, which had basically been mangled. A couple of views in either direction. Up, down the hill. The vehicle was clearly heading down.

Tire marks only after the point of impact.

Just like AJ Raymond.

Next Hauck leafed through the medical examiner's report. Severe blunt-force trauma, crushed pelvis and fractured vertebrae, head trauma. Massive internal bleeding. Dead on impact, the medical examiner presumed.

Hauck paged through the detectives' case reports. They had mapped out the same course of action Hauck had up in Connecticut. Did a canvass of the area, notified the state police, checked with the body shops, tried to trace back the tread marks for a tire brand. Interviewed the victim's wife, his employer. "No motive found" to assume it might not have been an accident.

Still no suspects.

Muñoz had gotten up and gone over to a canvas Hauck was working on by the window. He lifted it off the easel. "This is pretty good, Lieutenant!"

"Thanks, Freddy."

"May get to see you at the Bruce Museum yet. And I don't mean waiting in line."

"Feel free to help yourself to any you like," Hauck muttered, flipping through the pages. "One day they'll be worth millions."

It was frustrating—just like his. The Jersey folks had never found any solid leads.

It just came down to a coincidence, a coincidence Hauck didn't believe, one that didn't lead anywhere.

"Strike you as reasonable, Freddy?" Hauck asked. "Two separate 509s? Two different states. Each with a connection to Charles Friedman."

"Keep at it, Lieutenant," Muñoz said, flopping back over the arm of the heavy chair.

All that was left was the detail of the eyewitness depositions. *Deposition.* There was only one.

As Hauck opened it up, he froze. He felt his jaw drop open, his eyeballs pulled like magnets to the name on the deposition's front page.

"See what I'm seeing?" Freddy Muñoz sat up. He swung his legs off the chair.

"Yeah." Hauck nodded and took a breath. "I sure do."

The lone eyewitness to Jonathan Lauer's murder had been a retired New Jersey policeman.

His name was Phil Dietz.

The same eyewitness as at AJ Raymond's hit-and-run.

CHAPTER FIFTY

He had slipped up. Hauck read over his testimony once, twice, then again.

He had slipped up big-time!

Immediately Hauck recalled how Pappy Raymond had described the guy who'd met him outside the bar and put the pressure on him. *Stocky, mustached.* In the same moment, it became clear to Hauck just who had taken those pictures of AJ Raymond's body in the street.

Dietz.

His heart slammed to a stop.

Hauck thought back to his own case. Dietz had described himself as being in the security business. He'd said he'd run down to the crash site after the accident. That he never got a good look at the car, a white SUV, out-of-state plates, as it sped away up the road.

Good look, my ass.

He'd been planted there.

That's why they'd never been able to locate any white SUV with Massachusetts or New Hampshire plates. That's why the New Jersey police couldn't find a similar vehicle there.

They didn't exist! It had all been set up.

It was a thousand-to-one shot anyone would have ever connected the two incidents, if Karen hadn't seen her husband's face in that documentary.

Hauck grinned. Dietz was at both sites. Two states apart, separated by over a year.

Of course, that meant Charles Friedman was connected, too.

Hauck looked back up at Muñoz, a feeling that he was finally getting somewhere buzzing in his veins. "Anyone else know about this, Freddy?"

"You said keep it between us, Lieutenant." The detective shrugged. "So that's what I did."

He looked back up at Freddy. "Let's keep it that way."

Muñoz nodded.

"I want to go over the Raymond file again. You get me a copy up here today."

"Yes, sir."

Hauck stared at the image of the gregarious, mustached face—an ex-cop—now morphed into the calculating countenance of a professional killer.

The two cases hadn't merged, they had basically crashed together. Head-on. And this time there were other people to see. His blood was racing.

You screwed up, he said to Dietz. *Big-time, you son of a bitch!*

THE FIRST THING Hauck did was forward a photo of Dietz's face to Pappy, who a day later confirmed that that had been the same man who'd been in Pensacola. That alone was probably enough to arrest Dietz right now for conspiracy to murder AJ Raymond, and maybe Jonathan Lauer, too.

But it didn't take things through to Charles Friedman.

Coincidence didn't prove anything. With a good lawyer, it could be argued that being at both crash sites was just that. He'd given his word to Karen to find out about her husband. Charles had been in Greenwich. Lauer worked for him. They both led to Dolphin. Dietz was in it, too. Hauck wasn't liking at all where this was leading. Tying Charles to Dietz would be a start. Right now he was afraid that if he blew the lid off everything, who knew where any of it would lead?

You should go back to Fitzpatrick, a voice in him said. Swear out a warrant. Let the feds figure this out. He had taken oaths. His whole life he'd always upheld them. Karen had uncovered a conspiracy.

But something held him back.

What if Charles was innocent? What if he couldn't tie Charles and Dietz together? What if he hurt her, Karen, her whole family, after vowing to help her, trying to make *his* case, not hers? Bring him in. Put the pressure on Dietz. He would roll.

Or was it her? Was it what he felt himself falling into, these cases colliding together. Wanting to protect her just a little longer until he knew for sure. What stirred so fiercely in his blood. What he lay awake thinking of at night. Conflicted. As a cop, knowing his feelings were leading him astray.

He called her later that day, staring at Dietz's file. "I'm heading down to New Jersey for a day. We may have found something."

Karen sounded excited. "What?"

"I looked through the file on Jonathan Lauer's hit-and-run. The only eyewitness there, a man named Dietz—he was one of the two witnesses to AJ Raymond's death, too."

Karen gasped. In the following pause, Hauck knew she was putting together just what this meant.

"They were set up, Karen. This guy, Dietz, he was at both accidents. Except they weren't accidents, Karen. *They were homicides.* To cover something up. You did good. No one would ever have put any of this together if you hadn't gone to visit Lauer."

She didn't reply. There was only silence. The silence of her trying to decide what this meant. In regard to Charles. For her kids. For her.

"What the hell am I supposed to think, Ty?"

"Listen, Karen, before we jump . . ."

"Look, *I'm sorry,*" Karen said. "I'm sorry about these people. It's terrible. I know this is what you were always thinking. But *I* can't help thinking that there's something going on here, and it's starting to scare me, Ty. *What does all this mean about Charles?*"

"I don't know. That's what I'm going to find out."

"Find out how, Ty? What are you going to do?"

There was a lot he had withheld from her. That Charles had a connection to Falcon. To Pappy Raymond. That he was sure Charles was complicit in AJ Raymond's death—and maybe Jonathan Lauer's, too. But how could he tell her any of that now?

"I'm going to go down there," he said, "to Dietz's home. Tomorrow."

"You're going down there? What for?"

"See what the hell I can find. Try and figure out what our next step is."

"*Our next step?* You arrest him, Ty. You know he set those poor people up. He's responsible for their deaths!"

"You wanted to know how this connected to your husband, Karen! Isn't that why you came to me? You wanted to know what he's done."

"This man's a murderer, Ty. Two people are dead."

"I know that two people are dead, Karen! That's one thing you don't have to remind me of."

"What are you saying, Ty?"

The silence was frosty between them for a second. Suddenly Hauck felt sure that by admitting he was not going down to bring Dietz in he was somehow giving away everything that was in his heart: the feelings he carried for her, the braids of red hair that had pushed him here, the echo of a distant pain.

Finally Karen swallowed. "You're not telling me everything, are you, Ty? Charles is tied to this, isn't he? Deeper than you're letting on?"

"Yes."

"My husband . . ." Karen let out a dark chuckle. "He always bet against the trends. A *contrarian,* he called himself. A fancy name for someone who always thinks he's smarter than everybody else. You better be careful down there, Ty, whatever you're planning."

"I'm a cop, Karen," Hauck said. "This is what cops do."

"No, Ty, cops arrest people when they're implicated in a crime. I don't know what you're going to do down there, but what I do know is that some of it is about me. And that's scaring me, Ty. You just make sure you do the right thing, okay?"

Hauck flipped open the file and stared at Dietz's face. *"Okay."*

CHAPTER FIFTY-ONE

Something strange crept through Karen's thoughts that night. After she hung up from Ty.

About what he'd found.

It lifted her at first. The connections between the accidents. That she'd actually helped him.

Then she didn't know what she felt. An uneasiness that two people linked to her husband had been killed to cover something up—and the suspicion, a suspicion Ty wasn't clearing up for her, that Charlie was involved.

Jonathan Lauer worked for him. The fellow who was run over in Greenwich the day he disappeared had had Charlie's name in his pocket. The safe-deposit box with all that cash and the passport. The tanker that had a connection to Charlie's firm. Dolphin Oil . . .

She didn't know where any of this led.

Other than that her husband of eighteen years had been involved in something he'd kept from her and that Ty wasn't telling her all he knew.

Along with the fact that much of the life she'd led the last eighteen years, all those little myths she'd believed in, had been a lie.

But there was something else burrowing inside her. Even more than the fear that her family was still at risk. Or sympathy for the two people who had died. Deaths, Karen was starting to believe, against her will, that were inextricably tied to Charles.

She realized she was worried for him, Hauck. What he was about to do.

It had never dawned on her before, but it did now. How she'd grown to rely on him. How she knew by the way he'd looked at her—that day at the football game, how his eyes lit up when he saw her waiting at the station, how he had taken everything on for her. That he was attracted to her.

And that in the most subtle, undetected way Karen was feeling the same way, too.

But there was more.

She felt certain he was about to do something rash, way outside the boundaries. That he might be putting himself in danger. Dietz was a killer, whatever he had done. That he was holding something back—something related to Charlie.

For her.

After he called, she stayed in the kitchen heating up a frozen French-bread pizza in the microwave for Alex, who seemed to live on those things.

When it was done, Karen called him down, and she sat with him at the counter, hearing about his day at school—how he'd gotten a B-plus on a presentation in European history that was half his final exam and how he'd been named co-chair of the teen Kids in Crisis thing. She was truly proud of that. They made a date to watch *Friday Night Lights* together in the TV room later that evening.

But when he went back upstairs, Karen stayed at the counter, her blood coursing in a disquieted state.

Strangely, inexplicably, there had grown to be something between them.

Something she couldn't deny.

So after their show was done and Alex had said good night and had gone back upstairs, Karen went into the study and picked up the phone. She felt a shifting in her stomach, schoolgirlish, but she didn't care. She dialed his number, her palms perspiring. He answered on the second ring.

"Lieutenant?" she said. She waited for his objection.

"Yes?" he answered. There was none.

"You just be careful," she said again.

He tried to shrug it off with some joke about having done this a million times, but Karen cut him short.

"Don't," she pleaded. "Don't. Don't make me feel this all over again. Just please be careful, Ty. That's all I'm asking. Y'hear?"

There was a silence for a second, and then he said, "Yeah, *I hear.*"

"Good," she said softly, and hung up the phone.

Karen sat there on the couch for a long time, knees tucked into her chest. She felt a foreboding worming through her—just as it had on the small plane that day as the propellers whirred in Tortola, Charlie waving from the balcony, the sun reflecting off his aviators, a sudden sensation of loss. A tremor of fear.

"Just be careful, Ty," she whispered again, to no one, and closed her eyes, afraid. *I couldn't bear to lose you, too.*

CHAPTER FIFTY-TWO

The interstate that ran barely a mile from where Hauck lived in Stamford, I-95, turned into the New Jersey Turnpike south of the George Washington Bridge.

He took it, past the swamps of the Meadowlands, past the vast electrical trellises and the warehouse parks of northern New Jersey, past Newark Airport, over two hours, to the southern part of the state, north of the Philadelphia turnoff.

He got off at Exit 5 in Burlington County, finding himself on back roads that cut through the downstate—Columbus, Mount Holly, sleepy towns connected by wide-open countryside, horse country, a universe away from the industrial congestion back up north.

Dietz had been a cop in the town of Freehold. Hauck checked before he left. He'd put in sixteen years.

Sixteen years that had been cut short by a couple of sexual-harassment complaints and two rebukes for undue force, as well as some other issue that didn't go away involving an underage witness in a methamphetamine case where Dietz had been found to apply excessive pressure for her testimony, which sounded more like statutory rape.

Hauck had missed all this. What reason had there ever been to check?

Since then Dietz was self-employed in some kind of security company, Dark Star. Hauck had looked them up. It was hard to figure out just what they did. Bodyguards. Security. Private contract work. Not exactly installing exclusive security systems, or whatever he had said he'd been doing in the area when AJ Raymond was killed.

Dietz was a bad guy.

As he drove along backcountry stretches, Hauck's mind wandered. He had been a cop for almost fifteen years. Basically, it was all he knew. He'd risen fast through the bureaucracy that was the NYPD. He'd made detective. Been assigned to special units. Now he ran his own department in Greenwich. He'd always upheld the law.

What was he going to do when he got there? He didn't even have a plan.

Outside Medford, Hauck found County Road 620.

On each side there were gently sloping fields and white fencing. There were a few signs for stables and horse farms. Merryvale Farms—home to Barrister, "World's Record, quarter mile." Near Taunton Lake, Hauck checked the GPS. Dietz's address was 733 Muncey Road. It was about three miles south of town. Middle of nowhere. Hauck found it, bordering a fenced-in field and a local firehouse. He turned down the road. His heart started to pick up.

What are you doing here, Ty?

Muncey was a rutted blacktopped road in dire need of a repaving. There were a few houses near the turnoff, small clapboard farmhouses with trucks or the occasional horse van in front and overgrown, weeded yards. Hauck found a number on a mailbox: 340. He had a ways to go.

At some point the road turned into dirt. Hauck bounced along in his Bronco. The houses grew farther apart. At a bend he came upon a cluster of RD mailboxes, 733 written on one of them. The postal service didn't even come down any farther. A tremor shot through Hauck as he knew he was near. Boundaries, he knew he'd left them behind long ago. He didn't have a warrant. He hadn't run this by the office. Dietz was a potential co-conspirator in two homicides.

What the hell are you doing down here, Ty?

He passed a red, fifties-style ranch house: 650. A film of sweat had built up on his wrists and under his collar. He was getting close.

Now there was a huge distance between homes this far down. Maybe a quarter mile. There was no sound to be heard, other than the unsettling crunch of gravel under the Bronco's wheels.

Finally it came into view. Around a slight bend, tucked away under a nest of tall elms, the end of the road. An old white farmhouse. The picket fence in front was in need of repair. A loose gutter was hanging down. What lawn there was looked like it hadn't been mowed in months. Except for the presence of a two-seater

Jeep with a plowing hitch attached in the driveway, it hardly looked as if anyone even lived here. Hauck slowed the Bronco as he drove by, trying not to attract attention. A Freehold Township Police sticker was on the back of the Jeep. A number on the column of the front porch confirmed it:

733.

Bingo.

The dilapidated two-car garage was shut. Hauck couldn't see any lights on inside the house. Cars would be few and far between down here. He didn't want to be spotted driving by again. About fifty yards past, he noticed a turnoff, more of a horse trail than a road, barely wide enough for his car, and he took it, bouncing over the uneven terrain. Partway in, he cut a left through a field of dried hay, his path concealed by the tall, waist-high brush. A couple of hundred yards behind, Hauck had a decent view of the house.

Okay, so what happens now?

From a satchel Hauck removed a set of binoculars and, lowering the window, took a wide scan back at the house. No movement. A shutter hung indolently from one of the windows. No indication that anyone was there.

From the same satchel, Hauck took out his Sig automatic, safety off, checking that the sixteen nine-millimeter rounds were loaded in the clip. He hadn't drawn his gun in years. He recalled running into an alley, firing off three rounds at a suspect fleeing from a building, who had sprayed his TEC-9 at Hauck's partner in a weapons bust as he was running away. He'd hit the guy in the leg with one shot. Brought him in. Received a commendation for it. That was the only time he had ever fired his gun on the job.

Hauck rested the gun on the seat next to him. Then he opened the glove compartment and took out the small black leather folder that contained his Greenwich shield. He didn't quite know what to do with it, so he placed it in the pocket of his jacket, and took out a two-liter bottle of water and drank a long swig. His mouth was dry. He decided not to think too hard on what he was doing here. He took another sweep on the house with the binoculars.

Nothing. Not a fucking thing.

Then he did what he'd done a hundred times in various stakeouts over the years.

He uncapped a beer and watched seconds tick off the clock.

He waited.

CHAPTER FIFTY-THREE

He watched the house all night. No lights ever went on. No one ever drove up or came home.

At some point he looked up the phone number Dietz had given him along with his home address and dialed it. After four rings the answering machine came on. "You've reached Dark Star Security. . . . Please leave a message." Hauck hung up. He turned the radio to 104.3 Classic Rock and found the Who. *No one knows what it's like to be the bad man. . . .* His eyes grew heavy, and he dozed off for a while.

When he woke, it was light. Nothing had changed.

Hauck tucked the gun into his belt. Stretched on a pair of latex gloves. Then he grabbed a Maglite and his cell phone and stepped out of the Bronco. He pushed his way through the dense hayfield until he found the trail.

He decided that if Dietz was somehow there, he'd arrest him. He'd call in the Freehold police and work out the details later.

If he wasn't, he'd take a look around.

He made his way down the dirt road to the front of the dilapidated house. There was a sign on the scrabbly lawn: PRIVATE PROPERTY. BEWARE OF DOG. He climbed up the steps, his heart beginning to pound in his chest, his palms slick with perspiration. He stood to one side of the door and peeked in through a covered window. Nothing. He drew a breath and wondered if he was doing something crazy. *Here goes. . . .* He put a hand on the grip of his automatic. With the other he took his Maglite and knocked on the front door.

"Anyone home?"

Nothing.

After a few moments, he knocked again. "I'm looking for some directions. . . . Anybody home?"

Only silence came back.

The porch was a wraparound. Hauck decided to follow it around the side. On the lawn, just off the dirt driveway, he spotted a condenser box hidden in a bush and went over and lifted the metal panel. It was the main electrical feed to the house. Hauck pulled it, disabling the phone line and the alarm. Then he went back to the porch. Through the window he could see a dining room with a plain wooden table inside. Farther along he came upon the kitchen. It was old, fifties tile and linoleum, hadn't been updated in years. He tried the back door.

It was locked shut as well.

Suddenly a dog barked, the sound penetrating him. Hauck stiffened, swallowing his breath, feeling exposed. Then he realized that the bark had come from a neighboring property, a faraway woof that rifled through his bones, hundreds of yards off. Hauck looked out at the obstructed fields. His blood calmed. *Nerves . . .*

He continued around the back of the house. He passed a locked shed, a lawn mower with a protective tarp covering it, a few rusted tools scattered about. There was a step up to a cedar back porch. An old Weber grill. A bench-style outdoor table. Two French doors led to the back of the house. The curtains were drawn.

Hauck stepped carefully and paused for a moment, hidden by the curtains, in front of the door. It was locked as well. Panels of divided glass. A bolt drawn. He took his Maglite and tapped on one of the panels near the doorknob. It jiggled in its frame. Loose. He knelt down and hit the panel one more time, hard. The panel split and fell in.

Hand on his gun, he held there for a moment, waiting for any noise. Nothing. He doubted that Dietz had a security tie-in to the local police. He wouldn't want to take the chance of anybody needlessly poking around.

Hauck reached in through the open panel and wrapped his hand around the knob. He flicked the bolt back and twisted.

The door opened wide.

There was no alarm, no sound emanating. Cautiously, Hauck stepped inside.

He found himself in some kind of shabbily decorated sunroom. Faded upholstered chairs, a wooden table. A few magazines scattered on the table. *Forbes. Outdoor Life. Security Today.*

Heart pounding, Hauck took hold of his gun and went back through the kitchen, the floorboards creaking with each step. The house was dark, still. He looked into the living room and saw a fancy new Samsung flat-screen.

He was in. He just had no idea what he was searching for.

Hauck found a small room between the living room and the kitchen that was lined with bookshelves. An office. There was a small brick fireplace, a countertop desk with papers strewn about, a computer. A bunch of photos on the wall. Hauck looked. He recognized Dietz. In uniform with other policemen. In fishing clothes holding up an impressive sailfish. Another on some kind of large black-hulled sailing ship with a bare-chested, dark-haired man.

Hauck sifted through some of the papers on the desk. A few scattered bills, a couple of memos with Dark Star letterhead on them. Nothing that seemed to shed any light. The computer was on. Hauck saw an icon on the home page for Gmail, but when he clicked on it, up came a prompt asking for a password. Blocked. He took a shot and clicked the Internet icon, and the Google News homepage came on. He pointed the mouse and looked around to see what sites Dietz had previously logged on to. The last was the American Airlines site. International travel. Several seemed like standard trade sites. Farther down was something called the IAIM. He clicked—the International Association of Investment Managers.

Hauck felt his blood stir.

Harbor Capital, Charles Friedman's firm, had been queried in.

He sat in Dietz's chair and tried to follow the search. A Web file on the firm came up. A description of their business, energy-related portfolios. Assets under management, a few performance charts. A short history of the firm with a bio page of the management team. A photo of Friedman.

That wasn't all.

Falcon Partners, the investment partnership out of the BVIs, had been queried, too.

Now Hauck's blood was racing. He realized he was on the right track. The IAIM page merely provided a listing for Falcon. There was no information or records. Only a contact name and address in Tortola, which Hauck copied down. Then he swung around to the papers on Dietz's desk. Messages, correspondence, bills.

There had to be something here.

In a plastic in-box tray, he found something that sent his antennae buzzing. A photocopy of a list of names, from the National

Association of Securities Dealers, of people who had received licenses to trade securities for investment purposes. The list ran on for pages, hundreds of names and securities firms, from all across the globe. Hauck scanned down—*what would Dietz be looking for?*

Then, all of a sudden, it occurred to him just what was unique about the list of licenses.

They had all been granted within the past year.

As Hauck paged through it, he saw that several names had been circled. Others were crossed out, with handwritten notes in the margins. There were hundreds. A long, painstaking search to narrow them down.

Then it hit him, like a punch in the solar plexus.

Karen Friedman wasn't the only person who thought her husband was alive!

There was a printer-copier on the credenza adjacent to the desk, and Hauck placed the security list along with Dietz's notes in it. He kept looking. Amid some scattered sheets, he found a handwritten note on Dark Star stationery.

The Barclays Bank. In Tortola.

There was a long number under it, which had to be an account number, then arrows leading to other banks—the First Caribbean Bank. Nevis. Banc Domenica. Names. Thomas Smith. Ronald Torbor. It had been underlined three times.

Who were these people? What was Dietz looking for? Hauck had always assumed that Charles and Dietz were connected. The hit-and-runs . . .

That's when it struck him. *Jesus . . .*

Dietz was searching for him, too.

Hauck picked up a scrawled sheet of paper from the tray, some kind of travel itinerary. American Airlines. Tortola. Nevis. His skin started to feel all tingly.

Dietz was ahead of him. *Did he possibly already know where Charles was?*

He placed in a copy of the same sheet in the printing bay and pressed. The machine started warming up.

Then suddenly there was a noise from outside the window. Hauck's heart slammed to a stop.

Wheels crunching over gravel, followed by the sound of a car door slamming.

Someone was home.

CHAPTER FIFTY-FOUR

Hauck's blood became ice. He went over to the window and peeked through the drawn curtains. Dietz's office faced the wrong direction; there was no way to determine who it was. He removed the Sig 9 from his belt and checked the clip. He was completely out of bounds here—no warrant, no backup.

Inside, Hauck was just praying it wasn't Dietz.

He heard a knock at the door. Someone shouting out, *"Phil?"* Then, after a short pause, something that made his pulse skyrocket. The sound of a key being inserted in the front door, the lock opening. A man's voice calling.

"Phil?"

Hauck hid behind the office door. He wrapped his fingers around the handle of the Sig and stood pressed against the door. He had no way out. Whoever it was had already come inside.

Hauck heard the sound of footsteps approaching, the creak of bending wood on the floorboards. *"Phil? You here?"*

His heart started going wild. Panicked, his mind flashed to whether or not his Bronco might have been seen. He realized that sooner or later whoever this was, if he made his way around the house, would notice the smashed rear windowpane. Would find his way back to the office. Whoever this was had access. On the other hand, Hauck was there totally unlawfully. He had no warrant. He hadn't notified the local police. He would be cited just for bringing in his gun. The footsteps came closer. He wasn't sure what to do. Only that he'd gotten himself into a sizable amount of shit, and it was getting deeper by the second. The man was walking around the house. *Should he make a run for it?*

Then something happened that sent Hauck's pulse into a frenzy.

The fucking printer began to print.

The pages Hauck had fed into the tray, they were suddenly going through. The hum of the machine was like an alarm bell.

"Phil!"

The footsteps got closer. Behind the door Hauck gripped his Sig, pressing the muzzle up against his cheek. The machine continued to print. He couldn't stop it! *Think, think, what to do?*

Hauck froze at the creak of a nearby floorboard as whoever it was came around the corner. He peeked inside the office. Hauck held, rigid as a board.

"Phil, I didn't know you were here. . . ."

The man paused, remaining in the doorway. The pages continued to feed into the machine one by one.

Hauck held his breath. *Shit . . .*

A second later the heavy office door slammed into his chest, taking him by surprise, the Sig flying out of his hand.

Hauck's eyes darted after the gun, the door barreling into him again, striking him in the side of the head, dazing him, the gun clattering across the floor.

The man crashed the door into Hauck one more time, this time following it into the room, mashing Hauck's right hand in the hinge. Hauck finally threw the brunt of his weight against it and rammed it back with all his might, sending the man reeling into the room.

The man had close-cropped hair and a large nose, his cheek bloodied from the blow. He glared at Hauck. "What the hell are you doing here? Who the fuck are you?"

Hauck stared back. He realized he had seen him before.

The second witness. The guy in a warm-up jacket at AJ Raymond's hit-and-run. A track coach or something.

Hodges.

Their eyes met in a stunned, glaring gaze.

Hodges's eyes were equally as wide. *"You!"*

Hauck's glance darted toward the gun on the floor, as Hodges took the nearest thing available, a decorative scrimshaw horn Dietz kept on a side table, and lunged in Hauck's direction, slashing the sharp point of the horn through Hauck's sweatshirt and tearing into his skin.

Hauck cried out. The horn dug through his chest, his ribs on fire.

Hodges slashed at him again, Hauck flailing desperately for the other man's arm to block the blow, pinning it back, while Hodges pushed with all his might with his other hand against Hauck's neck.

He kneed Hauck sharply in the side of his chest, his wound.

"Aaagh!"

"What are you doing here?" Hodges screamed at him again.

"I know," Hauck grunted back. "I know what's happened." Blood seeped through the ripped, damp fabric of his sweatshirt. "It's over, Hodges. I know about the hit-and-runs."

Straining, Hauck forced back his attacker's fingers, reaching for the handle of the horn. It fell, skidding away.

Hauck faced him, clutching his side. "I know they were set up. I know they were done to protect Charles Friedman and Dolphin Oil. The police are on the way." He was still dazed from the first blows, short of breath. His neck was raw and throbbing where Hodges had squeezed it. "You're done, man."

"Police . . ." Hodges echoed skeptically. "So who the fuck are you, the advance guard?"

Eyes ablaze, he darted to the fireplace and grabbed an iron poker there and swung it at Hauck as hard as he could, narrowly missing his head by inches and striking into the wall behind him, shards of dug-out plaster splintering over the floor.

Hauck dove headfirst into him, knocking Hodges back against the desk, heavy books and photos tumbling all over them, the printer crashing down from the shelf.

They rolled onto the floor, Hodges coming up on top. He was strong. Maybe a few years back Hauck could've taken him, but he was still dazed from the body blows of the door and the gash on his side. Hodges fought like he had nothing to lose. He kneed Hauck deeply in the groin, sending the air rushing out of him, and grabbed the iron poker lengthwise with both hands, pinned it across Hauck's chest like a vise, forcing it into the nook of his neck.

Hauck gagged, sucking in a desperate breath.

"You think we did it to protect him?" Hodges said, squeezing him, his face turning red. "You don't know a fucking thing." He continued to press the poker into the cavity of Hauck's neck. Hauck felt his airway closing on him, a clawing tightness taking over his lungs. Intensifying. He tried to roll his attacker off, knee him, but he was pinned and the iron rod was squeezing the life out of him. He felt the blood rush into his face, his strength waning, his lungs about to burst.

Hodges was going to kill him.

Straining, he tried with everything he had to push the poker back. His breath was desperate, his lungs clutching for blocked air. The blood was almost bursting through his head.

That's when he felt the hard mound of the gun pressing sharply into his back. Hodges had him pinned, but somehow Hauck forced a shoulder up and reached, one arm dangling back, the other vainly trying to pry Hodges's grip away from his throat. Fingers grasping, Hauck found the warm steel of the muzzle, spun it around under his body for the grip.

"Stop," he gasped, "lemme talk. Stop."

"How did you get here?" Hodges shouted at him. "How did you find out?" It was as if an iron hoe were being clawed inside Hauck's throat. Finally he managed to wrap his fingers around the Sig's handle. With the gun still underneath his body, he maneuvered it around.

"How?" Hodges demanded, pinning Hauck's legs with his thighs and pressing the last gulps of air out of his chest.

All Hauck could do was raise himself ever so slightly, creating the tiniest space for him to slide his gun hand around, as Hodges now saw what he was attempting. And so, exerting himself even harder, he pinned Hauck's arm back with his knee, jamming the poker tighter into his larynx.

Hauck's lungs were about to explode.

His shoulder was pressed back so tightly there was no way he could aim. He managed to wrap his finger around the trigger, but the muzzle was jammed in against his body. He had no idea where it was even pointed, only that his strength was waning, his air disappearing. . . . No more time.

He braced for the explosion in his side.

And fired—a muffled, close-in pop.

Hauck felt a jolt. The concussive shock seemed to reverberate inside both of their bodies. He tensed, expecting the rush of pain.

None came.

On top of him, Hodges grimaced. The iron rod was still pressed into Hauck's neck.

There was a sharp smell of cordite in Hauck's nostrils. Slowly, the pressure on his throat released.

Hodges's eyes went to his side. Hauck saw an enlarging flower of red oozing from under his shirt there. Hodges straightened, his hand reaching to his side, and drew it back, smeared with blood.

"*Sonofafucking bitch . . .*" he groaned.

Hauck pushed his legs, and, glazy-eyed, Hodges rolled off him. Heaving, Hauck gulped precious, needed air deep into his lungs. His side felt on fire. There was blood all over him—whose, he wasn't sure. Hodges crawled his way to the door.

"It's over," Hauck gasped, staring over at him, barely able to point his gun.

Clumsily, Hodges dragged himself up. A damp scarlet blotch seeped out of his shirt. He clamped it with his hand. "You don't have a fucking clue," he said, coughing back a heavy laugh.

He winced. Stood there, waiting for Hauck to pull the trigger. Exhausted, Hauck could barely raise the gun.

"*You're dead!* You don't know it yet, but you're dead." Hodges glared at him. "You have no idea who you're fucking with!"

Hunched over, he staggered out of the room. Hauck could do nothing to stop him. It took everything he had just to pull himself up, coughing air back into his obstructed air pipe, his clothes drenched in sweat. He lurched outside after Hodges, clutching his ribs. Everything had gone wrong. He heard the sound of Hodges's truck starting up, spotted droplets of blood leading off the porch to the driveway.

"*Hodges!*" Hauck came down the steps and leveled his gun at the truck. It backed out of the driveway and sped off down the road. Hauck took aim at the rear tires, his finger pulsed. "Stop!" he called after him. *Stop.* He didn't even hear his own voice.

But he just held there, watching the truck ramble down the road, his gun aimed into the retreating cloud of dust.

It took everything Hauck had to focus on a single thought.

That he was involved in something—something that had blown up in his face.

And that he was no longer representing anything. Not all the oaths, not the truth, not even Karen.

Only his own base desire to know where it led.

CHAPTER FIFTY-FIVE

His side was on fire.

His neck was swollen twice its size. He could barely swallow.

Every time he breathed, his ribs ached like he'd been through ten rounds with a heavy weight. His chest was covered with a bright red welt.

He didn't know what he had done.

He'd gone back in and grabbed the papers he'd copied out of the copier. Then he headed to his car.

As he drove back, Hauck's first thoughts centered on Jessica—how lucky he was just to be alive.

Stupid, Ty, just plain stupid. He tried to size up the situation. Everything he'd done had been outside his jurisdiction. Breaking into Dietz's house. Taking in his gun. Not informing the local authorities. And Hodges . . . he would live. But, Hauck realized, that wouldn't be the half of it. Dietz would know—and so would whoever he worked for. This thing could explode. Of course, they had no way to know he was doing this on his own. Or, the thought calmed him slightly, that Karen was in any way involved.

That was the only fucking thing about any of this that was good.

It took him over three hours to drive back home. He got back in the early afternoon. He threw himself on his couch in exhaustion and examined his side, his head rolled back, trying to make sense of what he had done. He had broken laws. A shitload of them. He had put Karen in danger. The oaths he had taken in his life, to uphold the law, to do the right thing, they were all pretty much shattered now.

Hauck peeled off his bloodstained clothes and tossed them in a ball in the pantry. Just lifting his arms made him feel incredibly sore. The gash on his side had caked with blood, the skin torn where Hodges had slashed him. Bright red welts were all over his neck and chest. He looked in the mirror and winced. He didn't know if he needed medical attention. His head was heavy. He just wanted to sleep. He felt alone. For the first time in his life, he didn't know what to do.

He eased himself back onto the couch. There was just one person he could think of to call.

"Ty . . . ?"

"Karen, listen, I need you," he huffed. "Up here." It was more of a plea than a statement. He caught his breath and sucked in air.

"Ty, are you all right?" Karen's voice was alarmed. "I was worried. I tried calling you. You didn't answer."

"Karen, something happened. . . . Just come on up. Please." In close to a daze, he told her where he lived.

"I'm on my way. You don't sound good, Ty. You're scaring me. Just tell me, is there anything you need?"

"Yeah." He exhaled, his head falling back. "Disinfectant. And a whole lot of gauze."

HAUCK STAGGERED TO the door when he heard her knock. In a pair of gym shorts and a robe to conceal his wounds. He grinned, pale, his expression saying something like, *I'm really sorry for getting you into this.* Then he sort of leaned into her.

She looked at him, horrified. "What the hell's happened, Ty?"

"I found Dietz's place. I staked it out all night. I didn't think anyone was there. This morning I went in."

"He was there?"

"No." Hauck took the bag of medical supplies he'd requested out of her hands—disinfectant, tape, and gauze. He stepped back over to the couch with a bit of a limp, eased himself down. "Hodges was, though."

Her eyes screwed up. "Hodges?"

"He was the other witness at AJ Raymond's hit-and-run. I guess they were in this together. Partners."

"Together in what?"

That was when Karen's gaze focused on the welts on Hauck's neck, and she gasped. *"My God, Ty, what have you done?"* She drew back the collar of his terry robe, eyes wide, gently running her fingers across the bruised skin, inspecting the torn knuckles, aghast, carefully taking his hands in hers.

"This side's worse." Hauck shrugged, guiltily, letting his robe fall open to reveal the matted blood and tracks of torn flesh underneath his arm.

"*Oh, my God!*"

"It was all set up," he said, trying to explain. "Abel Raymond. Lauer. Those accidents, they were hits. Dietz and Hodges killed them both. To cover it all up."

"*What!?*" There was a pall of confusion on Karen's face, but also something deeper—*fear*, knowing that somehow what he wasn't totally divulging related back to her. That Charlie was involved.

"What happened to Hodges?" she asked, grabbing the disinfectant and ripping open the box of gauze.

His expression was stonelike. "Hodges was shot, Karen."

"*Shot?*" She put the things back down, the color draining from her face. "Dead . . . ?"

"No. At least I don't think so."

He told her everything. How he had gone inside the house figuring it was safe, and how Hodges came in, surprising him, in Dietz's office. How they'd struggled, Hodges slashing him with the horn, clamping the iron poker across his neck, how Hauck thought he was dying. How he'd shot Hodges.

"*Oh, my God, Ty . . .*" Karen's eyes were wide and empathetic. The consternation on her face had turned to real fear. "What did the police say? It has to be self-defense, right? He was trying to kill you, Ty."

Hauck kept his gaze trained on her. "I didn't call in the police, Karen."

She blinked. "*What . . . ?*"

"I had no right to be there, Karen. The whole thing was illegal from the start. I didn't have a warrant. There isn't an open case against them. I'm not even on goddamn duty, Karen."

"*Ty . . .*" Karen's hand shot to her mouth as she started to realize the situation. "You can't just pretend this didn't happen. You shot someone."

"This man tried to kill me, Karen! You want me to call the police? Don't you understand? Your husband was in bed with these people, Karen. Dietz, Hodges. When Charlie left Grand Central that morning, he made his way up to Greenwich. He stole the credit card off of someone who died on the tracks. There was a call to AJ Raymond, Karen, from the diner across the street. Charlie made that call, Karen. Your husband. Either he was directly involved in the murder of AJ Raymond or he damn well helped set it up."

"*Charlie . . . ?*" Karen shook her head. "You can't think Charlie's some kind of killer, Ty. No. *Why?*"

"To cover up what Raymond's father stumbled onto in Pensacola. That they were falsifying shipments of oil in one of the companies Charlie controlled."

Karen shook her head again defiantly.

"It's true. Have you ever heard of Dolphin Oil, Karen? Or something called Falcon Partners?"

"No."

"They're subsidiaries, owned by his company. Harbor. Offshore. You want me to call in the police, Karen? If I do, they're going to issue an immediate warrant for his arrest. There are ample grounds—fraud, money laundering, conspiracy to commit murder. Is that what you want me to do, Karen? To you *and* your family? Call in the police? Because that's what's going to happen."

Karen put a hand to her forehead and shook her head reflexively. "I don't know."

"Charlie was tied to them. Through the investment companies he controlled. Through Dietz. He's tied in to both murders, Karen—"

"I don't believe it! You can't expect me to believe my husband's a murderer, Ty!"

"*Look!*" Hauck reached over and grabbed the papers he had taken from Dietz's office and put them in front of her face. "His name is all over the place. Two people are dead, Karen. And now you have to listen to me and make a decision, because there may be more. This guy Dietz, he's looking for Charlie, too. I don't know who the hell he is or who he's working for, but he's out there, Karen, and somehow he knows Charlie's alive, just like we do, and he's searching for him, too—I found the trail! Maybe they're trying to shut him up, I don't know. But I guarantee you if he finds him, Karen, before we do, it won't be to tearfully look him in the eyes and ask how he could've possibly done this to you."

Karen nodded haltingly, a tremor of confusion rattling her. Hauck reached over and took her hand. He wrapped his fingers around her tightened fist.

"So you tell me, Karen, is that what you really want me to do? Call in the police? Because the police *are* involved. *I'm* involved.

And after today, with what's happened, I can't just reverse the clock and go back empty-handed anymore."

Her eyes were filled, tears reflecting in them. "He's the father of my kids. You don't know how many times I've wanted to kill him myself, but what you're telling me . . . a murderer? No, I won't believe it till I hear it from him."

"I'll find him for you, Karen. I promise I will. But just be sure that with what's happened now, these people know I'm onto them. We're in it now. If that's something you don't think you can face—and I'd understand it if it was—now's the time to say so."

Karen looked down. Hauck felt a finger wrap around his hand, her pinkie, cautious and tremulous. It squeezed. There was a frightened look in her eyes, but behind it something deeper, a twinkling of resolve. She looked at him and shook her head again.

"I want you to find him, Ty."

Her face dipped, ever so slightly, close to his, her hair tumbling against his cheek. Her breath was close and halting. Their knees touched. Hauck felt his blood spark alive as the side of her breast brushed his arm. Their lips could have touched right there. It would have taken only a nudge, and she would have folded into him—and a part of him wanted her to, a strong part, but another part said no. The hair on his arms tingled as he listened to her breathe.

"You knew this all along," she said to him. "About Charlie. That this led back to him. You held it back from me."

"I didn't want you to be any more hurt until I was sure."

She nodded. She locked her fingers inside his hand. "He wouldn't kill anyone, Ty. I don't care how foolish it makes me look. I know him. I lived with him for close to twenty years. He's the father of my kids. I know."

"So what do you want to do?"

Karen gently eased open Hauck's robe. He tensed. She ran her fingers along his chest. She reached for the bag of liniment she had brought. "I want to take a look at that wound."

"No," he said, catching her hand. "You know what I meant."

She held a moment, their hands still touching.

"I want to hear from his lips what he's done, why he walked away from us, from almost twenty years of marriage, his family. I want to find him, Ty. Find Charles. Something came up while you were down there. *I think I may know how.*"

CHAPTER FIFTY-SIX

It was the car.

She had already been through everything two times over, just as Ty had asked. Still, while he was down in Jersey, she felt she had to do something. To keep from worrying.

So Karen tore through Charlie's things all over again—the old bills, the stacks of receipts he'd left in his closet, the papers on his desk. Even the sites he'd visited on his computer before he "died."

A wild-goose chase, she told herself. Just like the one before.

Except this time some things came up. A file buried deep in his desk, hidden under a pile of legal papers. A file Karen had never noticed before. From before Charlie died. Things she didn't understand.

A small note card still in its envelope—addressed to Charles. The kind that accompanied a gift of flowers. Karen opened it, a little hesitantly, and saw it was written in a hand she didn't recognize.

It stopped her.

Sorry about the pooch, Charles. Could the kids be next?

Sorry about the pooch. Karen saw that her hands were shaking. Whoever wrote it had to be talking about Sasha. And what did that possibly mean, that the kids could be next?

Their kids . . .

Suddenly Karen felt a tightness in her chest. *What had these people done?*

And then, in that same hidden-away file, she came across one of the holiday cards they'd sent as a family before Charlie had died. The four of them sitting on a wooden fence at a field near their ski house in Vermont. A happy time.

She opened it.

She almost threw up.

The kids' faces, Samantha and Alexander—*they had both been cut out.*

Karen covered her face with her hands and felt her cheeks flush with blood.

"What the hell is happening here, Charlie?" She stared at the card. *What the hell were you involved in? What were you doing to us, Charlie?* All of a sudden, the incident in Samantha's car at school came hurtling back to Karen, her heart starting to race. Accusingly. She got up from the desk. She wanted to hit something. She touched her hand to her face. Looked around the room.

His room.

"Talk to me, Charlie, you bastard, talk to me!"

And then her eyes seemed to fall on it.

Amid the clutter of papers and prospectuses and sports magazines she had still never quite cleared from his office.

The stack. The neatly piled stack Charlie kept on the bookshelf. Every issue. A sure-as-hell fire hazard, Karen always called it. His little dream collection, dating back since he'd first acquired his toy, eight years earlier.

Mustang World.

She went over to it—the stack of magazines piled high. She picked up one or two, the thought now forming in her brain.

This was it! The one thing about him he could never change. No matter what name he was under. Or who he was now.

Or where.

His stupid car. *Charlie's Baby.* He read about the damn things in his spare time, checked out the prices, chatted about them online. They always joked how it was a part of him. His mistress that Karen just had to put up with. She called it Camilla, as in Camilla and Charles. Better than Camilla, Charlie always joked. "Better-looking, too."

Mustang World.

He constantly put the car up for sale, then never sold it. In the summer he drove it in rallies. Monitored the online sites. She didn't understand what these cards she'd found were about. They scared her. She didn't know for sure what he'd done.

"But that's the way," Karen said to Hauck as she went to dress his wounds now.

She reached into her bag and dropped a copy of the magazine on the table. *Mustang World.*

"That's how we find him, Ty. *Charlie's Baby.*"

CHAPTER FIFTY-SEVEN

One Police Plaza was the home of the NYPD's administrative offices in lower Manhattan, as well as of the Joint Inter-Agency Task Force that oversaw the city's security.

Hauck waited in the courtyard in front of the building, looking out over Frankfort Street, which led onto the Brooklyn Bridge. It was a warm May afternoon. Strollers and bikers were crossing the steel gray span, office workers in shirtsleeves and light dresses on their lunchtime stroll. A few years back, Hauck used to work out of this building. He hadn't been down here in years.

A slightly built, balding man in a navy police sweater waved to a coworker and came up to him, his police ID fastened to his chest.

"New York's Finest." The man winked, standing in front of Hauck. He sat down beside him and gave him a tap of the fist.

"Go, blue!" Hauck grinned back.

Lieutenant Joe Velko had been a young head of detectives in the 105th Precinct, and had gone on to receive a master's degree from NYU in computer forensics. For years he and Hauck had been teammates on the department's hockey team, Hauck a crease-clearing defenseman with gimpy knees, Joe a gritty forward who learned to use a stick on the streets of Elmhurst, Queens. Joe's wife, Marilyn, had been a secretary at Cantor Fitzgerald and had died on 9/11. Back then it was Hauck who had organized a benefit game for Joe's kids. Captain Joe Velko now ran one of the most important departments in the entire NYPD.

Watchdog was a state-of-the-art computer software program developed by the NCSA, powered by nine supercomputers at an underground command center across the river in Brooklyn. Basically what Watchdog did was monitor billions of bits of data over the Internet for random connections that could prove useful for security purposes. Blogs, e-mail messages, Web sites, MySpace pages—billions of bits of Internet traffic. It sought out any unusual relationships between names, dates, scheduled public events, even repeated colloquial phrases, and spit them out at the command center in daily "alerts," whereupon a staff of analysts pored over them, deciding if they were important enough to act on or to pass along to other security teams. A couple of years back, a plot to bomb the Citigroup Center by an antiglobalization group was uncovered by Watchdog, simply because it connected the same seemingly innocent but repeated phrase, "renewing our driver's license," to a random date, June 24, the day of an event there highlighted by a visit from the head of the World Bank. The connection was traced to someone on the catering team, who was an accomplice on the inside.

"So what do I owe this visit to?" Velko turned to Hauck. "I know this isn't exactly your favorite place."

"I need to ask you a favor, Joe."

A seasoned cop, Velko seemed to see something in Hauck's face that made him pause.

"I'm trying to locate someone," Hauck explained. He removed a thin manila envelope from under his sport jacket. "I have no idea where he is. Or even what name he might be using. He's most likely out of the country as well." He put the envelope on Velko's lap.

"I thought you were going to give me a challenge." The security man chuckled, unfastening the clasp.

He slid out the contents: a copy of Charles Friedman's passport photo, together with some things Karen had supplied him. The phrases "1966 Emberglow Mustang. GT. Pony interior. Greenwich, Connecticut." Some place called Ragtops, in Florida, where Charles had purchased it. The Greenwich Concours Rallye, where he sometimes showcased his car. A few of what Karen remembered as Charlie's favorite car sites. And finally a few favorite expressions he might use, like, "Lights out." Or "It's a home run, baby."

"You must think just because you elbowed a few firemen out of the crease who were trying to knock the shit out of me I really owe you, huh?"

"It was more than a few, Joe." Hauck smiled.

"A '66 Mustang. Pony interior. Can't you just log onto eBay for one of these things, Ty?" Velko grinned.

"Yeah, but this is far sexier," Hauck replied. "Look, the guy may be in the Caribbean, or maybe Central America. And Joe . . . this is gonna come out in your search, so I might as well tell you up front now—the person I'm looking for is supposedly dead. In the Grand Central bombing."

"*Supposedly* dead? As opposed to really dead?"

"Don't make me go into it, partner. I'm just trying to find him for a friend."

Velko slid the paper back inside the envelope. "Three hundred billion bits of data crossing the Internet every day, the city's security squarely in our hands, and I'm looking at an Amber Alert for a dead guy's '66 Mustang."

"Thank you, guy. I appreciate whatever turns up."

"A wide goddamn hole in the Patriot Act"—Velko cleared his throat—"That's what the hell's going to turn up. We're not exactly a missing-persons search system here." He looked at Hauck, reacting to the marks on his face and neck and the stiffness in his reach.

"You still skating?"

Hauck nodded. "Local team up there. Over-forty league now. Mostly a bunch of Wall Street types and mortgage salesmen. *You?*"

"No." Velko tapped his head. "They won't let me anymore. They seem to think my brain is good for something other than getting knocked around. Too risky on the new job. Michelle is, though. You should see her. She's a goddamn little bruiser. She plays on the boys' team for her school."

"I'd like to," Hauck said with a fond smile. When Marilyn died, Michelle had been nine and Bonnie six. Hauck had organized a benefit game for them against a team of local celebrities. Afterward Joe's family came onto the ice and received a team jersey signed by the Rangers and the Islanders.

"I know I've said this, Ty, but I always appreciated just what you did."

Hauck shot Joe a wink.

"Anyway, I better get on these, right? Top secret—specialized and classified. Joe stood up. "Is everything okay?"

Hauck nodded. His side still ached like hell. "Everything's okay."

"Whatever turns up," Joe said, "I can still find you up at your office in Greenwich?"

Hauck shook his head. "I'm taking a little time. My cell number's in the package. And Joe . . . I'd appreciate it if you kept this entirely between us."

"Oh, you don't have to worry about *that*." Joe raised the envelope and rolled his eyes. "Taking a little time . . ." As Velko backed away toward the police building, he cocked Ty a wary smile.

"What the hell are you getting yourself involved in, Ty?"

CHAPTER **FIFTY-EIGHT**

After his meeting with Velko, Hauck went to the office of Media Publishing, located on the thirtieth floor of a tall glass building at Forty-sixth Street and Third Avenue.

The publishers of *Mustang World*.

It took Hauck's flashing his badge first to the receptionist and then to a couple of junior marketing people to finally get him to the right person. He had no authority here. The last thing he wanted was to have to call in yet another old friend from the NYPD. Fortunately, the marketing guy he finally got him in front of seemed eager to help and didn't ask him to come back with a warrant.

"We've got two hundred and thirty-two thousand subscribers," the manager said, as if overwhelmed. "Any chance you can narrow it down?"

"I only need a list of those who've come aboard within the past year," Hauck told him.

He gave the guy a card. The manager promised he'd get to it as soon as he could and e-mail the results to Hauck's departmental address.

On the ride back home, Hauck mapped out what he would do. Hopefully, this Mustang search would yield something. If not, he still had the leads he'd taken from Dietz's office.

The Major Deegan Expressway was slow, and Hauck caught some tie-up near Yankee Stadium.

On a hunch he fumbled in his pocket for the number of the Caribbean bank he'd found at Dietz's. On St. Kitts. As he punched in the overseas number on his cell, he wasn't sure just how smart this was. The guy could be on Dietz's payroll for all he knew. But as long as he was playing long shots . . .

After a delay a sharp ring came on. "First Caribbean," answered a woman with a heavy island accent.

"Thomas Smith?" Hauck requested.

"Please hold da line."

After a short pause, a man's voice answered, "This is Thomas Smith."

"My name is Hauck," Hauck said. "I'm a police detective with the Greenwich police force, in Greenwich, Connecticut. In the States."

"I know Greenwich," the man responded brightly. "I went to college nearby at the University of Bridgeport. How can I help you, Detective?"

"I'm trying to find someone," Hauck explained. "He's a U.S. citizen. The only name I have for him is Charles Friedman. He may have an account on record there."

"I'm not familiar with anyone by the name of Charles Friedman having an account here," the bank manager replied.

"Look, I know this is a bit unorthodox. He's about five-ten. Brown hair. Medium stature. Wears glasses. It's possible he's transferred money into your bank from a corresponding bank in Tortola. It's possible that Friedman is not even the name he's currently using now."

"As I said, sir, there is no account holder on record here by that name. And I haven't seen anybody who might fit that description. Nevis is a small island. And you can understand why I would be reluctant to give you that information even if I did."

"I understand perfectly, Mr. Smith. But it is a police matter. If you would maybe ask around and check . . ."

"I don't need to check," the manager answered. "I have already." What he told Hauck made him flinch. "You are the second person from the States who's been looking for this man in the past week."

CHAPTER FIFTY-NINE

Michel Issa squinted through the lens over the glittering stone. It was a real beauty. A brilliant canary yellow, wonderful luminescence, easily a C rating. It had been part of a larger lot he'd bought and was the pick of the litter. Hovering over the loupe, Michel knew it would fetch a real price from the right buyer.

His specialty.

Issa's family had been in the diamond business for over fifty years, emigrating to the Caribbean from Belgium and opening the store on Mast Street, on the Dutch side of St. Maarten when Michel was young. For decades Issa et Fils had bought high-quality stones direct from Antwerp and a few "gray" markets. People came to them from around the world—and not just couples off the cruise ships looking to get engaged, though they catered to that, too, to keep up the storefront. But important people, people with things to hide. In the trade, Michel Issa was known, as his father and grandfather had been before him, as the kind of *négociant* who could keep his mouth shut, who had the discretion to handle a private transaction, no matter what its magnitude.

With the money trail between banks so transparent after 9/11, shifting assets into something tangible—and transportable—was a booming business these days. Especially if one had something to hide.

Michel put down the lens and transferred the premier stone back into the tray with the other stones. He placed them in his drawer and twisted the lock. The clock read 7:00 P.M. Time to close for the day. His wife, Marte, had an old-style Belgian meal of sausage and cabbage prepared for him. Later, on Tuesday nights, they played euchre with a couple of English friends.

Michel heard the outside door chime. He sighed. Too late. He had just sent his sales staff home. He didn't flinch. There was no crime here on the island. Not this kind of crime. Everyone knew him, and, more to the point, they were on an island, surrounded by water. There was absolutely nowhere to go. Still, he reproved himself for having to be rude. He should have locked the door.

"*Monsieur Issa?*"

"I'll be with you in a moment," Michel called. He glanced through the window into the showroom and saw a stocky, mustached man in sunglasses waiting by the door.

He twisted the lock of the security drawer a second time. When he went around into the shop, there were two men. The man who called out, sort of a circumspect smile in his dark features, stepped up to the counter. The other, tall in a beach shirt and a baseball cap, standing by the door.

"I'm Issa," Michel said. "What can I do for you?" He placed his left foot near the alarm behind the counter, noticing the taller man still hovering suspiciously by the door.

"I'd like you to take a look at something, Monsieur Issa," the mustached man said. He reached inside his shirt pocket.

"Stones?" Issa sighed. "This late? I was just preparing to leave. Is it possible we can reschedule for tomorrow?"

"Not stones." The mustached man shook his head. "Photographs."

Photographs. Issa squinted at him. The mustached man placed a snapshot of a man in business attire on the counter. Short, gray-flecked hair. Glasses. The photo looked like it had been cut out of some corporate brochure.

Issa put on his wire reading glasses and stared. "No."

The man leaned forward. "This was taken some time ago. He may look different today. His hair may be shorter. He may not wear glasses anymore. I have a suspicion he may have come through here at some point, seeking to make a transaction. This transaction you would remember, Monsieur Issa, I'm sure. It would have been a large sale."

Michel didn't answer right away. He was trying to gauge who his questioners were. He tried to brush it off with a modest smile.

The mustached man smiled knowingly at him. But there was something behind it that Issa didn't like.

"*Police?*" he questioned. He had arrangements with most of them. The local ones, even Interpol. They left him alone. But these men didn't look the type.

"No, not police." The man smiled coolly. "*Private.* A personal affair."

"I'm sorry." Michel shrugged his shoulders. "I have not seen him here."

"You're quite sure? He would have paid in cash. Or perhaps with a wire transfer from the First Caribbean Bank or the Maartens-Bank here on the island. Say, five, six months ago. Who knows, he may even have come back."

"I'm sorry," Michel said again, the specifics starting to alarm him, "I don't recognize him. And I would if he had been here, of course. Now, if you don't mind, I have to—"

"Let me show you this one, then," the mustached man said, firmer. "Another photo. You know how these things sometimes work. It may freshen everything up again."

The man pulled a second photo out of his breast pocket and laid it on the counter next to the first.

Michel froze. His mouth went dry.

This second photo was of his own daughter.

Juliette, who lived in the States. In D.C. She had married a professor at George Washington University. They'd just had a baby, Danielle, Issa's granddaughter, his first.

The man watched Issa's composure begin to waver. He seemed to be enjoying it.

"I was wondering if that refreshed your memory." He grinned. "If you knew this man now. She's a pretty woman, your daughter. My friends tell me there's a new baby, too. This is a cause for celebration, Monsieur Issa. No reason they should ever be involved in nasty business like this, if you know what I mean."

Issa felt his stomach knot. He knew precisely what the man meant. Their eyes locked, Michel sinking back on his stool, the color gone from his face.

He nodded.

"He's American." Michel looked down, and wet his lips. "As you said, he doesn't look the same now. His hair is closely shaved to his head. You know, the way young people wear it today. He wore sunglasses, no spectacles. He came here twice—both times with local bank contacts. As you said, maybe six or seven months ago."

"And what was the nature of the business, Monsieur Issa?" the mustached man asked.

"He bought stones, high quality—both times. He seemed interested in converting cash into something more transportable. Large amounts, as you say. I don't know where he is now. Or how to reach him. He called me on his cell phone once. I didn't take an address. I think he mentioned a boat he was living on. It was just those two times." Michel looked at him. "I've never seen him again."

"*Name?*" the mustached man demanded, his dark pupils urgent and smiling at the same time.

"I don't ask for names," Michel said back.

"*His name?*" the man said again. This time his hand applied pressure to Michel's forearm. "He had a bank check. It had to be made to someone. You did a large transaction. You had to have a record of it."

Michel Issa shut his eyes. He didn't like doing this. It violated every rule he lived by. Fifty years. He could see who these people were and what they wanted. And he could see, by the intensity in this man's gaze, what was coming next. *What choice did he have?*

"*Hanson.*" Issa moistened his lips again and exhaled. "Steven Hanson, something like that."

"*Something* like that?" The man now wrapped his stocky fingers around Issa's fist and squeezed. He was starting to hurt him. For the first time, Michel actually felt afraid.

"That's what it is." Michel looked at him. "*Hanson.* I don't know how to contact him, I swear. I think he was living off his boat. I could look up the date. There must be a record of it at the harbor."

The mustached man glanced back around to his friend. He winked, as if satisfied. "That would be good," he said.

"So that makes everything okay, yes?" Michel asked nervously. "No reason to bother us again. Or my daughter?"

"Why would we want to do that?" The mustached man grinned to his partner. "All we came for was a name."

STILL SHAKING, MICHEL closed up his shop and left shortly after. He locked the rear entrance to the store. That's where he kept his small Renault, in a little private lot.

He opened the car door. He didn't like what he'd just done. These rules had kept his family in business for generations. He had broken them. If word got out, everything they'd worked for all these years was shot.

As he stepped into the car and was about to shut the door, Michel felt a powerful force push at him from behind. He was thrown into the passenger seat. A strong hand pressed his face sharply into the leather.

"I gave you his name," Michel whimpered, heart racing. "I told you what you wanted to know. You said you wouldn't bother me anymore."

A hard metal object pressed to the back of Issa's head. The merchant heard the double click of a gun being cocked, and in his panic, his thoughts flashed to Marte, waiting for him at dinner. He shut his eyes.

"Please, I beg you, no. . . ."

"Sorry, old man." The pop of the gun going off was muffled by the Renault's chugging engine. "Changed our minds."

CHAPTER SIXTY

The first thing that came back was the data from *Mustang World*. The list of new subscribers Hauck had asked for.

Back at home, he glanced over the long list of names. One thousand six hundred and seventy-five of them. Several pages long. It was organized by mailing zip code, starting with Alabama. Mustang enthusiasts from every part of the globe.

From the bank trail he'd found at Dietz's, it seemed a valid assumption Charles might be in the Caribbean or Central America. Karen told him they'd sailed around there. The bank manager on St. Kitts had told Hauck someone else had been looking for Charles. He'd also have to have access to these banks at some point.

But as he flipped through the long list, Hauck realized Charles could be anywhere. If he was even in here . . .

Slowly, he started to scan through.

THE NEXT THING that he got was a call from Joe Velko.

The Joint Inter-Agency Task Force agent caught Hauck on a Saturday morning just as he had put on a batch of pancakes for Jessie, who was up with him that weekend. When she asked about the red marks on his neck and the stiffness in his gait, Hauck told her he'd slipped on the boat.

"I pulled up some hits for you on that search," Joe informed him. "Nothing great. I'll fax it out to you if you want."

Hauck went over to his desk. He sat in his shorts and T-shirt, holding a spatula as twelve pages of data came rolling in.

"Listen," Joe told him, "no promises. Generally we might get a thousand positive hits for any one that could actually lead somewhere—and *that* means merely something we can pass along to an analyst's desk. We call any correlations to key input 'alerts' and rank them by magnitude. From low to moderate to high. Most classify in the lower bracket. I've spared you most of the boiler-plate and methodology. Why don't you flip over to the third page?"

Hauck picked up a pen and found the spot. There was a shad-owed box with the heading "Search AF12987543. *ALERT.*"

Joe explained, "These are random hits from some online news-letter the computer picked up. From something called the Carlyle Antique Car Auction in Pennsylvania." He chuckled. "Real cloak-and-dagger stuff, Ty. You see how it says, '1966 Emberglow Mus-tang. Condition: Excellent. Low Mileage, 81.5. *Shines!* Frank Bottomly, Westport, Ct.'"

"I see it."

"The computer picked up the car and the connection to Con-necticut. This communication took place last year—basically just someone making a random query into buying one. You can see the program assigned a rating of LOW against it. There's a bunch of other stuff like that. Idle chatter. You can go on."

Hauck flipped through the next few pages. Several e-mails. The program was monitoring private interactions. Tons of back-and-forth chatter on classic-car sites, blogs, eBay, Yahoo.com. Whatever it picked up using the reference points Hauck had pro-vided. A few hits on the Web site of the Concours d'Elegance in Greenwich. All were assessed as LOW. There was even a rock group in Texas called Ember Glow that opened for the singer Kinky Friedman. The priority against that hit was labeled "ZERO."

There were twelve whole pages of this. One e-mail was literally a guy talking about a girl named Amber, with the comment, "She glows like an angel."

No Charles Friedman. Nothing from the Caribbean.

Hauck felt frustrated. Nothing to add to the list from *Mustang World.*

"*Dad?*" An acrid smell penetrated Hauck's nostrils. Jessie was standing by the stove in the open kitchen, her pancakes going up in smoke.

"*Oh shit!* Joe, hold on."

Hauck ran back into the open kitchen and flipped the black pancakes off the skillet and onto a plate. His daughter's nose turned up in disappointment. "Thanks."

"I'll make more."

"Emergency?" Joe inquired on the line.

"Yeah, a thirteen-year-old emergency. Dad screwed up breakfast."

"That takes precedence. Look, go through it. It's only a first pass. I just wanted you to know I was on it. I'll call if anything else comes in."

"Appreciate it, Joe."

CHAPTERER **SIXTY-ONE**

Karen pulled her Lexus into the driveway. She stopped at the mailbox and rolled down her window to pick up the mail. Samantha was home. Her Acura MPV was parked in front of the garage.

Sam was in the last days of school, graduating in a week. Then she and Alex were heading to Africa on safari with Karen's folks. Karen would have loved to be going along as well, but when the plans were made, months earlier, she had just started at the real-estate agency, and now, with all that was happening, how could she just walk away and abandon Ty? Anyhow, she rationalized, what was better than the kids going on that kind of adventure with their grandparents?

As the commercials said, *Priceless!*

Karen reached through the car window and pulled out the mail. The usual deadweight of publications and bills, credit-card solicitations. A couple of charity mailings. An invitation from the Bruce Museum was one of them. It had a fabulous collection of American and European paintings and was right in Greenwich. The year before, Charlie had been appointed to the board.

Staring at the envelope, Karen drifted back to an event there last year. She realized it was just two months before Charlie disappeared. It was black-tie, a carnival theme, and Charlie had gotten a table. They had invited Rick and Paula. Charlie's mother, up from Pennsylvania. Saul and Mimi Lennick. (Charlie had harangued Saul into a considerable pledge.) Karen remembered he'd had to get up in his tux and make a speech that night. She'd been so very proud of him.

Someone else invaded her thoughts from that night, too. Some Russian guy from town, whom she'd never met before, but Charlie seemed to know well. Charles had gotten him to donate fifty thousand dollars.

A real charmer, Karen recalled, swarthy and bull-like with thick, dark hair. He patted Charlie on the face as if they were old friends, though Karen had never even heard his name. The man had remarked that if he'd known that Charles had such an attractive wife, he would have been happy to donate more. On the dance floor, Charlie mentioned that the guy owned the largest private sailboat in the world. A financial guy, of course, he said—a biggie—friend of Saul's. The man's wife had on a diamond the size of Karen's watch. He had invited them all out to his house—in the backcountry. More of a palace, Charlie said, which struck Karen as strange. "You've been there?" she asked. "Just what I've heard." He shrugged and kept dancing. Karen remembered thinking she didn't even know where in the world he had known the guy from.

Afterward, at home, they took a walk down to the beach at around midnight, still in their tuxedo and gown. They brought along a half-filled bottle of champagne they'd taken from the table. Trading swigs like a couple of teenagers, they took off their shoes and Charles rolled up his pant legs, and they sat on the rocks, peering out at the faraway lights of Long Island, across the sound.

"Honey, I'm so proud of you," Karen had said, a little tipsy from all the champagne and wine, but clearheaded on this. She placed her arm around his neck and gave him a deep, loving kiss, their bare feet touching in the sand.

"Another year or two, I can get out of this," he replied, his tie hanging open. "We can go somewhere."

"I'll believe that when it happens," Karen said laughingly. "C'mon, Charlie, you love this shit. Besides . . ."

"No, I mean it," he said. When he turned, his face was suddenly drawn and haggard. A submission in his eyes Karen had never seen before. "You don't understand. . . ."

She moved close to him and brushed his hair off his forehead. "Understand *what*, Charlie?" She kissed him again.

A month later he was gone in the blast.

Karen put the car into park and sat there in front of her house, suddenly trying to hold back an inexplicable rush of tears.

Understand what, Charlie?

That you withheld things from me all our lives, who you really were? That while you went in to the office every day, drove to Costco with me on weekends, rooted for Alex and Sam at their games, you were always planning a way to leave? That you may have even had a hand in killing innocent people? *For what, Charlie?* When did it start? When did the person I devoted myself to, slept next to all those years, made love with, loved with all my heart—when did I have to become afraid of you, Charlie? When did it change?

Understand what?

Wiping her eyes with the heels of her hands, Karen gathered the stack of letters and magazines on her lap. She put the car back into gear and coasted down to the garage. It was then that she noticed something standing out in the pile—a large gray envelope addressed to her. She stopped in front of the garage and slit it open before she climbed out.

It was from Tufts, Samantha's college, where she was headed in August. No identifying logo on the envelope, just a brochure, the kind they had received early in the application process, introducing them to the school.

A couple of words had been written on the front. In pen.

As she read them, Karen's heart crashed to a stop.

CHAPTER SIXTY-TWO

A day later Hauck and Karen arranged to meet. They decided on the Arcadia Coffee House on a side street in town, not far away. Hauck was already at one of the tables when she arrived. Karen waved, then went to the counter and ordered herself a latte. She joined him by the window in the back.

"How's the side?"

He lifted his arm. "No harm, no foul. You did a good job."

She smiled at the compliment, but at the same time looked at him reprovingly. "You still should let someone take a look at it, Ty."

"I got a few things back," he said, changing the subject. He pushed across a copy of the list of *Mustang World* subscribers. Karen turned through a couple of pages and blew out her cheeks, daunted at the size.

"I was able to narrow it down. I think it's a good bet to assume that Charles is out of the country. If he has funds kept in the Caribbean, at some point he'd have to access those banks. There's sixty-five new names in Florida alone, another sixty-eight international. Thirty of them are in Canada, four in Europe, two in Asia, four in South America, so let's forget them. Twenty-eight of them were in Mexico, the Caribbean, or Central America."

Hauck had highlighted them with a yellow marker.

Karen cupped her hands around her coffee. "Okay."

"I have a friend who's a private investigator. I went to him for the information I showed you on Charles's offshore company in Tortola. We eliminated four of the names right away. Spanish. Six others were commercial—auto dealerships, parts suppliers. I had him do a quick financial search on the rest."

"So what did you find?"

"We scratched off six more because of issues like length of stay at their residence and stuff we could glean from credit cards. Five others listed themselves as married, so unless Charles has been really very busy in the past year, I think we're safe to can them, too."

Karen nodded and smiled.

"That leaves eleven." He had highlighted them page by page. Robert Hopewell, who lived on Shady Lane, in the Bahamas. An F. March—in Costa Rica. Karen paused over him. She and Charles and Paula and Rick had once been there. A Dennis Camp, who lived in Caracas, Venezuela. A Steven Hanson, who was listed at a post-office box in St. Kitts. Alan O'Shea, from Honduras.

Five more.

"Any of these names seem familiar to you?" Hauck asked.

Karen went through the entire list and shook her head. "No."

"A few have phone numbers listed as well. I can't imagine that anyone trying to be invisible would do that. Most are just post-office boxes."

"Assuming he's even here?"

"Assuming he's here." Hauck nodded with a sigh. "The one advantage we have is that he doesn't know there's any reason for anyone to assume he's alive." He looked at her. "But I have a couple more irons in the fire, before you even think of having to make that call."

"It's not that." Karen nodded, fretful, massaging her brow.

"What's wrong?"

"There's something I have to show you, Ty."

She reached inside her bag. "I found a couple of things last week, buried in Charlie's desk drawer, when you asked me to go through stuff. I should have showed them to you then, but they were old and they scared me. I wasn't sure what to do. They're from before the bombing."

"Let me see."

Karen took them out of her purse. One was a small note card still in its tiny envelope, addressed to Charles. Hauck flipped it open. It was one of those cards that would accompany a floral delivery.

Sorry about the pooch, Charles. Could your kids be next?

He looked back up at Karen. "I'm not sure I understand."

"Before he died"—Karen wet her lips—"*left . . .* we had another

Westie. Sasha. She was run over by a car, right on our street. Right in front of our house. It was horrible. Charlie was the one who found her. A couple of weeks before the bombing . . ."

Hauck looked back at the note. *They were threatening him.*

"And *this* . . ." Karen pushed forward the other item. She rubbed her forehead, her eyes strained.

It was a holiday card. A picture of the family on it. A happier time. *From the Friedmans.* Charlie, in a blue fleece vest and knit shirt, his arm around Karen, in a windbreaker and jeans, sitting on a stockade fence in the country somewhere. She looked bright-eyed and proud. Pretty. *Wishing you the season's best for the coming year . . .*

Hauck winced, as if a blunt force had punched him in the belly.

Samantha's and Alex's faces—they had both been cut out.

He looked up at her.

"Someone was threatening Charles, Ty. A year ago. Before he left. Charlie kept these things hidden away. I don't know what he did, but I know it has to do with the people at Archer and all this money offshore."

Someone *was* threatening him, Hauck thought, placing the cards on top of each other and handing them back to Karen.

"Then yesterday I got this."

Karen reached into her bag and came out with something else, this time a large gray envelope. "In the mail."

Her eyes were worried. Hauck thumbed the top open, slid out what was inside. It was a brochure. Tufts. Where Sam was heading in the fall, he remembered.

There was some writing on the front. The same forward-leaning script as on the floral note.

You still owe us some answers, Karen. No one's gone away. We're still here.

"They're threatening my children, Ty. I can't let that happen." He placed his palm over her hand. "No. We won't."

CHAPTER SIXTY-THREE

The cell call came in just as Hauck was getting ready to go into visit Chief Fitzpatrick, to request that a patrol car be assigned to watch Karen's house again.

"*Joe?*"

"Listen," the JIATF man said, "I have something important here. I'm faxing it out to you now."

The pages started to flow before Hauck even arrived back at his desk. "What I'm sending you is a transcript of a series of online conversations taken off a car-enthusiast site," Velko explained. "The first exchange took place in February." Three months earlier. Joe sounded excited. "I think we got something here."

Hauck started to read the transcript as fast as he could tear the pages from the machine. The first page was headed ALERT. In the shadow box, there was a transcript number and a date, February 24. There was also a listing of the key "trigger phrases" Hauck had given Joe: "1966 Ford Mustang. Emberglow. Greenwich, Ct. Concours d' Élégance. *Charlie's Baby.*" A few of his favorite phrases.

The alert box was marked "HIGH."

Hauck sat down at his desk and read, his blood pulsing expectantly.

KlassicKarMania.com:
Mal784: Hey, trading a 66 Ember Glow 'Stang in for a 69 Merc 230 Cabriolet. Any1 interested?
DragsterB: Saw one of those in a movie out last year. Sandra Bullock. Looked fine.
Xpgma: The car or the girl?

DragsterB: Real funny, dude.

Mal784: Lake House. Yeah, except mine's a ragtop, GT. 62,000 miles. 280hp. Near mint. Any1 interested? Take $38.5.

DragsterB: I know someone who might be.

SunDog: Where is it?

Mal784: Florida. Boynton Beach. Rarely sees the light of day.

SunDog: Maybe. Had one once myself. Up north. What's the VIN code? C or K?

Mal784: K. High performance. All the way.

SunDog: How's the inside?

Mal784: Orig Pony leather. Orig radio. Not a scratch. Little bastards have a way of getting under your skin, right?

SunDog: Had to sell. Moved. Used to show it around.

Mal784: Where?

DragsterB: This a private conversation? Anyone out there got a line on a set of Crager 16" rims????

SunDog: A few places. Stockbridge, Mass. The Concours in Greenwich. Once down your way, in Palm Beach.

Mal784: Hey, you used to be on here a while back? Different name, though. CharlieBoy or something, wasn't it?

SunDog: Change of life, man. Lemme see the car. Post a picture.

Mal784: Gimme your address.

SunDog: Put it on this site, Mal. I'll look.

That was all. Hauck read through the exchange again. Every instinct told him he was onto something. He flipped the page over. There was another exchange. This one was two weeks later, March 10.

Mal784: You don't know your Mustangs for shit, bro. Check out the VIN#. K's are higher horsepowers. Command higher price. Yours is a J. 27–28K tops.

Opie$: Okay, I'll check.

Mal784: You'll learn something. Some people don't know what they have.

SunDog: So, Mal, you still got that Ember Glow????

Mal784: Hey!!! Look what the tide dragged in. What happened to you, guy? I posted a shot, like you said. Never heard back.

SunDog: Saw it. Lights-out machine, no doubt. No luck, huh?
  Anyway, not for my life now.
Mal784: I can deal. My middle name.
SunDog: Not that. I'm more on water than dry land now.
  Then I got to find a way to get it through customs down
  here.
Mal784: Donde?
SunDog: Caribbean. No matter. Would only rot in the sun
  down here. But I may come back to you. Thx.
Mal784: You late, you wait, man. Putting it up through the
  auctions now.
SunDog: Best of luck. From an ol' short seller, another time.
  I'll keep checking.
Opie$: Hey, I just looked. What about VINS beginning with
  N?

"Ty, you read them yet?" Joe Velko asked.

Hauck shuffled the pages. "Yeah. I think we hit the jackpot
here. So how do we trace this dude, SunDog?"

"I already put out an IP user trace through the Web site's server,
Ty. You understand, I wouldn't be doing this if it wasn't for you?"

"I know that, Joe."

"So I went to the blog site. They didn't put up a lot of resistance. It's amazing what a government agency can do, post-9/11,
even without a subpoena. Got a pen?"

Hauck scrambled around the desk. "I'm feeling safer already,
Joe. Shoot."

"SunDog is just a user name. We traced it back to a Web address, which they supplied us. Oilman0716@hotmail.com."

CHAPTER **SIXTY-FOUR**

Hauck fixed on the name. *Oilman.* He knew without needing anything else that they had found him. Everything inside him told him this was Charles.

"Is this traceable, Joe?"

"Yes . . . and no. As you know, Hotmail is a free Internet site. Therefore you don't need anything but a given name to register, and it doesn't even have to be a real one to get that done. Or even a real address. But we can go back to them and trace what was on the application. And there's a communication history we can go back on. What I *can't* do, however, is narrow that down to a specific place."

Hauck's blood surged with optimism. "Okay . . ."

"The activity seems to be coming from the Caribbean region. Not to a specific location though, but on a wireless LAN. There's been activity picked up around St. Maarten, the BVIs. Even as far away as Panama."

"The guy's been traveling?"

"Maybe, or on a boat."

A boat. That made sense to Hauck. "Can we narrow *that* down?"

"With time," the JIATF man explained. "We can set up a surveillance and monitor future activity and triangulate a point of origin. But that takes manpower. And paperwork. And other countries involved. You understand what I mean. And I gather that's something you're not eager to deal with, are you, Ty?"

"No," he admitted. "Not if I can help it, Joe."

"That's what I thought. So this is the next-best step. We traced the application information through the Hotmail people. That much I can do, but after that you're on your own."

"That's great!"

"The address on the account is to a post-office box at the central post office on the island of St. Maarten in the Caribbean. I went as far as I could without getting anyone else involved and checked down there. It's registered to a Steven Hanson, Ty. That ring a bell?"

"Hanson?" At first it was a blank, but then something went off inside him. "Hold on a second, Joe. . . ."

He swiveled around the desk, rifling through a stack of papers. Until he found it.

The list of new subscribers from *Mustang World.*

He had narrowed it down to just a handful of names. From all over the region: Panama. Honduras. The Bahamas. The BVIs. . . . It took a few seconds, scanning the list. Hopewell, March, Camp, O'Shea.

But there it was!

S. Hanson. Date of subscription: 1/17. *This year!* The only address given was a post-office box on St. Kitts.

Steven Hanson.

A surge of validation ran through Hauck's veins.

Steven Hanson was Oilman0716. And Oilman0716 had to be Charles. Too much fit.

The car. The Concours. The little phrases. Karen had been right. This was the part of him that could not change. *His baby.*

They had found him!

CHAPTER SIXTY-FIVE

The doorbell rang, and when Karen went to answer it, she stood fixed in surprise. "Ty . . ."

Samantha was in the kitchen, polishing off a yogurt, watching the tube. Alex had his feet slung over the couch in the family room, alternately groaning and exulting loudly, engrossed in the latest Wii video game.

Hauck's face was lit up with anticipation. "There's something I have to show you, Karen."

"Come on in."

Karen had tried to shield the kids from all that was going on—her shifting moods, the worry that seemed permanently etched in her face right now. Her frustrated, late-night rummaging through Charles's old things.

But it was a losing fight. They weren't exactly stupid. They saw the unfamiliar circumspection, the tenseness, her temper a little quicker than it had ever been before. Ty's showing up unannounced would only arouse their suspicions even more.

"C'mon in here," Karen said, taking him into the kitchen. "Sam, you remember Detective Hauck?"

Her daughter looked up, her knees curled on the stool, dressed in sweatpants and a Greenwich Huskies T-shirt, her expression somewhere between confused and surprised. "Hi."

"Good to see you again," Hauck said. "Hear you're gearing up for graduation?"

"Yeah. Next week." She nodded. She shot a glance toward Karen.

"Tufts, right?"

"Yeah," she said again. "Can't wait. What's going on?"

"I need to speak with Detective Hauck a second, hon. Maybe we'll just go . . ."

"It's okay." She got down from the stool. "I'm leaving." She tossed her yogurt container into the trash and tossed the spoon into the sink. "Good to see you again," she said to Hauck, tilting her head and screwing her eyes toward Karen, like, *What's going on?*

Hauck waved. "You, too."

Karen flicked off the kitchen TV and led him toward the sunroom. "C'mon, we'll go in here."

She sat down on the corner of the floral couch. Ty took a seat in the upholstered chair next to her. She had her hair up in a ponytail and was wearing a vintage heather gray Texas Longhorns T-shirt. No makeup. She knew she looked a mess. Still, she knew he wouldn't show up like this, at night, unless it was about something important.

He asked her, "Do they know?"

"About what I found in the mail?" Karen shook her head. "No. I don't want to worry them. I've got my folks coming up next week for the graduation. Charlie's mom, coming in from PA. They're going to Africa on safari with my folks a few days later. Sam's graduation present. I'll feel a whole lot better the minute I get them on that plane."

Ty nodded. "I'm sure. Listen. . . ." He pulled some papers out of his jacket. "I'm sorry to bother you here like this." He dropped them on the table in front of her. "You might as well read it yourself."

Warily, Karen picked them up. "What is it?"

"It's a transcript. Of two Internet conversations. From one of your husband's car sites. They took place back in February and March. One of the outfits I gave the information you found managed to pick them up."

The tiny hairs on Karen's arms stood on end.

She read through the transcripts. *Emberglow. Concours. Greenwich.* Her heart picked up a beat each time she encountered a familiar phrase. Suddenly it dawned on Karen just what this was. *SunDog.* The mention of a change of life, in the Caribbean. A reference to Charlie's old screen name, *CharlieBoy.*

An invisible hand seemed to clutch her heart in its icy fist and not let go. She focused on the name for a long time. Then she looked up. "You think this is Charlie, don't you?"

"What I think is that there's an awful lot that sounds pretty familiar," he replied.

Karen stood up, a jolt of nerves winding through her. Until now it had been safe to feel that it was all some abstract puzzle. Seeing his face on the screen; finding the safe-deposit box in New York. Even the horrible death of that person on his staff, Jonathan . . . It all just led somewhere nebulous, somewhere she never thought she'd actually have to confront.

But now . . . Her heart raced. SunDog. Karen could actually see him coming up with something like that. Now there was the possibility that everything that had happened was real. Now she could read words and phrases he might have said and almost hear his voice—familiar, alive. Out there—doing the same things, having the same conversations he'd once had with her.

A pressure throbbed in Karen's forehead. "I don't know what to do with this, Ty."

"I had my contacts trace the name," he said. "It's a free Internet site, Karen. Hotmail. There's no name registered against it, just a post-office box out of St. Maarten. In the Caribbean."

Karen held her breath and nodded.

"The P.O. box was registered under the name of Steven Hanson."

"*Hanson?*" Karen looked anxious.

"Does it mean anything to you?"

"No."

Hauck shrugged. "No reason it should. But it did strike something in me. I checked it back against the list we got from *Mustang World.*" He handed her another sheet. "Look, there's an S. Hanson right here. No address, but a P.O. box. This one's in St. Kitts."

"That doesn't prove it's him," Karen said. "Only someone who's interested in the same kind of cars—from down there. Lots of people might be."

"Who's keeping an awfully low profile, Karen. Post-office boxes, assumed names. I did a credit check on the name down there, and you know what came back? *Nothing.*"

"That still doesn't mean it's Charles!" Her voice carried an edge of desperation in it. "*Why?* Why are you doing this, Ty? Why did you quit your job?" She came back to the couch and sat down on the arm, staring at him. "What's in it for you? *Why the hell are you making me face this?*"

"Karen . . ." He put his hand on her knee and gently squeezed.

"No!" She pulled away.

His deep-set eyes were unwavering, and for a second she thought she might just start to cry. She wanted him to hold her.

"You said there was an e-mail address?"

"Yeah. There is." He reached over and handed her a slip of paper. Karen took it, her fingers shaking.

Oilman0716@hotmail.com.

She read it over a couple of times, the truth slowly sinking in. Then she looked up at him with a half smile, as if stung, wounded.

"Oilman . . ." She sniffled, feeling lifted for a second, and at the same time let down.

A moist film burned in her eye.

"It's him." She nodded. "That's Charlie."

"You're sure?"

"Yeah, I'm sure." She exhaled, as if fortifying herself against the dam burst of tears about to come down. "That number, 0716—we always used it for our passwords. That's our anniversary—July sixteenth. . . . The date we were married. In 1989. *That's Charlie, Ty.*"

CHAPTER **SIXTY-SIX**

The house was dark. Karen sat in Charlie's office. The kids had long since closed their doors and gone to sleep.

Karen stared over and over at the e-mail address. Oilman0716.

Waves of anger and uncertainty coursed through her veins. Anger mixed with accusation, uncertainty at what she should do. She wasn't sure if she even knew what she was feeling inside, but the more she stared at the familiar number, the more all doubt was gone. She knew it had to be Charlie.

And that took something out of her. The last ember of faith she still had in him. In the life they'd led. Her last hope.

You bastard, Charlie . . .

Contact him? She didn't know what she could possibly even say to him.

How could you, Charlie? How could you have left us like that? We were a team. We were soul mates, right? Didn't we always say how we completed each other? How could you have done these horrible things?

Karen's head felt like it weighed a thousand pounds. She thought of AJ Raymond and Jonathan Lauer. Deaths her husband was tied to. It repulsed her, sickened her.

Is it all true?

Over the past year, she had learned to make her peace with the fact that her husband had died. She'd done whatever it had taken. And now he was back. *Alive*—just as she was alive.

She could confront him.

Oilman0716.

What could she possibly say?

Are you alive, Charlie? Are you reading this? Do you know how I feel? How we would all feel if the children even knew? How badly you've hurt me? How you cheapened all those years we spent together. Charlie, how . . . ?

She logged on to her own AOL account. KFried111. Twice she even summoned the courage to go as far as type in his address. *Oilman.*

Then stopped herself.

What was there to be gained from opening this all up? To have him say he was sorry. To have him admit to her that he was someone other than the person she knew. That he had done these things—while living with her, sleeping with her. Planned his way out. To hear the pretense that he had once loved her, loved them . . .

Why? What was to be gained? To drag her family through it all over again. This time it would be much worse.

A tear burned down Karen's cheek. A tear filled with doubt and accusation. She stared at the address on the screen and started to cry.

"Mom?"

Karen looked up. Samantha was in the doorway, in her oversize Michigan T-shirt and panties. "Mom, what's going on? What are you doing here sitting in the dark?"

Karen brushed away the tear. "I don't know, baby."

"Mom, what's happening?" Sam came over to the desk and knelt next to her. "What are you doing at Dad's desk? You can't tell me it's nothing—something's been bothering you for over two weeks." She put her hand on Karen's shoulder. "It's about Dad, isn't it? I know it. That detective was here again. Now there's a car outside down the street. *What the hell's going on, Mom?* Look at you—you're in here crying. Those people are bothering us again, aren't they, Mom?"

Karen nodded, drawing in a breath. "They sent another note," she said, wiping the wetness out of her eyes. "I just want you to have a day to yourself we'll all be proud of, honey. You deserve that. And then go on that trip."

"And then what happens, Mom? What the hell has Dad done? You can tell me, Mom. I'm not six."

How? How could she tell her? Tell her all? It would be like stealing her daughter's innocence in a way, the warm memory she carried of her father. They had mourned him, laid him to rest. Learned to live without him. *Damn you, Charlie,* Karen seethed. *Why are you making me do this now?*

She cuddled Sam by the waist and took a breath. "Daddy may have done some things, Sam. He may have run some people's money. Bad people, honey. Offshore. *Illegally.* I don't know who they were. All I know is now they want it."

"Want *what*, Mom?"

"Money that's unaccounted for, honey. That Daddy may have lost. That's the message they wanted you to pass along to me."

"What do you mean, they want it, Mom? *He's dead.*"

Karen brought her daughter to her lap and squeezed her, the way she did when she was little, even drawing in a breath of Sam's familiar fresh-scrubbed scent. She shuddered against what she was about to say.

"Yes, honey, he's dead." Karen nodded against her.

"There's stuff you're not telling me, isn't there? I know, Mom. Lately you're always down there rifling through his old things. Now you're here, in the middle of the night, in his office, in front of his computer. Daddy wouldn't do something wrong. He was a good man. I saw the way he worked. I saw the way the two of you were with each other. He's not here to defend himself, so it's up to us. He would never have done anything that would cause us harm. He may have been your husband, Mom, but he was our dad. I knew him, too."

"Yes, baby, you're right." Karen hugged her. "It is up to us." She stroked Sam's hair as her daughter folded into her.

It's up to us that this has to end. Whatever it was these people wanted from her. Sam had a life to live. They all did. What was this nightmare going to do—follow them *forever*?

Would you really want to know, baby, if I told you? What he'd done. Would you really want your memories and love destroyed? *Like mine.* Wouldn't it just be better, simply to love him, to remember him as you do? Taking you to skating practice, helping you with your math. Being there in your heart, as he was now?

"This is scaring me a little, Mom," Sam said, pulling close.

"Don't let it, honey." Karen kissed her hair. But inside, she said to herself, *It scares me, too.*

Damn you, Charlie. Why did I ever have to see your face on that screen?

Look at what you've done.

CHAPTER SIXTY-SEVEN

The day finally came for the kids to leave. Karen helped pack up their bags and drove them to JFK, where they connected with her folks, who had come up the day before, at the British Air terminal.

She parked the car and went inside with them to check in, where she met up with Sid and Joan. Everyone was excited. Karen hugged Sam with everything she had and told her to take care of her brother. "I don't want him to be listening to his iPod and get carried off by a pack of lions."

"It's a portable DVR, Mom. And in his case more likely a pack of baboons."

"Funny." Alex scrunched his face, elbowing her. He'd always had to be dragged a little to go on this trip, always moping about large bugs and contracting malaria.

"C'mon, guys . . ." Karen gave them both a big hug. "I love you both. You know that. You have a blast. And be in touch."

"We can't be in touch, Mom," Alex reminded her. "We're in the bush. We're on safari."

"Well, pictures then," she said. "I expect lots and lots of pictures. Y'hear?"

"Yeah, we hear." Alex smiled sheepishly.

The kids both put their arms around her and gave her a real hug. Karen couldn't help it—tears welled in her eyes.

Alex snorted. "Here goes Mom."

Karen wiped them away. "Cut it out."

She hugged her parents, too, and then she watched them go off, waving as they headed to security—Alex in a Syracuse baseball cap with his backpack containing his car magazines, Sam in a pair of sweatpants with her iPod, waving a last time. Karen barely held it together.

She thought of the warning she had just received and of Charles's e-mail. And how she wanted her kids to be safe—so what was she doing, sending them to Africa? Back in her car, she sat for a moment in the garage before turning on the ignition. She pressed her face against the steering wheel and cried, happy that her kids were gone but at the same time feeling very alone, knowing that the time had finally come.

The time to face him.

It's up to us, right?

THAT NIGHT KAREN sat over Charles's computer.

There was no more fear, no more question of what she had to do. Only the resolve that she now felt to face it.

The thought occurred that she should call Ty. In the past weeks, she had grown close to him, feelings stirring in her, feelings mixed in with the confusion over what was happening with Charles, that seemed better to deny. And she'd never given Ty an answer about what she was prepared to do with what he'd found.

She logged on to her e-mail account.

KFried111. A name Charlie would recognize in an instant.

She was giving him her answer.

It's just the two of us now, Charlie. And the truth.

What could she possibly say? Every time she thought about it, everything came back. The anguish of losing him. The shock of seeing him again on the screen. Finding the passport, the money. The realization that he wasn't dead but had abandoned her. Her daughter's fear after she'd been accosted in her car.

Everything came back, but Ty was right. It wasn't going to go away.

People had died.

Hesitantly, she typed in the address. Oilman0716. Karen had done it several times before, but this time there was no turning back. She wondered, with a faint smile, what he would think, how his world would change, what door she was opening, a door maybe better off shut.

Not any longer, Charlie.

Karen typed out two words. She read them over and swallowed. Two words that would change her life a second time, reopen wounds that had barely healed.

She clicked send.

Hello, Charlie.

CHAPTER SIXTY-EIGHT

In a spot called Little Water Cay, near the islands of Turks and Caicos, Charles Friedman flicked on his laptop. The satellite broadband beamed in.

An unsettling dread deepened in him.

First it had been a week ago on Domenica. A teller he sometimes flirted with there mentioned how someone had been into the bank the week before, a short, mustached man, inquiring of one of the managers about an American who had wired in funds. Describing a person similar to him. The man had even showed a photo around.

Then there was the article that he now unfolded in his lap.

From the *Caribbean Times*. Regional News section. About a murder on the island of St. Maarten. An old-line diamond merchant had been shot in his car. Nothing had been broken into or stolen. The man's name was Issa. He had been on the island for fifty years.

His diamond merchant. *His* contact. In the past year, he had made two transactions with Issa. Charles's eyes drilled in on the headline. A crime of that nature hadn't happened there in ten years.

Somehow they knew. It was getting too close. He'd have to change venues. They must have followed him through his network of banks, discovered that his fee account from Falcon had been drawn down. Now the death of this diamond merchant. It saddened Charles that he might be responsible for the old man's fate. He had liked Issa. Soon Charles would need funds. But it was getting too dangerous to show his face right now. Even here.

He always knew that it was always likely one day they would latch onto the trail of the money.

It had rained heavily during the night. A few puffy clouds still loitered in the crisp blue sky. He sat on the deck of his boat with a mug of coffee and fired up his Bloomberg account, his early-morning ritual. Checked his overnight positions, just as he'd been doing for twenty years, though now he traded only for himself. Soon he'd have to stop that as well. Maybe they could trace his activity—his investment signature was on every trade. Still, it was all he could do to keep sane. Now he would lose that, too.

His laptop came to life. His server announced that he had four new messages.

He didn't receive many e-mails under his new account. Mostly just spam that managed to reach him—mortgage solicitations and Viagra ads. An occasional electronic trading update. He didn't dare draw attention to his new identity. That's the way it had to be.

And that's what he was thinking, spam, as, sipping his coffee, he scanned the list of messages.

Until his eyes stopped.

Not stopped—*crashed* was more like it, his stomach seizing, into the address of the sender of the third one down.

KFried111.

Charles's feet fell off the gunwales. His spine arched, as if a jolt of high voltage had been shot through it. He focused on the name again, blinking, as if his eyes were somehow playing tricks on him.

Karen.

Heart pounding, he double-checked, just to make sure he hadn't managed to log on to his old e-mail address, which he knew was impossible. But what else could it be?

No, it was all correct. *Oilman.*

His throat went dry. Worse, then came the bowel-tightening realization that in a flash everything had just caught up with him. His past. His deceptions. What he had done. *How was this possible? How could she have found his name? His address?* No, he realized those weren't even the right questions.

How was it possible she even knew he was alive?

A year had passed. He had covered his tracks perfectly. He had no connection to his old life. He had never once run into anyone they knew—always his greatest fear. Charles's fingers were shaking. *KFried111.* Karen. *How would she have been able to track him there?*

A mix of emotions swept over him: panic, fear, longing. Memory. Seeing all their faces, missing them in this moment as much as he had missed them all so terribly those first months.

Finally Charles summoned the nerve. He clicked on the name. All that was there were two sparse words. He read them, the color draining from his face, his eyes welling up, stinging with guilt and shame.

Hello, Charlie.

CHAPTER SIXTY-NINE

When the call found him, Saul Lennick had just climbed into bed in his silk Sulka pajamas. He was glancing over a financial prospectus for a meeting he had in the morning, his attention diverted by the late TV news.

Mimi, who was in the midst of an Alan Furst novel next to him, sighed crossly, glancing at the cell phone. "Saul, it's after eleven."

Lennick fumbled for his phone on the night table. He didn't recognize the number, but it was from out of the country. *Barbados*. His heart picked up. "Sorry, dear."

He removed his reading glasses and flipped it open. "Can't this wait until the morning?"

"If it could, I would've," the caller, Dietz, replied. "Relax, I'm on a phone card. It can't be traced."

Lennick sat up and put on his slippers. He uttered a guilty sigh to his wife, pretending that it was business. He took the phone into the bathroom and shut the door. "All right, go ahead."

"We've got problems," Dietz announced. "There's a homicide detective in Greenwich who handled that thing we did up there. The one who interrogated me. I may have mentioned him before."

"So . . . ?"

"He knows."

"He knows *what*?" Lennick stood in front of the mirror, picking at a pore on the side of his face.

"He knows about the accident. He also knows about that other thing in New Jersey. He somehow broke into my house. He's linked me with one of the other witnesses. You beginning to get an idea what I'm talking about now?"

Under his breath Lennick gasped, "Jesus Christ!" He was no longer staring at the pore but at his face, which had turned white.

"Sit down. It gets worse."

"How the hell can it get worse, Dietz?"

"You remember Hodges? One of my men."

"Go on."

"He's been shot."

Lennick's chest began to feel like he was having a heart attack. Dietz told him how Hodges had gone to Dietz's house and found the cop. *Inside.* How the two of them had tussled.

"Now, listen, before you bust an artery, Saul, there's some good news."

"What can be good about this?" Lennick sat down.

"He has no grounds. The Greenwich detective. Whatever he's doing, he's doing it alone. It's not part of any official investigation. He broke into my house. He brought a gun in there and used it. He didn't make a move to arrest Hodges. You see what this means?"

"No," Lennick said, panicked, "I don't see what this means."

"It means he's completely out of his jurisdiction, Saul. He was simply sneaking around. Before I called you, I called up his station up in Greenwich. *The guy's on fucking leave!* He's freelancing, Saul. He's not even on active duty. If it came out what he did, they'd take his badge. They'd arrest *him*, not me."

A dull pain flared up in Lennick's chest. He ran a hand through his white hair, sweat building up underneath his pajama top. He immediately retraced the steps of what anyone could have known that could have led back to him.

He exhaled. It was all Dietz.

"Here's the kicker," Dietz went on. "I had someone I know up there keep an eye on him. At night he's been watching over a house in Greenwich in his own car."

"Whose?"

"A woman. Someone you know well, Saul."

Lennick blanched. "Karen?"

He tried to piece it together. *Did Karen somehow know?* Even if she had found out about the incident with Lauer, how would she possibly have connected it with the other? A year ago. She had found the safe-deposit box, the passport, the cash.

Did Karen somehow know that Charles was alive?

Lennick moistened his lips. They had to speed this up. He pressed Dietz. "How are things going down there?"

"We're making progress. I've had to do some 'off-road' stuff, if you know what I mean. But that never seemed to bother you before. I think he's on a boat somewhere. But somewhere close. I've traced him through three of his banks. He'll need money. I'll have him soon. I'm closing in.

"But, listen," Dietz said, "regarding the detective, he may have found certain things in my office . . . related to what I'm doing here. Maybe even about you. I can't be sure."

A police detective? Things were growing deeper than Lennick was comfortable with. That was surely crossing the line. Still, what choice did he have?

"You know how to handle these things, Phil. I've got to go."

"One more thing," Dietz said. "If the detective knows, there's always the chance that she knows, too. I realize you're friendly. That you have something to do with her kids."

"Yes," Lennick muttered blankly. He was fond of Karen. And, having been like an uncle to them since they were small, in charge of their family trusts, you could say he did have something to do with the kids.

But it was business. Lauer had been business, the Raymond kid had been business, too. The furrows on his face were carved deep and hard. They made him seem older—older than he'd felt in years.

"Just do whatever it is you have to do."

Lennick clicked off. He splashed some water on his face, smoothed back his hair. Shuffling in his slippers, he trudged back to bed.

The evening news had finished. Mimi had turned off the light. David Letterman was on. Lennick turned to her to see if she was asleep. "Shall we catch the monologue, dear?"

CHAPTER SEVENTY

Karen waited two days. Charles didn't reply.

She wasn't sure he ever would.

She knew Charles. She tried to imagine the shock and dismay that her e-mail must have caused.

The same shock he had caused when she saw his face up on that screen.

Karen checked her e-mails several times a day. She knew what must be going through him now. Sitting in some remote part of the globe, the careful construct of his new life suddenly crumbling. It must be killing him—retracing every step, running through a thousand possibilities.

How could she possibly know?

How many times, Karen imagined, he would have read over those two words. Replaying everything in his mind, racking his brain, all the preparations he had made. His bowels acting up. Not sleeping. Things always affected Charles that way. *You owe me,* she said to him silently, relishing this image of him, panicked, rocked. *You owe me for the hurt you put me through. The lies . . .*

Still, she couldn't forgive him. Not for what he'd done to her—to the kids. She no longer knew if there was love between them. If there was anything still between them, other than the memory of a life spent together. Still, it didn't matter. She just wanted to hear from him. She wanted to see him—face-to-face.

Answer me, Charlie . . .

Finally, after three days, Karen typed out another message. She closed her eyes and begged him.

Please, Charlie, please. . . . I know it's you. I know you're out there. Answer me, Charlie. You can't hide any longer. I know what you've done.

CHAPTER SEVENTY-ONE

I know what you've done!

Charles sat in the corner of a quiet Internet café in the harbor on Mustique, where he had put in, staring in horror at Karen's latest message.

A collection of dreadlocked locals drinking Jamaican beer and a party of itinerant German surfers in tattoos and bandannas. He had a pressing fear, even here, that everything was closing in on him.

I know what you've done!

What? What do you know I've done, Karen? And how? Hidden behind his shades, he took a sip of a Caribe and read the message over for the tenth time. He knew she would keep at it. He knew her. This was no longer something he could just ignore.

And how in hell did you find me?

What do you want me to say to you, Karen? That I'm a bastard? That I betrayed you? Charles could sense the anger resonating in her words. And he didn't blame her. He deserved whatever she felt. To have left them as he did. To have put them through that anguish. The loss of a husband, a father. Then, after it all finally subsided, to suddenly find out he was alive!

Answer me, Charlie.

What do you know, Karen?

If you knew, truly knew, you would understand. At least a little. That it was never to hurt you. That would have been the last thing in my heart.

But to protect you, Karen. To keep you safe. To keep Sam and Alex safe as well. You would know why I *had* to stay away. Why, when the door opened and the path presented itself, I had to "die."

Please, Charlie, please. . . . Answer me, Charlie.

The surfers were cackling loudly in German at something they had found on YouTube. A heavyset island woman in a colorful shift sat down across from him, towing a young daughter sipping on a Fanta. Charles realized he had spent so much of the past year hiding, in shadows, turning away from who he was. From everything he once loved.

But all of a sudden it was like he felt alive again. For the first time in a year! It was clear to him, you could never fully kill it. What was inside you. Who you are.

And now Charles realized that if he only touched this key, a flick of his hand, sent this message back, answered her, it reopened everything. The whole world changed again.

I know what you've done.

He took a swig of beer. Maybe it was time to move on again. To Vanuatu in the Indian Ocean. Or back to Panama. No one would find him. He had money there.

He lifted his shades. He looked closely at the words he had written. Pandora's box was about to open again. For her and for him. And this time there would be no closing it. No sudden bomb blast interfering—nowhere to hide.

The hell with it, he said. He finished the last of his beer. She had found him. *The iron fist in the velvet glove . . .* he recalled fondly.

She would never let up.

Yes, I'm here. Yes, it's me, he said. With one last reflection, he pushed the send key, sending his world spinning again.

Hello, baby. . . .

CHAPTER SEVENTY-TWO

Hauck had gone out for an evening run around the cove. He'd sat at home for a couple of days, and still he hadn't heard from Karen. The night was hot, sticky. The cicadas were buzzing. Finally he just had to calm the frustration that was bursting in his chest.

He knew it wasn't right to push. He knew how hard this had to be for her, to face her husband. It would be like a part of Norah suddenly brought up for him again. Ripping open wounds that hadn't healed. He wasn't sure whether to wait and see if she still wanted to find Charles. Or now that she knew the truth—at least parts of it—to simply pack it in. Bring what they'd found into Fitzpatrick.

He'd have to reopen the case. AJ Raymond's hit-and-run.

That's what had started him on it in the first place, right?

To his surprise, as he headed back down Euclid toward his house, he spotted the familiar Lexus parked on the street. Karen sitting on his front stairs. When he came to a stop, she stood up.

A slightly awkward smile. "Hey . . ."

She was dressed in a fitted black shirt worn out over nice jeans, her caramel hair a little messy, a chunky, quartzlike bracelet dangling loosely from her wrist. It was a warm summer night. She looked great to him.

"I'm sorry to barge in," she said, a look that was almost forlorn, little-girl-ish, coming through on her face. "I just needed to talk to someone. I took a chance."

Hauck shook his head. "You're not barging in."

He walked her up the steps and unlocked the door. He grabbed a towel off the kitchen counter and wiped down his face. He asked if she wanted a beer from the fridge.

"No. Thanks."

Karen was like a bundle of nerves, and she walked around like she was holding something deep inside. She went up to the easel by the window. He followed her over, taking a seat on the stool.

"I didn't know you paint."

Hauck shrugged. "You better look at it closely before you use that word."

She stepped up to the easel. So close that Hauck could smell her scent—sweet, blossomy—his pulse climbing. He held back the urge to touch her.

"It's nice," she said. "You're always full of surprises, aren't you, Lieutenant?"

"That's about the nicest thing anyone's ever said about it." He smiled.

"You probably cook, too. I bet you—"

"Karen . . ." He had never seen her so wound up. He swiveled around and went to grab her arm.

She pulled away.

"*It was him,*" she said. Her eyes were liquid, angry, almost glaring at him. "He answered me. It took three days. I had to write him twice." She put a hand to the back of her neck. "I didn't know what to say to him, Ty. What the hell *could* I say? 'I know it's you, Charles. Please answer me'? Finally he did."

"What did he say?"

"What did he say?" She sniffed, blew out a derisive blast of air. "He said '*Hello, baby.*' "

"That's all?"

"Yeah." She smiled, hurt. "That was all." She took a few steps around, as if she were holding back some torrent, checking out the view of the cove off the deck. She went over to a console against the wall. He kept a couple of pictures on it. She picked them up, one by one. A shot of the two girls when they were babies. He saw her staring at it. Another of Hauck's boat, the *Merrily.*

"Yours?"

"Mine." Hauck nodded. He stood up. "Not exactly like the sultan of Brunei's, but Jessie likes it. In the summer we go up to Newington or out to Shelter Island. Fish. When the weather's nice, I've been known to—"

"*You do it all, don't you, Ty?*" Her eyes were ablaze, flashing at him. "You're what they call a good man."

Hauck wasn't sure if that was a compliment. Karen compressed her lips tightly, ran a hand through her tousled hair. It was like she was ready to explode.

He stepped forward. "Karen . . ."

"'*Hello, baby,*'" she said again, her voice cracking. "That's all he fucking said to me, Ty. Like, '*What have you been up to, hon? Anything new with the kids?*' It was Charles! The man I buried. The man I slept next to for eighteen years! '*Hello, baby.*' What the hell do I say to him now, Ty? What the hell happens now?"

Hauck went to her and took her in his arms. This time as he had always dreamed of holding her tightly, pressing her close to his chest, hard. His blood almost burst out of his veins.

At first she tried to pull away, anger coursing. Then she let him, tears smearing on his shirt, her hair honey-scented and disarrayed, her breasts full against his chest.

He kissed her. Karen didn't resist. Instead she parted her lips in response, her tongue seeming just as eager to seek out his, something beyond their control taking hold of them, her scent deep in his nostrils—an intoxication, something sweet, jasmine—driving him wild.

His hand traveled down the curve of her back, his fingers crawling underneath the belt on her jeans. Arousing him. He drew it back, her blouse loose, finding the warmth of the exposed flesh of her belly, drew it past the breathless sigh of her breasts, and cupped her face in his hands.

"You don't have to do anything," he said.

"*I can't.*" Karen looked at him, tears glistening off her cheeks. "I can't be there alone."

He kissed her again. This time their tongues lingered in a sweet, slow dance. "*I just can't. . . .*"

Hauck wiped the tears off her face. "You don't have to," he said. "You don't have to do anything."

Then he picked her up in his arms.

THEY MADE LOVE in the bedroom.

Slowly, he unbuttoned her shirt, ran his hands over the black lace of bra, tenderly down to her groin, as she drew back, a little afraid, parts of her that hadn't been touched in a year.

Her breathing heavy, Karen tilted her head against his bare chest. "Ty, I haven't done this in a long time."

"I know," he said, gently pulling her arms through her sleeves, running his hand along her thigh, underneath her jeans.

She tensed with anticipation.

"I mean with someone else," she said. "I've been with Charles for twenty years."

"That's okay," he said. "I know."

He laid her back on the bed, drew her jeans out from under her firm thighs a leg at a time, slipped his hand underneath her panties, felt the tremor of anticipation there. The throbbing in her womb was driving Karen wild. She looked up at him. He had been there for her, steadied her, when everything else was just insanity. He had been the one thing in which she could believe. She reached up and gently touched his side, the marks healing, and kissed them, his perspiration sweet. Hauck, tensing, unbuckled his shorts. He was the one thing that held her together. Without him she didn't know what she would have done.

She put her face close to him. *"Ty . . ."*

He moved his body firmly over hers, his buttocks tight, arms strong, athletic. Their bodies came together like a warm wave, electricity shooting down Karen's spine. She arched her back. Her breasts, his chest came together, a hundred degrees.

Suddenly there was nothing holding them back. She felt this yearning rising up from her center. Karen let her head fall back, fall from side to side as he entered her, a tremor shooting through her from the tips of her fingers to her toes, like a current, a long-awaited prize. She cupped his rear and drew him into her deeply. A wildness taking over. Gasping, their bodies became a tangle of pelvises and thighs. She clung to him. This man had risked everything for her. She didn't want to hold anything back. They rocked. She wanted to give him everything. A part of her she had never given to anyone. Even Charles. A part of her she had always held back.

Everything.

CHAPTER SEVENTY-THREE

Afterward they lay on the bed, spent, Karen's body slick with lovely sweat, still radiating fire. Hauck cooled her, blowing on her chest, her neck. Her hair was a tangled mess.

"Must be your lucky day," she mused, with an ironic roll of her eyes. "Normally I never give out until at least the third date. It's a hard-and-fast rule at Match.com."

Hauck laughed, lifting a leg up on his other knee. "Listen, if it means anything, I promise I'll still come through with a couple of meals."

"*Whew!*" Karen blew out a breath. "That's a load off my mind."

She glanced around the cramped bedroom, looking for things about him she didn't know. A simple wooden bed frame, a night table with a couple of books stacked—a biography of Einstein, a novel by Dennis Lehane—a pair of jeans tossed over a chair in the corner. A small TV.

"What the hell is *that*?" Karen said, pointing to something against the wall.

"Hockey stick," Hauck said, falling back.

Karen propped up on her elbow. "Tell me I didn't just sleep with a man who keeps a hockey stick in his bedroom."

Hauck shrugged. "Winter league. Guess I never moved it."

"Ty, *it's fucking June.*"

He nodded, like a little boy discovered with a stash of cookies under his bed. "You're lucky you weren't here last week. My skates were in here, too."

Karen brushed her hand against his cheek. "It's good to see you laugh, Lieutenant."

"I guess we could say we're both a bit overdue."

For a while they lay like two starfish on the large bed, barely covered, just the tips of their fingers touching, still finding each other.

"Ty . . ." Karen raised herself up. "There's something I need to ask you about. I saw something when I came to your office that day. You had a picture on the credenza. *Two* young girls. When I saw you at the game that day, I met your daughter and you told me she was your only one. Then tonight I saw another of her, outside." She leaned close to him. "I don't mean to open something up—"

"No." He shook his head. "You're not opening anything up."

Facing the ceiling, he told her. About Norah. At last. "She'd be nine now."

Karen felt a stab of sadness rush over her.

He told her how they'd just come back from the store and forgotten something and had been in such a rush to get back there. There was his shift, he was running late. Beth was mad at him. They were living out in Queens then. He had bought the wrong dessert. "Pudding Snacks . . ."

How he had somehow left the car in a rush, his shift in half an hour, rushing back in to grab the receipt.

"Pudding Snacks," Hauck said again, shrugging at Karen, an empty smile.

"They'd been playing on the curb. Tugboat Annie, Jessie told us later. You know the song—'*Merrily, merrily, merrily . . .* '" He inhaled a breath. "The car backed out. I hadn't put it in park. All we ever heard was Jessie. And Beth. I remember the look she gave me. 'Oh, Ty, oh, my God!' It all happened so suddenly." He looked up at her and wet his lips. "She was four."

Karen sat up, and brushed her hand across his slick face. "You're still carrying it, aren't you? I can see it in your eyes. I saw it there the first time we met."

"You were the one who was forced to deal with something then."

"Yes, but I still saw it. I think that's why I thanked you. For what you said. You made me feel like you understood. I don't think you ever let it go."

"How *do* you let that go, Karen?"

"I know." Karen nodded. "I know. . . . What about your wife? Beth, right?"

Hauck leaned up on his side, hunched his shoulders sort of helplessly. "I don't think she's ever forgiven me. The irony was, she was the reason I was running back to the store." He turned and faced her. "You know how you always asked me why I'm doing this, Karen?"

She nodded again. "Yeah."

"And one reason is that I think I was drawn to you from the first time we met. I couldn't get you out of my mind."

Karen took his hand.

"But the other," he said, and shook his head, "that Raymond kid, lying there on the asphalt. I knew there was something about it from the get-go. Something about him just brought me back, to Norah. I couldn't put it away . . . his image. I still can't."

"Their *hair,*" Karen said, cupping Hauck's curled hand close to her breast. "They both had the same red hair. You've been trying to make up for that accident all this time. By solving this hit-and-run. By playing the hero for me."

"No, that part was just my plan to get in your pants," he teased, deadpan.

"Ty." She looked into his sorrowful eyes. "You are a good man. That part I could see the first time we met. Anyone who knows you can see that. We all do things every day—walk off the curb into traffic, drive when we've had a bit too much to drink, forget to blow out a candle when we go to sleep. And things just go on, like they always do. Until one time they don't. You can't keep judging yourself. This happened a long time ago. It was an accident. You loved your daughter. You still do. You don't have to make up for anything anymore."

Hauck smiled. He pressed his hand to her cheek and stroked Karen's face. "This from a woman who walked in here tonight having found out that her once-deceased husband was her new AOL pen pal."

"Tonight, yes." Karen laughed. "Tomorrow . . . who the hell knows?"

She dropped back onto the bed. Suddenly she remembered why she had come. The frustration that bristled in her blood. *Hello, baby . . .* It all overwhelmed her a little. She grasped his hand.

"So what the hell are we gonna do now, Ty?"

"We're gonna let it drop," he said, running his finger along the slope of her back and letting it linger on her buttock. "Anyway, it's not exactly conducive, Karen."

"Conducive? Conducive to *what*?" she asked, aware of the renewed stirring in her belly.

He turned toward her and shrugged. "To doing it again."

"*Doing it again*?" He pulled Karen on top of him, their bodies springing alive. She brushed her nose against his, her hair cascading all over his face like a waterfall, and then she laughed. "You know how long it's been since I've heard those words?"

CHAPTER SEVENTY-FOUR

In the morning Hauck put on coffee. He was out on the deck when Karen stepped outside after nine, wearing an oversize Fairfield University T-shirt she'd grabbed from the drawer, wiping sleep from her eyes.

"Morning." He looked up, his hand brushing against her thigh.

She leaned against him and rested her head on his shoulder. "Hi."

It was a bright, warm, early-summer morning. Karen looked across the row of modest homes to the sound. Boaters were readying their crafts in the marina. An early launch to Cove Island was going out. A few gray gulls flapped in the sky.

She went over to the railing. "It's nice out here." She nodded toward the painting, still on its easel. "Feel like I've seen this before."

Hauck pointed to a stack of canvases against the wall. "All the same view."

Karen raised her face to the sun and ran a hand through her tangled hair against the breeze. Then she sat down next to him, cupping her hands around the mug.

He said, "Listen, about last night . . ."

She put out her hand and stopped him. "Me first. I didn't mean to throw myself at you. I just couldn't face being alone. I—"

"I was about to say last night was a dream," he said, winking into her sleepy eyes.

"I was about to say something like that, too." Karen smiled back sheepishly. "I hadn't been with anyone else in almost twenty years."

"It was crazy. All that pent-up energy . . ."

"Yeah, *right*." She rolled her eyes.

He shifted himself around to her. "You know that yoga move, where you arch your spine back like that and—"

Karen slapped at his wrist, rebuking. "Oh, you're a stitch!"

Ty caught her hand. He looked at her, directly now. "I meant it, Karen. What I told you about why I started in on this. Because of you. But you knew that. I've never been much of a poker player."

Karen leaned her head on his shoulder again. "Ty, listen, I don't know if this is such a smart idea for us right now."

"That's a risk I'll have to take."

"There's just too much going on that I have to sort out. What we do about Charlie, my kids? My goddamn husband's out there, Ty!"

"Have you made up your mind?"

"About what? Help me out. It's like a fucking Costco of things to choose from."

"About Charles," Hauck said. "About what you want me to do."

Karen drew in a breath. There was something firm in her gaze, replacing the coiled anxiety of last night. She nodded. "I've made up my mind. He owes me answers, Ty, and I want them. *When* he first started lying to me. When whatever it was he was chasing became more important to him than me or the kids. And I'm not gonna turn the page on almost half my life without hearing them. From him. By letting him off the hook. I'm want to find the man, Ty."

AFTER SHE GOT home and took a shower and brushed out her hair, Karen sat back down at the computer. All the anxiety she'd been feeling last night had hardened into a new resolve.

She clicked onto AOL and found Charlie's reply to her. She read it over one more time.

Hello, baby. . . .

She started to type.

I'm not your "baby," Charles. Not anymore. I'm someone you've terribly hurt—beyond what you could

*ever imagine. Someone very confused. But you already
know that, Charles, don't you?*

*You knew that when you wrote me back. You must've
known that since the day you left. So here's the deal—I
want to see you, Charles. I want to hear why you did this.
Why you used us, Charlie, the people you supposedly
loved. Not over the Internet. Not like this. I want to hear
it directly from you. Face-to-face. Who you really are,
Charlie.*

She had to hold herself back.

*So you tell me—how. You tell me where I can meet you,
Charlie. You make it happen, so I can go forward in my
life—if that's something you at all might still care about.
Don't even think about saying no. Don't even think
about hiding, Charlie. Tell me how.*

Karen.

CHAPTER SEVENTY-FIVE

Charles was inside the South Island Bank on St. Lucia when Karen's message came in over his BlackBerry.

Her words stopped him like a shot of epinephrine into his heart.

No. He couldn't do this. He couldn't see her. This wasn't going to work. He had opened the door, but that had been a moment of weakness and stupidity. Now he had to slam it shut.

He had made out an account-transfer form. Filled in the routing numbers and the new accounts. He was cleaning house here, transferring the funds he kept to the Banco Nacional de Panama in Panama City and the Seitzenbank in Luxembourg, and from there on to safer ground.

It was time to be leaving.

Charles waited for a brightly clad local woman to finish, then sat down at the manager's desk. The manager was an amiable islander he had worked with before, who seemed pleased to see Charles again, as he did every few months.

And she was disappointed to see him closing out his accounts.

"Mr. Hanson," the manager said, dutifully fulfilling his request, "so it seems we will not be seeing you here anymore?"

"Maybe not for a while," Charles said, standing up. "Thanks." The two shook hands.

As he left, his mind weighing Karen's urgent message—resolving to tell her no, not to contact him anymore—Charles never noticed the manager reaching for a slip of paper he kept hidden in his desk. Or picking up the phone before Charles had even stepped out the door.

· · ·

KAREN WAS STILL at the computer when Charles's reply came in.

> No, Karen. It's way too dangerous. I can't let that
> happen. The things I did that you may think you know
> about . . . you simply don't. Just accept that. I know how
> you must feel, but please, I beg you, just go on with your
> life. Don't tell anyone you found me. No one, Karen! I
> loved you. I never meant to hurt you. But now it's too
> late. I accept that. But please, please, whatever you may
> feel, don't write me anymore.

Anger bristled through Karen's blood. She wrote back:

> Yes, Charlie, I'm afraid you ARE going to let that
> happen! When I say I know about what you've done, I
> don't just mean that you're alive. I know. . . . I know
> about Falcon and all the money you were managing
> offshore, Charlie. That you kept from me all those years.
> And Dolphin. Those empty tankers, Charlie. That person
> in Pensacola who uncovered your fraud. What the hell
> did you try to do to him, Charlie?

This time his reply came back in seconds—a tone of panic:

> Just who have you been talking to, Karen?

> What does it matter who I've been talking to, Charlie?

Now they were going back and forth, real time. Karen and the
man she had thought was a ghost.

> You're not seeing it. All that matters is, I know.
> I know about that boy who was killed in Greenwich.
> The day you disappeared. The day we were up here
> bleeding for you, Charlie. And I know you were there.
> Is that enough yet? I know you came up here after the
> bombing. The bombing when you were supposed to
> have been killed, Charlie. I know you called him under
> an assumed name.

How, Karen, how?

And I know who he was, Charlie. I know he was that man from Pensacola's son. What your own trader, Jonathan Lauer, probably found out himself and was trying to tell me. Is that enough yet, Charlie? Fraud. Murder. Covering it all up.

Seconds later Charlie wrote back:

Karen, please . . .

She wiped her eyes.

I haven't told any of this to the kids. If I did, it would surely kill them, Charlie. Like it's been fucking killing me. They're away now. On safari with my folks. Sam's graduation present. But people have been threatening us, Charlie. Threatening THEM! Is that what you wanted, Charlie? Is that what you wanted to leave behind?

She drew in a breath and went on typing.

I know there are risks. But we're going to take those risks. Otherwise, I'm going to pass all this on to the police. You'll be charged, Charlie. We're talking murder. They'll find you. If I could, believe me, so can they. And that's what your kids will think of you, Charlie. That you were a murderer. Not the person they admire now.

Karen was about to push send, but then she hesitated.

So that's the price, Charles, for my silence. To keep all this quiet. You always loved a fair exchange. I don't want you back. I don't love you anymore. I don't know if I have any feelings for you. But I am going to see you, Charlie. I am going to hear why you did this to us, from your lips, face-to-face. So you just tell me how it's going to get done. Nothing else. No apologies. No sorrow.

Then you can feel free to disappear for the rest of your miserable life.

She pressed send. And waited. For several minutes. There was no reply. Karen began to grow worried. What if she had divulged too much? What if she had scared him away? For good. Now that she'd finally found him.

She waited for what seemed forever. Staring at the blank screen. *Don't do this to me again, Charles. Not now. C'mon, Charlie, pretend that you once loved me. Don't put me through this again.*

She shut her eyes. Maybe she even dozed off for a while, totally enervated, spent.

She heard a sound. When Karen opened her eyes, she saw that an e-mail had come in. She clicked on it.

Alone. That's the only way it happens.

Karen stared at it. A tiny smile of satisfaction inched onto her lips.

All right, Charles. Alone.

CHAPTER SEVENTY-SIX

Another day passed while Karen waited for Charles's instructions. This time she wasn't nervous or afraid. Or surprised when she finally received them.

Just resolved.

Come down to the St. James's Club on St. Hubert's in the BVIs.

Karen knew the place. They had sailed around there a couple of times. It was a beautiful spot on a horseshoe cove, a cluster of thatched bungalows nestled right on the beach. Completely remote.

Charles added:

Soon. Days, not weeks, Karen. I'll contact you there.

There were many things Karen thought to say to him. But all she wrote back was:

I'll be there.

RONALD TORBOR WRESTLED with what to do. That very morning he had looked up and seen Steven Hanson, the American, standing in front of his desk.

Come to close out his accounts.

The bank manager tried to camouflage his surprise. Since the two Americans had been to his house, he had prayed he would never see this man again. But here he was. All the while they talked and conducted business, Ronald's heart was hammering out of his chest. As soon as the man left, Ronald rushed into the office bathroom. He splashed cold water all over his burning face.

What should he do?

He knew it was wrong—what those awful men had asked him to do. He knew it violated every fiduciary oath. That he would be fired if anyone found out. Lose everything he had worked for all these years.

And Ronald liked him. Mr. Steven Hanson. He was always cheerful and polite. He always had a good word to say about Ezra, whose picture was on Ronald's desk and whom Hanson had seen once before when Ezra and Edith had been visiting in the bank.

But what choice did he have?

It was for his son that he was doing this.

The mustached man had promised—if he ever found out that Ronald had screwed him, they would be back. And if they had traced Hanson this far, they could trace him further. And if they found out his accounts had been transferred out, it would be worse for them. Edith and Ezra.

Far, far worse.

Ronald realized there was a lot more at stake than just his job. There was his family. They had threatened to kill him. Ezra. Ronald had vowed he could not see that look of fear in his wife's eyes again.

Mr. Hanson, please understand. What choice do I have?

There was a pay telephone on the far end of the square outside the bank. Next to a bench, with an election poster on it, a picture of Nevis's corrupt incumbent minister over the slogan TIME COME FOR DEM TO GO.

He put a pay card in the slot and punched in the international number he'd been given. *Make sure I hear from you, Ronald*, the mustached man had said as he left, patting Ezra's head. "Nice boy." He winked. "I'm sure he'll have quite a future in life."

The call connected. Ronald swallowed back his fear.

"*Hello*," a voice answered. Ronald recognized its tone. Just hearing it again sent a shiver of shame and revulsion down his spine.

"It's Ronald Torbor. From Nevis. You said to call."

"Ronald. Good to hear from you," the mustached man replied. "How's Ezra? Getting along?"

"I've seen him," Ronald said without responding. "The man you're looking for. He was here today."

CHAPTER SEVENTY-SEVEN

"I'm going alone," Karen explained to Hauck.

They met for coffee again at Arcadia in town. Karen told him how Charlie had contacted her at last, and about his instructions. "He said just me. That was the deal I made. I've got to do it, Ty."

"No. You're not." He put down his coffee and shook his head. "That doesn't fly, Karen. You don't have any idea who else he may be involved with. There's no way I'm going to let you put yourself at risk."

"That's the deal, Ty. I agreed."

"*Karen.*" Hauck leaned in close, lowering his voice so people at the nearby tables wouldn't hear. "This man walked away from you and your family. You know precisely what he's done. You also know what he has to protect. This is dangerous, Karen. This isn't some high-school stunt. You told Charlie exactly what you'd un-covered about him. People have died. No way in hell would I let you go down there alone."

"You don't have to remind me what the stakes are, Ty." Karen's voice was strained, and growing louder. She looked at him plead-ingly. "When I came to you, I trusted you. I told you things I could never tell anyone else."

"I think I've earned that trust, Karen."

"Yes." Karen nodded. "I know you have. But now you have to trust *me* just a little, too. *I'm going,*" she said, her eyes lucid, unwa-vering. "This is my husband, Ty. I know him, whatever it may seem. And I know he would never harm me. I told him yes, Ty. I'm not going to lose this chance."

Hauck exhaled a deep breath, his stern gaze reflecting his resistance. He could stop her, he knew. He could blow the whole thing wide open today. Take the heat he had brought upon himself. But this was what he'd always promised her. From the beginning. To find Charles. And as he ran through his remaining options, he realized that in many ways he was already in too deep.

"It has to be somewhere very public," he said finally. "I have to be able to watch out for you. That's the only way."

She widened her eyes. "Ty . . ."

"That's not negotiable, Karen. If the situation seems safe once we know all the details, you can go see him. Alone. I give you my word. But I'm going to be around. That's the deal."

Karen's face carried an admonition. "You can't use me to get to him, Ty. You have to promise."

"You think I'm going down there to arrest him, Karen? What do you think, I'm going to call in Interpol and set up a sting like on *Miami Vice*?" He fixed on her. "The reason I'm going there is that I'm probably in love with you, Karen—don't you understand that?—or something pretty damn close. I'm going there because there's no way in hell I'm going to let you get in over your head and get yourself killed."

The look in his eyes was determined and unbending. The shining blue in them had hardened into more of an intractable gray resolve. For a while the two of them just sat there, Hauck bristling.

Then slowly Karen smiled. "You said 'probably.' "

"Yeah, probably." Hauck nodded. "And while I'm at it, probably a little jealous, too."

"Of Charles?"

"Of eighteen years, Karen. This is the person you built your life with, whatever the hell he's done."

"That part is over, Ty."

"I don't know what's over." He looked away for a second, then sucked in a frustrated breath. "Anyway, I said it, stupid as it sounded, what the hell."

Karen reached over to his hand. She pressed his palm inside both of hers, massaging the soft cushions. Eventually he met her eyes.

"You know, I probably love you, too." She shrugged. "Or something close."

"I'm overwhelmed."

"But if we do this, Ty, we can't do it like that. *Please*. This is the most important thing for me now. That's why I'm going down there. Afterward . . ." Karen pressed her thumb into his palm. "Afterward we'll see. Is that a deal?"

He wrapped his pinkie around hers and granted his reluctant agreement. "Do you know this place?"

"The St. James Club? We were there once. We pulled in at the dock for lunch." She saw his concern. "It's like in *Condé Nast Traveler*, Ty. It's not exactly the setting for an ambush."

"So when do you go?"

"*We* go, Ty. *We*. Tomorrow," Karen said. "I already booked the tickets."

"Tickets?"

"Yeah, Ty, *tickets*." Karen grinned. "You honestly think I thought you'd ever let me go down there on my own?"

CHAPTER SEVENTY-EIGHT

Rick and Paula were away. As were Karen's kids. She e-mailed the lodge where Sam and Alex were staying and told them she would also be away for a few days. She realized she should let someone know where she was going. She dialed a number and a familiar voice picked up, at home.

"Saul?"

"*Karen?*" Lennick sounded surprised but pleased. "How are you? How's that gang of yours?"

"We're all good, Saul. It's why I'm calling. I'm heading out of town for a few days. The kids are off in Africa, if you can believe it. On safari. Sam's graduation present. With my folks."

"Yes, I remember you talking about that," he said blithely. "It certainly pays to be young now, doesn't it?"

"Yes, Saul," Karen said, "I guess it does. Listen, they're a little hard to reach there, so I left your office number at their next lodge. You know, just in case anything comes up. I wasn't sure who else to call."

"Of course. I'm delighted, Karen. You know I'll do what I can do. So where are you heading? Just in case I need to reach you," he explained.

"Down to the Caribbean. The British Virgin Isles. . . ."

"*Excellent.* The island are nice this time of year. Any specific place?"

"I'll leave my cell number with you, Saul." She decided to hold the rest back. "If you need me, you can reach me there."

Saul was Charlie's mentor. He had overseen the shutdown of Charlie's firm. He had learned things about him. Archer. The offshore accounts. He'd never said anything about it to her. With a chill, Karen suddenly wondered, *Does he know it all?*

"I know that Charlie was up to some things, Saul."

He paused. "Just what do you mean, Karen?"

"I know he was handling a lot of money. Those accounts we spoke of, offshore. That's what those passports and the money were about, weren't they? You never got back to me, but I know you know that, Saul. You knew him better than I did. And you'd protect him, Saul, wouldn't you, if something came out? Even now?"

"I never wanted to worry you, Karen. That's part of my job. And I'd protect you, too."

"Would you, Saul?" Suddenly Karen felt she understood something. "Even if it threatened you?"

"Threatened me? How could it possibly threaten me, Karen. What do you mean?"

She was about to press him—ask him if he knew. Did he know that her husband was alive? Was Saul part of it? Part of why Charlie was hiding or, as a foreboding thought flashed through her, even the person he was running from? Was he a part of what came between them? *Saul?* He would have known about Jonathan Lauer. He never told her about that. Karen felt a nervousness snake through her, as if she had crept into a forbidden space, a closed vault, chilly and tightly sealed.

Saul cleared his throat. "Of course I would, Karen."

"Of course you would *what*, Saul?"

"Protect you, Karen. And the kids. Isn't that what you asked?"

Suddenly Karen felt sure. He did know. Much, much more than he was telling her. She could feel it in the quiver of his voice. Saul was Charlie's mentor.

He knew. He had to know.

And now Saul knew that she knew, too.

"You never told me." Karen wet her lips. "You knew that Jonathan Lauer had died. You knew he'd tried to contact me. You knew that Charlie was handling this money. Charlie's dead, right, Saul? He's dead—and you're still protecting him."

There was a pause.

"Of course he's dead, Karen. Charlie loved you. That's all you should be thinking about now. I think it's best to keep it like that."

"What did my husband do, Saul? What is it with you people? Why are you holding things back from me?"

"You enjoy yourself down there, Karen. Wherever you're heading. You know I'll take care of whatever needs to be done up here. You know that, don't you, dear?"

"Yes," Karen said. Her mouth was dry. A chill of uncertainty passed through her, a window left open to a world she once trusted.

"I know that, Saul."

PART *FOUR*

CHAPTER **SEVENTY-NINE**

The twelve-seater Island Air Cessna touched down on the remote island strip, its wheels barely finding the slip of land in the green-blue Caribbean Sea. The small plane coasted to a stop at the terminal, basically a Quonset hut with a tower and a wind indicator.

Hauck winked to Karen across the aisle from him. "Ready?" Two baggage handlers in T-shirts and shorts ran out as soon as the propellers stopped.

The young pilot in wraparound sunglasses helped passengers out onto the tarmac at the bottom of the landing steps.

"Nice flight," Hauck said.

"Welcome to paradise." He grinned back.

They had taken the morning flight down to San Juan from JFK, caught the American Eagle connection to Tortola, and now the cramped puddle jumper over the glasslike sea to St. Hubert. Karen had been quiet for much of the trip. She slept, fidgeted through a paperback she'd brought along. Anxious. To Hauck she could not have looked prettier in a tight-fitting brown tank and white capris, an onyx pendant around her neck, and tortoiseshell sunglasses perched on her head.

Hauck helped her off the steps and flipped down his own shades. Whyever they had come here, it was beautiful. The sun was dazzling. A cool trade wind off the sea caressed them.

"Friedman? Hauck?"

A local representative from the resort, dressed in an epauletted white shirt and holding a clipboard, called out to them.

Hauck waved him over.

"Welcome to St. Hubert." The young black man grinned amiably. "I'll be taking you to the resort."

They loaded their bags into a hotel Land Cruiser. The island seemed barely more than a large ribbon of sand and vegetation in the middle of the sea. Only a few miles from end to end. There was a small mountain splitting the island, some makeshift food stands, locals selling fruit and homemade rum, a few goats. A couple of colorful billboards for a local rent-a-car service and Caribe beer.

The trip to the hotel took a little more than fifteen minutes of bouncing over the uneven road. Soon they were pulling into the St. James's resort.

The setting was beautiful, lush with vegetation and tall palm trees. It took about two seconds to establish that this wasn't the type of place Hauck could afford on his own. A week here probably cost more than a month's pay. At the open-air front desk under a thatched roof, Karen asked for the two adjoining rooms she'd reserved in the hotel part of the resort. They had discussed it. That was okay with Hauck. This wasn't a holiday. It was important to remember just why they were here.

"Any messages?" Karen inquired as they checked in.

The pretty island desk clerk behind the counter scanned the computer. "I'm sorry, Ms. Friedman, none."

A bellman took them out to their rooms, each tastefully decorated with a large canopied bed and expensive rattan furniture. A large marble bathroom with a big tub. Outside, palm trees swayed right up to the terrace, which looked over the perfect white-sand beach.

They met on their adjoining decks, gazing out at the sea. There were a few tented cabanas dotting the beach. And a gorgeous white thirty-foot yacht moored at the pier.

"It's beautiful," Hauck said, looking around.

"Yeah," Karen agreed, inhaling the ocean breeze, "it is."

"No point in just sitting around until you hear from him." Hauck shrugged. "Want to meet for a swim?"

"What the hell?" Karen smiled. "Sure."

A short while later, Karen came down in a stylish bronze one-piece and a tie-dyed sarong, her hair pinned above her head. Hauck had on a pair of "designer" Colby College shorts.

The water was warm and foamy. Tiny white waves lapped at their feet. The beach was pretty much deserted. It was June and the resort didn't seem exactly filled. There was a small reef a couple of hundred yards out, a handful of sunbathers camped out on it. A young couple was playing paddleball. The sea was almost as calm as glass.

"God, it's gorgeous." Karen sighed, as if in heaven, wading in.

"Man," Hauck agreed, diving into the surf. When he came up, he pointed. "Want to swim out to that reef?"

"Swim? How about I race you?" Karen grinned.

"Race me? You know who you're talking to, lady?" Hauck laughed. "I'm still the third-leading all-time rushing leader for Greenwich High."

"Oh, I'm quaking." Karen rolled her eyes, unimpressed. "Watch out for sharks."

She dove in gracefully ahead of him. Hauck let her get a couple of strokes' head start, then went in after. He pulled hard, a few small waves breaking against him. Karen cut through the surf in an effortless crawl. He wasn't gaining. No matter how he pushed he couldn't seem to make up ground. Once or twice he tried to lunge and grab her legs. It took about three minutes. Karen beat him to the reef by a mile. She was already waiting as he climbed out, sucking air.

"I've been had."

She winked. "Atlanta AAU twelve-and-under freestyle champion." She shook the water out of her hair. "What the hell took you so long?"

"Ran into a shark," he snorted, grinning coyly at her.

Karen lay back on the fine sand. Hauck sat with his arms wrapped around his knees, looking back at the thatched roofs and swaying palms on the beautiful tropical isle.

"So what else do you do well?" he asked, feigning dejection. "Just so I know."

"Chili. Tennis. Large donors." She grinned. "I've been known to successfully raise a few bucks in my time. You?"

"Clear out a hockey crease. Get cats out of trees. Munch on doughnuts," he replied. "Catch the occasional blue."

"You paint," Karen said encouragingly.

"You saw it."

"That's true." She poked at him playfully with her toe. "You could call it that!"

Hauck watched the beads of water drying on her wet skin.

"So what happens?" Karen asked, her tone suggesting that the subject had changed. "After?"

"After?"

"After I see Charles. Then what happens to him, Ty? All those things he's done . . ."

"I don't know." Hauck exhaled. He shielded his eyes from the sun. "Maybe you can convince him to turn himself in. We found him—someone else could also. He can't run forever."

"You mean go to jail, right?"

Hauck shrugged.

"I don't think that would happen. I don't see that, Ty."

He tossed a pebble into the water. "First let's see what he has to say."

She nodded. They looked at each other a few seconds, neither of them wanting to put into words their fears for a future they didn't know. Then Karen prodded him again with her toe, smiled. "So . . . uh, double or nothing on the way back?"

"Not a chance. You should know, I don't take defeat very well."

"Your loss!" Karen chimed in with a conspiratorial grin, looking back at him as she pushed herself up and into the waves.

He jumped in after her. "On the other hand, I don't take being shown up particularly well either!"

Later they met for dinner. The dining terrace overlooking the cove was barely half filled. A few honeymoon couples and a couple of European families.

Hauck ordered a local spicy fish dish; Karen had lobster. Hauck insisted he pay, and ordered a fancy bottle of Meursault. Karen, already slightly tanned, was dressed in a black lace dress. Hauck knew the ground rules, but he could hardly keep his eyes off her.

Afterward they walked back along the pathway to the front desk. She checked her BlackBerry, disappointed. Then she asked at the desk for her messages.

Nothing there either.

"This was a nice day," he said.

Karen smiled sweetly. "Yeah."

Upstairs, he walked her to her door. There was an awkward moment until Karen leaned close and gave him a soft kiss on the cheek.

She smiled at him again, with a grateful twinkle and a wave of a finger, as she closed the door. But Hauck could see the worry in her eyes.

Still no word from Charles.

CHAPTER EIGHTY

There was nothing the next day either. Karen grew increasingly tense.

Hauck felt it, too. In the morning he went for a run outside the grounds, then came back and lifted some weights. Later he tried to distract himself with some departmental reviews he'd taken with him before he left.

In her room Karen checked her BlackBerry for messages a hundred times.

What if she had scared him off? she wondered. What if Charles had gone back into hiding? He could be a million miles away.

He would let her know, she told herself. He wouldn't torture her again.

In the afternoon Hauck swam out to the reef again, floated on his back for what seemed an hour. He thought about what Karen had said, what he would do regarding Charles—*after*. Back at home.

He knew he had to lay it all out. Dietz. Hodges. The money offshore. The empty tankers. Pappy Raymond. The hit-and-runs.

Everything.

Even if she begged him not to. There'd be an investigation. Into Hauck's behavior. He'd be suspended for sure. He might even lose his job.

He put it off and went back up to the room and lay down on the bed. His insides felt as if a jagged wire had been dragged through them. Charles's silence was killing both of them. And the thought of "what after." All of a sudden, the future, and everything it held, didn't seem so far off.

He tossed the stack of work papers onto the bed, slid open the sliding door, and stepped out onto the balcony.

He spotted Karen across from him on her terrace. She was facing the ocean, doing yoga, in tight leggings and a short cotton tank.

He watched.

She was graceful, moving from one pose to another as in a dance. The curve of her finely cut arms, her fingers reaching toward the sky. The steady rhythm of her breaths, her chest expanding and contracting, the delicate deep arch of her spine following the movement of her arms.

His blood stirred.

He knew he was in love with her. Not probably as he had kidded—but completely. He knew she had awakened him from a deep slumber, the sweet lure of something that had been dead inside him for a long time.

It was bursting through him now.

She didn't notice him at first, so intent was she in the precision of her movements. The arc of her leg, the lift of her pelvis, stretching. Her hair tumbling forward in its ponytail. The glimpse of her exposed midriff.

Goddamn it, Ty. . . .

She brought her arms back in a wide semicircle and seemed to open her eyes. Their gazes met.

At first Karen just smiled, as if she'd been exposed in some private ritual, like taking a bath.

Hauck saw the blotch of sweat on her top, the shoulder strap off her shoulder, the wisp of honey-colored hair that had fallen across her eyes.

He couldn't stand it anymore. It was like a fire blazing through him. Through the urgency of his nod. They didn't say a thing, but something wordless and breathless was communicated between them.

"Karen . . ."

He was at her door the very second that it opened, pushing it wide, taking her and forcing her back inside the room and up against the wall before she whispered, "What the hell do you want from me, Ty?"

He pressed his mouth on hers, stifling any objection, tasting the sweetness of her breath. Karen pulled his shirt out in the same necessity, tugging at his shorts. He cupped his rough palm to the curve of skin underneath her leggings, heat radiating out of every pore, unable to stop himself.

Her chest heaved. *"Jesus, Ty . . ."*

He yanked down her leggings. Her skin was slick and sweaty from outside. He lifted her there, setting her straight against the weight of the high-backed rattan chair, hearing her murmur, her arms around his neck, lifting, until he was inside her, like two starved people ravaging for food, her legs straddling his thighs.

This time there was no softness, no tenderness. Only a yearning that rose up from deep within their core. She buried her face in his chest and rocked in his arms. He clung to her as tightly as he had ever held anything in his life. And when it was over, with a last, unembarrassed gasp, he continued to hold her, pressing her shape against his, and letting her drop easily into the big chair, Hauck leaning up against the wall, sliding to the floor, spent.

"So much for the conditions." Karen groaned, brushing her damp hair out of her face.

"Didn't work too well. . . ." Hauck exhaled, raising a knee up off the floor.

"We could just leave," he said to her. "We don't have to wait around for him, Karen. I know there are things you want to hear from him, but the hell with it—all it's going to do is hurt you, Karen, whichever way it falls. We could just leave. Let Charles go back to wherever the hell he wants to."

Karen nodded. She forced a smile. "That doesn't exactly sound very policelike, coming from you, Ty."

"Maybe because I don't feel very policelike. Maybe because for the first time in five years I feel whole. I've spent my entire goddamn life trying to do the right thing, and I'm scared—for once I'm scared—of what seeing him will do. What we're doing here, Karen, this may be the biggest lie in the world. But whatever it is, it's a lie I don't want to end."

"I don't want to end it either, Ty."

A sharp ringing cut her off. It came from the table where Karen's bag was. Both sets of eyes flashed to it. She pulled her top over herself and ran and rummaged for her BlackBerry.

It was vibrating.

She looked up, anxious. "It's him."

Karen opened the message. " 'A boat will be at the St. James dock at eight A.M.,' " it read. " 'The captain's name is Neville. He'll take you to me. You alone, Karen. That's the only way. No one else. Charles.'"

She came over and passed the phone to Hauck. He read it for himself. Inside, he felt everything slipping away.

"He's my husband," Karen said. She slid down next to him. "I'm sorry, Ty, I have to go."

CHAPTER EIGHTY-ONE

Forty miles away Phil Dietz sipped a black cactus margarita in the Black Hat Bar in Tortola. There was a band playing Jimmy Buffett and Wyclef Jean, a throng of young people dancing, spilling beers, their carefree brains buzzing with rum. Dietz noticed a pretty gal in a low-cut halter sitting at the other end of the bar and thought, what the hell, he might just make a move as the evening developed, even if, by the looks, he had to pay. He'd earned it. He'd charge it off on Lennick's account, he decided. Sort of a celebration, because tomorrow the fun was over. It was going to get native again.

He'd found his man.

It had been a breeze to track the itinerary of Karen Friedman. Lennick had alerted him. He knew that the fish had caught the line. If she was heading to the BVIs, it was likely she'd pass through San Juan, so he called with a question about the reservation. Airlines still gave out shit like that. Made his job easy. So he had Lenz, who had driven the hit car in Greenwich, but whose face was unknown to them, watching out for her in Tortola. He tracked the Island Air single-engine to St. Hubert's. There was only one place they could go there.

What he hadn't planned on was the cop. Dietz knew this wasn't exactly a lovers' getaway. Charles wouldn't be far behind.

He had led them there.

Whatever would happen next, that part was right up Dietz's alley. Charles would show himself soon. He had Lenz installed at the club, keeping a watchful eye on them. Dietz had a small plane rented. The rest was routine. What they paid him for. The kinds of skills he'd honed his whole life.

Dietz took another sip of his drink. The girl with the boobs in the halter smiled his way. He grew aroused.

He knew he wasn't exactly handsome. He was short and stocky and had military tattoos up and down his thick arms. But women always managed to notice him, and they were drawn to him in a hard-edged way.

He thought of the cop. He complicated things. If they knew about Dolphin, they might have found the old geezer in Pensacola. And if they had, coupled with Lauer, maybe it wasn't as much of a fishing expedition down at his house as he'd thought.

Charles knew things. More than they could let him divulge. He had been sloppy, but the sloppiness was going to have to end.

Dietz scratched his mustache and pushed out his cigar. *Time to pay up, Charles.*

But in the meantime he had this little diversion. He took another look at the girl and finished off his drink. He flipped open his cell phone. One last call.

He dialed the number that was in his memory. A gravelly, accented voice picked up. *Always play both ends against the middle,* Dietz thought. He'd been told to give a progress report, stay in touch.

"Good news," Dietz said, keeping an eye on the girl. "I think we've found him."

"Excellent," the voice replied. "Was it through the accounts?" The banks, the electronic transfers. The diamond merchant they had painstakingly tracked.

"No need," Dietz said. "Ultimately, I found another way. His wife led us right to him."

Dietz stood up and tossed a twenty on the bar. Tomorrow . . . tomorrow it was back to business. He'd take care of Hodges, too. But tonight . . . The girl was talking to a tall, blond surfer dude. He passed by a group of bone fishermen, bragging about their catch. When he got in front of her, she looked up.

"Where are you?" Dietz asked into the phone.

"Don't you worry," the brusque voice replied. "I'm around."

CHAPTER EIGHTY-TWO

The morning broke hazy and warm.

Karen woke early and ate a light breakfast in her room. She sat out on the balcony and sipped her coffee, watching the sun rise over the calm sea. Trying to settle her nerves. A flock of birds circled out by the reef, honking and diving for an early meal.

Around seven-thirty she saw a white launch pull up at the St. James's dock. A captain jumped off. She stood and tried to relax her restless stomach. *Here goes. . . .*

She put on a print sundress and a pair of espadrilles. She clipped her hair up off her neck and applied a touch of blush to her cheeks and gloss to her lips, just to make herself look pretty. Then she packed her bag, sun cream, lip balm, a couple of bottles of water. She took along some pictures of the kids she'd brought with her.

Downstairs, Ty was waiting on the walkway to the beach. He gave her a supportive wink. What else was there really to say?

"I have something for you," he said, taking her under the loggia to a private spot where he sat her down in a wooden beach chair. He pressed a small disk into her palm. "It's a high-powered GPS receiver. Hide it in your purse. That way I can find you. I want you to call me on the hour. *Every hour.* Just so I know you're safe. You promise you'll do that for me, Karen?"

"Ty, I'll be fine. It's Charles."

"I want you to promise," he said, not a question this time, more of a command.

"Okay." She relented and smiled at him. "I promise."

From his pocket Hauck took out something else—a dark, metal object, small enough to fit into the palm of his hand—that made her shudder. "I want you to take this along, too, Karen."

"No."

"I mean it, Karen." He pressed it into her hand. "Just in case something happens. It's a Beretta .22. The safety's off. It may be nothing. But you don't know what you're walking into. You said it yourself—people have died. So take it. *Please.* Just in case."

Karen gazed at the gun, her heart quickening. She tried to push it back. "Ty, please, it's Charles . . ."

"It's Charles," he said, "and you have no idea what else you're walking into. Take it, Karen. It's not a request, it's an order. You can give it back to me this afternoon."

She stared at the gun, and it reminded her that no matter how she tried to play this, he was right—she was a little scared.

"I'm reluctant to bring it, 'cause I just might use it on him," she chortled. But she tucked it into her bag.

"Karen, listen." Ty lifted his shades. "I do love you. I think I have from that first day I came to your house. You know that. I don't know what happens after this, between you and me. We'll work that out. But now it's my turn, and I want you to hear me clearly. You be careful, Karen. I want you to stay as public as you can. You don't go anywhere with him—*after.* You don't take any risks, you understand?"

"Yessir." Karen nodded, a small smile creeping through the nerves.

"What the hell would you want me to say, Karen? I'm a cop."

The captain of the boat, a black man of about thirty in surf shorts and a baseball cap, jumped off the launch. It was called the *Sea Angel.* He seemed to be checking his watch.

Karen said, "I think I have to go."

She leaned close to him, and he hugged her. She gave him a kiss on his cheek and squeezed him tightly. "Don't worry about me, Ty." She stood up and did her best to smile. "It's Charlie. We'll probably be drinking a beer in some café by ten."

She hurried toward the dock, turning once and waving, her heart pounding all the same. Ty came out and followed her a few steps over the sand, a wave back. Then she ran up the dock to the *Sea Angel*'s captain, an affable-looking man. "You're Neville?"

"Yes, ma'am," he said. He took her bag from her. "We should be heading out." He noticed Ty, taking a step or two toward them. "He said just *you*, ma'am. Just you or we don't go."

Karen took his hand and jumped aboard. "It *is* just me. Go *where?*"

Neville stepped aboard, tossing the bowline back onto the dock. "He said you would know."

CHAPTER **EIGHTY-THREE**

She did know. Somewhere deep in her heart. It came to her on the water, the islands growing familiar. With a rising anticipation in her blood.

They headed west. As they cleared the reef, the twin-engine launch picked up speed. Karen went to the back of the boat. She waved at Hauck, who had come out onto the pier. A minute later the boat skidded around a bend, and he disappeared.

She was in Charlie's hands now.

It was a beautiful ride. Lots of white-beached islands, small, uninhabited slivers of sand and palms. The water was a soft green-blue, dotted with whitecaps. The sun beat down on them, clear and warm. The craft kicked speedily over the waves, leaving a wide wake, the captain clearly at home in the local waters. Karen's hair whipped in the salty breeze.

"Do you know Charles?" she shouted to Neville over the loud engines.

"You mean Mr. Hanson?" he said. "Yes. I man his boat."

"This one?"

"No, ma'am." Neville grinned broadly, as if amused. "Not at all."

The boat passed inhabited beaches. A few towns tucked into coves. Places they had been to. All of a sudden, she knew why Charles had asked her to come here. Once in a while, they shot past a beautiful yacht in the open sea. Or little fishing skiffs, manned by shirtless fishermen. Once Neville grinned and pointed out toward the horizon. "Sailfish."

Whatever agitation Karen felt, it began to ease.

The ride took fifty minutes. The launch started to come closer to tiny, uninhabited islands.

Suddenly she realized that Neville had been right. A bizarre familiarity began to overtake her. Karen recognized a beach restaurant they had once pulled into—no more than a large thatched hut with an open-kettle grill, where they had had lobsters and chicken. A few small boats moored there. Farther along, a lighthouse she remembered, striped blue and white. The name came back to Karen.

Bertram's Cay.

Now she knew where he was taking her. A last gulf of open blue sea and she saw it.

Her heart expanded.

The isolated cove where they'd once sailed, where the two of them had anchored. She thought of Charlie and his floppy hair and Ray-Bans at the helm. They had to swim into the beach, brought a basket of food and some beer, lay around like beachcombers on the fine white sand, protected by wavy palms.

Their own personal cove. What had they called it? The Never Mind Lagoon.

Where the hell did Charlie and Karen go? everyone would ask.

Karen went up to the bow as the boat slowed, and she shielded her eyes. Pulse quickening, she scanned the small horseshoe beach. Neville guided the launch, which must have drawn around three feet, to within a few yards of the beach.

It looked the same. Just as when they'd discovered it eight years earlier. There was a yellow inflatable raft drawn up on the sand. Karen's heart beat faster. She looked around. She didn't see anybody. Just heard a caw—a few gulls and pelicans hovering above the trees.

Charlie . . .

She didn't know what she was feeling. She didn't know what her reaction might be. Karen took off her sandals, crept up on the bow, steadying herself on the railing. She glanced back at Neville, and he gave her a cautioning hand to wait as he coasted in a little closer and came around sideways. Then he nodded for her to go. *Now . . .*

Karen jumped off, her bag strapped around her shoulder. The water was warm and foamy, coming halfway up her thighs, soaking the bottom of her dress. She waded in to the beach. She didn't see anybody there. She turned around to look as Neville started to back the *Sea Angel* away from the shore. He waved to her. Karen spun around again and for the first time actually began to feel afraid.

She was alone. On this totally deserted strip. Hardly even on a map.

What if he never even came for her?

She realized she had not called Ty. *Stay in a public place,* he had insisted. Public? This was the most deserted spot in the whole fucking world.

Karen stepped tentatively up the low dune. The morning sun had baked the sand, and it felt warm and fine underneath her bare feet. There was no sound, only some chirping from the trees and the soft lapping of the tide.

She went to grab her phone from her bag as a tiny tingling of fear rippled on the surface of her skin.

She heard the brush move and then his voice before she saw his shape.

Soft, eerily familiar. It sliced through her.

"Karen."

She felt her chest tighten, and she turned.

CHAPTER EIGHTY-FOUR

Like a ghost, Charles stepped out of the thick, close brush.

Karen's heart came to a stop.

There was a strange tentative smile on his lips. He looked at her and took off his sunglasses. "Hello, baby."

A knifepoint of shock stabbed through her. "Charles . . . ?"

Staring back at her, he nodded.

Karen's hand shot to her mouth. She didn't know what to do at first. Her breath was stolen away. She just stared. He looked different. Completely changed. She might not have recognized him if she'd passed him on the street. He had on a khaki baseball cap, but underneath Karen could see that his hair was virtually shaved. He had a stubbly growth over his cheeks, his eyes hidden. His body looked leaner, more built. And tanned. He wore pink and green floral beach trunks, water sandals, and a white tee. She couldn't tell if he looked older or younger. Just different.

"Charles?"

He stepped toward her. "Hello, Karen."

She stepped back. She didn't know quite what to feel. She was a jumble of confused emotions, suddenly seeing the man with whom she had shared every joy and important moment in her adult life, whom she had mourned as dead, and feeling the disgust that now burned in her for the stranger who had abandoned her and their children. She felt herself rear back. Just hearing his voice. The voice of someone she had buried. Her husband.

Then he stopped. Reflexively, she took a couple of awkward steps to narrow the distance. His gaze was tentative, uneasy. She stared through him like an X-ray. "You look so different, Charles."

"Comes with the territory," he shrugged, a thin, wiry smile.

"I bet it does. Nice touch, Charles, this spot." Continuing to walk toward him, absorbing the sight of him, like sharp, uncomfortable light slowly settling into shade.

He winked. "I thought you'd like that."

"Yeah." Karen stepped closer. "You always had a good antenna for irony, didn't you, Charles? You sure outdid yourself here."

"Karen"—his complexion changed—"I am so sorry. . . ."

"*Don't!*" She shook her head. "Don't you say that, Charles." Her blood was hot now, the shock over. The truth came back to her, why she was here. "Don't you tell me you're sorry, Charles. You don't understand where sorry even begins." A powerful current of anger and disbelief roared through her. She felt her fists close. Charles nodded, accepting the blow, removing his sunglasses. Karen stared, teeth clenched, narrowing her gaze into his familiar gray eyes.

She slapped him. Hard, across the face. He flinched, taking a step backward, but didn't cover up.

Karen hit him again—harder, confusion boiling over into unleashed rage. "How could you? *Goddamn you, Charles!* How can you be standing here in front of me?" She raised her hand and struck him again. This time in the chest, with her fist, sending him reeling back. "Goddamn you to hell, Charles! How could you do this to me? *To us?* To Alex and Sam, Charles, your family. It killed us. You took a part of us with you, Charles. We can never get that back. But *you,* you're here. . . . You'll never know. We mourned you, Charles, as deep as if it were a part of ourselves that had died." She pounded his chest again, tears of anger glistening in her eyes, Charles now deflecting the blows, which continued to rain on him, but not moving away. "We cried for you every day for a goddamn year. We lit candles in your memory. *How can you be standing here, Charles?*"

"I know, Karen," he said, bowing his head. "I know."

"*No,* you don't know, Charles." She glared. "You have no fucking idea what it is you've stolen from us. From Sam and Alex, Charles. And for what? But *I* know. I know exactly what you've done. I know what a lie you've lived. I know what you've kept from me. Dolphin. Falcon. Those tankers, Charles. That old guy in Pensacola . . ."

His eyes fixed on her. "Who have you been talking to, Karen?"

She hit him again. "Go to hell, Charles. Is that what you want from me here? You want me to tell you what I know?"

Finally he caught her arm, his fingers wrapping around her wrist.

"You say you know! You don't, Karen. You've got to listen to me and hear me out. I never meant to hurt you like this. God knows, in a million years, I never meant for you to find out. Whatever I did, I did it to save you, Karen. All of you. I know how you must hate me. I know what it must feel like for you to see me here. But you have to do one thing for me, Karen. Please, just hear me out. Because whatever I did, and why I'm standing here *now,* taking my life in my hands, I did for you."

"For me?"

"Yes, for you, Karen. And the kids."

"All right, Charles." Karen sniffed back tears. They moved out of the sun, near the brush. They sat down in the sand, cooler there. "You've always been able to charm me, haven't you, Charlie? Let me hear your best shot at the truth."

He swallowed. "You say you know what I've done. The offshore trading, Falcon, Dolphin Oil . . . It's all true. I'm guilty of all of it. I ran money for years I never told you about, Karen. I ran into some problems. Liquidity problems. Big ones, Karen. I had to cover myself. I panicked. I concocted this elaborate fraud."

"Those empty tankers . . . You were falsifying oil."

Charles nodded and sucked in a breath. "I needed to. My reserves were so low, if the banks found out, they would call in my loan agreements. I was leveraged up eight to one, Karen. I had to create collateral. Yes."

"Why, Charlie, why? Why did you have to do these things? Didn't I love you enough, Charlie? Wasn't I there for you? Didn't we have a good enough life together? The kids . . ."

"It was never that, Karen. It had nothing to do with you." He shook his head. "You remember years ago when I got overleveraged and Harbor was about to go under?"

Karen nodded.

"We would have been totally underwater. I would have had *nothing,* Karen. I would have ended up on some trading desk again, with my tail between my legs, trying to work myself back. I would've spent years paying off that debt. But it all came at a price, Karen."

"A price?"

"Yeah." He told her about the funds he'd been overseeing. "Not the birdshit little accounts I had at Harbor." The private partnerships. Falcon. Managed offshore. "Billions, Karen."

"But it was dirty money, Charles. You're a money launderer. Why don't you call it what it is? Who did this to you, Charles?"

"I'm *not* a money launderer, Karen. You don't understand— you don't judge these kinds of funds. You run them. You manage the money. That's what I do, Karen. It was our way out. And I took it, Karen, for the past ten goddamn years. I didn't know where the hell it all came from or who they fucking robbed or stole it from. Just that it was there. And you know what? I didn't care. They were accounts to me. I invested for them. It was the same, the same as the Levinsons and the Coumiers and Smith fucking Barney. I've never even met these people, Karen. Saul found it all for me. And what do you think, there aren't others? There aren't people doing this every day, respected people who come home every night and toss the ball with the kids, and watch *ER,* and take their wives to the Met. People like me! It's out there, Karen. Drug financiers, mobsters, people siphoning off their country's oil pipelines. So I grabbed it. Like anyone else would have. It was our way out. I've never laundered a penny, Karen. I just managed their accounts."

Karen looked at him—like a laser, looked through him. The truth, like some haze in the sky, melting away. "You didn't just manage their accounts, Charlie. That sounds so good, doesn't it? But you're wrong. *I know.* . . . This is what Jonathan Lauer wanted me to know, Charlie. After you so conveniently 'died.' But now *he's* dead, Charlie. For real. He's not coming back on some island. Like you . . . He was set to testify at some hearing a few weeks back, but he was killed, run over, just like that innocent boy in Greenwich, Charlie."

Charles averted his face.

"The one you went to see, Charlie, after Grand Central, when you stole that person's identity. The kid you helped kill, Charlie. Or *did* kill for all I know. I have no fucking idea.

"What was he going to do, Charlie, turn you in? Blow your little scam out of the water? You're not some money launderer— you're a whole lot worse, Charlie. These people, they're not coming back. Not to mention how many thousands were ruined or murdered in the name of all this money you so sacredly invested. Oh, Charlie . . . *what the hell did you do?* How did you lose your way?

This was your big way out, right, baby . . . ? Well, look at you! Look at what the hell it's done."

Charles stared at her, eyes pleading. He shook his head and moistened his dry lips. "I didn't do that, Karen. What you think. I swear. You can hate me if you want, just hate me for the things I've done." He took off his cap and ran his hand over his shaved scalp. "I didn't kill that boy, Karen. No matter what you think. I went up there to try to save him."

CHAPTER EIGHTY-FIVE

"Save him?" A surge of anger flared up in Karen. "Like you were going to save *me,* Charlie?"

"I went there to stop him, Karen! I knew what they were threatening to do."

"*Who,* Charles?" Karen shook her head in frustration. "Tell me who?"

"I can't spell it out for you, Karen. I don't even want you to goddamn know." Charles's face dimmed, and he drew in a harried breath and puffed his cheeks, slowly exhaling. "I had met with him once before. Near his shop. I tried to persuade him to convince his bullheaded father to simply let things go. If it got out, what we were doing with the tankers, it could unravel everything. You don't have a fucking clue where it would go. So I went there. Back to Greenwich. After the bombing. I was totally rattled. Part of me saw this as a chance to simply disappear. I should've died there anyway. These people had threatened me, Karen. You have no idea. Another part of me just wanted to make this whole thing go away.

"So I called him. Raymond. To come and meet me. I rang him from across the street, using the dead guy's name. And I sat there, in that goddamn booth, not knowing what I was going to do or what I was going to say. Just thinking, this whole thing has to end. *Now.* These people are bad. I can't have this poor kid's blood on my hands.

"And then I saw it." Charles looked through her, staring blankly. "I saw that kid through the goddamn window, coming toward me, crossing the street, flipping open his phone. . . . I saw the car, a black SUV, coming down the Post Road parallel to him, picking up speed.

"The vehicle veered around the corner. The kid, these locks of red hair in a ponytail, realizing what was about to happen. That moment I knew that the door had closed for me, Karen. I had lost all that money. Falsified my reserves. These bastards wanted blood. And now I had this kid's blood on my hands." He looked at her. "You have to see it, Karen, I was at risk. *You* were at risk, the kids. . . . There was no turning things back for me. I wasn't going to spend ten years in jail. I might as well have perished in that train. So I did."

"For what, Charles? To protect those monsters?"

"*You don't understand.*" He shook his head at her. "I lost over half a billion dollars, Karen! Every day I watched, having to cover my long contracts, the spread between my position growing larger. Our life sliding away. I crashed through my reserves. I could no longer cover my loans. They were going to kill me, Karen. I needed to hold them off. So I started to fake things. I had these goddamn tankers crisscrossing the fucking globe—Indonesia, Jamaica, Pensacola. . . . All empty! And this goddamn bullheaded fool in Pensacola who wouldn't go away . . ."

Karen touched his arm. He flinched slightly. "You could have told me, Charles. I was your wife. We were a family. You could have shared this with me."

"How could I *share* it with you, Karen? They sent me Christmas cards with the kids' faces cut out. Would you have liked me to share that? They killed Sasha. They sent me this note saying the kids were next. *How about that, Karen?* These kinds of people, you don't just send them out a report promising you're going to make it up next quarter. Our home, that fancy life of ours—it all came at a price, Karen. Should I have *shared* that? Who I was? What I did? These people are killers, Karen. That's the deal I made."

"The deal you made? Goddamn it, Charlie, look at it now. Look at us. Are you happy with it?"

Charles drew in a deep, painful breath. "You know, I thought about leaving a hundred times. Taking us all. I even went as far as to get us passports. Fake ones. You remember, when I had us all take pictures? I said they were for visas to Europe, a trip we never took?"

Karen blinked, biting back tears. "Oh, Charlie . . ."

"So tell me," Charlie went on, "should I have come to you, Karen? Is that the life you would have wanted? If I told you what I was and what we had to do, uprooting the kids, you, in days. Taking them out of school in the dark, away from everything they knew. Put all of you at risk. Made you all a part of this, too. What would you have said to me, Karen? Tell me, honey, would you have gone along?"

Charles looked at her, his gaze reflecting a shattered ray of understanding, answering the question for her. "These people have the means to track anyone, Karen. You would always have been at risk, the children. . . . When the bombing occurred, it was almost like a gift. The answer suddenly seemed so clear. I know you can't see it like that. I know you think there were ways I could have dealt with this, and maybe there were. But not one that was safer, Karen. Not for you."

"But it hasn't been safe for us, Charlie." Harried, she told him about the visit of the people from Archer that first scared her, then the man who accosted Sam in her car. And recently how she'd been sent that brochure from Tufts, where Sam was going to go, with the words *We're still here.* They keep demanding all that money."

"Just who have you been talking to, Karen?"

"No one, Charlie. This detective who's been helping me. Saul. That's all."

Charlie's jaw went tight. He took her hand. "How did you find out about me here? How did you first know I was alive?"

"I saw your face, Charlie!" Karen's eyes shone moist and wide, and she looked at him, fighting back a rush of tears.

"My face . . . ?"

"Yes." She told him about the documentary. How for a year she'd grieved for him, kept the parts of his life intact that she couldn't put away, tried to heal the hole in her heart. "You don't know what it was like, Charlie." And then the documentary, on the anniversary. How she forced herself to watch but it was too much, and she went to shut it off.

And then the instantaneous flash of him. On the street. After the explosion. Looking away from the camera. "I saw you. Rushing by, in the crowd. I must have watched it a thousand times. But it was you. Impossible as it was for me to believe. I knew you were alive."

Charles leaned back, his palms outstretched behind him. He chuckled, almost amusedly at first, in disbelief. Their lives, separated by death, crossing in a captured moment, despite a thousand precautions. "You saw me."

"I didn't know what to do. I was going crazy, Charlie. I didn't tell the kids. How could I, Charles? They love you. They would die."

Moistening his lips, he nodded.

"Then I found your safe-deposit box."

His eyes grew wide.

"The one with your other passport, Charlie. In a different name. And all that money."

"You found it how?"

Karen told him about the framed note sheet she'd received. From after the blast. Someone had found it at Grand Central. With all that scribbling on it. "Part of it was the information on the box. I had nothing else to go on, Charlie."

Charles looked back at her. His face in shock. Almost ashen. A notepad. That had led her to him. Something that hadn't been destroyed in the blast. Then he stiffened. His eyes grew hooded and dark. He squeezed her hand, but this time there was a coldness there, the pressure firmer than just support.

"Who else knows about this, Karen?"

CHAPTER EIGHTY-SIX

Anxious, Hauck decided to take a run, leaving the hotel's grounds and heading up along the coast road in a steady jog. He had to do something. Sitting around watching the GPS, letting his mind wander to inescapable conclusions, he was going insane.

The GPS had stopped a while back. Fixed. 18.50° N, 68.53° W. Some tiny sand reef in the middle of the Caribbean. Twenty miles away. About the least public place she could be. He had told her to call him and let him know she was going in.

That had been two hours ago.

In his job Hauck had been partnered on dozens of stakeouts and surveillances. Waited anxiously in cars while partners put themselves on the line. It was always better to be the one to go in himself. Still, he had never felt so helpless or responsible as he did now. He ran up the long, unevenly paved road that traveled the circumference of the tiny island. He had to do something.

Move.

His strong thighs picked up the pace. There was a large rise that loomed in front of him, green with vegetation and sharply ascending, jutting out of the sea. Hauck headed up the hill toward it, his heart rate rising, a sheen of sweat matting the back of his T-shirt, building up on his skin. The sun baked down on him. Whatever breeze there was remained on the beach.

Every once in a while, he stopped and checked the screen of the GPS, which he had strapped to his waist. Still 18.50 and 68.53 degrees. Still at the same spot. Still no word. It was going on two hours now. He had tried to call. Just her recording. Maybe there was no signal where she was. What could he do, set out in a boat after her? He had given her his word.

So he ran. The seascapes were beautiful, vistas of wide-open stretches of green-blue water, a few verdant knolls rising precipitously from the beaches, an occasional white boat dotting the sea, the hazy outline of a distant island on the horizon.

But Hauck wasn't absorbing all that. He was angry at himself for letting her go. For succumbing. The muscles in his thighs burned as the topography rose. He took off his shirt and wrapped it around his waist as sweat coated his skin. *C'mon, Karen, call. . . . Call!* His lungs grew tight.

Another hundred yards . . .

Finally he reached the top of the rise. Hauck pulled to a stop, doubled over, feeling angry, helpless, responsible.

He shouted out to no one, "Goddamn it!"

He doused himself with water. He seemed to be at the highest point. He looked back in the direction he had come from and saw the resort, tiny, far off, seemingly miles away.

Something caught his attention out on the sea.

Off the opposite side of the island. Hauck put his hand over his eyes to shield them from the sun.

It was a huge black ship. A sailing vessel. Like something he'd never seen before. Vast—it must have been as long as a football field, ultramodern, with three gleaming, metallic masts reflecting the sun. He was mesmerized.

He reached into his pouch and took out the binoculars he'd brought along. He looked out at the water and zeroed in.

Spectacular. Sleek and sparkling black. The name was on the stern. He focused.

The Black Bear.

The boat filled Hauck with awe, but also with a sense of unrest. From the edges of his memory, he knew he had seen it somewhere before.

He took out his cell phone and snapped a picture.

He *had* seen it—he tried to recall.

He just couldn't place where.

CHAPTER EIGHTY-SEVEN

"Listen, Charles, this is important." Karen reached out and touched his arm. "We're not the only people who know you're alive."

He ruffled his brow. " 'We'?"

She nodded. "Yes, 'we.' " Karen told him about Hauck. "He's a detective. From Greenwich. He was trying to solve the Raymond hit-and-run that happened the same day. The boy had your name and number in his pocket. He looked after me a bit in the days when we weren't sure if you had died. Then all these crazy things began to happen."

"What kinds of crazy things?"

"People were suddenly trying to find you, Charles. Or at least all that money. I told you, they were talking about millions. They were coming to the house. Then they threatened Samantha. At school. I didn't know who else to turn to, Charles."

He looked concerned. "People as in *who*, Karen?"

"I don't know. We didn't find out. The police, or Saul. But that doesn't really matter now. What does matter is, this detective, Hauck, *he* found out. Listen, Charles, they seem to be looking for you, too. Not just for the money. *You!* They're tracing you through these bank accounts down here. This person, his name is Dietz. . . . Do you know him?"

"*Dietz?*" Charles shook his head.

"He was a part of the Raymond hit-and-run. He was a witness, in Greenwich. But the thing is, he was also there at Jonathan Lauer's, too! They were both arranged hits, Charles. Not accidents. But you know that, don't you? You know what they were trying to protect. And now I think they're down here, Charles, trying to find you. They somehow know, Charles. You're in danger."

Charles pushed up his cap and massaged his brow, as though running back in his mind through a series of events, and the conclusion he seemed to come to alarmed him. "They know about the fees," he said, looking at her glumly.

"What fees, Charles?"

"A lot of money, Karen. Money I *earned*," he said, "I didn't steal. One and a quarter percent, on a couple of billion dollars. Accumulating over the past eight years. I always kept it offshore. It was for our island," he said. "Remember? *We're talking over sixty million dollars, Karen.*"

Karen's eyes grew wide.

"I never cared about the money, Charlie. I never cared about your stupid island. That was never going to happen. That was just our stupid dream." She looked at him. "What I cared about was *you*, Charlie. I cared about us, our family. These people are onto you. They can trace you, as I did. What are you going to do, Charlie, run from them the rest of your life?"

He hung his head, ran a troubled hand across his scalp. A wistful smile appeared in his gray eyes. "You know I came back once, Karen. Sam's graduation. I looked up the date on the school's Web site."

"*You were there?*"

He nodded fondly. "In a way. I took a car up and watched you come out after the ceremony from across the street. You had on a short yellow dress. Sam had a flower in her ear. I saw my folks there. Alex . . . He's gotten so tall. . . ."

"You were there!" Karen felt a pang grab at her heart. "Oh, Charlie, how long can you let this mess keep going on?"

"I don't know. I don't know," he said. Then, "Tell, me"—his eyes brightening—"how's his lacrosse?"

"*His lacrosse?*" Tears of confusion formed in her eyes. "I don't know, Charlie, he's second string, attack. He's on the bench mostly. Sam had a good year, though. She scored the winning goal against Greenwich Academy. She—" Then she caught herself. "Oh, Charlie, why are we doing this? You want to know how it was? It was hard, Charlie. It was fucking hard. Do you know how they would feel if they could see you here now? It would kill them, Charlie. Sam, Alex—they would die."

"Karen . . ."

Some strange force impelled her, and she leaned toward him, Charlie scared and confused, and they both took the other into their arms. It felt so strange, to have his arms wrapped around her. So familiar, yet so awkward. Like a ghost. "It's been hell, Charlie. First with you gone, then . . . You hurt me so." She pulled away, something between pain and accusation flashing in her eyes. "I can't forgive you, Charlie. I'm not sure I ever will. *We had a fucking life, Charles!"*

"I know it's been hard, Karen." He nodded, swallowing. "I know what I've done."

Karen sniffled back some tears and wiped her eyes with the heel of her hands. "No," she said, "no, you don't know. You don't even have a clue what you've done."

He looked at her. For the first time, he seemed to look her *over.* Her face. Her figure. How she looked in her dress. A faint smile came to his eyes. "You still look good, Karen."

"Yeah, and you don't wear glasses anymore?"

"Lasik." He shrugged. "Occupational necessity."

She smiled. "Finally drummed up the nerve, huh?"

"You got me."

Karen's smile broadened, a ray of sun reflecting brightly off her freckles.

"I want you to be happy, Karen. I want you to move on. Learn to love somebody. You ought to have happiness in your life."

"Yeah, well, you picked a wonderful time to suddenly have all this concern for me, Charlie."

He smiled ruefully.

"Listen, Charlie, it doesn't have to be like this. You can turn yourself in. This detective, Hauck, he's here with me now, Charlie."

Charles looked concerned.

"You can trust him, Charlie. I promise. He's my friend. He's not here to bring you in. You can explain what you did. You didn't kill anyone. You falsified collateral, Charlie. You lied. You can give back the money. Pay a fine. Even if you have to spend time in jail, you can get back your life. The kids, they deserve their father, Charlie. Even if we can't go back the same, they'll forgive you. They will. You can do this, Charlie."

"No." He shook his head weakly. "I can't."

"Yes you can. I know you, Charlie."

"I can't do it, Karen. I'll be in jail for twenty years. *I can't.* Besides, I'd never be safe. Nor would you. This is better, whatever it seems." He looked at her and smiled. "And just to be honest, Karen, neither of us would want to explain this to the kids."

"They would want their father, Charlie." She drew in a breath. "What are you going to do, run for the rest of your life?"

"No." He shook his head. Then a light of understanding seemed to go on in his eyes. "Listen, there are some things, Karen. You say these people are looking for me. If anything happens to me, I have these safe-deposit boxes, in different places around. St. Kitts. Panama. Tortola . . ."

"I don't want your money, Charles. What I want is for you to—"

"Ssshh . . ." He took her hand and stopped her. Squeezed. "You still have the Mustang, don't you?"

"Of course I have it, Charlie. That's what you said. In your will."

"Good. There are things you'll want to know. Important things, Karen. If anything should happen to me. The truth. The truth has always been right inside my heart. You understand that, Karen. Promise me you'll look. It'll explain a lot of things."

"What the hell are you talking about, Charlie? You have to come in with me. You can testify against these people. You can go into custody if you have to. But they're going to find you, Charlie. You just can't keep running."

"I'm not going to keep running, Karen."

"What do you mean?"

He glanced at his watch. "It's time to be getting back. I'll think about what you said. No promises." He got up, looked out at the water, and waved. On the *Sea Angel*, Neville signaled back. Karen heard the engine start. Farther out, a larger craft had come into view from around the bend. "That one's mine," Charlie pointed. "Pretty much my home for the past year. Check it out on the way back. You might get a kick out of the name."

Karen's heart kicked up, worried, as she watched her launch putter in. She was positive there was something she had failed to say.

"Promise me about the car."

"Promise you *what*, Charlie?"

"You'll need to get in." He took her by the shoulders and put a hand softly to her cheek. "I always thought you were beautiful, Karen. The most beautiful thing in the world. Except for maybe the color of my baby's eyes."

"Charlie, I can't just leave you here."

He took a glance up at the sky. "You have to leave me, Karen."

Neville coasted the *Sea Angel* back in near the shore. Charles took Karen by the arm, led her into the warm cove water. She went ahead, wading into the lapping surf, reaching for the bow. Grinning, Neville pulled her up onboard. She turned back to Charlie. The small boat began to move away. She looked at him standing on the shore. A wave of sadness swept over her. She felt she was leaving something there, a part of herself. He looked so lonely. She was sure she was seeing him for the last time.

"*Charlie!*" she called out over the engine.

"I'll think it over." He waved. "I promise. If I change my mind, I'll send Neville back for you tomorrow." He took a step into the shallow water and waved again. "The Mustang, Karen . . ."

Then he flipped his dark Ray-Bans down over his eyes.

Karen held on to the railing as the *Sea Angel*'s twin engines kicked up, creating a wake. Neville backed the craft around, and Karen ran to the stern as the boat picked up speed, the sight of Charlie on the beach growing smaller. He waved to her one last time. Karen finally gave herself over to the urge to cry. "I did miss you," she said softly. "I did miss you so much, Charlie."

As the *Sea Angel* sped away from the cove, it passed within close distance of Charlie's boat—larger, the kind he'd always dreamed of, heading in. As they drew near, Karen was able to make out the name, written in an ornate gold script on the wooden hull.

Emberglow.

It almost made her laugh, as warm, fond tears welled in her eyes. She took out her cell phone and framed a shot to remember, not knowing what she would do with it, or who she would ever show it to.

Karen never noticed the small plane circling high in the sky above her.

CHAPTER EIGHTY-EIGHT

Karen didn't arrive back at the hotel until well into the afternoon. Hauck was in his room by then, seated in a cane chair, his feet propped on the bed, going over some work to distract himself. His worst fears had faded. Karen had called in as soon as she hit open water to let him know she was all right. She sounded vague, even a bit distant emotionally, but she told him she would say more about it when she got to the hotel.

There was a knock on his door.

"It's open," he said.

Karen stepped into the room. She looked a little weary and conflicted. Her hair was tousled, out of place. She dropped the bag she was carrying onto the table by the door.

He asked, "So how did it go?"

She tried to smile. "How did it go?" She could read it—anyone could read it, what he was really asking. *Had anything changed?*

"Here," she said, placing the gun he'd given her on the table by the bed. "He didn't kill those people, Ty. He committed fraud with those tankers to cover up his losses, and he admitted he went up to Greenwich after the bombing like you said—with that man's ID. To *meet* with Raymond, Ty, not to kill him. To try to get him once and for all to convince his father to stop."

Hauck nodded.

She sat down across from him on the edge of the bed. "I believe him, Ty. He said he saw the whole thing happen and that he realized there was no turning back. These people had threatened him. I showed you that Christmas card. The note about what they did to our dog. He thought he was saving us, Ty, however it sounds. But everything he said—it fits."

"What fits is that he's up to his ankles in a shitload of trouble, Karen."

"He knows that, too. I tried to get him to come in. I even told him about you. I told him he hadn't killed anyone, that all he'd done was commit fraud, that he could give back the money, pay a fine, do some time, whatever anyone would want. Testify."

"And . . . ?"

"And he said he'd think about it. But I'm not sure. He's scared. Scared to face what he's done. To face our family. I think it's just easier to run. When the boat pulled away, he waved. I have the feeling that was his answer. I don't think I'll see him anymore."

Hauck drew his legs back, tossed his papers on the table. "Do you want him to come back, Karen?"

"Do I want him back?" She looked at him and shook her head, eyes glazing. "Not the way you're thinking, Ty. It's over between us like that. I could never go back. Nor could he. But I realized something there. Seeing him, hearing him . . ."

"What's that?"

"My children. They deserve the truth. They deserve their father, whatever he's done, as long as he's alive."

Hauck nodded. He understood that. He had Jessie. Whatever he'd done. He drew a breath.

Karen looked at him, aching. "You know how hard it was for me to do that, Ty?"

Something held him back. "Yeah, I know."

"To see him." Her eyes filled up. "To see my husband, in front of me again. To hear him out. After what he's done . . ."

"I know how it was, Karen."

"How? How was it, Ty?"

"What is it you want me to do, Karen?"

"I want you to hold me, goddamn it! I want you to tell me I did the right thing. Don't you see that?" She let her hand fall to his leg. "Anyway, I realized something else out there as well."

"What was that?"

She got up and sat down on his lap. "I realized I do love you, Ty. Not something close." She smiled, sniffing back a tear. "The whole shebang."

"Shebang?"

"Yeah." Karen nodded and drew herself close across his chest. "Shebang."

He wrapped his arms around her, squeezing her face against his shoulder. He realized she was crying. She couldn't help herself. He held her, feeling her warm body and the lift in his own heart as hers beat steadily against him. The dampness of a few warm tears pressed against his neck.

"I do," she whispered, cuddling against him. "Impossible as that may seem."

He shrugged, bringing her face gently against his chest. "Not so impossible."

"Yes it is. Totally frigging impossible. You don't think I can read you, mister? Like an open book." Then she pulled away. "But I can't let him simply disappear again. I want to bring him home to the kids. Whatever he's done. Their father's alive."

Hauck wiped a bead of moisture from her freckled cheek with his thumb. "We'll find a way," he said. "We will."

She kissed him lightly on the lips, rested her forehead against his. "Thank you, Ty."

"Not so impossible to me," he said again. "Of course, for the kids maybe . . ."

"Oh, man!" Karen shook her head, brushing a wave of hair out of her face. "Am I gonna have a bunch to explain when they get back or what?"

THAT NIGHT THEY stayed together in his room. They didn't make love. They just lay there, his arm around her waist, her body tucked closely to him, the shadow of her husband hovering ominously, like a front coming in across the sea, over their calm.

Around one, Hauck got up. Karen lay curled on the bed, sleeping heavily. He drew the covers off and pulled on his shorts and stepped over to the window, looking out at the moonlit sea. Something gnawed at him.

The Black Bear.

The boat he'd seen. It was in his sleep. His dreams. A dark presence. And it had come to him in his dream, where he had seen it before.

Dietz's office. A photo pinned there.

Dietz's arms wrapped around the shoulders of a couple of cronies, a sailfish dangling between them.

Dietz had been on it.

CHAPTER EIGHTY-NINE

Charles Friedman sat alone on the *Emberglow,* which was now moored offshore near Gavin's Cay. The night was quiet. His legs rested up on the gunnels, and he was halfway through a bottle of Pyrat xo Reserve rum that was trying to help him make up his mind.

He should just take off. Tonight. What Karen had told him, about people on his tail, worried him. He had a house he'd bought, on Bocas del Toro, up in Panama. No one knew about that. No one would trace him there. Then from there maybe on to the Pacific if he had to . . .

The way she had looked at him. *What are you going to do, Charles, run the rest of your life. . . .*

He shouldn't involve them now.

Yet a new stirring rose up in him. The stirring of who he was, who he'd been. Seeing Karen had awakened it. Not for her—that part was over. He'd never again regain her trust. And didn't deserve it. That, he knew.

But for the children. Alex and Sam.

Her words echoed: *They'll forgive you, Charles . . .*

Would they?

He thought back to the sight of them leaving the graduation. How hard it was just to look, aching, and then drive on. How deeply the sight of them burned in his memory, and the longing in his blood. It would be nice to reclaim his life. Was that a fantasy? Was it just a drunken hope? To seize it back, no matter what the cost. Who he was. From these people.

Why do they get to win?

What had he done? He hadn't killed anyone. He could explain. Serve time. Pay back his debt. Steal back his life.

Seeing what he'd lost made Charles realize just how sorry he was to have let it go.

Neville was on shore. At a sailors' party. In the morning they were supposed to head to Barbados. There he would leave the boat, fly to Panama.

Seeing her had suddenly made things hard.

A year ago he'd had a similar choice to make. He had watched the boy get killed. Run over in front of his eyes. Watched in horror as the black SUV drove away. Something inside told him there that he could never turn back. That that world was closed to him. The grave already dug. *So why not use it?* For a moment he'd given some thought to calling a car. Directing the driver to head up the Post Road. To his town—Old Greenwich. Then down Soundview onto Shore—in the direction of the water. *Home . . .* Karen would be there. She'd be worried, panicked, hearing word of the bombing. After he hadn't called. He would say he'd been confused. Confess everything to her. Dolphin. Falcon. No one would have to know where he'd been. That was where he belonged.

Instead he had run.

The question continued to stab at him. *Why do they get to win?*

The image of Sam and Alex shone in Charles's mind with the answer: *They don't.* He thought of the joy he'd felt with Karen, just hearing her speak the sound of his own name.

They don't. Charles put down the rum. The answer suddenly clear in his head.

He ran below. He found his cell phone in his cabin and left a detailed message for Neville, telling him just what he needed him to do. The words kept ringing: *They don't.* He went to the small pull-out counter he used as a desk, switched on his laptop. He scrolled to Karen's e-mail address and typed out the quick, heart-felt words.

He read it over. Yes. He felt lifted. He felt alive in his own body again for the first time in a year. *They don't.* He thought of seeing her again. Holding his kids again. He could reclaim his life.

He pressed send.

A noise came to him from up on deck, like a boat tying up. Neville, back from his reveling. Charles called out the captain's name. Excited, he headed up to the deck. His heart was racing. He ran out from under the bridge. "Change of plans—"

Instead he stood facing two men. One was tall, lanky, in a beach shirt and shorts, holding a gun. The other was shorter, barrel-chested, with a small mustache.

Both were looking very satisfied, as if a long search had ended and they were staring at a prize they'd waited to see for a long time. The man with the mustache wore a grin.

"Hello, Charles."

CHAPTER NINETY

"Ty, wake up! Look!" Karen stood at the side of the bed, shaking him.

Hauck sat up. He'd been unable to get back to sleep for much of the night, troubled by his realization about the boat.

"There's a message from Charlie," Karen said excitedly. "He wants us to come."

Hauck glanced at the clock. He saw it was going on eight. He never slept this late. "Come where?"

Karen, in a hotel robe, just out of the shower, shoved her Black-Berry in front of him as he tried to shake the sleep out of his eyes.

> *Karen. I've been going over what you said. I didn't tell you all I knew. Neville will be at the dock at ten and will bring you to me. You can bring who you like. Maybe it's time. Ch.*

She latched onto Hauck's hand and clasped it victoriously. "He's gonna come in with us, Ty."

They dressed quickly and met in the breakfast room down-stairs. That was where Hauck informed Karen, afraid of undercut-ting her excitement, that Charles would have to be arrested. Shaving, he had determined that the only way to make this work was to have Charles come back to the States with them of his own accord. Hauck could take him into custody there. Here, Charles would have to remain in a jail awaiting extradition. They'd have to produce a warrant, which meant going through everything with the people back home, including, in no small way, Hauck's own part and what he'd done. That could take days, weeks. The extradition could be challenged. Charles might get cold feet. And Dietz and his people were already circling nearby.

Shortly before ten he and Karen made their way to the dock. Neville, at the helm of the white-hulled *Sea Angel,* was just cruising in.

Karen waved to him from the pier.

"Hello, ma'am." The captain waved back as the boat pulled close. A dockhand from the hotel grabbed the line. He helped Karen climb aboard, Hauck following on his own.

"You're taking us to Mr. Friedman?"

"To Mistuh Hon-son, ma'am. That's what he ask me," Neville replied dutifully.

"Are we going back to the same place?"

"No, ma'am. Not this time. The boat is at sea. It's not far."

Hauck took a seat in the rear, and Karen sat across from him as the dockhand threw Neville the line. Hauck felt in his pocket for the Beretta he'd brought along. Anything could happen out here.

They headed west, never more than a quarter mile out at sea, hugging the coastlines of tiny, speckled islands. The sky was blue but breezy, and the boat bounced, the twin engines kicking up a heavy wake.

Neither of them said much on the journey out. A new uneasiness had settled over them. Charles could give Hauck the line onto AJ Raymond's killer, why he had started out in this from the beginning. Karen was quiet, too, maybe dealing with how she was going to explain all this to her kids.

About four islands east from St. Hubert, Neville brought the engines to a crawl. Hauck checked the map. It was a strip of land called Gavin's Cay. There was a town on the north side of the island, Amysville. They were on a barely inhabited part, on the south. They came around a bend.

Neville pointed. "There he is!"

A large white boat sat at anchor in an isolated cove.

Hauck steadied himself on the railing and headed up to the bow. Karen followed. The boat was maybe sixty feet. Probably slept eight, Hauck figured. A Panamanian flag flew from the stern.

Neville slowed the engines to under ten knots. He traversed around a reef expertly, obviously knowing the way. Then he picked up a walkie-talkie receiver at the controls. "*Sea Angel* comin' in, Mistuh Hon-son."

No reply.

Charlie's boat was about a quarter mile away. At anchor. Hauck couldn't make out anyone on deck. Neville picked up the walkie-talkie again. The tone was scratchy.

"What's going on?" Hauck called back to him.

The Trinidadian captain glanced at his watch and shrugged. "No one there."

"What's wrong, Ty?" Karen asked, suddenly worried.

He shook his head. "I don't know."

At a slow speed, they crept up on the bobbing craft from the port side. An anchor cable stretched underwater from the bow. No sign of life on deck. Nothing.

"When is the last time you spoke with him?" Hauck called to Neville.

"Didn't." The captain shrugged. "He left me a message on my cell phone last night. Said to pick you up at ten and bring you here." He brought the *Sea Angel* around to within about fifty feet.

Still nobody visible.

Hauck climbed as high as he could on the railing and peered over.

Neville coasted the *Sea Angel* closer in. He called out, "Mistuh Hon-son?"

Only silence. Worrisome silence.

Karen placed her hand on Hauck's shoulder. "I don't like this, Ty."

"Neither do I." Hauck took the Beretta from his pocket. He grasped for the railing of the larger boat as the *Sea Angel* came abreast. He said to Karen, "Just stay where you are."

He jumped on board.

"*Hello?*" The main deck of Charlie's boat was completely empty. But in troubling disarray. The seat cushions were upended. Compartment drawers were open. Hauck noticed an empty bottle of rum on the deck. He bent down and picked his finger at a small stain he noticed on one of the displaced cushions, and didn't like what he saw.

Traces of blood.

He turned to Karen, who was still on the *Sea Angel* with a worried look on her face. "Stay on board."

Shifting the gun off safety, Hauck climbed down to the cabin below. The first thing he encountered was a large galley. *Someone* had been here. The sink was filled with mugs and pots. Cabinets were open, pawed through, condiments strewn all over the floor. Farther along, toward the stern, Hauck ran into three staterooms.

In the first two, the beds had been tossed, drawers open, empty. The larger one looked like the Perfect Storm had hit it. The mattress was askew, sheets ripped all about, drawers rifled through, clothes thrown everywhere.

Hauck knelt. His eye was caught by the same traces of red on the floor.

He went back up on deck. "It's clear," he called to Karen. Neville ran a line and helped her climb aboard. "No one's here."

"What do you mean, no one's here? Where the hell is Charles, Ty?" said Karen, agitated now.

"Zodiac's still here," Neville said, pointing to the yellow inflatable raft, the one Karen had seen the day before, meaning that Charlie had not taken it ashore.

"Who knew he was here?" Hauck asked Neville.

"No one. Mr. Hanson kept to himself. We just moved our location yesterday afternoon."

Karen's face grew tense. "I don't like this, Ty. He wanted us to come to him."

Hauck gazed across the bay, toward the island, maybe about two or three hundred yards away. Charles could be anywhere. Dead. Taken. On another boat. He didn't want to tell Karen about the blood, which complicated things.

"Where's the nearest police station?" he asked Neville.

"Amysville," the captain replied. "Six miles or so. Around north."

Hauck nodded soberly. "Radio them in."

"*Oh, Charlie . . .*" Karen shook her head, exhaling a troubled breath.

Hauck went up to the bow and examined the overturned forward seat cushions, looking at the drops of blood. They seemed to lead right to the edge. He leaned over the side. The anchor line went under the surface from there. Hauck ran his hand along the cable. "Neville, hang on!"

The captain turned back from the bridge, the radio in his hand.

Hauck asked, "Do you know where the anchor switch is?"

"Of course."

"Raise it up for me."

Karen inhaled nervously. "What?"

Neville stared quizzically himself, then flicked a switch at the helm. Instantly, the anchor cable began to slowly wind back up. Hauck leaned over as far as he could, holding on by the railing.

"*Stay back,*" he said to Karen.

"Ty, what do you think is going on?" she asked, a rising anxiousness in her tone.

"Just stay back!" The anchor motor whirred. The tightly threaded cable rewound. Finally something broke the surface. Like a kind of line. Fishing wire. Seaweed wrapped around it.

"Ty . . . ?"

A grave dread ran through Hauck as he looked it over.

The wire was wound around a hand.

"Neville, *stop!*" he called, throwing up his own hand. Hauck turned back to Karen. The solemn feel in his gaze communicated everything.

"Oh, Jesus, Ty, *no* . . ."

She ran to the side to look, panicked. Hauck came back over and caught her, tucking her face firmly into his chest, hiding her from the ugly sight.

"No . . ."

He held on to her as she flinched, trying to break away from him. He motioned to Neville for him to raise the line a little higher.

The cable wound a few more turns. The hand that came out of the water locked tightly around the cable. Slowly, the rest of the body began to emerge.

Hauck's heart sank.

He had never seen Charles except in Karen's photos. What he was staring at now was a swollen, ghostly version of him. He hid Karen's face away and held her firmly to his chest.

"Is it him?" she asked, eyes averted, unable to look.

Charles's bloated white face rose above the surface—staring widely.

Hauck raised his hand and signaled for Neville to stop.

"*Is it him, Ty?*" Karen asked again, fighting back tears.

"Yeah, it's him." He nodded. He pressed her face close to his chest and held her as she shook. "*It's him.*"

CHAPTER NINETY-ONE

A launch of white-uniformed officers from the town of Amysville arrived an hour later with a local detective on board.

Together, they raised him.

Karen and Hauck stood by, watching Charles's body pulled up on deck, stripped of the oily seaweed and debris that had clung to him and the wires that had bound him to the anchor line.

Hauck identified himself as a police detective from the States and spoke with the local official, who was named Wilson, while Karen stood by, holding her face in her hands. Hauck identified her as Hanson's ex-wife and said they had gotten back in touch after a year and had come to visit. They both said they had no idea who would want to do such a horrible thing. Robbers, maybe. Look at the boat. That seemed easiest, without opening everything up. Whatever happened next, Hauck determined it was important that he control the investigation from the States, and if they came entirely clean with the local authorities, that wouldn't happen. They gave their names and their addresses back in the States. A brief statement. They told the detective what line of work Hanson had been in—investments. Hauck knew, once they checked, that Charles's new name wouldn't yield much.

The detective thanked them cordially but seemed to regard their stories with a skeptical eye.

Two of his men lifted Charles over to a yellow body bag. Karen asked if she could have a moment. They agreed.

She knelt down next to him. She felt she had already said her good-byes to him so many times before, shed her tears. But now, as she looked into the strange calm of his face, the puffy, bluish skin, recalling both the anguish and the resigned smile he had displayed on the beach the day before, the tears began to flow, all over again. Unjudging this time. Hot streaming rivers down her cheeks.

Oh, Charlie . . . Karen picked a piece of debris out of his hair.

So many things hurtled back to her. The night they first met—at the arts benefit—Charlie all decked out in his tux, with a bright red tie. The horn-rim frames he always wore. What had he said that charmed her? "What did you do to deserve to sit with this boring crowd?" Their wedding at the Pierre. The day he opened Harbor, that first trade—Halliburton, she recalled—everything so full of hope and promise. How he would run along the sidelines at Alex's lacrosse games, living and dying with each goal, shouting out his name—"Go, Alex, go!" clapping exuberantly.

The morning he'd called to her up in the bathroom and said he had to take the train into the city.

Karen brushed her fingers along his face. "How did you let this happen, Charlie? What do I tell the kids? Who's gonna mourn you now, Charlie? What the hell do I do with you?"

As much as she tried, she could not forgive him. But he was still the man with whom she'd shared her life for almost twenty years. Who'd been a part of every important moment in her life. Still the father of her kids.

And she had seen, in the repentance of his eyes yesterday, a picture of what he so desperately missed.

Sam. Alex. *Her.*

What the hell am I gonna do with you, Charlie?

"Karen . . ." Hauck came up behind her and placed his hands softly on her shoulders. "It's time to let them do their job."

She nodded. She put her fingers on Charlie's eyelids and closed them for the last time. That was better. That was the face she wanted to carry with her. She lifted herself up and leaned ever so slightly against Hauck.

One of the officers stepped over to Charles and zipped up the protective bag.

And that was all. He was gone.

"They're going to let us go," Hauck said in her ear. "I gave them my contact info. If stuff comes out, and it's likely it will, they'll want to talk with us again."

Karen nodded. "He came back to the States, you know." She looked at him. "For Samantha's graduation. He sat there in a car across the street and watched. I want him home, Ty. I want him back with us. I want the kids to know what happened. He was their dad."

"We can request that the body be sent back once the medical examiner has gone over it."

Karen sniffed. "Okay."

They climbed back onto the *Sea Angel* and watched Charles being lifted into the police launch.

"Those people found him, Ty. . . ." Karen fought back a rising anger in her blood. "He would've come back with us. I know it. That's why he called."

"They didn't find him, Karen." The troubling image of the large black schooner he'd seen grew vivid in his mind. "*We* did. We led them directly to him." He looked over Charles's ransacked boat. "And the real question is, what the hell would they be looking for?"

CHAPTER NINETY-TWO

Maybe they had been, Karen finally admitted as she went over and over the horrible image of Charles the next few days.

Maybe they had been set up. Maybe they did lead them directly to him.

Who?

Hauck told her about the black sailing ship he'd seen the day before. That he'd also seen on Dietz's wall. Karen even remembered a plane circling high above the island as she and Charles said good-bye, though it hadn't registered at the time.

Still, none of that mattered to her now.

Seeing Charlie—his poor, bloated body, whatever he'd done, whatever pain he'd caused, that's what haunted her. They'd spent half their lives together. They had shared just about every joyful moment in each other's life. As Karen reflected, it was hard to even separate her life from his, they were so intertwined. The tears returned, and they came back with mixed, hard-to-understand emotions. He had died all over again for her. She could not have imagined, having lost him a year ago, then having held in such pent-up anger toward him, that it could be so cruel. The who or the why—that was for Ty to solve.

They flew home the following day. Hauck wanted to get back into the country, before the investigation there rooted out that Steven Hanson had no past. Before they would have to explain things in full.

And Karen . . . she wanted to get out of that nightmare world as quickly as possible. When they got home, Hauck left her with her friend Paula. No way she could be alone. She had to finally open up to someone.

"I don't even know how to begin," Karen said. Paula took her hand. "You just have to swear, Paula, this is something between *us*. Us alone. You can't tell anyone. Not even Rick."

"Of course I won't, Karen," Paula vowed.

Karen swallowed. She shook her head and let out a breath that felt like it had been kept inside her for weeks. And it had. She looked at her friend with a flustered smile. "You remember that documentary, Paula?"

THAT SAME AFTERNOON Hauck went into Greenwich. To the station. He bypassed saying hello to his unit and went straight to Chief Fitzpatrick's office on the fourth floor.

"Ty!" Fitzpatrick stood up, as if elated. "Everyone's been wondering when we'd see you again. We got a few doozies waiting for you if you're ready to come back. Where you been?"

"Sit down, Carl."

The chief slowly retook his seat. "Not sure I like the sound of that, guy."

"You won't." Before he started in, Hauck looked his boss firmly in the eye. "You remember that hit-and-run I was handling?"

Fitzpatrick inhaled. "Yeah, I remember."

"Well, I have a little more information I can add."

Hauck took him through everything. From the top.

Karen. Charles's number in the victim's pocket. His trip down south to Pensacola. Finding the offshore accounts, how they all tied back to Charles. Soberly, he took Fitzpatrick through his escapade down at Dietz's house. The chief's eyes grew wide. Then his scuffle with Hodges . . .

"You must be fucking shitting me, Lieutenant." The chief pushed back from his desk. "What sort of evidence did you have? What went on down there—not to mention not reporting back immediately that you fucking *shot* someone—was totally illegal."

"I don't need a handbook refresher, Carl."

"I don't know, Ty." The chief stared. "Maybe you do!"

"Well, before that, there's more."

Hauck went on and told him about the second hit-and-run in New Jersey. How Dietz had been a witness at that one, too.

"They were hits, Carl. To keep people silent. To cover up their investment losses. I know that what I did was wrong. I know I may have to be cited. But the accidents were set up. *Murders,* Carl."

The chief put his fingers over his face and pressed the skin around his eyes. "The good news is, you may have found enough to reopen the case. The bad news is—it may be part of the case against *you.* You know better, Ty. Why the hell didn't you stop right there?"

"I'm not quite done, Carl."

Fitzpatrick blinked. "Oh, Jesus, Mary . . ."

Hauck took him through the last part. His trip to St. Hubert. With Karen. How they'd located Charles.

"How?"

"Doesn't matter." Hauck shrugged. "We just did." He told his boss about finding Charles's body on the boat. Then how he'd slightly misled the investigators there.

"Jesus, Ty, were you *trying* to break every fucking rule in the book?"

"No." Hauck smiled and shook his head, finally done. "Just seemed to happen naturally, Carl."

"I think I'm gonna need your badge and gun, Ty."

BEFORE HE LEFT, Hauck went over to a computer on the second floor. Members of his squad came up to him excitedly. "We got you back now, LT?"

"Not quite," he said with an air of resignation, "not just yet."

He did a Google search—something that had been bugging him for days.

The Black Bear.

The search yielded several responses. About a dozen wildlife sites. An inn in Vermont.

It took to the third page until Hauck finally found the first real hit.

From the Web site of Perini Navi, an Italian boatbuilder.

> *The Black Bear.* Luxury sailing yacht. The 88-meter clipper (290 ft.) is the largest privately owned sailing yacht in the world, using the state of the art DynaRig propulsion concept. 2 Duetz 1800 HP engines. Max Speed 19.5 knots. Sleek black ultramodern design with three 58-meter carbon fiber masts, total area under sail 25,791 sq.

ft. The boat has six luxury staterooms, complete with full satellite, Bloomberg, communications, oversize plasma TVs, full gym, 50" plasma in main salon, B/O sound system. A 32" twin-engine Pascoe tender. Sleeps 12 with a crew of 16.

Impressive, Hauck thought, scrolling on. A page later, in an online boat-enthusiast magazine, he found what he was looking for.

Hauck pushed back from the computer. He paused a long time on the name. It hit home. Once he'd even been out to the house. *Some house.*

The Black Bear was owned by Russian financier Gregory Khodoshevsky.

CHAPTER NINETY-THREE

We led them to him, Karen.

The whole first day back, after telling Paula and swearing her to secrecy, Karen racked her brain for how that might be.

Led whom?

She hadn't told anyone where they were going. She'd made the reservations herself. Sitting around trying to divert her thoughts from Charles, she backed through everything from the beginning.

The documentary. The horror of seeing his face on TV. Then the note sheet from his desk she'd been sent—with no return address. Which led to the passport and the money.

Then the men from Archer, the creep who terrified Sam in her car. The horrible things Karen had found in Charles's desk—the Christmas card and the note about Sasha. Her mind kept unavoidably flicking back to him. On the beach. Then the boat.

What was anyone trying to find there, Charles?

"Who? Charlie, *who*? Tell me?" Who were you running from? Why would they want to keep after you now? She knew that Ty had gone into the office, come clean. They'd have to reopen the hit-and-runs. They'd be able to find out now who his investors were.

Tell me, Charlie. How did they know you were alive? They must have seen the fee account drawn down, he had said. Followed the bank trail. A year later, what did they need from him? What did they think he had? All that money?

Karen let her mind run as she gazed out the office window. She'd been answering a couple of e-mails she'd received from the kids. Which excited her, made things feel normal. They were having a fabulous time.

The garage doors were open. She noticed Charlie's Mustang, parked in the far bay.

Suddenly it came back to her. Just what Charlie had said: *The truth, it's always been right inside my heart, Karen.*

Something did *happen to you, Charlie.*

Why weren't you able to tell me? Why did you have to hide it, Charlie, like everything else? What did he say when she pressed him? *Don't you understand, I don't want you to know, Karen.*

Don't want me to know what, Charles?

She was about to sign off on her message to the kids when her mind wandered back once again.

This time her whole body seemed to rattle.

The truth . . . it's always been right inside my heart.

Karen stood up. A sweat came over her. She looked out the window.

At Charlie's car.

You still have the Mustang, don't you, Karen?

She thought he was just babbling!

Oh, my God!

Karen ran out of the office, Tobey trailing after her, and out the front door to the open garage.

There it was. On the rear fender of the Mustang. Where it had always been. The bumper sticker. She had seen it, passed it by— every day for a year. The words written on it: LOVE OF MY LIFE.

Written on a bright red heart!

Karen's whole body seemed to convulse. "Oh, Charlie," she moaned out loud. "If you somehow didn't mean it like this, please don't think I'm the biggest fucking idiot in the world."

Karen knelt beside the rear bumper. Curious, Tobey nuzzled up. Karen pushed him away. "Gimme a second, baby, please." She crouched down, her back to the ground, reached up underneath the chrome bumper, and felt around.

Nothing. What did she expect? Just a bunch of dust and grime, her hand showing black streaks all over it. She pretended she wasn't feeling like a total fool.

It'll explain a lot of things, Karen.

Karen reached up again. This time farther. "I'm trying, Charlie," she said. *"I'm trying."*

She groped blindly just behind the "inside" of the heart.

Her fingers wrapped around something. Something small. Fastened to the inside of the fender.

Karen's heart started to race. She pushed herself farther underneath and stripped the object away from the edges of the chrome.

Whatever it was peeled off.

It was a small bundle, tightly bound in bubble wrap.

Karen stared incredulously at Tobey. *"Oh, my God."*

CHAPTER NINETY-FOUR

Karen brought it into the kitchen. She went through the pantry drawer and took out a package blade and cut at the tape, carefully unfolding the protective wrapping. She held it in her hand.

It was a cell phone.

Not any phone she'd ever seen before. Thinking back, she remembered that Charlie used a BlackBerry. It had never been found. Karen stared at it—almost afraid to keep it in her hands. "What are you trying to tell me, Charles?"

Finally she pressed the power button. Amazingly, after all this time, the LCD screen sprang to life.

HANDSET LOCKED.

Damn. Disappointed, Karen placed it down on the counter.

She ran through a mental file of what Charlie's password might be. Several possibilities, starting with the obvious. She punched in their anniversary, 0716. The day Harbor opened. His e-mail name. She pressed enter.

Nothing. HANDSET LOCKED.

Shit. Next she punched in 0123, his birthday. Nothing, again. Then 0821. Hers. Wrong—a third time. So Karen tried both of the kids' birthdays: 0330. Then 1112. No luck. It began to exasperate her. Even if her thinking was right, there could still be a hundred variations. A three-digit number—eliminate the zero for the month. Or a five-digit number—include the year.

Shit.

Karen sat down. She took a notepad from the counter. It had to be one of them. She prepared to go through them all.

Then it hit her. What else did Charlie say that day? Something about "You're still beautiful, Karen."

Something about "the color of my baby's eyes."

Charlie's Baby.

On a whim Karen punched in the word—the color of his "baby." *Emberglow.*

To her shock, the LOCKED icon on the readout disappeared.

CHAPTER NINETY-FIVE

Saul Lennick sat in the library of his home on Deerfield Road, on the grounds of the Greenwich Country Club.

He had Puccini's *Turandot* on the sound system. The opera put him in the right mood, as he was going over the minutes of the most recent board meeting of the Met that he'd attended. From his leather chair, Lennick looked out at the expansive garden in back, tall trees, a pergola leading to a beautiful gazebo by the pond, all lit up like a colorful stage set.

His cell phone trilled.

Lennick flipped open the phone. He'd been awaiting the call.

"I'm back," Dietz said. "You can rest a little now. It's done."

Lennick closed his eyes and nodded. "How?"

"Don't worry your buns off how. It seems that your old friend Charlie had a penchant for the late-night swim."

The news left Lennick relieved. All at once the weight he'd been carrying seemed to rise from his tired shoulders. This hadn't been easy. Charles had been his friend. Saul had known him twenty years. They'd shared many highs and lows together. He'd felt sadness when he first heard the news after the bombing. Now he just felt nothing. Charles had long ago grown into a liability that had to be written off.

Lennick felt *nothing*—other than a frightening new sense of what he was capable of.

"Were you able to find anything?"

"Nada. The poor bastard took it to the grave, whatever he had. And you know that I can be highly persuasive. We searched his boat from top to bottom. Ripped out the fucking engine block. Nothing."

"That's okay." Lennick sighed. "Maybe there never was anything. Anyway, it was due." Perhaps it was just a fear. *Survival,* Lennick reflected. It's truly astounding what one can do when it becomes threatened.

"There may still be a problem, though," Dietz said, breaking into his thoughts.

"What?" The detective, Lennick recalled. Now that he was back.

"Charles met with his wife. Before we were able to get to him. She and the cop, they found him."

"No," Lennick agreed sadly, "that's not good."

"They talked for a couple of hours on this island. I would've tried to do something down there, but the local cops were all over. He knows about both accidents. And Hodges. And who can guess what your boy Charles may have said to her?"

"No, we can't let that linger," Lennick concluded. This was something he had let fester far too long. "Where are they now?"

Dietz said, "Back here."

"Hmmph . . ." Lennick had gone to Yale. In his day he'd been one of the youngest partners ever at Goldman Sachs. Now he knew the most powerful people in the world. He could call anybody, and they would take it. He had the fucking secretary of the treasury on his speed dial. He had four loving grandkids. . . .

Still, when it came to business, you couldn't be too careful or too smart.

"Let's do what we have to do," Lennick said.

CHAPTER NINETY-SIX

"I was placed on disciplinary leave," Hauck said at Arcadia, warming his fingers around his coffee cup.

Karen had called him an hour earlier. She'd told him she had something important to show him. He met her in town.

"What about your job?" she asked.

"I'm not sure." Hauck let out a breath of resignation. "I'm not exactly up for Officer of the Year. I told them everything," he said, then smiled. "The whole shebang. There'll be a review. The problem is, I didn't help my case with what I let go on down in New Jersey. Still, we have the hit-and-runs. . . . I'm pretty sure Pappy Raymond will testify it was Dietz who forced him to back off the tankers. That'll have to do—until something else plays out."

"I'm sorry," Karen said. She placed a hand on his. Her eyes were sparkling, round. And they came with a smile. "But I think I may be able to help you, Lieutenant."

"What do you mean?" His heartbeat picked up, looking at her.

She grinned. "Something else played out."

Karen reached inside her bag. "A present. From Charlie. He left it for me to find. He mentioned something about it when he was walking me back to the boat on the island, about things I would want to know if anything happened to him. About the truth being somewhere inside his heart. I thought he was just babbling. I never even gave it a second thought until I saw it."

"Saw what?"

"The heart." Karen beamed triumphantly. "Charlie's Mustang, Ty. His *baby*."

She held out the phone. He looked at her a bit uncomprehend-ingly.

"It was taped inside the rear bumper of his car. That's why he didn't want me to get rid of it. He had it hidden there all along. It's what he wanted me to find."

"What, Karen?"

She shrugged. "I wasn't sure either. So I checked through the entire contact log. It didn't tell me much. Maybe you'll find a number or two you could trace. Then I thought, a cell phone—*pictures*. Maybe he had some photos in there, you know, implicating someone. There had to be some reason for him to have hidden it there. So I went into Media . . . into Camera." Karen flipped open the phone. "But there wasn't anything there either."

Hauck took it. "I can have someone go through it at the lab."

"Don't have to, Lieutenant—I found it! It was a voice record-ing. I never even knew these things did that, but it was there, next to Camera. So I clicked." Karen took back the phone and scrolled into Voice Recording. "*Here.* Here's your something else, Ty. A present from Charlie. Straight from the grave."

Hauck looked at her. "You don't seem very pleased about it, Karen."

"Just listen." She pressed the prompt.

A tinny voice came on. "*You think I like having to be here.*"

Hauck looked at Karen and Karen said, "That's Charles."

"*You think I like the predicament that I'm in. But I'm in it. And I can't let it go on.*"

"*No,*" a second voice replied. This one Hauck was sure he'd heard somewhere before. "*We're in it together, Charles.*"

Karen looked at him, the shock evaporated, replaced by a glint of vindication. "That's Saul Lennick."

Hauck blinked.

The recording continued. "*That's the whole problem, Charles. You think you're the only one whose life you're going to drag down because of your own bungling. I'm in this straight as you. You knew the stakes here. You knew who these people are. You want to play at the big table, Charles, you've got to put up the chips.*"

"*I got a holiday card back, Saul. Where the hell else could it have come from? For God's sake, my kids' faces were cut out.*"

"*And I have grandchildren, Charles. You think you're the only one whose neck is on the line?*" A pause. "*I told you what to do. I told you how to handle this. I told you you had to shut up that redneck fuck down there. Now what?*"

"It's too late," Charles replied with a sigh. *"The bank, they already suspect—"*

"I can handle the bank, Charles! But you . . . you have to clean up your own mess. If not, I assure you there are other ways, Charles."

"What other ways?"

"He's got a boy, I'm told, who lives up here."

Pause.

"It's called leverage, Charles. A concept you seemed to grasp quite clearly when it came to taking us down the well."

"He's just an old geezer, Saul."

"He's going to the press, Charles. You want them sticking their noses into some national-security story and finding out what they will? I'll make sure the old man doesn't talk. I've got guys who specialize in this kind of thing. You clean up your balance sheet, Charles. We've got a month. A month, Charles, no more fuckups. You understand what I'm saying, Charles? You're not the only one with his head in the noose here."

A hushed reply. *"I get it, Saul."*

Hauck stared at Karen.

"It was Saul," she said, tears fighting their way into her eyes. "Dietz, Hodges—they work for him."

He covered her hand. "I'm sorry, Karen."

A sadness darkened Karen's face. "Charlie loved him, Ty. Saul was there at every turn in our lives. Like an older brother to him." She clenched her teeth. "He fucking spoke at Charlie's memorial. And he could do this to him. . . . It was *Saul,* Ty. Jesus Christ, I even went to him when the Archer people came. When Sam got accosted. It makes me sick."

Hauck squeezed.

"I went to him, Ty—before we left. I didn't tell him exactly where I was going, but maybe he could have put it together." Her face was ashen. "Maybe we were followed, I don't know."

"You didn't do anything wrong, Karen."

"You're the one who said we led them to him." She lifted the phone. "This is what they were looking for when they trashed the boat. Charles could have told him he had evidence. Before the bombing. Insurance. Then somehow they found out he was alive."

She let out a breath, one filled with a feeling of betrayal and anger. "So what are we going to do?"

"You're going to go home," Hauck said. He looked at her firmly. "I want you to go and pack some clothes and wait for me to come over. If these people followed us to Charles, they must also know that you met with him there."

"Okay. What about you?"

He reached for the cell phone. "I'm going home to make a copy of this, just in case. Then I'm going to call Fitzpatrick. I'll have a warrant for them by tomorrow. Before this goes one step further."

"They killed Charles," Karen said, her fists curling slightly. She handed the phone over. "Make it worth something, Ty. Charlie wanted me to have this. Don't let them win."

"I promise, they won't."

CHAPTER NINETY-SEVEN

Karen drove home.

Her fingers trembled on the wheel. Her stomach had never felt quite so hollow or so uncertain. Was she in danger now?

How could Saul have done this to her? To Charles?

Someone she'd trusted like family over the past ten years. Someone she'd run to for support herself. It almost made her retch. He had lied to her. He had used her to get to Charlie, just as he'd used her husband. And Karen knew she had brought it on herself. She suddenly felt complicit in everything that had happened.

Even in Charlie's death.

Her mind flashed to Saul, standing up at the memorial, speaking so lovingly about Charles. How it must have amused him, Karen seethed, for fate to have intervened so beautifully. To get such a potential liability out of the way.

And all the while Charlie was alive.

Did Charlie know? Did he ever realize who it was who was after him? He thought it was his investors, in retribution. *These are bad people, Karen.* . . . But Dietz and Hodges, they worked for Saul. All along it was just his frightened longtime partner. Trying to protect his own cowardly ass.

Oh, Charlie, you always did get it wrong, didn't you?

She turned onto Shore, heading toward the water. She thought of going straight to Paula's but then remembered what Ty had told her. She turned onto Sea Wall. No sign of anybody. She pulled the Lexus into the driveway of her house.

The house lights were off.

Karen hurried in through the entrance off the garage and flicked on a light as soon as she got into the kitchen.

Immediately something didn't feel right.

"Tobey!" she called. She straightened the mail she'd left on the kitchen island. A few bills and catalogs. It always felt a little different with Alex and Sam out of the house. Since Charlie was gone. Coming back to a darkened house.

She called again, *"Tobey?* Hey, guy?" He was usually scratching at the door.

No answer.

Karen removed a bottle of water from the fridge and went into the house with the mail.

Suddenly she heard the dog—but somewhere distant, yelping.

The office, upstairs? Karen stopped, thought back. Hadn't she left him in the kitchen when she went out?

She headed through the house, following the sound of the dog. She flicked on a light near the front door.

An icy jolt traveled up her spine.

Saul Lennick sat facing her in a living-room chair, legs crossed.

"Hello, Karen."

CHAPTER NINETY-EIGHT

Her heart crawled up her throat. She looked back, frozen, the mail falling to the floor.

"What the hell are you doing here, Saul?"

"Come over here and sit down." He motioned, patting the cushions of the couch next to him.

"What are you doing here?" Karen asked again, a tremor of fear tingling across her skin.

Something in her shouted that she should immediately run. She was near the door. *Get out of here, Karen. Now.* Holding her breath, her gaze darted toward the front door.

"Sit down, Karen," Lennick said again. "Don't even think of leaving. I'm afraid that's not in the cards."

A figure stepped out of the shadows from down the hallway to her office, where Tobey was loudly barking.

Karen froze. "What do you want, Saul?"

"We have a few things to go over, you and I, don't we, dear?"

"I don't know what you're talking about, Saul."

"Let's not pretend, shall we? We both know you saw Charles. And now we both know he's dead. Finally dead, Karen. C'mon. . . ." He patted the couch as if he was coaxing over a niece or nephew. "Sit across from me, dear."

"Don't call me 'dear,' Saul." Karen glared at him. "I know what you've done."

"What I've done?" Lennick's fingers locked together. The avuncular warmth in his eyes dimmed. "What I'm asking you isn't a request, Karen." The man down the corridor moved toward her. He was tall, wearing a beach shirt, his hair gathered up in back in one of those short ponytails. Somehow she thought she'd seen him before.

"*I said come here.*"

Her heart starting to pound, Karen moved toward him slowly. Her mind flashed to Ty. How could she get word to him? What were they going to do with her? She lowered herself onto the couch where Lennick had indicated.

He smiled. "I want you to try to conceptualize, Karen, just what the figure 'a billion' really means. If it were time, a million seconds would be about eleven and a half days. *A billion,* Karen—that's over *thirty-one years*! A trillion—" Lennick's eyes lit up. "Well, that's hard to even contemplate—thirty-one *thousand* years."

Karen looked at him nervously. "Why are you telling me this, Saul?"

"*Why?* Do you have any idea just how much money is on deposit offshore in banks on Grand Cayman and in the British Virgin Islands, Karen? It's about 1.6 trillion dollars. Hard to imagine just what that is—more than a third of all the cash deposits in the United States. It's almost as much as the GNP of Britain or France, Karen. The 'turquoise economy,' as it's referred to. So tell me, Karen, a sum so vast, so consequential, how can it be wrong?"

"What is it you're trying to justify to me, Saul?"

"*Justify.*" He was wearing a brown cashmere V-neck sweater, a white dress shirt underneath. He leaned forward, elbows resting on his knees. "I don't have to justify anything to you, Karen. Or to Charles. I have ten Charleses. Each with sums under investments just as large. Do you have any idea who we represent? You could Google them, Karen, if you wished, and find some of the most prominent and influential people in the world. Names you would know. Important families, Karen, tycoons, *others* . . ."

"*Criminals,* Saul!"

"Criminals?" He laughed. "We don't launder money, Karen. We invest it. When it comes to us, whether from the sale of an Old Master painting or from a trust in Liechtenstein, it's just plain old cash, Karen. As green as yours or mine. You don't judge cash, Karen. Even Charlie would have told you that. You multiply it. You invest it."

"You had Charles killed, Saul! He loved you!"

Saul smiled, as if amused. "Charlie *needed* me, Karen. Just as, for the purpose of what he did, I needed him."

"You're a snake, Saul!" Tears trembled in Karen's eyes. "How is it I could be hearing you like this? How could I have gotten it so wrong?"

"What do you want me to admit, Karen? That I've done things? I've had to, Karen. So did Charles. You think he was such a saint? He defrauded banks. He falsified his accounts—"

"You had that boy killed, Saul, in Greenwich."

"*I* had him killed? *I* kept fucking around with those tankers?" Lennick's face grew taut. "*He lost over a billion dollars of their fucking money, Karen!* He was playing a shell game with his own bank loans. Loans I set up. *I* killed him? What choice did we have, Karen? What do you think these people do? Pat you on the back? Tell you, 'Jolly good run of it, we'll do better next time'? We're all at risk here, Karen. Anyone who plays this game. Not just Charles."

Karen glared at him. "So who was *Archer,* Saul? Who was that man in the back of Samantha's car? Did they come from you? You bastard, you used me. You used my children, Saul. You used Sam. To get to my husband, your friend. *To kill him, Saul.*"

He nodded, a bit guiltily, but his eyes were cold and dull. "Yes, I used you, Karen. Once we discovered that Charles was somehow alive. Once we realized that all the fees that had remained in his accounts offshore after he supposedly died had been withdrawn. Who else could it have been? Then I found that note sheet on his desk with the numbers of that safe-deposit box. I had to find out what was in them, Karen. We weren't getting anywhere tracing the accounts. So we tried to frighten you a bit, that's all. Put you in play, in the hope, slim as it was, that Charles might contact you. There was no other choice, Karen. You can't blame me for that."

"You preyed on me?" Karen gasped, her eyes wide. *Why, Saul, why?* "You were like a brother to him. You got up and eulogized him at his memorial—"

"*He lost over a billion dollars of their money, Karen!*"

"No." She gazed at him, this man who had always seemed so important, so wielding of control. And in a strange way, she suddenly felt she was stronger than him, no matter who was standing behind her. No matter what he might do. "It was never, ever about the money, was it, Saul?"

His face softened. He didn't even try to hide it. "No."

"It wasn't all that missing money you were looking for, why your people trashed his boat." Karen smiled. "Did you find it, Saul?"

"We found whatever we needed, Karen."

"No." Karen shook her head, emboldened. "I think not. He beat you, Saul. You may not realize it, but he did. You had that young boy killed. To protect your own interests. To keep silent what his father had managed to find out. Because you were behind it all, weren't you, Saul? The big, important man pulling all the strings. But then when you realized that Charlie's accounts had been drawn down, you suddenly understood he was alive. That he was out there, right, Saul? Your friend. Your partner. Who knew the truth about you, right?"

Karen chuckled. "You're pathetic, Saul. You didn't kill him for money. That might even give you some dignity. You had him killed out of cowardice, Saul—fear. Because he had the goods on you and you couldn't trust him. Because one day he might testify. And it was like a ticking bomb. You would never know when. One day, when he simply got tired of running . . . What do they call that, Saul, in business circles? A deferred liability?"

"*A billion dollars, Karen!* I gave him every chance. I put my life on the line for him—*my own grandkids' lives!* No—I couldn't have that hanging over me, Karen. I could no longer trust him. Not after what he'd done. One day, when he got tired, tired of running, he could just come in, make a deal." Saul's gray eyebrows narrowed. "You get used to it, Karen. Influence, power. I'm truly sorry if when you look at me, you don't like what you see."

"*What I see?*" She stared at him, eyes glistening with angry tears. "What I see isn't someone powerful, Saul. I see someone old—and scared. And pathetic. But guess what? *He won.* Charles won, Saul. You knew he had something on you. That's why you're here now, isn't it? To find out just what I know. Well, here it is, Saul, you fucking, cowardly bastard: He made a tape. Of your voice, Saul. Your clear, conspiring voice going over what you were getting ready to do to that boy. How'd you say it? With your people, who take care of these things? And right now—and I hope you find the same amusement I do in this, Saul—that tape is in the hands of the police, and they're swearing out a warrant against you. So whatever you and your lackeys had in mind to do to me, there's no point anymore. Even you can see that, Saul, not that that would cause you to lose even an hour of sleep. It's too late. *They know.* They know it's you, Saul. They already do."

Karen stared with a fierceness burning in her eyes. And for a second, Saul looked a little weak, unsure of what to do now, the arrogance melting. She waited for the composure to crack on Lennick's face.

It didn't.

Instead he shrugged and his lips curled into a smile. "You don't mean that detective friend of yours, Karen. Hauck?"

Karen's glare remained on him, but in her stomach a worm of fear began to squirm through.

"Because if that's what you had in mind, I'm afraid he's already been taken care of, Karen. Good cop, though—dogged. Seems to genuinely care about you, too." Saul stood up, glanced at his watch, and sighed.

"Unfortunately, I don't think he's even alive now, as we speak."

CHAPTER NINETY-NINE

Hauck headed home from the coffeehouse in Old Greenwich, about five minutes up the Post Road. He planned to copy the recording onto a tape, then take it over to Carl Fitzpatrick, who lived close by in Riverside, that very night. Karen had found exactly what he needed—evidence that was untainted. Fitzpatrick would have to open everything back up now.

In Stamford he veered off the Post Road onto Elm, soaring. He crossed back under the highway and the Metro-North tracks to Cove, toward the water, Euclid, where he lived. There were lights on across the street from his house, at Robert and Jacqueline's, the furniture restorers. It looked like they were having a party. Hauck made a left into the one-car driveway in front of his house.

He opened his glove compartment, pulled out the Beretta he had given Karen, and shoved it into his jacket. He slammed the Bronco's door shut and bounded up the stairs, stopping to pick up the mail.

Taking out his keys, he couldn't help but smile as his thoughts flashed to Karen. What Charles had told her before he died, how she'd put it all together and found the phone. Wouldn't make a half-bad cop—he laughed—if the real-estate thing didn't work out. In fact . . .

A man stepped out of the darkness, pointing something at his chest.

Before he fired, Hauck stared back at him, recognizing him in an instant, and in that same instant, his thoughts flashing to Karen, he realized he'd made a terrible mistake.

The first shot took him down, a searing, burning pain lancing through his lower abdomen as he twisted away. He reached futilely into his pocket for the Beretta as he started to fall.

The second struck him in the thigh as he toppled backward, tumbling helplessly down the stairs.

He never heard a sound.

Frantic, Hauck grasped out for the banister and, missing it, rolled all the way to the bottom of the stairs. He came to rest in a sitting position in the vestibule, a dull obfuscation clouding his head. One image pushed its way through, accompanied by a paralyzing sense of dread.

Karen.

His assailant stepped toward him down the stairs.

Hauck tried to lift himself up, but everything was rubbery. He turned over to face Richard and Jacqueline's and blinked at the glaring lights. He knew something bad was about to happen. He tried to call out. Loudly. He opened his mouth, but only a coppery taste slid over his tongue. He tried to think, but his brain was just jumbled. A blank.

So this is how it is. . . .

An image of his daughter came into his mind, not Norah but Jessie, which seemed strange to him. He realized he hadn't called her since he'd been back. For a second he thought that she was supposed to come up or something this weekend, wasn't she?

He heard footsteps coming down the stairs.

He put his hand inside his jacket pocket. Instinctively, he fumbled for something there. Charlie's phone—he couldn't let him take that! Or was it the Beretta? His brain was numb.

Breathing heavily, he looked across the street again to Richard and Jacqueline's.

The footsteps stopped. Glassily, Hauck looked up. A man stood over him.

"Hey, asshole, remember me?"

Hodges.

"Yeah . . ." Hauck nodded. "I remember you."

The man knelt over him. "You look a poor sight, Lieutenant. All busted up."

Hauck felt in his jacket and wrapped his fingers around the metal object there.

"You know what I've been carrying around the past two weeks?" Hodges said. He placed two fingers in front of Hauck's face. Hazily, Hauck made out the dark, flattened shape he was holding there. A bullet. Hodges pried open Hauck's mouth, pushed in the barrel of his gun, all metallic and warm, smelling of cordite, clicked the hammer.

"Been meaning to give this back to you."

Hauck looked into his laughing eyes. "Keep it."

He squeezed on the trigger in his pocket. A sharp pop rang out, followed by a burning smell. The bullet struck Hodges under the chin, the smile still stapled to his face. His head snapped back, blood exploding out of his mouth. His body jerked off of Hauck, as if yanked. His eyes rolled back.

Hauck pulled his legs from under the dead man's. Hodges's gun had fallen onto his chest. He just wanted to sit there a while. Pain lanced through his entire body. But that wasn't it. That wasn't what was worrying him.

Dread that fought its way through the pain.

Karen.

Using all his strength, Hauck pushed his way up to his feet. A slick coating of blood came off on his palm from his side.

He took Hodges's gun and staggered over to the Bronco. He opened the door and reached for the radio. He patched into the Greenwich station. The duty officer answered, but Hauck didn't recognize the voice.

"This is Lieutenant Hauck," he said. He bit back against the pain. "There's been a shooting at my house, 713 Euclid Avenue in Stamford. I need a local team dispatched there."

A pause. "Jesus, Lieutenant Hauck . . . ?"

"Who am I speaking to?" Hauck asked, wincing. He twisted the key in the ignition, closed the door, and backed out of the driveway, crashing into a car parked on the street, and drove.

"This is Sergeant Dicenzio, Lieutenant."

"Sergeant, listen, you heard what I just said—but first, this is important, I need a couple of teams, whoever's closest out there, sent immediately to 73 Surfside Road in Old Greenwich. I want the house secured and controlled. You understand, Sergeant? I want the woman who lives there, Karen Friedman, accounted for. Possibly dangerous situation. *Do you read me, Sergeant Dicenzio?*"

"I read you loud and clear, Lieutenant."

"I'm on my way there now."

A blade of fear knifed through Karen as the blood drained from her face. Disbelieving, she just shook her head. "No, that's a bluff, Saul." *Ty couldn't be dead.* He'd just left her. He was headed to the station. He was going to come back and pick her up.

"I'm afraid so, Karen. We had an old friend of his awaiting his arrival at home. He might even have been carrying something of interest to us on his person. Am I right, dear?"

"*No!*" She stood up. Her blood stiffened in denial and rage. "*No!*" She went to lunge at Lennick, but the ponytailed man who had crept up behind grabbed her by the arms and held her back.

She tried to wrench them away. "*Go to fucking hell, Saul!*"

"Maybe later." He shrugged. "But in the meantime, Karen, I'm afraid it's simply back to my house for a late dinner. And you . . ." He smoothed out the wrinkles from his sweater and straightened his collar. He had a look on his face that was almost sad. "You know I don't take any pleasure in doing this, Karen. I've always been fond of you. But you must realize there's just no way we can afford to let you go."

At that moment the French doors to the backyard opened and another man stepped in—shorter, dark-haired, with a graying mustache.

Karen knew him instantly from the descriptions. *Dietz.*

"All clear," he said. Karen noticed that his shoes were caked with dirt and sand.

Lennick nodded. "Good."

Fear swelled up in Karen. "What are you going to do with me, Saul?"

"A little late-night swim, maybe. Overcome with grief and dismay at finding your husband alive—then dead again. It's a lot for anybody, Karen."

Karen shook her head. "It's not gonna hold up, Saul. Hauck's already been to his boss. He told him everything. About the hit-and-runs, Dietz, and Hodges. They're gonna know who did this. They're gonna come after you, Saul."

"After *me*?" Lennick headed toward the door as Karen struggled against the man who pinned her arms. "Don't worry your little head about it, dear. Our friend Hodges is going to have a rather difficult go of it tonight himself. And Mr. Dietz here"—Lennick nodded conspiratorially—"well, I might as well let him explain his situation to you himself."

She pulled against her assailant's grip, tears of hate burning in her eyes. "How did you ever become such a reptile, Saul? How can you ever look at my children again after this?"

"Sam and Alex." He brushed his thin hair back. "Oh, rest assured they'll be very well taken care of, Karen. Those kids will have a lot of money coming to them. Your late husband was a very wealthy man. *Didn't you know?*"

"*Rot in hell, Saul!* You bastard!" Karen twisted around as he closed the front door.

He left. Karen started to sob. Hauck. Charles. Never seeing Sam and Alex again. The idea of Saul "grieving" over her. The anger burning inside her that her kids would never know. She thought of Ty, and a sharp sadness came over her. *She* had gotten him into this. She thought of his own daughter, who would never know.

Then she turned to Dietz, petrified. Hot tears and mucus were running down her face.

"You don't have to do this," she begged.

"Oh, don't get yourself into such a state," the man with the mustache sneered. "They say it's like falling asleep. Just give yourself over to it. It's sort of like sex, right? Do you want it rough? Or do you want it easy?" He chuckled to his partner. "We're not exactly savages here, are we, Cates?"

"Savages? No," the man holding her said. He kneed her in the back of the legs, and Karen cried out, her weight crumbling. "C'mon. . . ."

Dietz picked up a roll of packing tape that was sitting on the table. He tore a piece off and placed it firmly over Karen's mouth. It cut off her breath. Then he ripped a longer strip and wrapped it tightly around her wrists. "C'mon, doll. . . ." He took her by the arms. "Shame about your boyfriend, though. I mean, after busting into my house like that—I'd have liked to have done that one *myself.*"

They dragged her through the open French doors out onto the patio in back. Karen could hear Tobey barking wildly from where he was locked up, fighting them, forced into the dark against her will, his helpless yelps filled her not only with worry but with a rising sadness, too.

Why the hell do they get to win?

They pulled her off the deck into the backyard. There was a path behind her property through a wooden gate that led to the town road to Teddy's Beach, restricted to local residents, just a block away.

Teddy's Beach. Suddenly a new fear swept through Karen's body. That beach was tiny and deserted. It had a protective rock-wall jetty, and other than a few teenagers who might've gone down there at night to make a bonfire or smoke some pot, Karen realized that it would be totally deserted. And blocked from the other homes.

That's what Dietz had meant when he'd said "All clear."

Goddamn it, no. She kicked Dietz in the shins with the point of her shoe, and he spun, angry, and smacked her in the face with the back of his rough hand. Blood spurted out Karen's nose. She choked on it.

Dietz glared at her. "*I said behave!*"

He hoisted her over his shoulder like a sack of flour and ripped off her shoes. He thrust the barrel of a gun up into her nose. "Listen, bitch, I told you what the choice was. You want it easy—or rough? You can fucking decide. Me, I can do it either way. My advice is to lie back and enjoy the ride. It's gonna be over before you even know it. Trust me, you got a much better ticket than your boyfriend."

He carried her through the tightly wooded path, thorns and brambles scratching her legs. Her only hope was that someone would see them. She screamed and fought against the tape, but she could barely make a sound. *Please, let someone be down here,* she begged, *please. . . .*

But what would that even get her? Probably only a bullet in the head.

They came out of the woods onto the end of the town road. Totally dark and deserted. No one. The salty breeze crept into her nostrils. A few lights shone from houses in the distance, across the cove.

Dietz dropped her and pulled her by the arms. "Let's go."

No . . . Karen was crying. Fiercely, she wrenched her bound wrists away from him, but there was nothing she could do. Tears rolled down her cheeks. She thought of Ty, and the tears grew heavier and uncontrollable, choking her, making her unable to breathe. *Oh, baby, you can't be dead. Please, Ty, please, hear me.* . . . Her heart almost split in two at the thought that she had caused him harm.

They dragged her down through the sand, and she shook her head back and forth, screaming inside, *No!*

Cates, the ponytailed bastard, yanked her into the water.

Karen kneed him in the groin. He howled and then spun in rage. "Goddamn it!" and kicked her in the stomach. He dropped her at last, face-first, in the shallow water. Exhausted, out of resistance. Forcing Karen's face under the warm foam.

"Heard the jet stream's nice this time of year." Cates chuckled. "Shouldn't be too bad."

It took just minutes, Hauck's Bronco speeding down Route 1 with its top hat flashing, for him to pull outside the house on Sea Wall.

Two local blue-and-whites had already beaten him there.

Hauck noticed Karen's white Lexus parked in front of the garage. He grabbed his gun and slid out of the Bronco, favoring his right leg. Two uniformed cops, each carrying lit Maglites, were exiting the front door. He recognized one from the station, Torres. Hauck went up to them, clutching his side.

"Anyone inside?"

Torres shrugged. "There was a dog locked in one of the rooms, Lieutenant. Other than that, negative."

That didn't wash. Karen's car was here. If they had come after him, it seemed inevitable that they had come after her. "What about Mrs. Friedman? Did you check upstairs?"

"All over the house, Lieutenant. O'Hearn and Pallacio are still in there." The officer's eyes fell to Hauck's side. "Jesus, sir . . ."

Hauck headed past him into the open house, the patrolman left staring at the trail of blood.

He called out, "*Karen?*" No reply. Hauck's heart started to beat wildly. He heard barking. Officer Pallacio came down the stairs, with his gun drawn.

"Fucking dog." He shook his head. "Shot by me like a Formula One." He looked surprised to see Hauck. "Lieutenant!"

"Is anybody here?" Hauck demanded.

"No one, sir. Just Rin Tin Tin out there." He pointed out back.

"Did you check the basement?"

The cop nodded. "All over, sir."

Shit. Karen's car was here. Maybe she had gone to her friend's. . . . He racked his brain. What was her name? *Paula.* Hauck's gaze fixed on a roll of packing tape on a chair. A pile of mail and magazines were scattered about the floor. The French doors leading to the patio were ajar—Tobey barking like crazy out there.

He didn't like what he was feeling at all.

He went through the doors and looked out at the yard. The night was bright, clear. He smelled the nearby sound. The dog was on the deck, barking nonstop. Clearly upset.

"Where the hell is she, Tobey?" Hauck sucked in a breath. Every time he did, it killed him.

Limping, he made his way into the backyard. There was a small pool out there, a couple of chaises. Every instinct in his body told him Karen was in danger. She had talked with Charles. She knew. He should never have let her come back here without him. *Why would it make sense to silence only him?*

Farther along, his eyes were drawn to something lying in the grass.

Shoes. *Karen's.* The ones she'd been wearing earlier tonight. A pattering of nerves drummed up in him. The beating in his heart intensified.

"*Karen?*" he called.

Why would they be out here?

He looked further. There was some gardening equipment on the ground, a plastic watering jug. Near the end of the yard, he came upon a wooden gate—unlatched. It opened to a narrow wooded path. He went through it. Hauck suddenly realized what it was.

It led around to the end of the town road off Surfside.

To Teddy's Beach.

He heard a voice from behind him. "Lieutenant, you need any help out there?"

Clutching his gun, forcing the pain out of his mind, Hauck stepped along the path. He pushed a few branches out of his way. After thirty or forty yards, weaving behind other houses on Sea Wall, he saw the opening to the town road.

He cupped his hands over his mouth. "*Karen!*"

No reply.

Something on the ground caught Hauck's eye. He knelt, almost buckling from the surge of pain shooting through his thigh.

A sliver of fabric. Orange.

His heart stopped still. Karen had been wearing an orange top.

A tremor of dread rose up in him. He looked out toward the beach. *Oh, Jesus.* He did his best to run.

Her face was pressed under the surface, breath tightening in her lungs, flailing at him with her arms, Cates's strong hands pinning the back of her head.

Karen had fought him with everything she had. Clawing, trying to bite his arm, gasping to suck a gulp of precious air into her lungs. Once she even pulled him over on top of her, amusing Dietz, getting Cates all soaked, and he drew his fist to her face in a menacing rage. "Jesus, Cates, what a fucking woman!" she heard Dietz cackle.

Karen spit water out of her mouth and tried to scream. He dunked her under again.

Now it was ending. Cates had finally ripped off the tape from her mouth, and she was taking in water, gasping for breath with every last ounce of strength, coughing, but he cupped his hand over her mouth and forced her back down before she could scream.

And who would hear anyway? Who would hear in time? Her thoughts flashed to Ty. *Oh, please . . . please . . .* Now water was pouring in. She twisted away from his grasp a last time, gagging. This was it. She could no longer fight it. In desperation, Karen reached back, vainly trying to claw at the bastard's leg.

She heard him shout, "How's the temperature, bitch?"

A desperate will fought the urge to simply open her mouth, just surrender. Give herself over to the dark tide. She thought of Sam and Alex.

No, Karen, no . . .

Don't think of them. Please . . . That would mean this is it. *Don't give in.*

Then the denial inside her slowly relaxing, her mind wandering amid her last futile throes to an image that even in her greatest fear surprised her: an island, palms bending in the breeze, someone on the white sand, in a baseball cap, stepping toward her.

Waving.

Karen stepped toward him. *Oh, God . . .*

Just as the hand that pinned her under the dark water suddenly seemed to release.

HAUCK STAGGERED UP out of the grasses over the dune, his leg exploding in agony.

From thirty yards away, he spotted the man kneeling above her in the water, pressing her face down. Someone else—Dietz, he was certain—standing a few yards back on the beach, seemingly amused by things.

"Karen!"

He stepped forward, steadying his gun with two hands in a shooter's position, just as the man kneeling over Karen looked up.

The first shot hit him in the shoulder, jerking him backward in surprise. The second and the third thudded solidly into his print beach shirt, spewing red. The man toppled into the water and didn't move.

Karen rolled over and put a hand up in the soft tide.

"Karen!"

Hauck took a step toward her and at the same time spun on Dietz, who was scrambling along the sand, drawing his weapon. The bright moon had illuminated the first guy on the water, but it was dark. Dietz was like a shadow on the move. Hauck squeezed off a shot. It missed him. The next struck him in the knee as he tried to make a run toward the jetty. He pulled up, hobbling like a colt that had broken its leg.

Hauck ran, labored, toward Karen.

Slowly, she rolled over in the shallow surf, gagging, coughing up water. She pushed herself up on her elbows and knees. In horror, she stared at Cates's wide-eyed shape—next to her, faceup in the water, and backed away as if it were something vile. She turned to Hauck, tears and disbelief in her wet eyes.

But Dietz had moved into position behind her, placing her directly in Hauck's line of sight. He had his gun aimed at Hauck, momentarily shielded behind Karen.

"Let her go," Hauck said. He kept stepping forward. "Let her go, Dietz. There's no way out." He steadied his gun at Dietz's chest. "You might imagine just how much I'd relish doing this."

"You better be good." Dietz chuckled. "You miss, Lieutenant, the next one goes in her."

"I am good." Hauck nodded.

Hauck took a step toward him. More of a stagger in the sand. It was then he realized that his knees were growing weak and that his strength was waning. He had lost a lot of blood.

"No reason to die here, Dietz," he said. "We all know it was Lennick who was behind the hits. You've got someone to roll on, Dietz. Why die for him? You can cut a deal."

"*Why . . . ?*" Dietz circled behind Karen, keeping her in his line of sight. He shrugged. "Guess it's just my nature, Lieutenant."

Using her as a screen, he fired.

A bright streak whizzed just over Hauck's shoulder, the heat burning him. His wounded leg buckled as he staggered back. He winced, his arm lowering, exposed.

Seeing an advantage, Dietz stepped forward ready to fire again.

"*No . . . !*" Karen screamed, lunging out of the water to stop him. "No!"

Dietz shifted his gun to her.

Hauck hollered, "*Dietz!*"

He fired. The round caught Dietz squarely in the forehead. The killer's arm jerked as his own gun went off in the air. He fell back onto the sand, inert, landing like a snow angel, arms and legs spread wide. A trickle of blood oozed from the dime-size hole in his forehead into the lapping surf.

Karen turned, her face wet, glistening. For a moment Hauck just stood there, breathing heavily, two hands wrapped around the gun.

"You didn't leave," she said, shaking her head.

"Never," he said, with a labored smile. Then he dropped to his knees.

"*Ty!*"

Karen pushed herself up and ran over to him. Dark blood leaked from his side into his hand. Shouts emanated from behind them, flashlights raking over the beach.

Exhausted, Karen hugged him, wrapping her arms around him, a sob of laughter and relief snaking through her tears of fear and exhaustion. She started to cry.

"It's over, Ty, it's over," she said, wiping the blood off his face, tears flooding her eyes.

"No," he said, "it's not over." He collapsed into her, sucking back his pain against her shoulder. "There's one last stop."

The call came in just as Saul Lennick settled down for a late meal in his kitchen at his house on Deerfield Road.

Ida, the housekeeper, had heated up a pain du champignon meat loaf before she left. Lennick poured himself a glass of day-old Conseillante. Mimi was on the phone upstairs, going over donors for this season's Red Cross Ball.

He caught his face in the reflection from the window that overlooked Mimi's gardens. It had been close. A few days later, he didn't know what might have happened. But he had tidied it all up. Things had worked out pretty well.

Charles was dead, and with him the fear that anything might fall on Lennick. The heavy losses and the violations of the loans, those would be pinned on Charles. The poor fool had simply fled in fear. The cop was dead. Hodges, another loose end, would be dealt with the same way that very night. The old geezer in Pensacola, what did it matter what he went on about now? Dietz and Cates, as soon as he got the call, they would be rich men and out of the country. Out of anyone's sight.

Yes, Lennick had done things he never thought himself capable of. Things his grandchildren would never know. That was what his career was all about. There were always trade-offs, losses. Sometimes you just had to do things to preserve your capital, right? It had come close to all tumbling down. But now he was safe, his reputation unimpeachable, his network intact. In the morning there was money to be made. That was how you did it—you simply turned the page.

You forgot your losses of the day before.

At the sound of the phone, Lennick flipped it open, the caller ID both lifting him and making him sad at the same time. He washed down a bite of food with a sip of claret.

"Is it done?"

The voice on the other end made his heart stop.

Not just stop—*shatter.* Lennick's eyes bulged at the sight of the flashing lights outside.

"Yes, Saul, it's done," Karen said, calling from Dietz's phone. "Now it's completely done."

THREE GREENWICH BLUE-AND-WHITE police cars were pulled up in the courtyard of Lennick's stately Normandy that bordered the wooded expanse of the Greenwich Country Club.

Karen leaned against one, wrapped in a blanket, her clothes still wet. With a surge of satisfaction running through her, she handed Dietz's phone back to Hauck. "Thank you, Ty."

Carl Fitzpatrick himself had gone inside—as Hauck was under the care of a med tech—and the chief and two uniformed patrolmen pulled Lennick out of the house, his wrists bound in cuffs.

The banker's wife, dressed in just a night robe, ran out after him, frantic. "Why are they doing this, Saul? What's going on? What are they talking about—*murder?"*

"Call Tom!" Lennick shouted back over his shoulder as they led him onto the brick circle to one of the waiting cars. His eyes met Hauck's and cast him a contemptuous glare. "I'll be home tomorrow," he reassured his wife, almost mockingly.

His gaze fell upon Karen. She shivered despite the blanket but didn't break her gaze. Her eyes contained the hint of a wordless, satisfied smile.

As if she were saying, *He won, Saul.* With a nod. *He won.*

They pushed Lennick into one of the cars. Karen came over to Hauck. Exhausted, she rested her head against his weakened arm.

It's over.

The sound came from behind them. Only a sharp ping of splintering glass.

It took a moment to figure it out. By that time Hauck was screaming that someone was shooting and had pressed his body over Karen's on the driveway, shielding her.

"Ty, what's going on?"

Everyone hit the pavement or ducked protectively behind vehicles. Police guns came out, radios crackled. People were yelling, *"Everyone get down! Get down!"*

It all stopped as quickly as it began.

The shot had come from up in the trees. From the grounds of the club. No car starting. No footsteps.

Guns trained, the officers looked for a shooter in the darkness. Shouts rang out. *"Is anyone hurt?"*

No one answered.

Freddy Muñoz got up and got on the radio to order the area closed off, but there were a dozen ways to get out from back there. Onto Hill. Deerfield. North Street.

Anywhere.

Hauck pulled himself up off Karen. His eye was drawn to the waiting police car. His stomach fell. "Oh, Jesus, God . . ."

There was a spiderweb of fractured glass in the rear passenger window. A tiny hole in the center.

Saul Lennick was slumped against it, as if napping.

There was a widening dark spot on the side of his head. His white hair was turning red.

CHAPTER **ONE HUNDRED FOUR**

Illegal search. Breaking and entering. Unauthorized use of official firearms. Failing to report a felony act.

These were just some of the offenses Hauck knew he might be facing from his bed in Greenwich Hospital. Not to mention misleading a murder investigation in the BVIs, but at least, for the moment, that was out of the jurisdiction here.

Still, as he lay attached to a network of catheters and monitors, recuperating from surgeries on his abdomen and leg, it occurred to him that a continuing career in law enforcement was pretty much of a morphine drip right now.

That next morning Carl Fitzpatrick came to visit. He brought an arrangement of daffodils with him and placed it on the sill next to the flowers sent by the local policemen's union, shrugging at Hauck a bit foolishly, as if to say, *The wife made me do it, Ty.*

Hauck nodded and said, straightfaced, "I'm actually a bit more partial to purples and reds, Carl."

"Next time, then." Fitzpatrick grinned, sitting down.

He inquired about Hauck's injuries. The bullet to his side had had the good fortune of missing anything vital. That would heal. The leg, however—Hauck's right hip, actually—with all the running and limping around as he went after Dietz and Lennick, was basically shot.

"The doctor says those end-to-end rushes on the rink are pretty much a thing of the past now." Hauck smiled.

His boss nodded like that was too bad. "Well, you weren't exactly Bobby Orr." Then after a pause, Fitzpatrick shifted forward. "You know, I'd like to be able to say, 'Good work, Ty.' I mean, that was one sweet mother of a bust." He shook his head soberly. "Why couldn't you have just brought it in to me, Ty? We could have done it by the book."

Hauck shifted. "Guess I just got carried away."

"Yeah." The chief grinned, as if appreciating the joke. "That's what you could call it, getting carried away." Fitzpatrick stood up. "I gotta go."

Hauck reached over to him. "So be honest with me, Carl, what are the chances I'll be back on the job?"

"Honest?"

"Yeah." Hauck sighed. "Honest."

The chief blew a long blast of air. "I don't know. . . ." he swallowed. "There'll definitely have to be a review. People are going to look to me for some kind of suspension."

Hauck sucked in a breath. "I understand."

Fitzpatrick shrugged. "I don't know, Ty, whaddaya think? Maybe a week?" He curled a bright smile. "That was one fucking kick-ass of a bust, Lieutenant. I can't exactly stand behind the way you went about it. But it was sweet. Sweet enough that I want you back. So rest up. Take care of yourself. Ty, I probably shouldn't be saying this, but you should be proud."

"Thank you, Carl."

Fitzpatrick gave Hauck a tug on the forearm and headed to the door.

"Hey, Carl . . ."

The chief turned at the door. "Yeah?"

"If I *had* done it by the book . . . If I had come to you and said I wanted to reopen the Raymond hit-and-run. Before I had something. Tell me straight, would you have agreed?"

"*Agreed?*" The chief squinted in thought. "To open it back up? On *what*, Lieutenant?" He laughed as he went out the door. "No effing way."

HAUCK NAPPED A little. He felt restored. Around lunchtime there was a knock at the door. Jessie came in.

With Beth.

"*Hey, honey.* . . ." Hauck grinned widely. When he tried to open his arms, he winced.

"Oh, Daddy . . ." With tears of worry, Jessie ran over and put her face against his chest. "Daddy, are you going to be all right?"

"I'm okay, hon. I promise. I'm going to be okay. Strong as ever."

She nodded, and Hauck pressed her against him. He looked over at Beth.

She curled her short brown hair behind her ear and leaned against the door. Smiled. He was sure she was about to tell him, something like, *Nice job, Lieutenant,* or, *You sure outdid yourself this time, Ty.*

But she didn't.

Instead she came over and stood by the bed. Her eyes were liquid and deep, and it took her a while to say anything at all, and when she did, it was with a tight smile and a fond squeeze of his hand.

"All right," she said, "you can *have* Thanksgiving, Ty."

He looked at her and smiled.

And for the first time in years, he felt he saw something there. In her moist eyes. Something he'd been waiting for for a long time. Something that had been lost and had eluded him for many years and now, with their daughter's wet cheeks pressed into him, had been found.

Forgiveness.

He winked at her and held Jessie close. "That's good to hear, Beth."

THAT NIGHT HAUCK was a little groggy from all the medications. He had the Yankees game on but couldn't follow. There was a soft knock at the door.

Karen stepped in.

She was dressed in her gray Texas Longhorns T-shirt, a jean jacket thrown around her shoulders. Her hair was pinned up. Hauck noticed a cut on the side of her lip where Dietz had slapped her. She carried a single rose in a small vase and came over and placed it next to his bed.

"My heart." She pointed to it.

He smiled.

"You look pretty," he told her.

"Yeah, right. I look like a bus just ran over me."

"No. Everything looks pretty. The morphine's kicking in."

Karen smiled. "I was here last night when you were in surgery. The doctors talked to me. You're Mr. Lucky, Ty. How's the leg?"

"It was never exactly what you'd call limber. Now it's just completely shot." He chuckled. "The whole—"

"Don't say it." Karen stopped him. "Please."

Hauck nodded. After a pause he shrugged. "So what the hell is a shebang anyway?"

Karen's eyes glistened. "I don't know." She squeezed his hand with both of hers and stared deeply into his hooded eyes. "Thank you, Ty. I owe you so much. I owe you everything. I wish I knew what the hell to say."

"Don't . . ."

Karen pressed his fingers in her palms and shook her head. "I just don't know if I can pick up the same way."

He nodded.

"Charlie's dead," she said. "That's gonna take some time now. And the kids . . . they're coming back." She looked at him. Amid all these tubes, the monitor screens beeping. Her eyes flooded over.

"I understand."

She placed her head down on his chest. Felt his breathing.

"On the other hand"—she sniffed back a few tears—"I guess we could give it a try."

Hauck laughed. More like winced, pain rising up in his belly.

"Yeah." He held her. He stroked her hair. The fleshy round of her cheek. He felt her stop shaking. He felt himself start to feel at ease, too.

"We could try."

Two weeks later

Hauck drove his Bronco up to the large stone gate.

He lowered his window and leaned out to press an intercom button. A voice responded. "Yes?"

"Lieutenant Hauck," Hauck said into the speaker.

"Drive up to the house," the voice replied. The gates slowly opened. "Mr. Khodoshevsky is expecting you."

Hauck made his way up the long paved drive. Even applying the slightest pressure on the gas, his right leg still ached. He had begun some therapy, but there were weeks ahead of him. The doctors told him he might never again walk without the trace of a limp.

The property was massive. He drove past a huge pond. There was a fenced-in field—for horses, maybe. At the top he drove up to an enormous redbrick Georgian with a magnificent courtyard in front, an ornately crafted fountain in the center, with water spilling out of sculptured figures into a marble pool.

Billionaires ruining things for millionaires, Hauck recalled. Even by Greenwich standards, he'd never seen anything quite like this.

He stepped out of the car. Grabbed his cane. It helped. He climbed up the steps to the impressive front doors.

He rang the bell. Loud choral peals. That didn't surprise him. A young woman answered. Attractive. Eastern European. Maybe an au pair.

"Mr. Khodoshevsky asked me to bring you to the den," she said with a smile. "This way."

A young boy, maybe five or six, raced past him riding some kind of motorized toy car. "Beep, beep!"

The au pair yelled out, "Michael, no!" Then she smiled apologetically. "Sorry."

"I'm a cop." Hauck winked. "Tell him to try and keep it under forty in here."

He was led through a series of palatial rooms to a family room at the side of the house, featuring a curved wall of windows overlooking the property. There was a large leather couch, a recognizable contemporary painting over it that Hauck took to be immensely valuable, though he wasn't exactly sure about the guy's use of blue. A huge media console was stacked against a wall, a stereo that went on forever. The requisite sixty-inch flat-screen.

There was an old-time Western movie on.

"Lieutenant."

Hauck spotted a set of legs reclining on an ottoman. Then a large, bushy-haired body rose out of a chair, wearing baggy shorts and an oversize yellow T-shirt that read MONEY IS THE BEST REVENGE.

"I'm Gregory Khodoshevsky." The man extended a hand. He had a powerful shake. "Please, sit down."

Hauck eased against a chair, taking his weight off. He leaned on his cane. "Thanks."

"I see you're not well?"

"Just a little procedure," Hauck lied. "Bum hip."

The Russian nodded. "I've had my knee worked on several times. Skiing." He grinned. "I've learned—man is not meant to ski through trees." He reached for the clicker and turned down the volume. "You like westerns, Lieutenant?"

"Sure. Everyone does."

"Me, too. This is my favorite: *The Good, the Bad and the Ugly.* Never quite sure exactly who I identify with, though. My wife, of course, insists it's the ugly."

Hauck grinned. "If I remember, that was one of the film's themes. They all had their motives."

"Yes." The Russian smiled. "I think you're right—they all had motives. So what do I owe this visit to, Lieutenant Hauck?"

"I was working a case. A name came up that I hoped might mean something to you. Charles Friedman."

"Charles Friedman?" The Russian shrugged. "I'm sorry, no, Lieutenant. Should it?"

The guy was good, Hauck thought. A natural. Hauck looked back at him closely. "I was hoping so."

"Although, now that you mention it"—Khodoshevsky brightened—"I do remember someone named Friedman. He ran some benefit in town I went to a year or two ago. The Bruce Museum, I think. I made a donation. I remember now, he had an attractive wife. Maybe his name was Charles, if it's the one. So what did he do?"

"He's dead," Hauck said. "He had a connection to a case I was looking into, a hit-and-run."

"A hit-and-run." Khodoshevsky grimaced. "Too bad. The traffic up here is unbearable, Lieutenant. I'm sure you know that. Sometimes I'm afraid to cross the street myself in town."

"Especially when someone doesn't want you to succeed," Hauck said, staring into the Russian's steely eyes.

"Yes. I imagine that's true. Is there some reason you connected this man to me?"

"Yes." Hauck nodded. "Saul Lennick."

"*Lennick!*" The Russian drew in a breath. "Now, Lennick I did know. Terrible. That such a thing could happen. Right in the man's own home. Right here in town. A challenge, I'm sure, for you, Lieutenant."

"Mr. Friedman was killed himself a couple of weeks back. In the British Virgin Isles . . . Turns out he and Mr. Lennick were financial partners."

Khodoshevsky's eyes widened, as if in surprise. "*Partners?* Crazy what's going on around here. But I'm afraid I never saw the man again. Sorry that you had to come all the way out here to find that out. I wish I could have been more help."

Hauck reached for his cane. "Not a total loss. I don't often get to see a house like this."

"I'd be happy to show you around."

Hauck pushed himself up and winced. "Another time."

"I wish you good luck with your leg. And finding who was responsible for such a terrible thing."

"Thanks." Hauck took a step toward the door. "You know, before I go, there's something I might show you. Just in case it jogs something. I was down in the Caribbean myself a week ago." Hauck took out his cell phone. "I noticed something interesting—in the water. Off this island. I actually grabbed a snapshot of it. Funny, only a couple of miles from where Charles Friedman ended up killed."

He handed the cell phone to Khodoshevsky, who stared curiously at the image on the screen. The one Hauck had taken on his run.

Khodoshevsky's schooner. *The Black Bear.*

"Humph." The Russian shook his head, meeting Hauck's gaze. "Funny how lives seem to intersect, isn't it, Lieutenant?"

"No more," Hauck said, looking at him.

"Yes, you're right." He handed back the phone. "No more."

"I'll find my way out," Hauck said, placing his phone back in his pocket. "Just one last piece of advice, Mr. Khodoshevsky, if you don't mind. You seem to be partial to westerns, so I think you'll understand."

"And what is that?" The Russian looked at him innocently.

Hauck shrugged. "You know the expression 'Get out of Dodge'?"

"I think I've heard it. The sheriff always says it to the bad guys. But of course they never do."

"No, they never do." Hauck took a step toward the door. "That's what makes westerns. But just this once, you know, they should, Mr. Khodoshevsky." Hauck looked at him closely. "*You* should. If you know what I mean."

"I think I understand." The Russian smiled.

"Oh, and by the way"—Hauck turned, tilting his cane at the door—"that's one hell of a sweet boat, Mr. Khodoshevsky—if you know what I mean!"

EPILOGUE

"Flesh becomes dust and ash. Our ashes return to the soil. Where, in the cycle set before us by the Almighty, life springs up again."

It was a warm summer day, the sky a perfect blue. Karen looked down at Charlie's casket in the open grave. She had brought him back home, as she promised she would. He deserved that. A tear burned in the corner of her eye.

He deserved that and more.

Karen held tightly onto the hands of Samantha and Alex. This was so hard for them, harder than for anyone. They didn't understand. How he could have kept such secrets from them? How he could just walk away, whatever he'd done? Whoever he was?

"We were a family," Samantha said to Karen, confusion, even a measure of accusation, in her trembling voice.

"Yes, we were a family," Karen said.

She had come to forgive him. She had even come to love him again—in a way.

We were a family. Maybe one day they would love him again, too.

The rabbi said his final prayers. Karen's grip tightened on their hands. Her life came back to her. The day they met. How they fell in love. How one day she had said to herself he was the one.

Charlie, the captain—at the helm of the boat sailing in the Caribbean. Waving to her from their private cove at the end.

Her blood coursed with the warming current of eighteen years.

"Now it is our custom to pay our last respects to the dead by throwing a handful of dirt, reminding us that all life is transitory and humble before God."

Her father came up. He took the shovel from the rabbi and tossed a small patch over the casket. Her mom, too. Then Charlie's mother Margery, his brother steadying her arm. Then Rick and Paula.

Then Samantha, who did it in a quick, wounded manner, turning away, She handed the shovel to Alex, who stood over the grave for a long time, finally facing Karen and shaking his young head. "I can't, Mom. . . . No."

"Honey." Karen squeezed him tighter. "Yes you can." Who could blame him? "It's your father, baby, whatever he's done."

Finally he picked up the shovel and tossed in the dirt, sniffling back tears.

Then it was Karen's turn. She picked up the shovelful of soil. She had already said her good-byes to him. What more was there to say?

I did love you, Charlie. And I know you loved me, too.

She tossed it in.

So it was over. Their life together. *I just buried my husband today,* Karen said to herself. Finally. Irrevocably. She had earned the right to say that.

Everyone came up and gave her a hug, and the three of them waited a moment while the rest started to go down the hill. Karen looped her hand through Alex's arm. She wrapped her other around Samantha's shoulder, bringing her close. "One day you'll forgive him. I know it's hard. He came back, Sam. He stood outside on the street and watched us at your graduation. You'll forgive him. That's what life is all about."

As they headed back down the hill, she saw him under a leafy elm, standing off to the side. He was wearing a navy sport jacket and looked nice. Still with his cane.

Their gazes met.

Karen's eyes filled with a warm feeling she hadn't felt in many years.

"C'mon," she told the kids, "there's someone I want you to meet."

As they approached him, Alex glanced at her, confused. "We already know Lieutenant Hauck, Mom."

"I know you do, hon," Karen said. She lifted her sunglasses and smiled at him. "I want you to meet him again. His name is Ty."

ACKNOWLEDGMENTS

Each book is a mirror reflecting the outside world, and I'd like to say thanks to the following, all of whom have brought the outside world to life for me far more vividly through the creation of *The Dark Tide*:

Mark Schwarzman, Roy and Robin Grossman, and Gregory Kopchinsky, for their help on hedge funds and the movement of money across continents—all aboveboard, naturally.

Kirk Dauksavage, Rick McNees, and Pete Carroll of Riverglass, designers of an advanced security software far more sophisticated than that portrayed herein, for their help with information about ways the Internet is mined for national security. As one character says, "I feel safer for it."

Vito Collucci Jr., an ex–Stamford, Connecticut, police detective turned cable news consultant, and an author in his own right, for his help on police and investigative matters.

Liz and Fred Scoponich, for who you are and for the assists on classic Mustangs, too.

Simon Lipskar of Writers House for his support, and my team at William Morrow: Lisa Gallagher, Lynn Grady, Debbie Stier, Pam Jaffee, Michael Barrs, Gabe Robinson, and, mostly, David Highfill, who throws me just enough praise to make me believe I know what I'm doing now and then, and enough direction to steer clear of my worst traits. And also Amanda Ridout and Julia Wisdom over at HarperCollins in London.

Maureen Sugden, once again, for her diligence and steadfastness in waging the good fight against italics.

To my wife, Lynn, with me every step of the way, and who always lifts me up to do my best.

But mostly to Kristen, Matt, and Nick, whom I am more proud of now, for who they've become as adults in the world, than all the dance recitals, college acceptances, and squash matches of their youth. Your reflection is on every page.

DRAGON SWORD AND WIND CHILD

NORIKO OGIWARA

Translated by Cathy Hirano

Dragon Sword
AND Wind Child

Farrar   Straus   Giroux
New York

7-12

DRAGON SWORD AND WIND CHILD

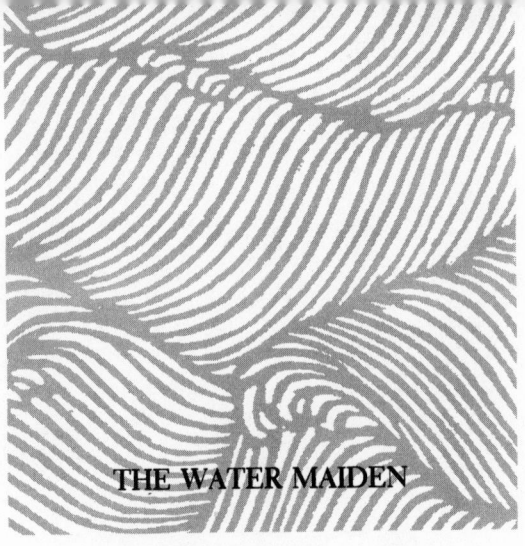

THE WATER MAIDEN

Like the swift flowing waters,
Parted by a rock in mid-stream,
We shall be united once again.

—The retired emperor Sutoku

1

In her dream, Saya was always six years old. Long fingers of flame rose up against the darkness, lighting the sky above. Fire, once a secure and comforting part of her world, now blazed spiteful and triumphant above the safe, warm refuge of her home. The glowing hearth; her room, permeated with the smells of cooking and familiar people; her very own wooden bowl; her mother's lap, soft and round, covered in rough-woven cloth—all were consumed by the flames. The child Saya had somehow managed to find her way to the marsh at the edge of the village, but she could go no farther. Crouched in a clump of dying reeds, she trembled with terror, choking down the hard lump of fear in her throat, unable even to cry.

The oppressive air of the swamp overwhelmed her with its thick, cloying stench of mud and decay. Water from the sodden ground had begun to well up between her toes, and her clothes were soaked. She was miserably uncomfortable, yet she could not move, for on the other side of the swamp, demons prowled in search of her. Peering through the reeds, she could just make out the shapes of the demons by the faint bluish light of their torches. There were five of them, widely disparate in size. Although she remained undetected, at any moment one of them might push aside the reeds, calling out, "I've found her!" The thought filled her with such despair that she almost wished they would find her then and there, just to end the agony of the suspense. The demons never wavered in their vigilance. They peered constantly back and forth, while the blue light from their torches skated across the inky-black waters like a lonely water insect.

The scene changed abruptly. Saya was inside a large building. Great, evenly spaced columns of cypress wood supported the stately roof, and a polished wood-floored corridor led off into the distance. Torches in iron brackets blazed comfortingly, dispelling the darkness. Somehow she had managed to slip through the demons' grasp and escape into a large shrine, yet one eerily devoid of any sign of life. She gazed up at the ceiling, then down at her bare feet. Gathering her courage, she began to move deeper into the sanctuary.

The only sounds that accompanied her as she walked past the innumerable columns were the echoes of her own footsteps and the hiss of the torches. The only sign of movement was her own shadow, which leaped ahead as she passed each torch. At the end of the corridor she could see a room from which shone a brilliant light. A solitary figure clothed in the white robes of a shrine maiden knelt before an altar of cypress wood decorated with dazzling white banners and a forest of dark green sakaki branches placed as offerings. Although Saya could not see her face, she knew the maiden must be beautiful. The white skirts of her robes spread out around her, and she seemed to be bathed in light. Her long, glossy black hair gleamed on her head and shoulders, cascading to the floor like a waterfall. But there was something wrong. Uneasy, Saya hesitated and glanced back the way she had come. Catching sight of her own shadow stretching behind her, she knew the source of her anxiety.

The shrine maiden had no shadow.

Saya was caught like a snared rabbit. Fleeing the fox, she had plunged straight into a trap. She opened her mouth to scream, but no sound came forth. Fear washed through her.

"Don't turn around! Please!" she pleaded silently.

She must not look upon the maiden's face. If she did, she would at once succumb to terror. She must not look, and yet she could neither shut nor avert her eyes.

"Please! Don't turn around! The demons will eat me!" she begged soundlessly.

The maiden, who had remained as immobile as a statue, began to turn slowly toward the desperate Saya. Her hair swayed gently about her face. Saya could see her pale profile, her eyes, and then her cool gaze upon her.

Saya sat up with a start, bathed in sweat, and felt fresh air caressing her face. She must have had the covers pulled up over her head. It was still dark and a few stars could be seen in the sky framed by the small west window. Her mother, who lay beside her, turned in her sleep and asked drowsily if she was all right. Her father continued to snore peacefully.

"I'm fine," Saya whispered. "I was just dreaming." Relieved that she had not cried out in her sleep, she pulled up her covers and rested her cheek once more upon her pillow.

"Same old dream?"

"No," she answered hastily. When she was a child, Saya had often woken with a scream to find herself crying hysterically. She had recently told her mother that her nightmare occurred less frequently as she grew older, but she had lied. In fact, the older she became, the more vivid and detailed her nightmare was, exercising an increasingly relentless hold over her.

This dream was Saya's one trouble in an otherwise peaceful life. It was a constant reminder that she was not native to the village of Hashiba, that the elderly couple she lived with were not her real parents, despite the fact that she did not remember any other home, let alone one beside a marsh. Nor did she remember the faces of her real mother and father.

Irritably brushing a stray lock of hair from her face, Saya bit her lip and fiercely told herself not to cry. It was anger that made her want to cry: anger at herself for continuing to have the same nightmare.

"I turned fifteen this year. I've lived most of my life in this village. I can't even remember any other home," Saya thought impatiently. "Who is that foolish girl still wandering about in that swamp? Well, it isn't me! It isn't me! I escaped all by myself and found another father and mother."

In fact, she had no memory of her escape. She had been told that she was found almost dead from starvation in the mountains by some villagers who had chanced upon her. A lingering high fever had kindly wiped away all memory of her suffering. Consequently, even though she knew that she must have been fleeing from the war in the east, the idea had no reality for her. The battleground was now very distant. Yet the indigenous people of the east still refused to worship the God of Light and continued to resist the army led by his immortal children, Princess Teruhi and Prince Tsukishiro. This concerned Saya very little. Three generations ago, the village chief of Hashiba had accepted the dominion of the God of Light. A shrine had been built in the forest with a burnished copper mirror placed as an emblem of his power. Since that time, the village had been blessed with peace and plenty, and its people were grateful.

"Surely the demons cannot enter a village protected by the sacred mirror. Why doesn't that girl come here?" thought Saya.

The terror that the demons in her dream had evoked was vividly revived and she shivered under her covers, thankful that she was now awake. This was the real Saya: the girl who slept in this bed, in this house, in the village of Hashiba. It was here that she would reach womanhood, marry, and care for her parents. She was fifteen. It would not be long now before these things took place.

Subconsciously, however, Saya knew that while the girl in her dream continued to flee from the demons, she would also continue to flee. But what could she do? Would it be better to let the demons destroy her? And what did her dream mean? She could find no answers to these questions.

The morning mist rising from the river cleared to reveal blue sky. Sunbeams played upon ripples of water, creating shimmering patterns of silver and gold. The sun's rays warmed the stones in the riverbed, flashing with dazzling brilliance as they glanced off crystals of quartz. The young girls of the village, gathering at the river to wash clothes, exchanged greetings and remarked on the warm weather. The villagers still wore their winter clothing of indigo and ocher, but already the top of the cliff on the opposite bank was robed in the moist green freshness of budding leaves and the vivid red of wild azaleas. Spring was here, and summer would soon follow, ushered in by the Day of Changing, when winter garments were put away in favor of summer clothes of white hemp cloth.

"Good morning." Climbing down the bank to the water's edge, Saya found most of her friends already there.

"Morning, Saya. What's the matter? There's no need to carry the world on your shoulders."

Saya blinked in surprise. In the dazzling light reflected from the water, the village maidens seemed like sprightly young minnows darting after bait with which to fuel their banter.

"What do you mean?" she asked.

"Come on now. You can't hide anything from us. You're walking like a dreamer. Out with it! Tell us who's troubling you so."

Saya was at a loss for words, in itself a sufficient circumstance to make all her friends laugh. "You've got it all wrong. It was just a bad dream," she finally said.

"A dream? That's easily remedied. Let me exorcise you. *To-*

gano no shika mo yume no mani mani. Now, don't dwell on it anymore. Thinking about evil dreams only increases their power."

"Tell us your dream. I'll interpret it for you."

"No!" Saya hastily emptied her basket and began rinsing the clothes in the water. The dream was something she could not share, even with her friends.

"Saya keeps her own counsel," remarked the girl who lived next door. "She's the only one who hasn't told us whom she wants as her partner at the Kagai."

"That's right. And we've all vowed to find out."

The Kagai, a festival of songs during which youths and maidens exchanged pledges of love, was to be celebrated at the next full moon, and, with the event so close at hand, it was the focus of the village girls' conversation. On the day of the celebration, the villagers would wear new summer garments. Then, from all the nearby villages, everyone but the children and the elderly would make their way toward Mount Itsuki, the highest peak in the area. In the center of a glade partway up the mountain, a bonfire would be lit, and the villagers would dance and sing around it until morning. Each youth would conceal a gift—a comb, a jewel, or a small box—in his pocket to present to the girl who responded to his song with one of her own. It was a time-honored ritual that provided release and enjoyment for everyone. But for the youths and maidens, the festival held a more important meaning: it would determine their future. The exchange of songs at the festival was the first step toward betrothal.

"You don't know whom I want for a partner? How slow you are!" Saya exclaimed. "Can't you guess?"

The girls' faces lit up with anticipation as they tossed the names of at least ten possible candidates in her direction.

"Too bad." Saya laughed, restored to her normal self. The lively exchange with her friends had chased away her gloom.

Putting her hand beside her mouth, she whispered confidentially, "Prince Tsukishiro." Her remark was followed by a storm of protest.

"That's not fair!"

"Saya! What nerve!"

"Besides, he won't be at the Kagai!"

"Don't be so sure of that," replied Saya, restraining a friend's hand as it tugged at her hair. "They say that the God of Light witnesses our vows at the Kagai. If so, then why shouldn't his son attend it?"

"Even if the Prince had a thousand bodies, he could not possibly attend all the Kagai in the land of Toyoashihara."

"And besides, he's at the battlefront right now, leading his troops."

"Wearing his silver armor," added Saya with a look of rapture. "Oh, how I would love to see him just once for myself. He must be more splendid than the full moon. Isn't it amazing that the children of the gods actually walk the earth?"

"You sound just like the shrine maiden. Are you going to remain chaste for the God of Light and live the rest of your life alone?"

"Such an honor would never be given to ordinary village girls like us anyway."

"You're right," said Saya, laughing. "I'll have to find a husband. After all, I'm an only child."

"That's more like it. Dreams are just dreams."

Although she knew she must face reality, Saya could not take the task of finding a husband seriously. Although there were numerous eligible youths in the village, not one of them appealed to her in that way. Saya suddenly felt ashamed of misleading her friends, for none of them suspected her true dilemma. "Well, if I can't find a husband, I'll ask the shrine maiden to accept me as a servant."

This remark resulted in further teasing. "What's the matter with her this morning? It sounds as if she's suffering from a broken heart. I suspected as much."

Her friends' speculations were interrupted by a voice from downstream, where the older women gathered. One of the women, pointing at the water, called loudly, "Don't just stand there talking all day. Get to work. Look! You're so careless you've let something float away."

The girls, turning together in the direction the woman indicated, saw a light green belt in the shallows slithering downstream like a luminous water snake. Saya leaped to her feet.

"Oh no! My belt!"

Without a moment's hesitation she gathered her skirt up to her thighs, and, ignoring the shocked expressions on the faces of her elders, set off after the belt, striding through the stream, her white legs flashing. Gazing after her determined figure, her friends burst out laughing.

"She'll never be a shrine maiden, that's for sure!"

Saya was mistaken in thinking that she would soon catch up with her belt. To her surprise, it slipped through the water without once catching on a rock or weed, drawing her after it. A colored belt was the one luxury owned by the village maidens, and she was not about to lose hers. Although the water was shallow, never reaching above her knees, the stones in the riverbed were loose, so one false step would cause a fall. But Saya was quick and agile, never faltering in her stride. Her nimble feet danced through the water, sending up a silver spray as she forged her way down the sparkling stream. Something about her suggested a wild creature, unfettered and free. Her waist-length hair tied at the nape of her neck danced upon her back like a lively tail. She was one of the slimmest of the village girls, but the slender limbs extending from her indigo smock were strong and tireless. Her small oval face with its expressive eyes drew people to her. She was impetuous, but under this rashness lay an intelligent awareness born of her early childhood experience of loss. She consciously strove to be polite and modest before her elders, doing her best to escape attention. Some adults indeed believed her to be a reticent and thoughtful young girl. But those who had been involved in her childhood escapades still talked about her as a leader among the village children. Both views reflected aspects of her character. In addition, there was the insecure, lonely Saya always in search of home, someone known only to Saya herself.

The river gurgled as it flowed along, winding around a craggy outcrop in the bank, where it turned and fed into a channel thickly lined with reeds. Saya stopped abruptly as she rounded the bend, surprised by the scene before her. Concentrating on following her belt, she had come much farther downstream than she had realized, reaching the stepping-stones of the ford. In the middle of the ford a figure was kneeling on one of the stones, busily fishing her belt from the water. He was small, a boy two or three years younger than herself, but his appearance was so different from that of the people of her own land that she hesitated to call out to him. He wore faded black clothes, almost too short for him, with fur leg guards, leather sandals, and a hat of braided sedges. Around his neck hung a handsome necklace of red stones that belied the worn and faded condition of the rest of his outfit. Saya had never seen such a boy before.

With the dripping belt held in one hand, he stood up and looked directly at her. Under a thatch of unkempt hair which seemed to have rarely seen a comb, his face resembled that of a saucy, stubborn puppy. He stared boldly at Saya as she stood in the middle of the river, her skirt still bunched in her hand, as at a rare and interesting sight. Then, with what Saya thought extreme impudence, he laughingly exclaimed, "Is this your belt? If you want it, you'd better come and get it." With the belt still in his hand, he sprang across the stepping-stones and clambered up the right-hand bank. Furious, Saya strode through the water, climbed onto the stones, and ran after him.

Noriko Ogiwara

"Give it back! What do you think you're doing?" Saya reached out to grab him by the shoulder, but the boy in black was faster, whirling out of reach to face her. He seemed to be enjoying her discomfort and was not in the least disturbed by her anger. Having been an unruly child herself, Saya recognized in the boy a formidable opponent. At that moment, however, three men, doubtless the boy's companions, came into view. Saya faltered and drew back.

She was filled with apprehension. They might be thieves or kidnappers. At the very least they were completely alien to the world that she knew. She would have screamed, but the men made no move to accost her. The three of them, wearing the same black clothes and fur leg guards as the boy, merely stood silently staring at her. To her frightened eyes there appeared to be not three but five or ten of them. Their large stature and cool composure certainly suggested the assurance of greater numbers.

Saya could have fled back to her friends but, to her own surprise, she turned once more to the boy and held out her hand, saying, "Give it back, please. That belt is mine."

The boy gazed coolly into Saya's face for a moment. Then a high-pitched fragile voice sounded from behind him. "Give it back, Torihiko."

Startled, Saya looked up. It was not, as she had first thought, one of his three companions feigning a woman's voice. Rather, among them stood a small white-haired old woman leaning on a cane. She was so tiny that Saya had not seen her at first. The boy called Torihiko smiled and, in surprising acquiescence, offered the belt to Saya.

"What an odd group of people," she thought.

She could not help but stare at them as she took her belt. Although all three men were large, on closer inspection only the one standing in the middle was truly gigantic. His companions were of more human proportions but still far superior to the village men in build. It was their air of confidence and power that made them impressive. They wore their hair in the common style, but their beards were thick, their skin was deeply tanned, and their eyes shone with an unearthly light. One wore a black leather patch over one eye, and this, coupled with the bright gleam in the other, made him appear particularly forbidding. The second was younger and slimmer, but his eyes, too, gleamed dangerously. The man in the middle surpassed ordinary men in girth and height, and his arms were as big as young tree trunks. Of the three, he had the kindest expression.

The old woman, on the other hand, was about the height of a five-year-old, giving her the appearance of a wizened child. Her cane was at least twice her height, and her head and eyes were overlarge in comparison with her spare frame. A halo of white hair like thistledown made her head appear even larger than it was. In this company, the boy seemed almost normal. All five of them gazed steadily at Saya as if they had been waiting for her.

The old woman suddenly blinked, froglike, and spoke. "Excuse me, but could you tell us if the house of Chief Azusahiko is far from here?"

"It's just over there," Saya answered quickly. "Follow the river and bear right when you come to the pine forest. You'll soon see it."

"Could you perhaps guide us there? We have been invited to the Kagai and wish to pay our respects to the chief."

"I see." Saya relaxed. "Are you the musicians for the festival?"

"Yes."

Suddenly their pride and their outlandish appearance were not so strange. It was common for traveling musicians and performers to wander from village to village at festival time. Until now Saya had seen musicians only during festivals, playing the koto or the flute, but no doubt they had all come from far away. It was the custom for musicians to be entertained at the home of the chief for several days before the festival and to continue their travels once it was over.

"I'd be happy to guide you, but I must go and collect my washing first. I'll be back shortly," Saya said.

As she was turning to leave, however, the boy casually remarked, "You have a small mark on your right palm, don't you?"

Saya turned back in surprise. She had a pale pink oval birthmark like a flower petal in the hollow of her palm. Normally, she never thought of it, but it annoyed her that the sharp-sighted boy had spotted it.

"I was born with it. What about it?" Saya answered somewhat brusquely, accustomed as she was to remarks about red birthmarks appearing on people who have seen a fire.

The boy continued to regard her. "You weren't born in this village either, were you?"

Saya frowned. Although deeply shaken, she kept her poise. "What makes you say that? Do birthmarks automatically indicate that a person was not born in this village?"

At that moment her ears picked up words muttered by the man with the eye patch to his neighbor. "She looks just like . . . You can tell by her . . . She has the face of the Water Maiden."

"The Water Maiden?" thought Saya. "Who is that?" She stiffened. Although she had never heard the name before, it filled her with a sense of foreboding that she could not shake. Her heart pounded and the blood drained from her face as though she had been touched by an icy finger. Aware that the old woman was watching her, Saya asked hoarsely, "Where do you come from?"

Half hoping that they were from the east, Saya awaited the reply. Perhaps they knew something about her true origins. But the old woman answered indifferently, "From the west. And some of us from the south. There are many small but prosperous villages hereabouts." The old woman's inner thoughts could not be read in her wrinkled face. All her energy seemed to be concentrated in her gleaming eyes, but these, too, betrayed no flicker of emotion. Saya's disappointment kept her silent. The old woman suddenly asked, almost as an afterthought, "Have you ever heard of Princess Sayura?"

"Princess Sayura? No."

"Mmm, I thought not. I thought not." The old woman nodded to herself. "It was so many years ago now, although her death in the palace of the Prince of Light seems like yesterday to me."

"Was she related to you?" Saya was puzzled. The old woman spoke of the Princess as if of her own daughter, yet the palace in the capital city was the home of Prince Tsukishiro and Princess Teruhi. Only those of very high rank could enter there.

The old woman did not reply, and the boy smothered a laugh. Saya suddenly felt ashamed and a little angry, as if she was the only one who had missed something obvious.

At that moment she was hailed by cheerful voices from the grassy riverbank. Out of curiosity, several friends had followed after her. "Saya! Are you all right? Did you get your belt?"

The girls, who had come running up to the top of the bank, stopped in their tracks, eyes wide with surprise as they caught sight of the strange group of people. Grateful to her friends for rescuing her from an awkward situation, Saya explained in a rush, "These people found it for me. They're the musicians for the festival. I'm taking them to Chief Azusahiko. Won't you come, too?"

The girls' faces brightened. Anything out of the ordinary was a welcome diversion. Laughing excitedly, they returned to collect their washing.

"What odd people!"

"Somehow they remind me of the Ground Spiders."

"You're exaggerating. That's not a very nice thing to say."

"But really, they say that the Ground Spiders are either long of leg and arm or very short. They sleep in nests in the trees in summer, and in winter they live in caves. That description fits the strangers perfectly, doesn't it?"

Everyone laughed. None of them had ever met a Ground Spider, although they knew that it was a derogatory name given to the frontier people who refused to worship the God of Light. The term was now commonly used to refer to those among their own people who looked strange or different, and as such, it aptly expressed the strangeness of the musicians' appearance. Saya laughed, too. But her smile froze as she recalled her friend's words: "long of leg and arm or very short." At last the reason for her sense of unease and foreboding crystallized. She glanced quickly behind her at the sober black figures on the grassy riverbank. The disparity in their sizes was almost comical. And there were five of them. Five.

Suppressing the sudden racing of her heart, Saya told herself fiercely, "It can't be. It's just a coincidence. They can't be the ones in my dream. Not on such a sunny day as this. Not in broad daylight. It can't be."

2

"Promise?"

"Yes. I promise," Saya said solemnly. "I swear before the God of Light that I will not accept gifts from, or reply to, the songs of Akihiko, Muraji, Toyo, Ohiro, and—um, let me see—Mahito."

"All right, then. That's settled." Although the girls spoke in a jesting manner, they were serious. Beneath their feelings of excitement and anticipation was an insecurity they could not totally suppress. The surrounding mountains were robed in vibrant green, displaying a breathtaking brightness that seemed to imbue even the white of the maidens' garments with a fresh green hue.

The girls were intoxicated with their own youthful beauty. Aware that the pure white of their clothes, the alpine roses in their hair, and the azalea adorning their sashes became them now more than at any other time, they vacillated between bashfulness and pride.

"It looks as if I've lost out," Saya remarked to the girl beside her.

"Well, what can you expect if you won't choose someone for yourself?"

"There's no need to worry about Saya, though. She won't have any trouble finding a partner!" interjected a girl who wore a bright yellow sash.

"Why do you say that?"

"Why, she asks! Saya, you're unbelievable!" responded a girl crowned with a wreath of green leaves. "Don't you know how attractive you are? Just the other day someone said that you don't look like an ordinary village maiden."

"So what do I look like?" Saya retorted.

"Cheer up. They said you were beautiful."

"That's it, then. You must be a princess. Princess Saya."

"Oh, stop it!" Saya exclaimed irritably. She was in no mood for joking about herself after what she had overheard the one-eyed musician saying. "She looks just like . . ." What did it mean? Was she really that different from everyone else?

The girl beside her gave her shoulder a friendly shake and laughed. "Don't worry! Nobody who sees you all scruffy with dirt is going to mistake you for a princess."

Meanwhile, on the southern slope of Mount Itsuki, in a glade surrounded by a forest of oak, horse chestnut, and chinquapin, and marked by a large camellia tree, the village youths were busy laying wood for an enormous bonfire. The old women of the village devoted themselves to preparing food for the Kagai, wrapping each delicacy in oak leaves. Decorations of woven straw and folded paper were placed at regular intervals around the circumference of the glade to mark the festival site, and a barrel of sake was placed beneath each marker. The men were already flushed with the effects of the wine. Although the camellia flowers had begun to fade, a little farther into the wood alpine rose bushes with silver-backed leaves bore large red blooms, while golden and white brier roses bloomed like stars along the mountain stream.

"We must adorn ourselves with the choicest flowers, for we are the bearers of spring," said a girl who wore a cord dyed red with madder tied around the middle of her sash.

"Yes. We are the ones who entice the gods to return to the land after spending the long winter in the mountain peaks. At least, that's how it was in the past."

"In the past?" Saya asked.

"Before the shrine was built honoring the God of Light. They say that is why the shrine maiden resents our continuation of the Kagai festival. But who wouldn't be gloomy if she had to sit up all night long with no one for company, as she does!"

"What gods came down from the mountain?"

"I don't know. The Kagai is just a legend now. But it's a good tradition. I'd hate to see it disappear."

Another girl, fixing a posy of yellow roses in her sash, remarked flippantly, "But the old gods are dead. They couldn't withstand the brilliance of the God of Light. The only ones who follow them are the Ground Spiders."

"Oh! Well, I certainly don't want to entice any god of theirs!" said the girl with the crown of green leaves.

"Of course not. There's only one person you're interested in enticing," Saya remarked dryly, causing several of the girls to laugh.

As she picked the golden roses that resembled miniature wine cups, Saya was enchanted by the idea of beckoning gods from the mountain. It seemed sad that they should be preparing themselves in this way when there were no longer any gods to greet.

The sun sank slowly behind the peak of a distant mountain while the blue sky deepened to red, then purple, and finally to indigo. The moon, like a disk of beaten copper, climbed in the eastern sky, and at its appearance the bonfire was lit. A great cheer arose from those assembled. The flames leaped higher and higher, rising to a pillar of fire that lent the glade a midday brightness. Saya blinked and stared as the smiling faces illumined by the firelight blended with the shadows crouching at their feet. The festival was about to begin. The chief made his way to the front and urged the villagers to enjoy themselves. A man of integrity, untainted by ambition, the chief was greatly respected by his people, despite complaints from some that he was too dry and dull. As his speech ended, the music began. With a shiver of apprehension, Saya stole a glance at the musicians' platform. All five were there.

She had not seen them since the day they had met on the riverbank. No longer garbed in dusty black, they wore robes of the finest hemp cloth, perhaps a gift from the chief, with garlands of leaves in their hair. They were even more imposing than before, surrounded now by an aura of dignity. The largest of them beat the big drum, the two other men played the hand drum and reed pipes, while the boy played the flute and the old woman the koto, leaning over so far that she almost straddled the instrument. Although they looked even more sinister to Saya, she could have no complaint with their music, which rang clear and bright over the glade, slipping effortlessly into the hearts of the people and heightening their exhilaration.

"What excellent musicians!" Saya overheard someone saying in an impressed voice.

"Saya! Don't just stand there. Hurry up and dance. If you stay there dreaming, you'll lose out to the girls from other villages!" Saya started from her reverie to find a girl beside her tugging at her sleeve. Nodding her thanks, she set off at a run.

The people circled the fire several rings deep, their bodies swaying and their feet stamping in a simple rhythm as they danced around the fire. The heat of the fire joined that of the dancers, reaching fever pitch. Although some laughed loudly or played the fool, the drumming of their feet overwhelmed them with its power, until everyone danced in perfect unison, shaking the very mountains with the beat of their footsteps, which echoed from the tops of the trees. The moon reached its zenith, its silver face gazing down upon the spellbound dancers, who breathed in time with the pulsing of the fire. It was a perfect evening: the full moon shining hazily through a mist of downy deutzia flowers; crystals of pale light scattered in the night sky.

The dancing reached its peak and then slackened as the rhythm of the dancers' feet was broken. The youths and young maidens no longer had ears for the music, absorbed instead in searching for an answering look among the ranks of the opposite sex. Married couples, recalling their days of courting, re-declared their mutual love. Here and there songs were already being sung, songs of enduring love for a husband or wife. Those who had found a partner slipped from the ring of dancers and moved toward the shadows of the trees in order to exchange their gifts.

As for Saya, she was just now beginning to regret the vow she had taken. It had never occurred to her that the boys whom she had sworn to reject would, one after the other, seek her out as a partner. She had played and fought with them as children, but after their initiation into the ranks of the youths, there had been few opportunities to meet. And even if they met, they only greeted one another from afar. She had not realized that these same boys had grown into broad-shouldered young men who regarded her as a woman. At last Saya realized that she had been tricked by her friends.

"They don't even deserve to be called friends," she thought. She knew, however, that they were truer friends than she herself had proved to be, for their attachment to the boys they had named was sincere. She had no one to blame for her predicament but herself. "What am I doing here?" she thought. For she, too, yearned to find someone: to face one man and, with her hands in his, pledge her heart. She was so filled with disappointment when she turned to face her next suitor that she could have wept. Before her stood Mahito, the last of the five youths named by her friends.

"Not you, too?"

Mahito was the former bully of the village. He was three years older than Saya and had once been a source of trouble and mischief in the neighborhood. Since then, however, he had become a handsome young man, the stubbornness receding from his oval face. Even his pug nose had somehow become attractive. Turning toward his tall figure, Saya felt as though she had been touched by invisible fireworks.

When she remarked that he had certainly never shown any kindness to her in childhood, Mahito laughed. But his eyes remained serious.

"That's because I knew that when you came of age I would have to go down upon my knees before you and beg you to declare your love for me at the Kagai."

Dazed, Saya could only stare at him in bewilderment. "But you just ignored me last year and the year before that."

"Last year was last year. This year, Saya, you are the most beautiful girl in the land. I can't bear to stand by and see you claimed by someone from another village. Let me hear your reply. Make it yes."

The alpine rose perched above her ear tilted as she bowed her head. She had already exhausted her repertoire of refusals. Along with many love songs, all the young women had memorized several songs that would gently put off unwanted suitors. These were traditional songs that she should have known by heart, yet now she could not remember any. What was she to do? Should she refuse him, and possibly hurt him, with a hastily improvised song? Or should she . . .

As she was agonizing over her response, a third voice rose in song nearby:

> *"I have come upon you in a crowd,*
> *You whom I long to meet in a quiet place."*

Saya and Mahito gasped in shock and spun around. For a third party to interrupt before a girl had replied was a direct challenge to the first suitor and, as such, would certainly lead to a confrontation. People with any common sense adhered to established etiquette. Mahito was understandably incensed, and an angry flush suffused his face.

"Just who do you think you are? You're asking for trouble!"

"Stop!" Saya recalled his earlier career as a bully in the village and hurried to intervene. The interloper was a slender young boy. Saya peered closely at his face in amazement and disbelief. It was none other than the impertinent boy who was supposed to be playing the flute. "You! What do you think you are doing!"

"Get home to bed, brat. You don't belong here!"

Torihiko watched the two of them, smiling complacently. If he had not been so young, his expression could have been described as bold and fearless. "What about the song, Saya?" he urged. "If you answer one of us, there will be no need to fight."

Saya hastily recollected herself and looked from one to the other. Then in desperation she sang:

> *"If you truly love me, then come.*
> *For surely you will find me waiting,*
> *Alone, in the quiet wood."*

"Saya!" Mahito cried in disbelief. "Why? Why did you answer him?"

"I'm sorry. I just couldn't answer you. Go and seek the girl whose eyes are fixed on you alone. I know you will find her." And she turned away as if to escape, feeling deeply unhappy.

"Why must I always be alone?"

A sigh escaped her lips. She was disillusioned with everything: with the Kagai, for which she had waited so eagerly; with the thought of love and courtship. Watching the interplay of light and shadow made her dizzy, and she turned to head deeper into the shadows of the forest to calm her heart in the concealing dark. Not until she had passed the boundary of the glade marked by the straw and paper ornaments did she realize that the boy had accompanied her. She glared at him.

"Just in case you are wondering, I have no intention of accepting any gift from you. You're just a child! Why did you leave the musicians' platform?"

The boy gave her a look of resigned exasperation. His eyes gleamed in the faint light that filtered through the branches. "And I thought you might even thank me! After all, I came to your rescue when you were in trouble."

Saya thought him an odd boy. How had he known that she was in trouble? Had he been watching her the whole time?

"Your name is Torihiko, isn't it?" Saya said slowly.

"Yes."

"How did you know I wasn't born in this village?"

"I just knew," he said, clasping his hands behind his head and looking insufferably smug. "After all, we came here to find you."

Struggling to keep calm, Saya snapped, "If you continue to make fun of me, I'm going to lose my patience. I'm not in a particularly good mood, as you may have noticed."

"Oh my, you frighten me," Torihiko responded, although he adopted a slightly less irreverent attitude. "But it's the truth, you see. We came looking for a girl who disappeared from a village burned at Princess Teruhi's command nine years ago. The girl was six years old and had a red birthmark on her right palm. That mark was proof that she was born clasping a stone, that she was the rightful successor, the rebirth of Princess Sayura."

"Stop," Saya whispered.

"Princess Sayura is one of the highborn among those who serve the Goddess of Darkness; she is the one who guards the Dragon Sword—"

"Stop!" Saya shouted, cutting him off in mid-sentence. She shook her head violently, sending a flower flying from her hair. "I don't want to hear any more! Go away! I said go!"

Torihiko winced as though wounded by this outburst, and said reproachfully, "You could refrain from yelling at me as though I were some unwanted cur. I may look like a child, but I have lived considerably longer than you."

Saya turned on her heel and began to run back to the gathering, back to the familiar faces of people who understood laughter and tears. But no matter how far she ran, she seemed to move deeper and deeper into the gloom of the forest. The glade with its bright fire lay but a few steps away, just past the trees, but still it did not come into view. Changing direction made no difference. No matter which way she ran, only the silence of the mountain forest rose up to greet her. She finally came to a halt and leaned against a tree trunk, breathing deeply to control her panic.

"Calm down," she thought. "At times like this, it is useless to struggle."

"There is nothing to fear." It was the voice of the tiny old woman. "You have the power to believe. You can accept what Torihiko has told you."

"There—you see," Saya told herself.

She pressed her back against the tree, preparing herself for whatever might come. The five musicians stood before her, wrapped in a pale phosphorescent glow. Saya knew then that she was finally facing what had filled her with terror for so many years. She could no longer escape. She drew a deep breath and exhaled slowly. She was no longer afraid. Perhaps her calm arose from sheer desperation, or perhaps her nerves were just numb. No, her nerves were far from numb. Rather, her entire being was consumed with a smoldering rage. Staring evenly at the five figures, she said coldly, "So you are the demons, after all."

The old woman stood in front and regarded Saya steadily. "No, we are not demons," she answered calmly. "We are at least as close to you as the people gathered for the Kagai."

"And our feelings can be hurt, too," added Torihiko, who stood directly behind the old woman.

"This is Lady Iwa," said the man with the patch. "And I am Lord Akitsu." Gesturing toward the largest of them, he continued, "This is Lord Ibuki, and over there are Lord Shinado and Torihiko. We are, all of us, servants of the Goddess of Darkness."

"They are Ground Spiders!" Saya thought.

The possibility that she, too, might be a Ground Spider made Saya wish that the earth would open up and swallow her. "No!" her heart rebelled. "No, no!" How could she be, she who loved the light of day, the flowers, the sky, the clouds? She who loved all things that lived beneath the sun?

"Saya, listen," said Lady Iwa. "Do you know the legend of how the earth and heavens were formed? The story of the God and Goddess who gave birth to the world? Combining their powers, they created the land of Toyoashihara, and hundreds of thousands of gods to populate it. Gods inhabited the mountains, the rivers, the rocks, the springs, the wind, and the ocean, and shook the earth with their laughter. But the last child born to the Goddess was the fire god, and she was so horribly burned that she fled and concealed herself in the underworld. In his grief and anger, the God of Light killed the fire god and went to the Land of the Dead to retrieve the Goddess. But he was horrified at the sight of her decaying body and returned to the world above, sealing the entrance with a huge stone and severing his ties with her forever. From that time onward the gods were divided into those of heaven and those of the underworld, who despised one another."

"They divided into the forces of Light and Darkness," Saya said sullenly. "Anyone born in Toyoashihara knows that much. The Goddess cursed the land and vowed she would kill one thousand people each day. The God responded that he would build one thousand five hundred birthing huts a day. It is he who bathes this world in light, nurturing all life. And his children are Princess Teruhi and Prince Tsukishiro."

"Does he really nurture all life?" the old woman countered in a strangely gentle voice. "Surely it is the earth that nurtures life. And it is water that revives the parched earth. Water falls from above, quenching the earth's great thirst, and then flows into the underworld. That is the road to the Goddess, the road that all living things on the earth will one day tread. Our land of Toyoashihara is dependent upon the eternal flow of water. If this cycle is disrupted, the flow of life will stagnate and become fouled. Evil and corruption will be left unchecked."

Feeling a sudden sadness, Saya looked up, but Lady Iwa's eyes were lowered. Saya was surprised that this old woman who resembled some kind of apparition should arouse sympathy in her. It was her vulnerability rather than her ugliness that impressed Saya. She looked like a clumsy fledgling not yet able to fly, waiting pathetically for rescue.

Lady Iwa continued. "In his hatred and anger, however, the God of Light sealed off the road to the underworld. And through his immortal children, Princess Teruhi and Prince Tsukishiro, he rules the earth, hunting down and destroying the gods of the mountains and rivers that he conceived with the Goddess. He intends to destroy all the gods and rule the earth alone, to claim Toyoashihara through slaughter and plunder."

"No! That's not true!" Saya protested hotly. "It's not true. It's not evil to shed light on all regions of the world and to unite it under one ruler. The war is caused by willful people who refuse to recognize the importance of his light. It's because some people reject peace—"

She was cut off by a voice of steel. It was the first time that she had heard Lord Shinado speak. Although he was the youngest of the three men, there was something in his bearing and mien reminiscent of a keen-edged sword.

"How can you be so heartless? This God of Light that you so praise murdered your own father and mother. Your village was razed by soldiers on horseback bearing torches in their hands. By the time we reached it, there was not one living soul left. Do you think that his two immortal children are able to understand the pain of those whom they have destroyed? They feel as much pain as a dewdrop evaporating in the morning sun. Yet you would still worship them? Will you choose comfort and ease without any thought of revenge against the enemies of your own parents?"

Saya shuddered. Surely it was this that she had most feared. But there was something within her that would not yield, that would never give in, and at that moment she realized she was stronger than she had known.

"I don't want to hate," she replied in a small voice. If she was afraid, it was only of Lord Shinado himself, for she was certain of what she said. "I have a new mother and father. They found me and raised me with love and tenderness. I am not heartless. It is just that I prefer to love rather than to hate."

"Hmmm. She reminds me of Princess Sayura, she does," muttered the huge Lord Ibuki. Although he was talking to himself, his voice reverberated like thunder.

Lady Iwa nodded in agreement. "Yes, she said the same thing. We are not saying that you should not be drawn to the Light. But we must fight. We must prevent the God of Light from destroying all the gods of the land. He has no regard for or understanding of human feelings. He strives to purify the entire earth and to descend upon it. But he neither knows nor cares whether there will be any people left alive when all the gods of river and mountain have disappeared from the land. He cannot comprehend what this would mean to us."

Lord Akitsu raised his jet-black brows and gazed at Saya. "Saya, you who hold the power of water, lend your strength to ours and help us fight. You are weak, but you are closest to our mother, the Goddess. You are even capable of grasping the Dragon Sword."

All five of them watched her intently from the depths of the shadows, awaiting her reply. Her heart was in turmoil, but she knew it would be useless to try to deceive them. At last she expressed what was in her heart. "I hate war. I cannot do it."

Their disappointment struck her keenly, and somehow she felt a need to defend herself. "Why didn't you come sooner? I've lived here, in a village of the God of Light, for nine years. Every day I have worshipped Princess Teruhi and Prince Tsukishiro. It's impossible for me to change now, so suddenly."

After a short pause, Lady Iwa replied, "In youth no one realizes that the trees that stretch higher and higher toward the sky are, at the same time, sending their roots deeper and deeper into the earth. And we, the reborn, because we are granted a new life, must each time experience the ignorance of youth. For this reason we cannot tell others of their mission until they have sufficiently matured. It has been the custom to gather together when the time comes and to seek them out. In your case, however, you are right. You disappeared without a trace, and it took much longer than we had expected to find you. Still, despite the danger, we have come into the domain of the God of Light to find you. But we cannot blame you for that."

The old woman groped in her pocket and pulled out something in her tiny hand, extending it toward Saya. "We must leave you now, or our pursuers will soon be upon us. But this is yours. Whether in the end you use it or not, it belongs to you."

Without a word, Saya held out both hands to receive it. Still glowing faintly with the phosphorescence of the old woman's palm, it was a small stone no larger than the tip of Saya's finger. It was not round but well worn and curved like the outer rim of an ear. Through a hole in the tip ran a thin cord. The stone was glossy, and milky blue, like the color of a spring sky.

The murmur of voices and leaves rustling gently in the wind returned, and Saya began to realize that she had been in a space without sound. As if awakening from a dream, she looked about her and saw a glimmer of firelight from the glade between the black silhouettes of the trees. The five musicians were gone. No doubt she would never meet them again. They had vanished as suddenly as they had appeared, without any attempt to force her to obey their will. Clutching the amulet in her hand, Saya thought distractedly, "I must go. I must get back to my own people."

But as her feet began to move, she realized that there was nowhere to go. Her parents were at home, and her friends were scattered about with eyes only for their partners. The night was far advanced, and the sound of high-pitched laughter drifted across the glade from the banquet areas of each village. No one else was alone.

A yawning gulf suddenly separated Saya from everyone here. She had always had a premonition that she did not belong but, unwilling to accept it, had managed to ignore it. Now she could no longer deny the truth. The demons had been gentle, but only because they had made so strong an impression upon her. Turning away from the brightly lit glade, Saya headed deeper into the forest. And as she walked, the tears she had held back for so long began to fall.

Her tears had no end. She wept as she walked, and walked as she wept, oblivious of her direction. Saya, who rarely cried, did not know how to stop. When, hiccuping and exhausted, she finally sat down on a fallen log, she seemed to hear a nearby tree speak to her in a grave voice.

"Why do you weep?"

The voice was pleasant, like the sound of a breeze through the treetops, and it sounded so natural that she replied without thinking, "Because I am all alone."

"You could find no lover?"

"More alone than that."

At that moment she heard another voice whisper tensely from the far side of the thick grove of trees. She craned her neck in surprise and peered into the darkness.

"It is just one of the village maidens crying. There is no cause for concern," the first voice answered quietly.

The shadows beneath the cedars were so thick that it was impossible to tell if anyone was there. Saya sniffed loudly, an action she regretted immediately, and asked suspiciously, "Who are you?"

At last she saw something move and a figure stepped out from the trees into the moonlight. He was tall and graceful, like a young cypress tree. Beneath the white light of the full moon, it was clear that he was more than just an ordinary man. Saya caught her breath and froze. She had thought that nothing more could surprise her after the events of the evening, but now she doubted her own eyes, sure that she must be dreaming. On his head he wore the same silver helmet that she had so often imagined, shining with the radiance of a hundred moons.

Before her stood Prince Tsukishiro himself.

3

Prince Tsukishiro stood like a silver statue bathed in moonlight in a trough of darkness amid the rustling leaves. Though he seemed to be a phantom, at the same time his presence was palpable to Saya. As surely as the mountains around them existed, his feet were firmly upon the ground. Saya felt the hair rise along the nape of her neck and realized for the first time that this sensation could be inspired by feelings other than fear.

The Prince was dressed for battle, armored in breastplate and helmet, with silver gauntlets covering his hands, a quiver slung across his back, and a long sword resting at his hip. The clothes beneath his armor were white, his shirtsleeves bound by cords ornamented with small beads. His face under the raised visor was fine-featured, with an aquiline nose and indescribably gentle eyes. Even as he exuded an air of refinement and grace, he radiated a fear-inspiring strength, an overwhelming power such that, just by standing there, he caused the night to change its shape and the forest its fragrance in submission to him.

Saya was so lost in admiration of his beauty that she completely forgot he could see her clearly, too. By the time she came to her senses and covered her face with her sleeve, Prince Tsukishiro had already had plenty of time to inspect her.

"Why do you hide your face?" he chided gently.

"I was crying." How embarrassing. She blushed behind her sleeve to think how frightful she must look.

"I know. You cried a long time." His voice held the hint of a smile. It had a beautiful timbre.

"Lift up your face." His tone was gentle, but his words commanded. Unconsciously, Saya obeyed.

As she gazed up at him, he said, "Are you not the Water Maiden?"

Saya felt as though she had been slapped in the face. Her eyes grew to twice their size. "How . . . how do you know that name?"

His eyes were hidden now in the shadow of his visor. But his voice remained gentle. "I know a maid with a face like yours. No, I knew her . . . a long time ago. It was just for a short while, but she lived in my palace."

"Who am I?" thought Saya gloomily. "Am I just the shade of Princess Sayura?" She clasped her hands together tightly to keep them from trembling and replied in a small voice, "Yes. Some demons came to me tonight and told me of that name. They told me that I am one of the people who serve the Goddess of Darkness. But until today such a thing had never occurred to me. I was raised in Hashiba and have always worshipped at the shrine of the mirror. In spring before the planting, I pray to the moon, and in fall before the harvest, I pray to the sun. I don't know what to do. I long to be blessed by the Light, even now. But can this still be possible for me? I have always—"

Despite her efforts, her voice broke. She was amazed that she still had tears left to weep. "Go on, Saya," she told herself fiercely. "Say it now, or never." Summoning all her courage, she continued, "I have always loved you, Lord . . ."

For a moment, Prince Tsukishiro gazed down at her silently. The armored soldiers of his party slowly approached and formed a guard behind him. Saya felt her courage seep away as she watched.

In the next instant, however, the Prince, undoing his chin strap, removed his silver helmet. He shook his head with pleasure, and the beads woven into the long, looped braids on either side of his head made a pure clear sound. "So young!" thought Saya. He looked much younger than she had imagined.

"What is your name?"

"Saya," she replied, her eyes fixed upon his face, begrudging their every blink.

"We came here following the thick spoor of darkness. We found not our enemy, but gained instead something infinitely precious," the Prince said gaily. Then he asked, "Tonight they should be celebrating the Kagai in Hashiba. Is it near here?"

Saya nodded distractedly, still overwhelmed.

"Guide us there. I wish to see the Kagai. For countless months I have traveled over mountain and valley, only for the sake of war. No, we will not go on foot." The Prince turned and called out, "Bring me my steed."

The people of Hashiba, including the chief himself, were dumbstruck. Legend had come true. A god had indeed come to the Kagai. The only horses in the village were sleepy plow horses. No one but the chief owned a saddle horse, and even his mount looked like a different species from the majestic gray stallion with star-dappled flanks that seemed to float suddenly into the circle of firelight. And the one who rode him, one whom even the shrine maiden had only glimpsed distantly in the shrine mirror, far exceeded the people's imagination.

The milling crowd, held back by the stern-faced warriors who guarded the Prince, gazed in open-mouthed astonishment. It was the sight of the slender girl, a maiden from their very own village, perched sideways on the gray stallion in front of the Prince, that most astounded them.

Prince Tsukishiro's retinue advanced slowly, parting the wall of people, and came to a halt before the chief. By this time the chief had scrambled from his seat and prostrated himself on the ground, his face pressed flat against the earth. The shrine maiden, keeper of the mirror, had done likewise. Seeing this, the villagers came to their senses and followed suit, hurriedly throwing themselves upon the ground.

Prince Tsukishiro looked over the backs of the crowd of silent worshippers who filled the glade. The crackling and popping of the bonfire echoed strangely and sparks danced in the night sky. The Prince spoke. "On with the festival! You need not fear. I have come to watch the Kagai. Dance and sing, drink and be merry. Find yourselves good mates. I will celebrate your vows. Strike up the music."

Thus commanded, the chief raised his face a fraction and spoke in a trembling, muffled voice. "It is an unexpected honor that the Prince of the people of Light should deign to attend our humble festival. We desire to obey his will, but unfortunately the musicians have disappeared . . ."

"No musicians?" Prince Tsukishiro said in a puzzled tone and looked at Saya questioningly. Saya was unable to reply and shrank in embarrassment. In fact, she was longing to get down from his horse, standing as it was in the midst of the prostrated forms of her own people.

"How can you celebrate without music? Never mind. I will play for you," the Prince said casually. With uncanny grace, he slipped to the ground, lifting Saya down after him; then, drawing out a flute, he leaped lightly onto the musicians' platform. Crossing his legs and brushing the hair back from his face, he took a deep breath and began to play a clear, ringing melody.

No one could believe it: that the festival would continue to music played by the Prince of Light himself. They thought it inconceivable that they should celebrate the Kagai in the presence of the hallowed Prince whom they worshipped. But before they knew it, they were dancing and the festival continued even more merrily than before. The sound of the flute melted their hearts like magic and filled their hands and feet with joy. They wept and laughed and clapped in time with the music, drunk with excitement.

Saya, watching from where she stood behind the platform, suddenly became aware that no one was able to look Prince Tsukishiro in the face. When they glanced up at him they turned their heads away immediately as if his countenance were too bright to behold. But their smiling faces glowed as if a torch had been lit in their hearts. Passionate vows were exchanged in the clearing.

"Am I the only one who can look at him?" wondered Saya. It was a strange thought, but, at the same time, her feet were itching to move. She, too, wanted to dance with abandon around the fire. Just as she leaned forward to go, she felt a hand on her shoulder. She turned in surprise to find Chief Azusahiko. He looked at her intently and said, "You are the daughter of Otohiko

and Yatame. How on earth did you entice the Prince of Light
to our festival? But this is not the time for asking such questions.
You must not leave his side tonight. You must serve him diligently. Offer him wine, fish. You understand, don't you?"

And so it was that Saya bore the tray of offerings to the Prince
when he rested from his music-making. As he relaxed with one
knee raised, watching the festival, his handsome features softened
into a smile when he saw Saya standing shyly before him.

"Come," he said. Saya stepped onto the platform and offered
him a cup. As she poured the wine, Prince Tsukishiro asked,
"Did you receive a gift from someone tonight?"

For an instant Saya thought of the amulet, but immediately
dismissed it. The Prince was asking about the Kagai. The amulet
was certainly not a betrothal gift. "No."

"In that case, will you accept mine?"

Saya raised her head in surprise. The Prince's gaze was deep
and unfathomable. But she supposed that when they were feeling
relaxed, the Children of Light must jest, too.

"As the Prince of Light wishes," Saya replied noncommittally,
and he smiled faintly.

"Your heart is pure. It has not yet been tainted by the Darkness.
It is fortunate that I found you so soon. I will protect that purity.
Come and be a handmaiden at my palace. Will you not accom-
pany me to Mahoroba, Saya?"

The handmaidens served the immortal Children of Light in
their palace in the capital of Mahoroba. The position was the
highest honor which a shrine maiden could attain, reserved for
the daughters of selected families of the most powerful clans.
Saya was taken aback. "But that's impossible. I have no training.
And my family—"

"There is no need to concern yourself with your origins," the
Prince said lightly. "It is a peculiarity of the people of Toyoashihara to be so concerned about lineage. It does not concern

our celestial father, ruler of the heavens. And I have heard that the Goddess of Darkness does not consider lineage when it comes to the rebirth of her people. Is that not so?"

"Ahh . . ." Saya could only stammer, nonplussed.

A decorous smile touched the corners of the Prince's lips, but there was little joy in it. "The people of Darkness are reborn. The Children of Light are ageless immortals. In neither case is the God or Goddess concerned with kinship or lineage."

The Prince drained his cup, revealing his shapely white throat. Saya, sensing some derision in his words, wondered whom he was mocking.

Setting down his cup, the Prince commanded, "Look at me."

Saya obeyed, but could not read his expression, for his noble features surpassed the splendor of the moon in the sky above.

"That qualifies you as my handmaiden. Do you not understand?" the Prince said softly. "The people of Toyoashihara never look me in the face. They cannot. It is impossible."

He turned his face toward the people of Hashiba, who were enjoying the festival. Couples, friends, all were laughing merrily.

"I understand." This time Saya was able to bow her head in assent. She sensed vaguely that some sorrow enveloped Prince Tsukishiro.

"Come to Mahoroba, Saya. Whatever happens, I want you by my side," the Prince said more forcefully perhaps than he had intended.

In the instant before she agreed, scenes from her nine years in Hashiba sprang into Saya's mind: the peach tree behind her house, her playmates, rice flowers, frogs on the embankment, frosty mornings, midsummer afternoons, her mother and father pounding straw, light through the window. Sorrow and joy were so intermingled that she felt emotionless. She heard her own voice as if from a great distance.

"As the Prince of Light wishes."

For a brief moment the Prince's face was brightened by a joyful look befitting his youthful countenance. "How fortunate that I found you. And how glad I am that it was I and not my sister," he said with a curious intensity.

As soon as she had agreed to accompany him, Saya felt a sudden lightening of her heart, a great sense of relief. It was as if she, who had wandered for so long, had at last found a thread that she could grasp.

"I will follow him," she thought. "I am lost no longer."

4

That night would surely be talked about for generations to come. The tale of the Kagai at Mount Itsuki spread far and wide: that Prince Tsukishiro had left the battlefield just to grace the festival; that a mere village girl was to become his handmaiden, an unprecedented appointment. Everyone gossiped in astonishment. Hashiba became famous overnight, and Chief Azusahiko suddenly found himself a successful and prominent figure. The Prince had sent priceless fabrics for Saya's court clothes, and gold to purchase all her needs. As he had also sent rich gifts for the chief to distribute, the village had prospered in fact as well as name. Saya was amazed at the turn of events that found her cosseted and protected by the chief, but felt empty of all emotion.

She stared in disbelief at the fine silks and wondrously dyed woven cloth which had arrived in numerous trunks and now filled the tiny house with a rainbow of color that seemed totally out of place. "Are these all to be made into clothes for me?" she demanded.

"Yes! We're going to have to ask the village women for help. I can't possibly sew them all before you leave!" her mother said, half laughing, half crying, as she caressed the shimmering fabrics with her gnarled fingers. "I never thought to cut such valuable cloth in all my life."

"Let's leave some of it here, then," said Saya. "Surely it's not necessary to make it all into clothes at once."

Yatame shook her head. "No, it's not as simple as that. I won't have you made miserable among the great princesses."

"Mother!" Saya laughed dryly. "I certainly cannot hope to rival any princess. Once a village maid, always a village maid."

"No. You're different," her mother said emphatically. There was a small silence.

"Somehow I always knew," she continued, "that you wouldn't exchange vows at the Kagai with an ordinary man and come back to me. Of course, it was my dream that your children would be born in this house, that we would make a happy, noisy family. Maybe I did hope a little. But the sky didn't fall when they told me the news."

Saya looked at her mother. She was an old woman, her face creased with wrinkles and her back bent by hard work in the fields. For Yatame, who had lost her son in an accident and had adopted Saya in her old age, the birth of her grandchildren was the only thing she had to look forward to.

"I'll come home soon," Saya said quickly. "Maybe they'll send me back."

At this Yatame snorted, bristling with pride. "What a foolish thing to say! If you came back, how could I show my face to the rest of the village? I certainly wouldn't let you in the door. Now let's get to work on these clothes. Just because you will become a handmaiden doesn't mean I'll let you remain idle."

It was unusual for Otohiko to drink, but when he came home that night and watched Saya hold up a half-sewn kimono against herself for him to see, he asked for some sake. Through the chief, the Prince had bestowed such riches on his house that the old couple could never use them all. It was so sudden that it seemed unreal.

"The chief told me that there is no greater joy than a dutiful daughter." Otohiko laughed as he raised his sake cup. "Azusahiko is probably regretting the day he foisted that little monkey of a girl he found in the mountains on me, and wishing he had taken care of her himself. You weren't a very pretty sight then, you know. Black from head to foot, just skin and bones wrapped in a few rags, two big eyes staring out from a thicket of bamboo grass."

Saya laughed bitterly. "Just like a spawn of the Ground Spiders. Why did you take me in?"

Otohiko looked at Saya from under his bushy gray brows. "You were just a little child, whose child we didn't know, wandering lost with no one to turn to. Who wouldn't reach out a hand? Anyone who could refuse to help wouldn't be human. Saya, you and your friends use the term 'Ground Spiders,' but they are people of Toyoashihara just like us, even though we were separated after the God of Light appeared."

"I know," Saya replied in a small voice. She felt her chest constrict. She wished to express her gratitude, to apologize for leaving without properly returning their kindness. But the formal words for such an occasion would not come.

"Father . . ."

As if he had guessed her thoughts, Otohiko smiled, the wrinkles crinkling at the corners of his eyes. "You are our child. You are a child of Hashiba. I am proud of you. You should also be proud—no matter where you go, to Mahoroba or elsewhere."

Saya walked along the river for one last look. Tomorrow she would leave. It was a clear early-summer evening before the start of the long rainy season. The willows with their leaves unfurled swayed in the wind and frogs croaked. The breeze already smelled of summer with the fragrance of brilliant green leaves and the scent of grass from the warm fields. The last rays of the sun rested on the tips of the mountains, and downstream the water gleamed red where it reflected the sky. Standing on the stones at the edge of the water with not a soul in sight, Saya strained to see the river's end.

How often she had played here; how often she had dreamed of places unknown, people unknown, gods unknown. On little leaf boats she had set her dreams sailing, never once thinking that she would leave this village. Mahoroba was said to lie far to the west of the end of the river. She had never before thought of its location in relation to her village. She had only imagined a misty palace somewhere far away in the direction she would now journey.

She gave a small sigh and removed the amulet on its cord from around her neck. The sky-blue stone, warmed by her skin, seemed to breathe. She laid it in her right hand, as she had done so often, against the birthmark on her palm. She found it difficult to believe a baby could be born with this squeezed in its tiny fist. But she could not deny its beauty. How proud she would have been if only it had been a betrothal gift.

"I'll throw it away."

She had already made up her mind. That was why she had come to the river. She would return the Water Maiden's stone to the water. She did not need it. She could not carry this shadow with her if she was to become a handmaiden at Mahoroba. She must bury all connections to the people of Darkness here.

Grasping the amulet in her right hand, Saya raised her arm. "Like this, as far as I can!" she thought.

But she could not throw it. She almost felt that someone was holding her arm. She faltered, stunned at what she had tried to do. Then she glanced furtively around as if she had done something wrong.

Dusk was beginning to creep along the river. Her sharp eyes detected a figure coming down the path along the bank farther upstream. Saya hurriedly concealed the amulet in her sleeve. She would have been ashamed to have someone discover her trying to throw it away. The figure seemed to be approaching her. "Who can it be at this time of day?" she wondered, peering intently. It was not difficult to guess. Although the face was hidden in the twilight, the outline was unmistakable: the hair piled high; the long skirt reaching to the ankles, which no ordinary person wore; the thick short figure, shoulders rounded by middle age. It was the shrine maiden, keeper of the mirror. Saya bowed hastily.

"Good evening, honorable priestess," she said, puzzled. She had never seen the shrine maiden walking alone. If that was true of the daytime, how much stranger was it to see her walking thus at dusk.

The shrine maiden halted and looked down at Saya haughtily. She was always haughty, even looking scornfully upon the chief at times, but now her gaze was particularly frigid. And the words she spoke were astonishing. "I am no longer shrine maiden. I have returned the mirror."

An icy fury filled her voice. Saya shuddered.

"So suddenly? But why are you resigning? You are the only shrine maiden in the village."

Standing stiffly erect as if the hair piled on the top of her head would fall should she bend, the woman replied, "Because you, Saya, received Prince Tsukishiro. It was you who made obeisance before him, you who offered the wine, you who received his words of celebration, and you who were chosen as handmaiden. And I? When the Prince of Light came to our village, I, the keeper of the mirror, was unable to attain his presence, and received not one word of acknowledgment. Do you expect me to remain meekly guarding the mirror after that?"

Unconsciously, Saya took a step backward.

The shrine maiden continued. "I am leaving. But before you go to Mahoroba, I have something to tell you."

She took a deep breath and suddenly her expression changed drastically. Saya thought that the woman had somehow achieved a strange transformation, with her eyes dilated and her mouth split grotesquely wide. Saya watched with fear, but was still unaware that this was a face filled with murder.

The shrine maiden shrieked as one possessed, "You are evil! You are of the Darkness! Did you think I did not know? How cleverly you have tried to deceive Prince Tsukishiro. Do you think that I will surrender you to him? Do you think that I will let you go?"

With surprising agility, she drew a dagger from her sash. The fading light glowed dull red along the short blade.

"I'll send you back to the Darkness here and now!"

Saya dodged the blade instinctively, but was too dazed to comprehend that she was confronted with death. It was only when she saw her sleeve hanging in tatters, slashed where the knife had caught it, that she was jolted to her senses and felt terror sweep through her like a wave of nausea.

"Stop! Please! I serve the Light!"

The shrine maiden shrieked in a voice like grinding metal, "Silence! How dare you presume to make such a claim?"

"It's true! I serve the Light with all my heart," Saya cried as she dodged the approaching blade once again. Then, turning, she began to run. The older woman's feet were slow and Saya should have outdistanced her with ease. Suddenly, however, she tripped on a rock. She fell hard on the sharp gravel but, looking behind, had no time to feel pain. The woman was already upon her. The black silhouette of her demonic form towered above Saya as she brought the blade down with a triumphant cry.

"She will kill me," thought Saya. Just as she closed her eyes, a piercing scream rent the air. Realizing that she herself had not cried out, Saya opened her eyes in surprise to see the shrine maiden cowering behind her sleeve, shielding herself. Two black shapes swooped down and attacked her repeatedly. Blood spurted from her arm, and once again she screamed. The sound of beating wings mingled with her cry. Birds.

The attackers were two crows.

The woman swung her dagger, but struck only empty air. The crows were swift and cruel. Saya saw blood dripping from one eye in the woman's contorted face. Her screams and gasps grew fainter, gradually changing into sobs. Finally, exhausted, she sank to the ground and lay prostrate, clutching her head in her hands. Only her shoulders moved, rising and falling with each ragged breath.

Through all of this, Saya had not moved. The blood on the stones lost its color in the twilight, looking like a black stain. She felt sick. Her ears rang, and she thought she would faint if she tried to stand. The crows, which had stopped attacking as soon as resistance ceased, settled on a large round rock a slight distance from Saya, where they began preening themselves as if nothing had happened.

The crows stole surreptitious glances at Saya from their crafty, gleaming eyes while she stared back at them. Satisfied with their appearance, they flapped their wings and sharpened their beaks on the rock. Then one of them calmly croaked, "Sa-ya . . ."

"Stu-pid . . ." the other added.

Saya's mouth dropped open in amazement. A different voice spoke behind her.

"Are you still too scared to move?"

There, small and slight, stood Torihiko, seemingly out of nowhere. He wore his old black clothes, and his uncombed hair was tied in a careless knot.

"Are you all right?" He stared at Saya, his hands behind his back. He wore an expression of feigned innocence and did not look in the least concerned.

Saya said hoarsely, "What are these?"

Torihiko eyed the crows. "Ah, my birds. This is Big Black and this is Little Black."

Then, leaping from stone to stone, he approached the cringing woman and gazed down at her. "Why don't you hurry home, lady, and attend to your wounds? I am sorry, but I cannot escort you myself. Because you tried to kill Saya, you see?"

"Ohhh!" The shrine maiden groaned loudly and staggered to her feet, one hand pressed tightly to her eye. Her hair had long since fallen into complete disarray.

"So! Spawn of evil. You have shown your true self," she hissed, gasping for breath. "Just wait. Princess Teruhi will surely . . ."

"You sent the mirror back, did you not? So how will you report this?" Torihiko said calmly.

"Just—just remember. You cannot fool Princess Teruhi. She knows who the new handmaiden is. I already sent her a full report. Assuredly—"

"Are you still blathering?" Torihiko interrupted impatiently. "I would think it would be rather inconvenient to lose your other eye as well."

His offhand manner held a chill that sent shivers up Saya's spine. The woman closed her mouth sharply and, hurrying off, was swallowed by the twilight.

Saya finally brushed the hair from her face.

"That woman will have only one eye for the rest of her life," she reprimanded him.

"It's all the same if you are going to die soon anyway," Torihiko said, unconcerned. "She certainly came to the river with the intention of killing herself. But, judging by the energy she displayed just now, she may be so angry that she'll change her mind."

Torihiko spoke as flippantly as if talking about the weather. Gazing at him, Saya wondered if this was a characteristic of the people of Darkness or just a quirk of his personality.

She sighed. "I thought you had already gone. What about the others?"

"They left. Only I stayed. Because I was a little worried, you know."

Torihiko took a wooden box from his belt. The crows immediately flew to him, landing on his shoulders and cocking their heads in anticipation. Torihiko opened the lid and, taking out some finely cut shreds of dried meat, fed the crows by turns.

"And it was just as I thought, wasn't it? I hear you're going to Mahoroba?"

"Yes," Saya murmured, feeling somewhat uncomfortable.

"Now, why do you never learn? You are driving yourself into a corner. You are going to tag along after Prince Tsukishiro just for the sake of his pretty face."

"That's enough! It's none of your business!" Saya spoke sharply, blushing deeply. "That—that isn't it at all. I love the Light. I want to live under the sun. That is why I accepted the chance to be his handmaiden. But someone like you would never understand!"

Torihiko folded his arms, the two solemn-faced crows perched one on either shoulder. "Now, take Princess Teruhi; she's got the same pretty face. But she is dreaded by everyone. She'll be more than you can handle. She may look young, but she's older than your great-great-grandmother. Not only that: there are bound to be at least fifty thousand or so ladies like the woman who was just here. Do you still want to go? Saya, you're throwing yourself into the midst of your enemies, in a place where no one will help you, where no one will comfort you."

Without replying, Saya stood up and brushed the dirt from her clothes. Blood was oozing from a scrape on her knee. Her mother would surely scold her. Well, no matter. It would not show. From tomorrow, she would be wearing a long skirt.

"I cannot turn back now," Saya said simply. "No matter what happens, I have to find out who I am. I cannot stay here in the village anymore, waiting for the answer. I will go to Mahoroba and see what happens. If I suffer for it, it is by my own choice. You can do as you please; I will not interfere. Just let me do as I please."

The crows, mocking her, croaked, "Stu-pid . . ."

"Sa-ya . . ."

She looked at them indignantly. "Get rid of those birds, will you."

"But they're clever," Torihiko said with a laugh. "They're trying to remember your name."

After a slight pause, Saya said, "Thank you for rescuing me. From here on, I will take care of myself."

"Stubborn old mule," Torihiko murmured with a shrug of his shoulders.

"Pardon me?"

"Nothing." Torihiko looked up at Saya affectionately, but he spoke like an adult. "I understand, I cannot change your mind. I had better say no more. Just remember: it was your own choice. Because you are sure to start doubting once you reach Mahoroba."

THE PALACE OF LIGHT

At eventide, I gaze beyond the clouds,
lost in thought,
Dreaming of my beloved so far away.

—Anonymous

1

Mahoroba derived its name from its location at the center of the lands of Toyoashihara from which a road had once led to heaven. Said to have been formed by the foot of the God of Light when he returned to his celestial home, the long valley, running north to south, did indeed resemble a huge footprint, as though someone had trodden in the midst of the mountains. Within this imprint nestled the extensive buildings of the Palace of Light and a multitude of lesser manors that housed the palace's subjects, together comprising the capital. The journey had lasted many days, during which time Saya had become accustomed to horse and saddle. She had even ridden on a ferry with the horses. What surprised her most as she crossed the mountain wall was the orderliness of the mountains hemming the capital; that and the way their vivid green slopes crowded in on every side, cutting off the sky. Comparing Mahoroba to her childhood home in the east, and to the countless mountains and rivers they had crossed in between, was like comparing a smooth bowl produced upon a potter's wheel to a rough-hewn wood carving. Here one would find no reedy marshes that took half a day to cross, no precipitous cliffs of red rock rising sudden and sheer in one's path. Everything was delicate and orderly, as if cradled tenderly within the palm of a giant hand. "The vengeful gods of the earth do not reside in this land. That is what makes it Mahoroba," Saya thought.

Nature wielded no power here; rather, power was vested in human hands. The roads, the cultivated fields, the buildings of men, which usually appeared insignificant before the creations of wind and water, had reached their zenith in Mahoroba. The entourage rode past irrigated rice paddies, the water levels of which were carefully regulated. The pale green of the young rice seedlings and the dark purple of the irises along the embankments seemed to melt into the humid haze. A fine silken rain fell continuously, though it posed no hindrance to their progress. Despite the heavy clouds hanging overhead, the sky was bright and glowed like dull nickel. The capital was also clad mysteriously in a light robe of early-summer rain. They passed many people wearing rain cloaks of straw who, on seeing the procession, scrambled off the road and knelt in the mud, not daring to raise their heads until the horses' hooves had passed.

Finally a huge gate set in a tall stockade came into view through the misty white haze. The gate was roofed, sufficiently large to house many people, and heavily guarded. Saya, expecting to see the main hall once she passed through the gate, was surprised to enter a large square from which the road stretched still farther before them. Countless tall buildings, each behind its own wall, lined the road.

"Well," Saya whispered to herself, "how many layers will it take to satisfy them? Mahoroba is just like a set of nested boxes."

They passed through two or three more gates. All she could see was earthen walls, pillars painted cinnabar red, and guards; the place seemed unnaturally still. It was so imposing that Saya, who was nervous anyway, was overwhelmed. When they passed through the last gate, however, the surroundings suddenly brightened. Despite the fact that it was midday, torches burned in metal brackets. The immense main hall, the Palace of Light, soared above them, with two wings extending to either side of its stately structure. People waiting to welcome them thronged the main steps and crowded along both wings of the hall.

Prince Tsukishiro urged his dapple-gray stallion forward to where his herald, who had preceded them, stood waiting respectfully. The horses of his aides halted next, and Saya and the others fell in behind them. When they had dismounted and arranged themselves in an orderly fashion, Prince Tsukishiro uttered a formal greeting in clear, ringing tones.

"We have long been parted, O revered sister. We have returned from the war in the remote lands of the barbarians to the east."

Saya's eyes were drawn to a resplendent figure standing at the top of the main steps. Long golden hairpins fastened her hair in numerous loops, and the ornaments adorning the pins swayed gently, framing her face. White pearls shone on her robes of layered crimson and purple, over which she wore a silver shawl of gossamer silk: a celestial robe. In her ears were charming earrings of jade. More dazzling than these, however, was the beauty that radiated from the Princess herself.

"Let us rejoice at your safe and swift return," replied Princess Teruhi, her scarlet lips brighter than the pillars of the hall. Her gaze and the clear ringing tone of her voice, unusual in a woman, were identical to her brother's. "And how handsome is your figure garbed in armor, my brother, even in the rain."

A wry smile briefly touched Prince Tsukishiro's face. "And you, my sister: the beauty of your figure in a woman's robes surpasses that of your golden armor shining in the midday sun. Even more so when to behold you thus is as rare as a rainbow at dawn."

Princess Teruhi responded to these words with a slight scowl. "Let us leave such banter for later. You had best remove your armor, dry yourself, and rest after your tiring journey. And your companions, too."

Having received her greeting, the entourage began leading their horses to the stables. As she was going through the palace doors, however, Princess Teruhi looked back as though remembering something, and said, "Tsukishiro, when you are finished, we will meet in your hall. And have your new so-called handmaiden attend us."

What followed for Saya was unpleasant. She was placed in the hands of an elderly lady-in-waiting and led off in the opposite direction from the Prince's hall. Although she realized it was outrageous to hope that she might always be near the Prince, she still felt forsaken. Prince Tsukishiro was her sole support, and without him she found everything around her intimidating. She was taken through countless stately buildings connected by passageways to a room which she was told was hers, but it was so far removed that she was sure she would never find her way back to the gate. Feeling like a prisoner, she could find no joy in the room's rich furnishings, its silk screen and fine straw mat. And worse, unlike the other servants at Mahoroba, the lady-in-waiting looked old. She gave the impression of having once been beautiful, but sharp wrinkles were etched in her face, and she had a rigid arrogance, as though assuming that whatever she took for granted was also taken for granted by everyone else. She looked Saya over from head to toe with scornful eyes and, allowing no protest, dragged her back into the passageway. This time she led her to the bath. Saya, who had always washed in the river, and was therefore totally ignorant of baths, found herself in a room with black wooden walls, a large tub, and a main bath from which steam was rising. Two young servant girls waiting in the room approached the astonished Saya, removed her clothes, and drove her into the tub, which they had filled with steaming water. Next they took a rough cloth and began to rub vigorously. The lady-in-waiting stood watching, commanding the girls to rub harder, despite the fact that Saya already felt herself to be subjected to punishing abuse. Unable to endure it any longer, she shook herself free, scooped up hot water in both hands, and poured it over the girls. Shocked, the lady-in-waiting shrieked,

"What do you think you're doing? This is no place for such unladylike behavior!"

"It is unnecessary to skin me alive."

"But you are covered in grime."

"That's not true!" Saya replied.

Perhaps realizing that Saya was not one to give in easily, the two girls relaxed their efforts somewhat. Even so, Saya was sure that her skin had been rubbed raw, but when the heat of the bath had cooled she found that it was not as sore as she had expected. Next they brushed her hair endlessly, clothed her, and tied her sash unnecessarily tight. By the time they had finished and she had returned to her room, it was already dark.

"Well, you look a little better," the elderly woman commented. "Would you like some color for your lips? You're a bit pale."

"No thank you," Saya replied, still fuming. "I'd rather have some food. I haven't eaten for ages."

She was acutely aware that the supper hour had long since passed. Delicious smells had come from the kitchens near the bathing rooms. Having ridden all day without a meal since morning, she was so hungry that it was no wonder she was pale.

"There's no time for that. It is the hour at which I was commanded to bring you to His Highness's presence," the lady-in-waiting replied imperiously. Sensing an undercurrent of spite in her words, Saya said, "It is of no consequence. I will just ask Prince Tsukishiro himself."

The lady-in-waiting drew herself up haughtily. "Surely you would not dare to sully His Highness's ears with such vulgar concerns."

"Oh no. I will simply tell him that I haven't had a bite to eat since we reached the palace."

"Well!" The lady-in-waiting broke off abruptly and, leaving the room, ordered a servant to bring a tray of food immediately. Returning, she continued, "How childish you are! You are not in the least attractive. I cannot imagine how you managed to catch the Prince's eye."

She was silenced, however, when Saya retorted, "And I suppose your attractiveness has caught his eye?" and remained with her back turned, uttering not another word. Besides a bowl of soft rice, the tray brought by the servant held numerous dishes, of which some, such as the fish, mushrooms, and greens, were familiar, and others, such as the dried abalone and sea cucumber, were not. Although Saya left the less appealing dishes untouched, she found the rice delicious.

Urged by the lady-in-waiting, Saya rose and was led hastily through numerous galleries and connecting passageways toward the Prince's hall. Built of plain wood, it was large enough to host a gathering of Saya's entire village beneath its roof. Entering through the double doors studded with gleaming rivets, they passed along a floor of polished white cedar smooth enough to skate on. In the innermost chamber, a canopy hung above the Prince's seat and curtains of fine silk with five-colored cords touched the floor. Before this were placed bearskin seats, each with an armrest attached, for receiving guests. Some fruit was placed upon a small lacquered table. Candlestands stood in the four corners of the room, each before a silk screen, making the pictures stand out brightly. Four strange animals unlike any creatures in this world were depicted there.

Parting the curtains, Prince Tsukishiro appeared. He was totally at ease, wearing a long pale-yellow robe, with his hair hanging loose. The lady-in-waiting knelt before him and bowed low.

"I have brought the maiden."

"You are late," said the Prince with some displeasure.

"I beg your forgiveness, Your Highness. The preparations took time."

The Prince looked at Saya and inclined his head to one side as though contemplating something.

"Servant, remove that sash. Pale blue is better. This color is something my sister would wear."

Saya, who was wearing a crimson sash, blushed.

"To hear is to obey. I will return with another sash immediately," replied the old woman in such a way that only Saya could detect the rebuke in her voice, and quickly left the room. It was too late now to do anything about the woman's deliberate unkindness. Saya raised a miserable face and looked questioningly at the Prince. Surely by now he must be tired of the ignorance of this country girl, but he smiled at her and said, "You prefer light shades, do you not?"

"Yes."

Seating himself on a bearskin, he said, "A pale blue sash will suit you. You should wear one. After all, Sayura always wore that color."

Saya's relief had lasted but a brief moment. The Prince's final words robbed her of strength. She felt even more miserable than before, but it was useless to complain or give up now. She did indeed feel more comfortable wearing the light blue sash brought by the lady-in-waiting, and she determined to concentrate on this thought alone.

Shortly after, a young girl announced the arrival of Princess Teruhi. Noticing Saya's anxiety, Prince Tsukishiro said, "If you're nervous, wait behind that screen."

"Who wouldn't be nervous if the sun and the moon were to appear before their very eyes?" Saya thought as she concealed herself gratefully. She could not control her trembling. Although she was overcome by fear, at the same time she could not let the opportunity to see such a marvel slip away. Soon she heard brisk, masculine footsteps and Princess Teruhi appeared.

The Princess had removed her sumptuous robes and wore only the pale peach-colored inner layer. Pleated trousers with garters at the knees now took the place of the fine skirts she had worn before. It was no wonder that her stride was masculine. She had removed all her ornaments, and her hair hung loose except for two small loops above her ears. Her hair was so long that it fell down her back to the floor.

Looking up at his sister, Prince Tsukishiro said, "Well, well. So you have changed already."

"Of course. I can hardly move in such garments. And I certainly can't sit properly in them," Princess Teruhi replied as she crossed her legs firmly on the bearskin.

There was not a speck of difference between the two faces confronting each other. Yet Saya had never dreamed it possible that they could give such opposite impressions. Like day to night, the spirit of Princess Teruhi was in striking contrast to that of Prince Tsukishiro. The Princess radiated passion; the Prince, sorrow.

Saya could readily understand that people instinctively feared Princess Teruhi more. Her beauty was her intensity. It was a beauty that slew. The faint musky perfume of her aggressive spirit quickly pervaded the room.

Princess Teruhi smiled like a military commander and said, "Is there no wine? Bring the wine! Are we not here to celebrate your safe return, dear brother?"

Other than in her slender form, she gave no sign of being a woman: not in her gestures as she lounged against the armrest, nor in her speech. Yet her behavior was so natural that it was fascinating to watch.

"I am well aware of your wishes, my sister," Prince Tsukishiro replied, and before he had finished speaking, a young woman glided into the room bearing a tray with a slender-necked glass flask and wine cups. Saya had thought that there was little difference between the work of a village maiden and that of a court handmaiden, except that the latter would be charmingly dressed. The young girl, however, was more beautiful and elegant than anyone Saya had seen, almost trembling with pride as she served them, a pride that shone in her face.

Princess Teruhi stared keenly at the maiden and then said to Prince Tsukishiro, "This is not the girl that you brought back with you from the east. I told you to have her attend us."

"You can tell?"

"You underrate your sister."

Prince Tsukishiro said teasingly, "It appears that you have come only to see my new handmaiden, dear sister; not to celebrate my return."

Princess Teruhi stuck out her shapely chin. "And it is obvious that you returned despite the lack of progress in the war solely because of that girl."

Her eyes swiftly swept the room, so that Saya, although she hurriedly ducked behind the screen from which she had been peeking, was too late to escape notice.

"What are you doing there?" Princess Teruhi said sharply, her voice severe. "This is no time for playing hide-and-seek. If you are coming out, then come!"

Saya, her face on fire, reluctantly emerged from behind the screen. Prince Tsukishiro ordered the maiden serving them to leave the room. Then, as if to intercede, he said to the Princess, "She was late, actually. I had no time to tell her what to do."

Saya knelt and, placing her hands on the floor before her, bowed low, saying faintly, "I am honored to meet you. I am Saya, from Hashiba."

"Hashiba?" Princess Teruhi repeated dubiously.

"She was reportedly adopted by an old couple when she was a child," Prince Tsukishiro explained.

Princess Teruhi continued to direct her penetrating gaze at Saya, who could feel those eyes boring through her. "What am I doing here?" she thought.

Saya knew that the woman before her could be considered a

demon, a serpent who had murdered her parents. Yet Saya could not hate her. Although she trembled with fear, at the same time she could not help being drawn to the Princess's beauty.

After a brief pause, Princess Teruhi turned to Prince Tsukishiro and said, "I despair of you, brother. Again and again you find and you lose. And now once more the same thing. Are you not weary of it? Why is it that your nature harbors an attraction to such an aberration?"

Prince Tsukishiro answered softly, "Is it not extreme to call the Water Maiden who yearns for the Light an aberration? Look at her. Do you not want to scoop her up like water in your hands? She is youth, newborn."

With a slight frown, Princess Teruhi brought the wine cup to her lips. "I certainly feel no such desire. Why should I? Not for one who is the hand of Darkness; not for one who is our enemy. She dies, and then returns to life, again and again. That is why she can never escape from eternally repeating the same stupid mistake."

"Perhaps that is so," Prince Tsukishiro said in a low voice. "But might that not be a strength in this world? The reborn know defeat, and yet they know it not. They are naïve, and yet they are not. Without fear, they return to ignorance and continue to hope that they can move a mountain."

Princess Teruhi glared fiercely at her brother. "Where on earth did you acquire such weakness?"

"The outcome of the war in the east is clear. Surely it is permissible to acknowledge the good points in our foes," Prince Tsukishiro replied rather hotly. When his eyes flashed with anger, the resemblance between him and his sister was even stronger.

"Considering that we have the Dragon Sword, they are stubborn in their resistance. That is a fact of which I, fighting on the western front, am well aware."

The Dragon Sword. The name caught Saya's attention, for

she had heard it before. Torihiko had mentioned it. And surely Lord Akitsu had, too.

Princess Teruhi, her elbow on the armrest, with her chin resting in her hand, glanced sharply at Saya. "Look at the little one; her ears pricked up at that. Listen carefully, and you will make a good little spy."

"I came . . ." Saya mumbled, then, forcing herself, said clearly, "I came to the palace to cut any ties with such people."

"I am sure that you speak with all sincerity, but I doubt such a thing is possible," the Princess replied coldly. "I know that you cannot disrupt the Palace of Light, no matter what you might do. Yet, to me, the presence of one of the people of Darkness in our midst is offensive. If you were not one of Tsukishiro's handmaidens, I would have slain you at first sight." Princess Teruhi looked over her wine cup at the Prince and smiled. "Is that not so?"

Although she seemed to speak in jest, her tone was serious. Saya could not help trembling, but she mustered the courage to speak, knowing that to show her fear would only increase the Princess's enjoyment. "I have come here solely to serve Prince Tsukishiro."

Princess Teruhi looked taken aback, and Prince Tsukishiro laughed aloud.

"Now you see, sister. She is an interesting girl."

"An infant will reach out its hand even to grasp hot iron," the Princess said with a snort. "It realizes its mistake only once it has been burned. Whether this child will still appeal to you then is another question."

"I have no intention of letting her get burned," Prince Tsukishiro replied. "I will keep her just as she is."

"Well said," Princess Teruhi sneered. With a scornful smile upon her face, she resembled a sleek and elegant feline. "And I shall see with my own eyes whether or not such a thing is possible.

Why do you concern yourself so over this child of Darkness? I cannot tell whether you are brave or foolish to boldly invite a mortal enemy to your side. Of one thing I am certain, though." The Princess leaned forward and looked coolly at Prince Tsukishiro. "Whenever you tire of the war, you find the Water Maiden and bring her home."

"Teruhi!" Prince Tsukishiro scowled.

Princess Teruhi's eyes gleamed with satisfaction as if to say "I told you so." "I do not understand you, brother. How can you tire of the war that prepares the earth for our father's coming? I have certainly never desired to rest from this task, anxious only for its speedy accomplishment. If it were not decreed that we should govern Mahoroba alternately, I would remain at the battle front. Yet you persist in this perversity, suddenly deserting the battlefield in your attraction to the people of Darkness."

Prince Tsukishiro looked grim. Although he did not show his feelings as much as his sister, his smile was cold.

"There is no need to hurry, sister. There is neither god nor demon who can divert the will of the illustrious God of Light. What is the will of our divine father is the destiny of this world. His arrival will surely occur."

"You are hard-hearted, brother. It is difficult to believe that we are children of the same father," said Princess Teruhi, disgruntled.

"No, I am his child. And what you call my perversity is also of him," Prince Tsukishiro replied quietly.

"Our celestial father does not desire you to sully your eyes with Darkness!" Princess Teruhi shouted, slamming her wine cup down on the floor. Her anger flared like a sudden blaze of flame. Unconsciously, Saya recoiled and gradually began edging away.

"What business does the God of pure Light have with them? Only by the extermination of Darkness will a new and shining world be created. It is for this purpose that our divine father will descend to the earth."

"I did not intend to propose anything to the contrary," Prince Tsukishiro parried. "You always speak the truth, my sister."

Having lost a target for her anger, Princess Teruhi folded her arms and scowled at her brother. "Why is it that you always go round in circles? I have despaired of the youngest member of our family, who is a total failure, but your actions have yet to satisfy me. Why?"

Prince Tsukishiro regarded his sister with an unfathomable expression. Finally he said, "We get along best when we do not spend much time together. When you are at Mahoroba, I am at the battlefield in the east. And when I am at Mahoroba, you are at the battlefield in the west. Has it not been thus since ages past? Yet originally you were our divine father's left eye, and I, his right. Both of us should be looking at the same thing."

Princess Teruhi rose indignantly. Her long hair swept the floor. "Nay, brother, you and I look at all things with our backs turned to each other," she said bitterly, looking down at him. "As you have said, now that you have returned to Mahoroba, I should leave as soon as possible for battle in the west. However, I did not foresee such a sudden return, and thus a mountain of work still remains. We will have to endure each other's presence a little longer until I have completed the work at hand."

With those words, Princess Teruhi stalked out of the room. Only her sweet perfume lingered behind.

After a time Prince Tsukishiro sighed quietly. "It is always the same. We rejoice at our reunion and the very same day we begin to quarrel." Although his whispered words were sorrowful, the Prince smiled when he looked at Saya. "It would seem that the people of Darkness are not the only ones who excel at repeating the same thing over and over again."

"Repeat, repeat. What is it that they say I repeat?" Saya wondered absently. A spool for winding thread came to mind. And the girl who held the spool in her hand as she wound over and over again was someone with a face unknown: Princess Sayura.

"Everywhere I go, they tell me that this is not the first time; that it is a repetition, a rebirth. It's not fair. It's not fair at all, when for me it is all new. In everything I am just groping in the dark."

She was upset at being talked about as if she were some kind of puppet. And at the same time it did not make sense.

"After all, I thought very carefully about what I should do and decided what seemed right for me . . ."

"Do you intend to sleep all day? It's time to get up." Saya jumped at hearing the lady-in-waiting snap at her. "Everyone has gathered in the morning room. The sun rose long ago."

Saya blinked. She did not feel that she had slept at all, yet the morning sun poured through the latticed window and spilled across the wooden floorboards. She could hear sparrows chirping.

"The morning room?" Saya asked, rubbing her eyes.

"We gather together to pay obeisance to the immortal Prince of Light, and then break our fast. If you do not wish to eat, there is no need to rise."

"I'm coming."

She was starving.

After dressing hurriedly, Saya followed the lady-in-waiting along the terrace, but suddenly a horrid suspicion entered her mind.

"Uhm, will you be taking care of me from now on?" she asked.

"I have been so commanded," the lady-in-waiting replied with obvious displeasure. "Most of those honored to become hand-maidens employ both a manservant and a child servant, but as you have none, the extra tasks fall upon my shoulders."

"Oh dear," Saya sighed to herself.

The morning room was long and narrow, situated under the eaves alongside a corridor. Trays were arranged in two rows, and young women with their long black hair neatly tied at the nape of the neck sat before them. Someone at the head of the table had already begun the morning ceremony and the room was hushed. There was a dais at the front with an ornately decorated seat, but the Prince was not present. It seemed that he did not necessarily attend. Saya slid neatly into the last empty place. There were about forty people. A dazzling light poured in from the corridor, and the girls sitting in rows appeared as fresh and elegant as lotus flowers blooming in the early morning. The diverse colors of their garments—white, light blue, pale mauve, grass-green—reflected the season, refreshing the eyes. Most of them were maidens in the first blush of youth, but as far as Saya could tell, she was the youngest.

The ceremony ended, and Saya, mimicking the actions of the others without really understanding, began to eat, but the food stuck in her throat. One after another the women directed cold stares in her direction. And although they whispered among themselves, not one of them spoke to her. Not only that, but they rose one by one and left after barely picking at their food, as if they wished to get away from her as quickly as possible. Saya was soon sitting on her own in the middle of a row of empty seats. While she wondered whether or not to lay down her own chopsticks, she sensed someone approaching. Looking up, she found the two older women who had been closest to the dais standing and looking down at her. Although both were past their prime, they preserved a well-polished beauty. The woman robed in purple appeared to be the older of the two.

"You are the novice who arrived yesterday. His Highness informed us. I am the senior handmaiden and this is my assistant."

"I am Saya," Saya said hastily, placing her palms formally upon her knees.

The assistant, who was wearing indigo and white, raised her sleeve to her mouth, decorously hiding a smile. "It would seem cheap to call you by such a name, don't you think? As if you were a mere servant . . ." There were hidden thorns in her voice. "Let's see. As light blue suits you so well, how would it be if we call you Lady Blue? Would that be acceptable?"

"Yes." Saya nodded uncertainly.

The senior handmaiden continued, "You have reportedly received no training for your new position. We have been commanded to instruct you in etiquette, comportment, prayer, and oracles every day from the end of the morning meal until the evening chores. You must be able to perform your duties by the time of the purification ceremony, which will take place at the end of the sixth month of the lunar calendar. We will be very busy, but you are willing, are you not?"

Feeling their gaze upon her, Saya started and answered hurriedly, "Ah, yes. I entrust myself to you."

She was then guided to a drab-looking building, which she later learned was where handmaidens of lower rank worked, and there she remained without setting foot outside until dusk. She practiced walking for the entire day. She walked from one corner of the room to the other hundreds of times, and by the end she was so exhausted that she could barely stand. The senior and assistant handmaidens, however, paid no heed.

"Tomorrow let us begin practicing how to carry a tray. Come here promptly after your morning meal," and with those words they left. Their departure, like that of the women in the morning room, was incredibly swift. No doubt she would soon undergo training in how to leave a room, Saya thought in exasperation.

As the lady-in-waiting did not seem likely to come and get her, she tried to find her own way through the intricate passages of the enormous complex. At one point she almost collided with some servants who were hurrying along with trays, but otherwise she managed to find her way back to the familiar roof of her quarters without incident. An unexpectedly large number of people passed to and fro along the galleries and passageways. The majority of them were servants: serving girls and child servants wearing ankle-length aprons. The handmaidens ministered to the personal needs of the Prince and Princess, preparing their meals, sewing their clothes, purifying the royal throne. In return, however, they were not required to lift a finger on their own behalf. All their needs were taken care of by other servants. Beneath these servants were more servants, and beneath them again more servants, so that Saya wondered how many people the palace supported as their numbers multiplied. She could not begin to guess.

Walking along the passage after finally locating her own room, she suddenly became aware of voices coming from behind the reed screen of the neighboring room. Several of the handmaidens were gathered there.

"Even some of the servant girls are of better birth than she."

"They say that she didn't even bring a manservant with her. She just sneaked into the palace without a proper ceremony."

"His Highness is occasionally subject to strange moods, you know."

"Anyone with a grain of sense would have restrained themselves, and declined his offer. How brazen!"

Unconsciously, Saya stopped walking. She could have coughed to let them know that someone was there, but practicing how to walk all day had dampened her spirits. The voices continued.

"Did you hear that she actually ate that evening?"

"What! Even though her Highness the Princess is here? Even though the Prince is always ill-tempered when Her Highness resides within the palace walls?"

"Unusual things attract only while the novelty lasts—like girls of lowly birth."

"Let's not let it go to her head. It's ridiculous that she should be considered one of us."

Saya decided to listen no more and walked quietly away.

"Well, I never expected them to welcome me with open arms,

after all," she told herself. "I'm quite satisfied to be a girl of lowly birth. Just think how much better that is than if they knew I was one of the people of Darkness. If they knew that, they wouldn't stop at anything."

She recalled the face of the village shrine maiden as she raised the knife above her head. Would these beautiful, elegant girls become like that? The thought was too depressing, and she shook her head to chase it away. But that night, memories of her home in Hashiba flooded her mind and she could not sleep.

2

Dismal days of drizzling rain continued.

Saya practiced continually, but was puzzled to find that the more she learned, the more distant she felt from the Prince of Light. On the day she had first innocently looked into his face, she had imagined that she could at least partially understand his feelings, whereas now, in Mahoroba, although he was but a stone's throw away, he was fast becoming increasingly awesome and unattainable. He closeted himself within his hall, so that she rarely saw him, and even when she glimpsed him from afar, he never noticed her.

Saya sat on the edge of the porch gazing out through a curtain of rain falling from the eaves. Clouds hung low in the sky, the trees were soaked with rain, and the surface of the pond surrounded by moss-covered rocks in the inner garden was clouded. Though it rained, she never got wet. Any outside business was taken care of by servants responsible for the outer area. How miserable to be imprisoned by damp floorboards and wooden posts, watching the rain like an indifferent bystander! If she could just get her feet wet, just step in a puddle, she would feel how the earth and the plants rejoiced in this weather.

She could not understand why the elite of the palace made such a fuss about getting their hair or feet wet. Without touching the rain, how could they know its variety and the joy it imparted? Of course, depending on the type of cloud, some rain was hard, cold, or bitter. But summer rain was usually sweet and gentle. Each time it fell, it bore a unique and different fragrance from the distant heavens.

On this particular day, the senior handmaiden had suddenly canceled the lesson, and Saya had nothing to do. She was so bored that she felt mold would sprout inside her. Watching a snail crawl along the top of the wet railing, she returned unconsciously to the problem that plagued her.

"Why am I here doing this?"

The other handmaidens continued to exclude her and did not forgo even the most trivial excuse to make things unpleasant, but Saya regarded this objectively as an endurance test. This was not the first time she had experienced such rejection. When she first arrived in Hashiba, all the neighborhood children had ostracized her. No matter how polite, how reserved she was, she could not change them. In the end, it was time that solved the problem. Now, if she neither exaggerated her situation nor whimpered about it, someday the door would open to her. And Saya had no intention of brooding over it. No, the cause of her depression was the unattainable Prince Tsukishiro.

Although she strove not to let the gossip that she had followed the Prince out of vanity bother her, she recognized that it was partly true. The pain in her heart, however, gradually informed her that it was much more than just partly true. The night of the Kagai when they had exchanged look for look seemed like a dream of long ago. She had believed that she alone could touch his heart, and that his was the only gaze that would ever move hers. Responding to his kind words, she had left her home, but her belief had been nothing but the conceit of an ignorant girl, and it hurt to know that the moon, which illuminates the world from on high, could not be grasped even by her hand.

"Why did I believe that I loved him so much?" Saya asked herself. "I followed him here, even brushing aside those who had come so far to meet me." Deep in her heart, she knew that she had fallen for his face. She sank into reverie, remembering the Prince's gently smiling countenance, his handsome profile as he gazed into the bonfire at the Kagai.

"I followed him because he seemed so lonely. Forgetting every-thing else, blindly. But I should never have presumed that it was possible for me, a lowly village girl, to alleviate his sorrow, when his grief is not that of mortal men."

As she became more depressed, she unconsciously withdrew the azure stone from her bosom. Unable to throw it away, and fearful lest someone like the lady-in-waiting should find it, she always carried it with her, and strangely enough, whenever she felt unhappy, looking at the color and curved shape of the stone always comforted her. It was a warm pastel blue, gentle yet at the same time imbued with hidden strength. Gazing at it, Saya thought, "I wonder why the amulet of the Water Maiden who drifts in darkness is such a bright blue, the color of the sky. It's odd."

That day she could not finish her supper. Considering that she felt a pain in the pit of her stomach whenever she saw the senior handmaiden and her assistant, it seemed strange that she could not eat today when there was no lesson. But the lessons, in which sparks often flew, were still preferable to boredom. Anger at least gave her energy. Leaving her food virtually untouched, an unusual thing for her to do, she rose and, for the first time, realized that the other handmaidens never ate much.

"Perhaps everyone here is suffering from melancholy," she thought.

All the handmaidens were as slender as willow branches swaying in the breeze. Saya had always tended to be thin, and although she had filled out somewhat since her childhood, her friends in the village still teased her about her small chest, her narrow waist. Here, however, she seemed to compare favorably with the rest.

Returning to her room, she found the lady-in-waiting already there. Saya braced herself when she saw her kneeling respectfully. The woman had not come for some time, and whenever she did appear, it was mainly to complain or reprimand.

"What is it?"

"I have come to accompany you. Please follow me," she said with some reluctance, and rose. Saya was startled. The lady-in-waiting had uttered such words only once before. After hurriedly smoothing her hair, Saya traveled along the dark passages by the light of an oil lamp held in the lady-in-waiting's hand. Her assumption was correct. She was led far into the palace to the Prince's chamber.

Although a full month had passed, the Prince and his surroundings remained unchanged. It was as if only a day had passed since she had first come. The only difference was that this time the Prince wore white. The Prince himself looked at Saya as though he had met her just recently. Saya felt she alone had aged.

"Just as I thought, that sash is much better," the Prince said with satisfaction, leaning on the armrest, his long hair flowing over his white robe. "And you have dressed well, much better than last time."

"A month has passed, O Prince of Light." While she felt it was useless to remind him, she could not stop herself, although a month must seem no more than the blink of an eye to one who lived forever.

"You have grown even more beautiful in that short time," said the Prince. And immediately Saya felt glad that she had said it.

"Come." Prince Tsukishiro invited her to seat herself on a bearskin. A simple repast had been prepared.

"Would you care for some wine?" the Prince asked. Saya, surprised, accepted the jade-colored wine cup he offered and took a tiny sip. The wine had a slightly bitter taste.

Although both the Prince and the Princess drank wine, they rarely touched their food. The places set for the Prince in the morning room and the evening room were merely a formality, for he never attended. The Children of Light had no need of sustenance from the earth. This thought made Saya a little sad. They were different: they had no connection with the land.

"Why do you cast down your eyes?" Prince Tsukishiro asked curiously.

Saya was surprised that he needed to ask. "I am being instructed in matters of etiquette, Your Highness," she replied. Unintentionally, a note of reproof had crept into her voice, as if she felt her efforts deserved praise. "I have learned many things."

"Etiquette can be very tedious at times," Prince Tsukishiro said. "Customs are formed, and the descendents of men are trapped therein. The generations pass without a chance to weed out the foolish from the essential; a regrettable situation."

Reaching out his hand, Prince Tsukishiro touched Saya's chin and raised her face. Saya felt as if the sky would fall in her shock that the Prince of Light had touched her.

"And you, Water Maiden, aren't you here having transcended those very conventions?"

Unable to speak, Saya could only stare at Prince Tsukishiro's fresh, handsome countenance. To her surprise, her chest constricted and she felt tears well in her eyes. Yet she could not look away, for she had no idea when she would be able to see him again. In a hoarse voice, she managed with great effort to put her thoughts into words. "All I have is now. I cannot transcend anything. I know nothing of the past. I am simply Saya, Your Highness."

"That is your strength. You are able to start afresh," said the Prince almost enviously. "On the night of the Kagai you consented to accept a gift from me, did you not?"

"Yes," Saya replied in a small voice. "And I have come to Mahoroba. But"—her voice became even smaller so that it was difficult to catch her words—"I now realize my conceit."

Prince Tsukishiro looked somewhat taken aback. "Did you think that I would break my promise?"

"No, of course not." Saya shook her head, wiping the tears that fell. "I don't know how to say it. But . . . I didn't realize what it meant to become your handmaiden."

"Little Water Maiden," Prince Tsukishiro said softly, "it seems you really do not understand. That is my fault for not knowing how to hurry."

Running his hand through his hair, the Prince leaned forward, looking at Saya with a merry gleam of mischief in his eyes. "I told you I wanted to give you a betrothal gift. You cannot imagine that I brought you to faraway Mahoroba just to clean and dust. Like this . . ." Prince Tsukishiro took Saya's hand in his and laid his other hand upon it. "I thought that surely you realized that a man and woman who join hands on the night of the Kagai exchange more than just a jewel or comb."

Certainly Saya should have known this.

Her mother had spoken of it obliquely, and her friends had whispered about it. The gift was a symbol of permission to exchange love, and it was love that was most important. It was sacred and mystical, and, looking into each other's eyes, lovers would know how to express it. But the Prince's words took Saya completely by surprise, and her mind, in her confusion, went totally blank. She was so befuddled that she felt like an owl that had fallen out of its nest in midday.

"I—" Gripped by an instinctive fear, Saya tried to pull away.

But Prince Tsukishiro would not release her hand, and her fear, whose cause she did not know, increased. Although he appeared slender and elegant, the Prince's grip was like iron.

"There is nothing to fear. You are the one who said you loved me. Am I wrong?" Prince Tsukishiro spoke quietly, but there was something suppressed in his voice. Saya could sense it, too, in his dark eyes, in his sigh. Flustered, she sent her eyes darting around the room seeking help, but they found only the screens with their overwhelming images of outlandish creatures. Feeling faint, she closed her eyes and was pulled closer to the Prince. She caught the fragrance of anise from his stiffly starched clothes.

At that moment a voice echoed unexpectedly in the room. "Really! You said you would keep the girl just as she is. But no sooner have the words left your lips than you behave like this!"

Feeling Prince Tsukishiro's grip relax, Saya gathered her courage and sprang away. For an instant she was grateful to the speaker, but her savior, Princess Teruhi, stood with folded arms, looking upon them coldly.

Prince Tsukishiro, however, did not seem surprised.

"I thought you would come, dear sister."

"Of course. For I told you that I would see with my own eyes whether you kept your word," said Princess Teruhi, advancing. As usual, she was dressed in trousers, and tiny gold bells attached to the garters below her knees jingled softly as she walked. Her sharp yet sweet scent wafted toward them. "Unlike you, I keep my word."

"Have you made some progress with your work?" asked Prince Tsukishiro, and the Princess glared at him fiercely.

"I am sure that you would love to be rid of me as soon as possible, but the priests wish me to perform the purification ceremony. I will proceed to the campaign in the west thereafter."

"You are certainly more suited to perform the purification, sister."

"Is that sarcasm?" Princess Teruhi snubbed him and, sweeping her hair out of the way, sat down. Her gestures closely resembled her brother's, but she radiated such energy that even his brightness faded beside hers.

Turning to find Saya huddled in the corner, having brought her fear somewhat under control yet unable to leave, Princess Teruhi smiled.

"At times like this, the Water Maiden usually flees without a backward glance. This one seems to have the nerves of a chicken who forgets the heat once the scalding broth has passed its throat. It appears that when you and I are together, her curiosity gets the better of her and she is unable to leave."

Prince Tsukishiro defended her. "That's because she has done nothing of which she need be ashamed."

"She is just a child!" Princess Teruhi snorted, giving the Prince a searching look. "Do you really intend to make such a little innocent your bride?"

Prince Tsukishiro raised his eyebrows. "She will not remain naïve forever. She is not like us, someone who never changes."

"I see. So she will grow feeble and shrivel and die before your very eyes," said Princess Teruhi in a mocking tone, but her eyes blazed fiercely. Only the Prince could withstand the intensity of her gaze, so terrifying that it could make goose bumps rise even on an uninvolved observer.

"That will never be, brother," she said in a low voice. "The Water Maiden will never live long enough to grow old. Soon she will take her own life and slip like water through your fingers. Do you understand, Tsukishiro? I will not tolerate a repetition of this useless behavior. I was not made to live on this earth in order to watch such folly. I will not allow you to make that girl your wife. I will destroy your foolish obsession with my own hands."

Prince Tsukishiro raised his head abruptly. His expression was grimmer than Saya had ever seen it. "What can you do? Although you are better at destruction than at anything else, you cannot see where my passion lies. How then, sister, will you destroy something you cannot see?"

Princess Teruhi's cheeks were tinged with red. She looked breathtakingly beautiful, and dangerous. "And how do you know what I cannot see?"

"Your eyes, my sister, are so fixed on our celestial father's brightness that they can see nothing else."

"Are you saying that you do not love our father, the God of Light?" cried Princess Teruhi in a ringing tone.

"Of course I love him," Prince Tsukishiro replied in as stern a voice as his sister's. "I, too, look for the day when the land of Toyoashihara will be transformed into a land of pure light befitting the coming of our celestial father. That is why we are here, you and I, the demigods bequeathed to the earth."

"And one other, though that one be a failure," Princess Teruhi murmured.

Prince Tsukishiro paused for a moment and then continued. "Even for us, however, a long time has passed since we first stood upon this earth. I never imagined that the purification of Toyoashihara would take this long. And recently I have begun to wonder what our celestial father truly desires . . ."

Princess Teruhi shook her head. "And I cannot help thinking that if you did not repeatedly fall into the snare of the people of Darkness as they strive to make you their ally, they would have been exterminated long ago."

The Princess rose, hands on hips. "You asked me what I can do. Do not forget that it was I who seized the Dragon Sword. If we can but slay the Goddess of Darkness with the Sword, her people will be destroyed along with her. It cannot be long now. As for that girl, she is the last of the Water Maidens."

Prince Tsukishiro looked at his sister, his face an emotionless mask. "As I said, you cannot see the object of my passion."

His voice was very quiet. Princess Teruhi returned his gaze

with a baffled expression, then turned her back on him abruptly. "Of all things, I like least the frivolous words of men," she said and left without a backward glance.

With a start, Saya pressed the palms of both hands to the floor and bowed low. "Forgive me, but I beg your leave to depart. Please pardon my discourtesy," she mumbled hastily and dashed out of the room.

Peering through the darkness, she ran along the wood floor of the gallery, brushing the entangling train of her skirt roughly aside. Perhaps the noise of Saya's steps reached the Princess's ears, for she turned at the corner of the gallery and looked back, allowing Saya to catch up.

"P-please!" Saya leaned against a pillar and gasped for breath, thankful for the darkness. Without it, she could not have spoken thus to someone who inspired such fear in her. "Please! Tell me. How did Princess Sayura die?"

A faint light like starlight seemed to float from Princess Teruhi's clothes as she stood in the darkness. But Saya could see only her slender silhouette, and not the expression on her face.

"Please!"

"Well, well. You are brave, or perhaps 'foolish' would be more apt," said Princess Teruhi, as though scrutinizing her.

"Is it true that Princess Sayura took her own life?"

"Quite true," Princess Teruhi replied. Her tone was masculine, forthright, and unhesitating. "Your people considerately die one after the other. As soon as the odds look bad, you kill yourselves. Of course, you are reborn, but I will never recognize that as a strength. To die is to escape. It is weakness. Try standing in the shoes of we who may never hope to, nay, are not permitted to escape from our difficulties. Do you understand? Because next time you throw yourself into the pond, I will wrap a rake in your hair and drag you out. Be prepared."

Having said this, she walked away. With her departure, Saya

was left in pitch darkness. She slumped down onto the cold floor. Her head ached in confusion. But one thing she had clearly understood.

"Prince Tsukishiro's gaze is not directed at me. Not now, not ever. He does not see me."

At first she had thought he was seeing Princess Sayura rather than herself. But it was not so. Princess Sayura, too, must have known that his heart was not hers and had thus grown weary of life. While drawn to the Water Maiden, in reality he was gazing far into the distance, and even the Prince himself did not understand.

But Saya did, and most likely Princess Sayura had also known. The object of his gaze was Teruhi's reflection glimpsed in the water's surface. A sharp intuition, like the sixth sense of a small animal, gave Saya this insight. That the immortal twins quarreled every time they met was not simply because they did not get along. It was because they revolved around each other like orbiting stars. Just let an outsider try to intrude upon such an unfathomable love-hate relationship, to break the intense bond in which the violence of their feelings caused them to repel each other!

"No mortal can possibly ease the Prince's pain, the rift created by the gods, when heaven and earth were sundered. No one can but the two immortals themselves, the sun and the moon who each represent one half of the other."

Saya knew that she had at last discovered the truth, but it did not help her. She could only meditate on the emptiness of her two open hands.

"Perhaps we should call for the physician? For Lady Blue," the senior handmaiden said to her assistant after Saya had left. The assistant, who was putting away the writing desk, turned and smoothed her hair.

"But she has become much more pliable. With the ceremony

soon to take place, a great weight has been lifted from my shoulders."

"Ah, but it makes me nervous when she is so well behaved day after day. There was a time when she ate a shameful amount, yet recently she hardly touches her food. I wonder if she is ill."

"I see what you mean. It could be." The assistant pondered the problem awhile.

"It would not be good for our reputation if people thought that she had become ill because we harassed her," the senior hand-maiden said, but the quick-witted assistant had already thought of a plan.

"A physician would perhaps be overdoing it. But what if we gave her a child servant? Until now Lady Blue, having no servant of her own, has had to do everything for herself. Perhaps this would ease her burden."

The other woman nodded in agreement. "An excellent idea. And perhaps if she had her own servant, the other girls would be less inclined to treat her as a serving girl."

"Well, as to that, who knows," said the assistant with a faint sneer.

Life was dreary; everything seemed tiresome. This was partly because of the change in climate, for the rainy season had been followed by intense summer heat that beat relentlessly down upon her. But more than anything else, Saya, who had never before lost her appetite from heartbreak, was defeated by herself. Her confidence in every area had evaporated and she no longer even hoped to continue as a handmaiden.

"Perhaps if I fall ill and die, Princess Teruhi will not revile me," she thought, but it would be too galling to become ill among the cold-hearted people of the palace, to be regarded as a nuis-ance. Her longing for her eastern home was keen. There, when the heat became intense, they had swum freely in the river, had brought out a bench at night and slept under the stars. But neither the cool refreshing breeze nor the moisture of the dew reached the deep recesses of the palace. There was only the sun glaring down on the hard dry earth. Summer in the palace hung heavy and stagnant.

One sleepless night, Saya thought she really would die. Although she still had no clear understanding of death, she felt that her soul was flailing wildly as if trying to leave her physical frame and all the confusion it entailed. It no longer mattered whether it was Saya who discarded or Saya who would be left behind. She knew only that if she could just get away from her body, she could get relief, could flee into the bracing freedom of emptiness. Like a bird, something within her beat its wings, poised for the moment of flight.

"If I am to die anyway, I don't want to leave my body lying here," thought Saya. "A purer place—yes, in cool, peaceful water . . ."

She imagined her hair spreading out like a fan on green water, swaying pleasantly like water weeds. "That would not be so bad. It would be a lovely scene."

She sat up abruptly on the woven straw mat. All was quiet and it seemed that the night watch was far away. When she stealthily opened the double doors, the three-quarters moon hung in the midnight sky, casting a clear light. A perfect reflection floated serenely on the still surface of the old pond surrounded by a thick grove of trees. A small black shadow, like that of a little urchin, crouched at the top of the porch steps, blocking her path.

"Who's there?" Saya whispered hoarsely. "What do you think you're doing in front of my room?"

"I have been sent as your new servant," the shadow replied. "I have come to serve you."

"I do not recall summoning you. Get out of my way."

"I have some skill as a physician. I was told that you were feeling unwell."

"I have no need of a physician either," Saya replied firmly.

"Really?" The child's tone suddenly changed. It was a voice she had heard before. Saya caught her breath in amazement.

"Torihiko! Is that really you?" Kneeling down, she could see his large mouth opened in a grin, and his sparkling acorn eyes. Still she could hardly believe it. This boy always appeared at the most extraordinary times.

"Officially I am your servant, Lady Blue," Torihiko said gaily. "The senior handmaiden told her footman, the footman told the guard, the guard told a servant, and the servant grabbed an appropriate-looking person from outside the gate. It seems that even the notorious palace guard has a few holes in its armor."

"But this is insane!" Saya's voice rose and she hastily lowered it. "I don't like it. The two of us together—think what would happen if your identity were known. Even if we tell them we are not plotting, no one would believe us. Why did you come? You know how dangerous it is!"

"I came because I am plotting, of course," Torihiko said coolly. "Why are you always so slow? You heard about the Dragon Sword. Naturally, I came to retrieve the Sword that will determine our destiny."

"Well, it has nothing to do with me," Saya said, and then, suddenly drawing in a sharp breath, she stood up. "You . . ." she said in a low voice, clenching her fists. "You surely didn't plan this all along, that I, an innocent, should come to the palace, just so you could get your foot in the door?"

"I thought I told you before to remember that it was your own choice," said Torihiko, laughing. Saya had no reply to that and peered at him moodily.

"It's all right, Saya. You don't have to do a thing. It's even all right if you love Prince Tsukishiro. You still won't give me away, right?"

Saya primly turned aside. "Don't be so sure. I am a member of the palace now. Who knows what I will do . . ."

"Are you really happy here, as a handmaiden?" Torihiko asked Saya, his voice filled with an unexpected concern. Once again Saya was unable to reply. Before she could stop them, tears began to flow and she reproached herself, wishing she could do something about this new habit of hers.

Torihiko watched her silently while she struggled to control her weeping, and then said calmly, "Let me speak as a physician, Lady Blue: the primary cause of your melancholy is that for too long you have lacked contact with the earth, with water, with green and growing plants. You are not the kind of person who can live apart from these things. Like a wild bird in a cage, you will lose the will to live. You have to get outside."

"Yes." Saya nodded like a little child. "That's true. I've been longing to do just that. I've been longing to do all the things they've said I mustn't do. Just now I could not control my urge to dive into that pond."

"Then don't try to control it. Go for a swim," Torihiko suggested simply. "It's sticky and humid tonight. A swim would be perfect. I need one, too. I stink of sweat."

Saya's eyes grew round. "But it's the palace pond. You wouldn't dare do such an outrageous thing," she started to protest when suddenly her sense of mischief overcame her. It was the first time in a long while. "But then it's so out of the way that the guards won't see us. Maybe no one will ever find out."

"Of course they won't find out. No one here would ever dream of doing such a thing."

At Torihiko's lighthearted urging, Saya stepped from the porch to the ground in her bare feet. The sweet pleasure of earth against her soles. The pungent fragrance of grass and trees in the dead of night. And best of all, the summer darkness wrapping her in a close embrace. There could be no sweeter pleasure than to do what was forbidden. Suppressing her excitement, Saya stole like a nocturnal creature through the shadows until she reached the grove of trees in the depths of the garden. In the darkness, the trees dreamed that they were still part of a deep mountain forest. Enticed by a gentle breeze, the grove was enveloped in the ancient song of the pine, the long-ago tale of the cedar. The moss on the bank was warm and damp; it felt as if she were standing on the back of an otter. Looking at the moon floating on the water's surface, Saya was unable to suppress her laughter. Torihiko was undressed first. He slid into the pond and parted the water with easy graceful strokes.

"You swim like a frog," Saya commented as she slipped into the water.

The water was softer on the skin than river water and filled her with exhilaration. It was the first time she had ever swum at night, but there was nothing to fear. The pond lacked any current and seemed to have been purified by the moonlight. Saya swam like a fish, gliding this way and that, forgetting all her cares. She could now laugh at the troubles that she had previously thought would cause her to waste away. Torihiko's appearance seemed another rich joke. Whatever would be would be.

"Wouldn't it be wonderful just to turn into one of the fish in this pond?" said Saya as she floated on her back. As if in response, a huge carp immediately leaped beside her. For an instant his scales and fins flashed like silverwork in the moonlight. Saya laughed aloud.

"Did you see that, Torihiko? It was the king of the pond."

"Why don't you give him our greetings? Tell him we apologize for swimming in his pond without asking his leave," Torihiko said from the far bank. Pretending to obey his command, Saya dived neatly underwater. Naturally, the water was dark, but, surprisingly, she could see—or rather, she could see the carp. His body seemed to glow with a faint light. He was of a magnificent size, longer than Saya's arm and fit to be called a king. His whiskers were long, too, and his face seemed very ancient.

She could see all this clearly because the fish had swum up close to her, apparently curious. He seemed to know no fear. Then, waving his fins in front of her nose, he spoke.

"So I am not the only one who wishes to become a fish on a summer's night. But if that is your wish, why not turn into a carp? Your body is much too awkward to enjoy swimming properly."

Saya thought it was Torihiko teasing her. In her surprise, she exhaled and had to swim quickly to the surface. When she turned her head, Torihiko was standing on the bank squeezing water from his hair.

"Torihiko!" she screamed without thinking. A sharp stab of fear went through her as she was suddenly pulled under, swallowing a great mouthful of water. She came close to drowning, but Torihiko, who was watching in puzzlement, pulled her out. When she finally lay clinging to a rock, racked by coughs, a light appeared between the trees. Torihiko blinked his eyes in surprise. Two forms stood at the top of the bank: Princess Teruhi, with a torch in her hand, and a manservant carrying a rake.

"I thought I warned you that I would wind a rake in your hair and drag you out," Princess Teruhi said, her voice charged with anger. "Do you wish to drown yourself so badly that you would risk such a humiliating fate?"

"I was just swimming," Saya gasped, still coughing. In her close brush with death, she had mislaid all courtesy. "Get out of my way and let me out, please. There's an evil spirit in this pond. Let me out of here."

"Oho, an evil spirit, she says." Princess Teruhi feigned an exaggerated interest, as if baiting her. "You certainly have some nerve to claim that there is an evil spirit in the Mirror Pond in the very midst of the Palace of Light."

Saya, her coughing finally under control, was slipping on her clothes, her hair streaming with water, but she said defensively,

"It's true. A carp came and talked to me. He looked straight at me and asked why I didn't become a fish like him."

The manservant had his back turned to Saya out of propriety, but his shoulders suddenly began to shake. He seemed to be having difficulty suppressing his mirth.

Princess Teruhi, however, did not laugh. Her eyes narrowed for an instant; then, nonchalantly, she said, "You never cease to entertain us. If you are going to walk around half-asleep, you could at least do it more quietly."

"It wasn't a dream. I would never dream such a crazy thing," Saya said hotly, and then quickly held her tongue as Princess Teruhi's gaze suddenly grew fierce.

"It was a dream. Do not mention it again," the Princess snapped, her voice shaking with anger.

"What on earth could it have been?"

The next morning, Saya still puzzled over it. Her grief and her desire to kill herself seemed unreal now; the evening had ended in farce. Yet, while the desire to die had certainly vanished like a dream, the carp's voice still echoed in her ear. Torihiko, of course, assured her that it had not been he.

"A long time ago, it is said that even the trees and the plants could talk. But in this day when the gods have become so few, it's impossible, no matter how we might wish otherwise. And I can't imagine that one of the gods could possibly still be alive in the middle of the Palace of Light. This is the last place a god would be." Torihiko shrugged. "It must have been your imagination. No doubt it was caused by an empty stomach."

"Even you think so?" Saya said indignantly. But when she thought about it, she was starving. Her appetite seemed to have returned. Once again her normal self, she hurriedly headed for the morning room.

"If I hear that voice again, I'll recognize it," she thought.

She continued thinking while she ate. It was not an evil voice. Rather, it was a young voice: distinctive, guileless, and, considering that she had heard it for the first time, somehow familiar. "Princess Teruhi behaved strangely. It must be because she had an idea whose voice it was. She knows something. There must be something there."

CHIHAYA

I long to fetch water from the mountain brook,
bedecked with Japanese rose,
But alas for me that I know not
the way which I must go.

—Prince Takechi

"The sacred ritual of purification is essential for the elimination of the evil and defilement that unavoidably cling to those who live upon this impure earth, and for the attainment of heavenly purity. Above all, the biannual purification ceremony is essential to preserve the honor of the Palace of Light through the cleansing of the entire area."

The senior handmaiden lectured a group of five or six younger novices, including Saya. "On that day the Prince and the Princess, followed by all those in important positions, will assemble beside the Nakase River at the West Gate and wash all defilement into the river. Therefore you must on no account fail in your task. As the handmaidens of Princess Teruhi's hall will also be performing the ceremony at the river, you must endeavor not to disgrace us." The senior handmaiden placed particular emphasis on the final words. There was considerable rivalry between the attendants of the Prince and those of the Princess. Although Saya sat respectfully, listening with one ear to the lecture, in fact her mind was wandering.

"Her Highness will leave for the battlefield in the west after the end of the month," she thought. "Prince Tsukishiro will be alone. I wonder if his feelings will change once Princess Teruhi is far away. Will he be able to turn to me with his whole heart?"

She was well aware of the futility of such hope. But unrequited love means just that: the inability to live without hoping despite the knowledge of futility. She was gradually becoming aware of her own anxious anticipation.

"If only the ceremony would come soon . . ."

Having emphatically explained the role that the girls must perform, the senior handmaiden asked them in a different tone of voice, "Do you understand the meaning of purity and of defilement? As handmaidens, you must understand better than anyone else the meaning of the bounty bestowed upon us by the illustrious God of Light."

She called on one of the girls to answer. With shining eyes and flushed cheeks, the girl responded readily. "The bounty bestowed by the illustrious God of Light is the transformation of Darkness into Light. Darkness refers to those things which die and decay. The God of Light will descend to purify this earth, which is defiled by Darkness, and to confer eternal life and beauty."

"That is the shrine maidens' creed. Even I could have said that," Saya thought. "I've heard it so often this last month that I'm sick of it."

"Exactly," the senior handmaiden said with a satisfied nod. "The Palace of Light is the sole spot in all the lands of Toyoashihara that mirrors the purity of heaven. You may rest assured in your good fortune at being chosen as handmaidens. If you continue without shirking in your efforts to purify yourselves, someday you may approach the perfection of the Prince and Princess of Light."

She placed a hand proudly on her bosom. "Through the blessed bounty of the God of Light, this is my sixty-fourth year of service as a handmaiden."

At this the girls, who had been sitting with eyes cast down, hoping for the lecture to end, raised their heads simultaneously in astonishment, doubting their own ears. Saya was no exception. Although she had heard rumors that the senior handmaiden was older than she looked, she could not believe she was that old. Even if she had entered service at the age of fifteen, she should long since have been stooped with age.

The senior handmaiden looked at the girls' amazed expressions with pleasure and smiled. "It is essential that you offer yourselves, both body and soul, in service to the God of Light. Through this the road will be opened to you. First you must endeavor to purify yourselves from all defilement."

She gave no indication of being past her prime as she swept her train elegantly aside and glided from the room. Cold and rigid as she was, her beauty was unrivaled. The girls, dumbfounded, watched her departure.

But once she had gone, they immediately gathered together, as though released from a spell, and began to gossip.

"Is it true? Can we really maintain our youth through purification?"

"I've heard that it's true. For it seems that there is no rite as terrible as the purification ceremony."

"Terrible?"

"Because of the human sacrifice."

"No!"

"Shhh!" One of the girls put her finger to her lips. "It is forbidden to speak of it. But they say that the Nakase River is also called the River of Bones. Because ashes and bones are washed away in the river."

"My! How horrible!"

"In other words . . ."

The girls gathered in a corner of the passageway suddenly fell silent. They had remembered Saya.

"Let's go," one of them said loudly, and, turning cold glances in Saya's direction, they quickly left. Saya was disappointed. She wanted to know the rest of the details. It bothered her that someone was to be sacrificed in the ceremony.

"I guess I shouldn't have expected the purification to be a mere ritual like the purification ceremony at our village festivals. After all, this is the Palace of Light."

While she stood thinking, she heard indignant voices raised from the corner of the passageway. It was the girls who had just left.

"My! Did you see that? The serving boy who just went by?"

"He didn't even bow to us."

"Whom does he belong to? Imagine! He was walking across the bare ground!"

As Saya expected, Torihiko came running into view. His outward appearance was proper, his forelock neatly trimmed and his clothes of cool blue linen, but he was cutting across the garden without using the walkway.

"Stop walking across the ground," Saya said with a frown. "Thanks to you, my reputation will be further sullied."

Laughing indifferently, Torihiko perched on the railing and perfunctorily slapped the dirt from the soles of his feet. "That would be silly, when there is a good shortcut. It's only fifty-three steps from your room to here. Do you know how I got here?"

How he remembered she could not tell, but within the space of a few days, Torihiko had mastered the entire layout of the enormous palace and flitted about wherever he pleased.

"Let's go back to my room. Along the walkway," Saya said dampeningly. "I have something to say to you."

Checking to see that no one was near, Saya lowered the reed screen over the door and said, "You know about the purification ceremony, don't you?"

"Sure. Just another five days to go." Torihiko lowered himself to the floor and sat with his knees drawn up under his chin.

"Because I'm a handmaiden I will be one of those performing the ceremony. Purification means to cleanse away the Darkness, you know."

"Yeah."

"Will everything be all right? The entire palace is to be purified."

"There's nothing for you to worry about, Saya. Just do what you would normally do. You have Prince Tsukishiro, and besides, you have never been tainted with the Darkness."

Saya became exasperated. "It's you I'm talking about, Torihiko. Will you be all right even if you undergo purification? Won't you be found out?"

Torihiko tilted his head and rolled his eyes upward. "Well, now—hmmm. I suppose I would not come out safely. I expect I would be singled out just like a bird who doesn't belong is pecked out of the flock."

"It's no joke. You speak so carelessly."

Torihiko grinned broadly at Saya's anger. "I never intended to stay very long in the palace. I'm too conspicuous. For the moment, people are merely offended by me, but that won't last long. That's why I have to make my move as soon as possible and finish my business here."

"Your business?"

Torihiko lowered his voice and said, "To retrieve the Dragon Sword."

"It isn't just an act. He really is a daredevil," Saya thought. For he intended to seize the Sword from the palace all on his own.

"I have a pretty good idea where the Sword is kept. This palace is built with the main hall in the center; Teruhi's hall and Tsukishiro's hall on either side are mirror images. Even the servants' wings are in exactly the same locations. But there is one difference. There is a narrow path leading some distance off from Teruhi's hall. It disappears into a dense grove; I could not see where it leads, but according to some people there is a shrine for the God of Light at the end which only the Princess and certain selected handmaidens are permitted to enter. That shrine strikes me as suspicious."

"And you intend to sneak in there?" asked Saya, who had unconsciously become involved. Torihiko raised a thoughtful face.

"Someone must be stilling the Sword. But as yet I cannot figure out who it could be. The Sword is not safe enough to just leave lying around. It must always be accompanied by a special priestess to still it. There can't be many such priestesses. In fact, I can't believe that there could be one here at all. After all, the Dragon Sword belonged to the people of Darkness for countless generations, and the Priestess of the Sword was always the Water Maiden."

"The Water Maiden?" Saya raised her voice in surprise.

"That's right." Torihiko nodded. "You probably didn't know, but the Dragon Sword is the same one that the God of Light used to slay the last-born son of the Goddess, our mother. Fury, malice, and damnation were seared into the Sword when it was stained with the blood of the fire god. It has the most fearsome power existing in the world today. The Dragon Sword owes allegiance to neither the Darkness nor the Light."

Torihiko's eyes glowed with excitement. "In other words, it is the one weapon that could destroy even the God of Light himself."

"But that's extraordinary," Saya whispered. "Who could possibly slay the God of Light?"

Torihiko suddenly shook his head. "You're right. Nobody can touch the Dragon Sword, except for the Water Maiden, who is able to still the curse of the fire god. Even Princess Teruhi had to abduct Princess Sayura, the most recent Water Maiden, in order to capture the Sword. That is how Princess Sayura came to Mahoroba."

"Ah, I see," Saya sighed. "So that's how it happened."

"Everyone did his best to rescue her. But it was no use, whether Princess Sayura liked it or not."

Saya remained silent. She could understand what Princess Sayura must have felt, yet at the same time she did not want to.

Torihiko scratched his head. "I heard all this from Lady Iwa. That old lady, she alone remembers everything. For you and me, it all took place in a former life."

"And I . . ." Saya spoke hesitantly. "Do I also have the power to still this terrible Sword?"

"Probably." Torihiko threw her a quick glance. "Are you willing now to get it back?"

"Not in the least," Saya replied emphatically. "I would gladly give it away."

"I see. Too bad," Torihiko said without any apparent regret. "If that's the case, I will just have to do as Princess Teruhi did and steal the priestess along with the Sword."

"That's outrageous!" Shivers ran up Saya's spine. Torihiko was just like the boys who set off to explore the mountain behind her home, boasting that they could do the impossible. But in this case, Torihiko's life was at stake.

"Don't underestimate the Palace of Light," Saya warned. "And besides, Princess Teruhi is of a totally different class. Quit this foolishness and leave immediately. If you go now, you will make it in time."

"I'm doing what I want," Torihiko said teasingly. "That's what you said, too. Just leave me alone, you said."

"But you will surely be killed!" Saya found herself shouting.

What Torihiko was thinking she could not tell, but the eyes he raised to Saya's face seemed full of compassion. "It would be strange for one of the people of Darkness to fear death. Don't worry. I do not intend to throw my life away needlessly."

"Don't worry, he said. How could I not worry?" Saya changed the position of her pillow. No matter how she tried, she could not sleep. The night wore on and a slight breeze blew through the half-open latticed shutters. Shell wind chimes hanging from the eaves made a dry sound as they swayed, faintly disturbing the still darkness. Lying anxiously awake, her eyes wide open, staring up at the darkness where it nestled against the ceiling, she felt she could see the faintly colored, shapeless forms of the dreams of those sleeping within the palace flitting across it. While she followed their aimless paths, she had a sudden shock of realization, as if she had stumbled across a large gaping hole.

"Torihiko was lying when he said he wasn't afraid of dying. No one, not even one of the people of Darkness, wishes for death."

The more she thought about it, the stronger her conviction grew.

"He came here knowing that the purification ceremony would soon take place. For me, to help me. It was Torihiko who saved me from the shrine maiden's blade. Twice he has pulled me back from death. How foolish of me to forget."

She was stung by remorse.

"No matter what he says, I'll make him leave. If I don't, it is the same as standing by and letting him be killed. Though he speaks brazenly, after all he is still younger than I. He can't be so eager to die. He can't be indifferent to death."

"Look at that. What are they?"

"I don't like it. What could they be up to?"

Saya heard surprised voices outside her door. Thinking from their disgusted tone that it must surely be Torihiko, she rose and went outside. But the boy was nowhere in sight, and two handmaidens were looking up at a tree in the garden.

"Is something wrong?" Saya asked.

One of them pointed to a red pine. "They've been sitting there like that for over an hour. We saw them last time we passed by. They give me the creeps."

"Perhaps it's an omen."

Saya looked and saw two large crows, black eyes gleaming, perched saucily upon a branch high in the gnarled pine tree. Then, as if they could understand the speech of the two frowning handmaidens, they suddenly began to screech. Their cry was deep and menacing. The two girls jumped in fright and fled. Saya remained staring at the crows. Although she could not tell, it was just possible that . . .

"Sa-ya," the crows cried indistinctly.

Saya, looking about quickly in consternation, ordered them to hush. "You're Little Black and Big Black, aren't you? You can't stay here."

But the two crows ignored her words and flew happily to the boxwood tree in front of the eaves. Saya stepped back. Seen close up, the sharpness of their huge beaks was fearsome.

"Food," they cried somewhat plaintively.

"Get it from Torihiko. Go on now," Saya said severely.

But the crows bobbed their heads up and down as if trying desperately to shake out the words, and finally cried, "No food."

"None."

The crows shook their wings discontentedly. Saya tried to think of something handy to feed them, but before she could, she heard voices behind her. The two handmaidens had brought a guard.

"Over there. Shoot them. Quickly."

Saya waved her hands frantically at the crows. "Flee! Hurry!"

Beating their wings, Big Black and Little Black took to the air. By the time the guard with his bow and arrow turned the corner, the two birds had flown over the roof.

"That's strange," thought Saya. "Come to think of it, I haven't seen Torihiko since yesterday . . ."

After that, Saya waited and waited for Torihiko to come, but it was no use. She waited until the sun began to set and then made up her mind to go to the senior handmaiden.

"My servant hasn't appeared since last night. Could something have happened, perhaps?"

The senior handmaiden was untying a scroll by the light of a lamp and avoided raising her eyes to meet Saya's. "To whom are you referring?"

"I cannot find my servant," Saya persisted.

The older woman rested the scroll on her knees and looked over her shoulder coldly. "Is that so?" she said in an expressionless tone. "Then let us summon another servant as soon as possible."

"Has something happened to Torihiko?"

The senior handmaiden gazed remotely at Saya, whose tone of voice had become unconsciously harsh, and replied, "Such shameful behavior. What are we to do if someone who claims to be a handmaiden makes such a fuss about a servant or two? It seems that you did not devote yourself attentively to my instruction. I thought I told you about the need of a sacrifice for the purification ceremony."

"I did listen attentively," Saya replied. "All defilement is transferred through the purification rite to the sacrificial offering within a metal cage, and after cleansing by fire, it is washed away in the river. I know the procedure. But what I want to know is—"

"Exactly. That is the answer to your question," the senior handmaiden said. "He has been chosen as the sacrificial offering by Her Highness, Princess Teruhi."

Saya stood with her mouth agape, unable to utter a word. As the meaning gradually penetrated her mind, the blood drained from her face. "But that—that's—"

"It is not something of which to speak lightly," the senior handmaiden admonished her sternly. "You have no right whatsoever to complain. After all, it was I who found that boy for you in the first place. All servants of the palace dedicate themselves body and soul to Their Royal Highnesses. You must realize that those who are chosen, despite their lowly birth, are gloriously honored."

She picked up the scroll once more. "You may leave. And do not trouble me any further."

Although the woman had turned away, Saya was unable to move from the spot. Collecting her scattered wits, she asked,

"Where might he be, he who has been chosen for the sacrifice—"

The senior handmaiden turned her head, showing undisguised contempt. The deep cleft between her brows marked her face with a startling ugliness. "Are you deaf?"

Saya could do nothing but retreat under that threatening glare. With her head reeling, she staggered out onto the porch. She grasped the railing and fought down her horror.

"What a terrible place I have come to. The palace is a dreadful place—a dreadful place."

She had thought that the ritual for purification was perfectly normal when they had been instructed in the procedure. Even the references to a human sacrifice had not concerned her much until Torihiko had been selected as the victim. But now she fully realized that the handmaiden's true role as priestess was to transfer people's defilement to another human being, to burn that person alive, and to wash the remains into the river!

Twice a year for countless generations, the purity of the Palace of Light had been maintained through this means.

"I will be killing Torihiko with my own hands."

At this thought she gave a moan of despair. Prince Tsukishiro's hall, shielded by a fence, towered in front of her, its ornamental crossbeams soaring against the red evening sky. The senior handmaiden's room was the closest of the attendants' quarters to the Prince's hall. Staring across at it, Saya felt that the fence that rose black and tall between herself and the Prince had never been so high.

"I must find out where Torihiko is. Somehow . . ."

It was time for the evening meal. She decided to make her way to the kitchens around the back. The servants gathered in the courtyard to the north of this building to take their supper. Thick clouds of steam and heat billowed from the earthen-floored kitchens where the sweat-drenched cooks labored beneath soot-blackened beams. Saya was astonished at the size of the ovens and pots used to feed the populace. They had gathered around an enormous pot to ladle a stew containing all sorts of things into large bowls. The child servants were eating the same fare, and they nursed their bowls carefully as they escaped into the cool back garden. Table manners were unknown and no one scolded them. Filled with the friendly clamor of people enjoying their meal, the place was in a lively uproar. To Saya, their meal appeared much more appetizing than her own. It was like what she had eaten at home in Hashiba.

Catching sight of a group of boys sitting on some rocks, totally engrossed in shoveling food into their mouths, Saya walked toward them. They must surely know Torihiko.

"Have you seen Torihiko?"

One of the boys raised his face to look at Saya and almost spilled the contents of his bowl in his surprise at seeing a long-robed handmaiden standing before him. "Nah. I dunno—I mean, he has not yet arrived, ma'am."

"Stupid. He won't never come," the boy beside him muttered.

"Oh. Right."

"He's probably being made to clean the shrine in punishment."

Saya, feigning ignorance, asked, "Why won't he come?"

"Someone from Princess Teruhi's hall took him away. I think there was some complaint. He was always wandering around that place even when he had no business there."

Across from Saya, one boy whispered to another, "He boasted that he would sneak into the shrine. If Her Highness knew that, he would get a hundred lashes."

The boys knew nothing of the sacrifice. Saya felt a pang of sorrow. Who would ever tell them? If they knew that one of their friends was to be burned alive, they would not continue to serve here.

Leaving the kitchens behind, she felt a faint spark of anger kindle in her breast. This was no childish anger, flaring and fading with her changing moods, such as she had known before. It was the first true anger that she had ever felt.

The lady-in-waiting appeared in her room and knelt before her, saying, "I have come to accompany you."

Saya was startled but immediately bit her lip and said, "I am ready."

The lady-in-waiting drew in her chin, faintly surprised by Saya's tone. "Is something wrong?"

"No. Nothing," Saya replied flatly, and saw a vexed expression cross the other's face. Tonight Saya had the advantage. She was not to be trifled with by the likes of this woman. The two passed wordlessly along the corridors.

"I have brought Lady Blue," the lady-in-waiting announced through the door and then withdrew.

Saya stepped forward, knelt with both hands on the floor before her, and bowed low.

A bark of laughter broke the silence. Saya raised her face and saw Princess Teruhi at Prince Tsukishiro's side, leaning languidly toward him.

"I was curious to see what face you would wear tonight," the Princess said with a mocking laugh. "You have spirit at least, and that is something. I hate whimpering."

Saya cast her eyes down demurely but felt a sudden hostility within her. After all, didn't Princess Teruhi always come between her brother and Saya? Every time Saya had been summoned to his hall it was so.

"Your Highness," Saya said, turning to Prince Tsukishiro. Unlike his sister, the Prince did not mock her but, rather, seemed sympathetic.

"Come," he commanded, and Saya approached him deliberately from the side opposite to Princess Teruhi. "I have heard that your servant has been chosen as the sacrifice. How-

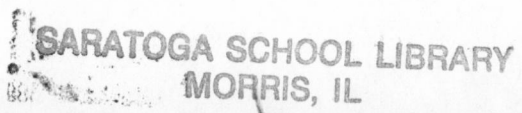

ever, you must surely know the reason for this choice."

Saya's fingertips, placed decorously before her on the floor, trembled. But she said in a brave voice, "I intended to dismiss him this very day. I will not allow him to come near the palace again. So please, grant him your pardon."

"Do you really believe such a thing is possible?"

Saya looked squarely at Prince Tsukishiro. "Yes, I do. Like the shadow of an insect straying within these walls, he is unworthy of your notice. It is possible for you to overlook him, just as you allowed me to enter this palace."

Prince Tsukishiro laughed wryly. "That you can say such a thing so innocently is very fetching. But it is not possible to free the sacrifice. You must be purified."

Saya was checked by the Prince as she was about to speak. "This is your test. As long as you remain attached to that servant, you cannot be cleansed of Darkness. By completing the purification ceremony in public, you will become a true handmaiden and attain your rightful station."

Throughout, Prince Tsukishiro's voice remained gentle. "I intend to make you my bride. This is permitted to a handmaiden. Once the end of the month has passed, we will have a formal ceremony. Your station will exceed even that of the senior handmaiden."

Saya was speechless with astonishment. "I—you mean me?"

"Is it not to your liking?"

"But I am not qualified."

Prince Tsukishiro gave a captivating smile. "Once again you protest. Yet you are the unrivaled Princess and priestess of your own people."

She could not tell him that she protested because she did not believe he loved her enough to be his wife. It was no ordinary man but the Prince of Light who was asking her to be his bride. And, she thought gloomily, what sacrifice might she have disregarded had his gaze been only for her?

"She will surely reject your offer," Princess Teruhi said, gazing around the Prince's shoulder at Saya. "The people of Darkness are always more concerned for their comrades than for themselves. If her friend is killed she will never open her heart to you again."

Prince Tsukishiro said without looking at her, "Sister, Saya and Sayura are different. Saya is a child of Hashiba. She is not kin to Darkness."

"I despair of you."

"I am a child of Hashiba," Saya said, contemplating the words. "My father told me to take pride in that. And I intend to do so."

Prince Tsukishiro nodded. "That is best. Be purified. As a child of Hashiba, as one of the people of Light. And your undefiled youth will last longer than that of any other."

Princess Teruhi looked at Saya like a cat teasing a mouse. "Tonight the moon rises late. It is a fleeting summer's night," she said brightly. "I shall stay here till daybreak and talk the night away. Handmaiden, you may leave us. I summoned you merely to see if you wore a tearstained face. You had best strive to purify yourself and cleanse yourself of defilement. If you understand that, go. Inform my servants that I shall not be returning to my hall tonight."

Saya bowed, her face as rigid as stone. "I beg leave to depart."

When she had fled from the room, Prince Tsukishiro looked reproachfully at Princess Teruhi. "Was that spite? You are unkind."

"To take one such as her for your bride dishonors the name of the Palace of Light," Princess Teruhi retorted angrily.

Prince Tsukishiro laughed and shook his head, then took the glass flask and poured some wine into his sister's cup.

"Sister, do you not see that this is one way to destroy an enemy? Think what a blow it will be to the forces of Darkness if I make the Water Maiden mine. You wish to kill her, but if you do, she will only return to the Darkness and be reborn again. Instead,

I will protect and nurture her innate attraction to the Light."

"Well, after all, I am just a woman whose sole talent is destruction," Princess Teruhi replied sarcastically, turning away. "Anyway, the trap is set. If she shows her true colors as one of the people of Darkness, I will brook no argument from you. I will throw her into the iron cage along with the sacrifice and burn them both alive. That way I will feel much easier about leaving for the campaign in the west."

"Well, it does not matter." Prince Tsukishiro raised his cup slightly. "I cannot argue with you. Not if you really intend to spend the night here."

"Of course. Do you think I would fight with you?" Princess Teruhi replied and, gazing at the Prince, suddenly laughed unreservedly. "We should be able to pass the night without quarreling. For the end of the month draws near."

"Yes, the end of the month draws near," Prince Tsukishiro repeated. "The moonless, sunless night approaches once again, the night that comes but once a month to our illustrious palace."

Hearing the concealed hope trembling in his voice, Princess Teruhi grinned rakishly. For a brief moment his concern conveyed to her the fragrance of falling blossoms. Stretching out a graceful arm, she caressed his cheek with her hand, and placed her lips which carried her sweet breath upon his.

2

Saya was so furious that she felt like kicking something as she walked along the passageways. Princess Teruhi toyed with her heart as with a bauble. " 'Inform my servants,' she says. Does she think she can use me as she pleases? I am not her servant. I'll go back to my room and sleep."

But as she walked, her initial anger cooled and changed to an aching pain that snaked its way through her. Strangely enough, it was not the malicious words of Princess Teruhi that had wounded her, but rather Prince Tsukishiro's proposal to make her his bride. It had been her greatest wish, although she had scarcely dared to dream of it. If only it could be achieved by other means.

Yet she still believed in the righteousness of the immortal Children of Light, and could not cease to worship them. Their splendor remained unclouded, and even their brutality, their disregard for other lives, was pure. For them, human sacrifice was as simple an act as wiping the dust from one's chair before sitting down, and they probably viewed the total extermination of the people of Darkness in the same way. They felt neither rancor nor prejudice. But for the same reason they could never feel any love for the creatures of the earth. Never.

"Or for me either. Even if his intention to make me his bride is sincere."

Although it was painful to acknowledge, she could no longer deny it. Now when she imagined herself as Prince Tsukishiro's wife she felt chilled to the bottom of her soul.

"Is this what it means to purify oneself?"

Depressed, she entered her room. The light was out and it was pitch-dark. She fumbled about for the lamp stand and took out the flints from the box beside it. But as she was about to strike the flints together, she stopped. In the darkness, Torihiko's face came vividly to mind, as did his mocking laugh, his affectionate gaze, his nimble limbs. She remembered his face the time he had snatched her green belt from the river, his easy stroke when swimming in the moonlit pond. Even supposing that the supreme God of Heaven had commanded that these things should be erased from the face of the earth, how could she not oppose it? Torihiko was someone she knew, someone whose blood pulsed in his veins, who moved, who raised his voice in laughter.

"If to be like the immortal Children of Light means to forget Torihiko, to remain calm and indifferent, then it is impossible for me. If I do that, the me I know now will die, too. I cannot be purified. I belong—to the people of Darkness."

Without realizing it, her hands, which gripped the flints, had fallen to her sides; her knees buckled, and she sank to the floor. She was amazed at herself and asked her heart once more to be sure. But the answer was clear, intensified by its release from long restraint.

"I belong to the people of Darkness."

Saya could not help but feel sorry for herself, a fledgling who had seared its wings trying to soar to the moon; but the knowledge that there was something she must do brought strength to her limbs. Quietly replacing the flints in their box, she thought carefully. "If I do not light the lamp, everyone will think that I am still at the hall. If I am to do anything, it must be now. Tomorrow the three days of purification will begin and the guard about the palace will become even tighter."

Torihiko must be held in the shrine he had told her about. She could not think of any other place he might be. Fortunately, Princess Teruhi was far away in Prince Tsukishiro's hall . . .

Saya felt a twinge of doubt. Had Princess Teruhi purposely emphasized the point that she would remain in the Prince's hall? Was it a trap?

"I can only try it and see."

Once roused, she could not imagine being able to sleep. She took out a long dark purple cloak from the chest of drawers in the corner and, wrapping it about her, stole carefully out of the room.

The rustling of the cloak against her skirt, which she was usually not conscious of, made her nervous. Although she regretted wearing it, it was too late now. Once past the main hall, she was in unknown territory. The palace grounds were strictly divided into Princess Teruhi's in the east and Prince Tsukishiro's in the west. Although the handmaidens lorded it over others within their own area, one step outside and they would be regarded with glances colder than those afforded the servants. She knew the layout of the two halls was identical; but lacking Torihiko's sense of direction, she often had to stop and think. She also had to take care that she did not cross the path of the palace guards who patrolled the gardens.

Still, she did not feel much danger. This was owing in part to her excitement, and also to her realization that the dark was an ally. In fact, she should have understood this the night she swam in the pond. Despite the darkness, her sight had remained keen, and even the blackness into which shadows seemed to melt had not frightened her. Her parents, believing that an indescribable demon lived in the dark, had forbidden her to go out at night, and she had been afraid. But now, knowing that only she herself was concealed by the darkness, the black curtain of night was a friendly robe that protected and enveloped her. As she became accustomed to the dark, she also became extremely sensitive to light, always noticing the guards with their torches before they saw her. With each encounter, her confidence increased.

"Torihiko used to sneak about just like this."

She felt she could understand him. Although it made her feel slightly guilty, she could not deny that she felt a tingle of pleasure.

She made her way undetected to Princess Teruhi's hall. Skirting the handmaidens' quarters, she climbed over a hedge and, heading toward the grove of trees, soon came across a wooden fence more than twice as tall as she. The fence was solid, built without a single crack between the boards, and it surrounded a large area. No doubt the shrine was within this fence. She walked alongside it until she came to the rear of the enclosure, but her heart sank when she saw the entrance. A bright watch fire burned near the gate, which was bolted with a heavy bar, and two guards bearing spears stood motionless before it as though rooted to the spot.

She hid in the nearby bushes and stared at the gate for a while, but finally turned away, realizing that even if she stayed here all night, there was nothing she could do. It would be impossible to sneak in without some sort of plan. Cursing herself for her lack of foresight, Saya was retracing her steps to the hedge of the garden near the handmaidens' quarters when she suddenly froze in her tracks. Someone else was moving about without a light in the middle of the night. And there was more than one person.

"Have they seen me?" she wondered.

For the first time that night she felt the cold sweat of fear, and she concealed herself under the garden hedge, pulling her cloak about her. The figures in the darkness continued on, however, showing no sign of looking for someone. Soon they stopped and gathered together to perform some task. It was not hard for Saya to guess what they were doing. The dry scraping sound of a bucket, the muffled sound of water deep underground, echoed in the stillness of the night. A well. The figures who had come into the garden had gathered at the edge of a well and were drawing water with awkward, jerky movements. To judge from their laborious efforts and their figures, they were quite old. Curious, Saya drew a little closer, following along the hedge. As she had suspected, they were three old, hunchbacked women.

They poured the water into an earthenware jar until one of them whispered hoarsely, "That's enough. It's overflowing."

"Oh, already?" another exclaimed in surprise, dropping the bucket to the bottom of the well with a loud clatter.

"The water of the star well must not be carelessly wasted."

"It was just a little."

Yet another of the women gave a deep sigh. "Hasn't Her Highness returned?"

"Not yet. Tonight we must carry the water."

"Will she not come back?" the woman lamented. "It seems to me that we are not equal to the task at our age. It is difficult for these old bones to climb those steps."

"I wonder if the one within will struggle tonight."

"Those bonds cannot possibly be broken. Her Highness has tied them with exceeding care."

"But still . . ."

"The poor thing. Our blindness is a blessing."

One of the women picked up the water jar. "Well, the water is drawn. It is time to go to the shrine."

Saya's heart began to pound violently. These old women must be the priestesses who, along with Princess Teruhi, were permitted to enter the shrine. Although she was amazed to see anyone so aged and decrepit within the palace, she was even more surprised that all three of them were blind. The existence of such women was a shock to Saya, who had grown accustomed to the fact that all the inhabitants of the palace down to the lowest servant were perfect in face and form. She did not know whether the old women had lost their sight in order to be allowed to enter the shrine or had been specially selected because of their blindness, but in any event, it was obvious that the shrine was extraordinarily sacrosanct.

Staring after the priestesses as they returned to their quarters, tapping their canes along the ground, Saya racked her brains.

"How am I to get in?"

A short while later the old women reappeared. This time all three were wrapped in long white shroud-like garments. The cloth covered their heads, and a fold at the front concealed even their faces. Only their canes protruded from the front of the garments. They looked like white pillars of cloth feeling their way along. Darkness made no difference to them. From the confidence in their steps, Saya suspected that they had trodden this path for countless decades. When she saw that the procession was heading for the wooden gate out of the garden, she crept under the bottom of the hedge and waited beside it. One priestess and then another passed directly in front of her. The last, weighed down by the water jar, was slightly slower than the others. Saya reached out her hand and deftly hooked the hem of the woman's garment with her finger. The priestess, who held the water jar in one hand and her cane in the other, was unable to restrain a cry of dismay when she felt her wrap slipping.

"What's wrong?" The two women in front halted.

"Nothing, nothing. Don't trouble yourselves. I just caught my hem on a branch protruding from the hedge. It seems that the gardener hasn't been doing his job," the last priestess said in some embarrassment. "You go on ahead and have them open the gate of the shrine. I'll soon catch up."

The two continued on while the remaining priestess set down her water jar and stooped to gather her wrap. There was no time to hesitate. Biting her lip, Saya raised her arm high and brought her fist down upon the nape of the woman's withered neck. It was a trick that she had learned in the days when she had played with the village boys, guaranteed to make an opponent's head swim without inflicting injury. She had never had the opportunity to use it in a real fight and thus she had no idea that it would be so effective. The old priestess sank to the ground without a murmur. It was almost shamefully easy.

"I'm sorry," Saya apologized silently. She swiftly dragged the priestess through the wooden gate and, laying her in the shadows as comfortably as possible, covered her with her own cloak. She then wrapped herself in the priestess's garment, picked up the cane and the water jar, and hurried to the shrine enclosure.

The first two women were waiting there. The gate was open. Saya approached them in a cold sweat, taking great pains to mimic the walk of an old woman, but it seemed that her efforts were unnecessary, for as soon as they saw her cane the guards at the gate bowed respectfully and let her inside without question. To her great relief, they did not attempt to touch her. She crossed the threshold and stepped within the shrine enclosure.

The grounds within the fence were paved with uniformly round white pebbles that glowed faintly in the starlight, and they appeared even more extensive than they actually were. Amazed at her own boldness, Saya stole surreptitious glances at the sacred precincts from the shadow of her wrap, her eyes full of wonder. The shrine stood near the back of the sanctified garden, its side facing her, and small storehouses were built around it. Behind it rose the dark grove of cedars, their sharply pointed tips thrusting up into the night sky. A cool breeze carried their tangy fragrance and the wild perfume of honeysuckle. Saya thought that she must be near the foot of the mountains. Even in comparison with the rest of the palace, an exceptional aura of purity pervaded the area. The empty white garden looked like a river from heaven which had descended into the depths of the night and upon which the shrine floated. The regular sound of the priestesses' footsteps on the round pebbles dissolved into the overall tranquillity. Saya shuddered, feeling an uneasy foreboding, as though she would never be able to return again to where she had come from. The water jar was heavy in her arms, and the water slopped up and down as if to aggravate her uneasiness.

The procession finally reached the shrine. The building appeared small to one used to the large buildings of Mahoroba. But it was tall for its size, with a raised floor as high as a granary's. A grown man could easily walk between the round columns under the floor. The space beneath the building was as spotless as the garden, and the central column was encircled by a rope of braided straw and surrounded by sakaki branches set in the ground. In the narrowest side of the shrine were double doors, with a single, treacherous-looking ladder leading up to them. The ladder was just a narrow log not even the width of her foot, and shallow notches provided the only footholds. And of course there was no handrail. The priestesses stood side by side at the bottom of the ladder and prayed soundlessly. Saya, casting a sideways glance in their direction, mimicked them. After standing this way for some time, one of the priestesses said, "You must not be timid. As Her Highness is not here, it is you who must take the water inside."

"We implore you not to fail in your duty," the other priestess added.

At last Saya realized that she alone was expected to perform the acrobatic feat of walking up the log. She stepped forward, wondering how on earth a blind old woman carrying a swaying water jar could possibly do it. One slip of her foot and undoubtedly she would fall. She swallowed hard as she looked up its length, then, summoning her courage, placed her foot upon it. She would have to do it before she lost her nerve. Success or failure depended upon her mettle. She did not fall. Her body lurched and swayed, but somehow she made it. The doors were of white wood studded with rivets, like the doors of the palace. She pushed against them with the force of her ascent and they opened without a sound, as if beckoning her within.

The bright light of torches struck her eyes. Torches in iron brackets burning with an intensity too great for mere illumination were ranged in two rows stretching to the far end of the shrine. Raising her eyes, she saw high ceiling beams blackened with soot, while the floor beneath her feet was so smoothly polished that she could see her reflection. She frowned, struck by a strange uneasiness. She felt that somehow this had all happened before.

"But that can't be."

She closed the door and began walking cautiously. The farther she went, the more her uncertainty about herself and her surroundings increased. She felt as though she were walking on a cloud. Her shadow, summoned by the light of the torches, fled before and after her, whispering. But when she stopped to listen, she seemed to lose touch with herself and she was afraid.

"Relax. What did you come here for? Wasn't it to rescue

Torihiko?" she reasoned with herself. At that moment she saw before her a brilliantly shining altar . . . a forest of sakaki branches placed as offerings . . . snow-white banners . . . an altar of cypress wood gleaming bright as day. Saya caught her breath and stood riveted to the spot, memory flooding back.

"It is the altar from my dream. This is where I met the shrine maiden."

A quiet terror crept up through the soles of her feet, and she began to shake as if with fever. It was a fear the very quietness of which seemed to push her to the brink of insanity. Her reason, no longer to be governed, fled, and Saya was suddenly a girl of six again. Her rigid body refused to move. And there before her very eyes, like her dream come to life, was her worst nightmare, her greatest fear: a white-robed, black-haired shrine maiden kneeling before the altar with her back to Saya. This time, surely, it was a dream from which she would never wake again . . .

3

For an instant Saya must have lost consciousness. The water jar slipped from her hands and fell to the floor. It shattered, drenching her from the knees down, and the cold shock of the water brought her back to her senses. Stepping aside, she realized with a jolt that this was not her dream, and became aware of what she was doing. Saya raised her eyes from the puddle of water and met the gaze of the shrine maiden, who had turned around to face her.

"See. She has a shadow. She's only a human being," Saya told herself calmly. "Now what were you so frightened of?"

The girl looking up was as young as Saya and certainly gave no cause for fear. Like the maiden in Saya's dream, she was clothed in pure white and had long, glossy hair, but her face held nothing but innocent surprise. She did not even show any sign of caution toward this stranger. And just as in Saya's dream, she was beautiful. Taller than Saya, she was endowed with a refined grace, and her slender face had a comeliness that was rare to behold. Her gaze was clear and her expression seemed melancholy but not mournful. Her hands and feet were tied with thick hemp ropes, just like a prisoner's. Unbelievably, Saya's eyes followed the ropes which tethered the girl's feet to a pillar. The old women had not been talking about Torihiko, after all.

The white-robed girl did not seem to be troubled by her plight but rather stared steadily at Saya with a naïve gaze. Finally she spoke.

"These days it is difficult to distinguish between dream and reality. I feel I have met you somewhere before, but where could it have been?"

Saya uttered a cry. "That voice. It's the same. It was you."

It was a voice she would never forget: the voice of the carp that night in the pond.

"You are the one who pretended to be a carp and talked to me, aren't you? Thanks to you, I almost drowned, you know."

"Oh yes!" The girl's face lit up in a smile of recognition. "I met you in the mirror pond, the night I was dreaming I was a carp. You were swimming there, too."

Overcome with curiosity, Saya went right up to the maiden and knelt before her, peering into her face.

"Who on earth are you?" Saya demanded.

"I am Chihaya," the girl replied. "I am the third-born child of the God of Light. The last of the immortals."

Saya gasped in surprise. No one knew of any immortal children besides Princess Teruhi and Prince Tsukishiro. But when she thought back, she remembered that Princess Teruhi had let slip something about another sibling. Even so, it was incredible. Deep within the palace grounds lived one more immortal of whom no one knew. And this one was bound!

"Why are you tied up like that?"

"You mean these?" Chihaya replied, unperturbed by Saya's suspicion. "My sister tied these knots for me. Because I dream. While I dream, my body must be kept here."

"Dream? You mean like the carp dream?"

"A carp or anything else. I can become anything—a bird, an insect, a furred creature. My sister never lets me outside because I am a disgrace to my family. So instead I learned to pass the time in this way."

There was no resentment or discontent in her voice, only a hint of resigned loneliness.

"Ah, that's it," Saya thought as she listened. "Her voice resembles Prince Tsukishiro's. That's why I thought it sounded familiar the first time I heard it."

For the same reason she could now understand Chihaya's beauty. Yet Chihaya lacked the dauntless gallantry that characterized her brother and sister. Instead she appeared somewhat forlorn.

Chihaya continued. "But my sister is displeased with my dreaming, too. Perhaps that is to be expected, though, as I seem to cause so much trouble. I don't remember, myself, but when I see how the priestesses dread me, I assume that I must appear to lose my sanity while I dream." She tilted her head and said meditatively, "Or perhaps I am insane to start with. I'm not really sure."

She told her story with such indifference and lack of self-pity that Saya was drawn to her.

"You look perfectly sane to me," Saya said sympathetically. "If you took off those ropes and went outside, you would look even saner."

Chihaya's eyes grew wide with surprise. "What a funny thing to say. And who are you, who says such things?"

"I am Saya. I am one of your brother's handmaidens," Saya said with a hint of irony directed at herself.

"Saya," Chihaya repeated, testing the sound of the name. "Saya, you remind me of my sister."

Saya looked at her in astonishment. "What makes you say that?"

Chihaya answered innocently, "You aren't old."

"Ah, I see. You don't know much."

"Perhaps. But then, when it comes to things experienced outside this physical frame, I know more."

Saya could not decide whether to confide in this girl. She might be one of the immortal Children of Light, but she did not seem to be an enemy—although she did seem a bit of a simpleton.

"Actually . . ." Saya mustered her courage and began. No matter which way the wind blew, she would still be in danger. "I came here looking for the servant who is to be sacrificed at the purification ceremony. He must be here somewhere. Perhaps you might know. He's the one who was swimming with me in the mirror pond and he is my friend. Can you tell me where he is?"

"He isn't here. The sacrifice is kept at the West Gate," Chihaya replied readily. "There is a small iron cage called the hut of abomination beside the river just in front of the West Gate. I saw the place when I flew over the river as a bird this morning. Your servant is there."

"The West Gate!" Saya exclaimed and then quickly lowered her voice. "It can't be!" She wanted to cry, but she realized that no one had told her Torihiko was in the shrine. For a variety of reasons, she had simply assumed he was. When she thought about it objectively, it was obvious that an impure sacrifice would never be permitted within the shrine, but would, rather, be taken to the river where the ceremony was to take place. She cursed her stupidity. But it was too late to gnash her teeth or weep. The West Gate was at the opposite end of the palace from the shrine that she had so painstakingly entered.

"So all my efforts were for naught. What a miserable fate."

Chihaya looked curiously at the dismayed Saya, who sat with her head buried in her hands.

"Why do you want to meet your servant this late at night?"

"I belong to the people of Darkness," Saya replied, reckless in her despair. "That boy, Torihiko, does, too. He mustn't be killed. But I, who should have helped him, have foolishly come to the wrong place."

"You mean the people who serve Mitsuha, the Goddess of Darkness?" Saya was shocked at Chihaya's lack of inhibition and stared at her in amazement. She would never have dreamed that the honorific title of the Goddess would be mentioned in such a sacred place as this. Even in the village of Hashiba, it was taboo to refer to the Goddess by name.

"You have just increased the need for purification," Saya said, which made Chihaya laugh.

"Me? Purification? If so, my sister will surely faint from shock."

Saya snorted. "Princess Teruhi faint? Now, that I'd like to see, if it were possible."

She stood up. Time was swiftly passing while she sat here chatting. Even if the effort was wasted, she could not bear to spend the rest of the night sitting idle.

"I'm going to go to the West Gate and see," Saya said to Chihaya. "Although there is little hope, I will do what I can. One of the people of Darkness called me heartless. Now I know that it was true."

"How unfortunate that I cannot help you," Chihaya said placidly yet sincerely. "All I have is the knowledge of my dreams. If you were a mouse, I could tell you the fastest way."

Saya smiled. "Thank you. I wish I were a mouse and could speed under the floor and swarm up the walls. Then I could rescue Torihiko without anyone's ever knowing."

She was amazed by Chihaya's reply. "Have you ever tried to become one?"

"No."

"Well then, you might be able to if you tried."

Saya, who had already turned to leave, looked back over her shoulder. "I am not like you. It is not something one can do just by willing it."

"Are you sure?" Chihaya asked. Saya was nonplussed. "That night in the pond, you were already half fish. That's why I was curious and spoke to you. You could even hear me talk although I was a fish. The other handmaidens cannot do that."

"But," Saya murmured, blushing as she remembered, "but it's impossible. I don't know how."

"Well, maybe I can teach you."

Saya looked hard at Chihaya's tranquil face. And as she looked, she began to feel that they were not so different after all. If anything, Chihaya's idea was no more crazy than the one of leaving the shrine and making her way across the entire palace. Inspired, she sat down. "Then teach me. I'll try anything."

Saya stared at a young gray mouse that Chihaya had summoned. The mouse was bewildered to find itself sitting on the bright floor for a reason it could not fathom.

"Engrave the image of this mouse in your mind so that you will not lose the way back to your soul," Chihaya said. "Then close your eyes and leave your body. It will remain behind while you catch the mouse. Returning is much easier than leaving, so there is no need to concern yourself about the rest. I will watch over your body. Now then, you must try very hard. You cannot leave your body if you move slowly."

Saya closed her eyes and imagined a log ladder before her. She felt as if she were groping along its narrow edge without the aid of a handrail. She sensed someone kindly supporting her, however, urging her along; probably Chihaya. Then suddenly it became clear.

"Ah, I know. I know how to do it."

She had to find the place where her soul resided, longing for release, and open the door to set it free. Exhilarated, she leaped into space. And with a little help from Chihaya, she slipped inside the mouse.

At first it was so strange that she thought she could not tolerate it. She could not see any of the things that she should be able to see. But that was only natural, because from a mouse's perspective, Chihaya's face was far in the distance. On the other hand, her sense of smell was exceptionally keen, informing her that there were two creatures looming like small hills nearby. She had to run about a bit to help calm herself down.

"So you did it. I thought you could," she heard Chihaya say happily from somewhere far above her. Then, regaining her self-control and recalling that time was running out, she ran through a hole in the wall, went under the floor, and sped to the West Gate along the path that Chihaya had carefully described to her.

Saya met many mice along the way, but whenever they saw her they backed away and made room for her to pass, as if afraid. Despite her borrowed body, she was still Saya, and apparently other mice could detect the difference. Perhaps she looked as though possessed by some evil spirit. But for Saya, who was racing against time, this was fortunate. She continued running as fast as her mouse legs could carry her, stopping only to sniff out the proper direction.

Eventually the smell of water began to pervade her senses. A large body of water was flowing outside the palisade. A river. The Nakase River wound alongside the West Gate, then snaked toward the south. The mouse's sensitive nose could detect even the width of the river and the speed with which it flowed, so that Saya felt she could see it with her eyes. The gate was just over there. Grateful that the mouse's body was still full of energy, Saya ran under the palisade and made her way through the brush along the bank. At the bottom of the bindweed-covered bank was the

river. Numerous watch fires burned around the site of the purification ceremony, and it was cordoned off with braided rope.
The place was thick with guards.

Although it was frustrating not to have an unbroken view,
because of the mouse's nearsighted vision, the hut of abomination
seemed to be in the center of a circle of lights. Saya boldly
approached it. The shadows of the stones along the shore concealed her gray fur. Even though she passed by the feet of one
of the guards, he did not notice her.

"So this is the hut of abomination."

She raised her head and wiggled her long whiskers. It was a
small structure covered with tightly woven bark and straw, and
from the outside appeared somewhat similar to the birthing huts
in the village of Hashiba made for women in labor. But a pungent
metallic stench told of the cold iron beneath the straw. Sticks
had been set in the ground around the hut, and they were joined
by a thin string hung with little gold bells like those Princess
Teruhi wore on the garters of her trousers. The contraption resembled a bird rattle set out in the rice fields in fall to chase away
sparrows, but Saya, ignoring it, passed underneath. Without her
even touching it, the bells began vibrating, making a faint but
clear sound. Hearing the noise, one of the men cried, "On your
guard, men! Some evil has entered this place."

Saya's heart skipped a beat and she leaped into the air in panic,
scurrying to conceal herself within the nearest shadow. She realized then that it was the hem of a long garment that hung from
the waist of a man who sat perched upon a folding stool. Immediately beside her she smelled an old man's bony ankle.

"But, honorable priest, we did not notice anyone approaching."

"I am not mistaken," the man sheltering Saya replied. "Search
the entire vicinity. Someone is lurking nearby. In the name of
Her Highness, search every shadow. Nothing must hinder the
purification ceremony."

"Thank goodness," Saya thought. She calmed her racing heart. The old man ordered the others about while he himself remained seated and showed no sign of moving. It never occurred to him that the intruder might be concealed under his hem. While he glared dourly under lowered brows toward the gate, Saya slipped behind him and climbed up the wall of the hut.

As she parted the straw and scrambled through, her feet touched the iron bars. It was indeed a merciless cage. The sacrifice would remain trapped within these bars while he was burned alive. Just the thought of it made her hair stand on end. It was pitch-black inside, but she could sense a huddled human form.

"Torihiko! Torihiko!" she shouted in a loud voice. It seemed as though she did not use the creature's mouth but rather called Torihiko from some other place. He responded immediately. He raised his face from the ground and seemed to be peering around in search of her.

"Saya?" he whispered faintly. "Where are you?"

"Here. Are you all right?" Saya's voice trembled with concern. Her nose told her that Torihiko was badly hurt.

"They broke my legs so that I couldn't escape."

"How cruel!" Saya's tiny body shook with indignation.

"How did you get here? How did you get through all the guards? I can't believe you did it."

"Never mind that," Saya replied, not wishing to go into details. "Let's think of a way to get you out of here. We can't let them burn you alive without putting up a fight."

Torihiko remained silent for so long that Saya was afraid even his sharp wits had been defeated. Finally he spoke.

"I don't understand girls. It would have been so much easier to help me get the Sword in the first place than to come all the way here now."

"So that's your greeting, is it?"

Why was he always so cheeky?

"But it's true. This place will be guarded continuously until the purification ceremony is completed. The Prince, the Princess, everyone in the palace is watching this spot. To try to escape would be the same as taking on the entire palace army. It's impossible. I can't even move," Torihiko said as if merely stating the facts. "Saya, take the Sword and escape. Do in my stead what I was unable to do."

Saya struggled to keep her voice calm. "Look, that Sword won't die if I leave it behind. But you most certainly will."

"I won't die," Torihiko replied cheerfully. "I will just return to the Goddess of Darkness. I will be born again somewhere and come to find you."

"And just when will that be? Don't talk nonsense!" Saya said, so angry she could cry. "Do you think we will ever meet again? Even if we do, it won't be me anymore, and I will have forgotten all about you. I won't live forever."

Torihiko seemed surprised. "Saya, you're strange. You'll never be able to fight if you think like that."

"But I am not Sayura. You have never met her, and neither have I. She is somebody else. Don't you understand that?"

"The Water Maiden certainly is different, really strange."

"It's you that are strange," Saya retorted.

"It's because you think like that that you are always attracted to the Light."

Saya was about to reply harshly but recollected herself. "This is no time to argue. Just remember what I said. It's true."

Torihiko reached out his hand and groped in the direction from which Saya's voice came. But of course he did not find her; his hand came up against the iron bars. "Saya, where are you really?" he queried uncertainly. He looked suddenly like the wounded boy he was, and Saya regretted not being in her own body so that she could grasp his hand in hers.

"I'm right here. But this is not my body. The body I am using now is that of a mouse."

"A mouse?" He stretched out a finger, and for the briefest of moments Saya allowed him to stroke her fur.

"Now do you see?"

"How did you do it?"

"The person who was the carp in the Mirror Pond taught me. She was in the shrine. Her name is Chihaya, and she is the youngest of the Children of Light. She's a little odd, and is kept tied up."

"In the shrine? One of the Children of Light?" Torihiko gasped, at a loss for words. "You mean you went into the shrine?"

"Yes. That's where my body is."

"Then you must go back immediately. Now!" Torihiko said, breathing harshly. "That girl must be the Priestess of the Sword. She is the one who stills the Dragon Sword. Now I know why she was able to do so. She is one of the Children of Light. If you but reach out your hand, you can take the Sword. I can't believe it."

"But rescuing you comes first."

"Saya, if anything can triumph over the combined forces of the entire palace, it is the Dragon Sword," Torihiko said in a subdued tone, and once the words were spoken he seemed somewhat afraid. "If you use the Dragon Sword—although the thought itself is terrifying—this iron cage will be no obstacle. Even the Children of Light would probably be unable to withstand it."

Torihiko's fear, the first he had ever shown, transmitted itself to Saya, and she wondered just what kind of weapon this Sword was.

"I understand. If taking the Dragon Sword is the only possible means left—"

"Saya, you have unwittingly put yourself in grave danger," Torihiko said seriously. "I don't know who Chihaya is, but it's dangerous to trust her. She is your rival. There cannot be two priestesses for the same sword."

"She seemed very nice. And she doesn't know that I am the Water Maiden," Saya said slightly anxiously.

"In that case, seize the Sword before Princess Teruhi discovers you. You should have the ability to remove it without wakening it."

"I'll try. Wait for me."

"Beware of Chihaya. Don't let her deceive you."

With Torihiko's warning following her, Saya raced off. While she ran she began to think that she was indeed gullible to have accepted Chihaya's words at face value. Not only was she one of the Children of Light but Saya had even told her that she belonged to the people of Darkness. Despite this, she had left her defenseless body with Chihaya in the perilous shrine.

"Perhaps it is I who am the simpleton."

Although the guards were still searching everywhere, they were not looking for anyone as small as a mouse, and Saya passed them with no trouble. Once she had crawled beneath the safety of the palace roof, she ran all the way along the beams. As she passed Princess Teruhi's hall, she noticed that the Princess's chamber was empty. Was she still with Prince Tsukishiro? Or had she gone somewhere else? The two old women were still offering prayers before the shrine. She would have to think about them also. Had the third priestess in the shadow of the wooden gate regained consciousness yet? Swarming up a column beneath the floor and crawling through the hole in the wainscoting, she finally returned to her starting point.

"There's my body!"

Just as Chihaya had said, it was much simpler to return. It was as if her body, waiting impatiently, summoned Saya and sucked her inside with such speed that her head swam. She opened her eyes and felt sensation returning to her limbs. And was scared to death at her predicament. She was lying flat on her back, her arms and legs flailing wildly in a desperate struggle to escape the menace bearing down upon her. And holding her down, restraining her, was Chihaya. Perhaps because of the struggle, Chihaya's beautiful hair was in disarray. Saya's blood ran cold, but at last she maneuvered herself into a position from which she could push Chihaya away.

"What do you think you're doing?" Saya exclaimed in a quivering voice.

Chihaya looked suddenly relieved. She relaxed and sat down where she was, saying, "Oh good. You're back."

"What were you doing?"

Chihaya raised her arm and wiped the sweat from her forehead. "The mouse in your body panicked and tried to run outside—without understanding anything."

"You're lying!"

"I'm not lying."

"You're lying! You're lying!" Saya cried furiously. She was so flustered that she could not control herself. The blood rushed to her face and she felt as if her cheeks were burning. She began to edge away.

"You're a liar. You—you—" In a choking voice she finally managed to say, "You're a boy!"

Chihaya looked perfectly calm. He did not even appear concerned about his wildly disheveled hair. He replied seriously, "I don't recall ever claiming to be a girl."

"But you're dressed like one. Look at you!"

Chihaya looked down at his long white sleeves. "This is what my sister made me wear to fulfill my duties as the Priestess of the Sword."

"It was true that I shouldn't trust you," Saya said, her cheeks growing even redder as she stared at his face, so beautiful that it was infuriating to think it belonged to a boy. "What were you trying to do to me?"

"Nothing."

"But you had your hands on me."

"You were kicking and struggling, so I tried to hold you still."

He did not seem to be hiding anything. Rather, he seemed perplexed by the extent of Saya's anger.

"Now I finally know what they mean when they say I struggle when I dream. Once the soul has left the body, it can no longer hear you."

Saya, recollecting that Chihaya's hands and feet were tied, relaxed somewhat.

"Well, once was sufficient for me," she grumbled. "I am never going to become another creature again. It makes me shudder to think that something that is not me was moving around inside my body."

Saya looked at Chihaya and wondered whether he did not care about his own body. What was he thinking of, to allow himself to be dressed in women's clothing, to give up his freedom, and to leave his body behind while he dreamed? She might under-stand if he were grotesque to look upon, but he was not.

"It seems you are the black sheep of your family. Well, I am the same for the people of Darkness," she said candidly, and then shrugged her shoulders, laughing at herself. Now that Saya had calmed down, she could be more objective. When she thought about it, the fact that he was bound was fortunate, for it meant the odds were in her favor.

"The Dragon Sword is kept here, isn't it?"

"Yes."

"Will you show it to me?"

"So you really did come to take the Sword? My sister warned me that the people of Darkness would try to get it." There was some disappointment in Chihaya's voice.

"Yes. I must have the Dragon Sword in order to rescue Torihiko."

"I have heard that no one is able to touch the Sword."

"I am supposed to be able to because . . ." Saya said somewhat dubiously, "because I am the Water Maiden."

"The Water Maiden?" Chihaya said, his eyes widening in

surprise. For the first time the dreamy Chihaya became animated. "Are you the real Priestess of the Sword?"

"According to some people," Saya replied modestly.

"Now that you mention it, you spilled the water of pacification. Despite that, the Sword did not roar."

"Roar?"

"Yes, it roars, and it howls, too. Because it yearns to be reborn."

Saya's mouth dropped open. "Just what kind of sword is it?"

"I don't really know what the Dragon Sword's original form was," Chihaya said seriously, raising his bound hands to indicate the altar. "But if you wish to see what it looks like while sleeping, it is there. You seem to have the right. It is placed within the coffer on the altar."

Saya looked up at the shining altar and approached it. When she had climbed to the third step, she saw before her a rectangular receptacle of stone, black as ebony. Despite its flawlessly polished surface, it was so black that it reflected nothing. She peered fearfully over the edge to find the box lidless and filled with clear water. And in the bottom lay a naked blade. The strong light of the torches reached into the water's depths, and the Sword gleamed faintly where it rested on its jet-black bed. The metal was blue-black and longer than any sword Saya had ever seen. The pommel was round and dark, and crimson stones were set in the hilt.

It reminded Saya of something lurking in wet grass against which one must always be on guard. "Like a serpent. A poisonous serpent," she thought. Although it had an unearthly beauty, she felt no affinity for it. She looked back at Chihaya.

"If I take the Sword, what will happen to you?" she asked almost teasingly.

"My sister will certainly despair of me," he answered after some thought.

"Then will you try to stop me?"

"If it is possible, maybe," Chihaya muttered without conviction. "Although I have never fought anyone before."

"Really? Never?" Saya said, descending the stairs and staring hard at his face. "Was it not decreed that the Children of Light would fight continually from the day they came down to this earth? And if you are truly a child of the God of Light, then you must surely have lived much longer than I."

"My sister is ashamed that I am his son. She often says that she wishes it were not so. She says that although I am a child of the God of Light I am a misfit, obsessed with death. My dreaming is proof of that."

"Well." Saya drew in her breath. Then she asked timidly, "Do you wish to die?"

"I do not know." Chihaya shook his head. It seemed that he lacked conviction about everything. "But when I am alone, I think of how my father followed the Goddess to the underworld. If he wanted so badly to have her by his side, how did they come to hate each other? And when I think of that, I begin to wander away from the palace. That is why my sister will not allow me to go outside." He sighed softly. "I am a failure as a Child of Light. That much I do know."

"Why?" Saya looked into his eyes. "Why do you call yourself a failure? Why don't you try and realize your desire? You are as securely trapped as Torihiko. But you have folded your wings by your own volition."

Confused, Chihaya lowered his head. "Because my sister always speaks the truth. She says that if I leave this place, some terrible evil will occur."

"Well, if you're talking about people calling you evil, I have been called that, too. But that's not the point. What do you, not Princess Teruhi, wish? You try to escape through dreaming, but wouldn't you rather walk upon the earth with your own feet? Don't you long to see with your own eyes the marks the Goddess left in Toyoashihara long ago?"

Chihaya could only blink under Saya's barrage of questions. Stray wisps of hair hung about his face and accentuated his bemused appearance. Saya smiled. It was the kind of smile she had shared with her friends when they played together in the mountains around Hashiba. She said in a warm voice, "I feel I can understand you. We are opposites, and yet we are very similar. We are both drawn to something beyond the confines of our own peoples. I longed to be one of the people of Light, and your brother brought me to this palace. So why shouldn't you, if you so wish, go to see the Land of the Dead? Even if in the end, as for me, it doesn't work out."

Saya pointed to the altar. "Let me take the accursed Sword and I will destroy the iron cage in which Torihiko is held. And at the same time I intend to destroy my own cage, the foolish cage of my illusions. Then I will return to the people of Darkness."

Marveling at the strength that he detected like a clear stream in her voice, Chihaya whispered, "You are truly the Water Maiden." There was nothing with which he could check the flow. The freshness of rushing water was in her face, in her gaze. Saya laid her hand upon Chihaya's arm and said, "Let us take the Sword and go together. I want to break the cage and sever the cords that bind you with the same blade."

4

"The moon has risen over the mountain," Princess Teruhi said abruptly. "Our dalliance is over. Release me."

She rose brusquely when Prince Tsukishiro pulled himself wordlessly away, and parting the curtain, she stood beside a column on the balcony. Near the horizon at which she gazed, a thin sliver of moon like a white crescent of fingernail looked down upon them. Although it was almost too ephemeral to be called light, the moonlight struck her figure as she stood with her back to the Prince, bathing her in coldness.

"Security at the West Gate troubles me. Surely they could not have let our prize slip through their fingers."

Prince Tsukishiro sighed and said, "I know that as long as there is light in this world you live only to serve our divine father, but is everything else a mere trifle to you?"

"Is there anything wrong with that?" Princess Teruhi asked, turning to face him.

The Prince continued, "Then what are you going to do when our father comes once again to rule this land?"

Princess Teruhi was caught off guard for an instant but replied unhesitatingly, "I will continue to do what I have always done. I will worship and obey him. To behold once more his illustrious face from which we have so long been parted will be the realization of my heart's desire."

Prince Tsukishiro raised himself on one elbow and looked at Princess Teruhi. "How sentimental. Sister, you are as blind as the priestesses of the sacred shrine."

"I am tired of your constant grumbling."

"Sometimes I almost feel sorry for our youngest brother."

Princess Teruhi glared at him as he ran his fingers through his hair, and said sharply, "Do not bring Chihaya into this just to please your fancy. Do you claim to be able to understand his degenerate mind?"

"No, I do not," Prince Tsukishiro said frankly. "Although I would feel easier if I could. Chihaya's eyes are fixed on something else; the path he follows differs from our own. Why do you think our divine father made one child so different?"

"Surely it was an accident," the Princess replied sullenly. "I cannot believe that our father would intentionally produce such a useless nuisance for a son."

Prince Tsukishiro folded his fingers together and said thoughtfully, "I used to think so, too: that he was not what our father intended. But recently I have begun to think that the opposite might be true—that Chihaya might in fact be the true will of our father, which has been concealed."

"What do you mean?" Princess Teruhi looked at her brother intently.

"You and I were born to act as our celestial father's two eyes. We have been placed upon this earth to watch over it for him. But Chihaya was born from our father's nose, through which his breath flows. Thus he is closer to our father's innermost being. For he was born from a sigh that expressed our father's true feelings."

Princess Teruhi gave a short laugh. "That boy? He who will never grow up and whose only talent is dreaming? What part of our miserable young brother do you claim expresses our father's feelings?"

Prince Tsukishiro hesitated. Then he said, "That boy loves the Goddess. He is constantly seeking the entrance to the place where we immortals can never go."

Princess Teruhi leaped like a startled deer and bore down upon Prince Tsukishiro with a menacing glare. "I will not permit such a thing to be suggested again, even by you, brother." Shaking with rage, she shouted, "You speak as though our divine father still wishes to meet the Goddess of Darkness."

Prince Tsukishiro regarded his sister calmly. "If . . . just if this were so, what would become of us?"

"Impossible! Stop talking nonsense," Princess Teruhi snapped decisively, waving her hand impatiently as though brushing the thought away. "Chihaya's attraction to the Darkness is necessary only to give him the power to still the Dragon Sword. Because that is the only thing he is good for. It demonstrates our father's true intention that the loathsome Sword shall become as useless as Chihaya. It is unthinkable that the will of the God of Light should be clouded in any way. Chihaya's dream wandering is his compensation for stilling the Sword along with himself. All we need to do is let him dream as much as he desires. The Sword is powerful and thus needs a guardian. He protects the Sword and we will protect him. Is that not sufficient? Why do you fret like this and repeatedly voice such doubts?"

"You are right. It is doubt," Prince Tsukishiro whispered. "Whatever the case, it does not alter the fact that Chihaya's power has been sealed inside him."

Princess Teruhi knelt, placing her hands on Prince Tsukishiro's shoulders. She frowned, looking into his face. "You are strange, you know. Within but a short space of time, victory will be ours."

Recollecting himself, Prince Tsukishiro smiled faintly. "I shall return to the present. It is just one of those whims that you, my dear sister, so dislike."

The expression of concern vanishing from her face, Princess Teruhi turned away. "This happens because you insist on bringing that Water Maiden into the palace," she said angrily. "The air becomes impure and you begin to doubt. It is unnecessary to waste your efforts trying to purify her. The only solution is to destroy her."

Striking her knee with her fist, she rose and picked up her sword, which she fastened at her waist. "I am going to see what is happening at the West Gate."

"Saya will not be there."

"Can you be so sure?"

"I will go with you, then." Prince Tsukishiro stood swiftly.

At that moment a roar shook the silence of the sleeping palace. Like a giant bubble, it rose from the depths of the night and then burst. It was like the growl of an enormous creature or a rumble of thunder from the edge of the earth. The instant the sound reached them, the trees, the grass, even the columns of the palace quivered momentarily. The sound was low-pitched, but the earth itself trembled with terror and the air seemed filled with apprehension.

The twins started and recoiled, looking at each other.

"The Dragon Sword cries," Princess Teruhi whispered. "Did the old women neglect to bring the water of pacification?"

"What can Chihaya be up to?" Prince Tsukishiro asked. "The Sword has not made such a clamor since he began to watch over it."

An expression crossed Princess Teruhi's face such as had never before clouded her countenance. "It cannot be. That girl!"

Saya gripped the Sword gingerly in both hands, staring at it blankly. The Sword had begun to shriek when she had yelled at the guards accosting them to keep away. The sound shook the air with a disturbing resonance, pulsing in a way that set her nerves on edge. Needless to say, the guards paled and fell back.

"Why is it doing this?" Saya asked in bewilderment, struggling to suppress her desire to fling the Sword away.

"Saya, calm down," Chihaya said anxiously from beside her. "If you allow yourself to become upset, you will be overcome by the Sword."

How could he possibly expect her to calm down, Saya wondered. The place was in an uproar, and she could hear the angry voices of the guards calling for reinforcements. It was clear that within moments the entire palace guard would be ranged against them. To sneak quietly away, taking Chihaya with her, was now utterly impossible.

"Let's go to the West Gate. There's no point in trying to hide any longer," Saya urged desperately, and they broke into a run. The narrow streets of Mahoroba were hemmed in by an intricate network of fences and buildings that obstructed the view, and so they repeatedly encountered soldiers responding to the alarm. Without exception, however, the soldiers blanched and fell back, unable to stop the fleeing pair. Not only did the Sword continue to shriek, making the palace rumble, but it gradually began to glow. The stones in the hilt blazed like murky red lidless eyes, glaring at those who crossed their path, and blue-white sparks fell from its tip. A bluish light radiated along the entire length of the Sword, illuminating Saya from the chest up and making her look like a madwoman. Even the bravest men trembled at the sight.

Saya and Chihaya ran without stopping while behind them a clamor rose in the streets and lights came on in every wakening mansion.

"Just a little farther," Saya prayed.

They had almost reached the West Gate. But only a few paces behind them were the people of the palace. If a night bird had been watching the two race from one side to the other, they would have appeared to be drawing the people toward the gate in order to expel them from the city.

The brightly lit West Gate came into view. Saya and Chihaya halted, gasping for breath. Between the gate's two pillars waited the Prince and Princess, arms folded. And they were surrounded by soldiers who stood fearlessly with bowstrings drawn.

"Saya," Prince Tsukishiro shouted thunderously. The rebuke in his voice struck her forcefully. "Control yourself. Such behavior does not become you."

The howling of the Sword ceased abruptly. A stillness pervaded the night, as if a curtain had suddenly been parted, and Saya stood immobile in shock. The Sword weighed heavily in her hands, and when she gradually lowered the tip of the blade it was so long that it almost touched the ground. The light that glowed within was beginning to fade, and at the same time the wild agitation in Saya's heart began to subside.

"Well, you certainly could not have chosen a more spectacular way to get here, little one," Princess Teruhi said, her hands on her hips. Although she spoke softly, Saya could feel the anger seething beneath. "Did you wish to disturb the peace of the palace? Where did you learn such behavior?"

"Let Torihiko go. That is all I wish," Saya said hoarsely. "I do not intend to harm anyone. Just let us go."

"Go? Where do you plan to go?" Prince Tsukishiro said in disbelief. "Do you think you can turn your back on me and return home? If you think the people of Hashiba will welcome you back with open arms, you are gravely mistaken. And you cannot possibly intend to go to the people of Darkness. For of all things, you most loathe your tainted birth among those who worship the Goddess."

"Yes," Saya whispered, "yet that is where I belong."

"Look at me," the Prince commanded harshly. Biting her lip, Saya raised her head. Prince Tsukishiro's face was rigid and hard but, more than anything else, sad. And as he stood there, his commanding presence still embodied all that she loved.

"I thought that I had given you all that it was in my power to give. I thought that you had vowed to cherish it. What could have been lacking that you should turn from me in this way? You always leave me. What is it you seek that I cannot see?"

Saya was on the verge of tears. Prince Tsukishiro's apparent sincerity was unbearable. "I am not turning my back on you. I love you—and I surely will continue to do so. But . . ." Shaking her head, Saya fixed him with a sad and hopeless gaze. "That which I am seeking and which you cannot see is the source of my soul, of life. This is something which the people of Darkness can never forget. So please forgive me, but I cannot stay here."

The Sword began to hum faintly.

"Let me pass."

Princess Teruhi spoke. "If you wish to go, then go. But I will permit neither Chihaya nor the Sword to pass through this gate."

Chihaya fell back a step under his sister's gaze.

"Why have you done what is strictly forbidden?" Princess Teruhi said in a tone that would have caused even stone to tremble.

"Why, when I strove so hard to keep you from the eyes of men, have you left the shrine?"

Certainly the people of Mahoroba milling at a distance all had their eyes fixed on Chihaya. It was obvious that he was no ordinary person, with his robe like a white bird alighting from above and his long black hair flowing like a river of night. With an uncertain expression on his face, he looked more like a celestial angel descended from heaven than a youth.

"Sister," he whispered hoarsely.

"I command you. Take the Sword from that girl and return to the shrine immediately," Princess Teruhi demanded. "I do not know how she managed to lure you out, but you cannot live anywhere else. Without us to protect you, you will not even be able to dream."

"Don't listen to her. You can think for yourself now," Saya said sharply at his side. The Dragon Sword began to glow again. Sparks sprang soundlessly from the blade, and the red stones awoke and glared threateningly.

Chihaya remained silent for a while; then, looking Princess Teruhi in the eye, he held up his hands. "Sister, I have cut the bonds that held me. Once I desired to cut them, it was simple to do so. And I realized that until now I had never even wished to be free."

"And that is how it should be," Princess Teruhi replied, lashing out at him. "You have never realized the peril you represent. Even if you knew, there was nothing you could have done but curse yourself and suffer needlessly. I did not wish to expose my own brother to such a fate. To remain in the shrine is your sole hope for happiness."

"Liar!" It was Saya, not Chihaya, who screamed. Shaking with indignation, she said, "I know. You can only use people, regardless of whether they are your own kin or not."

Light suddenly gushed from the Sword like a rushing stream and traced a thick line up into the sky. Within seconds, a swirling cloud had formed, a cloud that responded to the Sword. Above the heads of the gasping crowd the sky split in two, and from the cleft flashing orange light spilled forth. With an appalling roar the light struck the ground, a warm moist wind sprang up, and, before their very eyes, the palace burst into a pillar of flame. With a cry of terror, the crowd crested like a wave and broke, scattering like baby spiders from a broken nest. "Water! Water!" someone shouted.

Saya, shocked beyond fear, stood rooted to the spot, staring at the dancing flames. Then she realized that she could no longer bear the Sword. She had reached the limits of her courage.

"Chihaya," she whispered. "Take it. Please. I cannot still the Sword. I am too weak."

Chihaya looked at Saya in surprise. "But that can't be . . ."

"Please," Saya begged him. She did not want to tell him, but everything was growing dark and stars were dancing at the edge of her vision. "I think I'm going to faint. Please, before I fall."

Chihaya hastily put an arm around her and gripped the hilt of the Sword next to her hand. Princess Teruhi, turning her eyes from the fire and seeing them thus, gave a triumphant smile.

"That's it. Now take the girl and go back to the shrine. When the fire is out, we can take our time deciding her punishment."

Chihaya looked at the exhausted Saya and the Dragon Sword. When he gripped the hilt a little more firmly, Saya's hand fell limply away. He alone now held the Sword, and though it still glowed faintly, its humming was gradually subsiding. But from the quivering in the palm of his hand he could feel its impatience to move again.

"Sister." Chihaya raised his voice above the noise of the fire. "Yes?"

"I wish to return this girl to the people of Darkness."

A slightly puzzled expression crossed Princess Teruhi's face and changed gradually into speechless astonishment. "You what! Do you intend to take her yourself?"

"Yes."

"That is truly what you wish?"

"Yes."

"No! I will not allow it!" Princess Teruhi screamed in a shaking voice. "You're insane! Don't you know that if you do this, you can never return? You will have to fight against, to revile your own brother and sister. If you take but one step outside this gate, your fate will seize you. It is clearly written in the stars."

"I do not desire to fight you or my brother. But no matter what the consequences, I cannot stay." Chihaya spoke calmly, but the Sword in his hand grew increasingly bright. "The Water Maiden has broken the dam and released what was contained behind it. I wish to go and seek the Goddess, as my father intended."

"Tsukishiro, come!" The Princess cried desperately for help. "Stop him, stop Chihaya! The Dragon Sword will be reborn."

Prince Tsukishiro was directing the soldiers' efforts to extinguish the fire but he turned, paling, at her words. And saw Chihaya, the Sword grasped in one hand and Saya supported with the other, attempting to pass through the gate. Realizing that it was too late to run after him, he set an arrow to his bow as swiftly as a hawk. Aiming for his brother's heart, he pulled the bowstring taut. But at that instant the ground quivered as though about to heave upward. With a great rumbling and a blinding light, the earth shook with quake after quake, so that not a soul was left standing. The burning palace collapsed under the shock, and an anguished cry arose from the people as they were assailed by showers of sparks. The entire vault of heaven glowed dull purple. It was as if the world were turning upside down.

Prince Tsukishiro scrambled to Princess Teruhi's side and shielded her from the scraps of burning wood that fell from the sky. For a long time the two remained prostrate on the ground; but when the earthquakes had finally abated they raised their faces and looked up at the sky. Above their heads a dragon danced.

An enormous blue-white dragon danced wildly in pain, or in exultation.

Reckless, blind, it sped from cloud to blue-black cloud with chilling lack of purpose. Below, all the roofs of the palace had crumbled, belching forth flames, and the deafening roar of dry wood burning drowned out the cries of the people scattering in terror. Smoke as black as soot spouted into the air, whirling and spreading across the sky, which flickered with lightning.

"The curse of fire has been unsealed," Princess Teruhi whispered to herself, "that which brings evil to both the Darkness and the Light."

She turned her eyes absently to the West Gate beside her, which was now burning furiously, and then to the hut of abomination, which was likewise engulfed in flames.

Prince Tsukishiro tightened his grip on her shoulder. "Let us go to the river. We are in peril here."

5

She could hear the sound of water: the low murmur of a great river. Opening one eye and then the other, she saw that it was dawn. A faint white light touched the horizon. Saya lay on soft grass beside the riverbank. She felt as though she were waking from a bad dream but she could not remember what it was. She was not afraid but instead was filled with a forlorn helplessness, the feeling of a lost child. Where was she? Seeing Chihaya beside her, she smiled with relief. The air was clear and still and she could hear the sweet chirping of an early bird.

"Ah. So you are all right."

"Yes. And you too," Chihaya replied. His soot-smeared clothes were scorched and covered with little holes. There was a black smudge on the bridge of his nose, but he was unaware of it. He no longer looked like a heavenly maiden. Saya was dismayed to see the ends of his beautiful hair singed into frizzy brown tufts. She suddenly realized that the edges of her own clothes were also burned in numerous places.

"What happened?" Saya asked. "Where is the Sword?"

"The Palace of Light was burned to the ground. Smoke is still rising in the northern sky, so I suppose that it is still burning. As for the Dragon Sword, it is here. Having finished its rampage, it sleeps." Chihaya pointed to the Sword lying upon the grass, its darkened blade grim in the pale morning light.

"It seems so far," Saya said in surprise, looking up at the sky to the north. "We've come a long way from the palace, then. How did you do it?" She tilted her head, perplexed. "And what about Torihiko?"

Chihaya hesitated and seemed unwilling to reply. Saya frowned anxiously but at that moment sensed someone approaching her. Startled, she turned to see a tiny figure appear from the shadow of the bank.

"Lady Iwa!" Saya exclaimed, surprised at this unexpected encounter.

"These people came to our rescue, taking us on their raft. After that we were carried along by the river until we reached this spot," Chihaya explained.

Unable to wait for the old woman's short legs to carry her toward them, Saya ran to greet her. She bent down and looked into her face, demanding impatiently, "Lady Iwa, Torihiko—what happened to Torihiko?"

Lady Iwa's eyes filled with gentleness as she stroked Saya's cheek. "The brave boy was courageous to the end. He said to tell you not to cry but to wait for him."

"Then . . ." Saya lost her voice and whispered, "There—in that cage . . . like that?"

"We tried to help him, we and that youth over there. But

when the Dragon Sword is dancing, there is little that can be done. Now, now. There is nothing to grieve about. He is but resting awhile with the Goddess."

"How can you tell me not to cry?" Saya screamed, venting her anguish at the old woman. "Why do you think I took the Sword in the first place? Why do you think I turned my back on Prince Tsukishiro? For Torihiko. All of it was for him—to see him alive and well again."

She burst into tears and threw herself upon the grass. Even stamping the earth with her feet could not have assuaged her feelings. Torihiko had been burned alive in the iron cage, leaving only this show of courage behind. He, who could have been saved if she had just been a little stronger—if she had just tried a little harder—had died alone because of her utter failure.

The sky lightened, the sun shone down, evaporating the morning dew, and still Saya's face was wet with tears. Chihaya approached softly to see how she was. He seemed perplexed by her weeping.

"Is something wrong? Are you hurt somewhere?" he asked hesitantly.

"You cannot understand because you have nothing to lose," Saya said between sobs. "I lost him. I will never see Torihiko again. He is not here anymore."

Chihaya felt a shadow cross the sky and looked up. Black wings stood out like a stain on the blue sky.

"Crows. Two crows."

"It must be Big Black and Little Black." Saya looked up and felt fresh tears start to her eyes. "They are still looking for Torihiko."

"Sa-ya," one of the crows called familiarly and, folding its wings, dove down out of the sky. Landing on the grass with such force that it hopped right up to Saya, it tilted its glossy black head. "Boy, am I tired! I searched all over for you. I never dreamed you had come this far."

Stunned at this fluent speech, Saya stopped crying and stared.

"It's me," the crow said, hopping onto her knee. "Didn't you get my message? I told you not to cry but to wait for me."

"Torihiko!" Saya shrieked, but was unable to continue. The crow resembled a little demon with shining black eyes, and, looking at it, she was too astounded to know if she was happy or sad.

"I had to think about it: whether to go to the Goddess or not. Then I thought, the Goddess won't cry if I'm not there and Saya will, so I let it pass this time. I don't mind being a crow, and I'd rather stay with you. It wasn't very nice for Big Black, but I think he'd understand."

Saya looked at Chihaya, at a loss as to how to respond. "You?"

Chihaya nodded. "But he will never be able to return to his original form because his body was burned."

"No matter," Torihiko cried in a cheerful crow voice. "Did you know, the life-span of a crow is as long as that of a human being?"

REVOLT

Corpses fill the sea
and the mountain grasses deep.
I shall die by my emperor's side;
a peaceful death I will not seek.

—Shokunihongi

1

The infiltrators from the people of Darkness—Lady Iwa, Lord Shinado, and two others—discarded their raft once they had successfully rescued Saya, Chihaya, and Torihiko, and headed into the mountains. They followed the ridges, spending the night on a mountain peak. The next day a panoramic view of the road ahead was laid out far below them as they began their descent. The dense forest of pine and chinquapin ended abruptly at the foot of the mountain, beyond which shone a broad expanse of water, bluer than the sky that met it.

"Is that the sea?" Saya asked Torihiko, who was perched upon her shoulder. Although she had never seen it before, even she could guess that much.

"Yes, it is. We'll take a boat from that inlet," Torihiko answered.

When once again they entered the shadow of the forest, they could no longer see the ocean, but the gradually increasing head wind carried the booming sound of waves crashing on rocks. Saya felt uneasy and the angry moan of the ocean set her nerves on edge. Perhaps it was because it somehow resembled the voice of the Dragon Sword. But the call of the sea brought rain rather than fire. In the late afternoon the clouds began to thicken, and by dusk raindrops had already begun to fall. The wind buffeted the travelers, and a driving rain lashed their faces and showed no sign of abating.

Lord Shinado addressed Lady Iwa. "What bad luck. We cannot put to sea in this weather. We must wait out the storm onshore."

"There is no need for concern. We do not seem to have been followed. Let us seek shelter in the village in the cove."

"Would it not be wise to avoid the eyes of men? If this storm continues for several days . . ."

"Of that you need have no fear. It is but a tiny storm, just a little crow's temper tantrum. Tomorrow it will have spent itself," the old woman replied confidently. "We reached here in a night and a day. Surely it can do no harm to sleep in a little more comfort tonight."

Saya was relieved at Lady Iwa's reply. They had traveled in great haste, before she had had a chance to recover from the shock of the strange events in the palace. Her head was filled with a thick fog and everything seemed unreal. Her aching feet, her drenched clothing—all seemed like an endless nightmare whose keynote was a dull, aching pain. She desperately needed time and rest to return to reality.

By the time the travelers had reached the shore, it was dark. Trudging along the bay, so buffeted by wind and rain that they could not carry a torch, they finally stumbled upon a row of houses. The yellow light of an oil lamp leaking around a door seemed the warmest, most welcoming sight in the world. One of the men negotiated with the master of the house, and when it was finally settled that the men would sleep in the shed and the women in the house, Saya could have cried in relief. The low-eaved hut, which stood over a sunken floor of sand and earth, was a fisherman's home, and a pungent fishy smell assailed them as they entered. A net with scraps of seaweed clinging to it was kept in the house and the fisherman was mending it. Fish had been slit open and strung together around the smoke hole to dry.

Perhaps because of the salt air, the round wooden pillars were badly decayed and the house creaked and shuddered with every gust of wind, though it did not come tumbling down. Despite their meager life, the many red-faced children were cheerful, and willingly served the guests bowls of hot soup with strips of dried fish in it. Saya, however, could not even taste the soup that passed her lips. Her eyelids drooped before she could tell whether or not her wet body had dried. Leaving the circle of laughing conversation, she lay down in a corner and listened to the raging wind howl outside the thin wooden wall. It drowned out the voices within and bellowed, as if demanding something in a great loud voice of its own.

"Who? Where? Why? When? How?"

"Who could it be?" Saya wondered vaguely, but as she listened to the endless questioning she fell into a deep sleep.

When she opened her eyes the next morning, the fisherman and his family had already finished breakfast and left the house. They had been up since before dawn. Bereft of even the smallest child, the house appeared very large and empty. Lady Iwa sat alone beside the hearth, her small hands moving busily as she worked on something. Saya crawled from her sleeping place and looked out the open door. The storm had passed as though it had never come, and the sky was wide and clear. The fisherman's family stood side by side and greeted the sun as it rose above the rocky crags in the distance. Saya's heart ached as she watched their still figures from behind.

Lady Iwa called to her. "There's some porridge for you in the pot. You should eat it while it's still hot."

Saya turned away from the door as if shaking herself free and removed the lid from a large cauldron hanging on the hearth hook. This was the sort of breakfast she used to eat at home. Sitting down with a bowl in her hand, she looked at what Lady

Iwa was doing. The old woman had patiently hollowed out two pieces of wood and was now binding them together with wisteria vines.

When Saya asked what she was making, Lady Iwa casually replied, "A sheath. A sheath for the Sword. You cannot carry the blade unsheathed forever."

"Hmmm," Saya murmured noncommittally and glanced at the Sword, which lay nearby, thickly wrapped in cloth. The thought of it depressed her: the Dragon Sword, dreaded by all, even by Lady Iwa and Lord Shinado. And despite the fact that she felt not the least affinity for it, the Sword had been forced upon her on the grounds that it must be guarded by its priestess. Having no alternative, she had wrapped it in cloth and carried it on her shoulder, but there was never a more burdensome piece of baggage. It was constantly becoming entangled in thickets as they traveled along the mountain paths.

"By what fate did I become the Priestess of the Sword? Will I have to carry this thing with me for the rest of my life? What on earth is going to happen next?"

Saya wanted to ask these questions of Lady Iwa but was too timid. While she was rolling the questions about on the tip of her tongue, she sensed someone standing in the doorway. Looking over her shoulder, she saw a youth whom she did not recognize and stared up at him suspiciously. But when she was able to make out his features against the light she cried out in astonishment.

"Chihaya? I didn't recognize you."

Surely Lord Shinado had arranged it. Chihaya wore a faded indigo jacket and knee-length trousers like those the fisherman and his children wore. His singed hair had been evenly trimmed and fastened in loops on either side of his head. Although he was perhaps a little too pale, to the casual observer he looked like an ordinary boy. Saya was so pleased by this that she laughed aloud. She was glad that Lord Shinado had shown he was aware of Chihaya's ragged appearance. Since their first meeting, she had stood in awe of Lord Shinado. His dark, severe features and his piercing gaze seemed to judge others without hesitation, and she felt that although he had come to her aid, he would never forgive her for following the Light without a second thought. She had not yet had the courage to explain the details of how Chihaya had happened to leave the palace with her. And it seemed that Chihaya had no inclination to explain himself either. She wondered at his reception by the people of Darkness. They did not reject him as he followed along, but neither did they turn to him and question him. Rather, they ignored him, behaving as if they had not noticed his presence. Saya herself had had no energy left to think about others, yet in a corner of her mind she had been worried. Now, however, she knew that Lord Shinado and the others had accepted Chihaya as part of their group. She said teasingly, "You look good. That outfit suits you."

But Chihaya did not seem to hear her. He had not the slightest interest in his own appearance. Instead, he began speaking eagerly about something completely different.

"The children ran off saying that there is a sea monster."

Saya blinked in surprise. "A sea monster? What's that?"

"I don't know. They said it was washed ashore by the storm."

Saya, infected with Chihaya's innocent excitement, turned to the old woman. "Can we go and see?"

"It's just a shark," Lady Iwa said. "You can go, but the sea is still rough, so be careful."

Saya flew out the door. The narrow spit of sand below the shallow terrace curved gently out to the headland, and waves pounded against it as though attacking the shore. Where the waves swelled and broke with a roar, scattering white foam, the water was a somber brownish green, but out to sea it was a sparkling blue. The sharp-peaked crests rose steeply and raced toward land. Although at a distance the ocean had looked like a misty blue vision, at close range it seemed like a live and cunning creature on which one could not turn one's back. The smell on the wind was unfamiliar and it, too, seemed shrewd and intelligent. And yet she felt that she had known this scent before she was born. Birds wheeled in the sky above, their plaintive cries carried on the wind.

The smell of the sea was even sharper as they walked along the beach. It was strewn with debris from the previous night's storm: brilliantly colored seaweed, driftwood, various species of small fish, jellyfish, and starfish, half of which Saya did not recognize. Women and children, baskets in hand, gathered them busily. Saya wanted to stop and lend a hand, but she could not, for Chihaya continued walking without even glancing at them.

"Isn't the sea new to you?" Saya asked.

"It's the first time that I have seen it with my own eyes, but . . ." he replied.

Saya knew what he meant by this and did not bother to question him further.

Soon they saw a group of boys chattering excitedly. Knee-deep in the surf, they were gathered around a large black object that lay stranded on the beach. Coming closer, Saya saw that it was a huge shark twice as long as a man's height. It lay sideways with its pectoral fin piercing the sky, looking like a small hill with a flag upon it. Its belly was the hideous color of a corpse, and the long teeth which protruded from its jaws sent shivers up Saya's spine. Its eye, small compared to its body, stared blankly at the sky. She grimaced at the sight. No matter how she looked at the shark, it seemed like a monster from another world, and not something that should be exposed thus to the light of day. She felt nauseated but was not sure if it was from disgust or from pity.

Beside her, however, Chihaya whispered in awe, "What a beautiful creature."

Saya looked at him in astonishment. "Beautiful?"

"Beautiful, and strong. Look at the line of his body. Think how fast this fish could swim underneath the waves . . ."

Chihaya pointed at its pectoral fin, and at that moment the fin suddenly moved. Then the shark's flank undulated and its thick tail thrashed weakly against the sand. The children shrieked and leaped away.

"It's still alive!"

"Let's go get Father."

Although she did not scream, Saya clutched Chiyaha's arm so hard her nails dug in. "Look out! It's alive! Move back."

Chihaya, however, stood rooted to the spot. His eyes were wide, staring at the shark. Saya, realizing that something was wrong, tried to shake him, but his body was so rigid it did not budge.

"Chihaya!" she screamed, putting her mouth to his ear. But her voice did not reach him. He was listening to a different voice.

"I send thee greetings and encouragement, O young and solitary god. I am the God of the Sea who abides beneath the eternal waves in the ocean's depths. This great fish is the bearer of my message."

"Are you one of the many gods of the earth?" Chihaya asked.

"One might say that that is so, and yet one might say that it is not. For I am beyond the reach of the powers both of Darkness and of Light. In that sense, I am most like thee."

After pondering this for a moment, Chihaya said, "I think you have mistaken me for someone else. I am—"

But the God of the Sea paid him no heed.

"I send thee this message of encouragement, for I have seen thee upon my shore. I am merely an onlooker, powerless to lend a hand concerning thy bitter fate, and I can do no more. There are but two paths that lie before thee, and both are cruel. To slay thy parent, or to be slain by him—a hard choice indeed."

Chihaya was taken aback and pondered the meaning of his words.

"Although some may claim that it is not my concern, this shore borders on my territory. I will be watching the road that thou dost travel. O solitary god, unique in Toyoashihara, I send thee this message, for I also am alone. Tread with care, so that thou mayst have no regrets."

"Wait!" Chihaya cried. "Tell me . . ."

But the ancient voice faded away and instead he heard Saya's voice calling his name so loudly that his ear hurt. He blinked and saw before him Saya's face pale with anxiety.

"What?"

"I said move back!" Saya snapped at him.

Chihaya moved back a few paces but said, "If it's because of the shark, it just died."

Saya glanced over her shoulder at the motionless form and then stared suspiciously at Chihaya. "How did you know that? Surely you didn't try to possess that monster? Because if you did, I will have nothing more to do with you."

Chihaya shook his head. "I couldn't have. That fish was a messenger from the God of the Sea."

Saya's mouth dropped open in a childish expression. "What did you just say?"

Chihaya looked at the fish that had breathed its last, and frowned slightly, saying doubtfully, "I heard the voice of the Sea God. But I think he talked to me because he mistook me for someone else. He must have made a mistake." Puzzled, he looked at Saya and said in a low voice, "I think he mistook me for the Dragon."

A chill gripped Saya, and as she stood speechless, two fishermen approached from the other side of the beach, led by the children. They, too, stared at the huge shark, but when they saw that it was dead, they touched it with their hands and said, "This is a servant of the Sea God. We must prepare an altar and present suitable offerings."

Saya looked from one weathered face to the other in surprise. "Do you worship the gods of the earth?"

"Of course. For those who live by fishing could not survive if they were cursed by the lord of the sea."

"But didn't you worship the sun this morning?" Saya asked, and the fishermen laughed, their faces untroubled.

"Aye, and surely we would not forget the blessings of the Light. Isn't that so, young lady? The most important thing is to live a life full of thanks and praise. Our work is so perilous that even though we worship all the gods in the world, many of us still die untimely deaths."

"They are fortunate," Saya sighed after leaving the fishermen. "I wonder if the people of Darkness could not live like that, without fighting. You know, when I think of what lies before us, I'm afraid."

Brushing her windswept hair from her face, she turned to Chihaya with a pensive look.

"I don't want to be swept up in this war whether I will or no, to fight against the God of Light. But nothing can be done to stop it . . . Oh, I don't even know *that*. Have you thought about what you're going to do once we reach the stronghold of the people of Darkness?"

"No," Chihaya replied promptly.

"And you worry me, too."

Saya sighed again. She was used to the fact that Chihaya's way of thinking was difficult to understand. But it troubled her not to know what he, a Prince of Light, intended to do once he was among the people of Darkness. Nor did she know how the latter would receive him. She did not even know how she herself would be received. Although she was of the same race, she knew next to nothing about these enemies of the Light.

"I worry you?" Chihaya said in surprise. "What about me could worry you?"

"That is what worries me!" Saya said in exasperation.

The sun had risen high in the sky and the tide had reached its lowest ebb when Torihiko came gliding on the wind in search of them. Saya and Chihaya were helping dig up shellfish on the beach, and the children opened their mouths in astonishment to see a huge crow land purposefully on Saya's shoulder. She quickly walked away and turned her back to them so that their conversation could not be overheard.

"We leave by boat this afternoon," Torihiko said. "Her Ladyship said not to wander too far from the Sword."

"I know," Saya replied somewhat sulkily.

"I'll be leaving ahead of you. Flying is faster, so they told me to let Lord Akitsu know when you will be arriving."

Saya suddenly felt alone and helpless, and she looked at the black bird. "You're not coming with us?"

"Now that I've got wings they think of even more ways to keep me busy. Wouldn't you know it!"

"Where on earth are we going anyway? Across the sea?"

"No, it's not far from here. We're only going by boat because it's easier to go around the point and enter by the shore. The mountains are very rugged from here on, and it's impossible to approach by land. Lord Akitsu resides in a hidden valley. It's called Eagle's Manor." Torihiko broke off and hunched his shoulders, preening his feathers with his beak, and then continued smugly, "Of course, it's not much of a fortress if you have wings. Old Akitsu will be surprised to see me."

Saya bit back the words that sprang to her tongue. It seemed that Torihiko was almost enjoying his new form. He certainly seemed to have no regrets. And if he did, she knew he would never be caught lamenting his decision in front of her.

"Take care" was all that she said.

"See you later." Watching him fly into the sky, his spirits high, Saya wished that she could have even half of his talent for making the best of necessity.

2

They boarded two boats at noon that summer's day and rowed out into the dazzling sea. The two men accompanying them propelled the boats, sculling with practiced hands. Saya, who rode with Lady Iwa, shaded her eyes with her hand and watched the other boat some distance away, musing idly that the grim figure of Lord Shinado and the slender, fragile form of Chihaya could be mistaken for a slave dealer taking home a newly purchased slave girl. Although the little boats rolled and pitched, there was no fear of capsizing, and they forged ahead, trailing a wake behind. After they had skirted the point at a distance, the height of the cliffs gradually decreased and a dense black forest at the top came into view. They approached the shore carefully, passing several reefs where the waves broke white, and suddenly the bluff revealed a hidden cove. As they passed between cliffs, the rock ledges of which were lined with the nests of seabirds, the sea was suddenly transformed, becoming smooth and tranquil. Under the blazing sun, shore and forest were wrapped in silence and an air of brooding mystery. Or perhaps this impression was the result of Saya's anxiety at the thought of those who awaited them. She felt that the entire cove was watching in hushed expectancy. But there was no sign of anyone waiting to ambush them when they landed on the empty beach near a river that flowed into the cove. They found a path alongside it and began to ascend in the sweltering heat. No one spoke, and the only sound to be heard was the chirring of the cicadas. Soon the path entered a valley and became increasingly rugged.

Chihaya looked up and Saya, following suit, glimpsed tiny forms at the top of the cliff ahead, where the canopy of leaves was thinner. They seemed to wave and then disappeared. Saya, wondering if they would have to climb that far, suddenly felt she had had enough. It was a windless afternoon, hot and humid even in the shade; certainly not the season for sweating one's way up a rocky cliff. However, she need not have worried. They had gone only a few paces farther when they were met by a group of brawny men.

"Please pardon the delay and accept our humble apologies for not meeting you sooner. We had to be sure that you were not followed." The bearded leader of the group bowed his head respectfully. There were at least twenty men with him. They all wore black headbands and protective vests of hard leather over their bare tanned chests. Although they appeared respectful for the moment, Saya felt that underneath they were rough brigands. Lord Shinado accepted their greeting solemnly.

"Thank you for your trouble. Bring the litters here."

Two litters without canopies, each supported on long poles and carried by four men, were immediately brought forward. As Saya gazed at them curiously, Lord Shinado urged her to get in.

"Me?" Saya said in surprise. It had never occurred to her that she would ride while the lord walked. Confused, she looked from left to right, saying, "I—I'll walk. I'm not that tired."

But Lady Iwa said from the other litter, "It's all right. Get in. You are, after all, the Princess of our people."

Having no choice, Saya sat upon the litter, but in the end she found it much more tiring than walking, for she held herself rigid the whole way lest she should burden the bearers.

Finally a large plateau backed by a rock wall shaped like a folding screen appeared before them. Saya could see cool green meadows and cultivated fields. As they advanced, she noticed that the houses were built in rows along the bottom of the cliff and in front of them people were raising their voices in greeting. She recalled the day that she had entered the Palace of Light and the people who had greeted them in an orderly fashion in the fine rain, but this was a much more boisterous crowd, with children and dogs racing about.

"Look! She has come back at last."

"The Princess of the Sword has returned to us!"

"There she is, the mistress of the sacred Sword."

Wherever she passed, she heard these words on everyone's lips. Immensely thankful for the braided hat with its thin silk veil hanging from the brim, which had been lent to her to keep off the sun, she hid herself as much as possible within its shade. Of any reception she could have received, the worshipful adoration of these people was the most unsettling. Wondering what on earth Torihiko had told them, she struggled to conceal her discomfort.

Lord Akitsu's hall came into sight at the far end of Eagle's Manor. The space before the entrance formed the largest courtyard in the valley, and the back of the hall was set against the vertical cliff. The structure was built with a high raised floor resembling a wide shelf running horizontally across the cliff face. It did not appear very large. Indeed, Saya knew of much grander structures than this even among those owned by mere vassals in the capital of Mahoroba. But she later learned that she was mistaken, for the largest and most important sections of the dwelling were to be found within the cliff itself.

The one-eyed lord came to greet them at the gate. Although he smiled, his face was stern, like a rock long weathered by blizzards. In one hand he grasped a gnarled staff, on the top of which Torihiko perched nonchalantly as if part of its ornamentation.

"Well met." Lord Akitsu addressed Saya in a deep resonant voice, the beautiful timbre of which belied his looks. "You are indeed brave. How much more do we know this now."

Saya, wondering perversely what they would think if she burst into tears as she wished to do, sensibly remained silent, her head bowed.

"Lord Ibuki will join us in a few days. Then we will all be gathered together once more. But first you must rest yourselves in my hall."

Lord Akitsu beckoned them inside. His one shrewd eye missed nothing, and though he feigned uninterest, he watched Chihaya closely. He waited until Lady Iwa passed him and then addressed her in a low voice so that none should overhear, "That one. He can't be . . ."

"But he is," Lady Iwa replied, looking up at him.

Even Lord Akitsu was unable to hide his surprise, and he stared after Chihaya's receding figure. "That boy? One so young?"

"Yes, he is but a child not yet fully developed." Blinking her heavy, sparsely lashed eyelids, Lady Iwa whispered, "And that is precisely why he may yet become ours."

The room to which Saya was led was long and narrow, with one wall of stone, and she felt that she had indeed been placed upon a shelf, but it was much cooler and more pleasant than she had expected. Perhaps because she was tired, Saya sat drowsily where she had been left, and was slow to realize that a young woman was kneeling respectfully at her side. She was a round-cheeked, cheerful person, and although her hair was arranged on top of her head, it looked as if it had been fastened only with much effort, and many obstinate locks had defiantly escaped.

"My name is Natsume. I have been assigned to attend to your needs. Please do not hesitate to tell me your wishes," she said in a clear, crisp voice. Not much older than Saya, she nevertheless radiated a calm confidence.

"Really? Oh, I'm so glad!" Saya exclaimed, jumping to her feet. "I'm so glad that I am not to be attended by an old woman. Will you be my friend?"

Natsume's eyes widened slightly, but her face instantly broke into a smile as she replied, "Yes. Gladly, if I am acceptable to you."

"Are you married?" Saya asked, wondering if they had the same custom here in which married women wore their hair up.

"Yes. I was married this spring," Natsume replied, her cheeks turning a charming pink.

"How nice. What's your husband like?"

Still blushing, Natsume began to laugh. "Really, my lady! One of these days, I will tell you. After all, he, too, serves the lord of this hall."

Natsume was a dedicated worker, completing her tasks briskly and efficiently, and taking care that Saya should experience no inconvenience in an unfamiliar place. She seemed to find great joy in her work, so that just watching her was a pleasure. Saya, now having someone with whom she could be totally at ease after such a long and lonely time, took full advantage of Natsume's attentions and did not leave the hall for the next few days. She learned that Chihaya also had a servant and lacked for nothing. It was unusual, however, for Saya, unlike Chihaya, to remain indoors ignoring a new people and a new land. Although she herself did not realize it, she had not escaped unscathed from the string of events that had led her here. The scars of the experience had made her timid. Moreover, the reverent glances that the people of Eagle's Manor directed toward her confused her, causing her to withdraw.

Still, she was young and quick to recover. After several days had passed, her natural curiosity began to reassert itself. She could no longer endure the boredom of being cooped up in her narrow room all day and was just trying to think of some excuse to go out when Natsume returned from preparing the evening meal. "The other one, perhaps he is looking for something?" she said.

"What other one?"

Natsume blushed. "I do not know his name, but, you know, the handsome one."

"Oh, you mean Chihaya." Puzzled, Saya looked at the discomfited Natsume. "What about him?"

"I saw him beside the main building, and as he seemed to be looking for something I spoke to him, but he left as though he did not hear me."

"That's strange."

She could not think of any reason for such behavior. Yet the fact that Chihaya was walking about alone did not bode well. Saya rose. "I'll go and see. Take me to the place where you saw him."

She did not see Chihaya anywhere when she reached the courtyard adjoining the kitchen to which Natsume had led her. They walked a little farther until they came near the outer wall, and there they found Chihaya surrounded by several guards in front of the guardhouse.

"I was afraid it might be something like this," Saya thought. The guards, catching sight of Saya and Natsume running toward them, released Chihaya's arms and bowed their heads respectfully to Saya.

"My lady! We did not expect the honor of your presence in such a shabby place."

Although she had known her appearance would have some effect, she was disconcerted by their sudden humility. She felt somehow that it was not right that she, who until a short time ago had been an insignificant girl, should now be treated in this way. At the same time she could not reprove them for showing respect.

"Has this person caused you trouble?" Saya asked as she went to Chihaya's side.

"He ignored our challenge and began to approach the armory, so we ordered him to stop. He does not even attempt to answer our questions," one of the guards replied.

"Well!" Saya looked at the dreamy-eyed Chihaya. "What did you want in the armory?"

Chihaya's gaze, which had been roving far away, finally fixed itself upon Saya's face. "Nothing," he said. "I just wondered if there wasn't some way to get to the top of the cliff."

Upon hearing this, the guards' expressions once again grew grim. "And what business do you have up there? Only the sentries are permitted to stand at the top."

Saya hurried to defend him. "I assure you he had no sinister intent. He is just not accustomed to being in such a place as this."

"We are aware that he is a guest, one of your company, my lady, but we cannot ignore such suspicious behavior," said a serious-looking man who appeared to be their leader. "If anything should happen . . ."

"What do you intend to do with him, then?"

"Those who behave suspiciously must be imprisoned and interrogated."

Saya gasped in shock. "I give you my word that he can be trusted. I will talk to Lord Akitsu myself, so please, won't you let him go this time?"

The leader of the guards looked uncomfortable and finally said, "So you say, but this is our duty, my lady. If we are remiss, we will lose our lord's trust. Forgive us."

Saya bit her lip in consternation. But at that moment a voice came from behind them. "If the Lady of the Sword says so, why not let him go?"

Turning around, she saw Lord Shinado standing behind them, watching. His lean figure, while not particularly remarkable, conveyed more force than all the guards combined. He, too, was an honored guest at Eagle's Manor and, having nothing to do, seemed to have happened along at just that moment.

The head of the guards answered him in a spirited tone. "We beg your pardon, Lord Shinado. But he ignored our challenge as if he could not hear us. With such an attitude, the authority of the fortress will be undermined."

"There is no need to make a fuss over it. He does not have the intelligence of ordinary men, that is all. Like the lady, I will vouch for him, so let him go."

"Ah, I see. Is that how it is?" The guard looked hard at Chihaya, and his expression turned to one of pity. "If that is the case, let us overlook it as something that will not happen again."

"Why, of course," Saya said hastily. And at her urging, Chihaya came away quietly. As they walked back toward their lodgings, Saya glanced uneasily out of the corner of her eye at Lord Shinado walking beside her. She was at a loss as to whether to thank him. She appreciated his having come to her aid, yet she was vexed at his particular choice of words.

Lord Shinado, his face stern, likewise gave Saya a sidelong glance, and then said curtly, "Don't let Chihaya behave in such a way that he betrays his lineage. Most of our people are not yet ready to accept a Prince of Light into their midst. If he is going to walk about as he pleases, he might just be better off in prison."

Saya was about to make some retort, but Lord Shinado had already left her side and, turning his back on the hall, walked away. Saya angrily vented her feelings to Chihaya. "Don't you care what he says of you? He called you a fool."

"Oh, really? I didn't notice." Chihaya's response was so absentminded that Saya shut her mouth in futility.

"Why did you want to go to the top of the cliff?" she asked, overcoming her irritation. Chihaya's expression was instantly transformed into lively enthusiasm, so that he seemed a different person.

"Something was there early this morning. It was too far away to touch my mind but I know something came. Something that I have never seen before—like the shark."

Seeing his transfiguration, Saya realized just how little the argument with the guards had registered on his mind. And when she stopped to think about it, Chihaya had been extremely taciturn both during the journey to the valley and since their arrival. In fact, she suddenly realized that she had never seen him talk with anyone other than herself. This knowledge served further to increase her anxiety about the future.

"Could it be that Chihaya really didn't hear the guards, rather than just ignoring them?"

That night, Saya was summoned by Lord Akitsu and told much the same thing she had been told by Lord Shinado, although Lord Akitsu chose much gentler words to express his meaning. He wished to know, however, why Chihaya had suddenly taken it into his head to venture to the top of the cliff.

"I'm not sure, but he said that there was something up there, something that attracted his interest," Saya said thoughtfully. "Despite his usual absentmindedness, he is very sensitive in unusual ways, so I believe that there was indeed something there. Chihaya's senses seem to be different from those of other people. When we were on the beach the other day, he said he heard the voice of the Sea God."

Lord Akitsu listened intently to Saya's words. "Is that so? Yet I do not think that any god resides on the top of this mountain. Except for the sentries, there are not even any human beings. Only deer and mountain goats inhabit that area."

"It could perhaps be something like that," Saya said hesitantly, "because Chihaya is drawn to beasts rather than to people."

"Hmm." The one-eyed lord nodded as he thought to himself. Then, as if he had suddenly thought of something agreeable, he said, "In that case, tomorrow I shall climb to the top with him. I had just been thinking that it was about time to do something like deer hunting to keep my body from getting stiff. Has he ever used a bow? No, of course not. Anyway, I will guide him. Why don't you come, too, if you like?"

3

Early the next morning, Saya fastened the garters of her trousers and set out in high spirits. When she had said, half in jest, that she would need trousers in order to follow the hunt, Natsume had actually produced a pair. In Hashiba, women were not permitted to wear such things, and in the Palace of Light the mere mention of it would doubtless have invited chastisement. Saya, however, had always wanted, at least once, to stride boldly forth like Princess Teruhi, unencumbered by long skirts. Natsume had laid out an outfit of white trousers and jacket with a light green border and red garters adorned by little bells. "You're welcome," she said in response to Saya's fervent appreciation. "In times of war, all the women of Darkness must don men's attire and fight as bravely as the menfolk. We all have one such outfit to wear should the need arise."

"And you, would you fight, too, Natsume?" Saya asked in surprise. Fighting seemed as appropriate to Natsume's gentle nature as fangs to a fawn.

"If the enemy attacks us, then I will defend what must be defended," Natsume replied, adding somewhat harshly, "for the army of Light gives no quarter to women and children."

When Saya went outside, Torihiko flew down from a branch and alighted on her shoulder. "Well, well. You're wearing trousers."

"Of course. Don't I look dashing?"

"About as dashing as Chihaya," Torihiko replied. "His arm is at least as thin as yours. His bow is weeping. Look."

She looked and saw Chihaya dressed in hunting attire with a bow and a quiver of arrows, but no matter how often she looked, he appeared only to be carrying them for someone else. Beside him Lord Akitsu stood smartly equipped, every inch an experienced huntsman, with a falcon perched on his forearm. When Saya approached with Torihiko, the lord frowned slightly and glanced over his shoulder at them. "Torihiko? Do you intend to join us? You'll complicate things by upsetting Madarao."

The falcon, a cord fastened to one leg, screeched and repeatedly opened and closed its wings. It seemed poised to fly at the crow at any moment, but in fact was terrified of him. Chihaya was staring intently at the falcon.

Torihiko calmly parried Lord Akitsu's thrust. "Now, that surely can't matter. Considering the number of beaters you dispatched, you most certainly intend to hunt bigger game today than falcon bait."

"You're incorrigible. Well, never mind. Just don't get so close that Madarao breaks his jesses and escapes."

"You think I'd come close to you? I'm going to be with Saya." Bobbing his head up and down, Torihiko said to Saya, "I'll teach you how to shoot with bow and arrow. I used to be quite famous with the short bow."

The hunting party left the gate and, cutting across Eagle's Manor, set off along a mountain path. Torihiko told Saya in a low voice that there was actually a direct path to the top from the rock wall behind the hall.

"It's a secret. Lord Akitsu is a shrewd man. He thinks of everything, although he doesn't let on," Torihiko said softly. "Take that falcon, for example. It's not necessary for the hunt. He brought it along to attract Chihaya's attention. He's hoping to break through Chihaya's reserve in that way."

Saya realized that Chihaya had been so engrossed in the falcon that he had followed the lord ahead, leaving them behind. She shrugged. "Well, I hope that at least they can become friends."

The leaves were thick on the trees in the forest and the dense undergrowth of thickets and creepers made visibility poor. It was certainly not the best season for hunting, but the lord and his company did not seem to mind. As they moved farther and farther ahead, Saya gave up trying to keep pace with them to the site of the kill, stopping instead at the edge of the forest to practice archery with Torihiko. She stayed there till the sun rose high in the sky, lightheartedly shooting at a wooden target. Through the trees, the faint sound of the beaters' whistles and drums could be heard intermittently. The beaters had left before dawn and now were gradually tightening their circle, driving their prey in the direction of the river, where the archers waited. Hearing without really listening, Saya thought not of the excitement of those waiting with bows drawn but rather of the trembling of the living creatures who sought to flee from the sound of approaching death. Run! Run! Run! To those fleet of foot, sharp of hearing, the reward of life will be given.

"Is something wrong?" Torihiko asked, bringing Saya back from her thoughts.

"No. Nothing."

"Saya, no matter how you look at it, you will never be a famous archer. For one thing, you have no concentration," Torihiko said frankly. But at that moment there was a slight movement at the edge of Saya's vision. A bright reddish brown form passed swiftly and silently on the other side of the target.

"Shoot! Shoot! Shoot!" Torihiko screeched, flapping his wings, beside himself with impatience, but it never occurred to Saya to shoot. The form that she glimpsed through the thicket was a spectacular stag. Stately eight-branched antlers soared on his proud head. The fur at his throat was silver, while his back was dark, proclaiming him to be a long-lived veteran of many hunts. The stag glanced questioningly at her with glistening black eyes, and then disappeared once more without apparent haste. He bore himself with a spellbinding grace. Saya gazed after him for some time and then said to Torihiko, "He was like a god. If someone had said he was one, I would have believed it."

It grew hot, and at about the time that the hunt should have been going through the pass, Torihiko, who had flown off to check on their progress, returned in a fluster.

"Saya, Chihaya's run away! Everyone has stopped chasing game to chase him."

"What?" Saya raised her voice in astonishment. "I don't believe it. Chihaya?"

"Lord Akitsu said to come quickly. Hurry!"

Saya rose and ran after Torihiko.

Lord Akitsu was in the middle of the forest, far above the hunting site along the river's course. Seeing the breathless Saya, he spoke before she could question him. "I don't know what happened. He suddenly threw down his bow and quiver and ran off. I have never seen anyone move so fast in my life. We still haven't managed to catch him even with so many people searching."

"When did this happen?" Saya asked. "Until when was Chihaya with you? Or should I say with Madarao?"

"Madarao is now with the falconer, looking for Chihaya. But it seems that the falcon no longer holds his interest. He ran off after he saw the deer. A stag more than eight years old, a rare sight to behold, leaped out in front of the beaters, but before we had a chance to shoot, Chihaya ran off."

"After the stag?"

"No, in the opposite direction."

Saya shook her head. "But why?"

"You mean you don't know either?"

"I don't know that much about Chihaya."

"One thing I'll give him credit for, he's amazingly fast. I can't believe he's a human being," Lord Akitsu growled. "I was totally deceived by his outward appearance."

Saya, who was now quite worried, pleaded, "Please don't accuse him of anything until we find out what has happened. I'm sure there will be a simple explanation for this. In some ways he's just like a little baby."

The lord nodded but continued to frown. "I understand. But if he will not come meekly, we may have to catch him with a net like a wild animal. Although I intend, as far as possible, to see that he comes to no harm."

In a short while the men who had attempted to capture Chihaya reported that he had slipped through their circle and disappeared. It seemed that the manhunt would continue for some time. Although there was one possibility that worried her, Saya was so uncertain that she decided to keep quiet until she could see Chihaya for herself. The sun sank steadily lower in the sky. Lord Akitsu finally turned to her and said, "The mountain path is treacherous after dark. Go with my servant and return to the hall. There's no need to worry. We will surely find him and bring him home."

Torihiko stayed behind, saying that he would help the manhunt as long as his bird's eyes could be of use. Saya could not defy the lord's wishes, although she deeply regretted leaving.

"If only I had stayed with him," she thought bitterly. She descended the steep mountain path in silence, rebuking herself for her deliberate slowness in joining Lord Akitsu's company because of her lack of interest in the hunt. As they approached Eagle's Manor, she noticed a crowd of people in the distance.

"What is it?" she asked her companion, but he did not seem to know either. As they drew near, however, he said with relief, "Ah, Lord Ibuki has arrived. I must explain why our lord could not come to welcome him."

By this time Saya was able to make out the giant of a man who stood conspicuously in the middle of the crowd. Beside him even the tallest men looked like children clustered around their father. Cutting through the wall of people, she and the manservant came out in front of Lord Ibuki. He noticed Saya at once. His bearded bearlike face lit up and broke into a broad grin. "Well, well. If it isn't Saya, the Water Maiden! I'm glad to see you looking hale and hearty."

But Saya could think of no reply, for her eyes were riveted not upon Lord Ibuki but upon the squirming, struggling figure in his arms. Until then she had not seen it, as it had been obscured by the crowd. Covered in scratches, it flailed desperately at its captor, but Lord Ibuki did not budge, whether kicked or hit. When it finally began to use its teeth, however, the lord hoisted it upon his shoulder in exasperation. Marveling at this feat, Saya found her voice again.

"Chihaya!"

Her companion, too, blurted in surprise, "Where did you find him? Lord Akitsu is searching the entire mountain for him right now."

Lord Ibuki blinked several times and rubbed his face with his free hand. "Ho . . . Well, actually, thinking that I'd like to bring a little present with me, I went into the forest, but instead of game this thing sprang out. I couldn't really leave him there tangled in the brambles. But what a surprise to learn that he is the object of Akitsu's search." Lord Ibuki glanced at his shoulder, where Chihaya struggled wildly. "Such a handsome lunatic is a pathetic thing indeed."

"Please—just put him down."

Saya looked closely at Chihaya when he finally stood before her. He seemed to have been caught in a thorn bush, as he was a terrible mess. His hair hung in disarray, his clothes were in tatters, and blood oozed from countless scratches covering his face and limbs. But more than anything else, it was the eyes staring out through his matted hair that made her catch her breath. No one, not even Saya, was reflected there. His eyes shocked her, for in them resided only ignorance, despair, and naked terror.

"Lady, I will return to the mountain and report that Chihaya has been found," the manservant said. He turned to leave but stopped when Saya shouted, "No! No! This is not Chihaya!"

"What are you saying—" he began.

Saya interrupted him. "This is not Chihaya. What stands before us is a deer—a stag whose body has been possessed by Chihaya."

Lord Ibuki blinked again, as if he hoped that by blinking he would gain enlightenment. "Hmm. I'm having some difficulty following what you're saying."

"Chihaya has possessed a stag. Without thinking of the consequences, in the middle of the hunt."

This was the result of borrowing others' forms. Saya recalled the time when Chihaya had restrained her struggling body. Then a mouse's spirit had resided within her, and even now the thought gave her the shivers. When she held out her hands, Chihaya fell back and lowered his head, ready to charge her with nonexistent antlers.

"Don't be afraid. It's I," Saya spoke in a soothing voice. "Don't you remember? I didn't shoot you with my bow and arrow. I promise not to hurt you. Instead, I will help you. Calm down now, and I will help you return to yourself."

As she spoke softly and repetitively, Chihaya's breathing became slower, and he relaxed, looking timidly into her face. When she held out her hand once more, he sniffed it first, like a wild creature, and then came meekly to her.

"That's it, easy now." Saya stroked his twig-tangled hair lovingly. Abruptly she turned to the servant. "Go quickly to Lord Akitsu and tell him I want him to catch the stag with the eight-branched antlers. But the stag must not be shot, because that is the real Chihaya. Ah, but it would be faster to take his body with us."

She was suddenly filled with impatience. She began to think that at any moment Lord Akitsu or one of his men, ignorant of the truth, might shoot the great stag as he carelessly approached them. It would be just like Chihaya.

"We must make haste! Please, show me the shortcut that leads to the top of the cliff. We must hurry, or it will be too late."

Looking around her, Saya realized that none of them had as yet grasped the situation. But Lord Ibuki said, "Do as she says. It is the Lady of the Sword who speaks. Even if we do not understand, she surely has a good reason."

The servant seemed to accord him special respect, for upon hearing these words he obeyed immediately. But then it would be difficult not to accord special respect to one whose barrel chest towered high above him. The servant led Saya and the others toward the side of the lord's hall. There they saw a cave hidden by the building. It was a natural hollow that had been further shaped by the hands of men, and steps had been carved in the rock at the far end, leading upward. The servant, bearing a torch, beckoned them. "This way."

Although Saya herself did not mind, it required great effort to lead the terrified Chihaya along the passageway. She stayed by his side, stroking him to soothe and keep him from suddenly breaking free, and they could proceed only one slow step at a time. Lord Ibuki followed them, but he had to fold himself in two to keep his head from scraping the roof. Even so, the sound of his head hitting stone echoed countless times in the narrow cave.

After enduring these conditions for some time, they finally felt a breeze and saw the night sky. Stars twinkled. The sentry challenged them sharply but let them pass when the servant quickly uttered the password.

"Did you see a great stag? One with stately antlers?" Saya asked, squinting against the glare of the watch fire. But the sentry shook his head. Chihaya, however, appeared calm and turned his face to the wind. "Let us wait a little. If he is not a complete fool, he will come here in the end." Before she had finished speaking Saya sensed something moving among the trees at the edge of the light cast by the watch fire. As they turned toward it, two black eyes glinted in the firelight and the tall black shadow of branching antlers wavered.

"Chihaya!" Saya's voice rose to a shriek, though she had meant to speak quietly. "Come back here! Quickly!"

The stag leaped suddenly. But its movements were awkward. It was limping. Saya felt a stab of pain in her heart at the sight of a broken arrow shaft sticking out of its hind leg.

From beside her, Chihaya suddenly spoke. "Ahh. I am tired!"

While the startled Saya turned to look at him, the stag bounded into a thicket. "Stop!" Saya shouted hastily after it. "You're hurt! Let me dress your wound."

The stag did not return but disappeared into the darkness.

"Do you realize how much trouble you caused everyone?" Saya scolded Chihaya furiously after they had returned to the hall. In her relief, she was suddenly filled with anger. "Every one of us was running about the mountain after you. Me too. Not only that, but the entire population of Eagle's Manor is now convinced that you're crazy. And just think of that poor stag!"

Chihaya watched her face as though she were talking about someone else, finally remarking, "So Saya gets angry, too, just like my sister."

"And who wouldn't be angry!" Saya retorted sharply. "How can you treat your own body so carelessly! That is why you have no empathy for the poor stag. Doesn't it even bother you that you inflicted such wounds upon yourself when you were not in your body?"

Chihaya looked at the numerous gashes upon his arms. "Oh. I'll fix them."

"Well, you cannot fix the stag. It may even die because of that wound," Saya said, so vexed that tears came to her eyes. She could not forget the gaze of the creature that had trusted her and come to her side. Chihaya had been twice as attractive then as now, she thought.

"All right, all right. From now on, I will think carefully before I dream. Or I will ask you first."

"I don't want you to dream ever again," Saya said. "You are no longer in the shrine. No one is binding you or hiding you, so there is no excuse for you to leave your body in the care of a wild creature while you go out to play. You should be ashamed. You must take responsibility for yourself. You must have realized what a dangerous game you were playing when you were hit by that arrow."

"Mmm." Chihaya nodded, but he did not appear repentant. "That was the first time I have ever become such a large creature. It is difficult to control something so big and strong. When faced with danger, I found it impossible to stop its limbs. But when it ran, it was splendid! Really splendid! It springs from a rock and the next instant knows exactly where to land—not by sight but by feel—through its hooves. When it runs at full speed, the whole world changes. The ground becomes transitory, the wind thickens, and both become like water . . ."

It was rare for Chihaya to speak at such length, and before Saya knew it, he had lain down on his side, still talking, and with a soft thud as his head hit the woven rush mat, had fallen fast asleep. He fell asleep more easily than a gambler loses a fortune. Saya's anger died as she gazed at his face.

It was the face of a sleeping child. An untroubled face, with tightly closed eyelashes casting long shadows, and lips slightly parted. He was innocence itself.

"Lady." Natsume addressed her quietly from behind.

"Will you treat his wounds?" Saya responded. "Gently, though, so as not to wake him."

"I have brought herbs and hot water for just that purpose." Quickly completing her preparations, Natsume dipped a cloth in a basin of hot water and began to wipe the blood and dirt from his wounds. But a moment later she uttered a stifled cry.

"What—what's this?"

Saya looked over and she, too, doubted her own eyes. For beneath the crust of blood that Natsume had washed away, the skin was smooth and clear. There was not even a trace of a pink scar where the skin had healed. It might never have been cut.

The night had advanced when a strange girl came to Saya's room. She bowed and said, "The lords are meeting in my lady's inner chamber. They request the presence of Your Ladyship and Chihaya."

Saya recognized her as one of Lady Iwa's servants and said, "Chihaya is already asleep. Must he go as well?"

"Two places have been prepared. Your presence is desired," the girl replied politely but uncompromisingly, so Saya shook Chihaya awake and led him, yawning continually, where the girl guided them.

The "inner chamber" referred not to a room in the front of the hall but to one which had been carved into the cliff. There were probably countless such rooms hidden in this way. Saya pondered the strangeness of the building. Whether existing caves had been expanded or whether the rooms had been dug into the rock, they were the result of incredible labor. The walls of the corridor carved in the rock were smooth and unmarred, and not one of the supporting columns or the ceiling beams, set in a complex pattern, could have been easily executed. The strong-hold, lighted by the faint yellow glow of tallow candles, was pleasantly cool. No doubt in winter it would be warm. Perhaps it was even more magnificent than the palace.

At last Saya saw a light glowing through a silken curtain at the end of a passageway, and they arrived at Lady Iwa's room. Furs and silk hangings draped the quarried rock walls, and the floor was covered in thick woven fabric. Although the atmosphere was rather solemn, the room was spacious enough not to be oppressive. A faint, pleasant perfume pervaded it. An unusually large candle stood in the center, casting wavering shadows in four directions; perhaps it was the source of the fragrance. Each person sat upon a woven rush cushion. Lady Iwa was at the far end of the room, with Lord Akitsu and Lord Shinado to her right and Lord Ibuki and Torihiko to her left. The sight of Torihiko in crow's form claiming a seat all to himself was so absurd that Saya felt a little more at ease. The two nearest seats which completed the circle were vacant. Wine and food had been set before each place, but no one except Lord Ibuki appeared to have touched them. Even a whisper could be heard clearly. Saya realized then that no room could be more confidential.

Lady Iwa spoke. "The Sword and the Priestess of the Sword have both returned to us, completing our strength. We can now recover our power, which for decades has been inferior. All the omens are in our favor. My lords, you must exert yourselves. The will of the Goddess is with you."

The men all bowed respectfully. Saya was surprised to realize that the old woman, so small that Saya could have picked her up with one hand, commanded such authority. Although she spoke in her familiar husky voice, Saya suddenly felt as if the Goddess of Darkness herself were speaking.

Lady Iwa paused briefly and then continued. "However, there is one thing of which I must inform you. For countless generations the people of Darkness have fought the immortal Children of Light and their followers, at times attacking, at times retreating, for power has swung like a pendulum from one side to the other. Now, however, a new element has been added. At last he who until now was only foretold in prophecies has appeared: he who has the power to wield the Dragon Sword. Whether this is a good omen or not, I do not know. For it is an event that transcends fortune-telling. Since ancient times, the Water Maiden has been one of our people, invested with the power to still the Dragon Sword and lull its evil to sleep. At the same time, however, legend tells us that there is but one being capable of taking the

Sword in his hand and wielding it. That being is called the Wind Child. And having escaped from the Palace of Light, he is here, for the first time, before our very eyes."

Every face in the room turned toward Chihaya.

4

Saya and the lords stared in astonishment, their bewilderment increasing. Nothing could be harder to imagine than Chihaya wielding a sword. He was so sleepy that he appeared even more stunned than usual under their collective gaze, looking blankly off into space oblivious to Lady Iwa's words.

Lord Akitsu spoke in a choked voice. "Ah, hmm, you are certain, my lady—harrumph—that he is the Wind Child?"

"Chihaya turned the Sword into the Dragon. And you all know that it dealt a bitter blow to the Palace of Light. Is there anyone else who can call forth the Dragon and live?"

"He is an immortal, one of the Children of Light. They cannot die," Lord Shinado said brusquely.

"No. The Dragon has the power to destroy even the Children of Light. You must realize this if you consider why Teruhi and Tsukishiro never take the Sword in their own hands."

Lord Ibuki continued to look closely at Chihaya, but from his expression it was obvious that he still regarded him as a lunatic.

Torihiko said, "To tell Chihaya to wield the Sword would be the same as telling me to." He spread his wings. "In other words, it's impossible."

"Even if," Lord Shinado said belligerently to Lady Iwa, "even if he truly is the Wind Child, it would not change the fact that he is one of the people of Light. The Children of Light serve the God of Light. We would be hatching a snake in our bosom."

"That is not necessarily true," Lady Iwa replied, lowering her wrinkled eyelids and regarding him through half-closed eyes. "Princess Teruhi must have foreseen his potential long ago. She imprisoned him and concealed his existence. It can only have been because some harm would befall them if he woke to his power. Even after they had seized the Sword, they did not free him or give him the Sword to use; instead they required him to take the role of the Water Maiden. Princess Teruhi succeeded not only in stilling the Sword but in stilling Chihaya, who had the ability to wake it."

Lord Akitsu, who had been lost in thought, a grim expression on his face, asked suddenly, "But what will happen should Chihaya side with us and wield the Dragon Sword?"

"I don't know. It will surely bring great peril." Lady Iwa pressed the palms of her thin hands together. "But—and this is just a premonition—I cannot help feeling that the appearance now of the Wind Child is an omen that the end of this long struggle is approaching. I do not know what the outcome will be, but surely we must use drastic measures."

Lady Iwa sighed disconsolately and looked at Lord Akitsu. "Do you not agree?"

Lord Akitsu remained silent.

Lord Ibuki said abruptly in his booming voice, "If this little wisp of a boy must wield the Sword, then I am willing to teach him some swordsmanship. It may not help, but surely we would be foolish to decide before he receives some training."

After the previous strained exchange, his words were refreshing. Lady Iwa's wrinkled face relaxed in a smile. "Yes, you are right, Lord Ibuki. Although Chihaya has the power to use the Dragon Sword, he is still young and untried. In his lack of character development he perhaps resembles the Water Maiden here."

Saya ducked her head at being dragged into the discussion. Lady Iwa gazed directly at her. "Saya, you are the most recent of the generations of Water Maidens who have cared for the Sword. Do you agree to give it to the Wind Child?"

Saya thought of the Sword lying in her room, inlaid with red stones and sheathed in the scabbard that Lady Iwa had made. But no matter how she searched her heart, she could find no feeling of attachment to it appropriate for a priestess. It was a cheerless, cumbersome, accursed burden, and nothing would give her more relief than to have someone else shoulder it in her stead.

"Yes," she started to reply and then stopped. She remembered the thick black smoke rising over the great capital on the day the palace fell, and how she had so easily fainted. Was forcing the Sword onto Chihaya really the answer?

After searching for words, Saya said, "If Chihaya shows a little more reliability, I will gladly agree."

"That is sufficient." Lady Iwa nodded emphatically. "That is sufficient. Chihaya is still asleep. He has not yet roused himself from Princess Teruhi's sway. He needs your help. He does not know how to relate to people because he has spent too long alone. Right now you are the only person he is able to see properly."

Saya whispered to herself, "I don't think you can even say that he sees me properly."

"And likewise you are the only person at this time who is able to understand him. You must stay by his side and encourage him. It is fitting that you should make decisions and learn much together. For you have neither of you as yet developed your full potential."

After shaking the dozing Chihaya awake, Saya excused herself and led him back to their rooms. It seemed to her that, having succumbed to the coaxing of Lady Iwa, she now bore an even greater burden than before.

Although the days continued hot, the tone of the cicadas' song began to change. And raising her face to the cool breeze caressing the nape of her neck under the blazing sun, Saya could now catch sight of darting red dragonflies. But most of all, it was the dew at dusk and dawn that spoke of autumn to the flowers and plants. The season had begun to change. Saya, who had become friendly with the sentries and sometimes visited the top of the cliff, saw the reddish purple bush clover beginning to flower on the mountaintop, and thought of her home even farther east than the sky beyond the secluded mountains. The rice in the fields of Hashiba would be golden now. The busy season was approaching in which the harvest and the coming of the typhoons were the main concerns. The gayest festival of the year awaited them once the family had worked together to complete the harvest.

In the valley home of the people of Darkness the situation was entirely different. Here, too, activity increased with the changing of the seasons, but the harvest consisted of stones and wood for arrow shafts. There was a forge near Lord Akitsu's hall, and for the first time in her life Saya saw a foot bellows in action. Black iron ore brought from the bowels of the mountain turned red-hot in the well-stoked furnace, and the heat was further intensified by wind from the bellows. The ore, now glowing brightly, began to bend like a snake; then it was hardened, reheated, and beaten. Saya was not alone in her fear of the tremendous heat radiating through thick enveloping clouds of steam. The men beating the iron on the anvils seemed possessed by demons, their shoulder blades, tanned by the summer sun, rising and falling with their mighty efforts, their bodies drenched in sweat. And the results of all this labor were arrowheads and spear points, weapons of destruction; unlike the golden ears of grain that Saya had once harvested as she sang, these products led to death. Yet at the same time they spoke of a rugged heroism and inspired a strange excitement. The sound of the pounding hammer seemed to fill the people who heard it with eagerness.

"The war begins," she thought. Even the inexperienced Saya could understand that much. The mountain of arms that everyone was busily preparing was not just for hunting wildfowl or deer. The soldiers became even livelier, joking frequently. Saya enjoyed their banter, but in the bottom of her heart lay an uneasiness that disturbed her soul, as if she were awaiting an approaching typhoon.

Almost every night the lords or their advisers held councils of war in Lady Iwa's room within the stone hall. Day and night, scouts returned to report to Lord Akitsu.

"In two days' time we can reach the Asakura pastures. Warhorses are supplied directly from there to the Palace of Light. Let us first seize those pastures," Lord Akitsu announced one evening to all those assembled, after various suggestions had been made.

"Us? Take the pastures?"

As looks of surprise spread across the faces of the assemblage, the one-eyed lord continued. "Although we have mastered the strategy of surprise attack on foot by using the advantages of the terrain, we must prepare ourselves for the future. We will need cavalry. The time is coming when we must confront the forces of Light face-to-face on the plains."

"Are you saying that we have an even chance in a direct confrontation?" one of the older commanders asked in surprise.

"Exactly. From now on, we must ride the winds of fortune. Is that not so?" He turned to Lady Iwa for confirmation.

She nodded expressionlessly.

"Lady Iwa foresees that this campaign may be the final, decisive chapter in the war between the forces of Darkness and Light. This is our last and greatest opportunity to reverse the present state of affairs and to retrieve Toyoashihara from the hands of the immortals."

There was a stunned silence when he finished speaking, followed immediately by a buzz of excited whispering.

"Of course! We have the Dragon Sword. We may even have the power to overthrow the immortals themselves."

Lord Ibuki scratched his nose slowly and muttered doubtfully,

"The pastures? I wonder if they will have a horse large enough for me."

Lord Shinado, who sat to the right of Lord Akitsu, said in a confidential whisper, as if unable to contain himself, "You are surely thinking of Chihaya. That one could never keep up with us in battle."

Lord Akitsu smiled faintly and glanced at him. "I was thinking of Saya. But I suppose it's really the same thing."

"You intend to take the Princess to war with us?" Lord Shinado asked sharply, his expression harsh.

"We have no choice," Lord Akitsu replied. "We have no other way to keep the Wind Child at our side."

In a sunlit garden bordered by a fence, Lord Ibuki was yelling despite the early morning hour. He leaped about, wooden sword in hand, the agility of his movements belying his hulking frame. "Come on now! Move! Look! Here's my heart, here's my stomach. You can't even touch me when I'm wide open."

Chihaya lunged at him halfheartedly, but of course every blow was repulsed. Indeed, Lord Ibuki's great belly, slightly protruding, loomed directly before his eyes, but it was not so easily reached.

"I've never seen anyone so clumsy. Look sharp!"

Chihaya narrowly dodged a blow to his head. Even though Lord Ibuki was surely making allowances for his pupil's lack of skill, the blow would have resulted in more than a lump.

"But this stick is heavy."

"What are we to do if even a wooden sword is too heavy for you? Are you a man?"

Torihiko, who was perched on Saya's shoulder watching the practice, said, "It looks as though Chihaya's just fooling around."

"Well, it can't be helped. After all, he doesn't understand what it's all for," Saya replied. In fact, Chihaya's progress was so slow that she felt even she could do better. Though he had received blows hard enough to bruise as chastisement, he never once fought back in earnest. Even Saya, who did not really wish him to learn sword fighting, was concerned when she thought of sending him to war like this. Just in case, she was practicing in private with a wooden sword of her own so that she could help him should the need arise.

"You're working hard, my dear Ibuki," someone called out from the cool shade of a tree. Looking around, Saya saw Lord Shinado, dressed in a light blue jacket and trousers, his collar open, leaning his spare frame against the trunk of the tree.

"Ho!" said Lord Ibuki, wiping the sweat from his forehead with the back of his hand. "It's you. You are the best of us when it comes to sword fighting. Won't you teach this lazybones one of your secrets?"

As Lord Shinado was quite close to her, Saya could clearly see him as he turned his gaze slowly toward Chihaya. Unaware that he was observed, he let the feelings that he was usually careful to conceal cross his face for an instant: stabbing hatred and malice. Chilled, Saya prayed fervently that Lord Ibuki would not give him the wooden sword. Lord Shinado smiled coldly and shook his head.

"I haven't the skill to teach one who does not know death. For how could he ever understand the meaning of the words 'to fight for one's life'?"

"Ahh—I see." Lord Ibuki looked at Chihaya in surprise. Apparently, it was the first time this thought had ever occurred to him.

Lord Shinado added carelessly, "Why not try giving him a few mortal injuries? Then he might just become a little more like us."

He left the shade of the tree and began to walk away. He happened to glance in Saya's direction as he passed. Without thinking, the incensed Saya blurted out, "How can you say such horrible things?"

A look of faint surprise crossed Lord Shinado's face. Perhaps because she had caught him off guard, it made him appear vulnerable and easily hurt. For the first time, she realized that he was not as old as she had thought. Because of the grave expression he usually wore, he looked as old as Lord Akitsu, but in fact he might not even have been thirty.

After a brief hesitation, he replied in a low voice, "When I was about your age, my mother and father were slaughtered before my very eyes by Teruhi's troops. The entire village was massacred, wiped out. Though wounded, I escaped and vowed that someday I would take revenge on the Children of Light. If they could be killed by tearing them limb from limb I would gladly do it, but they are immortal. That is why I continue to fight, in the hope that the day will come to mete out suitable punishment to them. No matter how you may protest that the hands of that fool over there are clean, he is one of them. To demand that I stop despising him is to demand the impossible."

Turning his back on her, Lord Shinado added simply, "You should know. You have the same background as I."

Saya winced as she watched his departing form. "Our backgrounds are the same. So that's it," she thought. Perhaps that was why his words always seemed to sting her.

Chihaya continued practicing halfheartedly, showing no sign of improvement. One day, Saya, unable to bear it any longer, turned to Lord Akitsu, who had come to watch, and stated, "It's ridiculous to tell Chihaya to fight. It has never occurred to him to attack or wound someone. This whole business is foolish."

"But he's doing quite well." The one-eyed lord smiled and rubbed his chin as he watched the master and his pupil.

"What do you mean, 'quite well'?" Saya said acidly.

"You wish for proof, is that it?" The lord strung his bow with the swiftness of a seasoned archer. Then, drawing an arrow from the quiver on his back, he set it to the bowstring. "Watch. Don't make a sound."

Just as Chihaya sprang away from Lord Ibuki, the arrow flew whining through the air. Saya's breath caught in her throat, but in the same instant Chihaya nimbly dodged the arrow as if it were a bird in flight, and it whizzed past. After a slight pause, he looked toward them in surprise.

"You could have hit him!" Saya screamed. But Lord Akitsu shook his head.

"No. I knew he could dodge it. He must have acquired such instinct through his many experiences in animal form. That's why, despite his being a poor fighter, he is able to evade even Lord Ibuki's skilled sword arm. I just wanted to show you the kind of agility he displayed when he possessed the stag." Lord Akitsu smiled more grimly than before. "That youth conceals a power that neither he nor those around him comprehend. He is like the Dragon Sword."

Saya, however, was unable to take in his words. She was furious that he could shoot so casually at Chihaya.

"If that were your son, could you have shot at him with such lack of restraint? Even if you were certain he could dodge your arrow?"

Lord Akitsu seemed surprised at the anger trembling in Saya's voice. "Are you saying that there was any danger of killing him? But he—"

"Cannot die, right? I know. It is obvious that to you Chihaya is merely a weapon of war that has conveniently fallen into your hands. You are no different from Lord Shinado. Maybe you are even worse."

Saya turned her back on him and fled. She was uncertain why she had exploded in this way, but once she had vented her anger, she was overcome with sadness.

Torihiko followed her, flapping his wings. "Everyone is shocked. There is not a soul in this manor who would dare to criticize Lord Akitsu to his face."

Saya, without responding, took her wooden sword from where

it was leaning against the fence. She stared at it for a moment and then threw it to the ground with all her might. "I hate this! It would have been better if we had never come here."

Torihiko, who had hastily escaped to the top of the fence, looked down at her in concern. "What a temper! What's the matter, Saya?"

"I don't want to fight a war. I am to blame for involving Chihaya in it."

"But he wanted to come."

"It was my fault."

"No," Torihiko said, his black eyes glittering. "It was the Sword. We are all being made to dance by the Sword."

5

On the day of their departure, Saya was surprised to see Natsume dressed like a warrior complete with helmet. She had loosed her hair from its usual tall bun and wore it as the men did, in two loops at the side of her head tied tightly above her ears.

"I have no intention of entrusting you to the care of a man-servant, you know. After all, it takes a woman to understand another woman's needs."

"For me there is no choice. I must go to war. But there is certainly no need for you to come, too. It's absurd. Don't even consider it." Saya did her best to dissuade Natsume, because she knew that she was with child. She could not bear to think of her involved in battle.

"Stay here and defend what must be defended. You yourself said that is what you would do."

Natsume smiled, but it was the kind of smile that proclaimed she would not budge.

"I'll be all right. Please, let me go with you. I'm only in my third month, and I can still move easily. Any baby too weak to take such a little bit of movement is not worthy to be our child."

Seeing that Saya still hesitated, Natsume said frankly, "My lady, I wish to go for my own sake also. For in that way I can be with my husband, who will be one of Lord Akitsu's bodyguard."

Questioning her more closely, Saya learned that Natsume's husband, Masaki, was a friendly young guard whom she had met sometimes on top of the cliff.

"We often talk about you, my lady."

"That's not fair. You never told me. I never even thought he was married," Saya said, feigning disappointment and causing Natsume to laugh delightedly.

Having combed her long hair, Saya followed Natsume's example and fastened it in two loops at the side of her head. She then donned a pair of red trousers, tying each leg below the knee with a cord decked with silver bells. The trousers had been made especially for her. She alone of the people of Darkness was allowed to wear crimson, a sign that she was the priestess. Fastening a white headband around her forehead as a symbol of purity, she finished her preparations and, taking the sheathed Dragon Sword in her hand, went to bid farewell to Lady Iwa.

Lady Iwa sat motionless upon a mat in the middle of her room as though lost in meditation. The chamber seemed large and spacious, or perhaps this was only because of Saya's mood. When she became aware of Saya, Lady Iwa raised her eyes and gazed at her red and white apparel. Then she said quietly, "You leave for war, but a warlike spirit does not become you. Never forget that. Do you have the stone of appeasement?"

"Stone of appeasement? Oh, you mean Princess Sayura's amulet." Saya nodded and pulled the azure amulet from inside her collar, where it hung on a leather thong about her neck. "As you can see, I always wear it."

"It is not Sayura's. That amulet belongs to you," Lady Iwa

said somewhat sternly. "Never be without it, for it is a part of the Water Maiden, a part of you. Although you, who have not yet experienced its power, cannot be expected to understand, it is necessary for pacification. The Water Maiden's skill in appeasement is proof that she is priestess. It is because of this ability that she can still the Dragon Sword. And not only the Sword: she has the power to appease any god and call forth its peaceful spirit."

Saya's eyes widened in surprise. "Is that really true?"

"Only if you yourself remain unmoved," Lady Iwa replied dampeningly. "War stirs up wild emotions. In the midst of battle, it is difficult for one person to remain unmoved. You will surely experience such difficulties in the near future."

Saya reflected ruefully that she did not have much confidence in her ability in the first place, and that as for war, she was certainly not going by choice. If she had been permitted to remain behind, she would gladly have crawled into bed and stayed there. "Lady Iwa," she suddenly blurted out, "why must we fight? I still cannot understand. Why? Why must even Chihaya become involved in this war?" She knew once she had begun that she should not say it, but having started, she could not stop. She continued in a small voice, "I know that it is too late to say this. But Chihaya does not know how to say no. And because of that he will probably do as he is urged and try to fight. And I—I can't bear that."

Lady Iwa's large eyes gazed up at her like two dark pools. No matter how Saya tried, she could never glimpse what was at the bottom. But she thought for a moment that she caught a glimmer of sympathy within them. The old woman answered slowly, "I am one of the people of Darkness, and as such there is nothing I can say. For the sake of my people I would do anything, even become a demon. But . . ." She paused to reconsider, and then continued, "This is but part of one long river. Someday you will understand. If we do not follow the flow, we cannot hope to learn our destination."

Saya remained silent. She was now prepared to accept the old woman's words and engrave them upon her heart. When she uttered the formal words of farewell, the old woman nodded her head. "You are so young to be our one and only priestess. That grieves me, yet I cannot take your place. You must go. Surely there is some meaning in your very youth."

Leaving the inner chamber and walking into the courtyard, Saya saw Lord Akitsu, clad in black armor. With him was Chihaya, likewise dressed as a warrior. Saya flinched when she saw him. It was as though she were looking at Prince Tsukishiro that first time she had met him. Calming herself, she looked closely and realized that Chihaya wore a far from splendid iron helmet and black-lacquered armor with sturdy rivets. He looked bored, exhibiting none of the excitement one might expect in a youth. Still her first impression continued to plague her, throwing her into a strange mood.

"Saya, give him the Dragon Sword," Lord Akitsu said solemnly.

She stepped forward and spoke teasingly to cover her confusion at the sudden timidity she felt toward Chihaya. "Your armor looks heavy."

"Mmm," he agreed. When he took the Sword, however, he said, "But this sword is light. That's a help."

Saya saw the surprise on Lord Akitsu's face as she stood beside him. The Dragon Sword was a long, heavy broadsword. She sighed and thought, "In the end, it is I who drew Chihaya into battle. No matter how I may regret it, it is my own fault."

Several hundred soldiers had already gathered in organized ranks before the entrance to the hall. Black-helmeted, they carried black shields emblazoned with a vivid whirlpool, and each had a new bow or spear in hand. As Lord Akitsu stepped through the gate they gave a great cheer, greeting their general with a twanging of bowstrings and a beating of shields. Those who were to remain in the manor had gathered beyond the soldiers, and they, too, applauded. Saya attempted to slip through after Lord Akitsu but was so startled to be greeted with a similar uproar that she almost stopped in her tracks. She realized that she must now acknowledge her station. She was their priestess, and, garbed in red, she must exist for all of them as representative of the Goddess, just as Lord Akitsu could not exist only for himself. And in return, how many of them would not throw down their lives for her sake? It was terrifying to be thrust so suddenly into such a position. Knowing how unprepared she was, she worried about the future.

Under Lord Akitsu's command, they split up into groups when the sun had set and rowed out in small boats into the dark sea. The other lords and commanders parted with the army there, heading back to their homelands to raise troops. The greatest rising of the people of Darkness had quietly begun.

Three days later, Lord Akitsu and his soldiers were heading toward their strategic goal of the pastures, concealing themselves in the mountains' shadow.

"Saya!" Chihaya exclaimed in wonder just after they had crossed a mountain pass. "There are horses. A whole herd galloping."

Saya could see nothing. Before them lay only an unbroken line of low hills and quiet meadows beneath the darkening sky.

"Yes. A herd of rare and magnificent horses," said Lord Akitsu, despite the fact that he could not see them. "Wouldn't you like one?"

"Yes," Chihaya answered simply.

"This place is well guarded under the direct jurisdiction of the Palace of Light and ordinarily would be beyond our grasp. Now, however, they are preoccupied with rebuilding the palace and there are fewer guards. We will split into two groups and attack the barracks, all right?"

Saya tugged at Chihaya's sleeve. "Listen, don't even think of becoming one of those horses. This is important."

Chihaya nodded. "There were many horses in the palace stables but I never possessed one. It wouldn't do to confuse a trained war-horse."

Lord Akitsu asked Chihaya tensely, "You seem to be able to communicate with creatures. Can you call that herd of horses to you?"

"I couldn't call them all at one time."

"There must be a leader. If he came, the rest would follow."

"That I could do."

"Good." Lord Akitsu continued without pause, "First we must destroy the shrine mirror. While one group attacks the barracks, throwing our foes into confusion, the other group will skirt the wood and hit the shrine. Then this land will once again be ours. But as long as the mirror remains intact, we might as well be face-to-face with the immortal Children of Light."

The lord next looked at Saya. "I leave the work of appeasement to you."

Startled, Saya stammered, "But—but what should I do?"

"Just invoke the aid of the Goddess, as you would do to still the Dragon Sword. I have no intention of throwing the two of you into battle. I'll leave you under the protection of these stalwart guards. Move cautiously and do not leave Chihaya's side."

Under Lord Akitsu's rapid directions, the warriors moved as one, then split up and disappeared into the shadows. Saya caught sight of Masaki among the "stalwart guards" and felt somewhat relieved. His amiable young face, even in this place, seemed unchanged. But still Saya could not suppress her shivering or the goose bumps on her skin, and perhaps because of her pitiful appearance Masaki looked at her and came over to whisper, "Be easy, my lady. Our victory is certain. All you need do is remain calm."

Battle cries rose as flaming arrows arced through the air and the barracks' thatched roofs burst into flame. The battle had been joined. The sharp clash of metal on metal and the tumult of voices rose from the ground like a stagnant mist. Saya's group immediately began to move because they were in the rear guard of those attacking the shrine. They could no longer see Lord Akitsu and his men, who had rushed into the barracks brandishing their weapons. Saya kept her eyes on Chihaya's sword, but she could not tell if the occasional gleam of red in the hilt stones was a glow from within or merely a reflection of the fires of destruction.

Chihaya suddenly laughed aloud. Saya raised her head in surprise, for not only did he rarely laugh but their present circumstances were anything but amusing. "What's so funny?"

"I've never seen such a horse! He's fearless."

Chihaya's face, which glowed faintly in the flickering light of the flames, was animated and filled with eagerness. He frowned and turned to Saya, saying, "He's the leader of the herd. A magnificent horse. I wish I could show him to you, Saya. He's as black as coal. And on his forehead a single star—like the morning star."

Hearing his words, Saya thought for an instant that she could see a fleet-footed black horse with a star on its forehead, a proud, spirited young stallion roaming across the pastures. But she quickly pushed the image from her mind.

"Well, it's nice to be so carefree when everyone else is fighting for their lives!" she snapped. At that moment, however, she saw fingers of flame rise from behind the trees in front of her, whose black pointed silhouettes stood out in stark relief. The shrine had fallen.

She struggled to fight down a dizziness and something rising within her like a frightened bird. For Saya, the desecration of the grove, the defilement of the sacred precinct of the mirror, was painful. For an instant she felt the awful gaze of Princess Teruhi fixed upon her where she cowered in the shadow of the trees with Chihaya by her side.

"What is it, Saya? The Sword moans," Chihaya said, as if

noticing her for the first time. Her uneasiness had communicated itself directly to the Sword.

"The mirror has been broken." The words rushed from her as though she were delirious. "Something—something's coming!"

What it was she could not see, but it was palpable. From the midst of the darkness something radiating menace had suddenly arisen. Gradually it took shape—like a swarm of bees forming a cloud, like a lump of fat congealing. They must escape, now, a voice within Saya urged insistently.

"Hurry! Run! We must get away from here!"

The guards looked at her in consternation. "But it is dangerous to move. Stray arrows are still flying. It will be all right. Just a little longer."

These calm words, however, had no effect upon her terror.

"It's no good. You must flee! Or something terrible will happen!"

But Saya herself did not have the courage to turn her back on it, and in the end remained fixed to the spot, staring. Seeing it with her own eyes would in no way diminish her fear, but she could not bear the thought of being pursued by something unknown. At any moment it would materialize, ripping up the cedar trees in its path. And then, as though it could read her mind, it appeared with an appalling noise, smashing and rending as it came. The men surrounding Saya caught their breath.

It had taken the form of a creature the size of a small hill. It had the body of a giant bear on the rampage, and when it stood on its hind legs its face reached the tops of the trees. Its crescent-moon-shaped claws were much longer than any bear's, and a thick, hairless reptilian tail stretched out behind it, the scales gleaming in the evening light. Its face, wreathed in spines, was yet strangely human, a flat apelike visage hideous to look upon. The enormous monster came straight toward them, stamping its heavy feet and raking at the branches.

Gazing up at it, Saya could only hold her breath. What her eyes beheld was not a thing of this world, and before it any human cry for mercy seemed meaningless.

For a long moment they stood frozen to the spot and then Masaki, coming to his senses, yelled, "Stand fast! In the name of our lord, stand fast and protect the Princess."

The soldiers, startled by his voice, fitted arrows to their bows or held their spears ready. But Saya knew too well the uselessness of their resistance.

"Run! Run now!"

Whose voice it was she did not know, but the resolute urgency of that cry resounded strangely. She heard it as though unrelated to herself, but then suddenly someone grabbed her arm and yanked her roughly. As she opened her mouth to protest angrily at this treatment, she almost collided with the glossy flank of a jet-black horse. Before her, snorting and prancing, was a fierce stallion with a streaming mane.

Before she knew it, Chihaya had pulled her up onto its back. Then, feeling the horse's muscles moving rhythmically beneath her, she realized that they were flying across the dark meadow. The wind took her breath away and she buried her face in the horse's mane with the absurd thought that he was more like a shooting star than the morning star.

The monster pursued them. This was the only reason Saya managed to ride bareback on the speeding stallion without tumbling to the ground. Whether it was after her or Chihaya she could not tell, but it looked only at them and seemed filled with a malicious desire to harm them. Clinging to the horse's mane, Saya's legs ran with his in her mind. Flee! Flee! Flee for our lives!

But the creature was also fast. Its enormous form rushed toward them as though it were swimming through space. Rocks and trees were no more than level ground to its huge crushing feet. It came closer and closer even as she watched, and when the legs of the gasping stallion finally began to falter, it stretched out its long claws almost daintily toward their backs.

The stallion gave a piercing scream and the threesome that had been melded together were scattered in different directions like seeds scattering from a pod. As the horse tumbled head over heels, Saya felt herself thrown through the air and hurled onto a grassy slope; then she rolled for what seemed like ages. But when she finally raised her head, she saw she had not been thrown very far, and Chihaya was sitting up only a few paces distant from her. Moreover, the creature was but a stone's throw away. His nightmarish black form seemed about to engulf them.

"Unsheathe the Sword! Kill it before it kills us!"

It was not a conscious thought, but she knew she must have wished it, for the shining Sword was unsheathed with such speed that she could hardly believe Chihaya had done it. Then he threw it straight as an arrow toward the shadow towering like a mountain above them. Saya gazed up and saw the blade grow longer, twisting and thickening, engraving the image of the Dragon upon her mind. Its eyes gleamed bright crimson before the creature's murky darkness. Then the keenly honed blade moved like flashing light, slashing the monster's head and shoulders to tatters, until suddenly the creature lost its form and melted thickly into darkness. The Sword flashed once again, rising into the air, and as if seeking its next target raced toward Chihaya.

Saya, who had closed her eyes, opened them fearfully and saw that the night had once again returned to darkness, and Chihaya stood alone, trying to sheathe the Sword with awkward movements. Drenched with sweat as though she had been doused with water and shaking in every limb, Saya was only now aware of how terrified she had been. Unable to stand, she began to crawl toward Chihaya, but he checked her in an unexpectedly low voice.

"You had better not come too close."

Only then did Saya notice the bloody wounds that ran from

his shoulders down his back. The trail of the creature's merciless claws was apparent even in the starlight, as though Chihaya's flesh had been gouged with a sickle. Looking at Saya's pale, frozen face, Chihaya said, "It's nothing to worry about. Renewal will soon begin. The deeper the wound, the faster it begins."

"Renewal? You mean the return to youth?"

"Yes. The wounds will disappear. It is best to leave them alone."

Chihaya spoke as though it were nothing, but Saya, witnessing the immortality of the Children of Light, felt as bewildered as if she had come into contact with yet another monster, although one less fearsome. So this was how the Children of Light defied the passage of time and maintained a flawless, youthful form. In this way they rejected the natural flow of life and turned their backs on the road that all others followed to the Goddess.

Masaki and the other guards, who had been frantically searching for them, now raced up breathlessly. Asked if she was hurt, Saya shook her head and said, "No. I'm fine. I just got a few bruises . . ." Then, unable to bear it any longer, she broke down and began to sob.

Chihaya was in no condition to walk. He was placed, deathly pale, on a hastily prepared litter, but refused to allow anyone to touch his wounds. Walking quietly alongside the litter, Saya noticed that the black stallion, limping slightly, followed them hesitantly, like a dog worried about its master. But when he saw them enter the camp set up in the shade of the forest, he disappeared like the wind.

"Do you feel a little better?" Lord Akitsu asked, sitting down beside her. Saya nodded. Even with the bright fire burning directly in front of her, she still felt a faint chill in her shoulders, but perhaps because she had been persuaded to drink the medicinal wine that she had at first left untouched, she felt warm inside and slightly light-headed.

"How is Chihaya?" the lord asked.

"I think—I think he will be all right. He is sleeping like the dead right now."

"I had not the slightest idea that something like this would happen," the lord muttered as if to himself.

"What on earth was it? I have never seen anything so horrible in my life!"

Hearing the terror that still lurked in her voice, Lord Akitsu paused a moment before replying. "I cannot say for certain, but I think that what you saw was one of the earth gods."

Saya's eyes widened in surprise. "That monster was one of the gods of the earth?"

"Our job is to release those gods which have been harmed. The Children of Light subdued the earth gods and sealed them in the mirrors, then further confined them within the shrines they built. But if the mirror is broken and they are released, a strong god may even return. Many times we have freed the gods of the earth in this way, but never before has one of them borne us ill-will."

"Do you mean that this happened because Chihaya is one of the Children of Light?"

"I cannot think of any other reason," the lord said in a bitter tone. "To make matters worse, Chihaya used the Dragon Sword to kill the god we strove so hard to free. He has obliterated it much more surely than his brother or sister ever could."

Saya turned to face the lord. "But we had no choice. Who would not protect themselves when threatened by such a creature?"

Ignoring Saya's question, Lord Akitsu said in a low voice, "I wonder if Lady Iwa foresaw this. It seems that our plans are not to be implemented so smoothly. I cannot see how we are to make the Wind Child our ally."

SHADOW

Should frost chance to fall upon the field
Where the traveler seeks haven,
Shelter him, my son, beneath thy wings,
O cranes that cross the heavens.

—The mother of a member of a Japanese
envoy to China in the Tung dynasty

1

After he was injured, Chihaya slept for one full day, but by the next morning he was completely recovered and, saddling Morning Star, rode off. And from then on, Chihaya and Morning Star were as inseparable as two lovers. Morning Star was wild and spirited, approaching no one but Chihaya, while Chihaya never even glanced at another horse. The extraordinary pair showed no interest in the affairs of the group, creating instead an exclusive world of their own. At night they slept side by side, and as soon as the sun rose they set off for a morning gallop to drive the sleep from their eyes.

The weather became much cooler. Although the midday sun was warm enough to raise a slight sweat, sundown, which set the sky ablaze with color, brought with it a cool night. The red-and-gold-tinged clouds seemed to beckon the trees on the mountains, enticing them to follow suit. And the trees, eager to join the sky, put on their autumn colors. When the curtain of night had fallen, a myriad insects in the meadows set their wings humming. Faintly but earnestly they sang, warning that summer is followed by winter. It would have been well for all to listen to their song, since in their own fashion they proclaimed that light is followed by darkness, life by death.

The troops of Darkness remained in Asakura for a while to secure their hold on the pastures. Although the soldiers were thus afforded a brief respite, Natsume flew about as she helped prepare food for the troops. Saya followed her, trying to be useful, despite Natsume's protests, for she was much more comfortable being busy. She wanted to keep her hands occupied without time for thought.

Wherever she looked, she was confronted by unharvested crops trampled in the fields; the blackened shells of burned storehouses, their winter stores reduced to ashes overnight; grieving women laying their husbands to rest and, with their few remaining possessions on their shoulders, trudging along with faltering steps, leading their children away by the hand. Although Lord Akitsu did his best to be just to the people within the occupied territory, hundreds of soldiers were now devouring their food supply.

One afternoon, when they had some rare free time, Natsume said, "My lady, be so good as to behave like a lady sometimes instead of following me about like a serving woman."

"I see. You want to meet with Masaki," Saya replied. "Off you go, then. I'll just sit here by myself until nightfall."

"Whatever shall we do with you!" Natsume shrugged her shoulders, turning aside Saya's remark with a laugh, but then she added in the tone of one of superior age, "My lady, you truly care about the welfare of all those around you. But you should relax a little more. Like the other one, the guest in our midst. After all, I am only a serving maid."

Saya was surprised to be compared to Chihaya. "What? You mean I should imitate Chihaya and be excluded by everyone? No thank you."

Natsume burst out laughing. "I just meant it as an example. He keeps aloof from us all, as if he doesn't even see us."

"He's a bit dense."

"But he is very handsome," Natsume said with some admiration. "And recently he has become even more so—as if a light shines within him."

Saya cast her an anxious glance. But there was no hidden meaning in her words; Natsume was not implying that Chihaya was one of the Children of Light. She could not know.

It was true that Chihaya had changed since he was wounded. His face seemed more radiant than before, and Saya caught him smiling more often. He was still different, however, difficult to approach, and it was not only Lord Akitsu who puzzled over how to treat him.

"I'll have to tell that to Masaki," Saya teased, but Natsume remained unperturbed.

"He wouldn't be jealous. Chihaya is too different."

After Natsume had gone, Saya leaned against the fence at the edge of the pasture and rested her chin in her hands. Gently rolling meadows stirred by the breeze lay before her. Far in the distance she could see the tassels of luxuriant grasses swaying like silver waves. And there she caught a glimpse of Chihaya, the topic of their conversation, galloping across the meadow on Morning Star. Man and horse moved effortlessly, racing with exceptional speed and beauty, part of each other. Although Saya suspected that this could be only the result of horse and man changing places frequently, they had caused no harm, so she let them be.

"What am I doing here?" She had never imagined that she would still be asking herself this question having returned to her own people, her true origins. But finding herself caught in the midst of war, she was forced to ponder this once more. As though borne along by a tide, she had come to the front without understanding the purpose of the war. Surrounded by people who felt a burning sense of mission, people who had staked everything on the struggle, she secretly continued to wonder. Despite the confidence with which she had faced Prince Tsukishiro at the West Gate of the Palace of Light and told him that she must return to her own people, she now wavered in her conviction.

"I made an enemy of him, one against whom I must now

fight. I dealt him a terrible blow and enticed Chihaya, his own brother, over to the side of Darkness."

She remembered how her mother had frequently lectured her about not thinking ahead. Yatame had scolded her thus for climbing trees, for sliding down steep slopes.

"It's true. I never think ahead."

She looked up in sudden surprise at the sound of thundering hoofbeats. Before she knew it, Morning Star was almost at her side. Seeing the great stallion bearing down upon her at full speed, his dark flank glistening with sweat, she unconsciously stepped back from the fence, but Chihaya pulled on the reins, easily gentling the prancing horse, and jumped from his back. He looked over the fence at Saya and said, "The meadow over there is covered with gypsy roses in full bloom. Do you like flowers, Saya?"

In answer, she said in a small voice, "What do you think of every day?"

But Chihaya continued unperturbed. "Or would you rather see the akebi vines at the top of the hill? They are loaded with ripe fruit. By tomorrow the birds will have eaten it all."

"I like both," Saya replied. "I can like more than one thing, you know."

"Then let's hurry."

Saya frowned at his serious face. "Hurry?"

"Don't you want to come?"

She stared at Chihaya in disbelief, then looked at the black stallion by his side and said faintly, "I can't ride Morning Star. I've heard a mountain of stories from people who have been bitten or almost had their necks broken when they tried to ride him."

"But you've already ridden him!"

She had no response, for it was true.

"It's all right. Morning Star likes you. He wouldn't do anything to hurt you."

In fact, however, Saya hesitated because she herself did not really like this horse and was afraid he would sense her aversion. Such a creature must instinctively know how she felt. Strangely enough, Morning Star seemed taken with her. When the high-strung stallion flattered her by nuzzling her hand, she relented.

The black steed with the white star sped lightly across the fields with the two on his back. Unlike the full-speed gallop on the night that they had fled in panic from death, it was an easy gait that brought a surge of joy to her heart. They flew along, the wind whipping at her hair until it fell loose and streamed behind her, and she finally laughed aloud. The meadows were bathed in sunlight, giving off a scent of dried grass, and buzzards wheeled lazily in the clear expanse of sky. Together they gathered the dark purple akebi fruit, ripened and splitting, at the edge of the hill and then set off for the field of gypsy roses. The meadow was a mass of flowers spreading as far as the eye could see, exceeding Saya's expectations. The hollow was buried in pale purple, and the slender fragile stems swayed in the breeze, creating such beauty that she felt a pang of sorrow. She knew then that she would not pluck even one stem, for such beauty could never be captured in a bouquet.

While she stood speechless in the midst of the flowers, Chihaya waited, silently stroking Morning Star's mane. Many clouds had drifted peacefully across the sky by the time she finally spoke. "Why can't we live like the trees or the flowers? Flowers bloom for no one in particular when the time comes, and trees bear fruit without ever knowing war. If only we could live like that, too."

As if discovering something for the first time, Chihaya asked, "Don't you like war, Saya?"

Saya looked back at him in surprise. "Do you?"

Chihaya thought for a moment. "Well, I don't know whether or not I like it . . ."

Saya was about to scold him when he continued, "But if we had not come here, I would never have met Morning Star."

Placing his hand on the horse's shoulder, Chihaya gazed at him tenderly. Morning Star lowered his head and began browsing on some thistle flowers, heedless of the prickles.

"And it doesn't matter to you that storehouses were razed and people slain so long as you have Morning Star?" Saya pressed him.

Chihaya paused and finally said, "To attain something, you must lose something first. This must surely be the same for everyone. Just as I lost my other dreams the night that I found Morning Star."

Saya gazed at him inquiringly. "You mean you can no longer dream?"

Chihaya nodded slightly with a hard expression. It was the first time he had ever looked that way, as though contemplating a bitter memory. "I will never dream again. For I can never again forget who I am. I realized that when I could not escape from the pain."

Saya felt a stab of remorse. Knowing that Chihaya had the power of renewal, neither she nor Lord Akitsu had had much sympathy for him. It had never occurred to them that an immortal would feel the same pain as a mortal when wounded. Although he had borne an injury that would have killed an ordinary man, he had had to nurse his pain alone with none to comfort him.

Saya asked quietly, "Do you regret it—coming to join us?"

She thought that she could understand what Chihaya had lost. It was like the snow-white robe that he had first worn. When she had lured him out into the real world, it had soon become so soiled that it could never be worn again.

Chihaya, however, looked at her in surprise. "What should I regret? Morning Star is here, and so are you."

Saya was somewhat relieved, although a little annoyed that he put his horse before her.

Lord Akitsu continued to advance once he was certain that they had secured a sufficient foothold. The army traveled south and captured Kamioyama Pass, a strategic point on the road running east–west. This road was a major thoroughfare, along which passed all tribute from the districts connected to Mahoroba. Moreover, they captured the pass just as tribute for the year's harvest festival was being hurried toward the capital, and all of it fell into their hands. At the same time, it was necessary to destroy every shrine in the neighborhood and to shatter the mirrors within them in order to delay the news from reaching the forces of Light. Although Saya felt she would die of worry during this period, no other raging gods appeared, despite Chihaya's presence. It was unclear whether this was because of her ability to pacify the gods, but she chose to believe that it was the result of her fervent prayers.

Having at last located the enemy's position, the Palace of Light sent out a punitive force. The area around the pass was engulfed in fighting, so that none of the people of Darkness dared to approach it. Although the battle was prolonged, it was clear to all that the people of Darkness had the advantage. They were skilled in swift sorties and surprise attacks that took advantage of the mountainous terrain, in which they were perfectly at home. They materialized unexpectedly in small bands to attack and then disappeared again like phantoms.

The generals leading the army of Light, relying on the force of numbers, poured in constant reinforcements, but were finally forced to retreat. Saya and Natsume were removed from the front to Asakura when the fighting became intense. There they wrung their hands in anxiety. At the news of the victory, however, they rejoined the other troops, laughing with the soldiers and clapping their hands for joy. For the first time Saya understood how people can grow accustomed to war. Fleeting moments of joy such as these, intensified by the stark contrast between life and death, could make one almost mad with happiness. Friends joined by the bond of life became even closer, much more so than in everyday life. To Saya, there was no one more beloved than each and every returning soldier, garbed in rags, filthy or blood-smeared. Although she was surprised to find herself laughing so close to the carnage, her laughter was genuine, not a mere show to bring courage to the soldiers.

On such a day, the news came that Lord Shinado, who had been making for the western border, had completely routed an expeditionary force awaiting the arrival of Princess Teruhi, and that he was now pressing relentlessly eastward. The messenger, who had been dispatched immediately upon receipt of the news, returned within a few days with the report that Lord Shinado's forces would soon join Lord Akitsu's army.

"What speed! He is well named the 'keen-eyed hawk,' " Lord Akitsu said with a pleased smile. "This will surely have thrown the palace into a frenzy. But it's too late. By the time the immortals get moving, our army will be large enough to match them."

The soldiers were inspired by Lord Shinado's heroic feat, and morale soared. Saya, who stood listening to the soldiers sing stirring songs, their arms around one another's shoulders, was surprised to see the messenger, having finished reporting to the lord, heading toward her.

"Lord Shinado bade me bring this to you, my lady," he said. He gave her a package attached to a branch thick with dark green leaves. Taking it in her hands, she smelt a sharp, fresh fragrance. Several round yellow fruit nestled among the leaves. Mandarin oranges—she had heard of them, the poet's "ever-fragrant fruit." Opening the package, she found a necklace of bright green beads inside.

"Why this—for me?" she asked without thinking.

"I am not the man of whom you should ask that question, my

lady," the messenger answered in some embarrassment. Saya blushed and chided herself for her thoughtlessness. Yet she could not understand it. She had only talked to Lord Shinado a few times, and certainly the conversations had not been particularly pleasant.

The messenger bowed respectfully and said solemnly, "I was to ask whether Your Ladyship was in good health."

Saya, feeling strangely flustered, took the parcel to her quarters and put it away in her wicker trunk. "It's odd," she thought, "but I cannot feel glad. Why do I feel so awkward with that man?"

Several days later, Lord Shinado's army joined them as arranged and without incident. The troops displayed extraordinary mobility, demonstrating Lord Shinado's tactical skill. Saya saw the lord for the first time in a long while, but, far from alleviating her confusion, the sight of him only served to increase it. Although she realized that it was unkind, her eyes slid away from his gaze. It was impossible, however, to avoid him forever. Once quarters had been set up for the new soldiers, Lord Akitsu summoned Lord Shinado and Saya for a private consultation. When they reached his heavily guarded camp, Lord Akitsu carefully cleared people from the area and then related the details of Chihaya's encounter with the earth god to Lord Shinado.

"We cannot foresee what will come of this. It could happen again. Yet in all honesty I am at a loss as to how to hold Chihaya in check. What do you think?"

"It is unlike you to stand idle. Obviously an encounter between Chihaya and the gods of the earth can only bring harm," Lord Shinado said frankly.

"But we cannot disregard what Lady Iwa said. She called on us to find in Chihaya the one who would wield the Dragon Sword on our behalf."

"Killing the gods renders all our efforts meaningless. Even

disregarding that point, if we harbor someone like him in our midst, there is no telling when the wrath of the gods will fall upon us."

Lord Akitsu stroked his chin. "I, too, am concerned about that. But Chihaya has not yet caused us any harm."

"A Prince of Light who has not caused us harm?" Lord Shinado retorted sourly. "He is immortal. That alone is a rejection of all who live in Toyoashihara. He deserves to be cursed."

Unable to remain silent, Saya burst out, "Will you blame him simply because he does not die? Surely our people are not so narrow-minded as to shun him just because he differs in this one respect."

Lord Shinado said coldly and politely, "My lady appears to be mistaken. Perhaps you do not realize that the powers of renewal of the immortals threaten our very existence. They are trying to create a deathless land in Toyoashihara, removing obstacles such as ourselves as though they were pulling up weeds."

Saya was at a loss for words and regretted having opened her mouth. Lord Akitsu carefully brought the conversation back to the original topic. "Our present task is to somehow calm the wrath of the gods against Chihaya and continue our advance."

Lord Shinado drew his brows together. "The most effective way to appease the gods is to offer a sacrifice . . ."

"You know we cannot sacrifice Chihaya. He will not die."

"Have you ever thought of trying?" Lord Shinado retorted flippantly but then continued seriously, "Even if we don't go that far, Chihaya should at least be imprisoned, whether he is the Wind Child or not. Depending on how you look at it, he could in fact be considered our hostage."

"Hmm," the one-eyed lord grunted thoughtfully. It was obvious that this was not the first time that he had heard such advice. Furious, Saya screamed, "No! If you do that, we will lose Chihaya. Can't you see that?"

The two lords looked at Saya in surprise.

"Why do you think Chihaya came here in the first place? Why do you think he stays? It's because he was kept imprisoned the whole time he was in the Palace of Light. He could never feel the wind, the earth, the grass. Will we do the same to him as the people of Light did? Take away his freedom—use him—make no attempt to understand him?"

Lord Shinado said in a low voice, "Our first duty is to free the children of the Goddess of Darkness, the myriad gods of the earth. Concerning yourself with a Prince of Light when the gods wish otherwise is to invite their anger."

Saya turned away, sweeping back her hair. She spoke in a defiant tone. "If you are trying to say that I failed in my task of appeasing the gods, then you are correct. The fault is mine. I could not stop the Dragon Sword. If you are going to condemn Chihaya for this, then you have the wrong person. Why don't you seize me and offer me as a sacrifice?"

Lord Akitsu intervened. "There is no need to become so upset. Especially you, Saya, as priestess."

Seeing that Saya looked somewhat ashamed after this mild rebuke, he continued, "But I can understand your anger, too. Let us wait a little longer and see what happens concerning Chihaya. After all, so far trouble has arisen only once. Your power as priestess is certainly having some effect."

Although it had been a short meeting, Saya was exhausted and was about to hurry back to her quarters when she was suddenly stopped by a voice from behind. It was Lord Shinado. He stood, arms folded, beside a slender red pine tree. Saya stopped and turned, suddenly ill at ease. She remembered with embarrassment that she had not yet thanked him for his gift. "The other day, I didn't deserve such a—"

"Never mind that," the lord interrupted abruptly; yet he did not seem angry. Rather, his tanned face bore the expression of one deep in thought. "How can you defend one such as Chihaya?"

Hiding her surprise, Saya replied, "Because I have no reason to hate him. I feel sorry for him. He did not seem happy in the palace."

"Happy? Happiness, unhappiness depend upon our standards. We cannot fathom the immortals. You concern yourself too much with them. And your concern is in vain. Look carefully at Chihaya. He has not the compassion or the feelings of even an ordinary man."

His words struck a little too close to home and Saya retorted, "How can you judge that? I know him better than you."

"If you think about the meaning of the word 'compassion,' then it is obvious," Lord Shinado replied confidently. "It is impossible for someone who doesn't know death to know true fear, true separation, true sadness. It is impossible for him to understand concern for others, consideration, or the bond between hearts. It is the very fact that we have mortal frames that makes us long for one another when close, and love one another when apart. Isn't that so?"

There was no argument against this. Saya averted her gaze. She felt despondent, as though she had been severely reprimanded, yet she did not want to admit the truth of what he said to herself. Her eyes downcast, she said in a subdued tone, "But just because he does not respond, is that sufficient reason to reject him cruelly? I don't think that is what compassion means."

Lord Shinado stirred and unfolded his arms. Changing his tone suddenly, he said, "Why is it that whenever we speak together we end up arguing? Still, what you have just said is true."

When Saya raised her face, she found Lord Shinado gazing at her steadily. "I know it too well. For I am not without compassion myself."

Suddenly disconcerted, Saya opened her mouth but, even to her, her voice sounded lifeless. "Forgive me for my rudeness . . ."

"No, no. There is no need to apologize." He turned away and

as he left said in a low voice, "You should wear the necklace. The color of jade would surely suit you."

Saya returned to her quarters in confusion. Although Natsume asked what had happened, she could not bring herself to tell anyone.

2

The army of Darkness had become such an imposing force that it now proceeded east without any attempt at concealment. And all along the way, people joined its ranks, either won over to its side or subdued by its military might. Some powerful clans even removed the shrine mirrors themselves once they learned which way the wind was blowing. Something of which they had remained unaware while dazzled by the Light was now awakened by the storm of the passing of the army of Darkness. They began to realize that the earth had become exhausted during the long years of their infatuation with immortality and eternal youth, and the continuous offerings required. There were many who had groaned under the burden of tributes compounded by the annually decreasing harvests. By now there were none in Toyoashihara who did not know the names of Lord Akitsu, commander in chief, and his resourceful general, Lord Shinado. Their ranks swelled with deserters from the Light. The Prince and the Princess of Light remained in Mahoroba and sent general after general to oppose them, but nothing could stop the army of Darkness as it advanced toward the capital like a storm cloud covering the sun. At the same time, reports reached the army of Darkness that Lord Ibuki, who had been inciting small-scale insurrections in the east, had now assembled his battalions and was marching west to meet them.

Upon receiving this news, Lord Akitsu told his commanders,

"Once we have joined Lord Ibuki, our forces will be complete and we will be able to overthrow Mahoroba. The eastern front is heavily protected and there is as yet no crack in their defenses. The outcome depends on whether we can break through that wall to unite with Lord Ibuki's forces. If we succeed, our victory is almost assured. Now is the time to give full play to our military might."

Under his orders, an unprecedented and ferocious attack was launched. The army split into five, then eight, and advanced against the army of Light, which was strengthening strategic points. The army's movements were so complex that it seemed impossible that they could still be controlled. The battle raged for three days and three nights, and after a slight respite fighting erupted again and continued for another three days. Saya, of course, remained with the rear guard, but she was worried for Chihaya rather than for herself. He usually fought alongside Lord Akitsu, but when the army split and then split again she had no idea of his whereabouts. She had lost sight of him before in the midst of battle and he had always come riding nonchalantly back astride Morning Star; however, they had never yet been separated for this long, and she was uneasy.

The next day a rider brought the glad tidings that the two leaders, Akitsu and Shinado, riding side by side, had breached the last defenses of the army of Light. The anxious faces of the soldiers in the rear guard lit up. At the same time, however, a message from Lord Akitsu reached Saya that filled her heart with foreboding. She was requested to join him secretly at the front line.

She left immediately with the messenger, spurring on her mount. As they cut across the battlefield, where the smoke from smoldering grass still lingered, the heart-wrenching sight of the spears and helmets of fallen soldiers drew her eyes. Troops slowly making their way back as they cared for their wounded looked up in surprise at the sound of pounding hoofbeats. But Saya made no attempt to slow her horse, for if she allowed herself to see the young soldiers, dead or wounded, she would surely come to a halt.

The camp to which the messenger guided her was in a copse at the entrance to a valley, and the soldiers' shields were planted in a circle around it, just as they would have been during a battle. Horses were tethered outside this circle and Saya was startled to see Morning Star tied to a tree trunk, apart from the herd. "Well, what can have happened to your companion?"

Morning Star snorted when he caught sight of her. He looked disconsolate, but when without thinking she approached him, he suddenly bared his long teeth as though to bite her mount and she hurriedly withdrew.

Lord Akitsu himself came out to meet her and led her into a tent. Saya, too impatient for greetings, immediately demanded, "What is it? What has happened to Chihaya?"

The one-eyed lord looked exhausted, and even in the dim twilight his face was haggard. In a low, weary voice he replied, "It was two days ago. We were moving to a new position when we were unexpectedly attacked from behind. They shot arrows in our direction and fled—more like the way we used to fight—but Chihaya was hit. An arrow pierced his heart."

Saya paled but remained calm. "And what happened to him? He didn't die, surely?"

"Of course not. Renewal began. Although for some time he appeared to be dead . . ."

He lifted a curtain and allowed Saya to pass under it. It was dark within and she could see nothing until a lamp was lit. Then, as the flickering yellow glow illuminated the surroundings, she saw Chihaya's form lying half-hidden behind his armor.

"He seems to be just sleeping now. It's hard to believe until you actually see it—this return to wholeness."

Chihaya slept, a peaceful expression on his face, and his bare chest rose and fell gently. There was a faint red bruise on his left side that could no longer be called a wound.

"Oh, thank goodness. There was nothing to worry about, then," Saya said impulsively in a cheerful voice, but she regretted it as soon as she looked at Lord Akitsu. "Is something wrong?"

With a dark expression, the lord replied, "Everyone saw it. They saw Chihaya 'die.' If he returns as though nothing happened, they will demand an explanation from me. Rumors will spread instantly. The whole army will know that he is an immortal Prince of Light."

Startled, Saya stared at the sleeping Chihaya. But his face was still like an innocent child's, and as she looked, she felt reassured.

"It can't be helped. It's the truth. No matter how we try to conceal it, someday it will become known."

"Yes, that's true. But—but I don't have any confidence in my ability to protect him."

His voice was filled with anxiety and Saya looked closely at him in concern. His face, etched with deep shadows carved by the lamplight, was that of a man who had not slept for many days.

"What is it? What do you fear?"

The lord's voice was almost a whisper. "For the last two nights I have seen disturbing shadows. They circled the camp but did not attack us, probably because so much blood was spilled in the field. Angry gods thirst for the blood of sacrifice, but there was enough death to satiate any raging god. Now, however, the battle is finished. Tonight there is no substitute for the sacrifice."

Holding her breath, Saya whispered, "What is drawing them here?"

"It is Chihaya's power of renewal that most angers the gods of the earth. Just as death is defilement to the God of Light, so renewal is defilement to the gods of the earth, and they abhor it. You have managed to appease them well, but when the power of renewal is flaunted so clearly before them, it must be expected that they will bare their fangs . . ."

Saya glanced at the Dragon Sword lying beside Chihaya. Like him, it slept peacefully. The lord continued, "Unable to return to the rear guard with him, I summoned you. I wanted to hear your thoughts. We cannot fight against the gods in order to protect Chihaya. No matter how strong we are, it would be futile. Only you can stand before the gods. Only you have the power to appease their wrath."

For the first time, Saya realized that Lord Akitsu was afraid; he, a seasoned warrior, was overcome with fear. As for Saya, she was more than sufficiently terrified.

"Night is coming. We cannot remain here any longer. What shall we do? Should we leave Chihaya here and retreat? Or can you appease the wrath of the gods?"

In a hoarse voice, Saya asked, "If we desert Chihaya, what will happen to him?"

Lord Akitsu reached out a hand and took Saya by the shoulder, but before he could reply an anguished scream rose from somewhere near the tent. The sound quivered in the air, sending shivers up their spines.

"What's happening?" Lord Akitsu shouted to the soldiers outside.

"It's the horses!" cried one of his men. "The horses are screaming in fear."

The sound came again, and Saya put her hands over her ears, unable to bear it. She was afraid that she herself would start shrieking.

"Saya, calm down. If you allow yourself to become agitated, you'll wake the Dragon Sword," Lord Akitsu said sternly. Saya saw that the stones in the hilt of the sword were glowing red. But it was Chihaya, not the sword, who awoke. His eyes opened suddenly and he sat up in a leisurely fashion, stretching as if he had just awoken on a bright sunny morning. He stopped in mid-stretch, however, when he noticed Saya and Lord Akitsu staring at him wordlessly, and after looking closely at Saya, he spoke.

"You are afraid."

"You're so observant," Saya replied acidly. "We're in terrible danger!"

But at that moment a soldier rushed inside the tent. His face was as pale as wax and covered in sweat.

"A pack of wolves is closing in on us. Several soldiers were attacked and taken by surprise. We must retreat."

"Wolves? At this time of year?" Pushing past the soldier, Lord Akitsu left the tent. His guards stood in formation around the camp, their shields grasped in their hands. In the thick darkness between the trees, shadows squirmed toward them along the forest floor. Countless pairs of eyes glowed red in the torchlight. The menacing growl rattling low in their throats seemed to set the very air vibrating. Advancing to the edge of the forest, the creatures glared at the soldiers, their venomous tongues lolling and their yellow fangs bared and glinting in the firelight. Their eyes gleamed with savage intent.

One wolf, which had been inching slowly toward the soldiers, closed the distance between them and sprang. It leaped straight for the throat of its prey, but the soldier's sword swung true. As the wolf howled and rolled across the ground, the snarling of the pack grew louder.

Lord Akitsu, recognizing the profile of the guard who wiped the gore from his blade with a swift, practiced movement, called to him in a low voice.

"Masaki, is it you? How many were taken?"

"Three. They had no time to draw their swords."

In a heavy, cheerless voice the lord said, "We will be lucky if we lose only three. Listen. No more wolves must be slain. We will retreat without further resistance. These wolves are earth gods. Do you understand?"

Masaki looked back at him in surprise. "We will leave like this? Just run away?"

"That's right. We will show them that we bear them no malice and withdraw peacefully. I cannot set my men against the gods of the earth."

Lifting the curtain, the lord spoke quickly to Saya within. "We will retreat. I leave it to you whether you will escape with us."

Chihaya looked at Saya with a puzzled expression. "What's going on?"

"Get dressed, will you. We're going to flee," Saya replied. Of course they would take to their heels. She had no intention of standing alone to meet the anger and hatred of so many gods. But at the same time she could not desert the ignorant Chihaya. When the two of them tried to leave the tent, however, they froze in their tracks at a familiar dull roaring sound. The Dragon Sword had begun to cry out. The red stones blazed crimson.

"You mustn't draw the blade!" Saya said hurriedly. Chihaya's hand had gone instantly toward the sword as though controlled by another's will.

"It wants me to," Chihaya whispered. "The Dragon is awake. What is outside that can call the Dragon as it pleases?"

"Angry gods. But you mustn't draw the Sword!" Saya said earnestly. "Please! Pray that it will subside again."

"If I move, I'm afraid I will unsheathe it." Now Chihaya's face was tense. His voice was barely a whisper. "The Dragon is trying to move me."

"But the lady is not here," Masaki said.

"Never mind. We must retreat. We cannot stay any longer," Lord Akitsu commanded.

"But—"

"The Lady of the Sword knows what she is doing. She has her own thoughts as priestess, as Water Maiden. There is no need

for concern," the lord said gravely, but without as much conviction as he had hoped.

It was already too late. The malicious gods had surrounded
the tent where the two remained and were beginning to close in.
The rage emanating from the countless wolves was melded into
a single entity as if some giant being in midair were glaring down
upon the two of them.

"I don't have any ability to calm these gods," Saya thought in
despair. Their wrath was directed not only at Chihaya but also
at herself. She could feel their anger almost painfully, as though
piercing her skin. They could see into the depths of her soul,
and they knew. They knew that she still envied, was still drawn
to the Light: to the youth, beauty, and immortality of the Children of Light. They knew that she still worshipped them just as
surely as the senior handmaiden who rejected old age.

Chihaya, who had remained motionless, holding his breath,
suddenly raised his face sharply.

"What's wrong?" Saya said.

"Where's Morning Star?" Chihaya asked in a choked voice.
"Where is he? I can't feel him anywhere."

Saya raised her hands to her mouth and stared at Chihaya in
fright. Morning Star had been tied to a pine tree, unable to
escape, all alone.

"He was tethered to a tree outside the camp," Saya said, her
voice rising, and before she could stop him, Chihaya ran outside
the tent. Frantically Saya followed him, crying, "Wait!"

"Morning Star!" Chihaya shouted toward the dark forest, but
there was no answering nicker, only a gnashing of teeth and the
snarling and panting of bloodthirsty beasts.

Black shadows leaped one after the other like balls thrown from
every direction at Chihaya, who had stopped in his tracks. Although he instinctively dodged aside, he felt fangs grazing his
knees and shoulders and heard the sound of ripping cloth. His

legs were knocked from under him, and as he staggered, his hand went to the Sword.

Seeing the light gush forth, Saya screamed, "No!" but she, too, was attacked by wolves. By the light of the Sword she watched the foaming jaws and bloody fangs aiming for her throat as she cowered, mesmerized, unable to move.

The instant before the teeth of the leaping wolf met her throat a white arrow flew through the air and pierced the wolf's side. Saya gasped and turned to see Masaki casting aside his bow and drawing his sword as he rushed toward her.

"Are you all right? They don't seem the type to retreat before the power of your gaze."

"You . . ." Saya said in stunned surprise. "Did you not hear the lord's command?"

"If she heard that I had deserted you, my wife would disown me."

"But you will offend the gods."

"Two or three times more, what difference can that make when I have already slain one?" he replied with typical courage. "Now let's get out of here. Hurry!"

Saya, unable to reply, ran with him, but her thoughts were dark and gloomy: "Kind Masaki . . . foolish Masaki . . . you never should have come."

For she knew that mortal strength was not enough. Her heart broke at the thought of Masaki's needless death. These cruel and merciless gods would surely never forgive him.

Her vision was filled with leaping shadows. Many times she was knocked down, many times she felt fangs graze her skin, but each time she rose again and continued to run. It seemed the only thing she could do for Masaki. Soon, however, she was out of breath and only dimly conscious, her mind like a thick porridge, so that she no longer knew where she was running, and even began to forget why. Leaping shadows, shadows, shadows . . . interspersed with flashes of light that she could not place.

Leaping shadows, shadows, shadows—then flashing light—then more shadows, shadows, shadows. Only shadows . . .

When she regained consciousness and raised her head, the night had become hushed and still. It was the stillness that comes just before the dawn, when the night is coldest and silence reigns. And, standing so close that she almost cried out in surprise, was Chihaya. She could see his figure faintly by the greenish white light of the naked blade that he held in his hand.

"I finally know how to use this thing." Chihaya spoke as though he had been talking to her all along. "This Sword is a fang. All I have to do is become the owner of the fang. Like the wolves. As for wolves, I have been one myself."

Saya shuddered and found her voice. "What happened to them?"

"They've gone. They disappeared when I destroyed the one controlling them."

"I see," Saya whispered. "So you have slain another earth god." She intended neither praise nor censure but merely spoke what came into her mind.

"Saya." Chihaya spoke in a low voice, looking down at the Sword. "Morning Star is dead."

Saya nodded wordlessly. She could not offer him any easy words of comfort. Chihaya remained silent for a long time and then said sadly, "Morning Star was the only one who loved me for myself."

Through the mist on the treetops the night began to fade into dawn. Somewhere a deer called, searching for a mate in the autumn season. In the faint light, Saya wandered, dragging her feet, and found Masaki fallen facedown on the grass. His body had long grown cold, and dew clung to the blade still gripped in his hand. When she found him, it did not occur to her to weep. She was too exhausted. Instead, she sank down beside him and took his hand in hers as though to console him. One thought kept running through her mind: "What shall I tell Natsume? Natsume. How am I to tell her?"

When Lord Akitsu came in search of her, she was still sitting there. She saw him approaching, the somber expression on his face indicating that he had guessed all that had transpired. For the first time, tears traced their way down her cheeks.

"Why are they so cruel, these gods we worship? Why? Why must we fight for such gods as these?"

Lord Akitsu replied as though meditating on each word. "Cruelty is one aspect of all gods. But it is not the only one. Originally, the gods were loving and beautiful. These traits were twisted by the Light."

"I don't understand it. I don't believe it." Saya shook her head. "I hate the god who killed Masaki. I am glad that Chihaya destroyed it."

The lord looked down at Saya with a face full of pain. "Do you really think so, Saya? If so, then wait one year. Wait and then come again to this spot. You will surely find a totally different scene, a wasteland spreading out before you. Never again will this land bear fruit. Never again will flowers bloom. For the land has lost its spirit. Land unnurtured by the gods of the earth lacks the breath of life."

"Could it be?" Saya whispered. But she could not comprehend it. All she could think of was Natsume's unborn child.

When she returned to the camp, Saya was stricken with fever and remained bedridden for many days. In her delirium, she was plagued by constant nightmares, including her childhood dream, which, though she had not seen it for some time, had lost none of its terror. The white-robed priestess turning . . . It did not help to tell herself that it was Chihaya. Fear rose in her throat and she sank into despair, for what was done could not be undone.

"But I just saw her face," Saya thought over and over in her feverish rambling. "But I just saw her."

Finally one morning she awoke to sunlight. She felt as if waking for the first time in a very long while, and a mist had cleared from her eyes. It was almost noon, and the honey-colored sunlight poured through a small window high above. A man loomed beside her, blocking the sunlight. He sat hunched over as though his bulk would burst the tiny hut asunder. Looking at him, Saya smiled faintly.

"Lord Ibuki. So you reached us safely, then."

"Yes, many days ago," he replied in a thick rumbling voice, although for him this was an attempt to speak softly and quietly. "It seems your fever has abated. That's good. Very good."

"Surely it is due to the herbs that your lordship found for us," Natsume said gratefully. As always, Natsume worked diligently. She neither secluded herself nor wore mourning clothes. Saya would almost have preferred her to weep or rage rather than nurse her so devotedly, but Natsume never allowed a tear to show in front of Saya.

"I am an expert at tracking down medicinal herbs. I find them where no one would expect." Lord Ibuki patted his chest proudly with a large, heavy hand, although a less likely hand for plucking the slender stalks of herbs growing in rock crevices would be hard to imagine.

"Well, well. Wild pinks," Lord Ibuki remarked, noticing the bouquet in Natsume's hand. "You did a good job collecting those."

Natsume smiled meaningfully and glanced down at the pale pink flowers with their notched petals. "I didn't pick them. I don't know who it is, but someone has sent flowers every day since my lady fell ill."

Lord Ibuki gave her a strange look. "You don't know who it is, when the man who just left is one of Lord Shinado's servants?"

"Oh, really?" Natsume deftly feigned ignorance.

"What's this? What's this?" Lord Ibuki roared in his normal voice. "The devil! Who would have guessed from his looks that he was such a simplehearted—" Seeing the two girls staring at him, he stopped himself hastily. "Well, now. That's just between him and me."

Saya looked at the bouquet of gentians brought yesterday. The flowers were still a fresh blue. Her thoughts unconsciously returned to the field of gypsy roses she had once seen.

"Even though he saw an entire field covered with flowers, Chihaya never thought to pick them," she thought. "Instead, he took me to see the place where they were blooming."

"What's happened to Chihaya?" Her question was so sudden that Natsume and Lord Ibuki looked at her in surprise.

"Why, nothing. He's fine," Lord Ibuki replied hastily.

"Even without Morning Star?"

Seeing the disconcerted look on his face, Saya realized that Lord Ibuki knew nothing of Chihaya's whereabouts. Natsume seemed to hesitate and then in a strange tone answered Saya's question with one of her own.

"My lady, everyone has been talking about it, but is it true that he is a Prince of Light?"

Saya was caught off guard. So now everyone knew, she thought. "Yes, it's true."

"And that even though he was slain in battle, he came back to life as though nothing had happened . . ." Natsume's words trailed off.

Saya did not know what to say. "Yes, but—"

"Well, I never," Natsume said with forced cheerfulness, but was unable to keep her composure any longer. The hand in which she had held the bouquet of flowers was trembling. "Excuse me a moment," she whispered and left without a backward glance.

"She's a brave girl," Lord Ibuki said in a low voice. "She never utters a word of complaint."

Saya wondered where Natsume went to vent her grief.

Left on her own when Lord Ibuki departed, Saya went out on shaky legs to search for Chihaya. If Natsume had been there, she would certainly not have allowed Saya to go, but Natsume had not yet returned. Outside, the light was yellow and blindingly bright, and the wind felt uncomfortably cold against her skin. There were some soldiers training, their loud cries resounding, but Chihaya was nowhere to be seen. Nor was he among those returning with food supplies. After a while Saya cut across the dwelling area and, drawn by the shady darkness, made for the spring.

Fresh mountain water poured out of a rock, forming a brimming pool from which a narrow stream flowed downward. Lord Akitsu had chosen this spot as their temporary base partly because of this source. The banks were fringed with ferns, and above her head a tall, slender katsura tree raised its branches like a guardian spirit. Feeling suddenly exhausted, Saya collapsed upon a rock. She thought half-angrily, "That heartless wretch! Making an invalid walk all this way in search of him. When really he should have come to see me while I was sick."

Lord Shinado had said that Chihaya had no compassion. Although she did not want to admit it, she thought gloomily that he might be right.

She gazed at the clear water and suddenly felt thirsty. She leaned over the edge of the rock and bent to scoop up the water in her hands. There she saw the katsura tree reflected in the pond as in a mirror.

She began to laugh. After chuckling to herself for a moment, she looked up. "What on earth are you doing up there?"

On a large branch, Chihaya sat like a nesting bird. He looked down at Saya, his eyes blinking like an owl's. "How did you know?"

"Because you are reflected perfectly in the water. Come on down."

Chihaya rose slowly but slipped down swiftly to stand beside Saya. Looking at her more closely, he said, "You look thinner."

"I wasn't feeling well. But I'm all right now." Saya broke off abruptly, realizing that Chihaya was still dressed in the ragged clothes that had been torn by the fangs of the wolves. "What have you been doing all this time?"

"Sitting in that tree. I was thinking."

"The whole time?"

"The whole time."

Saya stared at him in surprise. "What can you have been thinking about for so long?"

Chihaya watched a leaf that he had shaken from the katsura tree riding like a small boat upon the water's surface. "Mostly I thought about the place where Morning Star has gone. All living things in Toyoashihara go there. Yet I alone return. I always come back," he said sulkily. "I thought about why I am denied entrance there when everyone else is allowed to go."

Saya was amused by his childishly petulant tone. "That's like crying for the moon. What a thing to begrudge us!"

"But what should I do when there is no destination for me, no matter where I go?" he asked earnestly. "Why was I made this way?"

After some hesitation, Saya replied, "I don't know. I don't even understand about my own self. But surely the God of Light and the Goddess of Darkness know."

"My father in the heavens?" Chihaya whispered. He sat down as if even more discouraged and hugged his knees to his chest. "Saya, if you want to meet the Goddess of your people you can go, right? But I cannot go to meet my father. Not like my sister or my brother."

"Why not?"

"Because I am different."

They looked at each other. Chihaya said quietly, "My sister used to say that my very existence was a disgrace to our divine father. Now I know what she meant."

Before Saya could speak, he drew the Dragon Sword from its scabbard. "Look at this. Then you will also understand."

Saya hastily smothered a scream of surprise. The naked blade did not glow. The polished metal merely reflected the rays of the midday sun, and the stones on the hilt remained dark. Chihaya laid the blade gently on top of the rock.

"Put it away quickly! It's dangerous!" Saya begged him anxiously.

"Would you like to pray for the Dragon to appear?"

"Don't be silly!" Saya said, raising her voice, but Chihaya shook his head, indicating that he had not spoken in jest.

"Even if you prayed, it would make no difference. The Dragon would still not appear. It would not raise its voice in even a single roar."

Saya looked at the Sword suspiciously. "What do you mean?"

"I mean that the Dragon no longer resides in the sword."

When Saya raised her wide-eyed face to his, Chihaya pointed to his own breast. "The Dragon is here."

"Where?"

"In me."

"Since when?"

"Since that night." Chihaya averted his eyes.

"The night the wolves came?"

"Yes. Perhaps you did not know, but that night the Dragon never appeared. The only one there was me. By the time I realized it, I had become one with the Dragon."

Saya caught her breath and whispered, "How could that be?"

"I don't know. I only know"—Chihaya's voice suddenly grew weak and small—"that I wanted to give the god who had slain Morning Star a taste of his own medicine."

Saya was at a loss for what to say to Chihaya. As Priestess of the Sword, how should she reply? She must choose her words very carefully. They might have grave consequences or they might not. They could not undo what had already been done. But her effect on future events would depend on which aspect she as priestess chose to pass judgment on. Misfortune could become good fortune, or good luck, bad. This much Saya knew. It was ironic, perhaps, but she had learned this at the Palace of Light.

"So that means that the Dragon Sword can never again rage as it wills without your consent?" Saya checked carefully.

"Yes." Chihaya nodded. "The Dragon is still in here. I can feel it constantly, like a nesting insect, a smoldering ember."

"Then you have captured the Dragon. You have sheathed it much more deeply and securely than before. That is good."

At these words Chihaya looked at her in surprise. "Good? To become the Dragon?"

"If you never let it out again, yes. If you yourself become its scabbard. If you are strong enough, you may even be able to keep it locked away forever," Saya said with conviction. "You just need to become stronger."

"Do you think I can?" Chihaya regarded Saya doubtfully. "Do I not offend you, Saya? You who used to shun the Dragon with such dread?"

"You are not the Dragon," Saya assured him brightly. "You have eyes, a mouth, you can think and talk. Become greater than the Dragon and grasp it by the neck. Surely you can do it. For you are the one Lady Iwa called the Wind Child."

Chihaya picked up the Sword and sheathed it in its scabbard. "If you say so, Saya," he said, smiling shyly. "Now I don't have to think about it anymore."

Saya smiled in return. "I was looking for you. There is something I want to tell you. Because I, too, have been thinking of many things since that night."

She broke off and looked at the tranquil scene around them. While she paused, Chihaya remained motionless, waiting for her words. Coming to her senses, Saya felt slightly embarrassed and shrugged her shoulders, saying, "It's nothing important. It's just that I have finally figured out what I myself must do. What I mean is this." She pointed to the katsura tree. "You think that this tree is beautiful, too, right? Soon its leaves will blaze with yellow. A splendid sight; and in winter when it has shed its leaves, it will be beautiful still in its majesty. And in spring, buds as adorable as newborn babies will burst gaily into leaf. And look, the water in this spring is pure and clear. The reason it is so clear is because fresh water is always pouring forth, allowing it no time to stagnate. The beauty of Toyoashihara is like that. It is found in birth and decay, always yielding one to the other. No matter how loath we may be to accept the changes, we cannot put out a hand to stop them. For if we did, in that instant its beauty and purity would vanish."

Turning to face Chihaya, she continued. "You, the immortal Children of Light, have a different beauty, eternal, unchanging. But this beauty belongs in the heavens; it is not meant for Toyoashihara. I don't want you to destroy Toyoashihara. I want you to understand that this land is beautiful just as it is. This is the reason my people are fighting. And that is what I must do, too."

She spoke as though talking to herself and then caught and held Chihaya's gaze. "You appreciate the beauty of Toyoashihara. I know, because you showed me the flowers. Because you understand, I want you to lend us your power to protect this land. I want you to come with us, to use the power you have over the Dragon for the sake of this country."

Chihaya remained silent, gravely pondering her words. Then he replied simply, "If you say so, Saya."

3

The forces of Darkness advanced inexorably, assembling at last at the mouth of the Nakase River. Across the river, only a stone's throw away, lay Mahoroba, where the God of Light was said to have descended to the earth. Although the army of Darkness, having had a long stretch of good fortune, now surpassed the might of the army of Light, the latter gave no sign of budging and the army of Darkness was unable to push across the river. Moreover, even if by fighting to the death they succeeded in breaching the enemy lines, it would be extremely difficult to capture the almost impenetrable fortress of Mahoroba. Lord Akitsu, favoring caution, held his eager troops in check and settled down on the opposite bank to study the enemy forces. He knew too well that as soon as they moved, the final battle that would determine control of the land would begin. Despite frequent provocation, the front remained deadlocked and the two opposing forces glared at each other across the river. While they waited, the mountainsides turned red, then yellow, and the first frosts covered the ground. The torches for the night watch were cut longer than before. The anxiety and impatience of the soldiers of Darkness grew with each day they waited, neither advancing nor retreating, as though waiting for a tautly stretched string to break. Their greatest concern was the conspicuous absence of both Princess Teruhi and Prince Tsukishiro at such a crucial juncture. The Princess's golden helmet and the Prince's silver one had always flashed at the head of the forces of Light, striking fear into their enemies. Their continuing absence was ominous, as though some evil plot were brewing.

Then one night a troop bringing up the rear position was suddenly attacked unawares. Despite heavy patrols that kept watch on the movements of the entire army of Light, no one had been seen crossing the river. Reinforcements arrived too late, and the army of Darkness received a crushing blow. Many supplies were lost, and many soldiers were killed or scattered.

But the loss in morale among the troops was much more serious than the loss of manpower and material goods. Speculation spread like wildfire, and some soldiers even declared openly that it was impossible to defeat the army of Light. Lord Shinado, who had hastily returned from the battlefield to report to the commander in chief, entered his quarters with a sour expression on his face, and, after consulting with Lord Akitsu, the commanders gathered for a council of war.

Saya was not invited. This alarmed her and she was unable to sleep. When she heard the results of the council next morning, however, she could not believe her ears. She rushed to see Lord Akitsu.

"Why are you going to imprison Chihaya? What has he done? Are you saying that he is responsible for this last defeat?"

"Saya." Lord Akitsu made an effort to speak calmly, but his face was dark and gloomy. "We are leading a great army. Yet you could also call it a motley rabble. Many of them have come far from their native lands, placing their complete trust in their leaders, rallying solely to the call of their commanders. It is impossible for us to accurately convey the real purpose of either Light or Darkness to such a mass of people from different home-lands and with such differing viewpoints. Good is good, evil is evil. Unless we make everything black-and-white, we cannot inspire them to follow us."

"And is it therefore just to imprison an innocent man?" Saya demanded fiercely. "I cannot believe that you would do this. After all, it is common knowledge that he is a Prince of Light."

"If we allow things to continue like this, his position will only deteriorate. Some accuse him of communicating secretly with the other side. Even if we absolve him from blame this time, every time something happens in the future they will point to Chihaya. I have feared this very thing all along—the spark of antagonism has been fanned into flame."

"But—" Saya broke off abruptly. "You are all selfish! Chihaya has fought as hard as anyone until now."

The grim expression on Lord Akitsu's face did not change. But his voice dropped almost to a whisper and was filled with pain. "I know. Can't you see that that is the very reason why fear and mistrust have spread so rapidly? The more Chihaya distinguishes himself, the more he displays the supremacy of the Children of Light, their limitless power, their immortality . . ."

Saya winced at his words as though struck by the palm of his hand. Confused and on the verge of tears, she asked, "Then what shall we do with Chihaya?"

"Forgive me." Lord Akitsu sighed. "Perhaps it is I who am afraid."

Saya was appalled, realizing that anything she might say would be futile. Lord Akitsu had passed judgment.

Near the spring of Ogidani, where the main army was stationed, was a cave carved by wind and rain. Formerly a dungeon for prisoners of war, it was now used to imprison Chihaya.

Solid oak bars were set into the entrance and stakes were driven in to hold them securely in place. Feeling more wretched than she could ever remember, Saya took the Dragon Sword from Chihaya's hands. However, he was unexpectedly calm as he faced her through the wooden bars.

"It's all right. It doesn't bother me as much as you think. I have just returned to being by myself again for a time. Surely they will come to understand after a little while."

As Saya left the cave, feeling worse for having received words of comfort from Chihaya, Lord Ibuki came after her. Hunching his burly shoulders in regret, he said, "I'm sorry. I couldn't convince them. The cowards just won't see reason."

"How feckless! Not you, Ibuki, but the rest of us, myself included," Saya said indignantly. "Chihaya said he would lend his power for Toyoashihara. That he would fight with us. And yet we turn around and behave so foolishly."

"Suspicion casts a difficult shadow. It hides the obvious from our eyes," Lord Ibuki said, frowning. "If we only knew the facts concerning this last incident, we might still convince them."

Saya vented her anger at him. "So even you think there is a possibility that Chihaya did it!"

"Of course not!" Lord Ibuki replied in surprise. "After all, I taught him how to use a sword, remember. And I have taught young soldiers swordsmanship for twenty years, yet never have I met such a poor fighter as he. Despite that—honestly, I can hardly believe that he is a Prince of Light. At any rate, when I put myself aside and cross swords with another man, I can see his character, no matter who he is."

A little calmer, Saya asked, "And what did you see?"

"Well, now. He is like a crane who has come flying from far away. Though he puts his feet and beak in the mud, his heart is still wandering above the clouds where he used to roam. How could someone like that possibly be capable of deceiving other people?"

Saya busied herself aiding soldiers injured in the attack, tending their wounds and rounding up the draft animals. As she was hurrying about, she noticed a commotion in the area where supplies were distributed. She could hear Natsume shouting something. Surprised, she threw aside her work and ran to the scene. When she arrived, panting for breath, she found Natsume, watched by a ring of soldiers, holding a filthy little girl and trying to wash her. The child screamed loudly, thrashing in Natsume's arms as the two scuffled together.

"No! No!"

"You're a girl, aren't you? At least wash your face!"

In danger of being kicked in the stomach, Natsume finally released the little girl, who rolled away and, glaring rebelliously, began rubbing dirt on her face with both hands.

"What's going on? Who is this child?" Saya asked. Natsume, drenched from head to toe with spilled water, looked back at Saya with an exasperated expression.

"The provisions corps found her unconscious and brought her back with them. They mistook her for a deer and shot at her, it seems. Fortunately, she was unharmed, but when she came to her senses, she went wild, as you just saw."

She appeared to be a girl of five or six years of age. She had an attractive face, but her hair was matted and she was covered in mud from head to toe. She seemed more like a wild creature than a human child the way she watched them suspiciously, reminding Saya of the time that Chihaya had become a deer.

"She was in the forest? Alone?"

"She must have been orphaned, have lost everything in the war. She won't even tell us her name or that of her family," Natsume said with concern. "What a troublesome find. What shall we do?"

Moved by the girl's plight, Saya looked at her carefully. The child stared at those around her and continued to rub her cheeks with her blackened hands as though they still bothered her. Saya could not help feeling that she was looking at herself so many years ago.

"Can't we take care of her? We can't just leave her here," Saya said, but Natsume and the soldiers looked troubled.

"I wish we could," Natsume answered in a low voice, "but we barely have enough provisions for the soldiers with our increased numbers. Even though it may be just a little bit, we have to draw the line somewhere . . . My lady, she is not the only child who has lost her parents in the war."

"But just this one," Saya appealed. "Please, couldn't we help just this one child?"

One of the soldiers whispered to his neighbor, "We could give her the portion of the immortal. He won't die even if he doesn't eat. It's a waste to feed him."

Saya turned her face toward them sharply. "Who was so bold as to say such a thing? You may leave my troop. I do not wish to share food or quarters with such a mean-spirited person."

Everyone looked at Saya in surprise. She had never spoken so coldly to a soldier before. Looking at each of them, she continued, "I will share my rations with this child. Then no trouble will be caused to anyone else."

Even Natsume stared at Saya in astonishment. Feeling a sudden estrangement, Saya turned back to the little girl, wondering if her efforts were in vain. The girl, the whites of her eyes shining in her dirty face, looked back at her as though she were the unusual sight.

"Come with me," Saya called to her warmly. "If you have lost your name, then I will call you Fawn, because you were mistaken for a deer. My name is Saya. That name was given to me when I was taken in, too—because the thicket of bamboo grass where I was found whispered, 'Saya, saya,' or so I was told."

Fawn returned to the fortifications with Saya and shared her quarters. Within a few days she had calmed down and adapted extraordinarily quickly to her new environment. She played without fear among the soldiers and flew about with such innocent curiosity that it seemed a baby sparrow had found its way into the camp. But no matter how often she was scolded, she never stopped rubbing her face with dirt. Saya, feeling that she must have some childish reason of her own for it, ceased to mention it.

For the people of Darkness, the gloom continued. Everything seemed to go against them, and the war dragged on in a stalemate that seemed without solution. An unseasonably cold and dismal drizzle set in; even the weather was depressed. Absolving Chihaya from the false charges laid against him was not going to be an easy task, and Saya watched the days pass with a heavy heart. Her only solace was the innocent play of Fawn. And she was not the only one beguiled by her charms. Despite her dirty face, she was a winsome child, and the soldiers were happy to have her with them. For many she brought back memories of their own beloved daughters. The cruel winter drew near, and the thoughts of the soldiers, tired of fighting, turned toward the warm hearths of their homes far away.

Looking out of her tent at the cold rain, Saya found her thoughts returning repeatedly to the damp rocks near the spring, the cave lashed by the north wind. Fawn, who was playing inside the tent, dragged something toward her. Glancing casually over her shoulder, Saya was startled to see her holding the Dragon Sword, which had been carefully concealed. How had she found it?

"What are you doing? If you touch that, you'll be struck dead by lightning!"

"No I won't. I like it. I want it."

Saya hastily snatched the Sword away. "You can't have it. It belongs to someone else. It cannot be yours, and it is not mine, either. We will just leave it alone until it is time to return it to its owner. Only a bad girl would play with it."

"Whose is it?"

Saya said heavily, "It belongs to the person in the cave."

Fawn's voice rose excitedly. "I know! The one everyone calls the Prince of Light. Too bad. I'll go find something else to play with."

The little girl ran out into the fine rain. Saya was about to stop her but thought better of it. She looked at the Sword in her hand and sighed, thinking that she had better find a different hiding place for it.

After a while Fawn saw some soldiers under a shelter gathered around a fire roasting chestnuts, and she squirmed her way in eagerly. One of the men sat her on his lap, and they continued talking without taking any notice of her.

"That's all very well to say, but how can you execute someone who doesn't die?"

"But it's obvious that he is betraying us to Princess Teruhi. I can't believe that she of the golden helmet is still with her own troops. She must have concealed herself somewhere and be communicating with that traitor. If we don't stop him soon, we'll be murdered in our sleep."

"I'd feel much easier myself if he were dead, but even if he received neither food nor drink he would still live . . ."

"It makes my blood boil. He sits in that flooded cell as though nothing bothers him."

"My brother was killed by the Children of Light."

"So was my father."

"Why should they alone return from death?"

Just then Fawn spoke with childish innocence, "But there is one way to get rid of them for good."

The men stared at her in surprise, for it had never occurred to them that she was listening. Fawn, in turn, was looking at them with wide eyes.

"What's the matter? You just want to make sure he dies, right? My father told me there is only one way."

The man holding her on his lap asked gently, "And what could that be, little one? What did your father say?"

Fawn giggled as if it amused her. "You eat him. You chop him up into little pieces like mincemeat and eat him. Then the Prince of Light will lose his immortality and those who eat him will gain eternal life."

A strange expression crossed the faces of her listeners. They exchanged covert glances, but none of them spoke. Only Fawn seemed unconcerned, concentrating solely on the chestnuts she was poking in the fire.

Lord Ibuki came to Saya. "Have you heard any distasteful rumors?" he asked her in an unusually dark tone of voice. "Some people are saying things that I cannot stand to hear. If I knew who started it, I'd have them hanged."

Saya put down her breakfast bowl and looked at him. "What kind of rumor? I don't know what you mean."

Fawn, sitting beside Saya with her nose in her porridge bowl, raised her face. "What does he mean, 'have them hanged'?"

"Keep quiet and eat your breakfast," Saya said and then turned to Lord Ibuki again. "What rumors? It's unusual for you to be so upset."

"Never mind. It's better not to know." Lord Ibuki shook his head and left. "I cannot bear to repeat them."

That afternoon Natsume entered Saya's tent with a troubled expression. Fawn was outside playing and Saya was alone.

"My lady, it is difficult for me to say this, but . . ."

"What is it? This is not like you."

"Well, actually it's about Fawn. I don't think it's good for her to be with you, my lady."

Saya looked at her inquiringly. "Is the food shortage that severe?"

"No, it isn't that." Natsume faltered, then, clasping and unclasping her hands repeatedly, finally said, "There is something evil about that child."

Saya was shocked and disappointed. "So all those who are not our kinfolk will be shunned. First Chihaya, and now Fawn?"

"No. You're wrong. I, too, feel that Chihaya has been treated unjustly," Natsume responded earnestly. "It is our shame that we have placed the blame on him. I understand how everyone feels—after all, I despised him, too, for a while wondering why he alone should come back from the dead. But that way of thinking is futile and mistaken. I know now that I can bear my grief without hating, thanks to this unborn child."

Natsume caressed her swollen belly tenderly; to Saya, her gesture seemed to embody the Goddess herself.

"Whether it is a boy or a girl, this child is Masaki. It is the same as Masaki returning to life. Now I can believe that."

"It is true," Saya said with feeling. "Bear the child well, Natsume."

A grateful smile touched the woman's face, but then her expression suddenly clouded. "That girl, Fawn, no matter how I try, I cannot get her to recall her parents. She is more like a little demon than a child born from a womb. Perhaps that is what bothers me about her."

"She certainly has an impudent streak, but she can be sweet, too, you know," Saya said.

But Natsume shook her head. The gentle-natured Natsume had taken an unusual aversion to the child. "Sometimes Fawn stares at me. She glares at me with indescribably cold eyes. That is the look of one who brings evil."

"Are you sure you're not exaggerating?"

But Natsume continued. "Even dogs treat a pregnant bitch gently, don't they? Although I can offer little service on the battlefield in this state, everyone treats me with kindness. It is not conscious; rather, they instinctively honor the evidence of life they see within me. I am grateful. And I do not intend to take advantage of it. It is just that that child's gaze differs too much from everyone else's."

Saya felt uneasy but at the same time could not feel that this was enough reason to censure a five- or six-year-old child. "She is too little and does not understand. Without knowing it, she is probably jealous of the baby."

"Perhaps that could be . . ."

Saya appealed to her. "Please don't hate Fawn. She is just like me when I was a child. When my parents in Hashiba adopted me, I'm sure I was just like that—bereft of loved ones, trusting no one, wild and rough. My parents took in just such a child and nurtured her lovingly. We should be able to do the same."

Natsume exhaled quietly. She seemed to reconsider. "Yes, I can understand what you are saying, my lady. I'm sorry to have troubled you."

Looking at Natsume's heavy form and drawn face as she rose, Saya thought that she had probably become oversensitive, owing to the changes in her body. "It cannot be good for her to be in such a brutal environment. If even I get depressed, it cannot be any good for Natsume."

Leaving Saya's quarters, Natsume walked behind them, where, distracted by a stray lock of hair, she stopped to remove a comb from her hair and fix her bun. Patting some stray wisps into place, she happened to look into a nearby grove of trees, and her hand froze with shock. In the crook of a tree, just at eye level, sat Fawn, swinging her legs back and forth. At a casual glance she appeared as cute as a doll, but the eyes that peered out from her grimy face were piercingly cold.

Speaking in a tone that did not match her childish voice, Fawn said, "You're a little too perceptive—perhaps because you carry two lives within you."

A faint, lopsided smile twisted her delicate lips. "It won't do to have you meddling when Saya is so trusting. Just a little longer and I will be able to make the soldiers of Darkness do exactly as I wish."

The color drained from Natsume's face. Backing away, she whispered, "Demon—you're a demon in disguise!"

"Far from it!" Fawn sprang lightly down from the tree. "By demons you mean the dirty little gods of field and mountain. You insult me. With extreme forbearance I have come to this squalid spot. But it's exhausting, a waste of my powers of renewal." Her bright pink tongue, like that of a kitten, flickered across her lips. "But two lives in one body—now, that would help wash away this defilement."

Natsume, who had continued to edge away, wheeled around. Her hair, which had loosened once again, fell down her back.

"You would flee?" Fawn inquired. "From whom will you seek aid? Who will believe you?"

Without waiting to hear more, Natsume ran for her life. Through the chill air, still damp with the recent rain, she ran as though possessed, trampling and scattering the sodden leaves, until she collided with a group of soldiers. They grabbed her in surprise and asked her what she was doing.

"What's wrong? If you trip and fall, what will happen to the baby?"

"Fawn—" Panting for breath, Natsume babbled like someone demented. "Help me. Fawn is coming to kill me!"

"You're overwrought, Natsume. Though it is no wonder," the soldiers replied sadly. "But even in the midst of this war you at least must stay calm. Just lie down awhile. We'll fix you a good herbal infusion."

No matter what she said, they merely tried to soothe her. Finally, unable to resist their sincere intentions, she was put to bed in a nearby hut, but as soon as they had gone, she fled once more.

Her feet, driven by fear, turned at last toward the spring. Passing the pool made by a simple dam, she began to climb. There, surrounded by the bare rock, was the cold, barred cave.

Chihaya gazed out through the bars at the distant river mouth, shrouded in mist. In his windy aerie he could clearly see the sandbar. Lonely waterfowl flew aimlessly beneath the low-lying gray clouds. His view was suddenly blocked by a shadow as he was attempting to capture the feelings of a bird. Surprised, he returned to himself and saw Natsume on the other side of the bars. She sank to her knees and grasped the bars of his prison as though in entreaty.

"Please! Help me! You must help me and the child I bear!"

Chihaya stared frowningly into Natsume's desperate face.

"Help you? Why?"

"The girl—she is trying to kill me. Nobody believes me. But you—I know you will surely understand. Because you are no ordinary man."

Chihaya looked troubled. "Yes. I am different from you. That is why I am in this prison."

"You have a right to be angered by our treatment. I and all my kindred are at fault. But this child within me is innocent. It has done you no harm. Please, for the sake of the child, protect me."

"But how . . ."

Natsume picked up a sharp stone and began to try to break the wedges that held the bars in place. "Please! Come out. These wooden bars should not stop you, Prince of Light."

Flustered, Chihaya whispered, "Don't do that. You'll get me in trouble. If it is known that I have left the prison, your people will never trust me again."

Natsume finally began to weep. The tears streamed down her cheeks and splashed on the rocks. "You will desert me, then? When no man can stand against her, and you alone can match her?"

"Don't cry! Please!" Now it was Chihaya's turn to become distressed. If he could just stop her tears, he was willing to do anything. "Calm down and tell me what you mean. I want to help you but I don't understand yet what is happening."

But as she opened her mouth to speak, she suddenly reared back, staring up into space. Her outstretched arms flailed in a swimming motion. Chihaya leaped to his feet, shocked at the sight of fresh blood, and there behind her he saw a little girl gripping the hilt of the Dragon Sword, which was plunged deep into Natsume's back, and bathing herself in the blood.

"Natsume!"

He thrust his arms through the bars to support her, but in vain. Natsume crumpled slowly to the ground. The light in her eyes was swiftly fading and already she looked at Chihaya without seeing. After a convulsive shudder, she turned her sorrowful eyes toward him one last time and whispered beneath her breath, "Masaki."

Then she collapsed upon the earth, dead. Chihaya gazed

speechlessly over her body to the blood-drenched child. She beamed a smile at him and then, without a word, turned and ran.

"Wait!"

When he unconsciously applied pressure to the bars where his hands gripped them, they popped out easily. He had no time to wonder whether it was Natsume's doing or his own as he rushed out of the prison in pursuit of the girl.

She leaped lightly from rock to rock before him as though dancing through the air, and in three strides she had descended to the edge of the pool. She stripped off her soiled clothing and dived into the cold water. Chihaya pursued her to the edge but there he stopped. The girl showed no sign of haste as she stood chest-deep in the water, washing. When she raised her clean face, her skin shone pure white. Though childish, her countenance was as flawless as a jewel. She looked up at him and once again smiled gaily, while Chihaya, taken aback, remained rooted to the spot. Next she began to wash her body. Each time she scooped the water, she grew taller. Her hair grew longer as he watched, and spread out upon the water. Her slender arms grew long and lithesome, her shoulders round and smooth, and her breasts swelled like ripe fruit. By the time she had finished bathing herself, she had undergone a transformation that would have taken a mortal a decade or more to complete. When she turned to climb out onto the bank, the water lapped just below her navel against the rounded hips and slender waist of a young woman.

She rose shamelessly from the water and stood before Chihaya with her wet body exposed. And indeed there was no need to conceal her perfect form.

"Sister," Chihaya whispered.

"An excellent cleansing. Now I feel better," Princess Teruhi said as she combed her hair with her fingers. "It is quite a skill to return to childhood. Perhaps because a child is weaker, one tires easily. Not to mention the bother of the lesser gods catching the scent of renewal."

"Why did you kill Natsume?"

"Because two lives in one body are a most effective means for purification."

"Sister!"

"You are angry? You?" Princess Teruhi said in surprise and looked hard at Chihaya. "You have changed. Even your appearance. I almost wouldn't recognize you. How can that be when those of our lineage never change? But never mind. I have come to meet you. Let's leave harsh words for another time."

She smiled a not altogether unkind smile. "It was for your sake that I went to such lengths to penetrate the encampment of the forces of Darkness. When all is said and done, you are, after all, my brother. If possible, I would rather not fight against you. Come back with me to the palace. Surely you have realized by now the foolishness of these people."

After a pause, Chihaya asked, "Was it you who directed this last attack, sister?"

"Yes. I slipped behind their lines in the guise of a girl and stirred the fools up a little. It was easy to twist them around my finger." Leaning her back against a rock and folding her arms, the Princess continued, "And it was I who made sure that suspicion blew in your direction. And I again who pierced you with the arrow. And just as I intended, the followers of Darkness have turned their backs on you. That is the sort of people they are. And now you will certainly be unable to remain here any longer. For they will soon come to carve you into little pieces."

"Why?" Chihaya looked at her in disbelief.

Princess Teruhi shrugged her white shoulders. "Because they are base and savage. I only planted the seeds. It is they who are at fault for reaping the harvest."

Bending down, she picked up the Sword, which lay on the

bank, and meticulously washed the blood off in the stream. Then, carefully inspecting the blade, she murmured, "It is only a sword, an empty husk. You have broken the seals one after the other. So now do you know yourself?"

"A little," Chihaya replied quietly.

"It would have been better had you never known," the Princess said with a sigh. "Then you also know why we must strive with all our might to destroy you. You are our father's child and, at the same time, his gravest threat. If you become our foe . . . But no, there is still time." She gazed at her brother partly in entreaty, partly as if to compel him. "Do not make me your enemy. If you return to the palace, I will protect you once again. I will protect you from your own self. That is what you need."

Chihaya hesitated for a long moment. Seeing that her brother's heart was wavering, Princess Teruhi waited motionless for his reply. After a while he spoke.

"I—I have already promised Saya," he said haltingly, "that I will use my power to aid Toyoashihara. I cannot break my word so suddenly."

Rage glittered in Princess Teruhi's eyes when she heard this. She said coldly, "Are you saying that you will set a vow made between children before an appeal from your own sister? You are still a fool. In that case, let us see whether you will still speak thus when the mob descends upon you."

Returning the Dragon Sword to Chihaya, she turned her back on him in fury. "At least you should protect yourself. I did not lie. We cannot live if we are cut into pieces. But even should you escape their clutches, I will surely come after you. Consider us no longer brother and sister. I have made my appeal, once and once only. There will be no second chance."

In the blink of an eye, she vanished. Even Chihaya did not know by what skill she achieved this. Confused and dazed, he looked at the Sword she had placed in his hand. At that moment a voice clouded with fury fell upon him from above.

"Hold! Murderer! How dare you slay a woman!"

Startled, he looked up to see two guards, their faces black with anger, standing with their spears at the ready.

"No. You've made a mistake. It wasn't I."

But his voice was drowned by the guard's whistle as it cut the air, sounding the alarm.

4

"Something terrible has happened!"

Lord Shinado rushed into Saya's quarters. His usually composed face was utterly transformed.

Saya had been sewing, thinking that it was about time for Fawn to return, but when Lord Shinado wrenched aside the curtain flap instead, she looked up at him in startled amazement. Struggling to calm his breathing, he said in a low voice, "Chihaya has escaped from prison. He was caught immediately, but he has been surrounded by a frenzied mob and we cannot reach him. They demand his immediate execution."

The needle and cloth fell from Saya's hands. "Where is he?"

"In the clearing by the pool. Lord Ibuki rushed to the scene and is doing his best to calm everyone down, but they are so enraged that they are liable to strike out even at him. As priestess, do you have the power to calm the wrath of mortal men?"

"I have no idea!"

There was no time for further exchange as the two ran toward the hollow ringed by a wood of alder trees, now packed with men shouting angrily. "Kill the Prince of Light! Carve him into pieces!" they cried. Saya was amazed, wondering what had given rise to this drunken delirium. The narrow-minded people had been swept into a vortex, no longer able to listen to reason. In fact they did not even see Saya or Lord Shinado, who found themselves roughly jostled as they attempted to pass through the crowd. The noise of the mob was melded into an unfamiliar language that spoke only of hunger and rage.

"They are like one enormous ravenous beast," Saya thought as she struggled to make her way through the seething throng. "They need something stronger than words to appease their hunger. But it must not be blood, or they will become no better than wolves. Oh, how I wish I could dump a bucket of cold water over every head."

She heard the sound of someone being struck above her.

"Where are your eyes? What do you think you are doing to the Lady of the Sword?"

A burly arm reached out and grasped Saya, plucking her from the midst of the crowd as though pulling a plant from the field. It was Lord Ibuki.

"Are you all right?"

"Yes. But what about . . ."

Saya brushed her disheveled hair from her face and looked around. Chihaya stood beneath a leafless tree surrounded by soldiers. His arms were tied behind him around the trunk of the tree and he gazed off into the distance, unaware as yet of Saya's presence. His face was gashed and his knees and chest were smeared with grime. The soldiers stood with their spears at the ready but more to protect Chihaya from the angry mob than anything else. Already several men were grabbing at the guards and arguing with them.

"Why do they demand his execution when he has the power of renewal?"

Lord Ibuki answered her in a strained voice, "They say that if he is cut into a myriad pieces and each is buried separately, he will not return to life. Whether it is true or not, I do not know."

Saya caught her breath. "Cut Chihaya . . . ?"

"No matter what he has done, the commander, Lord Akitsu,

should be the one to judge. It is not permissible for Chihaya to be butchered here in a so-called execution. We must take him to Lord Akitsu. Saya, can you help us calm this crowd?"

While she pondered what to do, she looked around and noticed a body shrouded by a straw mat lying at the feet of the guards who held back the surging crowd with their spears. The lifeless hand of a woman protruded from beneath the mat.

"Wait!" Lord Ibuki tried to intercept her, but it was too late. Saya flew to the corpse and, wrenching aside the mat, gazed on what lay beneath: the lifeless form of Natsume and, beside her, the Dragon Sword.

Unconsciously, Saya began to scream, and even when she became aware of what she was doing, she could not stop. Her high, thin wail rose clearly above the tumult of the mob, so that even the shouting men were startled.

"Natsume! Why? Why? Why?"

She threw herself upon the body, shaking it futilely while she continued to scream. For it was Natsume, who but a short time ago had smiled like the Goddess as she placed her hand upon her belly; Natsume, who had so confidently declared that Masaki would return. Saya could not bear the sight without screaming. She could not accept what her eyes beheld.

"Why? Who did this?"

"That Prince of Light; he took her as his victim," someone said. "That one who brings nothing but evil, he who does not die."

"Kill him!"

"Let us harbor this evil no longer!"

"Kill him!"

"They are not human! They need not receive judgment like us. They need not be spared like us."

"Cut him to pieces!"

The tumult rose once again like sulfurous water brought to the boil.

"Cut off his ears! His fingers! Tear him to pieces and make him die!"

Amid the clamor of voices that assailed her ears, Saya finally raised her face from Natsume and looked at Chihaya. He saw her now. When he caught her gaze, she saw his expression change. At first he showed only surprise, but as he stared at her, the expression on his face was gradually transformed into one of deep despair. As though he were a mirror, she saw upon his face her own expression reflected back at her. Yet even while she was stunned by this fact there was nothing that she could do.

Surrounded by an angry roar that filled their ears, they looked at each other as though they were strangers. True, the noise prevented speech, yet the yawning chasm across which they gazed separated them more surely than the noise. Saya, astounded at the enormity of her loss, turned her face away. If she looked at him any longer, she would soon see in his face distrust and hatred. That she could not bear. Even if they were but a reflection of her own feelings, she did not wish to see such things in Chihaya.

In the next instant, the circle of the crowd broke. Losing control, the men forgot themselves and, raising the weapons in their hands, rushed like an avalanche toward the tree where Chihaya was tied. Embroiled in the mob as they tried to check the sudden onslaught, the guards were struck, stabbed, or thrust aside and lost from sight. Saya, too, was tossed aside and almost trampled, but in the nick of time Lord Shinado snatched her out of the way. Half fainting, she regained her senses and, as soon as she could speak, cried out to him, "Stop them! Hurry!"

"Impossible," he answered, ignoring the half-crazed Saya as he strove to distance her from the jostling crowd. "It would require more than the strength of one or two men. I'd likely be killed myself in the effort."

"Stop them! If you don't," Saya pleaded, trembling, "it is they who will die."

"What?"

Lord Shinado stopped and looked at Saya. At that moment a blinding blue streak of lightning flashed across the sky, transforming the clouds, and in the same instant a deafening roar smote the earth, shaking the land of Toyoashihara. Not one man remained standing under the terrific impact, and people fell on top of one another. Lifting faces ashen with fear, they saw the tree where Chihaya had stood burst into flame. Blackened instantly from the tip down to the base of the trunk, where it was broad enough to put one's arms around, it burned fiercely and, with crimson flames blossoming on its charred branches, came crashing down, a harbinger of death to those below. The pitiful screams of those who could not escape rent the air. But the onslaught was not yet finished. Lightning flashed repeatedly in pursuit of them. The sky turned a murky black as if ink had been spilled across it, and a raging storm descended upon them. Violent winds assailed them along with a sudden torrential rain, while thunderbolts continued to fall, compounding the disaster. The lightning struck as though aimed and, with the water, took many lives. Scores of people fell as one. Within a short time the scene presented was more tragic than any previously witnessed on the battlefield. The dead fallen in the mud and the wounded who lay groaning were trampled by those fleeing in panic.

Saya was fortunate to have been outside the circle and to hide behind a rock, but she was helpless within a nightmare of driving rain. She could do no more than cower in terror. A god of appalling fury, one whom black clouds followed and lightning obeyed, even now raged above them, totally out of control.

Someone grasped her shoulder suddenly, and she almost jumped out of her skin. Lord Shinado stood beside her, likewise drenched from head to toe, his hair plastered to his scalp. He had been there all along, but in her fear she had forgotten him.

"Is this the truth, then?" he said in a low voice. His tone and expression were drained of energy. He, too, was afraid. "Chihaya has become the Dragon? The Sword and Chihaya are one and the same?"

Saya nodded, feeling her throat tremble with suppressed sobs. The rocks about them sent up clouds of spray from the driving rain, which formed countless silver rivulets. The brook had already burst its dam and had swollen into an ugly turbid brown stream.

"Stop him, Saya, please!" Lord Shinado pleaded. "If this continues, we will be destroyed before we ever have the chance to face the forces of Light."

Unable to restrain herself, Saya wailed, "How? How shall I stop him? When I know full well what we have done to him."

"But are you not the Priestess of the Sword?"

"We have lost him. Don't you understand?"

Saya longed to rebuke him. "Can't you see by looking at me?" she wanted to demand. "Do you not see how I fear, how I despair, how lost I am?" But she knew that her rage should be directed at herself.

A huge man came running through the torrent, his arms held high, illuminated by flashes of lightning, rain pouring off him. It was Lord Ibuki.

"So you are here, Shinado, Saya. Will you not lead those who can walk to refuge on the heights above? They are in peril here. They won't have a chance should the river overflow its banks."

"But the Dragon is above. The lightning is still striking."

"Have no fear. I will deal with him," Lord Ibuki said calmly. Lord Shinado and Saya both stared at him in shock.

"How do you intend to do what even Saya, the Priestess of the Sword, cannot?"

Lord Ibuki glanced at Saya. "That is Chihaya. Is that not so? If it is Chihaya, he is my pupil. It is my duty, as his teacher, to admonish him," he stated, slapping the wide hilt of his sword. As he turned away from them, Saya grabbed at him desperately.

"Wait! A sword is no match for his power. You will be killed. The Dragon has neither eyes nor heart. He cannot see you."

"How can we know that if we do not try?" Lord Ibuki said with a flash of white teeth. His was the face of a bold and seasoned warrior, but he was more than that. "I will not be slain so easily. I will tell him that if he wishes to bare his fangs against his comrades, he must kill me first."

Still clinging to him, Saya whispered, "Please don't go. If we lose you, too, what are we to do?"

Lord Ibuki only stroked her head with his large hand as though comforting a wayward child. Then, gently loosening her grasp, he climbed the rocks in the torrential rain to face the Dragon dancing amid the black clouds.

"Saya."

A familiar voice called her name. The storm had abated and the lonesome twilight imbued the land with stillness. The red rays of the setting sun finally pierced the clouds, which were only now beginning to disperse, casting a warmer blush on the tips of the crimson-leafed trees. Saya, who sat absentmindedly outside a small hut, turned her vacant gaze toward the voice, but saw no one, only the horses of Lord Akitsu and his men milling about.

"Hey, Saya!"

A little life came into Saya's face when she finally located the owner of the voice perched on the fence. "Torihiko!"

"I thought you had forgotten me. And I was only gone a short while," said the crow.

"Where have you been?"

"Here and there. I've mustered many troops. Even Lord Akitsu couldn't match their number. I'll have to be called Lord Torihiko hereafter," he joked, but seeing Saya remain glum, he flapped his wings. "Cheer up. The Dragon has been pacified, hasn't he?"

"But it was Lord Ibuki who pacified him."

"How is His Lordship?"

Saya shook her head wordlessly. Then suddenly she groaned as though no longer able to endure it. "Torihiko, I've failed."

"No you haven't!"

"I have. I'm useless. I can't do anything. Why am I, who am unable to accomplish even one vital task, the priestess?"

Torihiko gazed in concern at Saya, her face buried in her hands. "I should never have left your side."

After a short while an attendant came out of the hut and addressed Saya in a hushed voice. "His Lordship is conscious. He wishes to speak with you."

Saya followed the attendant and passed through the doorway. In the dim light of the hut, Lord Akitsu and the commanders sat in silence, their faces grave. Their expressions clearly indicated that there was no hope for Lord Ibuki's recovery. Her spirits drooping even further, Saya looked at his huge, prostrate form. His hair and beard were singed and burns covered his entire body; beneath the white cloth, she caught glimpses of painfully blistered skin. He had lost both eyes. The healer, unable to treat him, could only apply a cool damp cloth to his eyes in an attempt to relieve at least some of the pain. As Saya stood beside him, he moved his blackened lips and spoke.

"Is that Saya? The footsteps were light."

His voice was hoarse, barely audible, so unlike his natural booming tone. Clenching her teeth to hold back her tears, Saya knelt and replied, "Yes, it is I. Are you in pain?"

"No. It is not bad. Saya, I spoke with Chihaya. In the end, he knew me," he said as cheerfully as he could manage. "So I told him that I was relieved to see that he, who I had thought was the worst pupil I ever had, could now defeat even his own teacher."

"It was my fault, Lord," Saya whispered.

"Saya, do not reject him. Please. He could not control his own power, but raged blindly. He did not yet know what had befallen us. He is not evil. Certainly not. For we wounded him grievously."

"Yes. I know." Saya nodded. Her tears overflowed and would not stop. When she thought how she had lost all those dear to her, in vain, she wanted to rant and rave and pummel the earth. But she could only weep quietly. Lord Ibuki had already set his feet toward the Goddess and was only looking back at Saya on his way.

"If you reject Chihaya, he will surely reject himself. And that would be a terrible thing, for he will become true evil. He will become the Dragon. Forgive him. Though the death of Natsume hurt you, Chihaya has also been hurt. Forgiveness will become your strength."

"Yes," Saya replied through her tears.

"That is what makes you the Water Maiden." Lord Ibuki let out a long sigh as if suddenly tired. "Though I leave you to seek rest with the Goddess, I will never forget you. Tell Chihaya that I hope we meet again in some other guise."

He fell into a deep sleep. And then, as they watched, he quietly breathed his last.

When night fell, the sky cleared into a starlit vault. The quarter moon cast a fresh, clean light, etching shadows in the autumn thickets. A wake was held for Lord Ibuki; and after laying his body to rest within a newly built enclosure, his companions kept watch. There was none who did not mourn his passing, none who did not lament this appalling blow to their military strength. Saya sat a long while in a corner of the small hut thronged with people, but, unable to endure it any longer, she slipped out alone into the night.

White chrysanthemums floated forlornly in the light of the moon. The smell of frost was in the air. By dawn the ground would surely be covered in white. And to Saya the cold bite of the air on her skin seemed appropriate. Drawing near to a cherry tree that cast a dappled shadow in the moonlight through its sparsely leafed branches, she rested her throbbing head against its trunk and whispered softly, "It cannot be undone."

These words kept ringing in her head. No matter what she thought of, her thoughts always concluded with those words.

"I have lost Chihaya, and thus I no longer exist as Priestess of the Sword. What a fool I was. Natsume, Lord Ibuki—both have left me behind. Now what shall I live for? How am I to carry on?"

She suddenly felt someone walking silently toward her through the darkness. She moved away from the tree in surprise.

"Who is it?"

A small figure, about the same height as Fawn, walked toward her, silhouetted against the moonlight. But in the pale light her hair shone whiter than frost.

"Lady Iwa," Saya exclaimed, her voice loud at this unexpected appearance. "When did you arrive? Did word reach us that you were coming?"

"I am always with you. It is just that no one notices," Lady Iwa replied enigmatically, and then, coming up to Saya, asked her abruptly, "Daughter, why did you fear, when you knew long ago that Chihaya and the Dragon were one?"

Saya could not answer immediately. The old woman had casually pierced the heart of the matter. But as she gazed into the fathomless depths of Lady Iwa's eyes, Saya realized that the old woman already knew everything. Then it was not words that most adequately expressed her feelings. Like a heartbroken child breaking down before its mother, she suddenly burst into tears. "I did not believe it. I don't know what came over me. I saw Natsume and just lost control . . . To think that I could for a moment believe such a thing of Chihaya, when he had delivered the Sword into my hands on his internment in the prison. When the only person who could have taken the Sword from my tent was Fawn."

"Yes, and that child you took under your wing in all likelihood was Princess Teruhi herself. It is just the sort of thing that audacious woman would do."

"Natsume distrusted Fawn. But . . ." Saya murmured.

"The immortals are skilled at utilizing human frailties. Using your compassion, she infiltrated our lines and carried out her plan."

"Then if I had been stronger, Natsume and Lord Ibuki would not have died, isn't that so?"

Lady Iwa's large eyes blinked slowly. "It does no good to talk of what might have been."

"But I cannot be silent. I have been such a fool that I despise myself," Saya continued, unable to stop. "The one thing—the one thing I can never forget is the expression on Chihaya's face. I abandoned him at the most critical moment. How could I have looked at him like that? Lord Ibuki's words, which he spoke with such sincerity before he died, were too late. Chihaya is gone. It cannot be undone."

Lady Iwa waited until Saya's sobs had quieted, and then said gently, "You must not despair. That is the worst thing you can do when you recognize a mistake. Although there are some things in this world that can be amended and others that cannot, acknowledgment of this is different from not trying to make amends."

Saya finally wiped her eyes. "If I had even the slightest hope that I could make amends I would do anything—even if I were to have only the least of opportunities."

"Daughter," Lady Iwa said earnestly, "I do not believe that Chihaya has returned to the Palace of Light. Where he has gone I do not know, yet I feel he must be wandering somewhere not so far away."

"Could it be true?" Saya opened her tear-drenched eyes wide and gazed at the old woman. "Even after this, can Chihaya not despise us?"

"Yes, because he now knows himself. He is no longer a child

who will do as his sister bids him. He will think for himself and will make a move only after he has come to a decision. Of course, he will never come back to the camp of Darkness of his own accord—"

"But if I were to look for him, I might speak with him." Saya eagerly finished the sentence. "If there is such a hope, I will go. I will find Chihaya."

"Yes. It is possible that you may be able to take his hand once again. This time, however, you must choose your words with the utmost care, for Chihaya will never again simply do whatever you tell him."

But Saya took a deep breath and straightened her back. She no longer felt she had lost everything. "It will be enough to admit that I was wrong, if it means that we won't be alienated by misunderstanding anymore. I will go to seek Chihaya. That is what I must do."

Hearing the strong conviction in her voice, Lady Iwa closed her eyes and appeared to be lost in thought. She said in a slow, deliberate voice, "Saya, more than three hundred years have passed since the forces of Light began to rule this land. During that period we have struggled to resist them. Generation after generation, the Water Maiden was born, and each generation that same maiden was drawn to the Light and destroyed herself. I thought this must be the curse of the maid who keeps the Sword. Yet you found Chihaya. You are the first Water Maiden to meet the Wind Child. And I think that this will change everything. The Water Maiden in your generation has at last found her true self."

Saya looked at the old woman in awe. Such words instilled in her a vague apprehension. "I am thoughtless and have failed repeatedly so far. Are you saying that even though I was the first to meet Chihaya, if I fail now, I may destroy myself again?"

"Have I made you nervous?" Lady Iwa said with laughter in her voice, then asked her teasingly, "Do you still fear Chihaya?"

"No," Saya said defiantly, but Lady Iwa shook her head.

"No, no. You are lying. After all, he is the Dragon. It would be false not to fear him, and a grave error. But it is wrong to fear him completely. For he is not evil. If you deal with him honestly, you will be rewarded with honesty. He is the Dragon, but in order for him to transcend the Dragon you must fear, and transcend your fear."

THE EARTHEN VESSEL

O winds of heaven, bring up the clouds
and seal the vaulted sky
Lest these heavenly maids should wings possess
and away from us should fly.

—Bishop Shojo

1

The warriors seated in a circle watched Lord Akitsu carefully, waiting to see how he would respond to Saya's request. Lady Iwa remained outside the circle, sitting with eyes closed in a corner of the room.

Lord Akitsu spoke slowly, as if trying to postpone making a decision. "I understand what you are saying. And I realize that Chihaya was not to blame. But what can you hope to gain by going off in search of him? He will surely never rejoin our side. Our actions, and his, were such that we will never be able to face one another again."

"No. We are capable of forgiveness. If we can forgive him, then surely he will forgive us. Those who let his immortality blind them are even now regretting their actions, and most of all, everyone knows that we were manipulated by the deceit of Princess Teruhi," Saya said earnestly.

"Is it necessary for us to go to such lengths to regain Chihaya as our ally?" Lord Shinado demanded harshly.

"Yes. The Dragon Sword has always been kept by the people of Darkness. He is the Dragon Sword. He is our greatest, our most powerful source of strength."

"But you yourself said that we had lost him."

Saya flinched. "Yes. And that is why I—I myself—must go once more in search of him."

"Do you think you can just wander about looking for him without the slightest idea of his whereabouts?" Lord Shinado exclaimed. "In the midst of a war that is ripe for explosion? The forces of Light have laid ambushes everywhere. Such a quest is impossible!"

Torihiko, engrossed in preening his feathers, raised his head and stated, "I will accompany her. Even now those under my command are wheeling through the sky in search of him."

Lord Shinado frowned. "Torihiko, you are a military weapon we cannot spare. Do you intend to desert your post?"

"I have only to fly back here to maintain contact," the crow replied indifferently. "And I would have you recall that it was for Saya's sake that I remained in this world in feathered form."

Lord Akitsu gazed at Saya as though weary of thinking. "Can you not wait a little while longer, just until things settle down? We can ill afford to split up our forces at this time, yet I cannot send you out without protection."

"It must not wait. Please!" Saya leaned forward, pleading. "Let me go. If I have Torihiko with me, I can protect myself. I must leave now, for with each passing day Chihaya moves farther away."

Lord Shinado broke in. "What on earth do you see in Chihaya, that Prince of Light, that Dragon? It was indeed you who brought Chihaya to us in the first place, but what is the use of this devotion which prompts you to such a suicidal attempt to regain him? You act like some love-struck maid running after her lover. You are blind to everything else."

Saya, nonplussed, could only gape at him, she was so astonished by his words.

At that moment, Lady Iwa spoke from the corner of the room.

"You are right." The old woman had opened her eyes for the first time and was looking at Saya. "Because Saya is the Priestess of the Sword. That is what it means to be priestess. A priestess is one who, though of mortal frame, can wed a god."

The blood rushed to Lord Shinado's face and there was anger in his voice. "Are you telling me that the god Saya serves is Chihaya? I will never accept that, never! Not such a—"

"I did not say he was the god she serves," Lady Iwa interrupted swiftly. "But you must recognize that with the Sword between them, Chihaya and Saya form the opposing poles of one axis. They are like opposite sides of the same body. Whether they choose to give or to take, they seek in the other what is incomplete within themselves. Just as a god cannot exist without a priestess, so a priestess cannot exist without a god."

Lord Shinado did not utter another word. Granted just seven days, Saya was given a horse and provisions on the condition that Torihiko flew back daily to report.

After they had left the meeting, Torihiko perched himself on Saya's shoulder and said, "Lord Shinado's heart has certainly been broken. To me, it appears that he is the love-struck one— although I can sympathize with his unrequited feelings."

Saya gave a small sigh. "Well, I cannot pretend that I don't understand what you're talking about. But it's no good, though I am sorry for him."

"What do you think about what Lady Iwa said?"

"Such a thought had never occurred to me," she said hesitantly, her eyes downcast. "If Lady Iwa says so, then I suppose it must be true, but it doesn't feel real to me. After all, I hardly understand Chihaya myself. I have yet to guess correctly what he will do next."

She fell silent, but after they had walked a little farther, she added, "Yet at the same time, I think that probably no one else understands him better than I do."

The crow shrugged his wings. "Either way, it doesn't really matter to me, so long as you're happy."

"Either way?" Saya asked.

"Whether you are lover or priestess. Either way, it is not the business of a bird."

Ivy leaves redder than flame and clusters of red berries on the naked branches of shrubs vied for attention. A biting wind blew in gusts along the ground, and the trees shed their colorful leaves with each blast. The fallen leaves lay thick upon the forest floor, and day by day the scraggy branches of the trees were stripped bare. Birds left, birds came: migrating throngs at the end of their journey.

Torihiko gazed up at flocks of large white birds crossing the sky high above and said, "Those birds are no help. They won't join our ranks. They feel no attachment or loyalty to Toyoashi-hara because they come from across the sea."

"So somewhere across the sea is another land."

From her horse Saya gazed into the distance across a wide sandbar. The sea was very near. She could feel it even in the breeze. "Why don't we go over that way?"

"To the seashore? Do you think we might find him there?"

"Not particularly. I just feel an urge to see the ocean once more."

Grumbling about the trouble caused by this foolish whim, which would take her to where there was no hiding place, the crow flew into the air, returning almost immediately.

"I've just sent out some scouts. You'll have to stay here until they come back."

They waited for a while in front of a field of swaying reeds until Torihiko's scouts returned to report. They were a flock of about twenty greenfinches that appeared one after the other, beating their gray-green and yellow wings. Finding Torihiko perched on Saya's shoulders, the friendly round-eyed birds swooped down in a rush and perched without fear upon Saya's arms and fingers, chirping merrily.

"All right. I see. Let's go." After Torihiko had spoken with them, the flock rose once more into the air; Saya parted with them somewhat reluctantly.

She urged her horse forward until they came to the tideland. In this forlorn and desolate landscape only migrating snipe could be seen, resting their wings and poking their beaks in the mud. They could learn nothing from these birds, and as Torihiko judged open spaces to be too dangerous, Saya was forced to turn back and follow a path through the black pine forest along the coast. Finally, climbing up from the shore, she was able to glimpse through the branches white-capped waves crashing against the rocks at the foot of a sheer cliff.

She slept each night under the open sky and was on her own most of the days. Torihiko was extremely cautious, but nevertheless spent most of his time flying in all directions, searching for Chihaya. When night began to fall, Saya would tether her horse to a tree and gather dry branches to make a small fire. And often, though she had gone to the trouble of gathering a bed of dry leaves and curling up in it, she found she could not sleep. More than the cold or loneliness, the fear that she was heading in the wrong direction and traveling farther and farther away from Chihaya tormented her at night.

"Being alone helps one to realize many things, doesn't it?" Saya said to Torihiko when he flew down to join her. "It's strange. I always thought I was alone, but actually I never really have been, in the true sense of the word."

"Are you feeling lonely?"

Saya shook her head. "No, I'm not alone in that sense. But for some reason I feel I have returned to the person I was before I came to Hashiba."

From the first day she awoke in Hashiba, Saya had hated the frightened little girl in her dreams. She had despised her fear, her wretchedness; had rejected her, and scorned her helplessness. She had not wanted to recognize her as part of herself. But she was wrong. For was she not even now wretched, crushed by fear, pitifully pleading and searching for the warmth of love? She was no different from that little girl who wandered lost in the middle of the night. At last she had realized that she must accept and recognize this part of herself. For without accepting it, she could never transcend her fear, could never move forward.

"The place that that girl was searching for and never found may have been nothing more than my self," Saya thought quietly.

At night the wind carried the faint sounds of battle, and, peering through the trees, she could see torches flickering like fox fires on the distant shore. Although she knew from the reports gathered by Torihiko that the battle was still limited to local skirmishes, it was obviously bloody. Far removed from the tranquil peace of the passing autumn season, the final battle between Light and Darkness, on which the fate of Toyoashihara hinged, would soon commence.

The next morning an unprecedented number of gulls wheeled along the coast. Diving through the white-winged flock, an excited Torihiko flew toward her like an arrow. "We've found him!"

At his triumphant cry, Saya was amazed to find herself overcome with dizziness as a sudden surge of blood coursed hotly through her veins.

"Where is he?"

"On the beach at the foot of the cliff on the cape. Some foolish plovers mistook him for the body of a drowned man and never said a word."

The cliff protruded like a nose, and it was with great difficulty that Saya clambered down the rocks. At the bottom was a shallow cove with a pebbly beach. When she finally caught sight of Chihaya, she thought that she could not blame the plovers. He lay across the sand like a beached corpse, half-submerged in the waves that washed the shore. From the fact that he was half-buried in sand, and from the small crabs that scuttled nonchalantly over his body, it was obvious that he had not stirred for a considerable time. Seaweed had twined itself around his hands and feet, and his salt-stained clothing was charred and torn. With each step she took toward him, her heart beat more wildly. Perhaps there was a chance in a thousand, one in a million, that even a Prince of Light could die.

But when she came to a halt, hesitating to touch him, Chihaya opened his eyes and looked up at her.

"Are you awake?" The words that fell from her lips sounded ludicrous.

"I'm so tired," Chihaya whispered weakly. "I did not know that the bottom of the sea was so far away."

"You went there?"

"I wished to meet the God of the Sea . . . but I could not reach him."

"Can you stand?"

"Yes." Chihaya sat up slowly, but he seemed so weary that she had to help him walk.

"How did you find me? At the end I didn't care anymore and just let the tide carry me."

"Torihiko found you," Saya replied. "We've been traveling all over for the last six days. And it took another day to get here once we had found you. It will soon be dark. We've used up all seven of the days given us."

A little way along the narrow beach was a small hollow in the bottom of the cliff, enough to serve as a shelter from the weather, and Saya took him there. "I will carry the news to Lord Akitsu before night falls," Torihiko said to Saya. "If possible, I'll bring some help. It doesn't look as if we'll be able to make it up the cliff with him like this."

After watching the crow fly away, Saya went in search of dry driftwood. When she returned with the kindling she found Chihaya leaning against a rock as if asleep once more. But when she began rummaging in her bag for a flint he addressed her abruptly.

"You brought the Sword. I thought you loathed carrying it around with you."

She looked at the Dragon Sword protruding from her bag and smiled. "I used it as a talisman. I felt that if I had it with me, I would find you."

"Why did you come looking for me?" Chihaya whispered in such a low voice that it was barely audible.

"Because I wanted to apologize."

"Apologize?"

"For thinking that you killed Natsume."

"But what does it mean, to apologize?"

Saya looked at him, perplexed, and realized that he actually did not understand. "It means to say 'I'm sorry.' But don't you know that?"

"This is the first time I've heard of it," Chihaya said seriously. "What does it mean?"

"Well! What a predicament!"

For the first time Saya felt that she understood what the novices had been taught in the Palace of Light; why a priestess who lost favor with the gods was held responsible to the degree that she would take her own life. It was because the gods could not forgive. If one erred, one could not make amends. There was no second chance. For the immortal Children of Light, this was accepted as a matter of course. The words of Princess Teruhi came back to her: ". . . we who may never hope, nay, are not permitted to escape." To them, reflecting on one's mistakes must surely appear to be an aberration.

Saya suddenly felt unsure of herself and, with eyes downcast, began hesitantly to explain.

"To apologize is to tell someone that you realize you have done wrong, that you wish you had never done it. And then to beg them, in consideration of this feeling, to withhold punishment, to forgo their anger, and to ask them to forget the past and have no bitter feelings. It is indeed a selfish thing to do. But among our people, when we realize that we have done wrong, the first thing we do is apologize . . ."

Saya stopped, her voice fading away. Chihaya remained silent. Just when she felt sure that he could not understand, he asked abruptly, "Then, if I apologize, do you think I will be forgiven? By Lord Ibuki?"

"Lord Ibuki already forgave you, even before you could apologize," Saya replied gently.

"Can I meet him once more?"

"No."

"Then he died?"

Seeing Saya nod slightly, Chihaya said softly, "Then it is the same as not being forgiven."

"No, it isn't!" Saya said hastily. "That's not true. Before he died, Lord Ibuki said that he hoped to see you once more. In some other guise, he said. After all, we have the saying 'until we meet again.' "

"I do not understand." Chihaya turned his face away and pressed his forehead against his arms, which were folded upon his knees. "Everyone dies. Natsume died right before my eyes. Though she sought my aid, I could only watch her die. I am different. I cannot be like my brother or my sister, yet I am shunned by the people of Darkness. I only cause harm to Toyoashihara. Can you bring the gods or people back to life just by apologizing? It's impossible. For I cannot go to the Land of the Dead to apologize."

"If you think that you are all alone, you are wrong," Saya said. "I am here."

"But even you, Saya, who speak thus, you will die, too. You, too, will leave me."

"Yes, that's true. Someday." Then taking a deep breath, she said, "Yes, maybe even tomorrow. And that is why I came to apologize. Even if you can't forgive me—before I am parted from you, at least I want to do this much."

"Well, if you must apologize," Chihaya muttered, "you'd best go find someone who is angry and wants to punish you. I don't know who that may be, but it certainly isn't I. Who on earth could think of you in that way?"

"Well then," Saya began, and then suddenly realized that she could say nothing at all. She was overcome with a desire to laugh or cry but could do neither. Finally she said, "Let's eat. That will surely make us feel better."

The driftwood was permeated with salt and, as it burned, the flames at times turned grass-green. It was a novelty to see a steady fire burning, and the hollow in the rock became warm and bright. Saya divided all the remaining provisions in half: chestnuts, walnuts, and a bamboo flask of wine. When she offered Chihaya chestnut dumplings that she had roasted over the fire, he said, deeply moved, "It's a long time since I last ate. I had totally forgotten."

"But you always ate normally before, didn't you?" Saya asked in surprise. "Or did you stop eating, like Princess Teruhi and Prince Tsukishiro?"

"They don't eat because they wish to retain their youth. If they eat too much of the things of the earth, they don't feel right. When I was in the shrine, I was rarely allowed to eat." Then, as though the thought had just occurred to him, he added, "Maybe that's why. My sister said that I had changed."

"I don't think that's the only reason . . ." Saya faltered as she looked at Chihaya on the other side of the brightly dancing flames. And no wonder. For Chihaya looked just like what she had once imagined the Ground Spiders looked like.

"But then I think perhaps you have grown a bit taller. I noticed it when I was beside you earlier."

"Perhaps if I continue to eat like this I will even grow into an old man."

"Hmm." Imagining it, Saya unexpectedly burst out laughing. "If you were an old man forever, you would certainly suffer from aches and pains in your bones. The old people in Hashiba were always grumbling."

Chihaya did not laugh but whispered seriously, "The voice of the God of the Sea . . . it was the voice of an old man. A very, very old man."

"Why did you decide to visit him?" Saya asked. It was a question that had been worrying her.

"Because he knew me. He knew me much better than I knew myself . . ." Seeing the inquiring look on Saya's face, he continued. "Do you remember the other time we came to the seashore? The time I met the messenger of the Sea God on the beach?"

"You mean the shark? It was midsummer. It seems like so long ago."

"I thought then that he had mistaken me for someone else, and I didn't pay much attention to what he said. After all, old people are often forgetful—like the priestesses of the shrine. But it wasn't so. The God of the Sea knew I was the Dragon, even though I did not know it myself. And he said that there were only two paths before me: to slay my parent or to be slain by him."

"What?" Saya paled. "What does that mean?"

"That's what I wanted to ask him." Chihaya clasped his hands together. "But it was no use. I traveled along the sea floor until I came to a bottomless fissure, and though I descended into it, I lost consciousness partway down. It was a blackness more relentless than the night, one which the strength of neither Light nor Darkness can ever penetrate."

Saya shuddered as if she were there. "You are lucky you made it back."

"Perhaps I was sent back. When I regained consciousness, I was floating far out at sea. The ancient one said that we were both isolated, alone. Perhaps he meant that I should think for myself."

Chihaya had been staring into the dancing green flames, but

now he raised his eyes and asked, "What do you think, Saya? About slaying or being slain?"

"Does he mean the God of Light?"

"I think so."

Saya muttered, "I—I don't want to think of such a thing. Such a terrible, frightening thing!"

"But still, if there were only two paths . . . ?"

The flames lit up his eyes as though gold dust had been scattered in them. His soiled and tattered clothing, his sand-encrusted hair, made no difference. He was a Prince of Light, and the superiority of his being shone through his outer garments. Saya suddenly realized that no trace of girlishness remained in him.

"It is as Lady Iwa said," she thought. "Chihaya knows who he is."

She knew he had not asked her this question with any intent to follow her instructions. "If you must choose," she replied earnestly, "then I will tell you. I do not want you to be killed. If that is the choice, I would rather you killed the God of Light."

Chihaya smiled unexpectedly. It was the first time she had seen him smile in a long time, and it seemed as if the golden light deep within his eyes were strewn all about her. "Now I feel better. I will doubt no longer. If there is no way to avoid this fate, I will go out to meet it with sword in hand rather than standing by with arms folded—even if it means I must fight my own brother and sister. That is the road I must take."

Saya was surprised to catch herself returning his smile. When Chihaya expressed his decision, she felt as though a ray of clear light had pierced her heart. In that moment she realized that the problem was not hers to judge. The decision was Chihaya's alone, one which she must entrust to him no matter what.

"Now, of all times, I know that I can return the Sword to you. You, yourself, are the Sword that must be wielded, and you must follow your own path. You have no need of a priestess to still you. I am sure it is so, because, for the first time, I can see you for what you truly are."

Taking the Sword from her hands, Chihaya hesitated slightly and looked at Saya. "And what do I look like? My true self?"

"Don't you know?" Saya gave a little laugh. She was tempted to evade the question by leaving it at that, but thought better of it and said seriously, "There was never any time when you looked more like a Prince of Light. Dazzling to our eyes, powerful, pure, implacable—and beautiful. Yet at the same time completely different from Princess Teruhi or Prince Tsukishiro. You know how to grieve for those who have died, and you know enough to hate killing. Although you are immortal, strangely enough you have what we call compassion. You are even capable of forgiveness. And that is why, although you possess a terrible power, I have no fear of you. Now I understand why you are the one whom the Water Maiden has sought so long."

Chihaya looked as though he wanted to feel pleased but could not. "I have no right to be described like that. I have already slain countless people, and I don't know what I will do in future."

Stroking the hilt of the Sword, he hung his head and then continued. "What you have said is probably just another way of saying that I am different. If it comes to a confrontation with my father or with my brother and sister, then I will most likely fill you once more with dread."

"No. No matter what happens, I will not lose sight of you a second time. Just watch me," Saya said with conviction. "I will join you. If you are labeled 'different,' then I, too, will gladly be different. After all, I am the only person in the world who has found the Sword's true form."

The burning wood crackled and popped, and the green and gold flames wavered sharply, causing the shadows on the rock wall to dance. Outside the shallow cave it was completely dark. The only evidence of the outside world was the sound of the waves against the beach. The rocks and the sea had melted into the jet-black night. Neither moon nor stars could be seen. Saya was suddenly caught up in the illusion that the shallow cave was the one spot in the ever-changing land of Toyoashihara that remained unchanged, and that the two of them were at the center of the world. The world in constant motion swung like a busy pendulum, dancing through time. Yet before her were the eyes of Chihaya, which continued to hold her gaze, reflecting the light of the flames, rivaling the entire world.

As though a thin silk veil had suddenly been torn in half, she understood what all couples feel when they exchange glances, what they all know.

At dawn the eastern sky was dyed a deep crimson as if a huge barrel of blood had been spilled along the horizon between the water and the sky. Then, as the sun rose from the sea, round and full, the waves and the clouds turned to gold. The sun, haloed in white, was almost ephemeral in its paleness. Saya, who had gone down to the beach alone to watch the sunrise, wondered if this was an omen, but although it seemed uncanny, it was nevertheless beautiful. A pang of anxiety flitted through her heart, but in the next moment it was replaced by happiness.

"There is not one thing in this world that is not beautiful," she thought with satisfaction. Like the water lapping the shore at her feet, waves of happiness welled up and immersed her in a sea of bliss. She was so warm and snug within, she almost felt guilty. The freezing dawn wind that pierced her skin did not bother her at all, and she continued to sit on the windswept beach, wrapping both arms about herself as though hugging the warm glow within her breast.

Even when she had decided to look for Chihaya one last time, she had never imagined she would find such contentment as this. Last night she had suddenly realized the closeness of what she had always been seeking. It was so close that she had only to reach out her hand to touch it. What an amazing thing.

"Change is something we should be thankful for." Saya pondered the idea. And she would surely go on changing—she and Chihaya, both of them, for they had only just learned how to open the door that had been closed. That thought, too, was part of the happiness engulfing her.

A flock of gulls, gleaming white, flew across the brightening sky. The sea opened its blue bosom to welcome the new day. Saya realized that she could now accept Princess Sayura without resistance.

"By leaving her footprints in the palace, Princess Sayura led me to Chihaya. Princess Sayura, and all the Water Maidens before her, showed me the road to take . . . Together we have traveled along one path. But just as today is not a repeat of yesterday, so I am not Sayura. I am Saya. And I found Chihaya . . ."

"Saya."

Without her noticing, Chihaya had come up behind her. She looked up at his face bathed in the morning sun, bright and animated.

"Let's leave this beach. You should get back as soon as you can."

"But what about you? Are you all right?"

"I'm fine. I can move well enough. Let's go to the top. Your poor horse—his nosebag is empty."

Saya was surprised and then laughed. She could not recall having mentioned a word about her horse, which she had left tethered at the top of the cliff. "Well! You haven't changed."

She slung her lightened bag across her back and left the cave with Chihaya. Returning to the cliff and looking up, she saw the rugged rock face looming far up into the distance and found it hard to believe that she had actually climbed down it. She had been so impatient yesterday that she had not stopped to consider how she would get back up. There was no easier place, however, so, steeling themselves, they grasped the rock and began the long, grueling climb. Less than halfway up, their breath came in gasps, their clothes were drenched in sweat, and they could not drag themselves any higher.

They clung to a narrow ledge, too narrow to sit upon, and rested where they stood. Saya leaned her head against the rock and caught her breath; suddenly she was struck by the ludicrousness of their position. Chihaya was watching a bird wheel in the sky but turned to look at her when he heard her laughing whisper.

"What did you say?"

" 'No climb is too steep when with you, beloved,' " Saya repeated, but, seeing Chihaya's puzzled look, explained. "It's one of the Kagai songs. It means that no matter how steep the mountain, it doesn't seem so steep when I'm with you. It's a good song, don't you think? Everyone used to sing it."

Chihaya smiled vaguely. It was clear that he did not really understand. For the first time it dawned on Saya that there was still one major problem left.

"What does Chihaya really think about me?" she wondered. Not even she could imagine him bearing a betrothal gift and coming to ask for her hand like other men. This realization discouraged her, and Chihaya was left to puzzle over her sudden gloomy silence.

In any case, the most urgent problem was to master the cliff. After their rest, they patiently labored upward with renewed strength, the sun slowly climbing the sky at their backs, until at last they saw flat ground before them. It was already close to noon. They stretched out upon the ground for a while, unable even to search for the horse. But at last they rose and turned toward the forest. It was bright among the leafless trees, but no matter where they looked, there was no trace of a living creature; all was silent and still.

"How strange. I'm sure he was here. Perhaps I tethered him carelessly," Saya said, scratching her head.

"Let's look for hoofprints. I doubt he's gone far."

But just as Saya had begun to scan the ground, Chihaya said in a hard voice, "Run, Saya!"

"What?"

"I said run!"

He grabbed her hand and as she began to run, uncomprehending, armed soldiers appeared one after another from the shadow of a grove of withered trees. They were soldiers from the army of Light, copper disks emblazoned on their helmets. Pursued, Saya and Chihaya fled toward a gap in their ranks, but there they saw a group of horsemen riding abreast galloping head on at them. They turned back, but there was no avenue of escape. They ran to the edge of the cliff, and there they were surrounded. Facing the soldiers brandishing their swords, Chihaya drew the Dragon Sword. The soldiers naturally recoiled before its imposing shower of blue-white sparks, but not one of them broke ranks. As they glared at one another, a cool voice reverberated through the air.

"If you wish to fight, I'm sure that you are perfectly able. But before you do, take a good look at our numbers. Saya will most certainly die. Are you still willing?"

Looking up, they saw that among the horsemen, who held their bows ready, sat a lone unhelmeted figure, robed from head to foot in white. His face, like those of the shrine priestesses, was hidden in a fold of cloth. But the curve of his cheekbone, only partially revealed, and the tall dapple-gray steed he rode were well known to Saya.

"Prince Tsukishiro! What is he doing here?" she wondered.

Chihaya had also recognized him. The tip of the Sword, tinged with light, drooped slightly as though he was losing confidence. Prince Tsukishiro spoke again, his face still concealed. Somehow he seemed to be dressed in mourning.

"I saw you go to the bottom of the sea. Why did you come back? Why? Now we will be forced to deal with you."

"There was no place for me to go. That's all," Chihaya replied in a subdued voice. "But my fate is not to be killed by my brother."

"The time of our divine father's coming will soon be upon us. If your fate is to die, would you not rather it should be by my hand than his? Even Teruhi, when compared to our father, must be considered more merciful."

A nearby soldier suddenly grabbed Saya's arm and yanked her toward him. Before she could utter a sound, blue light flashed like lightning from the sword. The soldier released her with a scream and fell with a thud, not cut by the blade but with his hair and body engulfed in flame. Although the soldiers were thrown into confusion, the death of their comrade fanned their fear and rage, and in the next instant they set upon the two of them with a guttural cry. Saya, who had closed her eyes at the sight of countless blades and spears rushing toward her, felt someone catch her deftly as she reeled.

"Put down your sword. Do you understand? Or you will never see this maiden again."

The voice came from right beside her ear and, opening startled eyes, she found herself in Prince Tsukishiro's arms. Moreover, she was seated upon the saddle of his dapple-gray stallion. What could have happened in that one short instant? She was at least fifty paces from where she had been standing. Struggling frantically, she screamed, "Chihaya!"

She saw Chihaya turn and glare fiercely at the Prince across a forest of spears. "If you harm Saya, I will kill everyone. You, my father, everyone."

"That sounds like something the Dragon would say," Prince Tsukishiro said with contempt. "But think of the consequences before you speak. You cannot yet have developed such power. If we take the time, we can certainly tear you limb from limb. Unfortunately, I have no desire to engage in further combat here and now. I came here only to get Saya. Let us strike a bargain. If you let me take her, I will let you go. I vow that I will not harm her if you will retreat from this spot."

"No," Chihaya responded immediately.

"Then you had better bear this in mind: promises made by the Children of Light are eternal, whereas the lives of the people of Toyoashihara are fleeting."

Prince Tsukishiro leisurely moved one hand to Saya's chin. She tried to twist away, but her arms were pinned and she could not move.

"If I but strengthen my hold a fraction you will lose her. She will return to her own land, where you cannot follow."

"What do you intend to do with her?"

"Nothing in particular. This girl was originally one of my handmaidens. I thought to make her my bride."

"Don't be ridiculous! I will never become your bride," Saya snapped angrily. "What nerve! When you have no desire to—"

Prince Tsukishiro suddenly laughed.

She wanted to warn Chihaya to be careful, not to trust him. But she could not raise her voice. She looked at him in earnest appeal, but he did not notice her gaze and stood hesitating. Finally he said, "If you promise . . ."

"Very good. I promise." And as soon as the words had left Prince Tsukishiro's lips, he cast aside his robe. Before the white cloth had floated to the ground, he had grasped his bow and fitted an arrow to the string. The bowstring twanged and the arrow sank deep into Chihaya's heart.

"You monster!" Saya shrieked. Without a backward glance, Prince Tsukishiro wheeled his horse lightly around and galloped away with her.

"Liar! Is that how a Prince of Light behaves?" Saya continued to scream at him as she struggled wildly, trying to look back.

"I did not break my promise. I merely prevented him from pursuing us," the Prince replied calmly.

"But your soldiers—"

"Alas, they will not have time to cut him to pieces. For I saw your allies approaching."

Chihaya opened his eyes. There was a metallic taste in his mouth.

"He's come to."

The man who approached at the sound of Torihiko's voice was Lord Shinado. The soldiers of Light had vanished and Chihaya was now surrounded by soldiers wearing familiar black vests. He himself lay on the yellowed grass at the foot of a pine tree. He sat up quickly but was suddenly overcome by unbearable pain. Looking down, he saw that the wound in his chest still gushed blood, staining his clothes bright red. The other injuries he could bear, but this deep wound was a telling blow. He would have to sleep a long time, but before he allowed himself to sink into the oblivion of renewal there was something he must do.

"Saya—" He broke off and turned his head away, vomiting blood.

The lines on Lord Shinado's tanned forehead were deeply etched and his face was as rigid as stone. "Saya was taken. She exposed herself to the enemy in order to look for you and, just as I feared, has been captured. We were wrong to allow her to commit such folly."

Chihaya wiped his mouth, and stared up at him. "I will bring her back."

"You?"

"Yes, I."

Lord Shinado paused and then said in a low voice, "I don't suppose you'd like to hear what I think of you."

"I already know," Chihaya replied as he struggled desperately to rise. "You would like to carve me into pieces, as the soldiers of Light would have done. But wait. Before my brother took Saya he said that our divine father would soon descend. If that is true . . . My brother and sister, though they may deceive, do not utter outright falsehoods. It will mean disaster."

"What?" Doubting his own ears, Lord Shinado stooped forward to catch Chihaya's faint voice. "Do you mean the God of Light?"

Chihaya could barely manage to keep his eyes open; his face bore a ghastly pallor and beads of sweat stood out on his brow. The hand he pressed against his wound was already dyed red with blood.

"We knew that our father would someday descend from heaven. But for a long time even my sister, who reads the omens, did not know when. If our father sets foot upon the earth, the battle is finished. The forces of Darkness will have no hope of victory. Toyoashihara will belong to him. That is why there has been no noticeable movement from the army of Light."

Lord Shinado paled and said in a low voice, "If this is true, these are evil tidings indeed. Are you saying we are finished?"

"There is still time. We must penetrate the palace and prevent the ceremony of his arrival from taking place. I must tell Lord Akitsu. We must ignore everything else and attack at once . . ." Chihaya's voice faded and ended in a gasp but, gathering his strength, he continued, "Take me to the camp. It doesn't matter how. I know that you mistrust me, but I can show him a way into the palace."

"You have no need to ask. I will take you," Lord Shinado told him sullenly. "For if I did not, Saya's efforts would be in vain. For her sake, I would storm the palace immediately. At any rate, do something about that wound. Even though you may be immortal, it's unsightly."

But Chihaya gritted his teeth and shook his head. "First I must talk with Lord Akitsu. Once the healing begins, I will be unable to wake for some time."

Seeing Lord Shinado walking toward him where he perched in the treetops, Torihiko said, "I know. I know. You want me to fly to Lord Akitsu."

Lord Shinado stroked his chin irritably. "Damnation!"

"I know what you mean. We are right there with our men when Saya is whisked away and instead we rescue your hated rival. My wings feel heavy just at the thought of reporting it. But perhaps, having seen what happened to Chihaya, you feel a little revenged?"

"That's exactly why I feel so foul." Lord Shinado paced about even more irritably.

"Could it be—you don't mean that you actually feel some sympathy for him?" The crow looked down at him, his eyes bright with curiosity.

Lord Shinado glared up at Torihiko and then, averting his face abruptly, said, "Is that what they mean by immortality? To bear the agony of death countless times more than mortal man, despite the fact that the pain is no less?"

"It seems so," Torihiko replied, unusually sober. "It makes it seem much pleasanter to die."

Lord Shinado rose when he saw Lord Akitsu draw aside the curtain and step out. "How is Chihaya?"

"He has been carried within. He had exhausted his last ounce of strength. I've told them to let no one touch him." Lord Akitsu looked at him, the severe expression on his face slightly softening. "You have rendered us a great service. It was some feat to bring Chihaya back."

Lord Shinado shook his head and wiped his face as if to dispel an unpleasant memory. "I felt I was watching over his deathbed for the entire journey."

Lord Akitsu smiled faintly. "I, too, felt I was listening to his dying words. Even though I know he will not die, it is hard to believe."

Lord Shinado's expression remained grim. "Whatever the case, no mortal man has the strength to withstand that degree of agony. No man could have such a strong will. That much I learned."

Lord Akitsu nodded and his voice was tinged with awe. "And perhaps that is the very reason that he is endowed with the power to destroy even the God of Light. It seems that we were gravely mistaken. Chihaya is the last hope for the salvation of this land from subjection by the forces of Light."

"Will you raise the army?"

"Yes. Now let us call a council of war."

Lord Shinado accompanied the general as he began to stride away.

"If Chihaya's words are credible, our only ally is time. And I intend to believe him. We need three, four, five men. We must choose those who can infiltrate the Palace of Light and open the gates from inside."

"I will go," Lord Shinado said, as though it were already decided.

Torihiko flew in with a report. It was afternoon, the day after Chihaya had returned to the camp of the army of Darkness.

"The forces of Light camped upstream have all been recalled to the palace. They have begun to greatly fortify their defenses. In addition, young women are being summoned from all over the capital and are entering the palace. According to the ground thrushes, they are only being recruited as handmaidens, but I doubt there has ever been such a mustering before."

"It seems that the damage from the fire has left its mark," Lord Akitsu murmured. "Could it be . . . the purification ceremony at the end of the month? I wonder."

"You mean the God of Light may arrive at that time?" one of the generals asked with a shudder.

"Perhaps."

"Then there are only ten days left."

A murmur of voices rose within the tent. Lord Shinado stood

up impatiently and said, "Speed has always been our forte. Now we must move immediately. Any further delay will be fatal."

Lord Akitsu cast a sharp glance in his direction. "Very well, proceed. When do you leave?"

"Now."

"And your men?"

"We are five."

"Is that enough?"

"The more we take, the harder it will be to move."

"Well then . . ."

At that moment a voice came from beyond the curtain. "Will you not include one more in your party?"

Chihaya appeared. Wearing a new robe, he looked cool and collected, as if nothing had happened.

Lord Shinado frowned. "This task is not for you. You will be detected as soon as you set foot in the palace."

"There are plenty of ways to disguise oneself."

Lord Akitsu asked, "Are you well enough?"

Chihaya nodded. "Let me go."

After some thought, the one-eyed lord responded, "Our fate depends upon the opening of the gate. Those who infiltrate the palace hold the key to victory or defeat. We may need your strength. Go with Lord Shinado."

They left Lord Akitsu together, and Lord Shinado turned to face Chihaya angrily. "Show me your wound."

"It's better."

"Then show me."

When the lord reached out to grab the front of his robe, Chihaya stepped back to avoid his grasp.

"There!" Lord Shinado exclaimed roughly. "Don't go and tell me such an obvious lie. Who do you think you're fooling when your face is still so pale?"

"It's nothing. Just a scratch. It ought to have disappeared by now," Chihaya said defensively.

"It seems that even an immortal Prince of Light has his limits. But this time we cannot afford any mistakes."

"I know."

"We cannot allow anyone to hinder us," Lord Shinado snapped unsympathetically. "If you are going to be a burden, then stay here and sleep."

"Never."

Three soldiers of indeterminate age and no distinguishing features approached them. Lord Shinado introduced them, the members of the infiltration force, to Chihaya.

"Yahiro, Tsutsuno, Shiomitsu. These are skilled men. They can become trees or rocks. They have distinguished themselves as spies in our service."

Chihaya stared at the men with eager curiosity. "I have become furred creatures, birds, and fish, but never a tree or a rock."

Lord Shinado choked on his words, and then explained, "I was speaking metaphorically to indicate that they can remain undetected."

As they looked at each other nonplussed, Torihiko flew up to them.

"And, needless to say, Torihiko. These are the faces of those who will penetrate the Palace of Light. Torihiko is fine as he is, but you others must disguise yourselves and each find his own way into the palace. For we have more chance of success if we separate."

"Excuse me," the most senior of the three, whether Yahiro, Tsutsuno, or Shiomitsu it was hard to tell, interjected hesitantly. "It appears to me that this other personage must attract attention no matter how he disguises himself."

Before Lord Shinado could reply, Chihaya said, "Then I will disguise myself as one who attracts attention."

"What are you planning?"

Chihaya smiled impudently at their dubious looks. "Let me be chosen as a handmaiden. I'm sure that I can do that."

2

"Don't be so angry." Prince Tsukishiro had come to see how Saya was doing, only to find her sitting rigidly, face to the wall, her food untouched.

"Do you expect me to smile?" Saya retorted sharply. "When I have been taken captive by my enemies and brought here against my will?"

"Am I your enemy?"

"You seem to have lost your sense," Saya answered hotly, standing and facing him. "I can never be your bride. For I love all that lives in Toyoashihara more than I love the Light. You are my enemy, the one we fight. You may despise me if you like. For if I had had a bow and arrow, I would surely have shot you when you shot Chihaya."

Prince Tsukishiro had removed his armor and was garbed entirely in a soft shade of blue. Slim and graceful, he in no way resembled a warrior. She could scarcely believe it was the same man who had but a short while ago loosed the arrow. "Let me go," she demanded once again. "Either that or kill me. For I have no desire to live as a captive. Let me go back to Chihaya."

Smiling, the Prince shook his head. "They say that a maiden's heart is fickle, but to think that it would change thus in such a brief time!"

"Have you forgotten? I left the palace by my own choice."

"But you also left with the words that you still loved me."

Saya faltered and fell silent. It was true; moreover, whether she willed it or no, as he stood before her he struck a chord in her heart. He had not changed a fraction since the night of the Kagai when she had first met him. No matter how bloodstained his hands, he still inspired her with awe. Yet his eternal nobility was beyond her grasp. She whispered in a low voice, "Sometimes one realizes the truth only later."

"That's absurd." Prince Tsukishiro laughed. "You seem to be taken with Chihaya, but he, too, is a Prince of Light. While you claim to fight against the Light, you continue to be drawn to it. That is your nature."

Saya reddened. "Chihaya is not like you. He learns, he overcomes, he changes. And he intends to protect this land from your hands."

"He always was a useless fool. Whatever Chihaya may do, it is futile. He cannot save Toyoashihara."

"Can you be so sure?"

"Yes. For it is Chihaya himself who summons our celestial father." The Prince's voice echoed coldly in the room. "At the time of his birth, the God of Light placed seals within him. If those seals are broken, our father will descend. There is nothing Chihaya can do."

"It can't be!" Saya gasped, appalled.

Prince Tsukishiro looked at her sadly. "And you, Saya, you also summon our father. All of this was revealed in Teruhi's interpretation of the omens. She has been locked in her room for the last few days, reading the future."

Still not fully comprehending, Saya gazed at him, both hands held to her mouth, unable to move. She felt caught, bound by an invisible thread, as though she glimpsed a huge spinning wheel, spinning, spinning, unmoved by the desires of men.

Prince Tsukishiro spoke softly. "Teruhi intends to use you as the sacrifice in the purification ceremony. But I brought you here before she could find you. Come back to me. If you will give me your heart, I will give you the power of renewal, and so save you from being sacrificed. If it is your nature to change your affections, then surely you can do so once again."

Saya stepped back slightly. With her eyes riveted on the Prince's face, she slowly shook her head.

"Even though you could, by agreeing, prevent the descent of the God of Light?"

"Yes," Saya replied in a scarcely audible voice. "My heart moves of its own accord. I cannot control it with my mind."

Another voice unexpectedly endorsed her statement. "She's right. It's impossible."

Saya and Prince Tsukishiro caught their breath and turned. Leaning one arm against the doorway stood Princess Teruhi. She wore a snow-white robe over white trousers, and her long hair hung loose in disarray as though blown by a fierce wind. Her eyes glowed eerily, making her appear demented.

"It never occurred to me that you of all people would attempt to interfere, Tsukishiro. For what foolish whim do you intend to obstruct the arrival of our father?"

Concealing his consternation, Prince Tsukishiro asked casually, "How came you here, sister, when you have not set foot outside the shrine sanctuary for days?"

Princess Teruhi laughed abruptly in a high voice. "Don't be a fool. When I sought the omens for Saya's location, didn't they point directly to within this very palace? Well, at least you saved me the trouble of abducting her myself."

Her laughter ceased and she fixed her brother with a murderous glare. "If you have some explanation, you had better give it. Why did you seek to steal Saya away? You must have some reason, because you know full well she is our precious sacrifice."

Seeing that the Prince did not answer, she continued, "Do not think I will pardon your actions on the basis of your reply. Anyone who attempts to obstruct me now when we are about to fulfill our work upon this earth is my foe."

"You still do not understand, do you, my sister?" Prince Tsukishiro said softly. "I did not wish to disillusion you, but if you insist, then I will speak. I did it because I know the true reason for our father's descent. He comes to summon the Goddess of Darkness back to the realms above."

Princess Teruhi's eyebrows shot up. "What nonsense!"

"No. Although you are the omen reader, you have been so enraptured by our father that you ignored this one fact, which was concealed within all the omens. Perhaps it is more appropriate to say that you did not attempt to understand it. From the very beginning, our father's thoughts have always been centered upon the Goddess of Darkness."

"Our purpose on this earth was to cleanse it of all things tainted by the Darkness."

"Don't you see? To destroy the power of Darkness is to destroy death. To destroy death is to summon the Goddess before us." Prince Tsukishiro's voice was resigned. "Our celestial father intends to restore everything to its original state, to join earth and heaven once more in chaos and begin all over again. To return the Goddess to his side. The outcome is beyond our knowledge, but for myself, I wish to gaze on Toyoashihara just a little while longer, for it is beautiful in itself, just as it is."

An expression of shocked disbelief spread across Princess Teruhi's face. "The God of Light and the Goddess of Darkness are incompatible. It cannot be. They despise each other." Walking forward, she stopped directly in front of Prince Tsukishiro and demanded, "Then are you saying that all our efforts to purify the earth for so many years have been for the sake of the Goddess of Darkness?"

"It is not I who say so. It is the truth. Think carefully about why Saya should be chosen as the final sacrifice."

For a while, Princess Teruhi did not respond. Then she asked in a strangely quiet voice, "When did you know this?"

"I had an inkling of it some time ago," Prince Tsukishiro replied.

At that his sister suddenly shrieked, "I have had enough of you! Always, always you disappoint me!"

"Sister."

"How, then, could you continue to fight until now?"

The Prince whispered, "What else could we do but fight?"

Princess Teruhi gripped one hand in the other and bit down on her fingers in an attempt to control her trembling. "I don't believe it. I will not believe that the war we have fought is meaningless. I will not believe that our father's sacred eyes could be fixed on the filth of Darkness. The God in heaven is pure and stainless. We are here to worship and praise him." Her voice suddenly weakened. She murmured as though to herself, "Our celestial father must surely love us."

The Princess's eyes were hidden in the shadow of her tousled hair. Prince Tsukishiro reached out his hand and gently brushed a lock of hair from her face as though soothing a child. "Of course he does. We are our father's children."

Without raising her face, Princess Teruhi said, "You always speak so lightly."

"I just cannot bear to see you grieve."

After a brief pause, Princess Teruhi recovered and gave her head a shake. "There is still plenty to be done. The war is not yet finished, and the ceremony is long overdue. The palace has not yet been rebuilt, and changes must be made in the purification rite."

She looked at Saya and then at Prince Tsukishiro and said, "There will be no change in the sacrificial offering. In any case, you cannot give her immortality. This maid will be useful as bait, for you can be sure that Chihaya will come after her."

3

The room in which Saya was imprisoned was at the very top of the main hall that separated the two wings of the palace. No doubt the view would have been splendid, but there was only one tiny window near the ceiling, which functioned as a skylight.

Enclosed by four bare walls, she felt suffocated, and like a small bird beating its wings against a cage, she paced unceasingly about the room in search of an opening. Her search was futile, however, and she only succeeded in bruising her fingers. Although she wept occasionally, she did not abandon herself to despair. For, in parting, Princess Teruhi had said that Chihaya would surely come. Although the omens foreshadowed that which seemed beyond despair, Saya longed for Chihaya. No matter what happened, no matter what the future held, she could not suppress the hope that they would meet again, nor quell the desire to behold his smiling face just one last time.

The temperature dropped each night, and a piercing cold permeated the unheated hall. The guard, pitying her plight, gave her a fur to wrap herself in, but even huddled within it she was frozen. Several days passed where only the color of the sky glimpsed through the skylight told her of the changing of day to night. Then one particularly cold morning, as she sat curled up in a corner, her feet tucked as close to her body as possible, she heard the sound of the latch opening. Thinking it was the guard coming to collect her dishes, she thought that he would do well to notice the film of ice on the water in the pitcher. But to her surprise, the person who entered the room was none other than Princess Teruhi. The cold air turned her breath frosty white, but she wore only one robe of thin white cloth, which made Saya shiver just to look at. Princess Teruhi, however, seemed totally unconcerned, and her fair skin had the healthy glow of a peach.

She addressed Saya, who stared at her warily, in a clear, sweet voice. "So, we were about to turn the Water Maiden into an ice maiden. I'd forgotten that you need the warmth of charcoal. Never mind. It snowed."

Saya was well aware that the sleet of the previous day had turned to snow in the night. Some had even blown through the skylight. Wondering what the Princess had come to tell her, she waited suspiciously for her to speak.

"It's unusual for so much to fall in the first snow of the year. Come, let us go and look at it together." The sight of Princess Teruhi speaking so gaily called to mind the little girl Fawn. Saya was taken aback, but somehow this naïveté also suited her. Though unwilling, Saya's heart was drawn to her, and she followed after. Climbing gingerly down the steep stairs on numb legs, she found herself in an open-walled colonnade from which she could view the scenery in all directions to her heart's content. The storm clouds had gone, and beneath the bright silver sky everything was white as though wearing a new coat of paint. The snow was not deep, but it covered every inch of the ground, every crack and cranny. The black thatched roofs of the main hall and its red-lacquered columns were accentuated by the white snow's damp embrace. The ancient green pine trees brooded silently. Even the blackened remnants of the columns burned in the summer fire appeared beautiful in the snow. Sounds were muted as though absorbed by silk floss, and in the bright silent morning Mahoroba seemed a different world.

"I love snow, even more than flowers," Princess Teruhi said lightheartedly as she leaned against the balustrade. "How white the snow that falls from heaven! I love its coldness, a manifestation of purity. It soothes all troubles away."

"Children love snow, too. They romp about in it heedless of frostbite," Saya said.

"Do you also like it?"

"Yes. But I like flowers, too. And summer, and autumn . . . everything."

Princess Teruhi smiled faintly and looked at Saya. "You wish to tell me that you love Toyoashihara. But you know, in my own way, I, too, am striving for the good of this land." The Princess continued as though talking to herself. "While I am a child of the God in heaven, this is the only land I know. I often used to imagine when I saw snow fall that this place was like the palace in the heavens. But most likely I love this view simply because it is all I know."

Saya stared at the back of the Princess, who was once again gazing at the view. Her figure lacked its usual arrogance, appearing instead to be deep in thought. Saya addressed her frankly. "There is still time. Won't you stop the coming of the God of Light?"

"I cannot," Princess Teruhi responded in a low voice. "No one can bend the will of the God. I am only his child, a demigod."

"But you and your brother understand, don't you, that the will of the God to destroy Toyoashihara is wrong? For it is only in cherishing this land, in nurturing it, that he is truly our divine father."

Princess Teruhi thought awhile but then, instead of replying, asked Saya a question. "What is the Goddess of Darkness like? Is she beautiful? No, I cannot believe that one who receives all the defilement of the earth can be beautiful or pure. After all, our father was so seized with dread at the sight of her in the underworld that he sealed the opening with a stone. But why, then, does he summon her?"

Saya hesitated and shook her head. "I do not know. And only those who reside in the Land of the Dead know her form."

She was returned to her room, but the guard brought her a brazier.

"Princess Teruhi. She killed my parents; she killed Natsume and the child she bore; she has obliterated countless innocent lives. And she is undoubtedly planning to kill me and Chihaya without compunction," Saya argued with herself. She had more than enough reason to despise the Princess, yet she could only pity her. Like a naughty child, Teruhi destroyed whatever she laid her hands on without knowing what she had done. Perhaps she would only realize it with surprise after she had lost everything.

"But then it will be too late. I don't wish to succumb so easily. If only I had the power to defend myself." As her thoughts ran on fruitlessly, she heard the faint sound of wings. She raised her head but without much hope, for the sound was too much like the whisperings of her fancy. However, a glossy black beak and head peered through the bars of the window. Then, folding his wings and squeezing through, a crow dropped down to the floor.

"Here I am," he said.

A lump rose in Saya's throat, so that she could not respond immediately. "I—I knew you would come. But oh, I am so glad!"

"Actually, I would have been here much sooner, but I've become so well known that there are mist nets hung all around this place. It was hard work making a hole in them."

"Is anyone else with you?"

"Lord Shinado, Chihaya, and three others. They are all concealed within the palace in disguise: Lord Shinado, as usual, as a musician; the three others as servants or soldiers; and, best of all, Chihaya as one of Princess Teruhi's own handmaidens. We will open the gate tomorrow at sunset, and the army of Darkness will invade the palace."

"What about the purification ceremony?"

"It's scheduled for the day after. I have no intention of allowing you to be sacrificed. There was never such a revolting ceremony as that."

"Please don't let it happen. I don't want to be the one who summons the God of Light."

Suddenly she began to shake. It was a strange time to feel afraid, but her fear seemed to increase now that there was hope of rescue.

"Is Chihaya all right? A handmaiden of all things! Princess Teruhi must not be underestimated."

"Don't worry. Don't worry. He has disguised himself well. You wouldn't recognize him," Torihiko replied cheerfully, spreading his wings. "He isn't stupid. Although there were times when he seemed so."

"That's true." Saya tried to smile and realized that her cheeks had become stiff in the last few days.

"I am to mobilize all my underlings and take you out of here. Not bad, hey? It will be an amazing sight. I have such an army of birds it would take you your whole life to count them. And together we will lower you to the ground."

"Can you really do it?" Saya's eyes were wide with astonishment.

"Wait and see." And with a flap of his wings he flew up to the window.

"I'm so excited!" Now that her hopes were raised, Saya regretted her inability to help in any way. To simply sit and wait to be rescued seemed the least attractive role.

"That's the spirit. Once I've gone, the woodpeckers will come. It will be a bit noisy but be patient."

"Wait!" Saya called out impulsively, longing to participate in some way. She put her hand to her neck and, removing the Water Maiden's amulet, held it out to Torihiko. "Give this to Chihaya for me. Tell him to keep it until we meet again."

The crow flew down and grasped the blue amulet in his beak. "Right. I'll take it to him."

Once Torihiko had left, a flock of woodpeckers came, just as he had told her. They clung to the window frame and began patiently pecking at it with their beaks.

The next day was also cold. Much of the snow still remained. While Chihaya knelt on the verandah, pretending to gaze at the garden, Lord Shinado, having checked that no one else was about, passed casually by.

"A performance is to be held at noon," Lord Shinado whispered rapidly.

"But this is the period of abstinence!"

"Teruhi knows nothing about it. It's Prince Tsukishiro's plan."

Chihaya thought a moment before replying. "This will make it easier for us to act."

"Inform the other three. I plan to stay in my place until the last moment."

Without changing his expression, Lord Shinado proceeded along the passageway. Chihaya rose after waiting a little longer and went cautiously toward Tsukishiro's palace. People hurried constantly up and down the connecting passages. The palace, which had always been short-staffed, had been gradually losing its previous elegance since the fire. The complaint of the elderly that this was a degenerate age was not necessarily an idle one. Although the palace still retained an air of grandeur, something had been broken and irretrievably lost. Certainly the fact that the two immortals no longer paid attention played a major role in its decline. Princess Teruhi had not returned to her quarters for a long time, remaining closeted in the reconstructed shrine. Because of this, Chihaya had been able to pass himself off as a novice without being challenged, but it was not pleasant to see the handmaidens' quarters, where discipline had become lax.

"Even without fighting the army of Darkness, this place will fall into ruin. It would be better that way," thought Chihaya as he stopped in a corner of the gallery and watched the people passing by.

"Excuse me. If you have a moment, perhaps you could help me?"

An attendant he had never seen before suddenly addressed him. She was just a naïve maiden, probably a novice such as he was pretending to be. "I had not heard that there was to be a recital today and I have no idea what I am to do."

Red-faced, she was on the verge of tears. "No one here cares about anyone else. I have only recently entered service in the palace, yet they tell me I must dance. I don't even know which fan I am to use. And then they tell me that anyone who makes a blunder will be executed on the spot."

"In that case, fear no more," Chihaya reassured her. "I will teach you."

The girl's face shone. "How kind of you! Will you be one of the dancers, too?"

"No."

The girl looked up a little bashfully at Chihaya. "But how strange. You would make a much better dancer than I. You are so tall and beautiful."

"I am one of Princess Teruhi's handmaidens," Chihaya explained.

The girl covered her mouth in consternation. "Oh! I'm sorry. I shouldn't have asked such a thing of you."

Chihaya grinned and said, "But only you and I need ever know."

At noon the sun, a silver disk bereft of warmth, peered through the clouded sky. It remained cold, and a frozen landscape spread out in all directions. The sound of string and wind instruments hung in the frosty air, echoing mysteriously. Seats had been set up around the balcony on the south side of the palace, and Prince Tsukishiro, who had assembled the performers, watched the dancers in the inner garden while the musicians played on a platform set up on the terrace. The Prince himself, however, did not appear to be enjoying the music. Rather, he seemed deep in thought, his arm laid along the armrest as he stared at the performers. Their master's mood naturally infected the musicians, and despite the gay costumes of the dancers the music suddenly assumed a melancholy air.

"This is indeed farewell," thought Lord Shinado as he played his reed pipes. "Win or lose, this is the last performance for the forces of Light and Darkness."

"You there!" Prince Tsukishiro spoke without bothering to look at the musicians. "You're flat. Did you not know that I am musician enough to tell?"

Armored guards leaped out before they had fully grasped the meaning of his words, and surrounded the musicians' platform. Some musicians dropped their instruments in surprise, the music came to a sudden standstill, and the dancers stood trembling.

The soldiers stood over the musicians, their spears held ready, but, perplexed about which musician the Prince had indicated, one of them asked, "Who is the offending party?"

"He knows who I mean," Prince Tsukishiro replied. The commander queried the musicians, but no one responded.

Prince Tsukishiro said listlessly, "It does not matter. Behead them all, starting at the end."

A soldier grasped the shirt front of an old flute player, who had turned deathly pale, and hauled him from his place. As he drew his sword and held it aloft, Lord Shinado rose.

"It was I."

Before the soldiers could turn around, Lord Shinado jumped from the platform. The soldier who had been about to lop off the old man's head turned his sword toward him and attacked, but Lord Shinado swiftly parried the blow with his pipes. The hoop binding the pipes together was severed, and the bamboo reeds flew apart with a loud noise. Momentarily distracted, the soldier found himself pummeled with fists and feet, and dropped his sword. Lord Shinado grasped the fallen blade and desperately attacked the soldiers. Some fell back under the vigor of his assault.

"My bow," commanded Prince Tsukishiro, cool and collected as usual. Taking the proffered weapon, he shrugged one arm out of his sleeve and grasped an arrow. No matter how agile Lord Shinado may have been, Prince Tsukishiro could not miss at this range. By the time Lord Shinado was aware of him, it was too late. With a shrill noise the arrow was loosed. But at the same instant someone threw a fan. The arrow pierced its handle and, swerving slightly from its path, struck the column beside Lord Shinado. The people turned in disbelief to see that one of the five dancers was empty-handed.

Prince Tsukishiro turned as if astonished and said, "So there you are."

His dancer's jade-green and crimson hem billowed slightly as Chihaya leaped lightly over the people's heads and, as if scoffing at their incredulity, landed right beside Lord Shinado.

"You fool!" Lord Shinado said angrily. "We agreed that anyone who was discovered would be left behind."

"As an extra member, I never agreed to anything," Chihaya replied. "Besides I am in your debt."

"You are every inch a fool, my brother," Prince Tsukishiro said with bitter disappointment. "To come here, to this place, playing into our hands. Do you not realize that I am holding this performance for Saya's sake?"

Chihaya looked at his older brother in surprise.

"Teruhi will not use Saya for the sacrifice. If I know our sister, she will not let her live that long."

The flock of woodpeckers now numbered twenty or thirty, and they continued to chip away at the wood like carpenters. They had already begun to remove the second panel of wainscoting, and it looked as if Saya would be able to squeeze through. Suddenly, however, the birds became tense and silent. As they flew hastily away, Saya heard the sound of light footsteps. The latch drew back. Saya stood up hurriedly and tried to conceal the woodpeckers' handiwork with her body. Before her stood Princess Teruhi. Her expression was calm and peaceful.

"Saya," the Princess addressed her in a quiet tone. "Do you wish to preserve Toyoashihara no matter what the cost?"

"Yes," Saya replied.

"I have been thinking. I cannot help feeling that it is too heartless to return this land to chaos."

Saya's eyes widened. "If both sides think this way, then war is no longer necessary. Will you stop the coming of the God of Light?"

"Even if the God of Light descends upon the earth, if the Goddess remains in the Land of the Dead, Toyoashihara will be preserved. Is that not so?" Princess Teruhi said. "It is the meeting of the two divinities that must be prevented. Regardless of whether it is our divine father's will, the Goddess must not be summoned before him. I have decided to ignore just this one point of the omens. The purification ceremony will be conducted without you—because you, along with our celestial father, would surely summon forth the Goddess. I do not wish to see our father's eyes turned toward anything other than us at his arrival. I cannot bear that that should be the end of all our endeavors."

But just as a bright ray of hope was lit in Saya's breast, Princess Teruhi calmly drew a long-bladed sword from the scabbard at her waist. The winter sun lent the naked blade a cold light. Staring at the cruel steel held before her eyes, Saya paled and fell back, only to bump into the wall.

"Why?" she whispered almost inaudibly.

"You have asked me to stop the coming of my father. But to me it is the Goddess of Darkness that stands in the way. I do not want her to return. But I myself cannot disobey my father's command. No one can go against his will, no one except the Goddess of Darkness herself." Princess Teruhi continued to speak calmly. "That is why I wish you to return to the Goddess before the purification ceremony. Tell her to refuse our divine father's summons. I can trust you to do this, can't I? Because, in return, Toyoashihara will be saved."

"Are you saying that you will kill me here?" Saya's lips trembled. The icy blade filled her with terror, death in tangible form, and her entire youthful being rejected it with all its strength. She could not possibly die now. Not in this narrow room, so unprepared, without even seeing Chihaya . . .

Princess Teruhi's feet, pale and bare, approached her swiftly. "If I could, I would go myself to meet the Goddess. But that path can be trodden only by the people of Darkness."

"No!" Saya screamed as she watched the Princess raise the sword. In that small room there was no escape but still she tried to flee, groping along the wall, dodging aside. Seeking help, she called out for Chihaya, for Torihiko. But—

The tip of the sword described a graceful arc as it descended. It was a deft, a masterful stroke. For an instant Saya glimpsed the window and saw the white and distant sky. Then she saw Princess Teruhi's serene and beautiful face. "Even when she kills, her expression remains pure," Saya thought, recalling the shrine maiden in Hashiba so far away. And then she thought no more.

Like a priestess, Princess Teruhi knelt beside Saya's body where it lay upon the floor, watching as the last warmth fled from the dead girl's body. She almost looked as if she were praying. Into the still and silent room, however, a richly colored apparition suddenly floated and immediately became solid. It was Chihaya, still in dancer's robes but now holding the Sword. Gold ornaments shimmered on his clothes, but his feet were bare, his hair was in disarray, and he was gasping for breath.

"So you have finally learned how to travel between time," Princess Teruhi murmured without surprise. But Chihaya did not reply. He gazed only at Saya, at the girl who lay like a broken-stemmed flower.

"It seems that you are a moment too late. Saya has already left for another land."

"I will never forgive you," Chihaya whispered.

Princess Teruhi laughed. "Unfortunately, it is I who wish to say those words. As long as you remain a threat to our father, we cannot stand before him while you live. However, you have no doubt come prepared for this, have you not?"

Her hair stirred as though a wind had suddenly sprung up.

"The people of this land have no inkling of what would happen should the Children of Light loose all their power. You may be more terrible than thunder and lightning, but we are your older sister and brother. We are the sun and the moon. Watch and see what happens when the powers of the sun and the moon are unleashed together." Looking at Chihaya with a grim smile, she turned on her heel and slipped between time. Without a moment's hesitation, Chihaya raced after her.

Although the intervals between time are indescribable, they are not composed of nothingness. Rather, the shadows of many things hang suspended. Princess Teruhi, slipping between these like an arrow flying, looked like a golden shadow leaving a long trail. After a while Chihaya became aware of a gleaming silver shadow approaching from another direction. It was undoubtedly Prince Tsukishiro. The two shadows, silver and gold, drew closer and closer until they became one. At that moment a light burst forth as though the world between time had exploded. The light, whose heat and strength transcended that of incandescence, turned black, piercing, shattering, burning, and melting all in its path.

Without warning the sun darkened. Despite its being noon, shadows arose from all four corners of the land and covered the sky, turning the day to night more completely than any eclipse. The palace was thrown into confusion, and the soldiers rushed about, unable to remain at their posts. It was little different among the invading soldiers of the army of Darkness. The horses panicked and reared, and the soldiers cowered, breaking their ranks. As if this were not enough, violent earthquakes rocked the land. Landslides buried villages at the foot of the mountains, while a great tidal wave washed away fishing villages along the shore. Unable to stand, the people lay prostrate on the ground praying with heart and soul that this convulsion of the world would prove but a passing phenomenon.

"Has Chihaya been destroyed?"

"Not yet."

"Something must be protecting him. Could it be our father?"

"No. That cannot be."

"In any case, we cannot withstand this much longer."

Princess Teruhi and Prince Tsukishiro slipped between several intervals of time and continued to run. Whenever they reappeared on the earth they could hear the rumble of Chihaya's thunder beneath the dark sky. At last they came to a place at the end of the world where there were only rocks and snow. The air was surprisingly thin, and it was well below freezing. Snow crystals, driven by the wind, were reluctant to fall to the ground. Hot steam rose from a rock wall nearby, exposing fantastic formations in the black rock around the fissure.

"Where are we?" Princess Teruhi asked.

"At the mouth of Mount Fuji," Prince Tsukishiro replied, looking at the smoke. "It seems to have come to life somewhat with that last earthquake."

"I'm leaving. I do not wish to stay in a place like this."

Prince Tsukishiro said, teasing her, "Why not rest? This is the closest place to heaven."

"Don't jest. The stench of the underworld is so foul that I can barely breathe."

Receiving this irritable response, Prince Tsukishiro rose and slipped into another interval of time. "Then let us go somewhere pleasanter."

Princess Teruhi attempted to follow him but was suddenly flung back. Losing her footing on the slope from the shock of the impact, she almost slipped inside the mouth of the volcano. She paled when, leaning forward, she glimpsed the glowing red lava bubbling and belching smoke in the depths.

A voice spoke quietly. "Not even you, dear sister, could possibly survive if you fell in there, could you."

Princess Teruhi started and looked around. Prince Tsukishiro was nowhere to be seen. He was on another side of time, ignorant of her plight. Chihaya's shadow, blurred by the smoke, appeared before her. In his hand was the shining blue Sword. The Princess was unarmed, for there was no need of swords when battling between time. She cursed herself for her carelessness. Chihaya now stood immediately over her. The Princess looked up at him from where she lay at the edge of the volcano.

"You! So you can follow me even here?"

"I told you that I would never forgive you," Chihaya replied, and his sister smiled faintly.

"How masculine. I like that in a man."

As he turned the Sword toward her, she asked without any trace of regret, "I have just one question. What is protecting you?"

"Nothing."

"You did not fall even under the combined forces of Tsukishiro and myself. I cannot believe you could do that alone."

"I know of nothing," Chihaya began but then fell silent. Placing one hand on his breast, he touched the little amulet.

As Chihaya remained silent, Princess Teruhi sighed. "Won't you hurry up and get it over with. It is rude to keep your victim waiting."

"I've changed my mind," Chihaya said abruptly.

Princess Teruhi's eyes widened in surprise. "Are you mad?"

The expression on Chihaya's face as he gazed down upon his sister was one which, as a child of Light, she could neither believe nor comprehend.

"Even if I kill you, it won't bring Saya back to life."

Sheathing the Sword, he turned his back on her and disappeared.

When Chihaya stood before the open palace gate it was already late at night. Although the place was still filled with confusion, the battle was over and the palace was in the hands of the army of Darkness. Torihiko found him walking in the torchlight and flew up to him.

"The army of Light has been routed. Without their leaders, they disintegrated. We've won!" Torihiko said in a rush, then seeing Chihaya's face, he faltered. "Where have you been, Chihaya? The main hall collapsed in the fire, but the birds managed to carry Saya out."

When Chihaya still did not reply, Torihiko furled his wings wretchedly and said, "Go and see Saya, will you? She is lying in state over there."

Inside the fenced enclosure where she lay, grown men wept unashamedly, moved by the sight of Saya's small, pale form lying pathetically upon its bier, bereft of flowers in the midwinter season. Chihaya gazed at her steadily but knew that he would never find her here. She had already left, racing to a place where he could never join her, leaving him with her amulet, which she had given him until they should meet again.

Opening his closed fist, he stared at the pale blue stone and whispered to himself, "How can I return it?"

At that moment something moved at the foot of Saya's bier. It was so small that at first he did not think it was a person, but when he saw the white-haired head turn toward him, he recognized Lady Iwa. Opening her wrinkled eyelids, the old woman looked at him.

"That belongs to the Water Maiden. Without it she will come to grief."

Chihaya nodded slowly. "Saya protected me, when I could not save her, when I let her die all alone. Until now I thought that I was always alone. For as long as I can remember I was alone. Why didn't I realize sooner that Saya had come to me? Many times she came. Over and over again, even after she had died. Now I understand. Without Saya I am incomplete."

Chihaya's voice broke off, and Lady Iwa, looking at him curiously, said, "Oho, so you claim that you now understand that you need Saya?"

"Until I met her I was nothing," Chihaya whispered. "She called me forth. She taught me about Toyoashihara, and about myself. She helped me realize what I must do. But there are still so many things that I must learn. Without her I will remain a blind Dragon."

"But you will go on alone. Saya has already returned to the Goddess," Lady Iwa said bluntly. Chihaya remained silent but a spark of light, a faint stirring of anger, was kindled in his previously vacant black eyes.

"And why can't I follow her? Whether it be to the Land of the Dead or no, is it really impossible for me to follow where Saya has gone? Even our celestial father once went to see the Goddess in the underworld. So why shouldn't I? Saya always came looking for me. Now it's my turn to find her."

"How?" snorted Lady Iwa.

Suddenly at a loss, Chihaya looked down at the tiny old woman. "Isn't there some way?" he asked.

Lady Iwa turned away indignantly. "Supposing I did know . . . ."

Realization dawning on him, Chihaya knelt hurriedly upon the floor and, laying the Sword aside, prostrated himself meekly before her. "Please. Tell me. No matter what it takes, I wish to go to the Land of the Dead," Chihaya pleaded and then added, "If I could return Saya to life, I would begrudge nothing."

"Do you speak from your heart?"

"Yes."

"Then you should have said so from the beginning," Lady Iwa said, brightening, as she turned to face him. "I myself do not know of any trick that will take an immortal to the underworld. But Saya gave you the amulet. If the bond between you is strong enough, there may be a way."

"And what is that?" Chihaya leaned forward eagerly.

"I cannot guarantee anything," Lady Iwa warned him sternly.

"You may find Saya, and then again you may not. You may be able to return again, and you may not. The path of Darkness is shadowed and fraught with danger."

Chihaya answered positively, "It does not matter, so long as there is hope."

"In that case, swallow the amulet you hold in your hand. It is part of Saya. No matter how far the distance, it will be drawn toward her soul. Whether you reach her or not, how far you travel along the road to Darkness depends upon you."

The next morning, Chihaya was found lying cold and lifeless at the foot of Saya's bier. His breathing had stopped, there was no heartbeat, and no sign of renewal. Lord Shinado, who had just returned from pursuing the remnants of the army of Light, exclaimed, "But the children of Light cannot die. Surely he will come back to life again."

Lord Akitsu said in a low voice, "Yet I can understand his desire to follow Saya. Let us lay them side by side on the bier. Then Saya will be less lonely."

4

Saya was standing near a marsh. The summer grasses grew tall, and the heads of the cattails along the shore were brown. Pale blue dragonflies flitted lightly above the marsh, their figures reflected on the water's surface. The red glow of sunset lingered in the sky, while a soft twilight pervaded the scene. She heard a gentle voice that filled her with warmth.

"Where have you been, Saya? It's time to come home. Supper's ready."

"It's my mother's voice," Saya thought.

Turning around, she saw a path leading through a meadow dotted with evening primroses just beginning to open, and in the distance she could see houses, thin trails of smoke rising from the hearths. If she ran home, she would find the familiar hearthside, the bowl her father had made for her; and her mother, with her soft lap, would be there to greet her.

But she could not move. Instead she burst into tears.

"Why do you weep when you've come home at last? What makes you so sad? What is it that you wish?"

Still weeping, Saya pleaded, "I want to go back."

"Poor little thing. And just where do you want to go back to, when this is your home?"

Coming to her senses, Saya looked about her, trying to find the speaker. But Saya herself was the only person on the edge of the marsh. Wiping her tears, she whispered, "You are the Goddess of Darkness, aren't you?"

"Yes. This is the Land of the Dead. But when people return to this world, they bear such grievous wounds that it is hard for them to sleep peacefully. First I must ease their pain in this way."

"Won't you show yourself to me?" Saya asked, and a breeze like a sigh blew across the marsh grasses.

"All that you see here is I. I have no body. I discarded it long ago, when that one rejected me. Instead I now live in many forms at once."

"O merciful Goddess, the God of Light wishes to summon you to the world above, to take up your previous form," Saya said. Not knowing where to direct her words, she gazed at her own shadow on the water as she spoke. "The God in heaven gives no thought to we who live in Toyoashihara. He intends to destroy the land and return the world to chaos. But you are the loving Goddess. Surely you will have compassion for the world above?"

"There is no need to ask," the Goddess responded emphatically. "I gave birth to all that is in Toyoashihara. Where is the mother who does not love her children? I love Toyoashihara more than you do."

Saya finally smiled. "Thank you. Now I can be at peace."

"Then follow the path. Your long-forgotten mother awaits you." Urged along, Saya began to walk, but after a few steps she stopped.

"Something still troubles you, doesn't it?" the Goddess of Darkness said indulgently. "Tell me what you wish without fear, and I will fulfill your desire."

Saya hesitated awhile and then, gathering her courage, said, "I wish to see the field of gypsy roses once more. Will you show it to me?"

The summer scene became clouded and the marsh turned into an autumn meadow. A cool highland breeze caressed her cheeks and clouds swept across the sky. A mass of pale purple flowers swayed in the breeze, just as she remembered them. The breathtaking beauty of the flowers filling the hollow, perhaps even more than in reality, was identical to the memory that she treasured in her heart.

"What a fool I am!" The beauty of the flowers pierced her breast like a knife and she instantly regretted her request. What use was it to recall this meadow when Chihaya was not here? It was like rubbing salt into a wound. Saya stood filled with misery, too wretched to cry.

The autumn breeze swayed through the flowers, through Saya's hair, like a tender caress. When the burning agony of her loss had passed and died to a smoldering ember, a feeling of resignation began to grow within her, immersing her. For the swaying purple flowers, in their silence, spoke to her, telling her that this was a peaceful place, a place of rest; that there was no point in suffering.

"This pain is just an illusion. I should be ashamed of myself. It is pointless. Chihaya and I have been separated by a distance so absolute that we can never reach each other again. The only thing I can do is accept this fact," she thought listlessly. She could feel the Goddess coaxing her, soothing her. But she still clung stubbornly to her pain.

"If only I could set eyes on Chihaya just one more time; just once more and then I could forget him."

A figure appeared suddenly at the edge of the hollow.

It came down the slope, disappearing and reappearing in the tall grasses. She was so shocked that, as though her body were numbed, she could not move. No matter how merciful the Goddess might be, Saya had never dreamed that she would go to such lengths as this. Chihaya appeared, looking about him doubtfully. He seemed like a traveler in a foreign land. She stared at him without uttering a sound. But when he caught sight of her standing in the midst of the flowers he raced toward her.

A few seconds before he reached her, she was able to move at last. And leaping toward him suddenly, she collided against his chest. Just the touch of his physical frame seemed a miracle. Feeling that anything was permissible, she kissed him. Even if it was an illusion, she thought that if it was this satisfying, it did not matter.

"I came looking for you," Chihaya murmured in her ear, his arms still wrapped around her. "If I am with you, it does not matter if I never return to the earth again."

Saya thought, "That is just what I wanted him to say. Now there is nothing else I desire." She smiled.

"Did Torihiko give you the amulet?" she asked. "Keep it always—even if you forget me."

"It was thanks to the amulet that I came here," Chihaya replied. "Lady Iwa told me. She said that this stone was part of you, that it would find its way back to you. But I can hardly believe it worked so well."

It finally began to dawn on Saya that something was odd. This was not something that Chihaya would say if he were truly an illusion. She freed herself and stared into his face, her eyes wide. "You don't mean—you can't possibly have really come? You're not just a dream that the Goddess of Darkness is showing me?"

"Yes, I have really come, to the Land of the Dead."

"How?"

Chihaya stared back at her blankly. "But I just told you."

At that moment a strong gust of wind hit them, taking their breath away, ripping the flowers from their stalks, whipping the dead grasses into the air. Pummeled by leaves, they shielded themselves, looking up when the wind had passed to see the sky filled by dark black clouds twisting slowly like a tornado.

"I sense the presence of one who has no right to be here. Someone who, like oil in water, cannot belong. Who art thou? And why hast thou come uninvited?" The Goddess's voice shook the air, her earlier gentle tone utterly transformed to one full of threatening rage.

Chihaya, ignorant of the sudden change, answered unhesitatingly, "I am Chihaya. My father is the God of Light. I came here to meet Saya and if possible to take her back—" He broke off as Saya interrupted him.

"It was my fault, O divine Mother. Because I gave him my amulet, he has come in search of me."

"What hast thou done?" The Goddess's harsh voice was directed to Saya as well. "That amulet was given to thee as a sign of the Water Maiden. It should have been returned to me. Yet thou hast given it to one of the Children of Light and so exposed the path that we have taken such pains to conceal."

Saya paled in surprise. "I beg thy forgiveness. I did not mean—"

"The God of Light. I intended to forgive him: even though he feared and shunned me, turned his face from me and fled; even though he sealed the entrance to the path with stone and severed relations with me. He mercilessly kills my children who live upon the earth and causes me to suffer. Even this I intended to forgive. But now he invades my very home. Even my mercy has limits!" Her voice became increasingly menacing, filling her listeners with such dread that their blood ran cold, a dread which far surpassed that inspired by her children, the raging gods of the earth. Trembling and shaking, Saya managed to gain enough control to speak.

"Chihaya is not an instrument of the God of Light. He fought on our side."

"Don't waste your breath," Chihaya said beside her. "She will not listen."

They turned on their heels and fled, with the surging black cloud in pursuit. Tentacles of jet-black darkness as dense as mud reached toward them, when suddenly a voice called out to them.

"Make haste. Take Morning Star!"

Morning Star, the white star on his forehead shining, waited, his hooves pawing the ground. And holding him in check was Lord Ibuki.

"I'll distract her while you flee."

Without wasting time on words, they leaped astride Morning Star, who raced across the dark sky as though he had wings. The vault of the underworld was bejeweled with unblinking stars. Some were as large as walnuts and the faint light they cast was of different hues. The black stallion ran longer than they could tell, until he landed on a bare rock ledge. It was very dark, with no other light than that of the stars. Lord Ibuki was already there waiting for them.

"I did not expect to meet you so soon. And it seems you are creating havoc even in the underworld," he said frankly.

"I longed to see you again," Chihaya began in a choked voice. "There were many things I wanted to say—"

"I know, so there is no need to say them. This is not the time or place. You have angered the Goddess of this land. There is nowhere you can hide. Even here you are safe for but a moment." Wheeling about, Lord Ibuki asked Saya, "Where is your amulet?

At this of all times, you will need your skill at pacification. If you become the object of the Goddess's wrath, your suffering will be eternal. In this world, death will not be the end of it."

Saya said hurriedly to Chihaya, "You have it, don't you?"

"I brought it with me, yes, but . . ." Chihaya looked troubled and faltered, pointing to his stomach. "It's in here. I forgot to think of a way of returning it."

Saya and Lord Ibuki gaped at him in astonishment. Then Saya asked in a small voice, "What should we do now?"

Lord Ibuki groaned. "Don't ask me! After all, I am just a dead man."

From the left the stars began to go out one by one. A blackness so total that it seemed to crush the very sky began to gather above their heads.

"We must flee," Saya said, grabbing Chihaya's arm.

"It makes no difference whether we flee or not if in the end there is no escape," Chihaya said, gazing at the stars disappearing from sight. "Let us rather go to meet her. For it is only right that we should seek proper judgment."

"No!"

But Chihaya paid her no heed. Kicking his feet lightly against the rock ledge, he ran effortlessly into the sky.

"Lord Ibuki," Saya turned and asked desperately, "do you think that I can fly through the sky, too?"

"It's up to you. After all, this isn't the world above," Lord Ibuki replied.

When Chihaya had approached as close as he thought necessary, he addressed the black shadow.

"O great Goddess, Ruler of the netherworld, please hear me. Though I am the child of my father, I love you, and have always yearned for the Darkness. For—" Slender tendrils of darkness, like snakes, reached out and wrapped themselves around his neck, arms, and legs, and he felt them slowly tightening. Ignoring them, he continued, "Since the day I was born I have searched for a path to you. It was Saya who happened to show me a way, yet even without that, I so desired to meet you that—"

He was unable to continue, for the fingers of darkness squeezed him with a sudden bone-crushing force.

"Do not speak falsehoods. How can one with the power of renewal be attracted to what is destined to rot and decay? Even I myself did not come here of my own desire."

Chihaya tried to free himself, but it was futile. Although he knew he must not use the power of the Dragon, his anger at being unjustly accused was beginning to grow. Just as he thought he was about to explode he felt the touch of a small light hand. It was Saya.

"O merciful Goddess. Please quell thine anger," she said boldly. For Saya, this was her ultimate and most daring attempt to appease. "And if it does not please thee to do so, then accuse me also. For though I am a child of the Darkness, I love the Light and served at the Palace of Light. Though Light and Darkness are incompatible, even we, who cannot live without thy beneficent hand, love the Light. For it is one of the purest, most beautiful things to behold upon the earth.

"I met Chihaya in the Palace of Light. At first he was the keeper of the Dragon Sword—the Sword with which the God of Light slew the fire god when thou didst depart for the Land of the Dead. When I and my people learned that Chihaya was not one who stills the Sword, like me, but rather the Sword itself, we feared him. But this was wrong. For Chihaya, more than myself or anyone else, continued to be true to thee. Perhaps because he is the child of the Sword, the son of the Sword that the God of Light wielded in his grief for thee."

Her voice was absorbed by the air; even its vibrations were swallowed up. A silence like sleep filled the space. Then the Goddess of Darkness spoke quietly.

"Perhaps he grieved for me. But when he saw me in the

underworld he turned away his face and deserted me. Since then he has cursed me, shunned me, loathed me."

"No, for if he truly despised thee he would not contemplate leaving his palace in heaven far above to come to meet thee," Saya said, leaning forward. "Even now the God of Light still longs for thee—so much so that he will sacrifice all of Toyoashihara."

"Dost thou claim that this is why thou gavest this youth the amulet?" the Goddess asked.

"No," Saya replied, somewhat dampened. "I did not think. I just did not want to be parted from him. I gave it neither as priestess nor as Water Maiden. I just did it."

Realizing that he could now speak, Chihaya said, "I was commanded by my father to seek the Goddess of Darkness, and to bring her back to the earth."

Saya looked up at him in shock. "Chihaya!"

"This was sealed from me and I did not know it until now. I always wondered why I was given this body. But now I remember. I am my father's messenger."

"Then what will happen to Toyoashihara?" Saya whispered, but Chihaya turned to the Goddess of Darkness and continued.

"However, it was a dangerous message. For by giving me the power to reach the Land of Darkness, he gave me the potential to destroy him. If I had not reached you I would surely have turned on him and fought until one of us was slain. But I was able to come. Saya destroyed the wall of hate between the Darkness and the Light. Is my father's desire now clear to you?"

The Goddess whispered in a voice like wind through the trees. "O Child of the Sword, how like him thou art. Thou hast come all alone, without fear or timidity. But thou art different. For the amulet of the Water Maiden is now part of thee." She continued calmly, "Thou hast stilled my anger. When I see the two of you I can believe that he does indeed wish to meet me. I have clearly received thy message, Child of the Sword. Yet I do not intend to clothe myself once more in the body I discarded in order to go to him. Therefore, Prince, thou must return to thy father's side."

"Do you mean to send me back alone, empty-handed?" Chihaya said in a dissatisfied tone.

"Thy father did just that."

"Then I will remain here."

"That cannot be. For thou canst not remain in the Land of the Dead."

"I will never go back without Saya. Never." Chihaya grasped Saya's hand and said brusquely, "It is not enough to take back only the amulet; I will take Saya, too."

"But you can't. I really died," Saya protested. Suddenly they heard another voice beside them.

"It's all right. Return to Toyoashihara."

Saya looked about in surprise. "That voice . . ."

"Renewal requires a sacrifice. I will be that sacrifice. I have already lived too long. Surely it is no crime to seek a rest. Besides, you have something you must do. Return with Chihaya."

It was Lady Iwa. A strange and fragile voice, yet, to one accustomed to it, warmer than any other. But as Saya turned to question her, Chihaya pulled her away.

"Saya, let's go home."

When she came to her senses, her feet and hands were so cold that they were numb. Opening her eyes and wondering what the prison guard had done with her fur wrap, she found herself not in the palace but surrounded by the people of Darkness. Lord Akitsu and Lord Shinado were there; Torihiko, too. And with them, looking as if nothing had happened, was Chihaya.

"You're late. Where were you dawdling?" Chihaya said smiling.

"The Goddess of Darkness . . ." Saya whispered. Her throat felt strange and she couldn't speak.

With deep emotion, Lord Akitsu said, "It is just as Lady Iwa told us. She said that both of you would return."

"We met Lady Iwa. Lord Ibuki, too," and as she said it, she was hit by the realization that she had come back from the dead. It should not be possible, yet she was breathing. Blood pulsed through her veins. Sensation had returned. She could speak. She burst into tears and felt the hot teardrops scalding her frozen cheeks. Chihaya slipped his arm about her as though she would break and raised her to a sitting position. She thought regretfully that if only there were not so many people here, she could rest in his embrace and cry to her heart's content.

Lady Iwa's tiny corpse was laid out in the same hut, wizened and frail. The spirit which had made her seem so overpowering while alive had vanished.

"She was so old no one knew her age. Perhaps it was her time to die," Lord Akitsu said quietly. But Saya shook her head.

"No. She went instead of me; she took my place in the Land of the Dead. She told me there was something I must do."

"What was that?" Torihiko asked.

"The Goddess of Darkness stopped me as I was about to return and said—"

But before she could finish speaking, gold and silver dust fell shining between the cracks of the rough roof thatch. Before their startled eyes, the inside of the hut grew brighter than the seashore on a midsummer's day. Walls and people seemed to have lost their outlines. Terrified, they looked at one another.

"Is it the God of Light?"

"It can't be! The two Children of Light have not yet reappeared."

"Is it the end of Toyoashihara?"

"But we won, didn't we?"

Pushing aside the people as they shouted in confusion, Chihaya rushed outside the little hut. He opened the door on an incredible flood of light. The sky had turned pearl-white, and all other things seemed to have lost their hue. The mountains of Mahoroba looked like ghosts, and several rainbows clung to the mountaintops. The ground glittered like shattered crystal, so that it was impossible to discern its contours. And not a single shadow could be seen. Chihaya raised one foot to see if he could find his shadow but it was so bright he could barely see anything. Shielding his eyes, he raised his head little by little. Over the eastern row of mountains, he could just make out the upper half of a towering golden form framed by the rainbows on the mountain ridge. He felt Saya come running after him.

"Don't look!" he ordered her sharply. "If you look upon our celestial father you will be blinded. Don't open your eyes until I tell you."

Startled, Saya clapped both hands over her eyes, but she could still feel light burning gold and black against her eyelids. It had been a near thing.

From above their heads a voice that moved the heart like the vibration of a bass string on an instrument flowed over them.

"Dragon Child, didst thou fulfill thy task of summoning the Goddess of the netherworld to the earth?"

"No," Chihaya answered weakly. "The Goddess will not come."

"I saw thee descend into the Land of the Dead." The God's voice was tinged with displeasure. "Then for what purpose didst thou go? And why hast thou returned alone?"

Saya suddenly stepped forward, and with both eyes still covered addressed the God of Light.

"O my beloved."

Chihaya had put a hand on her shoulder to restrain her but withdrew it hastily. Saya's body was as rigid as stone, and she spoke in a trance. Moreover, the words she spoke were not her own.

"The maiden who stands here is unique, one who has returned from the Land of the Dead. For thy sake I have twice permitted the breaking of the sacred rules of Darkness: once when I allowed thy son to enter the Land of the Dead, and once when I allowed my daughter to return to the Land of the Living. In this way I have permitted myself the smallest measure of selfishness: to borrow this maiden's body and allow myself to meet thee for a fleeting moment."

"O beloved wife." The God of Light's voice trembled slightly. "A fleeting moment cannot suffice. I have come now like this to take thy hand once more. Show thyself, thy willowy form, with thy long black hair flowing."

The Goddess of Darkness replied sadly, "Dost thou still not understand? My body has long since crumbled into dust, as fate decreed. It was destined to be thus when earth and heaven were sundered."

"And that is why I intend to turn back time. Let us return earth and heaven into the original sea of chaos and return once more, side by side, to that time. I need thee."

The Goddess sighed faintly. "Thou didst send the Sword to me. Why didst thou attempt such a dangerous thing?"

"I have never once forgotten thee. Although I knew that thou didst despise me."

The Goddess of Darkness exclaimed in surprise, "But it was thou who didst despise me! After thou didst sever thyself from me, thou didst despise even my children who lived upon the earth."

"Because thou didst prefer to remain within that dark pit rather than be by my side."

"My beloved husband," the Goddess said, deeply moved, "Toyoashihara moves with the seasons. She needs a mother: someone to give birth, to nurture and love her. I cannot turn back or stop time. All of my children would die."

"Dost thou love Toyoashihara more than thou lovest me?"

"O beloved one." Her gentle tone softly but firmly restrained the God of Light, who seemed on the verge of rage. "I have received the Sword. And I now know of thy fierce longing, a longing so great that thou wouldst destroy even thine own tempestuous self. And therefore I can forgive all that thou hast done. And I will surely continue to forgive thee countless times hereafter. How great was our longing for each other. We were not so far apart as we had thought. The children of Toyoashihara realized this before we ourselves. Behold thy son and my daughter, who stand here before us. The union of these two, is it not the same as if we had taken each other's hand?"

Since the God of Light remained silent, the Goddess continued, "Cherish the land of Toyoashihara. I have lost my body, but my hand is in every corner of this land. I am reaching out my hand to thee in love. People make bowls by kneading water and clay and baking them in the fire. Even as water and fire, which are incompatible, can become united, thus can we, too, be joined as one."

The God whispered in a low voice, "An earthen vessel? It sounds like Toyoashihara: so easily broken, yet kneaded and fired again and again. And thou art telling me not to take this task away from them?"

"Yes. If thou dost allow thine anger to rule thee, if thou dost destroy this land in rage, the efforts of these two will have been in vain. Rather let them be a sign. Let them be a remembrance of us, thee and me."

"I understand thy wish," the God of Light said suddenly. Yet his voice was filled with sorrow. "But dost thou understand my loneliness as I sit alone in our great palace in heaven with no one at my side? Thou canst never know the coldness of that high and empty void."

The Goddess replied with sympathy, "But thou hast excellent children."

Chihaya finally realized that his brother and sister were also visible at the top of the hill. His eyes were at last adjusting to the light shed by the God. The two of them standing on a slight rise in front of their father looked like two heat waves burning. Princess Teruhi stood with her eyes downcast, and her cheeks were pure white and translucent. Before her father, whom she had come at long last to greet, she looked like a modest and reverent maiden. Prince Tsukishiro appeared to be looking toward Chihaya, but it was still too bright for him to tell.

The God of Light regarded the twins for a while.

"O children who have served me upon the earth," he said softly. "What do you wish in recompense for your services? Ask of me anything. Teruhi, what of thee?"

Princess Teruhi raised her face. In a serene, bright voice she replied, "I desire nothing. I only wish to accompany thee, Father, to thy palace in heaven."

"And thou, Tsukishiro?"

"I, too," Prince Tsukishiro replied.

"Then so be it. You shall both accompany me."

Finally the God of Light turned to Chihaya. Under his gaze, Chihaya felt himself blinded once again as everything about him was bathed in light.

"And thou, my youngest. What dost thou desire, Child of the Sword?"

Chihaya was somewhat surprised but answered frankly, "I wish to be granted mortality. If it is possible, I wish to be permitted to live as do the people of Toyoashihara, to grow old as they do, and finally to die and seek rest with the Goddess."

The God of Light paused before replying. But at last he spoke. "It is granted."

Seeing Chihaya's joyous face, the God said in an amused tone, "I never imagined that thou wouldst fulfill thy mission in this way: that thou wouldst ask for death from thine own father. But if that is truly what thou wishest, so shall it be."

Chihaya heard the voice of Princess Teruhi, who stood far

away on the hill, whispering in his ear. Perhaps she spoke through an interval in time.

"My foolish little brother, you choose a different path right to the end. But then, that is your nature. Deep in my heart I have always liked you. I could not be your mother, but my feeling for you was akin to that of a mother for her child."

A myriad memories raced through his mind, but Chihaya could not voice his thoughts. In parting he could only whisper, "For always, without change."

He heard Prince Tsukishiro's voice also from a distance. "If the Goddess of Darkness ever resumed her physical form, she would look just like Saya. I am not my father, but so I believe."

Chihaya looked at Saya, but she still stood with both eyes covered. He was tempted to speak to her but thought better of it, for it would be rude if the Goddess was still there.

The light gathered in the east and rose to heaven like a gleaming white pillar, then gradually faded from the rest of the land. The blue returned to the sky, the mountains regained their contours, the buildings once again cast their shadows. The light suffusing the clouds dyed everything a vivid gold, and in the next instant all had returned to normal. But the ground still glittered white. Snow had fallen while they had been absorbed.

When Saya finally opened her eyes, she saw only the silent snowy landscape. A flock of sparrows descended on a harvested field now wrapped in white and pecked at fallen grains under the snow. A dog began to bark somewhere but, daunted by the silence, ceased abruptly. Nothing had changed. It seemed she must have been dreaming.

"Has the God of Light gone?" Saya asked Chihaya softly.

"Yes. Everything is finished. Toyoashihara has been saved. My brother and sister have gone, too," Chihaya replied and then added after a slight hesitation, "My brother watched you until the very end."

"Well then, why didn't you tell me sooner?" Saya demanded. "We will never meet again. I kept my eyes covered just as you told me to."

"I didn't want to tell you," Chihaya said and burst out laughing.

"That's terrible!"

"Are you mad at me?"

"Of course!"

People began to poke their heads out of the buildings and come outside in groups. They looked about with expressions of wonder. They could hardly believe that nothing had changed, that everything had been restored. Torihiko flew up and shook the branch of a tree, dumping snow on everyone's head.

"It's finished, finished! No more Darkness, no more Light. No more friends or foes. Now we will have nothing to do. How about a snowball fight?"

"There is plenty to be done, fool!" Lord Shinado, who had snow down his collar, said, and shook his fist. "We have to build a new country—a country that embraces one ruler."

Lord Akitsu stood before Chihaya and Saya. "You are the new rulers of all the people. In place of the God and Goddess, you must be the father and mother of Toyoashihara. If you can live together in harmony, the earthen vessel will never be broken."

Saya could hardly believe her ears, she was so astounded, and it seemed that Chihaya was no different, for, with a puzzled frown, he asked Lord Akitsu, "Just what are you telling us to do?"

Lord Akitsu put his hand to his chin. "Well, first of all, you must have a wedding."

"Wedding?"

"Yes, I believe so."

"But I have not received a betrothal gift from Chihaya," Saya said from beside him.

Chihaya choked for an instant and then said, "I gave you the Sword."

"That doesn't count."

"But I have nothing else."

"That's true," Saya looked up in surprise as though she had just realized it. "Neither of us owns anything. Well, I have never heard of two such people with nothing being made rulers."

"We shall build you a palace," Lord Akitsu said. "We shall have a ground-breaking ceremony, bury the cornerstone deep in the ground, raise the main post, and build the roof high. Everyone will surely contribute their aid. By the time it is built, spring will be here."

Saya whispered privately to Chihaya, "I will invite my parents to the wedding. And I'll tell them that we'll give them so many grandchildren they won't know what to do with them."

"I heard that," Torihiko said, beating his wings above their heads and just dodging being hit by a snowball thrown by Saya.

Chihaya laughed but then asked, "By the way, what is a wedding? I've never heard of that before."

AFTERWORD

I have always wanted to read a Japanese fantasy. My first encounter with the literary genre of fantasy was of course the Chronicles of Narnia by C. S. Lewis. (I say "of course" because this is true of most people of my generation.) I first read these books when I was in the third and fourth grades and was captivated by a work whose scope encompassed seven whole volumes. This impressed me as much as learning that there was a sequel to *Anne of Green Gables*, and implanted a prejudice in my child's mind that good stories are long.

The Chronicles of Narnia were my salvation during adolescence, when I was filled with distrust toward adults. Reading them, I felt that the author had maintained his ability to enjoy and appreciate things on the same level as myself, yet at the same time had experienced much more suffering and sadness in life than I. "There are adults who mature in this way even after fifty," I thought. "That is the kind of person I would like to become." I was even eager to reach my fifties and prove to all that I had not lost the spirit of my girlhood.

While studying to enter the university, I read avidly and found many books I liked better than the Chronicles of Narnia, from which I was growing away. But I began to fear that I would never be able to enjoy children's literature in the way I had before. Although I was still reading fantasy novels, it bothered me that they were all translations. I thought I might never again be able to lose myself totally in another world.

"Then why not write something that you can lose yourself in?" a voice within me said. "Write the book that you most want to read without expecting someone else to do it."

I later realized that these were the words of C. S. Lewis. I had read them in the translator's notes for *The Lion, the Witch and the Wardrobe*. At that point I tried to write a little . . . and found that I could not stop. After ten years, I am still hooked.

So the stories I write are still long, and still fantasy. I still believe that a real writer writes even after turning fifty, and I cannot write unless the story is the one I most want to read. First encounters can thus have a powerful and lasting influence.

Dragon Sword and Wind Child is the story I have wanted to read for a long time. If the reader grasps even a little of my feeling, it will give me the greatest joy. Because I love ancient Japanese literature, it was as natural for me to write a fantasy related to ancient times as it is for water to flow downward. I became familiar with the *Kojiki* (*The Book of Ancient Matters*) in elementary school, and read it in the original in the university. But (after numerous failures) I realized that the *Kojiki* was complete in itself, leaving no room for fantasy. Some readers of *Dragon Sword and Wind Child* will have realized that motifs that seem similar to those in the *Kojiki* are actually of different origin. The idea for this story was born from *Norito* (*Shinto Prayers*) in volume 8 of the *Engishiki* (*Engi Period Chronicles*). The Goddess of the underworld in that chapter was filled with a charm I had not hitherto recognized.

Just to be able to write such a story was sufficient happiness for me. To have it published was a long-cherished private dream, one which I can hardly believe is actually being realized. The credit for this belongs to Rei Uemura, my editor at Fukutake Publishing Co. I would also like to express my appreciation to

Hiroshi Ito. In fact, these two were my faithful companions in the dark basement of Building 8 in Waseda University's Children's Literature Department. In addition to my heartfelt appreciation for these two friends, I wish to thank all the other unique and delightful people I met in the Children's Literature Department. In various ways they have all helped wed me to the literary profession, and it is thanks to their praise of my first efforts that I am still writing.

NORIKO OGIWARA
July 20, 1988
Hachioji, Japan